Kamau Brathwaite by Omowale Stewart

For the
Geography of a Soul

For the
Geography of a Soul:
Emerging Perspectives
on Kamau Brathwaite

edited by

Timothy J. Reiss

Africa World Press, Inc.

P.O. Box 1892
Trenton, NJ 08607

P.O. Box 48
Asmara, ERITREA

Africa World Press, Inc.

P.O. Box 1892
Trenton, NJ 08607

P.O. Box 48
Asmara, ERITREA

Cover design: Jonathan Gullery
Book design: Wanjiku Ngugi

Cover Art: "Peligroso", by kind permission of Ras Akyen Ramsay
Frontispiece: Omowale Stewart

Library of Congress Cataloging-in-Publication Data

For the geography of soul: emerging perspectives on Kamau Brathwaite / edited by Timothy J. Reiss.
    p. cm.
Includes bibliographical references and index.
  ISBN 0-86543-904-4 -- ISBN 0-86543-905-2 (pbk.)
  1. Brathwaite, Kamau, 1930---Criticism and interpretation. 2. Caribbean Area--In literature. I. Reiss, Timothy J., 1942-
    PR9230.9.B68 Z68 2001
    811'.54--dc21

                        2001002550

Contents

Abbreviations

In citing, the following abbreviations are used throughout this collection:

BB[1]:	*Black + Blues.* Havana: Casa de las Americas, 1976.
BB[2]:	*Black + Blues.* 2nd edn. New York: New Directions, 1995.
BP:	*Barabajan Poems 1492-1992.* Kingston and New York: Savacou North, 1994.
DS:	*DreamStories.* Harlow: Longman, 1994.
IS:	*Islands* (1969). Cited by page from TA (see below).
M:	*Masks* (1968). Cited by page from TA (see below).
Middle[1]:	*Middle Passages.* Newcastle: Bloodaxe, 1992.
Middle[2]:	*Middle Passages.* [New edn.] New York: New Directions, 1993.
MP:	*Mother Poem.* Oxford: Oxford UP, 1977.
RP:	*Rights of Passage* (1967). Cited by page from TA (see below).
SP:	*Sun Poem.* Oxford: Oxford UP, 1982.
TA:	*The Arrivants: A New World Trilogy.* Oxford: Oxford UP, 1973.
"TTR":	"Trench Town Rock." *Hambone* 10 (Spring 1992): 123-201.
TTR:	*Trench Town Rock.* Providence, RI: Lost Road, 1994.
X/S:	*X/Self.* Oxford and New York: Oxford UP, 1987.

Less frequently cited works use a short title referring to the combined bibliography at the end of the collection. A superscript numeral indicates the edition in the case of books or essays published more than once (ordered chronologically in the bibliography).

Preface

This collection was first conceived as a celebration honoring Kamau Brathwaite's work on the occasion of his seventieth birthday in the year 2000. As poet, historian, and cultural and literary critic Brathwaite's place in Caribbean and world cultural creation over the past forty years has been of immense importance. Indeed, he has now acquired something of a legendary and iconic status as a principal participant in the creation of one of the most "word-scatteringly" alive cultures on the globe, but also simply as a poet of utter integrity, a historian whose work has been germinal, an original and inventive cultural and literary critic, and, more recently, an experimental innovator in using the computer to express voice, nation language and the emotional and intellectual vibrancy of a blooming culture. His achievements in these areas have been matched by the singularly unusual way in which his work and simple presence in Caribbean cultural action have inspired other people's creativity–as many of the contributors to this collection attest.

Perhaps these achievements have been matched as well by the relative lack of critical attention his work has received for most of his career compared to that given to some others. It is true that Brathwaite has received important awards: honorary degrees, a Guggenheim and two Fulbrights from the US, Britain's Cholmondeley award for poetry, Jamaica's Centennial Award, a Gabriela-Mistral Inter-American special citation, the Commonwealth Prize for Poetry, the Casa de las Américas prize an unprecedented three times for poetry and criticism, Companion of Honour, the Neustadt prize for his contributions to world literature, the Pride of Barbados prize for his lifelong contribution to arts and culture in his native country, the International Poetry Forum prize and still others. Yet these outward marks of official public esteem have not until recently been translated into very much critical attention (with one or two farseeing exceptions). Too, they are countered by the considerable difficulty he has had in getting some of his more experimental work published. No doubt this is partly because it requires unfamiliar formats. Unfortunately, it is surely also because it queries "mainstream" habits of thought, questions canonical styles and tones, affronts and discomfits economic, political and aesthetic hegemonies exercised still from the self-styled "metropolitan centers," and continues to explore–indeed increasingly assails–the disasters these centers inflict on their surroundings, directly and through local surrogates. So this is a struggle whose essence will not quickly be resolved, but it can be hoped that at least as far as hindering publication is concerned it will very soon be at an end.

At the same time, this very struggle, its contentions, its occasional bitterness and grief, its not infrequent happiness, have produced a lineage of writers in the Caribbean and worldwide. As this collection shows, Brathwaite has profoundly influenced at least two generations of poets and other creative writers working in this lineage, using his work in and behind theirs. As this collection also shows there are finally increasing numbers of scholars in the Atlantic world writing *on* his work and using it in theirs. As this collection's bibliography shows, this influence is now becoming global: besides its importance through the Caribbean, from India to the United States, Britain to Nigeria, Japan to Belgium, South Africa to Germany and Canada to Columbia, scholars, critics and historians are increasingly looking to his theoretical and historical work, poets and their audiences to his creative.

The present volume offers perspectives on Brathwaite's writing and thought at the same time as showing how their formative impact on other writers is integral to that thought and writing and to the cultural wealth characterizing the Caribbean especially over the past fifty years. It does not offer biographical information, however, except sporadically and incidentally. Gordon Rohlehr's *Pathfinder* is rich in information (esp. 3-20), Stewart Brown gives a brief overview in the Introduction to his edited collection, *The Art of Kamau Brathwaite*, as does Jean Small in her praise "Po'm for Kamau," and Anne Walmsley offers many aspects in her book on *The Caribbean Artists Movement*, of whose eponymous organization Brathwaite was one of the three founders. The recorded *Acta* of two symposia honoring Brathwaite and his work provide more aspects (see bibliography 2.13.: the third such symposium was occasioned by the Neustadt prize and published in *World Literature Today*, edited by Djelal Kadir). He is listed in many encyclopedias, but those interested in the intellectual and emotional life founding his work should look in the work itself, in the two trilogies, *The Arrivants* and *Ancestors*, to be sure, but especially in *Barabajan Poems* and, more agonizingly, in *Trench Town Rock* and *The Zea Mexican Diary*. In all of these, save possibly the last, one person's life is seen as ineluctably enlaced in, shaped by, indicative of, indebted to, sociopolitical life and conditions. This deep sense of being trammeled in collective life has its strict counterpart in the experience other artists, thinkers and people in the street have of his work as grounding for them. To walk with him through streets of Bridgetown, Bathsheba, or simply a parish country-side is to be not seldom caught in the emotional embrace of people coming up to ask in tones I make no effort to imitate: "Aren't you Mr. Brathwaite?" "Let me shake your hand...." "I thank you...." "You give us our place...."

This, then, is an anthology of writings *on* Kamau Brathwaite and his work, but is also one that seeks to match the interests and dimensions *of* that work. It has three "paths." One involves creative work by his contemporaries and younger writers who think of him as a beacon. A second concerns literary and cultural criticism. The third treats matters historical. Like Brathwaite's work, these are neither a limit nor separate areas of practice. They are facets of one overarching practice of cultural creation. So the collection does not divide its writings by genre or discipline but tries to organize them by theme, matter, tone and, most simply, chronology of the work they consider, build on and perhaps even herald. They show the wide importance of Brathwaite's place in the contemporary creation of Barbadian culture in particular and of Caribbean culture in general; his role in efforts to understand the syncretic nature of this culture and its bonds with the many cultures from which it has been composed–not just African and European, but Amerindian, south Asian and east Asian; the images and themes he deploys in his writing to these and other ends; too, his recent efforts to create a new style of writing able to capture in print the cadences, tones, rhythms and motions of "nation language" and the local cultures it speaks (the computer/video style he calls "Sycorax"); the discovery of figures representative of Caribbean culture's self-assertion against attempts to seal it into someone (or somewhere) else's history–or History; his interventions not just in colonial and postcolonial politics of race and class but, more unusually in his context, in those of gender. These, and not the poem, the historical argument or the critical essay, are organizing principles of this volume.

After the editor's introduction, offering an overview principally of Brathwaite's literary work and attempting to set the general context and themes of this book, Linton Kwesi Johnson offers a humorous view of Brathwaite's poetic creation, at the same time marking his importance, some of his themes and his powerful influence. Maryse Condé then places Brathwaite's first trilogy in the context of the first major generation of Caribbean writers, comparing his work with Aimé Césaire's and suggesting something of the anguish, anger and contradictory omens involved for those who start to create a new cultural history and geography. Exploring the same poems, Pamela Mordecai shows how the poet limns certain themes and images to begin that cultural creation, while Velma Pollard suggests how central women are as creative figures and perhaps too as figures of the stable "folk" culture that has been basic to Brathwaite's understanding of poetry's, historiography's, and criticism's contribution to *any* cultural creation. Something of this–and of the cultural syncretism also suggested in the poems–is advanced via Olive Senior's three poems. Mark McWatt argues how the changing of rhythms in *The Arrivants*, the movement of meaning within and between images and themes make the trilogy into a single unit. All see *The Arrivants* as powerfully embodying the moving sweep of Atlantic history that has made the modern Caribbean. They see the trilogy, too, as heralding the grand creativity of the later work. John Chioles, precisely, takes these poems and that sweep to set them into one of the cultural traditions on which they draw (a European one from Plato and the myth of Atlantis) and against its longer legacy of slaveries and oppressions, while at the same time making a personal statement of amity and influence, echoing a transAtlantic passage and "taking" these poems towards Brathwaite's own later "Dreamstories."

To be sure, all these writings reflect in one way or another movements of exile, emigration and transoceanic passages. Too, all are statements of friendship and love, some engaging critically with the poetry, criticism and historiography, some being moved by one or the other into new ways of writing or new paths of research, some paying tribute by setting personal memories into a wider context of Caribbean, diaspora and world sociopolitical and cultural realities. One of these is Ralph Jemmott's, reflecting on the meaning of Brathwaite's teaching of history in Jamaica. For during the years when Brathwaite was working on the three sequences that became the epic *Arrivants*, he was traveling from Britain to Africa (spending seven germinal years in Ghana) and back to the Caribbean, teaching first in St Lucia in UWI's Extramural Department and then, although for a time back in London, in Jamaica in UWI's History Department. Jemmott was among the first students there to participate in the course that eventually became *The Development of Creole Society in Jamaica*, and he records how his professor's teaching signaled a completely new way of understanding Caribbean history, changing not only how he saw his own Barbadian social and political actualities but his emotions and affective relationships. Kamau effectively taught a new sensibility to his history students as he was doing at the same time to the readers of his poetry. This charismatic giving of self is feelingly recorded in Mervyn Morris's poem and then further still in John La Rose's memoir, recalling years from London and the foundation of the Caribbean Artists Movement, Brathwaite's role in the practicalities of creating cultural spaces, outlets, markets and all the nitty-gritty under whose absence so many earlier generations of artists from non-

"metropolitan" centers had suffered and been silenced, the role, too, of his wife Doris and her grievous death in 1986.

Rex Nettleford also remembers these years, and Brathwaite as a Barbadian teaching in St Lucia, then in Jamaica, an artist striving to place and create a Caribbean culture, fascinated with the creation of language and rhythm, utterly focused on changing a colonial–and colonized–culture and the means to do this through a sense of place, a making of art(s), a use of history and above all education. Cynthia James's three poems give a further sense of a particular geography, of growing to the demands and dangers of colonial and neocolonial societies, of the imperative of exile, the force of education and, yes, even the power of new poetic energies and forms. Nettleford refers to that energy as "kinetic" in Brathwaite's writings, whether in poetry, historiography or criticism. So, too, does Elaine Savory in comparing his poetry and his thinking about its purpose to William Blake's aims in both, reflecting not simply on the ways in which both make different art forms overlap, but on their concentration on the interplay of form and content and function, and, again, on the force of poetry to make and capture social change. She tends to see this more in Brathwaite's later poetry than in the earlier *Arrivants*, arguing that many may have had difficulty with the second trilogy because both the fact and nature of its interventions have become less familiar. For his part, Enrique Lima looks at *Black + Blues*, a collection forming a bridge between the two trilogies, and he, too, concentrates on a tie between Brathwaite's poetry and that of an earlier "metropolitan" poet. But he aims to show not how radicalities meet but how the Caribbean poet, "taking" an image from the other, radicalizes it in ways the other precisely could not, suggesting that Brathwaite unearths from "Eliot's" image contradictory marks of oppressive violence which he–but not the other–can hope to turn towards something ultimately liberating.

Such contradictions lead to equally contradictory reactions. One can be the kind of flight suggested in Erna Brodber's "Lace People"–at least as far as this small portion of the future novel suggests. Another can be those efforts at new cultural creation of which we have already seen so much. Aside from his poetry, his historiography, his criticism, his pedagogy, his share in forging new outlets and spaces, in these years, Brathwaite also asked how language reflected the particularities of history and geography. Throughout the seventies, he found, named and explored what many now agree in calling "nation language," a people's own expression of its own complicated social, political and cultural realities. Korah Belgrave gives some sense of how this actually *works* in the detail of the poems. She uses *The Arrivants* to this end, but principally *Mother Poem* and *Sun Poem* from the second trilogy. Increasingly of course one can look to all his writing, and especially now to his use of the "Sycorax" computer style to capture on the page the rhythms, cadences, silences and the rest of a spoken exchange, one functioning in its own space and sculpting its owns truths and actualities. This is the kind of effort reflected as well in Edward Chamberlin's essay on "tracking", suggesting the kind of quite new directions in which Brathwaite's work leads (if not it alone, of course). Arguing that tracking techniques are wholly analogous to reading, he denies recent western claims about how the movement from orality to literacy, or indeed more recently still from oral to print culture, made a sea-change in how the human mind functioned. This simultaneously queries certain favorite western notions about "civilizational progress" and its claims of "universality." Chamberlin draws considerably on Brathwaite's revaluation of the power of orature, oral culture and the nation language expressing it.

Such powerful contentions correspond to more precisely political asseverations about the role of cultural interventions in neo- and post-colonial conditions. Ngugi wa Thiong'o has of course been particularly concerned over the past twenty and more years specifically with the role of language in creating new cultural spaces and "centers." Not for nothing, indeed, was Brathwaite the first artist and thinker of the African diaspora whom Ngugi and his colleagues invited to the new Literature (not "English") Department at the University of Nairobi. Not for nothing was he named ("Kamau") in 1972 into a new language and an old tradition. Here, Ngugi writes of the role cultural action must have in creating new sociopolitical geographies–indeed, *a* new *global* sociopolitical geography. This theme is taken up with specific regard to the relation between "Africa" (real or mythical) and the Caribbean by Mervyn Alleyne, again in the context of language and its role in the creation of identity. Alleyne argues that "Africa" is present in the Caribbean more in diversities and contrasts than in unity.

Here is a source of fertile and complex argument. Thus J. Michael Dash plays Brathwaite off against Glissant as, in some degree, the seeker for some deeply unified syncretic culture against one who sees unity in "*relation*," in the play of mutual differences. Dash sees a fruitful exchange here that perhaps ultimately plays out to Glissant's "advantage." That these two thinkers and artists form a particularly forceful "dual" Caribbean voice is also suggested in Roberto Fernández Retamar's poem to Nancy Morejón, seeing them as somehow co-mediators between African, European and Caribbean cultures, whose contemporary vibrancy is the greater from the interplay of their voices. Morejón herself has elsewhere reminded us that Brathwaite does not just link English and French Caribbean voices, but that he may also be seen as a link with Spanish, the epic *Arrivants* trilogy being a "worthy heir of [Nicolás Guillén's] unsurpassable fluvial cuban poem called *West Indies, Ltd.*" ("Brathwaite" 28). In a way, Richard Clarke responds to the thought that Brathwaite supposes the possibility of some relatively unambiguous and solid (not to say *stolid*) singularity with a concept of a "dialectical creolization" drawn essentially from *Contradictory Omens*, but owing much as well to his reading of "nation language," the second trilogy, and the later "Sycorax" work. The issue has been a deeply divisive one, and I take the liberty of placing NourbeSe Philip's poem here to catch something of the strains of these struggles between visions of cultural dis-ease and internal combats of cultural contradictions. I like to think of Silvio Torres-Saillant's intervention as a further productive response to these fraught struggles and the contradictions they seek to resolve, one striving to make full use of Brathwaite's concept of "tidalectics," going beyond the familiar European notion of dialectic as defined clearly in Clarke's essay. Honor Ford-Smith's sequence of poems further underscores the personal emotional freight of these efforts.

Many of these writers, artists and thinkers now live as exiles or emigrés at least partly in response to these anguishing conflicts. This is all too often a jump from the frying pan into the fire, where new and unfamiliar wars take the place of those left behind. I think here, especially, of NourbeSe Philip's passionate response to Canadian attempts to close off local spaces (ones not a little reflective of that country's often neo-imperialist stance in the Caribbean itself). Writing from the same place, Pamela Mordecai proposes a rather milder reaction to the same impediments, at the same time rejoicing once again (in "Caliban") in the possibility that the poet may create the changes capable of overcoming these contradictions and barriers. And this brings on a series of essays and poems that may perhaps be seen as offering ways out of these hard conflicts, moving with the poet and historian into new creative discoveries and new historical understandings. Gordon Rohlehr explores *Mother Poem* as a vast construction offering new language, new figures (Sycorax especially), and a refound geography to move minds and practices away from these oppressions and the violences accompanying them. Rhonda Cobham explores *Barabajan Poems* as a continuation of these efforts, focusing, as do so many others, on the conjunction of new language, identity and sociopolitical and aesthetic change. Mary E. Morgan reads the Neustadt Prize as a confirmation of this direction taken by the poet and historian, concluding with examples of the direction Brathwaite's work is now taking. Joan Dayan reads this recent work, notably the second trilogy and the new dreamstories as continuing in this exploration, emphasizing anew the role taken by female figures in this development–an argument continued by Isis Costa in her creative contribution, following directly in the paths opened out by Brathwaite, moving them from the immediate Caribbean to North America (as do others here) and to Brazil. Cynthia James brings these explorations to *ConVERSations*, the most recent long work Brathwaite has published, while Opal Palmer Adisa ties them again to the personal and affective, expressing the effects of these charismatic explorations on a fellow artist and having recourse to something akin to his video style to do so.

With Hilary Beckles' essay, we return to a historian's exploration of the immense effect all this has had on Brathwaite's immediate context and the sociopolitical reality particularly of Barbados. Like others, Beckles shows that the poet's and historian's impact has not simply been in the aesthetic arena, but has indeed changed the everyday activities of his island and the self-understanding of those who live there. In Brathwaite's explorations, Beckles sees the catalyst for actual transformation and for changes still as yet only potential. Caliban's role has been and is *real*, it has mattered and continues to matter: hence what Beckles refers to as the continued "stoning" of one who refuses to be still. That refusal empowers others. That is the import of Elaine Savory's "miranda." It is also, I suggest, the further import of Patricia Penn Hilden's essay here and research into the considerable presence of North American native slaves in Barbados (and elsewhere in the Caribbean archipelago). The correction of false stories that have been told over the years about such exchanges is part of the actual important changes on the ground and the equally significant alterations in understanding that Brathwaite's work has been bringing about and which is now coming to fruition in the many ways this collection suggests. Lorna Goodison's poem closes by suggesting further the immense affective, social, political and aesthetic weight of the motions, exchanges, and mutualities these essays underscore. These writings and all the others suggest, too, the *personal* impetus and deep affection behind these efforts at intellectual comprehension and change.

Versions of some of the poetry have appeared before. Honor Ford-Smith's "The Archangel" appeared in her *My Mother's Last Dance* (Toronto: Sister Vision, 1996), "The Thief" [*sic*] in *Jamaica Journal* 26.3 (December 1998). Roberto Fernández Retamar's "Sólo tu Nancy Morejón" appears in his recent collection, *Versos* (Havana: Letras Cubanas, 1999). Cynthia James's three poems appeared in her *La Vega* (Tunapuna: privately printed, 1995). Elaine Savory's "miranda" first appeared in *The Caribbean Writer* 12 (1998): 63-72. Lorna Goodison's "Angel of Dreamers" is from her *Turn Thanks* (Urbana, Chicago and London: University of Illinois P, 1999) and appeared in *Caribbean Quarterly* 44.1-2 (March-June 1998): 183-6. All are here, like those that have not been in print before, because their authors wrote them to, in response to, or in the wake of Kamau Brathwaite.

Debts have been incurred in preparing this volume. First, I thank Kassahun Checole, publisher of Africa World Press, for his welcome and enthusiasm, and Ngugi wa Thiong'o for introducing us. Isis Costa was always ready with information. Rhonda Cobham brought in some of the contributors, graciously commented on the original project and on other details along the way. Only time, distance and prior commitments impeded more elaborate collaboration. Ronnie Pardo, too, made contacts easier and acted not seldom as a diplomatic and sensitively caring go-between. I much regret that personal circumstances prevented closer participation. Richard Clarke enabled me to bring in a couple of late contributors via UWI Cave Hill's celebratory symposium held on 12 May 2000, the day after Kamau Brathwaite's 70th birthday. Mervyn Awon made it possible to use Ras Akyem Ramsay's art on our cover. Ras Akyem graciously allowed it. Omowale Stewart was hugely generous with his time and talents, and patient with my photographic supplies and mailing delays. Contributors have been equally patient with my questions, proddings, occasional rewrites, comments and insistences. Kamau Brathwaite especially, along with Neil Astley, Richard Clarke, Jeniphier R. Carnegie, and Anne Collett, Louis James, Nancy Morejón, James Morgan, Christine Pagnoulle, Myriam Radlow, Graeme Rigby, Gordon Rohlehr, Robert A. Soza, Andy Taitt, Anne Walmsley and Erika Waters replied with alacrity and indulgence to various bibliographical queries. Silvio Torres-Saillant provided roots of his earlier bibliography on disk, saving me a lot of time. In this regard, Doris Monica Brathwaite's two bibliographical monographs remain of course indispensable bases. Ruth Backer gave essential help with moving things from hardcopy to computer storage, from one program to another and generally with keeping machines, communications and pocketbooks from blinking too hard. Roland Greene and the Comparative Literature Program at the University of Oregon and Jess Benhabib, Dean of the Faculty of Arts and Sciences at New York University, generously made funds available for certain aspects of this project. All have my gratitude. Most of all, I thank Patricia Penn Hilden for putting up with my obsessions and bringing light while I was gathering the pieces of this volume–doing so amid obligations and hardships of her own–and Kamau Brathwaite for his presence, his grace, his friendship.

(TJR)

Introduction:
Forging a Geography of the Soul[1]

Timothy J. Reiss

Through Kamau Brathwaite's work run three favorite metaphors. The earliest uses the iambic pentameter that had become a norm in English poetry from roughly the seventeenth century. The second represents the Caribbean islands as product of a child's (or god's) skipping stones in a great curve across the ocean from the coast of Guyana to the tip of Florida. The third transforms the waters buried deep in the porous rock that is Barbados into the welling of a buried culture whose very concealment has made it the more vital to the life above. The first concerns the constitution, practice and differentiation of a poetic voice; the second holds an individual's sense of a home place, a local geography; the third captures something like a collectivity's living cultural and political consciousness and its historical memory quickened *in* that place.

At the same time, each one works and plays with the other two. More than tropes in language, more than just representation, capture or comparison, the finest metaphors are alive and manifest vital actualities: the process of cultural creation making new experience of place. Such are these. Barbados *is* rock of the sort Brathwaite takes for what M. NourbeSe Philip calls an "i-mage", sign/concept of irreducible intuition of place and people "speak[ing] to the essential being of the people among whom and for whom the artist creates" (*Genealogy* 43). Beneath and in it *is* the fresh water making life on the island possible. As the poet/historian has also been able to show, Barbados *does* have a hidden culture, living remnant of Igbo consciousness, however much mixed with others, both African and native American.[2] Too, Barbados is geologically unique among the islands, and the more-than-metaphor grasps that singularity as it simultaneously situates it among its companion islands geographically, historically and culturally. Lastly, the skipping stones, as well, offer not just an image of place, but a rhythm and the curving shape of an imagination, sung and stamped by a calypso drawn to the measure of their multilingual islands:

> The stone had skidded arc'd and bloomed into islands:
> Cuba and San Domingo
> Jamaica and Puerto Rico
> Grenada Guadeloupe Bonaire
>
> curved stone hissed into reef
> wave teeth fanged into clay
> white splash flashed into spray
> Bathsheba Montego Bay
>
> bloom of the arcing summers... ("Calypso," RP 48)

These metaphors and rhythms ground a different poetry and a consciousness not best rendered by that pentameter whose exemplar Brathwaite finds in Thomas Gray's eighteenth century: "The Cúrfew tólls the knéll of párting dáy." He observes that before Chaucer no such dominant metre was to be found, but that since then poetic effort in the anglophone world has increasingly kept to its terms. (Whitman tried to overcome it by noise, "a large movement of sound"; cummings by fragmentation; Moore "with syllabics.") Yet it stays. And though S. T. Coleridge and T. S. Eliot praised "the generic variety its rhythmic pattern could accommodate" (Marks 300-1) and many have observed how flexibly it modulates, its grounding rhythm remains directive. "It carries with it a certain kind of experience, which is not the experience of a hurricane. A hurricane does not roar in pentameters. And that's the problem: how do you get a rhythm which approximates the *natural* experience, the *environmental* experience?" (Brathwaite, *History* 9-10). The needed rhythm is grounded and trammeled in the skipping stones and rock-concealed water, both bearing spirit of place. But that is not the only problem. With experience of place tied in form goes a bond of culture. So Coleridge argued at length that the poet's language was essentially bound in an experienced world, metre being "superadded" (in poetry over prose) yet inseparable from thought, content, emotion, expression and the poet's mind and particular sense of place (*Biographia*, chap. 18: 2.58-88; cf. Marks 141-9). The choice of "a form" and its rhythm, wrote Eliot of Shakespeare's sonnets, is that of "a precise way of thinking and feeling" (*Sacred* 57). Like Brathwaite, Philip applies the thought to a

Caribbean case, agreeing that the choice of language between what he calls "nation language," "Caribbean demotic and standard English...is a choice which often affects the choice of subject matter, the rhythms of thought patterns, and the tension within the work. It is also a choice resonant with historical and political realities *and* possibilities" (*Frontiers* 37). One would say it *always* affects, and indeed *effects*, all these.

In the essay just quoted, Brathwaite did not dwell on Gray's celebrated poem, and for good reason: he wanted to get on to the forms of a new voice. Here, though, we may grant it a bit more attention, and I would like to quote a bit more of its beginning:

> The Cúrfew tólls the knéll of párting dáy,
> The lówing hérd winds slówly ó'er the léa,
> The plówman hómeward plóds his wéary wáy,
> And léaves the wórld to dárkness ánd to mé.
>
> Now fádes the glímmering lándscape ón the síght
> And áll the áir a stíllness hólds,
> Save whére the béetle whéels his dróning flight,
> And drówsy tínklings lúll the dístant fólds...

If you look at where the accents fall in the first stanza, you see how the long vowels echo tolling bell and "lowing herd." You see, too, how these same long vowels combine with the assonance of the labial and nasal consonants (l and r, m and n) to trace the slow rhythmic trudge of animals and men tiredly returning home at day's wane. Fading landscape at dusk, evening quiet of late summer, wheeling beetles, tinkling sheep bells, the later "ivy-mantled tow'r", "mopeing owl", "rugged elms", "yew-tree's shade", and "swallow twitt'ring from the straw-built shed", are stereotypes meant to summon the image of an age-old country England to frame the elegy on humble folk that is the principal weight of the poem: "the short and simple annals of the poor" (l.32). They frame a nostalgic musing on those who might have been great churchmen, rulers or musicians, except only that "Knowledge to their eyes her ample pages / Rich with the spoils of time did ne'er unroll" (ll.49-50). So these remain a gem unknown in ocean cave (53-4), a flower "to blush unseen" and "waste its sweetness on the desert air" (55-6), "a village-Hampden," a "Cromwell guiltless," or "some mute inglorious Milton" (57-60).

The advancing expansive pentameter, Coleridge's "march of the words" (*Biographia*, chap. 15: 2.20), contains a particular history and cultural experience. "The madding crowd's... strife" may be called "ignoble" (73), but the nostalgia grounding the poem's theme depends on the achievements of those who supposedly formed and sprang from that crowd. Those achievements themselves are taken as due in some *essential* way to their embedding in this storied and edenic countryside. Not for nothing did James Froude, a bit more than a century after Gray, fall back on these terms to introduce what J. J. Thomas in reply called the "ghastly imaginings" in which he grounded "the dark outlines of [his] scheme to thwart political aspirations in the Antilles" (*Froudacity* 9, 6). Froude began by recounting the train journey towards his West Indian packet at Southampton away from the "destructive," "dishonest" and self-defeating London debates urging independence and separation for the Caribbean colonies of Britain's empire. As they rode past fields "deep with snow", under a "winter sky...soft and blue," frozen "ponds and canals" where "all was brilliant and beautiful," the "air cleared, and my mind also." "It was," he wrote, "like escaping out of a nightmare into happy healthy England once more." Against the background of this landscape (now wintry, in contrast to the tropical islands where he was going), and out of it, came not only bullish Froude himself, complacent in his righteous Englishness, but his "several gentlemen" traveling companions, "officers," "planters" and "young sportsmen." These would lay to rest the degenerate debates of the capital and firmly reestablish England's rightful hold on its Caribbean colonies (*The English* 16).

Gray's lowly Hampdens, Miltons and Cromwells, who, lost in poverty, misery and illiteracy, never did share this expansive culture, would nonetheless have done so if only they had had the wealth and learning to give them the necessary competitive edge. Gray gloried in a "loss" that proved the depth of English culture, with its myriad putative conquerors, preachers and poets scattered about the countryside. Froude nostalgically embroiders on its and their continuing power. Indeed, the Hampdens, Cromwells and Miltons raise before us the image of those churchmen, rulers and artists who were *not* silent or "wasted" in the desert or under the seas; those who *did* "wade through slaughter for a throne" and "shut the gates of mercy on mankind" (67-8), whether at home on those of a different class, abroad on those of a different race or everywhere on those of a different sex. Well might Eliot say that while the language of such as Gray may have become "more refined" than that of his poetic predecessors, "the feeling became more crude" ("Metaphysical" 30).

In Froude, what Thomas called his "flowers of rhetoric" quite deliberately hid the actuality of "a degrading tyranny" (*Froudacity* 6, 78) and their author's desire to see it extended, while expressing a savage racism that he did not at all try to hide. On one hand was "a strange rhapsody on Negro felicity," as Thomas again ironically put it (82). Here were noble natives under British colonial rule, untrammeled by sin or shame and living in a "happiness" that made them "the supremest specimen" of fortunate humanity, "the most perfectly contented specimens of the human race to be found upon the planet" (*The English* 49-50, 79; cf. 73, 78). Such, he wrote, were those of Barbados and Trinidad, where "a white community" could help lead "blacks" to such "progress as they [were] capable of making" (88), bringing them "along with them into more settled manners and higher forms of civilisation" (90), towards "a peace and order" that could not be "of their own creation" (98), but from which they could benefit because "a negro can be attached to his employer at least as easily as a horse or a dog" (106).

On another hand was the evidence of what happened when colonizers left, when once "docile, good-tempered, excellent and faithful servants...peel[ed] off such civilisation as they have learnt as easily and as willingly as their coats and trousers" (286-7). Haiti's "ghastly example" (81) was Froude's constant motif for representing what happened when "the inflammable negro nature" (104) was thus deprived of European guidance: an island of "cannibalism" (112-3), where "children [were] offered to the devil and salted and eaten" (164), where white people were not only excluded "from any share of the administration, but forbid[den from] acquisition or possession of real property in any form" (165-6), where "African Obeah, the worship of serpents and trees and stones..., witchcraft and poisoning" were rampant (126), where Port-au-Prince was just "the central ulcer" of disease rampant nationwide (342). No wonder, he intoned, "the better side...would welcome back the French" (344; cf. 120, 183-8, 333, 340-8). To be sure, Froude was not writing poetry–but besides "the flowers of rhetoric" for which he was celebrated, he likened English colonial power and expansion to a Homeric epic, asserting that the proper (and propertied) men of his storied English countryside were alone the worthy and legitimate inheritors of "the bow of Ulysses." This phrase and idea gave him both his subtitle and another recurring motif for a book which assumed that "these beautiful West Indian islands were intended to be homes for the overflowing numbers of our own race," an escape from "the lanes and alleys of our choking cities" into a new countryside of their own possession (362)–*rightful* possession since, according to the Homeric metaphor, they were *returning* home. Froude supplied what C. L. R. James later called "the prose-poetry and the flowers" to transmogrify violence, greed and prejudice (*Black* 63).

For we may perhaps see how the marching linear pentameter (or its equally normative counterpart of the French alexandrine, whose more or less clearly-set caesura and alternating masculine and feminine rhymes beat repetitively onward in what René Depestre in an aberrant moment called "the great adventure of the alexandrine and traditional forms")[3] corresponds to a broader cultural reality, one anchored in political theory and historical actuality. I mean the argument that what makes a "healthy" state, society and culture, is expansion. The idea dated at least from Niccolò Machiavelli's suggestion that the reason a society needed to think constantly of outward expansion was clear in its image as a place composed of endlessly active animals who would turn destructively against each other if not directed elsewhere. So Bacon thought "Forraine Warre" the vital regimen of nations, "like the Heat of *Exercise* [that] serveth to keepe the Body in Health"; so did Hobbes, Locke and many heirs. Bacon had linked the health of European nations rather precisely to their control of and expansion across the seas and the riches they brought, "because, the Wealth of both *Indies*, seemes in great Part, but an Accessary, to the Command of the *Seas*" ("Of the true Greatnesse of Kingdomes and *Estates*," *Essayes* 97-8). After Hobbes, the individuals whose threatened warring necessitated the founding covenant of civil society provided the very image and model of the states that those individual societies were to become. Reason, knowledge, will and power to act became their organizing axioms. The order of reason matched that of the world, the accumulation of material knowledge let such reason instrumentally adjust the world to its own benefit, will urged one to it and power gave the tools to make intervention sure.

What became called "literature" participated in these changes, adopting what I have called *epistemological*, *ethical*, *aesthetic* and *political* rolesthe last being initially the most important. Literature confirmed a (sometimes complicated) politics of singular authority, however embodied; it claimed to be ordered by a syntax that was both that of right language and that of universal reason; it portrayed and asserted an ethics of individual interest whose virtue lay in simultaneously benefitting the community; and it placed beauty in a personal "taste" that echoed general reason (Reiss, especially *Meaning*, but also *Discourse* Chapters 1-2). Literature's "guarantee" of political claim and historical practice ultimately helped "universalize" these developments, so that the assertion of a right to intervene in others' histories and cultures became grounded in Europe's claim to being the vanguard of human progress, with no less than an obligation (God- or History-given) to put others in the way of such progress. Such writing, then, echoed the project of those "worthies of England," Froude gloried, "who cleared and tilled her fields, formed her laws, built her colleges and cathedrals, founded her colonies, fought her battles, covered the ocean with commerce, and spread our race over the planet to leave a mark on it which time will not efface" (*The English* 35). To possess "these beautiful West

Indian islands," destroy or control whoever might be their inhabitants and to impose a culture (poetic and other) upon whoever remained or was brought were elements of a god-given right–indeed obligation.

The claimants do this of course only with deepest regret and a sensitive awareness that something has been lost. Gray's mid-eighteenth-century nostalgia was typical of that of many others: Oliver Goldsmith's, for example, in poems like *The Deserted Village* or *The Traveller*. And that such as Samuel Johnson made fun of Gray's linguistic archaisms changes not a whit the nostalgia's significance. Alexander Pope put it perfectly in his *Essay on Man* not so long before (1730-34), writing of the "lurking principle of death" that dwelt in the body as ever-present threat–loss: "The young disease, that must subdue at length, / Grows with his growth, and strengthens with his strength / ... cast and mingled with his very frame" (I.134-37). This death lurking in the heart of expansive Enlightened Reason finds its modern currency circulating among the very many (Max Horkheimer, Theodor Adorno, Edmund Husserl, Martin Heidegger, Georg Lukács, Claude Lévi-Strauss) who have argued that within this Reason lies a virus destructive not just of the European–western–world and its culture, but of all civilizations. Some think it means the need to find something quite new (or to take over others' "spirituality"); others to complete an unfinished, unperfected Enlightenment; yet others a rediscovery of what came before, of some supposed wholeness with the universe.

Whatever the solution, golden age or Eldorado lost meant golden age or Eldorado had to be found. With or without regret, expansive Europe would have to march out in file and find it. Death could not be allowed its victory. Just so did the degeneracy of Froude's London have its counter first in a glowing English countryside, then in the happy "singing, dancing, and chattering," noble if ignorant "coloured people" of a West Indies "old-fashioned" because its denizens had retained their sense of their places (*The English* 48-9). For the English, there, still knew they had just to rule or let things fall into the decay and death of "Hayti, where they eat the babies, and no white man can own a yard of land" (56). For whatever they might be, right reason and knowledge would first be Europe's. Others, Asian, African or American, untutored like Gray's inglorious Miltons and guiltless Cromwells, poor like his "rustic moralist" (84) or "hoary-headed Swain" (97), without power and the knowledge of right reason, would justly be put in order by the vanguard–unless they managed to ride the coach out and take power abroad. These were exactly the terms, we have seen, which Froude still used more than a century later. For after all, as James Thomson wrote of these others in the artful pentameters of his rewritten *Summer* of 1744:

> Ill-fated race! the softening arts of peace,
> Whate'er the humanizing Muses teach,
> The godlike wisdom of the tempered breast,
> Progressive truth, the patient force of thought,
> Investigation calm whose silent powers
> Command the world, the light that leads to Heaven,
> Kind equal rule, the government of laws,
> And all-protecting freedom which alone
> Sustains the name and dignity of man--
> These are not theirs. (*Seasons* 61-62: ll. 874-84)

One can but admire these "softening arts of peace" that by teaching us that we alone rightfully possess "the name and dignity of man" so readily justify the manipulation of those who therefore do not. The two iambs of "These are not theirs" readily modulate to beat out their phrase in rhythm prefiguring the opening of a not-yet-born Ludwig van Beethoven's Fifth Symphony, poetically glorifying an imperialism long since in place and due only to become an increasingly competitive race in the era following the expansive extravagancies of the hero for whom Beethoven's bars tolled, Napoleon Bonaparte. Witold Gombrowicz was not eccentric in tying Beethoven's "drama in history" to his music's "Form" as a gracious "evening stroll" through a fresh, "splendidly fertile" land of "forests, groves, stream and pools, flowery meadows and fields rustling with wheat" (*Diary* 2.183-5), unerringly bringing us back to Gray. Brathwaite analogously links the "Miltonic ode"'s "nobility" to that of the same romantic symphony, simply observing that "the models are important" (*History* 22-3). Mark McWatt, recalling Bacon, Thomson and so many others, catches these narrow bonds between poetry, history, expansionist despoliation and imperial rapine:

> the osmotic assault
>   of the history-mongering tribes
> of Europe, with their penchant
>   for names and other subtleties,
> fretting about "Indies" amidst the
>   righteous bleeding, as the ruddied
> occidental light, shipped home in galleons,
>   leapt from divine gold and silver. ("Then," *Language* 9)

I am not, need I say? proposing that pentameters or Beethoven create (or in themselves are) a tool of oppression, a title of hegemony. Nor was Brathwaite. Language and style no more make hegemony than revolution. But they do confirm and guarantee them. As Coleridge, Eliot and so many others have asserted, they are nonetheless the form of a particular pattern

of thought, bearer of certain structures of feeling and expression of specific kinds of practice. Formal models do matter. And that is one reason
why Eliot could speak of Gray's poem as "a good example of a beautiful
poem which is nearly all platitude."[4] In its very rhythm and metre it manifests patterns of thought, structures of feeling and kinds of practice crucial
to this experience that never had to learn to roar with the notes of a hurricane, to curve with stones skipping across the ocean, to limp with the life
of Legba or dance with the rhythm of Shango. In his 1992 "Columbus
poem," Brathwaite aims Colón westward into the future as a linear missile
whose sure systems become less assured when he looks out over the changed
history and geography for which he has been willy-nilly responsible. Not
for him the view of Keats' Cortez in Darien. Both the rhythm and the
"Sycorax" typography of the poem (a computerized typography using fonts,
spacings, word-breaks, icons and other devices to track the voice's rhythms,
volume, tones and accents) aim to undermine the patterns, structures, and
practices which Columbus was to come historically and culturally to embody and exemplify. Here Columbus regains his sight. His doing so recalls
a later admiral, directly at imperialist war with Beethoven's Bonaparte,
setting his telescope to his blind eye to avoid seeing his fleet-commander's
signal and decisively winning the battle the signal had ordered him not to
engage. Raising such blindness to heroic virtue, Horatio Nelson gave a
metaphor for imperialism's deliberate unseeing of difference and for
colonialism's internal blinding of the cultural mind. Brathwaite's Colón
recovers from these blindings.

Seeking different rhythms, using other metaphors, working in "nation
language," Brathwaite wants, he once said, 'a revolution of consciousness'
(Walmsley 242), different cultural realities. From them he raises a voice
that confronts and saps the heroic tradition of Nelson's telescope and rejects its justifying claims, while generously pushing away its vices and
abuses and striving to include its virtues in a new--yet old--*mestizaje* made
from Indio-American, European and African strands. "*Bajan culture*," he
writes in *Barabajan Poems* "is this shared collective xperience on a rock
of coral limestone, half-way from Europe, half-way (?back) to Africa; but
like Nelson's statue in both Trafalgar Squares - but I'm talking about *ours*
[Barbadian Bridgetown's, that is] - seeing, it see/ms, with only one & outer
eye of the plantation; while the other inner eye & world of art &
dream&meaning was for too long a time ignored, eroded, submerged; treated
not only as if it did not xist, but that it could not: *Carry on Big Inglan, Lil
Inglan is behine yuh!*" (21-2). Brathwaite's poetry turns away from that
internalizing of oppression to face its history and its causes--*causers*; to
forge a *home* culture from a forcibly fragmented language and a naturally

fragmented geography—where the wages of Western economies have been and are still further splinterings.

The move to change the voice and the cultural patterns it embodies is essential. The issue is not just the language of poetry, of course. John La Rose once commented on that 'imprisonment in English, in Spanish, in French, in Dutch which accordingly denies areas of experience which, if made available, would immediately disclose the total specificity of Caribbean life' (Walmsley 251). Voice, language, forms of expression capture and colonize the mind just as surely as more overt ways of seizure. As James Joyce's Stephen Dedalus put it in a famous passage: "His language, so familiar and so foreign, will always be for me an acquired speech. I have not made or accepted its words. My voice holds them at bay. My soul frets in the shadow of his language" (*Portrait* 189). For Dedalus, this linguistic oppression is never "resolved", Denis Donoghue notwithstanding, who will have it that a "resolution" comes "fifty pages later" when Stephen records in his journal his discovery that the word "tundish," criticized as outlandish by the Jesuit Dean of Studies and to be replaced by "funnel," was in fact "good old blunt English." "Damn the Dean of Studies and his funnel!" he exclaimed: "What did he come here for to teach us his own language or to learn it from us. Damn him one way or the other!" (Donoghue, "Fretting"). This is far from any "resolution." On the contrary, Stephen emphasizes the imposition of the colonizer's language as something the victim can never escape, ineluctably oppressed by being deprived of control over its representational possibilities and orders, but even, too, of any "comfort" in its ready availability as weapon, subversion or strategy of concealment. That the victim may know the language better than the victimizer still cannot put it in the former's control, tied as it is to the patterns and structures of a culture.

Ngugi has put the matter at the center of his creative and critical project. Many others have of course spoken of language as "instrument of oppression and source of humiliation," principal tool of culture letting you know that "it was your soul that was imprisoned" (Mphahlele, *Down* 167, 202). But these and others have a different mother tongue into which they can move. Brathwaite inevitably puts the issue differently: "It was in language that the slave was perhaps most successfully imprisoned by his master, and it was in his (mis-)use of it that he perhaps most effectively rebelled. Within the folk tradition, language was (and is) a creative act in itself" (*Development* 237). Similarly, Gomez observes how slaves sought to "attenuate" "the meter" of English "so that when spoken, the language would be as deracinated as possible" (*Exchanging* 172). Brathwaite (like Philip) is looking for something beyond deracination. For language is not and cannot be separated from a whole culture, and the West Indian case was graver still than such a one as the Irish to which Dedalus referred.

The modern peoples of the islands never had a tongue alive in and imbued with the place where they dwell. They were forcibly brought to lands whose own peoples had been largely destroyed. At the same time, the languages whence they came were robbed of their source, shattered and fragmented. Some argue that speakers of the same language were separated, those of different languages put together, forced to use the slave-owners' language. With their bodies, their words would have been "bought, sold, owned and stolen," leaving only a silence of which they were also robbed, forced as they were into an alien language, Philip stresses (*Looking* 43, 20, 57, 69; cf. *She Tries* 56). Others argue that there is no "hard evidence" for this and that on the contrary "there is every reason to believe that [same language users] were kept together," one result of which would have been to change alterations to English in ways traceable to specific idioms, its users being "taught one brand of English but [giving] back another" (Gomez 173, 177). Whichever the case–and no doubt no reason not to suppose both occurred–, the language Dedalus holds at bay is their only possibility: a language bent to a victimizer's will, desires and interests. "The place we occupy as poets is one that is unique," writes Philip, "one that forces us to operate in a language that was used to brutalize Africans so that they would come to believe in their own lack of humanity" (*Genealogy* 63). As Arwhal says to her narrator elswhere: "you need the word--whore words--to weave your silence" (*Looking* 53). Caribbean writers have to use "a language that was not only experientially foreign, but also etymologically hostile and expressive of the non-being of the African" (*She Tries* 15; cf. 16).

Brathwaite argued the consequences in 1963, characterizing anglophone Caribbean prose writers as producing, at home or abroad, "the same story, expressed in the same rhythms and a similar technique: frustration, bewilderment, lack of a center, lack of faith in the society into which they were born or in which they find themselves" (*Roots*[1] 36). It was a story of endless emigration, of flight from what James called "the cramping West Indies" (*Black* 397), no matter the direction in which it went. In this regard, one reads now, with the surprise that even a mere twenty years of changed awareness can bring, the pride with which Kenneth Ramchand viewed such emigration in 1971: "since 1950...every well-known West Indian novelist has established himself while living [in the English capital]. London is indisputably the West Indian literary capital" ("Introduction" 5). One recognizes economic and cultural pressures that still drive a Caryl Phillips (in *The Final Passage*, for example) to "establish himself" in London and indeed tell the same tale of exiled "frustration, bewilderment, lack of a cen-

ter, [and] lack of faith in [their] society," as that to which Brathwaite earlier addressed himself. The point, though, was the *pride*, regretful and
ambivalent as it was, that Ramchand could take in such emigration.[5] For
after all, as Philip also observes, colonialism and neocolonialism had forced
the exile (no longer just towards the old capitals of empire) by first colonizing minds with everything from material goods to imported culture to
language: "we not knowing that is exile we smelling when we excited for
so, we pressing we noses against the new clothes; we not knowing that the
literature and history, even the grammar we learning in school is part of the
contour map in we own geography of exile" (*Frontiers* 10). All too visible
clothes of a distant emperor. So generations "grew to maturity knowing,
almost simultaneously with awareness of self, that any future lay elsewhere,
overseas, abroad, anywhere else but home" (*Genealogy* 61).

In a very real way, one may characterize Brathwaite's own work as
historian, story-teller, cultural archivist, educator, essayist and poet, as a
lifelong effort to take up the gauntlet he threw down in his criticism. The
effort to find a poetic form that would not just pick at or disrupt the dominant pentameter but use an altogether different rhythm, one from another
place, another environment, another experience, was just the earliest of the
shapes that work took. It also led him from the rock of Barbados and the
curving stones of its habitat through Europe to Africa and eventually back
to the Caribbean. Its aim has been to discover, to invent (in that word's
double sense of finding *and* making: *invenire*) that Caribbean--especially
his own Barbados—as a *home*, not as a displacement or a surrogate for
something else, be it "little England" or robbed Africa. His aim has been to
create a written culture and especially a poetry able to write the cultural
rhythms, style, sensibility and language of a particular Caribbean geography much as Velma Pollard calls more recently for the narrower achievement of a "writing system for Jamaican creole" ("Afterword," *Considering*, 75). His aim has been, as Philip puts it, to "keep the deep structure, the
movement, the kinetic energy, the tone and pitch, the slides and glissandos
of the demotic within a tradition that is primarily page-bound" (*She Tries*
23), a *poetic* tradition. Without a different mother tongue, his aim has been
so to disrupt the forms, rhythms and structures of the colonizer's language
as effectively to make it the bearer of different cultural realities, speaker of
different ways of thinking, representative of changed histories and other
environments.

The first part and understanding of Brathwaite's geographical and historical story was told in *The Arrivants* trilogy. There, *Rights of Passage*
"tells the story" of the passage from Africa to the Caribbean as a displacement that remains a displacement, simply the obverse, in a sense, of the

coin that had Europe as center and exile on its other face. Indeed, that particular passage was quite evidently part of the same story. Here, Brathwaite echoes Depestre's gesture of passing through the immense wall of noise erected by a violent European history, to try and find again the sounds of a silenced Africa:

Dans mon coeur il y a quelque part	In my heart there is somewhere
Un mur du son	A wall of sound
Qui se dresse, géant, nuit et jour	That rises, gigantic, night and day
Entre le monde et moi.	Between the world and me.
Est-ce la mer traversée jadis?	Is it the sea crossed long ago?
Est-ce mon aïeul enchaîné	Is it my ancestor chained
Dans la cale d'un négrier?	In a slave-ship's hold?
Est-ce toi Afrique qui saigne	Is it you Africa who bleed
Dans mes profondeurs?	In my deepest parts?
Est-ce toi que je dois franchir	Is it you through whom I must pass
Pour être tout à fait moi-même?	To be altogether myself?

("Le mur du son," *Journal* 38)

Perhaps this will later be Philip's discovery of the sounds of silence. In *The Arrivants, Masks* told the further tale of a modern poet's return to Africa, less as a search for "roots" than as a way to compose cultural remains into something more "whole," whose masks become successive distancings from a self that will ultimately be thereby able to become part of a collectivity. Again, in a way, this repeats Depestre's search for new–lost–sounds: "Ouvrez la bouche de mes tambours / Et versez-leur à boire" (Open the mouths of my drums / And pour them something to drink) ("Mes tambours ont soif," *Journal* 41)... drums no less important to Brathwaite, as he describes their making–drawing skin from the death of a goat, barrel from the hard forest trees, sticks from the "stripped tree," accompaniment from the "Gourds and Rattles"–and at the last the "gong-gong" leading into its song (*Masks* 94-7):

> *Kon kon kon kon*
> *Kun kun kun kun*
> *Funtumi Akore*
> *Tweneboa Akore*
> *Tweneboa Kodia*
> *Kodia Tweneduru* ("Atumpan," M 98)

Can these take passage back to the poet's home in the *Islands* whence he came? The third part of the trilogy answers the question with another: can remnants that Africa may "put together" be anything but residual shards in these displaced islands? Yet it is as shards, pieces fit for recovery, creation, building that they can be fitted into a cultural space that is, precisely, Caribbean—a *home* space.

Brathwaite's poetry has never sought easy answers. There was certainly no hope here for one. This last "conclusion," if it were not to remain a pious wish, required broad cultural work. Already in the late 1950s, Brathwaite had started writing criticism of Caribbean literary work, and it has always accompanied his poetry and, equally importantly, his work as a historian. That latter work was clearly essential: to understand the place that was and is Barbados and its island companions and the African, European and American history in which it and they participated. This is not the place to examine the details of that work. What is important, here, is how it informs the poetry and criticism, infusing it with that very sense of an "environment," a place, of particular historical experience, which is and is not that of Europeans—or Africans, or other Americans (although it may be worth noting that the effort to make anew a culture's voice is seconded by an educative one, where he has made his scholarly work the basis of textbooks for schoolchildren of the Caribbean).

Suffice it to say, as the three metaphors with which I began suggest, that this work has always explored issues similar to that found in the poetry and criticism. One way to get at this, perhaps, and to give it a wider context, is to suggest that the ten years Brathwaite spent in Africa (mainly Ghana) enabled him to propose, like Depestre in the closing lines of "Mes tambours ont soif", that the ancient drums of a lost African past might themselves at last make the Atlantic passage:

O forêt qui a soif	O thirsty forest
O tambours haïtiens	O Haitian drums
Patience, frères,	Patience, brothers,
La rosée est en route	The dew is on its way
	(*Journal* 42)

The last line's reference to Jacques Roumain's celebrated 1944 novel, *Gouverneurs de la rosée* (Masters of the Dew), asserts coming control over one's own political and social destiny, over the geography of one's home. This is to make a passage akin, too, to that expressed by Lamming's Trumper, who comes back from the United States having discovered his group identity as a black. Memory, a sense of place, above all a culture-consciousness are embodied for Trumper in this recognition, so that the old "big bad feeling in the pit of the stomach," the dizziness and emptiness are forgotten: "A man who knows his people won't ever feel like that" (*Castle* 300-1). Brathwaite came close to paraphrasing these sentences in the characterization we saw of the anglophone Caribbean novel as marked by frustration, bewilderment and lack of a center. In West Africa, he found both the possibility of a new group belonging and a place which grounded many of the fragments he had found and was to find in the Caribbean.

But none of this is to say, as some critics have clamored, that he simplistically set Europe aside. "West Indian literature" had to be seen, he wrote in 1967, in its "proper context of an expression both European and African at the same time" ("Jazz and the West Indian Novel," *Roots*[1] 62-3). It is to say, however, that fragments of the one had to be set against, recovered from, built into the "imposure" of the other (*Contradictory* 61 and passim). Brathwaite was now prepared to go beyond both those he had once criticized and his own criticism. He would seek the home from a discovery of Caribbean geography and its meaning in history (skipped stones and their fall; rock hiding vital waters; windstorms of Africa–Saharan *harmattan*–that are now, after him, understood to affect the December-February droughts that strike the islands and the aforementioned hurricanes), by reconstructing the shards of fragmented cultural memory, by historical recovery, folk recall, and exploration in a poetry that would set out to find not only a Caribbean "content," but its own form of expression, its own rhythms and music. This last he would eventually draw from his work on jazz forms, his sensitivity to local sounds and images, and his deep awareness of the cultural importance of drumming rhythms, refound and remade from more distant rattles, gourds and drums. But he would also explore the wider more general possibility of "nation language": a language that would itself echo "the environmental experience."

For one–disastrous–way for the colonized mind to face down its colonizer is to do what some did to the normative pentameter: fragment it, take it apart, break it up: even though, as Brathwaite argues, to do so still leaves it as the only hegemonic form. And what the fragmenter risks getting, and indeed gets in the end, is "a frantic impoverished dialect." This is to cite Harris describing the speech of one of his protagonists, Hassan, in *The Far Journey of Oudin*. He is matched by Kaiser, who had but "a few words of formal English." Neither of them can possibly come close to grasping the "unearthly delicate writing on the sky." And to Hassan's imagined wish to go back to India, Kaiser responds by protesting: "What language had he save the darkest and frailest outline of an ancient style and tongue? Not a blasted thing more." "You have no language," says another, "you have no custom." That is why the Hindus' Indian father feels so distanced from them: "we got to forgive he," says one of them, "for the strict unfathomable way he got of looking at we like if he grieving for a language. In ancient scorn and habit at the hard careless words we does use. But is who fault if the only language we got is a breaking-up or a making-up language?" (*Guyana* 179-82, 155).

One cannot just "create a language" or "rescue...the word" from its possessors, as Eduardo Galeano writes. No doubt a writer's feel for "his or her people—their roots, their vicissitudes, their destiny--and the ability to perceive the heartbeat, the sound and rhythm of the authentic counterculture" must be intense ("In Defense of the Word," *We Say No* 141-42, 138). But what and where is such "*another* culture"? How can one recognize its "authenticity"? To say so much leaves yet unsaid the matter of *how* one might create or rescue language and word. One does neither *e nihilo*: one uses, combines, fuses and recombines myriad elements from the varied sources that forge everyone's homes or home. These elements already always exist, doing so in cultural experiences and environments whose ramifications may often escape notice. Whatever impoverishment is theirs, they remain remnants of a particular culture, and will do so until we know enough of *that* experience and ours to be able to use them otherwise. "Collective identity is born out of the past and is nourished by it" (Galeano, "Defense" 138). We must know the working of the elements composing that past and the identities arising from it. To think one can adopt them without preparation as if they were neutral is almost surely to fall back into the patterns customary to the words one supposed one was rescuing: not--perhaps--impoverished, but still colonized.

Brathwaite traced those difficulties—with anger—in *Black + Blues*. There, the angry breaking away from the consequences of colonization and oppression, of cultural "imposure," made use of his gradual uncovering of jazz forms, local sounds and images, the rhythm of the drum, the fragmented shards of cultural memory: to rejoin them into something potentially new. Anger, while it is surely the only appropriate response to the theft of a language and a culture, clearly risks rejecting altogether the very elements it must of necessity use: "like a rat/ like a rat/like a rat-a-tap tappin/ /like a rat/like a rat/like a rat-a-tap tappin/ /an we burnin babylone" ("Conqueror," BB[1] 19, 23). These lines were to be repeated in *Sun Poem* (1982), where they signal even more emphatically Caliban's revolt. *Black + Blues* then takes the reader through a triple sequence of understanding.

The opening anger stresses dismay and disgust of a poet forced to pick through "Fragments" marking the loss of his own culture and the sinister "gift" of the pieces permitted by another only to serve its own interests. Then comes the outrage of "Drought," facing the consequences of oppression: Caliban as "victim of the cities' victory" (BB[1] 30), London or Madrid, Paris or Amsterdam (La Rose's imprisonment in English, Spanish, French or Dutch); Caliban, too, confronting visions of a place that "is no white man lan'/ an' yet we have ghetto here" (32), the exile geography of Philip's anger, neocolonial Babylon of the island itself. This yields to the further outrage of being forced to violence to avenge what has been taken (a violence that usually destroys its own), and at the adulteration of African memories: "a forgotten kingdom" (43), a yearning still borne in pain. Yet, at the last, we find the hopefulness of "Flowers": the rediscovery of fragments, African and Caribbean, based in firm geography of place: "the seas drummers/ /softly softly on sound.../it is a beginning" ("Harbour" 83); in the symbol and existence of "Crab," who holds memory and geography together; and in the final hope of "Koker," with its "coastline" lying beneath "the sounds of stretched light...the don drumming light, against/sky that is their living monument" (90). Such could be a geography no longer of exile, where remnant drums of Africa meet those of North American jazz and blues and Caribbean pan.

Black + Blues captured the dismay, frustration, bewilderment, decentering and grief of Harris' characters in their linguistic and cultural deprivation, but found a way to tap new rhythms, a confident history and a solid sense of place(s) to start making something otherwise. In a way, it repeated in concentrated little the movement of *Arrivants*. We seem to be shifting here from what we may once more call, again after Ngugi and Mphahlele, a decolonizing of the mind, towards something that may be yet harder, something that requires remapping the terrain, reclaiming the soul. Brathwaite's second trilogy, *Ancestors* (as it is now called), consisting of *Mother Poem*, *Sun Poem* and *X/Self*, furthered these themes. The first was, so to speak, a discovery of the *place* of Barbados. The poet's quest to know and remember his mother is rediscovery of Barbadian geography, imbued with the Atlantic call of Africa and Europe, but essentially now *itself*, its own, with its own no-longer buried culture. Out of the submerged coral of the island comes its waters of life as out of various cultural practices, now *seen* for the first time, come submerged but ever-less fragmented cultural forms, completing the hope expressed at the end of *Black + Blues*. The poet himself gets a grounded (new, but also culturally old) name.

Sun Poem next pursued the poet's paternal "genealogy," confirming his place in the land less "mythically," through the family grounding of grandfather, father, son and memories of the boy's childhood. The son's name of Adam symbolized this rooting, discovery, and, no doubt above all, the poet's *invention* of the new. *X/Self* finally explored the poet's now affirmed grounding in past and present, in Europe and Africa, in violence and oppression as well as in tact, grace and renewal. The islands have become, too, a place of and for their *own* people: "not fe dem/not fe dem / de way caliban / done / / but fe we / fe a-we" (*X/Self* 84-5). This poem was to be reworked, rewritten, and lengthened as "Letter Sycorax" in *Middle Passages*, where the poet himself became and superseded the old Caliban of a past that still depended on fragments tied to a particular hegemonic memory (*Middle*[1] 76-88; *Middle*[2] 93-116). Answering (for example) Galeano's dilemma, this shift may prove as important a one for the Caribbean imagination as was Roberto Fernández Retamar's replacement of Rodó's Ariel by Caliban himself, following Fanon's acid rejection of Mannoni's oppressive (and repressive) European theme. The negation, aggression and denial with which Rodó's "Uncle Tom" was finally rejected yield here to new cultural creation.

Not for nothing did Brathwaite finish the second trilogy by rewriting "Shango," a poem that came towards the end of *Black + Blues*. There the poem had started : "huh/there is a new breath here/ /hah/there is a sound of sparrows" (75). "Xango" begins: *"Hail/* there is new breath here/ */huh/* there is a victory of sparrows" (107). The more European-like "hail" (befitting conquering Rome of the beginning of *X/Self*) was now combined with the thunder-god's "huh", noncommittal "sound" became the more optimistic "victory"–still perhaps not altogether freed of indecent hegemonies. But if these sparrows remain marked as the New Testament birds whose fall god would heed as much as a human's, in other texts we could see them become something altogether sharper: victims who turn against the oppressors their own instruments to be free to occupy their own geography and make their own history. Their victory may risk being understood as a version of a central tenet of a text crucial to the European imagination– "and the meek shall inherit the earth." But an earlier poem in *Mother Poem* takes this urgent "huh" to figure a break from European imposition.

Listening to a fundamentalist Baptist church service sung by those 'meek', the poet overhears an entire shift in culture. First iambic hymns move to the dactylic 'praaaze be to', ending in the single syllable, 'god', itself lengthening into a kind of guttural sigh ('ggg'). Little by little the verbal dactyls yield to a simple trainlike rhythm, followed by a long exhaled sigh: 'bub-a-dups / bub-a-dups / bub-a-dups / huh / bub-a-dups / bub-a-dups / bub-a-dups / hah', a sigh stretching to long 'shshshshsh' and at last able to be heard as 'shaaaaaango'. Christian colonization is already ruptured here in *loas* of a different continent and different cultures welling up in language with the rhythms and sounds of Shango, the menacing hiss of the Dahomeyan serpent god of the sky, Yoruba Oshumare or Haitian Damballah breaking through the song of a Baptist hymn in "Angel/Engine" (MP 97-103: a much longer "account"/"version" is in BP 177-202).

At the end of *X/Self,* even if only momentarily, the poet of the second trilogy seemed to have found a moment of that "tact and selfless grace" he found necessary for such peace and balance in the much earlier *Contradictory Omens* (61). It is in light of this that we should read the humorously-expressed sense of hope maintained in *Middle Passages* (even after the most catastrophic losses, personal and intellectual): "is a matter of hope.of keep hope alive.to continue the dream / cause we able.about our rightful place at the table," he wrote in "Duke. Playing Piano at 70" (*Middle*[1] 27; *Middle*[2] 24). Of this collection, Fenella Copplestone observed: "its menace is real, its compassion touches the deepest springs of sadness, and its mythology is potent and frightening. People die in his world" (Review).

But people also live there, and if the world has menace it is to those whose control is overthrown by it. For here death is not the lurking disease, at least momentarily endemic to Enlightened reason, recorded, we saw, in seeming unthreatening expansive linear pentameter. Death plays its accepted and unfearful part in the ineluctable rhythm of life, the balanced experience of tact and grace. The "menace" of this poetry (poor, but revealing, word) is of a site composed from fragments no longer just remnants of things lost, but living crystals recombined and fused into consciousness of a place that does now capture fully "the *natural* experience, the *environmental* experience" of which Brathwaite was writing twenty years and more ago.

It touches the deepest springs of sadness because the people who die there are vital, crucial to the remaking; their loss--one loss, anyway--is incomprehensible disaster: "without reason," he wrote in the dedication of *X/Self,* "all you hope gone/ev'rything look like it comin out wrong./Why is dat? What it mean?" But these lines come from the last part ("The Return") of *Rights of Passage,* first book of a trilogy whose last word was of hope–"making / with their // rhythms some- / thing torn // and new" (TA 69, 270)--so that the loss itself was now tied to the sense of place. Geography, poetry, self, history come together. The "missile" that was Columbus, that was the whole mighty power of an expansive culture imposed on Africa and the Americas, has yielded to a changed rhythm, a changed voice, the networked circle of Shango hidden in the watered rock beneath the still ongoing destructions of multinational capital, he writes in *Barabajan Poems* (187). Another major impingement of Europe on the Caribbean was of a different missile: a German torpedo sinking the *Cornwallis* in Bridgetown Harbour—but that was fifty years ago. Here, too, marks of European aggression were quickly swallowed by Barbadian waters, becoming a plaything for local boys (153-54, 347-61). This swallowing may also be a harbinger of creation and hope. It is a grieving but vital hope that Brathwaite—and others—have passed along. So Jean 'Binta' Breeze puts it:

> lang time we walking, chile
> lang time
> we shapin mountain
> wid we foot
> lang time
> we makiag waves
> wash rock
>
> an in de walking
> we still
> be doing
> revealing
> wat we is ('Caribe', *Spring Cleaning* 51-2)

Now the older poet returns to the uncle's workshop of his youth, to his limping Bob'ob. In the ruins of the old workshop, he discovers that Bob'ob had carved a forbidden African image–as surprising and mysterious as the carving itself, is its survival over the years in the ruins of Bob'ob's home (BP 155). Limping Bob'ob, holding a lost past of Africa, but also opening it unbeknownst to the poet, can be recognized as Legba, divine trickster god of Dahomey, once a force of primal energy, now "the limping/ crippled African god of the crossroads of beginnings & opening doors - as Bob'ob as Toussaint Louverture—the Liberator or 'Opener' of S Domingue into Haiti—himself a cripple—*fatras baton* they once called him...and whose French sobriquet—'Louverture'—was surely a direct translation of the Dahomey Legba (Open/Doorway) & why not?" (172). And what of the poet himself? New "Adam" of *Sun Poem*, inventor of new names, opener of culture, finder of lost presences, joiner of remnants–may he not fill the same role? And why not? He finds too that Bob'ob's ruined workshop has become a Zion meeting hall, a place of worship for a fundamentalist "Christian" group not happily accepted by authorities (166).

Now again, as in *Mother Poem*, listening outside, the poet hears the rhythm of their worship, their singing/chanting, and their movement/dancing slowly change, "the sound of their voices has gradually gone through an alteration of orbit & pitch . they are into the pull of an alteration of consciousness as if the tides of their lives have paused on the brin(k) of falling onto our beaches & instead have slowly lifted themselves up up up so that the cries that should have been breaking from their crests do not move anymore but glisten in the deep silence of their throats until they begin to sweep slowly backwards like away from our shore from our trees from our hills away from Barbados" (BP 181-2). Rhythm changes, dance moves, cadence slips into the hoarse measured breathing of Shango's visitation. Christian hymnal pentameters give way to a different syncopated drumbeat, that is also the echoed blues and jazz rhythms of the old trains, "sulphur and fire into a sibilant & quiet acceptance of her trans-formation like Aretha coming home in *Pullin*" (196-7: I cannot attempt here to capture Brathwaite's typographical play, his "Sycorax" computer style, echoing visually the changing sounds of voice and rhythm of dance). "Until there is at last what there always was / SHANGO / as she struggles to name almost names him the train comin in/ comin in / comin in wid de rain" (200-1; and see MP 98-103).

Barabajan Poems culminated for a moment the movement traced here. Bringing together the three metaphors with which we started, it transforms them into the vital essence of a culture. Legba, Shango, the rhythms, voice and history that together make a whole have come together with other shards of other cultures: steam trains and blues, Christian hymns and jazz, the "rattle and pain" of loss and deprivation (201) with the vivid hope of new names and endless depth of proverbial orality (268-83). Proverbs are another link with a local past still alive in everyday material exchange. They are, Achebe avers, "like citing the precedents in law." They set a present case in ancestral context, give "a certain connectedness" and help "banish the sense of loneliness, the cry of desolation" (*Conversations* 180). Brathwaite is here far indeed from Pope, Thomson, Gray and Froude–not to mention the falling snow of his Cambridge youth. He is very far, too, from those bewildered tales of emigration typical of the Caribbean writers of his youth–and still perfectly usual, we saw: both are, we have of course been suggesting, aspects of the *same*, very partial and interested, history–and place (which is not–not just, and not first–Caribbean). *Barabajan Poems* confirms the hopefulness of the lighted living coastline that ended *Black + Blues*, and affirms the embedded collective 'self' of *X/Self* into what seems a quite new cultural, natural, environmental surety.

This, though, seems a moment of "equilibrium", ambivalent as it was, that the poet has left behind him. On the whole, since 1977 when *Mother Poem* first appeared, his voice has grown bleaker. Publishing the complete trilogy in 2001, Brathwaite adds and subtracts poems, rewrites all in Sycorax, changing rhythms, cadences, tones, emotions. In particular, perhaps, he adds the "bittern poem", "Pixie", deliberately interrupting *Mother Poem*'s flow with the story of a child's flight from horror and consequent prostituting, marking a changing Barbados, a Barbados where the sparrows live in fear and the voice runs hoarse; where the child

>stripped even of her sweat &sweet & sleep & sarrow
>so many serpent esses in this silence where he waits

she watches. a whisper at the corner sounding scared
This scaly voice of sound. dry shak shak shackle podes scrape

Scrabble on the ravage concrete brown
(Mother Poem, Ancestors 53)

'He' is the policeman who prostitutes the child, the politician who prostitutes his island, the journalist on bended knee to both. The poem joins
newspaper report, letters (from Pixie/Stephanie) and commentary, narrating the corrupting of community and especially of childhood, law and order's
role in that corruption, indeed the community's making of it.

This story of the loss of innocence is new here, however "traditional",
even "Wordsworthian", it may be in other regards. Particularly damning is
the bleak indifference, even exploitation, that is the the story's context and
overwhelm its atmosphere. "Pixie", with the many other changes Brathwaite
has wrought in the trilogy's first book, tends to subvert the rural/urban
courtesies of *Mother Poem*'s earlier version, marking an erosion that "Pixie"
makes stunningly clear. *Mother Poem* retains its deep compassion and a
certain sense of tact and gentleness, but these are now joined by anger
deeper and more evident than before. Not only "Pixie" marks this change:
so, too, do the now more-urgent breach of standard English, changes in
rhythm created by Sycorax, assured handling of unfamiliar word-breaks–
deliberate sappings of an imposed language–, disruption of what had been
a certain "evenness" of tone, hugely increased variation of voice and cadence. Together they signal a loss of innocence that is not just the child's
but the island's–and surely the poet's as well. It picks up on the new anger
and something often close to despair apparent in such other writings of the
1990s as the anguishingly personal *Zea Mexican Diary* and the painful
Trench Town Rock, indicting local victim/thug and his colonial creator at
one and the same time. Yet the sunken warship turned boys' plaything now
finds its way into the long 'Bubbles' of *Sun Poem*, and if a poem like
'Clips', with its 'harf-arse' planter father/unfather, uneasy mixed blood
children and legacy of desperate stress, conveys an atmosphere of decayed
racism, sexual violence but compassion still for a history not altogether
lost but the *wrong one*, even so the sense of *place* making culture—from
histories of its own, among other ways—remains no less overwhelming.

Galeano wrote that "a literature born in the process of crisis and change,
and deeply immersed in the risks and events of its time, can indeed help to
create the symbols of the new reality, and perhaps...throw light on the signs
along the road" ("Defense" 139). Brathwaite, poet, historian and critic, has
brought us—and himself—somewhere else, into a "web," it may be, as
Harris puts it, "born of the music of the elements" (*Guyana* 7). The poet

offers a reply of grace and tact to inertias of a European literature whose forms still by and large correspond to needs fixed four centuries ago and query them, sap them, only with a great tentativeness of difficulty, striving against political, economic and cultural forces whose interests lie in pursuing and retaining a familiar and customary history into the present (pretending its conflicts over: Reiss, *Meaning* 338-47). This is indeed why Brathwaite argued the need not just to fragment, break up or in some other way "subvert" the pentameter, the King's or Queen's English it measured and the cultural meanings it transported, but to break with these altogether, drumming the rhythms of different histories, singing the marks of a different geography, in sadness no doubt but also in hope and in humor. Still another younger poet has picked up here on Brathwaite's practice and hopes, tying them to Jamaican urban and rastafarian life. Mervyn Morris reports the dub poet Oku Onuora saying at a public debate in 1986:

> Dub poetry simply means to take out and to put in, but more fi put in more than anything else. We take out the little isms, the little English ism and the little highfalutin business and the little penta-metre...that is what dub poetry mean. It's dubbing out the little penta-metre and the little highfalutin business and dubbing in the rootsical, yard, basic rhythm that I-an-I know. Using the language, using the body. It also mean to dub out the isms and schisms and to dub consciousness into the people-dem head. That's dub poetry. (Morris, *"Is English"* 38)

I have tried to suggest—as this collection does—that Brathwaite is already followed by a legion of artists and critics questioning and turning imposed or inherited cultural "instruments"—those practices, reasons, devices and stories that define a culture's self-understanding. He has of course never been alone in doing so either, and it is worth adding one more older voice to those of his contemporaries already heard, that of Claude McKay who like them (and Onuora) spoke in similar terms of "Babylon" imposing its isms, its doings and beliefs, via the familiar rhythms of its language:

> Around me roar and crash the pagan isms
> To which most of my life was consecrate,
> Betrayed by evil men and torn by schisms
> For they were built on nothing more than hate!
> (*Selected Poems* 49; cf. Morris, *"Is English"* 96)

Like these now many others, Brathwaite deeply questions and reworks–replays—many cultural instruments: those in particular we have seen. He has translated Philip's "*i-mage*," the irreducible intuition of a place and its people, creating "new *i-mages* that speak to [their] essential being" (*Genealogy* 43). He has done as much as any to confront colonial oppression, decolonize minds and reclaim a culture's soul. On all of these, finding new i-mages, decolonizing minds and reclaiming the soul, he wrote wistfully from his Barbadian and Jamaican cultural situations of an advantage he saw in Aubrey Williams' Guyanese one, not so stripped and destroyed as that of the islands:

> he could actually *see* the ancient art of the Warraou Indians. Living with them placed him in a significant continuum with it; for high up on the rocks at Tutatumari, at Imbaimadai, people who were perhaps of Mayan origin—the ancestors of the Warraou and others in the area—had made marks, or *timehri*: rock signs, paintings, petroglyphs; glimpses of a language, glitters of a vision of a world, scattered utterals of a remote *Gestalt*; but still there, near, potentially communicative. Sometimes there were sleek brown bodies that could have been antelope or ocelot; there were horns and claws of crabs. There were triangular forms that might have been the mouths of cenotes. But hints only; gateways to intuitions; abstract signals of hieroglyphic art. To confirm that these marks were made by humans, imprints of the etcher's palm were left beside the work; anonymous brands in living stone, imperishable witness from past to conscious present. ("Timehri"[2] 40)

Brathwaite has been in search of his own *timehri*—in Europe, Africa, Amerindia. Certainly, his pictographs are rather more "phonographs": sounds and whispers, cries and rhythms of cultures whose fragments— opposing claims to the contrary—do survive and are part even of cultures where they once seemed to have been lost. They were but submerged: rhythms of Shango in the hounfort; statue of Africa by uncle Bob'ob/Legba in a ruined workshop; hidden fresh streams in the limestone of Barbados-- like those imaged cenotes of Guyana or the Yucatan. Brathwaite has been retrieving, present already in his Caribbean world, what Harris calls "a complex mutuality of cultures" (*Womb* 18), breaking across old boundaries, forging new links with different homes, yet staying clearly enlaced in his own—enabling from his *timehri* not some hybrid mush, but new mutualities of distinct vernaculars. Brathwaite is foremost among those who offer a model and an image of such vital practices—crucial in our time— expressing in his life and in his poetry that "elation" which Walcott once applied, particularly, to two older poets, Saint-John Perse and Aimé Césaire: a "staggering elation in possibility" ("Muse" 17).

But this possibility is not just one of elation. These complex mutualities entail other sorts of responsibility, ones calling for the deep pity of a passion without sentiment—to adapt a phrase of Brathwaite's, making history and poetry outcries against violence and oppression, demands for other sorts of attention and justice. Such poetry he has made in the past, such poetry he is writing now, attending to present violences and suffering of desperate, postcolonial catastrophe. He has found and created experience natural to the place that is his, itself made a whole from what had been the blighted fragments he recorded in earlier poetry. This is to go beyond decolonizing the mind, becoming aware of the forms and content of colonization, so as to remove—or at least see past and between—the accretions of alien "imposure." It is to remap an environment, a history, a geography, a culture and an experience. It is to reclaim the soul.

Notes

1. This Introduction appeared more briefly as "Reclaiming the Soul: Poetry, Autobiography, and the Voice of History" in *World Literature Today* 68.4 (Autumn 1994): 683-90. A longer version, exploring connections with Césaire and using other of Brathwaite's more recent writings, will be Chapter Eight of my *Against Autonomy*.

2. Michael Gomez has collated the most reliable figures concerning the geographical origins of slaves imported to north America, many of whom came via Caribbean islands. Parts of Africa were exploited differently at different times, but overall, between the 1620s and 1830s, nearly a quarter of the slaves came from the Bight of Biafra, mostly Igbo–a proportion virtually even with that of slaves brought from the whole of West Central Africa, which included peoples from all down the coast and inland from modern Cameroon, Equatorial Guinea and Gabon through Congo to Angola (*Exchanging* 29, 114-5). Since the Bight of Biafra was a principal British trading area, these proportions could well be more lopsided for the British Caribbean.

3. "Lettre à Dobzynski," *Optique* 18 (August 1955): 46-50, here 48, quoted by Joan Dayan, "Introduction" 32. Aimé Césaire offered a sharp "Réponse à Depestre" in the same *Optique* (50-2). In a further "Réponse à Césaire" (*Optique* 24 [Feb. 1956]: 5-33), Depestre asked how colonized peoples, "American, and even Negro American," could take on "the adventure of English verse without a preliminary meditation on the forms utilized in Great Britain, from Chaucer to Dylan Thomas? Can one believe that Whitman rushed into the luminous swell of verse without having reflected upon that of Shakespeare?...In a word, does a revolutionary and human content really make a work of art? What would Rimbaud be without the carnal triumph of his verse?" ("Réponse" 16-17; Dayan 29: her translation). Brathwaite might agree but argue (like Philip

and others) that just because form *is* inseparable from "revolutionary" content is why "the adventure" is one that demands that poets find forms embedded in their own cultural reality.

4. T. S. Eliot, "Scylla and Charybdis," *Agenda* 23 (1985): 11. Quoted by Schuchard in Eliot, *Varieties* 53n20.

5. To friends in the incipient Caribbean Artists Movement Ramchand had written in January 1967 that Caribbean writers and artists should do their best to get home to the West Indies and do their cultural work there (as he did in 1968, right away starting with Brathwaite the journal *Savacou* for this proselytizing goal) (Walmsley 53-4, 190). He had been in Britain for some years, writing his doctorate at Edinburgh University (*ibid.* 28) and even after leaving, it was perhaps a lingering sense of being in a tradition without *home* support, with exile inevitable, that imposed pride in Caribbean achievement abroad (Walmsley 105, 172-3, 200-6).

Linton Kwesi Johnson: Two Poems

If I Woz A Tap-Natch Poet

"dub poetry has been described as... 'over-compensation for deprivation'"
(Oxford Companion to Twentieth-Century Poetry)

"mostofthestraighteningisinthetongue"
(Bongo Jerry)

if I woz a tap-natch poet
like Chris Okigbo
Derek Walcott
ar T.S.Eliot

ah woodah write a poem
soh dam deep
dat it bittah-sweet
like a precious
memory
whe mek yu weep
whe mek yu feel incomplete

like wen yu lovah leave
an dow defeat yu kanseed
still yu beg an yu plead
till yu win a repreve
an yu ready fi rack steady
but di muzik done aready

still
inna di meantime
wid mi riddim
wid mi rime
wid mi ruff base line

wid mi own sense a time
goon poet haffi step in line
caw Bootahlazy mite a gat couple touzan
but Mandela fi im
touzans a touzans a touzans a touzans

if I woz a tap-natch poet
like Kamau Brathwaite
Martin Carter
Jayne Cortez ar Amiri Baraka

ah woodah write a poem
soh rude
an rootsy
an subversive
dat it mek di goon poet
tun white wid envy

like a candhumble/ voodoo/ kumina chant
a ole time calypso ar a slave song
dat get ban
but fram granny

> rite
> dung
> to
> gran
> pickney

each an evry wan
can recite dat-dey wan

still
inna di meantime
wid mi riddim
wid mi rime
wid mi ruff base line
wid mi own sense a time

goon poet haffi step in line
caw Bootahlazy mite a gat couple touzan
but Mandela fi im
touzans a touzans a touzans a touzans

if I woz a tap-natch poet
like Tchikaya U'tamsi
Nicholas Guillen

ar Lorna Goodison

an woodah write a poem
soh beautiful dat it simple
like a plain girl
wid good brains
an nice ways
wid a sexy dispozishan
an plenty compahshan
wid a sweet smile
an a suttle style

still
mi naw goh bow an scrape
an gwan like a ape
peddlin noh puerile parchment af etnicity
wid ongle a vaig fleetin hint af hawtenticity
like a black Lance Percival in reverse
ar even worse
a babblin bafoon whe looze im tongue

no sah
nat atall
mi gat mi riddim
mi gat mi rime
mi gat mi ruff base line
mi gat mi own sense a time

goon poet bettah step in line
caw Bootahlazy mite a gat couple touzan
but Mandela fi im
touzans a touzans a touzans a touzans

July 1994

Hurricane Blues

lang-time lovah
mi mine run pan yu all di while
an mi membah ow fus time
di two a wi come een - it did seem
like two shallow lickle snakin stream
mawchin mapless hapless a galang
tru di ruggid lanscape a di awt sang

an a soh wi did a gwaan
sohtil dat fateful day
awftah di pashan a di hurricane
furdah dan imaginaeshan ar dream
wi fine wiself lay-dung pan di same bedrack
flowing now togheddah as wan stream
ridin sublime tru love lavish terrain
lush an green an brite awftah di rain
shimmarin wid glittahrin eyes
glowin in di glare a di smilin sun

lang-time lovah
mi feel blue fi true wen mi tink bout yu
blue like di sky lingahrin pramis af rain
in di leakin lite in di hush af a evenin twilite
wen mi membah ow fus time
di two wi come een - it did seem
like a lang lang rivah dat is wide an deep

sometime wi woz silent like di langwidge a rackstone
sometime wi woodah sing wi rivah sang as wi a wine a galang
sometime wi jus cool an caam andah plenty shady tree
sometime sawfly lappin bamboo root as dem swing an sway
sometime cascadin carefree doun a steep gully bank
sometime turbulent in tempahment wi flood wi bank
but weddah ebb ar flow tru rain tru drout
wi nevah stray far fram love rigid route

ole-time sweet-awt
up til now mi still cyaan andahstan
ow wi get bag doun inna somuch silt an san
rackstone debri lag-jam
sohtil wi ad woz fi flow wi sepahret pawt
now traversin di tarrid terrain a love lanscape

4

runnin fram di polueshun af a cantrite awt
mi lang fi di marvelous miracle a hurricane
fi carry mi goh a meetin stream agen
lamentin mi saltid fate
sohmizin seh it too late

April 1994

For We Who Have Achieved Nothing

Maryse Condé

Aujourd'hui, il est de bon ton de minimiser l'importance de l'origine africaine dans la culture des Caraïbes et de considérer la plantation comme le laboratoire qui généra le métissage qui la spécifie. Kamau Brathwaite fait partie de cette génération d'intellectuels antillais pour qui l'Afrique représentait la terre matricielle et que la quête des origines conduisit à la redécouverte de ses sources. Il appartient à cette génération dont l'imaginaire se construisit d'abord sur des clichés imposés par l'Europe et qui dut se déconstruire mentalement en pratiquant une traversée à rebours. Ce voyage de retour vers le continent dont il avait été dépossédé avant que de naître et dont l'absence le lancinait comme une blessure a donné naissance à quelques-uns des plus beaux poèmes dont puisse s'enorgueillir notre littérature: la trilogie *Rights of Passage* (1967), *Masks* (1968), *Islands* (1969), reprise plus tard sous le titre *The Arrivants* (1973).

Dans un interview parmi les essais qui composent *The Art of Kamau Brathwaite* (1995) réunis par Stewart Brown, le poète s'est clairement expliqué sur son choix de la trilogie:

> [I]t was really, écrit-il, a matter of raising an issue, replying to that issue and trying to create a synthesis. In other words, the first question, which is in *Rights of Passage*, is: How did we get into the Caribbean? Our people, the black people of the Caribbean—what was the origin of their presence in the Caribbean? And the antithesis to that was—well, the answer which emerged was that they came out of migration out of Africa, so that the second movement in the tril-

For We Who Have Achieved Nothing

Maryse Condé

It's good form nowadays to minimize the importance of African origins in Caribbean culture and to consider the plantation as the laboratory that produced the *métissage* characterizing it. Kamau Brathwaite belongs to that generation of Caribbean intellectuals for whom Africa represented the mother land and whom the search for origins led to rediscover African sources. He belongs to that generation whose imaginary was constructed first on stereotypes imposed by Europe and which had to deconstruct its mind by undertaking a passage in reverse. This return journey towards the continent of which he had been dispossessed before birth and whose absence stabbed him like a wound has given birth to some of the finest poems our literature can boast: the trilogy *Rights of Passage* (1967), *Masks* (1968), *Islands* (1969), brought together later under the title, *The Arrivants* (1973).

In an interview included among the essays composing *The Art of Kamau Brathwaite* (1995), edited by Stewart Brown, the poet has clearly expounded his choice of the trilogy:

> [I]t was really a matter of raising an issue, replying to that issue and trying to create a synthesis. In other words, the first question, which is in *Rights of Passage*, is: How did we get into the Caribbean? Our people, the black people of the Caribbean—what was the origin of their presence in the Caribbean? And the antithesis to that was— well, the answer which emerged was that they came out of migration out of Africa, so that the second movement in the trilogy was the answer to that question. Hence, *Masks*. And then, we came out of

8

ogy was the answer to that question. Hence, *Masks*. And then, we came out of Africa and went into the New World. Hence, *Islands*. (Mackey, "Interview"[2] 13)

Il découle de ces explications que la trilogie de Brathwaite peut effectivement se lire comme une réécriture poétique d'un Middle Passage à l'envers, c'est-à-dire une tentative de renouer les liens rompus entre la mère Afrique et ses enfants de la Diaspora: "The paths," se lamente-t-il, "we shall never remember / again: Atumpan talking and the harvest Branch- / es, all the tribes of Ashanti dreaming the dream / of Tutu, Anokye and the Golden Stool, built / in Heaven for our nation by the work / of lightning and the brilliant adze: and now nothing" (RP 13).

Rights of Passage est donc le volume qui signifie la perte et de l'angoisse; angoisse qui résulte de l'ignorance et peut-être de la peur de connaître son origine. Sa tonalité est sombre. Dans la mémoire collective ne se chevauchent que d'obsessives images, amères et persistantes comme celles de Ceddo du cinéaste Sembène Ousmane: "Flame burns the village down." Des plaintes le traversent qui rappellent celles de *Return to my Native Land* (1938) et en vérité, bien que tant d'années les séparent, le fait est bien connu, le nègre de Césaire trouve un frère en celui de Brathwaite:

> no dreams
> for us
> no hopes
> no scabs
> to heal
> in the hot
> sun neither
> no screams
> no whip rope
> lash (RP 28)

Brathwaite s'est expliqué sur sa relation avec Aimé Césaire et avoué qu'il connaissait très peu *Return to my Native Land* au moment où il écrivait cette première trilogie, "even though," dit-il plaisamment, "it had been written when I was nine years old and living in the same backyard of his sea" (Mackey "Interview" 26). La véritable découverte de Césaire sera plus tardive ainsi que les tributs à son oeuvre. Il ne s'agit donc pas dans *Rights of Passage* d'une influence du poète martiniquais sur ses poèmes, mais d'échos de souffrances et d'humiliations partagées par deux esprits nourris dans des terreaux culturels proches. Et ce, malgré les barrières de la langue et de la colonisation. Ces échos et ces similitudes, ces correspon-

Africa and went into the New World. Hence, *Islands*. (Mackey, "Interview"[2] 13)

It follows from these explanations that Brathwaite's trilogy can indeed be read as a poetic rewriting of a Middle Passage in reverse, as an effort, that is, to retie the broken bonds between mother Africa and her children in the Diaspora. "The paths," he laments, "we shall never remember / again: Atumpan talking and the harvest Branch-/ es, all the tribes of Ashanti dreaming the dream / of Tutu, Anokye and the Golden Stool, built / in Heaven for our nation by the work / of lightning and the brilliant adze: and now nothing" (RP 13).

Rights of Passage is therefore the book which signifies loss and anguish; anguish coming from ignorance and perhaps from fear of knowing one's origin. Its tonality is somber. In the collective memory only obsessive images tumble over one another, bitter and unbending images like those of the film-maker Sembène Ousmane's Ceddo: "Flame burns the village down." Laments traverse it that recall those of *Return to my Native Land* (1938), and indeed, although so many years separate them, it is well known that Césaire's nigger finds a brother in Brathwaite's:

> no dreams
> for us
> no hopes
> no scabs
> to heal
> in the hot
> sun neither
> no screams
> no whip rope
> lash   (RP 28)

Brathwaite has talked of his relation with Aimé Césaire and admitted that he hardly knew *Return to my Native Land* when he was writing this first trilogy, "even though," he amusingly says, "it had been written when I was nine years old and living in the same backyard of his sea" (Mackey, "Interview"[2] 26). His real discovery of Césaire will come later along with tributes paid to his work. So in *Rights of Passage* it's not a matter of the Martinican poet's influence on his poems, but of echoes of sufferings and humiliations shared by two minds nurtured in neighboring cultural humus. And this despite barriers of language and colonization. These echoes and these similarities, in a word, these agreements, constitute in advance tangible evidence of that Caribbean Artists' Movement that Brathwaite will

dences en un mot, constituent avant la lettre une manifestation tangible de ce Caribbean Artists Movement que Brathwaite crééra autour de 1970 avec Andrew Salkey et John La Rose et dont les convictions irrigueront toute son oeuvre. Cependant, en dépit de sa peinture négative du Nègre dans *Rights of Passage*, Brathwaite ne s'est jamais attiré les mêmes critiques que Césaire. On sait qu'en 1993, année de ses 80 ans, Césaire découvrit parmi ses cadeaux d'anniversaire l'ouvrage de Raphaël Confiant intitulé *Aimé Césaire: la traversée paradoxale d'un siècle*, ouvrage critique où son cadet accumulait les reproches les plus passionés, à la fois au plan poétique et au plan politique. Déjà, dans l'*Eloge de la Créolité* (1989), le même Raphaël Confiant auquel s'ajoutaient le romancier Patrick Chamoiseau et le linguiste Jean Bernabé, l'accusaient de n'avoir par la Négritude initié aucune pédagogie du Beau. En un mot, Césaire serait accusé, quoi qu'il en dise, de manquer de foi en l'homme Noir et de demeurer dans la dépendance intellectuelle de l'Europe. Nous ne nous engagerons pas dans l'activité stérile qui consiste à évaluer le degré de justesse de pareilles critiques. Ce qui semble important, c'est que Brathwaite y ait échappé entièrement, pour de nombreuses raisons. D'abord, immédiatement après *Rights of Passage*, parut *Masks*, célébration de la grandeur du continent retrouvé, ivresse de la découverte des richesses culturelles. Cette grandeur est principalement symbolisée par celle de la civilisation Akan dont Brathwaite intermêle audacieusement les sonorités avec celles de l'anglais:

Funtumi Akore
Tweneboa Akore
Spirit of the Cedar
Spirit of the Cedar Tree
Tweneboa Kodia
Odomankoma 'Kyerema says... (M 98)

A la question: pourquoi la civilisation Akan? la réponse est double. Elle s'inscrit en partie dans l'histoire littéraire. Nul n'ignore que le Ghana de l'Osagyefo Kwame Nkrumah, c'est-à-dire le Ghana post-colonial des années 60, fit fonction de centre du renouveau intellectual de l'Afrique. Brathwaite compte parmi les nombreux Caribbéens, Africains-Americains qui tels W. E. B. du Bois, Maya Angelou, Tom Feelings ou Julia Wright crurent, jusqu'à la chute du Rédempteur en 1966, tracer des jambages lumineux sur une nouvelle page de l'histoire du monde noir. La réponse s'inscrit aussi au plan de l'anthropologie. La civilisation Akan compte comme une des plus mystérieuses et des plus élaborées de l'Afrique de l'Ouest. Un de ses fondateurs fut le légendaire Osei Tutu. Si en une idéalisation facile, Brathwaite ne manque pas de lui rendre hommage,

create around 1970 with Andrew Salkey et John La Rose and whose convictions will irrigate all his work. Still, in spite of the negative portrait of the Negro in *Rights of Passage*, Brathwaite never incurred the same criticisms as Césaire. It is well known that in 1993, the year he turned 80, Césaire found among his birthday gifts Raphaël Confiant's work titled *Aimé Césaire: la traversée paradoxale d'un siècle*, a critical work where his junior amassed the most impassioned reproaches, on both poetic and political grounds. Already, in "In Praise of Creoleness" (English 1990), the same Raphaël Confiant, joined by the novelist Patrick Chamoiseau and the linguist Jean Bernabé, accused him of not having initiated with Negritude any pedagogy of the Beautiful. In a word, Césaire would be accused, whatever he may say, of lacking faith in the Black man and of remaining in intellectual dependency of Europe. We will not get involved in the sterile activity of trying to evaluate the accuracy (or not) of such criticisms. What seems to matter here is that for many reasons Brathwaite altogether escaped them. First of all, immediately after *Rights of Passage*, *Masks* appeared, celebrating the grandeur of the regained continent, intoxicated with the discovery of its cultural riches. This grandeur is symbolized chiefly by that of Akan civilization, whose sonorities Brathwaite audaciously intermingles with those of English:

> Funtumi Akore
> Tweneboa Akore
> Spirit of the Cedar
> Spirit of the Cedar Tree
> Tweneboa Kodia
> Odomankoma 'Kyerema says... (M 98)

To the question: why Akan civilization? the response is twofold. It is grounded in part in literary history. No one is unaware that the Ghana of Osagyefo Kwame Nkrumah, postcolonial 1960s Ghana, that is, acted as the center of African intellectual renewal. Brathwaite was among the many Caribbeans and African-Americans, like W. E. B. du Bois, Maya Angelou, Tom Feelings or Julia Wright, who until the Redeemer's fall in 1966 believed they could draw luminous strokes on a new page of the black world's history. monde noir. The reply is also grounded in anthropology. Akan civilization counts as one of West Africa's most mysterious and most elaborate. One of its founders was the legendary Osei Tutu. While Brathwaite does not fail to pay tribute to him by means of a simple idealization,

> Osai Tutu
> is coming

Osai Tutu
is coming

'Birempon Tutu
is coming

Whispers of dark
sasabonsam of darkness (M 141-2),

il occulte d'autres aspects de la civilisation Akan, à savoir les sacrifices humains qu'elle pratiqua sur une grande échelle.

Pour tenter de déchiffrer ces "primitifs" qui leur tenaient tête, les Anglais dépêchèrent à Kumasi, "city of gold / paved with silver / ivory altars / tables of horn" (138), un de leurs meilleurs ethnologues-administrateurs, Robert Sutherland Rattray. En dépit de cela, des années entières, ils durent guerroyer afin d'en venir à bout, d'annexer leurs terres, d'humilier l'Asantehene, leur chef suprême. (Sur ce dernier point, Kwame Nkrumah en fit de même, au nom de la démocratie et du progrès; en réalité pour détruire jusqu'au souvenir de son principal rival, J.B. Danquah). Les études prouvent que la culture Akan se perpétue dans les Antilles, via le transbord d'esclaves; en particulier à travers le cycle d'Ananse, le Dieu Créateur qui, dans la littérature orale, assume la forme bénigne de l'araignée. Cependant, Brathwaite ne limite pas son évocation à la grandeur de la civilisation Akan. C'est d'une célébration continentale qu'il s'agit quand, dans une saisie poétique, le poète récuse les dichotomies classiques entre Afrique musulmane, Afrique animiste, Afrique des savanes, Afrique des forêts et se veut un griot pan-africain. Pêle-mêle, des motifs associés à Ougadougou, Timbuctu, Volta, se dessinent au travers des poèmes:

This sacred lake
is the soul
of the world;

winds whirl
born in the soul
of this dark water's world. (M 105)

Selon Maureen Warner-Lewis, dans son article intitulé "Africa: submerged Mother," la présence du lac Tchad peut être perçue comme une métaphore signifiant la mère, l'île, et l'Afrique. "The lake or the pool," écrit-elle, "represents both the subconscious and the unconscious presence of that mother in the personal and ethnic psyche. One mechanism for re-connec-

'Birempon Tutu
is coming

Whispers of dark
sasabonsam of darkness (M 141-2),

he conceals other aspects of Akan civilization, notably its large-scale practice of human sacrifice.

In an effort to decipher these "primitives" who were resisting them, the
English dispatched to Kumasi, "city of gold / paved with silver / ivory
altars / tables of horn" (138), one of their best ethnologist-administrators,
Robert Sutherland Rattray. Despite this, they had to wage war for many
years to break them down, annex their lands, humiliate the Asantehene,
their supreme chieftain. (As to this last, Kwame Nkrumah did the same, in
the name of democracy and progress, in reality to destroy even the memory
of his principal rival, J.-B. Danquah.) Studies prove that Akan culture lives
on in the Caribbean, via the trans-shipment of slaves, particularly in story-
cycles about Anancy, the Creator God who, in oral literature, takes the
spider's benign form. Still, Brathwaite does not limit his evocation to the
grandeur of Akan civilization. The poet celebrates the entire continent when,
in a poetic frenzy, he challenges the classic dichotomies between muslim
Africa, animist Africa, Africa of the savannas, Africa of the forests, and
imagines himself a pan-African *griot*. Themes associated with
Ouagadougou, Timbuktu, Volta take form pell-mell through the poems:

This sacred lake
is the soul
of the world;

winds whirl
born in the soul
of this dark water's world. (M 105)

According to Maureen Warner-Lewis, in her article "Africa: submerged
Mother," the presence of Lake Chad may be seen as a metaphor signifying
mother, island, and Africa. "The lake or the pool," she writes, "represents
both the subconscious and the unconscious presence of that mother in the
personal and ethnic psyche. One mechanism for re-connection with this
pool of submerged consciousness is the ritual possession of the living by
African deities and ancestral dead" (57).

Through *Masks*, Brathwaite's intention seems luminously clear. *Islands*
breaks with this seeming clarity. This third volet comes across as the most

tion with this pool of submerged consciousness is the ritual possession of the living by African deities and ancestral dead" (57).

Jusqu'à *Masks*, l'intention de Brathwaite apparait lumineuse. *Islands* vient rompre cette apparente simplicité. Ce troisième volet se présente comme le plus complexe, car il perturbe la linéarité précédente. En effet, si *Rights of Passage* se situe comme le point de départ du voyage de retour vers la connaissance, *Masks* le point d'arrivée et l'appréhension éclairée de l'intimité, *Islands* emblématise un nouveau retour vers le point de départ. Puisque l'Afrique n'est plus niée, *Islands* devrait signifier une nouvelle naissance, impliquer un réenraçinement plus fécond dans la culture d'origine, aussi, une relecture de son environnement. Après la perversion doudouiste, Glissant a démontré l'importance de la réappropriation de son paysage par l'Antillais. Le paysage est Histoire. Comme il l'écrit dans le *Discours antillais* (1997): "Le renoncement à la poétique du paysage antillais transporte l'être dans un non-pays essential, transparent" (740).

Or dans *Islands*, n'apparaît pas la cohérence, voire la transparence que nous escomptions. Certes, des sections s'intitulent Rebellion, Beginning.... Certes, il ne manque pas de références aux religions autonomes des îles des Caraïbes, aux dieux, aux héros, aux lieux, aux places, comme si tous ces éléments composeraient une mythologie positivisée dont le Caribbéen n'aurait plus honte... . Certes, émerge par endroits l'amorce d'un Chant Général de foi:

> The islands' jewels
> Saba, Barbuda, dry flat-
> tened Antigua, will remain rocks,
> dots, in the sky-blue frame
> of the map. (IS 205)

Mais toutes ces notations, éparses et heurtées, qui s'opèrent dans un style fragmenté, n'édifient pas un contre-discours. Il semble que le poète s'attelle soudain à un autre labeur. Non plus la reconquête des racines africaines, mais la laborieuse prise en compte des réalités caribbéennes. Dans *The Art of Kamau Brathwaite*, Nathaniel Mackey fait observer: "A sense of the emergence of an alternative cultural order, of being present at the inception of a new dispensation, pervades *Islands*.... Language, the cornerstone of cultural order is accordingly prioritized" (134).

Là réside peut-être la difficulté première à appréhender *Islands*, non pas point de retour, mais périmètre d'un nouveau départ. Là réside aussi la puissance innovatrice de Brathwaite:

complex, for it disturbs the preceding linearity. Indeed, if *Rights of Passage* stands as the starting point for a journey back towards knowledge, and *Masks* as the point of arrival and of enlightened understanding of intimacy, *Islands* emblematizes a new return towards the starting point. Because Africa is no longer denied, *Islands* should signify a new birth, imply a more fruitful rerooting in the culture of origin, as well as a rereading of its overall setting. Following the exoticizing *doudouist* perversion, Glissant has shown how important it is for Caribbeans to reappropriate their landscape. Landscape is History. As he writes in *Discours antillais* (1997): "Yielding to the poetics of the Caribbean landscape takes being into an essential, transparent non-land" (740).

Now, in *Islands*, we do not find the coherence, even the transparency we were expecting. To be sure, sections are titled "Rebellion," "Beginning".... To be sure, references to the autonomous religions of the Caribbean islands are not lacking, to gods, heroes, places, localities, as if all these elements would compose concretized mythology of which the Caribbean would no longer be ashamed.... To be sure, here and there the beginning of a General Canto of faith comes into view:

> The islands' jewels
> Saba, Barbuda, dry flat-
> tened Antigua, will remain rocks,
> dots, in the sky-blue frame
> of the map. (IS 205)

But all these scattered and conflicted notations, occurring in fragmented fashion, do not build up a counter-discourse. The poet suddenly seems to harness himself for another labor. No longer reconquest of African roots, but that laborious accounting for Caribbean realities. In *The Art of Kamau Brathwaite*, Nathaniel Mackey points out: "A sense of the emergence of an alternative cultural order, of being present at the inception of a new dispensation, pervades *Islands*.... Language, the cornerstone of cultural order is accordingly prioritized" (134).

There lies perhaps the first difficulty in grasping *Islands*: not a point of return, but perimeter of a new departure. There, too, lies Brathwaite's innovative power:

> it is not
> it is not
> it is not enough
> it is not enough to be free
> of the whips, principalities and powers

it is not
it is not
it is not enough
it is not enough to be free
of the whips, principalities and powers
where is your kingdom of the Word?
....
I
Must be given words to shape my name
to the syllables of trees (IS 222-3)

Contrairement aux idées reçues, la revendication linguistique s'est fait entendre tardivement dans les Caraïbes. Il n'y a guère plus d'une quinzaine d'années que le problème de la langue se situe au coeur du débat de l'identité. Le reproche fait à Césaire d'y avoir été insensible, est puéril, car peu d'esprits de sa génération y songeait. Son attachement fétichiste à la langue de colonisation, son mépris de la langue "vernaculaire," de l'outil linguistique forgé par l'esclave malgré sa sujétion dans l'univers concentrationnaire de la plantation, était courant. Aujourd'hui, les théoriciens de la créolité sans prôner le retour absolu à la langue "vernaculaire" (bien que Raphaël Confiant ait publié cinq romans en créole), opteraient pour une déconstruction du français à partir des rythmes, des sonorités et des métaphores du créole. Brathwaite est un des tout premiers écrivains, en fait dès *The Development of Creole Society in Jamaica, 1770-1820*, à avoir pressenti la nécessité de la décolonisation linguistique. Des années plus tard, en 1989, il déclare: "I think the real challenge for the artist who knows his English and mediates between the two languages is to develop an English which increasingly reflects the nature of nation-language" (Brown, "Interview" 85).

Qu'est-ce qu'une "nation-language"?

C'est, pourrait-on dire, un décentrement volontaire du langage de la métropole vers la périphérie, la refonte d'une syntaxe et d'un vocabulaire qui tienne compte des pratiques langagières des îles. L'entreprise est malaisée et Brathwaite s'en plaint: "My tongue is heavy with new language / but I cannot give birth speech" (IS 221).

Mais elle seule assure la véritable reconquête de soi. Les spécialistes de Brathwaite insistent sur l'utilisation du jazz et des motifs de folklore dans ses poèmes. Il n'est pas niable qu'*Islands* se clôture sur une pulsion de Carnaval Jou'vert:

Nyame God
and Nyankopon

> where is your kingdom of the Word?
> ....
> I
> Must be given words to shape my name
> to the syllables of trees (IS 222-3)

Contrary to what is generally believed, linguistic claim has made itself heard late in the Caribbean. For scarcely more than fifteen years has the problem of language been at the heart of the debate about identity. To reproach Césaire with having been indifferent to it is puerile, for few minds of his generation dreamt of it. His fetishistic attachment to the language of colonization, his scorn of the "vernacular" language, of the linguistic tool forged by the slave despite his subjection in the concentration-camp plantation universe, this was general. Today, the theorists of creolity, without preaching complete return to the "vernacular" language (although Raphaël Confiant has published five novels in creole), would opt for deconstruction of French on the basis of rhythms, sonorities and creole metaphors. Brathwaite is one of the very first writers, since, indeed, *The Development of Creole Society in Jamaica, 1770-1820*, to have foreseen the necessity of linguistic decolonization. Years later, in 1989, he remarked: "I think the real challenge for the artist who knows his English and mediates between the two languages is to develop an English which increasingly reflects the nature of nation-language" (Brown, "Interview" 85).

What is a "nation-language"?

One could say that it is a deliberate decentering of the metropole's language towards the periphery, the recasting of a syntax and a vocbulary to take account of the islands' linguistic practices. The undertaking is difficult and Brathwaite laments: "My tongue is heavy with new language / but I cannot give birth speech" (IS 221).

But only that ensures the true reconquest of self. Brathwaite specialists emphasize the use of jazz and of folkloric themes in his poems. It cannot be denied that *Islands* closes on the driving force of Carnaval Jou'vert:

> Nyame God
> and Nyankopon
>
> and
>
> *bambalula bambulai*
> *bambalula bambulai* (IS 267)

and

bambalula bambulai
bambalula bambulai (IS 267)

Avec l'approbation de l'auteur, Gordon Rohlehr dans *Pathfinder* (1981) va jusqu'à dresser la liste des diverses références musicales qui servent de base aux textes. Nous n'en doutons point. Mais l'appropriation d'une oeuvre d'art demeure subjective. Il me plaît, quant à moi, de lire dans *Islands* les premiers éructations—balbutiements—sonorités de ce "nation-language" qui s'intensifiera à travers au fur et à mesure de l'oeuvre de Brathwaite et structurera, par exemple, *Mother Poem, Sun Poem* et *X/Self.*

With the author's approval, Gordon Rohlehr in *Pathfinder* (1981) goes so far as to draw up a list of the various musical references serving as basis for the texts. I do not question them in the least. But the appropriation of an art work remains subjective. For my part, I like to read in *Islands* the first eructations—stutterings—sonorities of that "nation-language" which will grow more intense throughout as Brathwaite's work progresses and will organize, for example, *Mother Poem*, *Sun Poem* and *X/Self*.

Trans. Timothy J. Reiss

Images for Creativity and the Art of Writing in *The Arrivants*[1]

Pamela Mordecai

Brathwaite offers, in his first trilogy *The Arrivants*, an extended symbolic "exploration" of the creative act. This essay considers particularly those symbolic tokens for creativity in which something I call "prismatic vision" and the refracted perception related to it are represented. Prismatic vision is a non-linear style of cognition proposed for Caribbean creole-speaking peoples. Cogently defined, it is the disposition to construe reality in some-times unresolved pluralities. The theory is that this cognitive style was induced in creole-speaking communities by the conjunction of cultures, under pressure from a unique social dynamism which focused their energy so that societies arose and altered with unusual speed, and creole languages consolidated in comparatively short periods of time. Prismatic vision is seen to inform the literature in various ways, from the micro-level where it may imbue a single symbolic token with refracting signifieds, to the macro level where it may dictate the complete symbolic infrastructure of a poem or story.

In Brathwaite's poetry, prisming is demonstrated in his construction and manipulation of various images for creativity, as well as in individual symbolic tokens. Nor does he regard the creative impulse as the preserve of the artist, for both the "doing" of the ordinary person and the building of the ideal society, are in his view creative.

"The Fine Webs"

If, as Baugh says, "Walcott's binding theme is Walcott" ("Ripening" 84), Brathwaite's preoccupation is with "others-than-himself" in the community. They are tied to him in symbiosis, so that it is appropriate for the poet-i[2] to typify the West-Indian person as (1) observed in community, and (2) studied in history. (Brathwaite is historian, poet, jazz aficionado, literary-aesthetic theorist, as well as trained teacher—a prism in himself!)

His images for the act of creating embrace creators and creations, and vary according to the poetry's immediate concern. Some are broad, flexible, amoebic: they recur in different poetic contexts and figurative combinations and represent a series of interrelated symbolic threads that provide a sort of supra-metaphorical structure, a web of meanings which becomes part of the poetic statement. Green images, sound/naming images, sea/river/water images, dust/pebble/rock images—all constitute threads in this web. Sea/river/water images often have a historical significance, for a sense of history infuses all Brathwaite's poetry.

Other images of "making" are more specific in their realizations. The narrative mother in *Mother Poem* is one such image. In this trilogy, the complex of images representing the creative act in one or other of its aspects includes: Tom, Francina, the carpenter, the ancestors; the fisherman, his voices and his net; the blacksmith; the shepherd; Ananse/spider and his web and conundrums; coral; the drum and other musical instruments. Of these, (1) Ananse/spider, his web and his conundrums, (2) the fisherman and his net, and (3) coral, are the most relevant to this discussion.

It is necessary to devise terms for discussing the trilogy. Because the three books make up a coherent epic piece, *poem* is used to refer to the trilogy. *Rights of Passage, Masks* and *Islands* are referred to as *books*. The sections ("Work Song and Blues," "The Spades," etc.) are called *sequences*, and the poems in the sequences are called *statements*. This use of *statement* and *sequence* is to some extent guided by the poet's comments in his "Preface" to *Mother Poem*. Divisions within the statements are called *sections* or *parts*.

"Ananse" is the title of the second statement in the first movement of *Islands*, the last book of *The Arrivants*. The glossary says that Ananse is "the spider-hero of the Akans (*sic*), earthly trickster, but once with the powers of the creator-gods" (TA 263). Although the Ananse image appears only in *Islands*, the related images of web, net, and spider occur throughout and, looked at across the trilogy, their cross-signifying imparts an important dimension to the unfolding work.

The present discussion first tackles the development of this thread of imagery, then considers coral and conundrum images. It also considers the fisherman and Tom since it turns out that they both belong to the Ananse/spider image sequence.

The web/spider images

The first example of the web/net/spider complex of images occurs in "Didn't He Ramble," the last statement in "Work Song and Blues," the sequence which begins the trilogy. The last example occurs in "Vèvè" at the end of the last book (see Table 1). Thus, this thread of imagery spans the trilogy and forms part of the poem's symbolic infrastructure. In addition, in some cases the images *themselves* bear the prismatic imprint.

The current interest begins with this "prismatic imprint" – the purely visual configurations of net, web and spider evident in everyday things resembling prisms. They perform in Brathwaite's poetry a role akin to the crystal—the quintessential prismatic image—in Walcott's work. Since for Brathwaite *all* making is creative, inspired, and therefore art, he never discourses on writing itself or art itself in the way Walcott does in his poetry. Thus, the same images serve for the creativity of human beings, of society, of the artist; for the personal recovery of ancestry, and the societal reclamation of heritage.

Aspects of the net/web/spider/Ananse sequence make connections with religion, ritual, indeed creation in its widest interpretations. The once creator-god-spider Ananse, in his reduced New World status, survives as the hero of traditional folk tales in the Caribbean, and is one of the clearest manifestations of cultural continuities. Ananse is thus an important player in the survival/revival of cultural continuities—for Brathwaite, a *sine qua non* for establishing any stable, resilient community.

There are other related significances for the spider. In vodun mythology he is symbolic of Legba, also known as Maitre Carrefour, guardian of crossroads and gateways, the spirit who controls access to the other gods and is thus usually the first to be invoked in vodun ceremonial. (Janus—important in Walcott's grammar of symbols—and Legba correspond, both being in their respective pantheons, guardians of doors and gateways.) A celebrant possessed by this god in the vodun ceremony affects the limp of an aged person and is supported by a crutch—a spider-like way of moving. Rohlehr, discussing Hic Tizzic as Mas-playing stilt dancer and image-of-the-poet-as-acrobat, and commenting on the transition from Carnival to Lent that sees Tizzic tumbling from his stilts, says: "The artist as Moko Jumby falls from his aspired height and becomes cripple, Legba faltering on his crutch, or Ananse crawling on broken legs" (*Pathfinder* 305).

Legba has lost status crossing the Middle Passage, for in Yoruba mythology he is a *divine* trickster figure. Henry Louis Gates points to the pervasive myths of Esu-Elegbara and the Signifying Monkey which crossed the Middle Passage to survive in Brazil, the Caribbean (especially Haiti and Cuba), and the United States. ("Esu-Elegbara" is the Yoruba designation; the more familiar "Legba" is Fon.) He sees these myths as serving "in their respective traditions as points of conscious articulation of language traditions aware of themselves as traditions, complete with a history, patterns of development and revision, and internal principles of patterning and organization" (*Signifying*, xx-xxi). Esu and Ananse are trickster figures. Gates says of the Esu figures, "as tricksters they are mediators and their mediations are tricks" (6). Both connect to language performance traditions; both enjoyed divine status in the African Old World. Gates further observes that the persistence of the Esu myths in the African Old (Nigeria) and the New World is testimony to the persistence of "shared belief systems maintained for well over three centuries, remarkably, by sustained vernacular traditions" (4). Ananse myths are a part of that persistence.

Table 1: Ananse/spider/net/web Images in *The Arrivants*

Book	Page #	Image	Context
Rights	23	net	Bring me now where the warm wind blows... where the showers fan soft like a fisherman's net thrown through the sweetned air
Rights	24	web spider	Long, too, for flowers: not for their spider-feet of roots that now transfix me, but for their touch of surfaces, of shapes, of colours,
Masks	119	net/web/ Ananse	Here green's net sticks wet, clings soft sweet comfort cunning like Ananse's tune- less, once Onyame's, trap of doom.
Masks	125	fisherman's net	I tossed my net but the net caught no fish.
Masks	148/9	Ananse/spider	Some- where under gravel that black chord of birth still clings to the earth's warmth of glints, jewel's pressures, spinning songs of the spider Kwaku Ananse who gleams in the darkness

			and captures our underground fears.
Islands	163	(net)	we float round and round
			in the bright bubbled bowl
			without hope of the hook,
			of the fisherman's tugging-in root;
Islands	164	spider/web	Creation has burned to a spider
			It peeps over the hills with the sunrise
			but prefers to spin webs in the trees.
Islands	165	Ananse/web/net	The whole song "Ananse" but especially
			(1) webs of sound
			(2) threading
			threading
			the moon
			moonlight stories
Islands	170	nets	His fingers work
			shuttle and twine
			...
			lapping his slack
			nets, embroideries
			traps for the brine.
Islands	173	spiders	How will the dry fruit warm
			at my fingers, the leaves'
			spiders spin green winning webs,
Islands	184	nets	the fisherman's boat is broken on the first white
			inland hills,
			his tangled nets in a lonely tree,
			the trapped fish still confused.
Islands	219	Ananse	Come in
			Brother Spider
			Creator of silver
Islands	232	spiders	...roots that scramble outward like spiders,
			tendrils that spin, weeds that hoot in their harness.
Islands	262	net/webs/	Sections 1 and 2 of "Vèvè"
		seine/cobwebs	

For Brathwaite, Legba and the other gods of vodun ritual are "near gods" as opposed to the "far gods" of the whiteman who are complained of in "Jah" in "Islands." As such they provide the means of another kind of re-creation: they are deities who provide access to *sunsum*, spiritual blood, sustenance and provision. Legba and Ananse are related, then, but insofar as the vodun connection resonates rather than functions as pursued, elaborated metaphor, this discussion will concentrate on those aspects of creativity which the spider is clearly and most frequently used to realize. It does not pretend explore this line of imagery exhaustively: the focus is on significances most relevant to the present argument.

The distribution of this complex of images (spider/Ananse/net/ web) in the trilogy is important: twice in *Rights of Passage*, three times in *Masks*, nine times in *Islands*. If *Rights of Passage* is a description of the fragmented experience of the new world blackman, and *Masks* describes his journey home and back in time to recover the continuities, *Islands* is a closely reported metaphorical blueprint for the coming into being of the integrated Caribbean island society. It is not surprising, then, that metaphors for creativity occur most frequently in the last book.

In this interpretation of the images, the fisherman's net is seen as the most important of the three tokens (Ananse/spider, net, web), for it symbolizes the comprehensive, ultimate realization of the new completed/completing creative work. Thus, it comes to embrace the other images of Ananse, spider and web which tend to express the old creating. The fisherman and his net symbolize new/New World creation, and on occasion the potential hoped for in that. In the first section of "Vèvè," the fisherman's net is "the seine [which] holds the sun" (TA 263). The seine is the heritage complex: the linguistic substrate driving the creoles; the historical continuities. The sun (as in "sunsum" also) is the personal-societal oneness achieved when behaviours that secure the heritage complex are employed.

One problem in tracking sets of images in Brathwaite's poetry is that of setting limits. The process of refraction enables an image or sequence of images to metamorphose. A comprehensive account of the imagery can lead to a work as substantial as Gordon Rohlehr's *Pathfinder*. Our limits allow us only to go beyond instances of the images represented in Table 1 to include three songs in the trilogy in which the images *do not* appear ("Cabin", "South" and "Anvil"), for reasons that will emerge in the discussion.

The first two images occur on consecutive pages (TA 23, 24) early in the poem. The first, in section 2 of "Didn't He Ramble," describes the idyllic landscape for which Tom, the archetypal shape-shifting protagonist of *Rights of Passage*, longs as he dies, in section 1, "alone, without the benefit of fire" (TA 22):

> Bring me now where the warm wind
> blows, where the grasses
> sigh, where the sweet
> tongue'd blossom flowers

where the showers
fan soft like a fisherman's
net thrown through the sweetened air

Bring me now where the workers
rest, where the cotton drifts,
where the rivers are
and the minstrel sits

on the logwood stump
with the dreams of his slow guitar. (TA 23)

Barring two short sequences in "Tom," the five pieces in "Work Song and Blues" up to this point are an anguished account of the journey of the blackman to the New World, and the horror of his contemporary situation. Of the two sequences in "Tom" that offer some "relief," one recalls the proud tribal history "we will never remember again" (TA 13) and the other describes Tom's aspirations (TA 14)—freedom of spirit and joy in the landscape—for his children. Section 2 (quoted above) follows on a section that reports the defeat of Tom-turned-emigrant in the temperate climes whither he has gone to seek a better life. This is the first expression in the poem of what the New World blackman regards as a positive, restoring environment. (Tom's vision is of course constrained by his experience.)

The only metaphor in section 2 is that of the "showers / fan[ning] soft like the fisherman's net"—significantly—"*thrown* through the sweetened air" (italics mine). The image yokes five counters: (1) the "showers" (2) "fanning" soft (3) "like the fisherman's net" (4) "thrown" (5) "through the sweetened air." The "soft-fanning showers" is another example of a "poor man's prism." The showers link back to the simple description of the idealized landscape of verse 1. The fisherman's net is also a gigantic forward-link to the heraldic fisherman in IS whom Tom "becomes" and to the vision of an integrated island society expressed in the images in sections 1 and 2 of "Vèvè." The act of "throwing" the fisherman's net (analogous to the "tugging in [of his] root" in "Jah" (IS 163) is a reiterated component of the image. It is the line- or net-in-motion that signifies. And the air is sweetened presumably by the blossoms whose spider-roots transfix Tom in the grave.

This softly hurled net of the fisherman defines the beginning and end of the poem: what at the beginning is wished for becomes what at the end almost is. Within the text, the variant forms of the image provide an intermittent account of the journey from Tom's devoutly wishing for a wholesome landscape to its periphrastic becoming in "The Stone Sermon" (TA 254-7). It is a story of communal making.

The second of these images to appear in *Rights of Passage* occurs in section 4 of "Didn't He Ramble." In this last section Tom continues to reflect on his circumstances and share his longings:

> And I no longer lonely now
> long for the drums to speak,
> the violins listen
>
> before they begin, the slow
> guitars converse.
> Long, too, for flowers:
> not for their spider-feet of roots that now trans-
>
> fix me, but for their touch
> of surfaces, of shapes, of colours,
> and of course the various
> scents that really give them
> meaning. (TA 24-5)

This is the first reference to the spider in the trilogy and the only one in the first book. The image occurs too early on for its full yield to be derived when first read. Tom has come north from the (island or rural) south, to New York/London; he is old and cold, in a small hired room, bedded down on damp newspapers, dying. Nostalgia prompts recollections. It is easy enough to understand his longing for flowers in these circumstances, but what is the significance of the "spider-feet of roots that *now* trans-/ fix" him? (Italics mine.)

There are some structural clues in the poem. First, there is the question of whether Tom's remembering is effected with the "fixed/ locked mem/ ory" which the narrator ascribes to "we/ who have cre-/ated nothing" in "Postlude/Home" (TA 79). It probably is: the lines in "Tom" which refer to the recalling of the glorious African past are ambivalent, as much a forgetting as a recalling: thus, we "dare to remember/the paths we shall never remember/ again" (TA 13). After this there are no more references to anything African in ROP until the rehearsal of African places at the beginning of "The Journeys," and that is a swift evocation of the first trans-Africa migration so as to anchor historically all subsequent journeys: the Middle Passage crossing, North American and South American migrations, and Atlantic recrossings. Thereafter, Africa goes into hiding, emerging at the end of "Postlude/Home," the penultimate poem, when a migrant descendant of Tom, reporting on the marginalized, catch-as-you-can lives of the emigrants, wonders whether "Tawia Tutu Anokye or/ Tom could'a ever/ have live/ such a life" (TA 80). The irony is that these are "just" the names of forbears; the *words* themselves are all that make the African connection.

It is the ritual incantatory account of the "Epilogue"—the poem is framed by a "Prologue" and an "Epilogue" variation of the prologue—which puts the whole experience into perspective. The personae in the poem, Tom and we-his-descendants, are not really part of what is symbolized by the thrown net of the fisherman. It is not (yet) our vision, or else we would not need to make the journey back (M) nor the return (IS). The spider-roots which make Tom chafe are the submerged continuities: he knows they are there but not what they are, even as he wishes good things for his children, un-aware of the fullness of that good.

Concrete elements, on which Brathwaite's poetry signifies often and powerfully, invite this reading. The line in which this image occurs is the longest in the two movements of "Work Song and Blues" which describe Tom in his New World context ("Tom" and "All God's Children"); *the only lines as long or longer occur in an unusually lengthy quintet in "Tom" which recalls the glorious past of the Ashanti nation* (TA 13). The length is unusual both for the statement, "Tom," and for the entire "Work Song and Blues" sequence, where only two other lines (in the section describing the transatlantic crossing in "New World A-Comin") are as long. So the line can be seen as visually representing the generational/temporal extension back to Africa—that is, Tom's roots. The unbidden image of the flowers' spider-feet irritates dim-memoried Tom, as he indulges his nostalgia; still, he cannot summon the flowers' beauty without their intrusion.

And they "trans-/fix" him. Tom is aware that the roots are forcefully connecting him with something. Brathwaite not only extends the line in which the image occurs, but he places "trans-" at the end of it, breaks the verse to create an actual (symbolic) space on the page, and begins the next verse with "fix me." There is another resonance: the roots of the flowers trans-fix = mesmerize Tom, making him uneasy but helping to locate him across the hiatus of time and culture effected by the Middle Passage. Brathwaite has very carefully fixed these spider-roots in the poem. They symbolize the submerged continuities, the African mind space, the way-of-seeing and of making that will enable us to create more than "nothing." When the image recurs in "Coral," that recognition and recovery have been made, not by Tom, but by his children, the about-to-be island society, symbolized as the "stone" about to be born in "The Stone Sermon." Coral comes to be pris-matic by its association with other plain man's prisms, including the multi-folded "brain" (brain-coral is a kind of coral), uncurling fist, and uncurling embryo. It transmutes into chalk, limestone, the land which takes every-thing into itself, into the soil and mud out of which things grow.

"Coral" uses the spider image to represent the means by which this indigenous material, the chalk-limestone-land-mud substance for making the society, is formed:

> mud is a milk of darkness that feeds
> orchids, roots that scramble outward like spiders,
> tendrils that spin, weeds that hoot in their harness. (TA 232)

The roots "scrambl[ing] outward like spiders" are the "tendrils that spin": they are creators, makers. Their role in the mud—a sustaining 'milk of darkness'—is to nurture extravagant tropical blooms out of the (mud) memories of the past, the submerged continuities. (The returning African, we recall, was obliged to "eat time like a mudfish" (TA 136).) The root-tendrils that spin are also "weeds that hoot in their harness." That "hoot'—of laughter and/or warning—is the noise of buried lore: myth and story, the wisdom of hearth and home, hunt and husbandry; rules for peace and stratagems for war. The two spider images, second and penultimate, provide another frame containing the symbolic movement of the poem. "Harness" expresses their repression as well as their potential as energy source.

This brings us to "South" and "The Cabin." "South" is a celebration of the fact of the "Caribbean" experience, rooted in the islands but foraying beyond that, stalled briefly in the "house in the forest...where shadows oppress" (TA 57) (Tom's cabin?), but returning triumphantly in memory and imagination to the island seacoast, the hallooing fisherman and the gulls soaring into the limitless morning. It is a poem which claims, with a powerful contained emotion, the island place as home. "South" claims a place for two reasons. First, this is the fisherman's landscape: twice fishermen's houses occur; the symbolic "path of pebbles" leads to them and the fisherman's voice alone enlivens the scene. In the statements "Jah," "Littoral" and "Vèvè," the fisherman, with his "tugging in root" and his flung-wide net, represents the wholeness of vision and recovery of heritage required of both rooted island person and integrated island society. Second, "South" relocates Tom's longed-for idyll in "Didn't He Ramble," making a kind of prescient promise of what the island society is on the brink of, at the end of the poem." Thus, via the fisherman, "South" becomes a link in the net/web/spider/Ananse chain of images.

"The Cabin" presents Tom's southern circumstances transplanted into the island context. Rohlehr (*Pathfinder* 51) says that the cabin in this poem is "a description of a Barbadian chattel-house" but Brathwaite has said it is a slave cabin from the American South, which at the time was the only mental picture of housing for slaves that he had. "The Cabin" describes what Tom tried to make and how it was lost. It insists that his descendants affirm and claim his effort, for the fisherman's "becoming" depends on exactly this.

These are images which point to the symbiotic relationship between culture as the sum of what the community has made, and the in-culturation of individuals who come to self-awareness as persons whom the community recognizes as potential makers, members who keep it going. (Brathwaite explored the role of the community in giving voice to the individual/artist in his early essay, "Jazz and the West Indian Novel.") Tom's descendants must accept who he was and what he did, for he is part of who they are. The image also confirms our reading of Tom's early discomfort with the spider-roots of the flowers he longs for. Those spider-roots are the same ones that "hoot" in the "harness" of his forgetting. As long as he fails to heed them, he forfeits ancestral wisdom and the self-identity which comes with it.

The spider image next appears in "Techiman." This time it appears in conjunction with the "net," and this time the spider is named; he is Ananse, the once-creator god:

> Here green's net sticks
> wet, clings soft sweet comfort cunning
>
> like Ananse's tune-
> less, once Onyame's, trap of doom. (TA 119)

Rohlehr comments that:

> The voice here seems already to be that of the *omowale*, the stranger returned after three centuries of disaster. He has seen the ambiguous Ananse replace Onyame as the presiding deity of the tribes; particularly of the emancipated Afro-West Indians, who needed to learn deception as a first principle of survival. Here he comments with hindsight on the birth of Ananse, who was even at the start, associated with both creativity and doom. (*Pathfinder* 138)

Brathwaite probably intends both dimensions—doom and creativity—to attach to the Ananse figure on this occasion; his splitting the word "tune-less" and careful, end-of-line location of "tune" suggest this. The intent to signal both dimensions may also explain why the spider image is more than once allied with the fisherman's net—the fisherman being, as I have pointed out, the new indigenous creator. But most Caribbean people associate Ananse with survival (by fair means or foul) or else see him as an ingenious meddler—no doubt an aspect of his once-creator status. In survival mode, he is a "long-head" David overcoming his Goliath-oppressors (snake, tiger, alligator) with his wits; he may also "work his brain," sometimes shamelessly, to indulge his appetites. As mischief maker, he is often held responsible, as David Ormerod puts it, for "the inherently flawed nature of reality"—ergo, "'Is Ananse mek it'" ("Bad Talk" 42). But in none of these modes is Ananse associated with doom, so if this meaning is intended, it may well escape the regional audience. Indeed, as the original "ginnal," he may be fairly regarded as the expert exponent of slaves' "sidewise crawling" survival strategy (Walcott, *Another Life* 59).

It is in the end a positive conception of Ananse that the next image invokes. The poet laments in "Jah" that "the land has lost the memory of the most secret places"; it is a cultural loss, so—

> Creation has burned to a spider
> It peeps over the hill with the sunrise
> but prefers to spin webs in the trees. (TA 164)

The "burning" which has reduced creation is as much an image of concentrated energy as it is of reduction. The "peeping" is empowered by conjunction with "sunrise": its look is surreptitious but it rises early with the sun and *chooses* to spin webs in the trees. The next statement, "Ananse," also portrays the creator-god in the New World as having a diminished but persistent and lively presence: his eye is "unwinking"; he is "thinking thinking"; his brain is green; "he squats on the tips// of our language"; he sits "threading/ threading/ the moon/ moonlight stories" (TA 166). Nor is he powerless, for his "doll's liquid gaze" is the stare of a voudoo fetish. Significantly, he hangs in the ceiling in the houses of the poor where "their brooms cannot reach his hushed corner" (TA 166). So he *endures*—in myth, as a way of thinking and making, "black beating heart of him breathing" (TA 166); "dry stony world-maker, word-breaker,/ creator" (TA 167).

When in "Sunsum" the returning stranger, bent upon finding his navel string, remarks:

> Somewhere under gravel
> the black chord of birth
>
> still clings to the earth's
> warmth of glints, jewel's pressures, spin-
> ning songs of the spider:
>
> Kwaku Ananse who gleams
> in the darkness
> and captures our underground fears (TA 148-9),

what is being identified by this capture also seems to have both creation and doom aspects. On the one hand, the race memory ("the black chord of birth") or something like it effects this capture in an effort to sustain the continuities ("clings to the earth's/ warmth of glints, jewel's pressures, spin-/ning songs of the spider"). The act in this case is restorative: Ananse presumably "captures our underground fears" in order to replace them with certainties about our culture and heritage. On the other hand, the image does have a sinister aspect, a resonance according to which Ananse captures our fears as being the object of them, scaring us. Such an interpretation can enrich rather than run contrary to the first: ironically we regard the creator-god Ananse, who can give us access to the wealth ("jewel's pressures") of lore, as being "only" able to "frighten di pikni."

At the level of imagery as "all the sense impressions in the poem," as well as at the most obvious declarative level, the next statement, "Littoral," is also ambivalent. Descriptions of the island adrift, "plundered by butterflies" are sensuous, evocative—and despairing at the same time. The image of the fisherman is pertinent: he is blind but he can "work/ shuttle and twine"; his "dark rejoices"; "he has his voices" (TA 170). The last section ends:

> How will the dry fruit warm
> at my fingers, the leaves'
> spiders spin green winning webs,
>
> shadows, lean working tissues
> for moisture, for light,
> tricking the raindrop, trapping the blight. (TA 173)

The spiders spinning green webs are clearly meant as a positive image: the webs are winning, are lean working tissues/for moisture, for light which will secure water by tricking the raindrop, and ensure the health of the plant by trapping the blight. They are images of possibility. But they are embedded in a question that is also a plea, for there are as yet no hands for this creative task—"Who will till the soil/cutting straight fervours into the rock/whose marrow, whose toil//butting into this sweat-sweetened rot/will soften these roots,//loosen the shoots under pebble and shale?" (TA 172)

"Eating the Dead" invites the spider into a strange announcement of beginnings. The ceremony marks the birth (of the new societies) but the poet presents the infant as virtually doomed in embryo. The statement also concerns the artist's role of envisioning the future for the society—a role he finds hard ("Illegal, illegitimate/ I cannot sing" [TA 211]) because he is outlawed by corrupt leaders who have sucked the islands dry and allowed the spread of deleterious influences. "Eating the Dead" perhaps carries too much symbolic weight in its few pages: metaphors come thick and fast and (reflecting the content?) have barely a chance to develop before others overtake them.

The poet knocks three times (on *black* doors) to begin the ceremony, then summons Ananse to assist in the ritual:

> Come in
> Brother Spider
> Creator of silver
>
> I need your speed
> and your enduring cunning (TA 219)

Gordon Rohlehr comments: "Ananse, the Creator... is chosen for his speed, his capacity to endure and his cunning which he has often employed to undermine the oppressor. Ananse will bestow webbed intricacy of design and the dexterity of mind... (*Pathfinder* 259)." The status of the "Brother Spider" here invoked is that of a god – hence the capitals, as in "Ogun," who is summoned next. The spider has in some wise resumed his original role as maker, for the ritual of the dead is a decisive point in the arrivants' story, prelude to the coming into being of the "curled embryo" (island society). Though not strictly speaking one of this set of images, the web/net/ spider resonance summoned by the word "roots" operates in the last three verses of section one of "Eating The Dead":

> Offer the flesh up
> time, ruins, relics
> leaping over the tips
>
> over the root tips of fingers   .
> offer the failures up
> sing cry *kanzo*
>
> from this red skin
> and cradle
> we begin. (TA 220)

By using the roots image (a visually prismatic one), Brathwaite attaches the significances associated with the image-set to the climax of the ritual marking the society's birth: "curled embryo that will grow/to sweat/ the eyes that will know// what greedy means" (TA 220).

This first section of "Eating the Dead" recalls all ancient sacrifice involving the consumption of the victim, vodun rituals included; it also recalls the Christian blood sacrifice of Christ on the cross and the Eucharist which re-enacts it. Brathwaite explains that the "Eating the Dead" ritual is "both *vodun* (*manger les morts*) and catholique (eucharist)." Rohlehr sees it as syncretizing Akan, European and Caribbean traditions (*Pathfinder* 257-8: earlier Brathwaite citation on 257): there is a sort of mixing of the bread/dead figures that operates when either token is used. So the poet conceives of the resources to be mobilized against corrupt political and mercantilist interests in spiritual terms, and conjoins traditions as he invokes divine power.

Perhaps the bloody "Eating the Dead" rituals foreshadow the destiny of the 'curled embryo'—a grim one. The poet does not hide the enormity of the creative task: "from the slow sinking mud of your plunder, grow" (TA 221). Propitiation and sacrifice are for the sake of renewal, despite the weight of the odds and the size of the task—one in which the artist has a central role.

The Net Images

The opening lines of "The New Ships" declare:

> I tossed my net
> but the net
> caught no fish (TA 125)

The sequence signals both the cultural rape of the diasporic blackperson-slave, coffled and hauled to the New World, deprived of heritage, and the fruitless search of the returned descendant for his point of entry into the old community. It is this fruitless search which provides the *raison d'etre* for the last book of the trilogy. The journey across the Middle Passage has been too long: as the poet tells us in "Jah"

> The sea is a divider. It is not a life-giver,
> Time's river. (TA 164)

The net—it is once again "tossed"—cannot secure for the *omowale* direct re-entry into the old community. The thrown net (as web of continuities + new syncretic device) is necessary, for without it the fisherman cannot be heroic maker; but it must also become the instrument of the forging of a new community such as the poet (in IS) hopes will develop.

The two remaining net images (TA 170, 184) which occur before those in "Vèvè" can be read in much the same way. What remains is to consider

the articulation of these images in "Vèvè" and to establish an explicit connection between the creative act as these images express it, and the creativity of art.

The relevant sections of "Vèvè" are these:

1.   But on the beach
            the fisherman's net is completed;
            the fine webs fall softly,

            sand shifting under his walking;
            the water is ready;
            twined spray through the air

            and the seine holds the sun
            and the line in his hand
            tightens steady.

            The net drifted downward,
            through times and reversals
            of shell-clinking water,

            through time and the hopes
            that were drowned in the deep
            sleeping sound of the bay.

            The fan sifted slowly
            through cobwebs of light
            catching softly the moons of his green
            spreading opening day.

2.   And so the black eye travels to the brink of vision
            but not yet;
            hold back the fishnet's fling of morn-
            ing (TA 263)

The six short verses of Section 1 of "Vèvè" offer an extraordinarily refined
and satisfying dénouement for the poem. In one sense the completed net is
the poem itself. Mervyn Morris's suggestion, with which Rohlehr concurs,
that the words, "the line in his hand/tightens steady," refer to "Brathwaite's
realization that he is getting better with each book" fits neatly with this
interpretation (Morris, "This Broken" 21; Rohlehr, *Pathfinder* 307). But
this sense is only part of a wider significance upon which the work—through
this and a number of other threads of imagery—has all along been intent.
Rohlehr sees the poem as concerned to make important statements about

the poetic-artistic "i" (*ibid.* 162, 303, 304-5, 306, etc.). The poem does do this, but it also makes a more general statement about art and the ordinary person's capacity for creativity.

Rohlehr is correct when he observes that in "Vèvè," which begins with a return to the fisherman/Ananse persona, "There is a sense of cyclic fulfilment as earlier themes are recalled. The fisherman's net merges with the spider's web, and both of these, images of the complex reticulation of the trilogy itself, are now complete" (*Pathfinder* 306). It is this enlarged significance for *both* the fisherman's net and the fisherman himself that need to be emphasized. The fisherman is the integrated island person, the new creator for whom a more perfect making is possible. The cast net is an image for that making. The fisherman is also (in a more muted resonance) the integrated society of which this new person is a member. Thus, the fisherman *is* the poet, but he is also the poet as everyman, the plain island person, Tom bereft of melancholy and confusion, no longer a reduced figure but liberated into creativity by meeting the conditions for wholeness set out in the last book. (I have elsewhere examined the use of the pebble/sand/stone/rock image in *The Arrivants* and described how Brathwaite arrives at these necessary conditions in the poem "Islands": Mordecai, "Image.")

The connection with Tom can be seen more clearly if one considers "Anvil," in which "The Cabin"'s first three verses, describing Tom's house, are repeated in their entirety. In "The Cabin" these verses are followed by a protest at the destruction of Tom's attempt at making and at the lack of respect in Tom's "descendants," who fail to recognize his contribution. In "Anvil", the verses are followed by sections chronicling: the savage state of colonizer/those whom colonization has ravaged (part 2); Tom's reluctance to carry through his rebellion, as well as the rationale for that reluctance (part 3); and the state of the Leopard, pacing his cage, silent, his terror unblinking (part 4).

Rohlehr's interpretation of the crucial Leopard section is significantly different from the one offered here. The difference turns on how the word "terror" is interpreted. In Rohlehr's version, "terror" is the fact of being terrified; in this one it is the fact of being terrified but also the capacity to create fear. Rohlehr's reading flounders on the interpretation of "nothing". Rohlehr says, "[Tom] bequeaths to succeeding generations not simply an imperfect image, but no image at all ('made/nothing. un-/made nothing')" (298). However this "nothing"—an enormous conundrum coursing through Brathwaite, Walcott and the regional literature—is as much its opposite ('everything'), as it is itself. Tom's "failure" to act must be contextualized by this understanding.

If we interpret it as the capacity to create fear, terror can provide a backward link to the contained savagery of Tom's descendants in part 2 as well as to the power with which Tom could have struck in part 3. That power has not been destroyed. It inheres still in both individual and community. It is self-contained. The symbol speaks to many things, among them, aesthetics, since formal elements contain resonant content in much this way, and politics, since it is the restraint of brutishness that permits society to exist. There are various other significances as well—geographical, biological, etc. Brathwaite's comment is finally ontological: matter contains energy in this way.

There is no question, then, as to whether Brathwaite thinks Tom chose rightly when he elected to hold back his impulse to destruction. The restraint can be seen as a metaphor for the distancing, the setting of space/time between powerful feeling and the action flowing from it. The uncertainty which Rohlehr indicates as to "whether Tom in failing to strike the slavemaster down is acting out of higher humanity or cowardice" is not the issue (298). The hammer poised, about-to-strike, and the Leopard, bundle of physical and nervous energy, power and rage, are both images of potentially destructive forces being held in check. That "time/ticks/still" implies that the forces have by no means been defused.

The poet sharpens the cutting edge of this conclusion against passages in which the unleashed power of the beast in its own habitat is celebrated (sections 2, 3 and part of section 4 in "Leopard"). Part of the success of both "Leopard" and "Anvil" is that the central images represent at once the ideas of the imprisoning of a noble energy and the necessary restraint of violent feelings—the basis of culture, civilization and art. Inherent in the duplicity is the notion that the one is somehow the other.

It is necessary to return to "The Cabin" and "Anvil." For the repetition of the initial (identical) verses underscores a relationship between them which only emerges if one considers the sections that follow in both. Part of what is suggested is that the descendants of Tom who are spoken of in "Anvil" should themselves come to recognize the necessity/importance/inevitability of the daring-not-to-do for which they have found it hard to forgive him. In his original reluctance Tom paved the way for the abused to express their rage through art instead of violence.

Rohlehr comments further on the significance of the fisherman:

> The fisherman/poet is now able to travel in spite of the shifting sand under his feet. He again becomes shepherd and Baptist traveller on mourning ground, like whom he realises that "the water is ready". The idea of the reconciliation exists not only in this fusion of perso-

nae—fisherman/ Ananse/Shepherd—but in movement, mood, rhythm
and image. (306)

The idea of reconciliation does indeed exist in the fused personae and in
movement, mood, rhythm and image. But the personae which fuse in the
fisherman are not only Ananse and the shepherd—and, as we have shown,
Tom—but all those who contribute to bringing into being the conditions
for integrity: Francina, the persona in "Cane," the grandparents in "Ancestors," the joiner Ogun. Thus is the fisherman this poet, and all other poets,
as well as every artist, as well as the artist-in-everyone.

It has already been pointed out that the fisherman's "fine webs fall[ing]
softly" and the "twined spray through the air" recall Tom's longing to be
brought

> where the showers
> fan soft like a fisherman's
> net thrown through the sweet-
> ened air (TA 23)

The total vision symbolized in the net proceeds backwards through time to
be historically inclusive as the tense in the poem changes—

> the line in his hand
> tight*ens* steady.
>
> The net drift*ed* downward,
> through tides and reversals
> of shell-clinking water
>
> through time and the hopes
> that were drowned in the deep
> sleeping sound of the bay. (TA 263: italics mine)

The "green/spreading opening day" (recalling, *inter alia*, "green/open(ing)
a crack" at the end of ROP) is the about-to-be day of enlarged integrated
perception for Caribbean person and society. But "moons" suggests the
returning cycles of earth time, so that a whole future opens up, generations
to be caught in the vision as it fans out. The "fishnet fling of morning" in
section 2 comfortably accommodates the broad parameters attributed to
the metaphor, as Brathwaite sustains the tidal progress of the poem to the
end.

Images in *The Arrivants* directly connected to Creativity

The symbol most readily connected with art and poetry which occurs in this context is Ananse. With his "memories trunked up in a dark attick," he:

> squats on the tips
>
> of our language
> black burr of conundrums
> eye corner of ghosts, ancient his-
> tories;
>
> he spins drum-
> beats, silver skin
> webs of sound
> through the villages;
> *　　*　　*　　*
> threading
> threading
> the moon
> moonlight stores (TA 165-6)

Rohlehr comments that "At this point of the poem Ananse is the incarnation of that folk-consciousness which preserved the proverb, the folk tales and riddles of wakes and moonlight nights, and created the pun in *Pierrot Granade, Ole Mas* and *Kaiso*" (186). This connection of Ananse with the oral tradition occurs well into Rohlehr's commentary on "Ananse," and he makes less of it than might be expected. This is perhaps because his interpretation of the images used in conjunction with the trickster/spider tend to have a negative cast. On four (of a total of seven) occasions when the spider/Ananse image occurs, it is in conjunction with thriving flora and fauna, the hopeful green of the trilogy. In addition the spider is more than once associated with silver and brilliance; as a "Creator of silver" (TA 219), as "curling silver" (TA 166), and as one who "gleams/ in the darkness/ ... underground" (TA 149). The Shepherd summons him as a power to assist in the ritual of "Eating the Dead." The image does have its negative aspects but it also evokes strong, positive associations with a continuing capacity for creativity, rooted in African tradition, that survived the Middle Passage then went underground to generate the stratagem of "sidewise crawling" and to preserve/create the Oral Tradition to which, in the very writing of the trilogy, the poet contributes.

The negative aspects of the image can be seen to contribute an appropriate complexity to the signifier—the born stone is, after all, confused, ambivalent, multiple-speaking. It is a "dark" past we are (or have been) ashamed of, as much as a black heritage of which we have learned to be proud; it is a harsh future we anticipate and we lack the hands to make it.

For certain, the spider's web-spinning signals the 'Nansi story tradition, regardless of what its other metaphorical contributions may be in the particular context. The returning stranger/blackman sees his navel string as a "chord of birth" which spins "songs of the spider" (TA 148). The spiders' songs are what most visibly remains of the grounding and rooting the *omowale* seeks. As we have noted, for many Caribbean people this is the first clear surfacing of their 'darker' heritage. It is also, for many, the beginning of the impulse to search—the journey the first trilogy records. We must not make too little of it, just as we should not make too little of Tom.

Brathwaite describes Ananse's gaze as "crystal." For Rohlehr the crystal gaze is "hard and inorganic" so that he considers the poet's choice of the word "chrysalis" to describe the vitality of Ananse's brain, a "miraculous echo" (185). But the crystal can equally be seen as symbolic of the refracted vision that the discontinuities of the Middle Passage and the flux of the new societies have bequeathed to the New World artist. The "glass," "quartz," once "stony water," are images for the Atlantic water (= history) which the New World Creators must dig (as "quarry" suggests) their way back through, if they are to recover the lost heritage. The images also recall Paul's "seeing through a glass darkly," where darkly signifies positively.

Ananse becomes a doll in two ways, each conveying a different aspect. In one respect he is the vodun fetish: in this guise he retains ritual power, albeit in a tradition which laws once proscribed and tourists now gawk at. In the other he is a doll in the sense of an object of play: in a situation where the continuities are lost and his status is diminished, he is, as the hero of folktales, "merely" this. The doll's gaze is liquid because the questing artists-cum- surviving traditions are fluid, in flux, looking for a shape. There is also the water of the Middle Passage which must be searched through in the quest for roots, and which, by a kind of metonymical association with the eye seeing it, confers its aspect on the vision. Crystal, thus interpreted, relates to the refracted perception we propose. The scraps of surviving heritage become facets of an energetic perception, a "green chrysalis/storing leaves," embryonic possibility of a more complete construing of reality and experience.

Finally, in respect of Ananse, there is the "black burr of conundrums." Rohlehr's explication of conundrums is useful: "The word 'conundrums' does not only through sound foreshadow the drum theme in the next few lines, but points to the association of the Ananse of the folk tales with word-play and riddles, as well as to the prevalence of punning in the Oral

Tradition of the West Indies" (186). Rohlehr also sees relationships between Brathwaite's style and Ananse "tactics," and makes an explicit connection between the spider and the poet-as-creator. In addition to this stylistic riddling, the conundrum—one of five symbolic devices in my taxonomy of prismatic forms—comprehends and points to multiplicities of meaning that are the basis of the riddle.[3] Truth in art is enigmatic: the riddle sends us off to discover an inadvertent meaning and to entertain many others before we come to that one. It is not so much the answer that instructs, but the quest to find it.

Notes

1. This essay is adapted from part of chapter three of Mordecai, "Prismatic Vision."
2. i is preferred in some places in the first trilogy, and is firmly embraced by the second. As Brathwaite makes his way to *Barabajan Poems*, the concrete elements of his poetry assume ever greater significance. The lower case i both enables traditional capital I to signify as well as underscores all use of capitals.
3. The other prismatic forms are: the litany; basic image as prism; extended image as prism, mixing image—or poetic mix (Mordecai, "Prismatic," chapter 4).

Francina and the Turtle and All the Others: Women in EKB

Velma Pollard

Francina

He chooses Francina, a simple woman. She who "used to scale/ fish in the market." He makes her save the "humpbacked turtle with the shell-fish eyes..." (IS 215).

Brathwaite, railing against the destruction of a park, something precious reserved for the use of the people, chooses a woman to be the rescuer. The turtle she saves is a symbol of what is dearest to him, to all people of similar mind–the island with all that is natural to it.

The poem rails against "the Mayor and Council/ thin brown impressive men." We meet them in the act of destroying the park to build a dance hall and a barbecue. We share the poet's outrage. The lake has become a parking lot. A macaw, monkeys and the "humped hundred/-year old turtle" must go. Francina rescues the turtle. She is the opposing symbol to what the city officials represent. A woman with no resources at all takes pity on the turtle which represents the real values of the islands. The city officials loudly declare that they will build

> the island; hotels where there were pebbles,
> casinos where the casuarinas sang,
> and flowing fields of tourists for our daily bread   (IS 214)

This progress, this building of the island is in fact the island's undoing. Francina's act of rescue is an indication of some small hope; if any one will follow it up. While it is significant that she is poor:

> ...How she think she could spare
> nine dollars an' thirty-five cents
> for a wrinkle-face monster you can't
> even eat, when she can't keep
>
> she body an' soul-seam together—
> I can't unnerstand it... (215),

it is even more significant that Francina is woman, nurturer, protector of the future for the next generation. It does not matter that she is not strong enough to fight powerful corporate men effectively. What is important is that she tries. The excuse, suggested with what sarcasm the poet can muster in these circumstances, is predictably not convincing:

> ... I suppose
> she got a nose for slimy things
> like eels an' red-tail lobsters
> though muh eyes can't see
> what she want wid a turtle that too old
> to be yuh father.... (215)

Her act remains heroic. The poem is "Francina" from the collection, *Islands*, third book of Brathwaite's first trilogy, *The Arrivants*. He selects for the task of saving a civilization, a simple woman, an outcast of society really, scorned by most men. The creature she rescues is a turtle. The shell ensures its protection and survival beyond the century it has already lived. The lines exude the gratitude her poet creator feels towards Francina and wishes the reader to feel as well. There is deep warmth and affection here.

Before Her

Before Francina (at least in order of publication) were the wise women gathering at evening in the small goods (grocery) shop in the village in "The Dust," a poem which has become a true classic, appearing in most Caribbean anthologies. These women represent the people who, in Brathwaite's own words in another context, "from the centre of an oppressive system have been able to survive, adapt, recreate; have devised means of protecting what has been so gained" (*Contradictory Omens* 64).

They speak the language of the West Indian street–an anglophone creole (here a Barbadian version). It is what Brathwaite labels "nation language." These women love, respect, care for each other. The latest arrival
greets each one by name and immediately addresses problems:

> Evenin' Miss
> Evvy, Miss
> Maisie, Miss
> Maud. Olive,
>
> how you? How
> you, Eveie, chile?
> You tek dat Miraculous Bush
> fuh de trouble you tell me about? (RP 62)

Life is not easy. Times are hard. Nature is sometimes unkind. But they
have forged philosophies which allow them to endure hardship without
complaining, propped up by the support they receive from each other and
by their faith in God to whom they constantly give thanks:

> we got to thank God
> fuh small mercies.
>
> Amen,
> Eveie, chile...
>
> an' agen
> I say is Amen. (63)

There is no hopelessness here. The main speaker among the women names
each blessing, lest we regard them as commonplace and pass over their
value. They include the possibility of a child for the man you love, healthy
offspring and a piece of land which is small but productive and your own.
Perhaps most important is the faith and hope they find in the unfailing
progression of time where nature's cycle repeats itself:

> ev'ry day you see the sun
> rise, the sun
> set; God sen' ev'ry month
>
> a new moon. Dry season
> follow wet season again
> an' the green crop follow the rain. (68)

This is the hope which allows them to endure the inexplicable tantrums of nature which make crops fail and visits other tragedies upon them.

These women bring to the world a message of survival in spite of misfortune, beauty in spite of ugliness and hope where one expects despair. This is the same message as that contained in the detailed description of Francina's saving the turtle. The difference is that where their actions are personal, protecting themselves and each other, hers is public. She is saving a world.

After Her

After her is a catalogue of women in *Mother Poem*, the first book of Brathwaite's second trilogy. Here he celebrates the endurance of woman who must nurture husband and children and on a grander scale, celebrates the Mother his island—Barbados.

"Calypso" (*Rights of Passage*) begins by explaining how the Archipelago of Caribbean islands came into being:

> The stone had skidded arc'd and bloomed into islands...
> ...curved stone hissed into reef
> wave teeth fanged into clay.... (TA 48)

But when the stone does not skid it connects with the water and forms quick concentric circles around itself. The mind can draw an imaginary line from the stone center to the circumference of the farthest circle, a line that unites them all. Francina is the stone at the centre. The largest circle is the island–Barbados; the circles in between are all the women of *Mother Poem*. And all are linked ingeniously to Francina and in some way to the women in the evening grocery shop.

The cycle/circle in "...Dry season/ follow wet season again" reasserts itself in *Mother Poem*. Rohlehr points out that mother is, "ultimately, a principle of renewal and rebirth" (*Shape* 191). Later, he comments that the sea is the major presence through which the perpetual ongoing movement of the life force is conveyed, and notes another cycle implied in the portraits of women ending with the death of the grandmother (193).

Francina is the kernel, the nam which is expanded into this major celebratory poem of woman. She has rescued the turtle, the symbol of the island and its future. There is hope if anyone follows the lead she has provided. In "Hex" (*Mother Poem*) we get a feeling of (temporary) despair. The poet loudly laments the signs of Francina's failure, on the body of the island:

> all the peaks, the promontories, the coves, the glitter
> bays of her body have been turned into money...
> for master for mister for massa for mortal baas... (MP 46)

And the Mayor and Council men, the evil male figures of destruction re-turn here, in the various guises of plantation authority figures. They are embodied in the figure of Money/Mammon which breaks the land and breaks people. Through the complaints of women we find that he haunts the futures of children. Brathwaite's women, these wives and mothers, lament his effect on their husbands, watching with tears how he breaks them just as the council men broke the future of the Island. He is the "thin skinned merchant" who, in "Alpha," represents "...the world Columbus found/...the world raleigh raided/...the plantation ground" where the husband works to death while the caring woman, the mother

> sits and calls on jesus name
> ...waits for his return
> with her gold rings of love... (MP 4)

He is the Mammon who breaks the courage of the husband of the woman who in "Twine" is full of regrets as she compares his past with his present:

> I know when I did first meet e
> he did strong...
>
> but if you look pun e now
> fragile, 'fraid o' e own shadow

and explains that after all what made him so: "he never get no pension from de people" (6). He is the merchant the woman in "Bell" sings about:

> the merchant own me husband
> an me husband never home (12)

She curses and blames him for her husband's illness. She too notes the pensionless condition:

> not a cent
> not a bline bloody cent
> not even a dollar a year for the rock he was wrackin
> not even a placket to help pay de rent (14)

Predictably the poet records her resilience. She complains. This is not what she expected. But "to help enns meet," she gets out and goes to work, "sellin shoes in de white people shop." She becomes a worker like the other women in *Mother Poem*.

Like "Miss Own" who keeps "body and soul-seam together" singing "sign a bill here" as she sells "calico cloth on the mercantile shame/rock" (15), or the woman in "Horse Weebles" who sells "biscuit an saltfish in de plantation shop at pie/corner so she can keep "body and soul-seam together" (38), this woman is a prototype of mother. She sells in the shop full time but she also is doctor and seamstress for her family and she still finds the time and the energy to express the concern which links her to all other women in late night grocery shops, repeating accordingly the lines of an earlier poem:

> evenin' miss
> evvy, miss
> maisie, miss
> maud, olive
> how you? how
> you, eveie, chile?
> yu tek dat miraculous bush
> fu de trouble you tell me about? (38-9)

Eventually the woman becomes old and tired. In "Moth-air" she has worked too long and too hard. Her sigh comes from deep within her:

> *boy me feet heavy*
>
> de tiredness passin
> like water clouds carryin
>
> rain... (86)

She is gravely ill. The doctor comes around prescribing diet and pills. What folk wisdom says about dying is happening to her. Her whole life passes through her mind: her own mother's illness, her lifelong service to children and husband, her feeding the children coming home from the beach, rushing them off to "sabbath day school," her bearing with silent endurance her husband's infidelities, all the while pretending not to know: "dese men doan know what a wo-/man does know..." (89). Near her end now there is no one to return nurture to her:

> ...she turns
> alone to the o-
>
> ven burn-
> in burn-
>
> in world
> without
>
> without
> end
>
> amen (93)

This is her end. The lines mark as well the endlessness of this kind of suffering that is the thankless reward for a life of sacrifice and hard work. There is a kind of passionate empathy here from the poet to this woman who is all women.

But *Mother Poem* will not end on a note of hopelessness, for Brathwaite is above all a poet of hope. Out of every "falling" situation he creates a "rising": future out of past, birth out of death. The line "the midwife encircles us all" ("Mid/Life" 111) is perhaps his most eloquent expression of this way of seeing. "Kounfort," the final movement of *Mother Poem*, indicates ways of comfort additional to those mentioned earlier, bound to the *hounfort* where world and spirit meet. In "Angel/Engine," for example, the woman finds her comfort in the church/*hounfort*, an Afro-Caribbean version where the prayers are loud and there is breathless trumping:

> praaze be to
> praaze be to
> praaze be to gg (98),

and where the faithful are assured a seat on the Zion train.

Finally in "Driftword," the last poem of the collection, all the mothers become one with the mother that is the island. The prototypical mother is drifting away. Through her "dead sea eyes" she sees the future generations who will save the island: those who

> ...will say no to distortions
> who will pick up the broken stones
> sloping them with chip and mallet out of the concave quarries... (112)

Because of this kind of hope she is at peace at her death–"she knows that her death has been born", and so is everyone else. On the page, that sense is achieved with Brathwaite's usual economy. He simply juxtaposes opposing notions:

> so that *losing* her now
> you will slowly *restore* her silent gutters of word-fall (17: my emphassis)

I like to think that the composite woman at the end of *Mother Poem* is the transformed Francina who goes gently out

> ...into the sunlight
> towards the breaking of her flesh with foam (117)

Three Poems

Olive Senior

PENNY REEL

It is Saturday, the night of penny reel dances, girls in
pressed hair, white muslin and sashes, turn to
high-stepping gentlemen as they weave out and in
eye passing each other on the go-round.

> The little dressmaker in the circle of light spilled from
> Home Sweet Home lamp shade, sits sewing
> at her straight-stitch treadle-foot machine, unwound
> by the laughter, the fiddle and fife of penny reel.

Near the very same spot on the edge of the park where
the stark shanty-town edges in, there's a
Merry-go-Round. Her children she locks up
inside and away from temptation till she earns

> enough pennies for their ride. She's not locked in.
> It's life she's locked into. Can't remember
> how she entered that ring. Can't see the revellers.
> In a tenement room, there're no windows to outside:

every door in a row facing in. No wheel and spin.
The treadle-foot machine the go-round she rides.
But sometimes (she's noticed of late)
there's slippage, as with silk from her customers,

> easy slide of her body to a pull from the outside.
> Alone save the children, how unattached she feels.

Out there, her Saturday night sisters weave
something from life. Each reel a new set so the dance

might continue. Who decides on our measure?
She addresses this to no one in particular.
Her man could be anywhere: penny-reeling,
at his gambling, the bar. Perhaps (she is hopeful)

tonight he won't come. Forever. No more scars
on her body criss-crossing like ribbons. No more
riding her. No more grinding her down. No more
turning her into Ol'Higue. If she knew how to stop

having children she'd do it. But there's no one to ask.
Her sisters are all at the dance. Penny reel.
Thread reels her in. Three a.m. and she's
sewing for a Sunday delivery. Though the fabrics

are dancing, kaleidoscoping her eyes, her feet keep
on moving the treadle. Up and down. O Saturday night
sisters moving out and in to that rhythm of life.
But like her customers,

they too dissolve in her mind into parts custom fitted,
tape ribbon the only measure she knows.
And she? Do they see her as more
than a figure kneeling down to adjust the hems

of their garments, straight pins in her mouth. Do they
know she is coming unstitched? Sometimes
they don't pay her on time. Sometimes never.
And there's that Merry-go-Round. If she knew

how to rain curses down she would do it. But there's
no one to ask how to creep into houses, rip
their clothing to strips, tie as ribbons to the maypole,
and swing. If only she knew how to stop herself

wanting to fly through the walls as her feet work
the treadle. If only she could stay plaited up
like the ribbons round the pole. Stop reeling off
into this other. Not the straight-stitcher looking after

the children but the one overlooking. The one
who rips her skin, strips and discards it, so that

bat-like, taking wing, she flies through the air,
homing only to sound, to movement, the scent

> of the dancers O my sisters who are reeling. She
> dives for their blood. To suck up their being.
> But the ribbons criss-crossed at the pole
> are unyielding to witches or to humans

who ribbon their skin. And because it is Saturday evening
the one time in the week these lassies and lads
are not grieving for homes left behind. Freed
from labour, from tenement rooms, they abandon

> themselves to each other. Keep dancing
> till the dawn when witches must return to their skin.
> Or be undone. Like the man coming in to curse her
> - 'Ol'Higue' - when she asks where he's been.

For it's dawn. She needles him with her eyes.
If she knew how to kill she'd do it but there's
no one to ask. Her sisters still dancing. She finds herself knotting a thread
round his neck. She jerks it. Bites.

> There, it's done. But it's only one garment. Many more
> till delivery. Sunday morning soon come.
> Thank God for the dawning and the whisper
> in the streets of the revellers passing, the girls

in crushed muslin, their hair now unpressed, the boys
still high-stepping. Easy passage tonight.
They have paid for the ride.
O penny reel dancers unreeling.

Notes to 'Penny Reel'

Penny reel = dancing round the Maypole, popular in bygone days in the colonies,
derived from the European May Day phallic ribbon dance round a pole. In
Jamaica, in working class districts where it became a popular social pastime,
dancers paid for each 'reel' or turn at plaiting and unplaiting the ribbons round
the pole, hence 'penny reel'. "Penny Reel O" is also the title of a once-popular
sexually suggestive folk song.

Ol'Higue = a witch who sheds her skin at night and flies in the shape of a bat to feast on blood. She must assume her skin (and human shape) before daybreak. The term 'Ol'Higue' is also applied to someone perceived as a nag.

EMBROIDERY

The women of the family took tea all together except for
Aunt Millie, Uncle Vincent's wife. She read books, she

wore makeup and jewellery even on weekdays. On Sunday
afternoons behind locked door, she had me put colouring

(Madame Walker's, IMPORTED FROM AMERICA) in her
hair. She was a *blue foot*, a stranger, not a *born-ya*. She

had crossed water. They did not know precisely where
Uncle V had found her. He was the eldest, family head.

A *sly dog* and purse-string controller, so no one said
anything. Aunt Millie smiled often but her mouth was

sewn up. Her reticence offering them few strands, the women
of the family enhanced them with embroidery

(washing lightly in vinegar to keep the colours fast). From
her straight nose and swarthy skin they plucked skeins to

compose the features of a Jewess, or herring-bone in
the outside daughter of a rich merchant or plantation owner.

Her mother was someone mysterious, whipped onto the scene
with a slanting backstitch. She once sang opera?

She was said to be of Panamanian or Colombian origin.
Something exotic enough—like a french knot—to mistrust

but work in. They reviled Aunt Millie's use of scent. From
the few words they extracted they thought they detected

a foreign accent. Sometimes they feathered in 'Haitian',
infilled with dark threads to signify the occult powers

of that nation – how else could she have snared such as
Uncle V? They thought she kept her distance because

she was all of the above and snobbish. *My dears, such airs!*
She and I were *What a pair*! Myself, orphaned with frayed

edges unravelling into their care. Everyone knowing my
pathetic history, I could wind myself up in Aunt Millie's

mysterious air, undulate in the sweet waves (artificially
induced) of her hair. She nurtured me on books and

reticence. The women of the family fed me cold banana
porridge (or so everything then seemed) told me tales

of girls who did and men who didn't marry them. Tried to
enmesh me in their schemes to undo Aunt Millie's disguise.

In the end they embroidered her an elaborate cover when
(I could have said) a plain winding sheet would have suited

her. For to me she gave her story, unadorned. The women of
the family willed me their uniform tension. Aunt Millie left

me her pearls. I sold them, became a *blue foot* traveller.
Kept no diary. Sewed up my mouth. Shunned embroidery.

Olive Senior

LACEMAKER *(Valencienne 1794)*

Attached to my bobbins like the spider
I, with no time on my hands, spin out
a lifeline to hang on. Then I make
the noose: to form the hole I capture air
tangible as breath in this damp cellar. Round it,
I weave the thread in finest silk which will age
(unlike me) to palest cream, ecru, ivory,
age into 'charming old lace'.

I envy the spider her speed. In inches my life
edges by - (Her Ladyship so many yards for her ruff,
My Lord, years of work for each cuff, My Lord Bishop
three-quarters of my life to trim his alb).

Like the spider I grow brittle and dry,
like its web (pale and strong) my lace
(kept moist for good tension) surges on
fine as foam on the ocean which I'll never see.

For my eyesight's opalescent as shell now,
my vision translucent as pearl
yet my skeletons of thread stay delicate as webs
(like the fly, it's the holes I'm mesmerized by).

When I die, I'll go to my grave in coarse linen,
no edging. But my virginal hands will not cease
from signing punto in aria: stitches in air.
Never cease from making nooses for My Lord, My Lady.

Meantime, the spider and I wait
for our traps to be sprung

for lace-trimmed heads
to swing in bloodied air

(What a waste
of good lace

What a waste
of my lifetime).

Looking Back at *The Arrivants*

Mark A. McWatt

My first publication after arriving at Cave Hill as a very green Assistant
Lecturer in the mid-70s was a review of Kamau Brathwaite's *Mother Poem*
in *Bim* magazine. The first paragraph of that review was not lacking in
effrontery:

> As a whole the poem sustains the reader's interest and there is much
> in it that is effective, but by some reverse alchemical process the
> golden poetic voice of the earlier poems has been transformed into
> that of a baser metal.... (137)

At that time I had not yet met the poem's author, but someone suggested to
me that he would be very displeased to read that and a few other sentences
in the first paragraph of my review. This bothered me and I consulted my
most approachable colleague at the time, Michael Gilkes, asking him what
he thought. Michael said that he had not yet read the review but that Kamau
was one of the most important and celebrated of Caribbean poets and why
did I think he would care two hoots what was said about his work by a
young Assistant Lecturer in his first published review. This advice was
meant to console me, of course. Two days later Michael Gilkes came up to
me and said: "I've now read your review and the first paragraph is not so
much annoying as puzzling: after the negatives of that introductory paragraph you go on to show precisely why *Mother Poem is* a wonderful volume of poetry." He then went on to give me a good piece of advice: "In
future, don't worry with introductory rhetorical flourishes, just get down
to the practical criticism." I hope I've been able to follow his advice since.

Gilkes had seen through me—realized that the offending paragraph was mostly insincere rhetoric and was there more because of the precious alchemical image than anything else. Fortunately for me its point was lost as the review moved on to an appreciation of the poems themselves. The pretentiousness and posturing of youth? Certainly, but I also consider now that part of the problem may have been my inordinate love and admiration for the first trilogy—*The Arrivants*—which is something I still feel and is why I want to look back here at *The Arrivants*, in an attempt to assess something of what those poems have meant to me over the years.

Before that, however, I should say that I have long since come to consider *Mother Poem* one of Kamau's finest volumes of poetry, probably the one I most enjoy teaching, particularly to Barbadian students, and that, having got to know Kamau quite well (soon after the *faux pas* of my first review), I have found him to be entirely tolerant, helpful and generous, not only in encouraging my academic writing (on himself as well as on other Caribbean writers) but also my own efforts at writing poetry.

I read *Rights of Passage, Masks* and *Islands* as separate volumes during my undergraduate years at university in Toronto and they were an important part of my own self-discovery as a West Indian and a great influence on my thinking about the West Indies and its history. For me *The Arrivants* is still the most important of Brathwaite's works. In this trilogy the reader encounters most of the poet's major themes and obsessions and many facets of complex imagination and craft. Perhaps the foremost theme is history itself. Everything that Kamau writes is touched and coloured by a sense of history; sometimes this is very subtle—particularly when the poems are excerpted or appear in anthologies, taken out of their context in the trilogy—but if you read attentively you can always detect, in the orbit of each Brathwaite poem, subtle displacements and perturbations caused by the gravitational tug of the author's academic discipline, and this often makes for a mysterious, numinous quality in the poems and great richness of meaning and emotional impact.

The first volume of the trilogy, *Rights of Passage*, begins with two poems which trace, in a rapid and highly evocative way, the large historical movements of a people across the continental desert to the west coast of Africa, and then the journey in chains across the sea to the new world. Here is the first stanza of the first poem, "Prelude":

Drum skin whip
lash, master sun's
cutting edge of
heat, taut

surfaces of things
I sing
I shout
I groan
I dream
about... (RP 4)

Thus are we introduced to the history of the New World Black man. The drum controls the rhythm of the poem as it does the rhythm of the life of the people, but in this poem it also reverberates with historical references: the stretched skin that is the percussive surface of the drum is or becomes also the skin of the black man which feels the slaver's lash and the fierce heat of tropical plantations. Thus the drum and its rhythm become part of the identity of the black man and, at the very beginning of the first journey, proleptically suggests the slave plantations many miles and years away. I can still remember vividly the excitement with which those drumbeat lines were read by me and probably by many of my generation in the late sixties. Now the technique is well known and ears well tuned to this poetic line and this rhythm (there are many imitators of Kamau among younger West Indian Poets), but then we were all like Keats looking into Chapman's Homer, savouring the wonder and newness of the poetry. However much the cruder Afro-Centrics and Cultural Nationalists among us may have beaten the African drum into a tiresome cliché, there's no denying the original power and freshness with which it was associated in those first Brathwaite volumes of poetry.

The other aspect worth pointing out in that first stanza quoted above is the way in which Brathwaite attaches an emotional freight to the historic references, indeed to history itself. The poetic form rescues the historical past from the dust-dry aloofness of the academic subject and reconnects it to the human subject in terms of fears and feelings. The four consecutive verbs at the end of the quoted paragraph—"I sing / I shout / I groan / I dream"—do not just fill in the emotional content of the particular historical reference, but also insist upon the varied and even contradictory nature of those emotional responses, as the verbs together indicate celebration, exuberance, pain and longing all at the same time. The dull continuum of historical time is thus compressed and conflated and its effects concentrated into paradoxical expressions and experiences. This is one of the aspects of Kamau's poetry that I value most—its sense of emotional and moral balance, achieved through its inclusiveness, through its paradoxes and seeming contradictions.

The first stanza of the second poem, "New World A-Coming", is as follows:

> Helpless like this
> leader-
> less like this
> heroless,
> we meet you: lover,
> warrior, hater,
> coming through the files
> of the forest
> soft foot
> to soft soil
> of silence:
> we met in the soiled
> tunnel of leaves. (9)

Note the seeming contradiction in the sequence of nouns "lover, / warrior, hater" which nevertheless captures accurately the serial masks of the European in Africa, his various roles over time and the modulation of emotional responses from attraction to conflict to rejection. Perhaps this is how we arrive, at the end of the stanza, at "the soiled / tunnel of leaves," where the very landscape or location has become morally tainted by the infamous acts that took place there. It's interesting the way the repetition of soft sounds reinforces the bitter leap from the soft physical soil of Africa to the harsh notion of the way in which the particular human encounter is "soiled" in a metaphysical sense – tainted for all time. Also the "tunnel of leaves," suggestive of forest pathways where the encounters took place, also conjures up the morally darkened tunnels that led from the slave forts (like Elmina) to the ships of the middle passage. Such moments, when ordinary language leaps into extraordinary referential plenitude because of historical resonances, are frequent in Brathwaite's poetry, particularly in *The Arrivants*.

It is worth remarking that the pain of these historical memories does not lead Brathwaite to proclaim implacable enmities. The poetic techniques we have been looking at ensure that the scope and vision of the poems are always larger than the individual hurts they may contain. As with Walcott at the end of "Ruins of a Great House," there's an inevitable movement towards compassion and understanding and a desire to learn from the experience. Hence we have the Uncle Tom figure in *Rights*:

> hoping my children's eyes
> will learn
>
> not green alone
> not Africa alone

> not dark alone
> not fear
> alone
> but Cortez
> and Drake
> Magellan
> and that Ferdinand
> the sailor
> who pierced the salt seas to this land. (16)

This passage at the end of the poem "Tom," apart from indicating the generosity of Tom's dream that his children will acquire from their bitter experiences the skill and technology to master the physical world in which they live, lifts the mood of the poem out of the helplessness it expressed earlier, the way the frustrations and the despair of the "Spade" in "Folkways," are alleviated and transcended by the rhythm of the "boogie woogie" train in the second section of the poem. This too is typical of Kamau and one of the reasons for cherishing these poems which taught a generation how to live with a painful past.

I'm suggesting that one discerns in *The Arrivants* the way drum rhythms, as well as phrases, themes and other aspects of content build into patterns which transcend individual poems or passages. The first two poems of *Rights* are about journeys across the desert and across the sea. Later on, in "The Emigrants," we see the Black man on the move again:

> These are The Emigrants.
> On sea-port quays
> at air-ports
> anywhere where there is a ship
> or train, swift
> motor car or jet
> to travel faster than the breeze...
>
> Where to?
> They do not know. (51)

These later journeys contain thematic, verbal and circumstantial echoes of the earlier journeys and come eventually to create an inevitable pattern of journeying and to suggest drift and placelessness. In this way Brathwaite achieves a more powerful emotional impact that transcends all individual historical moments. I cannot but feel myself that this is where history should go, to the level of large patterns and designs which are entirely comprehensible in terms of how they came about and what they mean to a people, but are free of niggling scholarly disputes, individual hurts and dry dates and other particularities. To enjoy *The Arrivants* is to celebrate Kamau Brathwaite *as historian* as much as poet; by packaging history in poems, he teaches West Indians about themselves painlessly and without shrill polemic. (Perhaps if other prominent Barbadian historians had chosen poetry as the medium in which to educate their countrymen about history and historical figures, much recent controversy might have been avoided and fewer reputations called into question.)

Another aspect of *The Arrivants* that has always interested me is the persona, the voice we hear in the poems. Of course there are times when the voice comes from historical or archetypal figures, like "Tom," literary and "folk" figures like "Caliban" and "Ananse," and from contemporary figures of town or village, like "Tizzic" or the women in "The Dust." But the voice is also that of a frequently undramatized but protean persona, who speaks to us throughout. What has always struck me is the range and the protean nature of Kamau Brathwaite's poetic voice in the trilogy. It can speak for a whole people, as in "Jah"; it can become the voice of the drum, as in "Atumpan" or, perhaps more interestingly, in "Tano":

> dam
> dam
> damirifa
> damirifa due
> damirifa due
> damirifa due
> due
> due
> due... (M 151),

or can express personal memories, as in "Ancestors" or "Ogun." There are times when the voice stutters and claims to be unfamiliar with speech, as in "Eating the Dead" (suggesting strategies of resistance or for recovering lost modes of expression), and times when it gushes Nation Language like a river in spate, as in "The Dust" or "The Stone Sermon." But one senses that behind this voice lie years of silence, of voicelessness. The poetry gives a people their history, but also their voice: the strategies for expression and self-discovery, for emerging from the "soiled" tunnel of the past. There's a sense in which the voice, the *breath* of the poems, is itself the interpellated subject, the one called into being or constructed by the specific ideological and discursive machinery that we all acknowledge – and this subject speaks for us all, with a voice that is our own, for, as Ashcroft, Griffiths and Tiffin contend:

Although ideology serves the interests of the ruling classes, it is not static or unchangeable, and its materiality has certain important consequences. For while ideology is dominant, it is also contradictory, fragmentary and inconsistent and does not necessarily or inevitably blindfold the 'interpellated' subject to a perception of its operations. (*Key Concepts* 222)

Brathwaite's poetic voice transmits its perceptions and strategies to its people.

Finally, there are times when the voice seems to be simply that of, if not Kamau Brathwaite, then "the Poet," the one planning future voices. To illustrate and celebrate this, I end with a passage from "Dawn" which seems to point, in terms of subject, rhythm and feeling, towards the second trilogy, especially towards *Mother Poem* and *Sun Poem*:

> Till the sun enters fine, enters fine, enters fin-
> ally its growing circle of splendour
> rising
> rising
>
> into the eyes of my father,
> the fat valley loads of my mother
> of water, lap-
> ping, lapping my ankles, lap-
>
> ping these shores with their silence:
> insistence of pure
> light, pure pouring of water
> that opens the eyes of my window
>
> and I see you, my wound-
> ed gift giver of sea
> spoken syllables: words salt on your lips
> on my lips... (IS 238)

DREAM ATLANTIS

John Chioles

The water of the mirror in the
Room was dark green. quiet as
translucence. in the light of a
limestone cave near the ocean
and it had been pasted on the wall.
like a mop. the shape of an island.
one of those lopped jagged half-
square Caribbean-shaped islands
like Trinidad or central Virgin Gorda

'*Da road int got no endin'*
    (Kamau Brathwaite, *Dreamstories*)

The torch that burned the sheep after the plague belonged to my grandfather. He brought it out at the end of summer to light the sacrificial pyre; an
armful of wheat stalks burning, a litany to local gods and saints, Augustine
out of Africa, others further up in the deep North. We took to the road then,
not knowing where it would lead. The torch went with us, the only sacred
element we carried, like water. Here, so many stades separating us, need
for the torch jumps time and brings it full force to the hull of this ship
where errant rats threaten my limbs. Grandfather's torch of white light
would spell survival, forcing the rodents to their nests and I could look at
the sea uninterrupted in the arms of its murky peplon. I can only come out
in the open at the hour of the wolf and stay till Phaethon's steeds make
their appearance behind us, as an aubade of lyrics cracks its cheeks follow-

ing us westward. The ship is full of travelers, but I don't dare see them. I only feel their presence and hear the strain of the steel beams under their weight. She's a rickety one, a wartime conversion to passenger status. That's what Hephaistos, the lame old-youth, a cook's aide, who brings me leftovers when he remembers, had said. But it's safe, he said in mock seriousness, it'll get us to the mountain-island before it sinks.

The Pillars of Herakles are still ahead and I fear of missing them if I stay below with the other stowaways. I should never believe any part of the other side, the lush islets of Atlantis, were I to miss these dark imposing pillars in this misty dawn. But miss them I did, for I waited too long to come out on top; an old book partly eaten away by the rats and the salt, thrown against the seams of the ship's hull where I found it, had absorbed all of my senses at the crucial moment. I began to read in amazement, not comprehending but sounding the words aloud, feeling a rush of music that dreams itself into adjacent curlicues of silent meaning, traveling a parallel time, as if I'm outside of the rickety ship, astride a dolphin, laughing together with the sleek animal and telling it, "faster, faster!" Now the book overwhelms me as I read myself in it, while the dolphin keeps laughing and will not let me return to the ship. I'm not afraid, for I feel certain I'm in good hands. And so I begin to read at first in timid sounds:

Phaedo says that he heard the story, when he was a boy, from his grandfather Critias, who had heard it from his father Dropides, who got it from Solon.

[The dolphin seems to snort knowingly at this.]

Solon brought it from Egypt, having learned it from a priest of Neith—that is, of Egyptian Athena—at Sais. Solon had been passing on to the priests of Neith some of his country's old stories, particularly the one about the Flood which Deucalion and Pyrrha (later, the parents to Pyrrho of wanderlust fame) survived, when a very aged priest exclaimed, "You Greeks are always children; there is not an old man among you!" meaning that the oldest Greek stories were but of yesterday. Floods and catastrophes were constant in that part of the world, the destruction of civilizations quite common. This was the Mediterranean after all. But Egypt had been spared the greatest horrors, and her priests had made records, which were still preserved in continuous series, of all that had happened, not only in Egypt, but in other parts of the world, during the successive periods terminated by the various Floods and other catastrophes. Among these records was one relating to the crowning city along the sea of Aegeus, which flourished before the greatest of the Floods. This Athens, the aged priest told Solon, Athena founded nine thousand years before his time-one thousand years before she founded Sais along the Nile; and the constitution of the antediluvian Athens was similar to that which the sister city of Sais still preserved, especially in the separation of the class of priests and the class of warriors from a third class, including the castes of artisans, shepherds, huntsmen, and husbandmen, husbanding for food and procreation with the god Eros willing.

> In the bleached
> stare of the one-
> eye'd beach,
> the fisherman
> sits, his head
> sleeps in the surf's
> drone, his crossed
> legs at home
> on the rough sand.
>
> His fingers work
> Shuttle and twine,
> soft clack between
> breakers and whine
> of the fine spume
> flying off rock,
> lapping his slack
> nets, embroideries,
> traps for the brine. ("Littoral," IS 170)

Now, the History of the Great War is an endless story in which the whole coast of Aegeus, so constituted, was engaged with the people of the Island of Atlantis in a love-hate relation; suffice it to say that this island, which was larger than Libya and Asia together, lay in the Ocean outside, off the straits now called the Pillars of Herakles. Beyond this island there were other islands in the Atlantic Ocean, by means of which it was possible to pass to the Continent on the farther side of that Ocean. In the Island of Atlantis itself there was a mighty dynasty of Kings (foreigners they were, tall with small heads and pale white faces) who ruled over the people, over many of the adjacent islands, over parts of the Transatlantic Continent, and over Libya as far as the Egyptian border, and, on the other side of the Mediterranean Sea, as far as Etruria.

The land rises slowly
fed by the ringed sun and the distant Amazon:
leaves, seed, silt, feathers,
broken wings, hooks, clutching eyes,
bugs, green-backed bats, leeches;
mud is a milk of darkness that feeds
orchids, roots that scramble outward like spiders,
tendrils that spin, weeks that hoot in the harness.

Here now are canoes, huts, yellowing corn husks, cassava,
hard harpoon heads, broken pots on the headland;
broken by time, by neglect, the touch boots
of Columbus, of pirate, the red boots of flame;
cracked soles of Africa, broken by whip,
bit of pain between teeth; broken by rain,
the new shoots of the green-dollar cane.

But the coral builds
quarries, explosions,
limestone walls,
bougainvillea churches, plantation halls ("Coral," IS 232-3)

This mighty Power, collecting all its forces, was moving eastward to add to its empire the remaining Mediterranean countries, Greece and Egypt, when Aegeus' city stood forth as their champion; and, leading the other coastal States, now deserted by the pointed heads, waged a decisive war against the invaders, and conquered them, and not only saved Greece and Egypt, but liberated the Western Mediterranean countries which had been enslaved. Then, sometime after, came the Deluge. Athens was overwhelmed, in a day and a night, by flood and earthquake; and the Island of Atlantis sank under the sea, leaving shoals which still render the navigation of the Ocean difficult in these parts.

[The dolphin is now shrieking at me, clearly expressing the desire to be heard. I cannot make out the tenor of his sounds; but I feel certain it is saying something about time, or is it perhaps the name Timaios that I hear in its sounds, the name I see in the book when I turn to it as I run ahead of myself. The dolphin is now an extension of the book; it sits inside the book and rides outside the ship all at the same time:]

He proposes to enter fully into its details, on the understanding that the citizens of the Ideal State constructed in the Republic are identified with the citizens of the antediluvian Athens; but first, Timaios must give his

*promised account of the creation of the world and of man, so that, when all
is said, we may have the full history of man—as created in the* Timaios,
educated in the Republic, *and acquitting himself nobly in the* Atlantis Myth.

[My sleek transporter is in full control of the story, which it calls a
myth; but I don't need the book to know a dreamstory when I see one.
Besides, all of these books, rat eaten or not, are given to fragmenting dreams,
dreaming mostly about the coupling of love and wisdom. My silk-skin
lover, transmitting more love and wisdom than I can handle, continues:]

The fragment begins, ...in the old time, the Earth was divided into provinces, each of which was directly governed by a God, or Gods. Thus Athens was assigned to Hephaistos and Athena, brother and sister, and the
Island of Atlantis to Poseidon. That's how Odysseus managed to destroy
the Cyclops: Poseidon was forever searching for his possession in the endless Ocean, too far away to be of help to his illegitimate son.

*The Athens of Athena and Hephaistos was constituted according to the
model set forth in the* Republic. *There were artisans and husbandmen, and
a class of warriors originally set apart by certain "divine men." The warriors dwelt together, and had all things in common, being supported by the
labor of the other citizens. Men and women alike practiced the art of warfare. The territory of the city, coextensive with Attica as it now is, was the
most fertile in the world. What is now a mere skeleton of mountains and
rocks was then filled in with rich soil, so that what are now mountains were
then only hills; and Pnyx, Acropolis, and Lycabettus formed one almost
level ridge of loam. On the top of this ridge, where the Acropolis now is,
the warriors lived round the Temple of Athena and Hephaistos, their winter quarters towards the north, and their summer quarters towards the
south. The number of these warriors, men and women, was always about
twenty thousand. They were the guardians of their own citizens, and the
leaders of the other Greeks were their willing followers. Such were the
dwellers along the shores of Aegeus; and they were famous throughout
Europe and Asia for the beauty of their bodies, brawny and brown, and for
the various virtues of their souls.*

A toss night between us
high seas
and then in the morning
sails slack
rope flapping the rigging
your schooner come in

on the deck.   buttress
w/ mango boxes.   chicken-

coops. crocus bag rices. i see you
older than i wd wish you
more tatter than my pride
cd stand   (BB[2] 6)

To Poseidon the Island of Atlantis was allotted. Near the center of the island, a fertile plain, and nearby, a mountain. In this mountain dwelt the earth-born Evenor, who had a daughter Cleito. Her Poseidon loved best, and enclosed the mountain in which she lived with concentric rings of sea and land, three of sea and two of land, so that it could not be approached, for at that time there were no ships. Being a god, he easily brought subterranean streams of Avater, one cold and the other hot, to this island-mountain, and made it fruitful. Here he begat ten sons. And he divided the whole of Atlantis among them into ten parts. To the first-born, who was named Atlas, he gave the island-mountain and surrounding territory, and also made him King of the whole of Atlantis, his nine brothers being governors under him in their several provinces. From Atlas were descended the Kings of Atlantis in long and unbroken line; and under them the island prospered greatly, receiving much through foreign trade, and itself producing all the richness of the world: metals, timber, spices, and all manner of food for man, and pasture for the elephants and other animals which abounded. Great works were also carried out by these descendants of the seafaring God... First they made a bridge across the rings of sea which enclosed the ancient metropolis, and began to build a palace on the island-mountain, to the size and adornment of which each generation added till it became a wonder. Then they dug a canal some 50 stadia long, 300 feet broad, and 100 feet deep, making a waterway for the largest ships from the ocean to their metropolis, which thus became a seaport. They also cut passages for ships through the two rings of land, and spanned the passages by bridges under which ships could go. The first ring of land, like the outermost ring of sea, was three stadia broad; the second ring of land, like the ring of sea which enclosed it, was two stadia broad; while the ring of water which immediately surrounded the island-mountain was one stade wide; the island-mountain itself being five stadia across.

A yellow mote of sand dreams in the polyp's eye,
the coral needs this pain.
Look closely:
the pearl has limestone ridges, hills,
out of grows the sun
and the fat valleys of Haiti,

72

deep mourning waters under the mornes.
The coral killers crust my wall of bone
make feet for footprints on the first beach;
cold sea of sound splinters the fishes' dawn;
it rings bells in the shingle
it curls messages into the shell
it cuts me coconut branches
it tugs, whorls, it pushes
me, it teaches me how to swim
at midday it sparkles with screams and the sprats' silver. ("Coral," IS 232)

The island-mountain and its palace they surrounded with a wall; and another wall they built round the circuit of the mid ring of land; and a third wall round the circuit of the outer ring of land; and also a wall on either side of the great bridge leading from the country without to that ring; and towers and gates they placed at the bridges which spanned the passages cut in both rings of land. The stone for the walls they quarried from the foot of the island-mountain and from both sides of the two rings of land, thus at the same time making cavities in the rock which served as covered docks. The stone was of three kinds: white, black, and red; and these three kinds, pieced together in one building, made it beautiful to behold. The outermost wall was coated with brass, laid on like ointment; the middle wall with tin, and the wall of the Acropolis itself with orichalcum glancing red like fire.

Even when I was a slave here
I could hear the polyp's thunder
crack of the brain's armour
the ducts and factories sucking
the rivers out, engineering
their courses, as if the stone
were a secret leaf, or a first curled
in embryo slowly uncurling. ("Coral," IS 232)

Within the enclosure of the Acropolis was first the holy place of Cleito and Poseidon, in which no man might set foot—the spot where the ten sons were begotten. It was surrounded with a golden fence. Here they brought the seasonable fruits of the earth, from each of the ten provinces, as offerings to each of the ten sons. Then there was the Temple of Poseidon himself, in length a stade, in breadth three plethra, and of proportionate height, on the outside coated all over with silver except the pinnacles, which were coated with gold—a spectacle of barbaric splendor; and within, the roof of

ivory inlaid with gold and silver and orichalcum, and all other parts—
walls, pillars, and floor covered over with orichalcum—and images all
golden; the God himself mounted on a chariot driving six winged horses,
his head towering tip to the roof of the temple, and round him in a ring a
hundred Nereids riding on dolphins.

[I could swear my salty friend muttered, "Against their will, I'll bet
you, hrumff.]

And there were other images too, which had been hung up by private
persons within the temple; and outside, golden statues of the demi-god
Kings and their wives, and many other statues presented by persons at
home and in foreign countries belonging to the Atlantis Empire. There was
also an altar in keeping with the temple, and there were magnificent pal-
aces to house the dignitaries hard by.

The numerous fountains of cold and hot water which Poseidon had
caused to spring in his island-mountain were housed and made to serve as
baths for the Kings, for private persons, for women, and for horses and
other beasts of burden; and the water not used in this way was conducted,
some of it to the beautiful grove of Poseidon in the island-mountain, some
of it by aqueducts across the bridges to the two rings of land, where also
there were temples and gardens and gymnasia and race-courses for horses—
especially in the outermost of the two rings, where there was a race-course
a stade wide running right round the ring. Along this grand course were the
quarters of the main body of the troops; a smaller number of trusted troops
were quartered in the inner ring of land, and the most trusted of all in the
Acropolis itself as bodyguard to the Kings.

The docks close under the island-mountain and the two rings of land
were full of warships and giant storage spaces; and when you crossed
these two rings and came to the outermost ring of sea, the harbor, you
found it, and the canal leading to the ocean, full of merchant shipping. At
the ocean-mouth of this canal the two semicircles met up with a wall that
ran always at a distance of fifty stades from the outermost ring of sea, and
enclosed a densely populated area.

> The stone had skidded arc'd and bloomed into islands:
> Cuba and San Domingo
> Jamaica and Puerto Rico
> Granada Guadalupe Bonaire
>
> curved stone hissed into reef
> wave teeth fanged into clay
> white splash flashed into spray
> Bathsheba Montego Bay ("Calypso," RP 48)

And that is only the royal city. The whole of Atlantis itself was a moun-
tainous island, save for the plain in which the royal city stood. This
plain was oblong, extending 3000 stades in one direction, and 2,000
inland through the center of the island. The mountains that enclosed it
were great and beautiful, and sheltered it from the north wind. A moat
10,000 stades long, one stade broad, and a hundred feet deep—a work,
it may be thought, of superhuman magnitude—was carried round the
whole oblong of the plain. The streams from the mountains poured into
it, and it had an outlet into the ocean. From the furthest inland part of
it parallel canals were cut through the plain at intervals of one hun-
dred stades, and these were connected by cross canals. By means of
this system of canals, timber and fruits were brought down to the city.
There were two harvests, one after the winter rains, and the other in
summer, raised by irrigation from the canals. The plain was divided
into 60,000 lots, each lot being a square with sides measuring ten
stades. Over those fit for military service in each lot was set a Leader;
and there were likewise Leaders of those who dwelt in the mountains
and other parts of the country—a vast population—according to their
settlements and villages. Each Leader was bound to supply a sixth part of
the cost of a chariot of war—in this way 10,000 chariots were furnished;
he was also bound to supply two horses with riders, and a light chariot for
a pair of horses, with a shield-bearer to go on foot with it, and a driver to
ride in it and drive the horses; each Leader was also bound to supply two
heavy armed soldiers, two archers, two slingers, and, as skirmishers, three
stone-throwers and three men armed with javelins, also four sailors to
help to man the fleet of 1,200 war-ships. Such was the armament of the
capital; and the nine provinces had also their own different armaments,
but it would be tedious to describe these and I refuse, for I will tire too
much with you on my back.

[It was at this moment that Hephaistos came from the kitchen agitated.
He noticed that I had not eaten the scraps of food he had brought me earlier. I told him that I was engrossed in this book. "Oh no, you didn't find
that piece of trash, did you? Meaningless fantasies," he said. "Yes, and I've
been talking with a dolphin as well." Hephaistos rolled his eyes and started
to tell me the story of his other crossing during the other war when the
German submarines were causing them grief. "There was a cabin boy just
like you who kept talking with the submarines and the fish." I told him no, no
I didn't want to hear anything or eat anything until I was finished. The poor
lame soul left me alone, seeing the state I was in.]

In each of the nine provinces, as well as in the capital, its own
Philosopher-King was supreme over the lives of the citizens and the
administration of the laws; but the dealings of the ten governments

with one another were determined by the Commandments of Poseidon, which were engraved by the first men on a Table of orichalcum, which was preserved in the Temple of Poseidon on the island-mountain. There, every fifth year and every sixth year alternately, a meeting was held for the discussion of affairs and the judgment of transgressions; and this is how they conducted their business: There were sacred bulls, which were kept within the precincts of Poseidon. The Ten, who were left alone in the precincts, after they had prayed to the god that they might take that bull which should be an acceptable sacrifice to him, began to hunt the bulls, without weapons of iron, with staves and nooses; and when they had taken one of them they brought him to the Table of the Commandments, and there struck him on the head and shed his blood over the writing, and afterwards burnt his members, and mingled a bowl, casting into it clots of his blood, one clot for each of the Ten. Then they drew from the bowl in golden vials, and poured a libation on the fire, and swore that they would give judgments, and do all things, according to the Commandments of their Father Poseidon written on the Table. When they had drunken of the vials, and dedicated them in the Temple, they had their feast; and after supper, when it was dark and the sacrificial fire had died down, they put on azure robes exceeding beautiful, and sat down on the ground about the embers, all the lights in the Temple having been extinguished, and there, in the darkness of night, judged and were judged; and when day dawned they wrote the judgments on a golden tablet, and laid it by, along with their robes, for a memorial. These include:

Remember the past to keep it sacred, since the Lord and your ancestors have given us only one eternity to keep sacred; be great cultivators both of soil and soul, because it's only in that way that there will be a tomorrow's harvest; if you live on an island love it, but remember no man is an island and that no island belongs to one man.

> Learn to build the pyramid
> Learn to dance the djoumba
> Learn to listen to the silence
> Learn to live alive in the desert
> Learn to make the drum w/the sacred skin of the goat or the sheep
> or the cow; w/the correct signal wood of the tree
> (coconut here in the Caribbean. ebony, cedar, mahogany)
> w/the beautiful skill of the palms of yr hands, yr wrist & the fingers
> Make the drum say make it sing
> Like the djoumbe, the conga, the kete, the nyabinghi, the funde, the
> Fontomfrom,
> Like the panam, the banja, like the atumpan.... ("Fragments" 7-8)

And now their minds are filled with poetry. It came to them in the night, entering their very being. The premier poet is the descendant of Atlas; he holds up the world now as a wordsmith, now as a musician. He is said to reside at a small island, living a simple life, passing his father's trade on to deserving souls so they might sing through all time. The poet stands tall and unassuming, shunning the glare of his illustrious ancestors. He lives at a place due south from the island-mountain, called Eleutheria, where he can fashion his words and songs and pass them on to the descendants of the seafaring God, pass them on at night in their dreams. And that is part of what the dolphin whispered at the end. Some of what it said appears in the book, I can read it before me, but as soon as I look away it becomes erased, and I cannot find it again.

Steel drum steel drum
hit the hot calypso dancing
hot rum hot rum
who goin' stop this bacchanalling?

when they come
with their cameras and straw
hats: sacred pink tourists from the frozen Nawth

we should get down to those
white beaches
where if we don't wear breeches

it becomes an island dance
*Some people doin' well
while others are catchin' hell*

o the boss gave our Johnny the sack
though we beg him please
please to take 'im back

so the boy now nigratin' overseas. ("Calypso," RP 49-50)

Hephaistos appears to have come back and is now sitting by me. I am sprawled at the bottom of the ship exhausted and do not know where I am or whether I'm still alive. I hear the kind man telling me that I must eat something, that we're approaching Newfoundland, and what will become of me in the new world, and more of such motherly laments. He has picked up the book and I hear him mutter, "Plato, J.A. Stewart Hm, must be an

Englishman. They're the only ones who still read Plato, them and the dolphins." I stir, "Is the war over, Hephaistos?" He laughs, "Yes, it's the mid-nineteen fifties, my boy."

> So my island drifts
> plundered by butterflies.
> The dog lifts his mourning to heaven. ("Littoral," IS 172)

In the lazy tumble of years, with the jagged bumblebee's flight, we linger in the global city, its Greenwich Village, crisscrossing the one-time graveyard, now a triumph of Atlantis raised from the ashes of the dream. Oneiric: the poet dreams disaster into submission on a bitter cold January morning; tulips of snow give Washington Square over to white flames (*pace* Henry James); the lanky figure, still a descendant of Atlas, cuts across: a stevedore's woolen cap comes to a point, a goatee compliments the downward slant, steel-rimmed glasses—every bit a Trotsky on a vulnerable day. We meet at *Pane e Cioccolato* for the coffee nectar of these parts. And there we ask ourselves many questions. But we leave the most important ones pass us by in knowing silence: What on earth are we doing here, which way is it to the bottom of the ocean, the Mountain-island and its gorges, the many names of Eleuftheria? And we both know that Diotima's love is the only thing that remains, the only fragment of the good life to contemplate. The January snows continue to burn white, like my grandfather's ritual torch long ago.

Pedagogy and the
Sensibilities of Race

Ralph Jemmott

The 1970 graduating History class of UWI's Mona Campus, we who were the first to study under Edward Kamau Brathwaite in the course, "History, Society and Ideas in the British West Indies during Slavery," may be particularly well-placed to recognise his contributions to Caribbean and world-wide scholarship. Participants included many who have gone on to occupy leading roles in education, publishing, politics and business in Jamaica, Barbados, and elsewhere. Being myself now focused on education, it seems appropriate that I write of what I believe his students took from him and his class by way of education and enlightenment.

The history faculty at Mona in the late 1960s was blessed with persons who were not only brilliant scholars, but good teachers. It included such stalwarts as Dr. Roy Augier, Professor Elsa Goveia, Dr. David Buisseret, Professor Douglas Hall, Dr. Woodville Marshall, Dr. Keith Lawrence, Dr. Walter Rodney and Brathwaite himself. Each teacher brought to our education their own particular influences. The imperatives of scholastic precision were inculcated by Roy Augier and Woodville Marshall, while the sense of academic gravity was fostered by Professors Hall and Goveia. With respect to professor Brathwaite as lecturer and teacher, I would want to address his contribution in the area of affective learning, that is, in the creating and nourishing of sensibility, particularly what I shall call "the sensibility of race," a positive repositioning of one's sense of ethnic identity. Formal education or schooling is about the fostering of knowledge, thinking or cognition and sensibility. The development of sensibility, or way of Being, is a dimension of education that is now more honoured in the breach than in the observance, concerned as we have become with the utilitarian aspects of formal schooling.

Sitting in Kamau Brathwaite's class at Mona, I recognised that of all the people in that class he and I alone had certain things in common, we were both Barbadian-born men, the three other Barbadians, Jackie Alleyne-Wade (now of the Cave Hill campus), Jean Belle (now of the Caribbean Development Bank) and Dr. Janice Mayers (now at Combermere School) were all women, and we, Dr. Brathwaite and myself had both attended Harrison College, a prestigious boys' school developed along the lines of the English public schools. I entered Harrison college in 1953 some four years after Brathwaite won the Barbados Scholarship in 1949. (As males we were both the products of the same society and the same type of Grammar school colonial education). This is significant and very much linked to my emphasis on the orientation of consciousness.

By the time I arrived at Mona, Dr. Brathwaite had gone off to Cambridge, lived for a while in Africa and had completed his doctoral work on the development of creole society in Jamaica. My own education to that point in terms of History as an academic discipline involved the normal British and European fare that was part and parcel of the Oxford and Cambridge Ordinary- and Advanced-Level syllabi. I left Harrison College in 1962 with painfully little knowledge of Barbadian or Caribbean History and an absolute ignorance of Africa and its people. In fact I am ashamed to say that like many young Barbadians of that time, my perception of Africa and Africans was based largely on the popular Tarzan movies and adventure films such as *The Snows of Kilimanjaro* which I regularly viewed at the Roxy Cinema·, situated only four houses below where I lived in the Bank Hall district, a working class suburban area of Bridgetown. The protagonists of history for me were the heroes of English and British Imperialist discourses, Robert Walpole, the Earl of Stanhope, Bute, the Duke of Wellington, Admirals Nelson and Rodney, Robert Clive and Warren Hastings in India. This peculiar indoctrination if you will, had started earlier at the Wesley Hall Primary School when the History teacher told us about a Sir John Hawkins (the teacher who first aroused my interest in and love of History was Mr Walter Trotman and he was a very good teacher). I think that those of us who left Wesley Hall at the tender age of ten all assumed that Hawkins was "a great man." He was white, he was English and he was a Knight, Sir John. The point is that the teacher as far as I can remember said little or nothing about the horrors of the Slave Trade and the complicity and infamy of Hawkins's participation in it. I was only ten at the time, but adults in Barbados were guilty of what George Lamming has called the same "tragic innocence." A colleague at Harrison College had a cousin with the curious name of Cecil Rhodes Bell. In an obituary notice last year, I came across another Barbadian named "Cecil Rhodes" something, both named by their black parents after the racist imperial British explorer. Talk about a "tragic innocence." Lamming recently and rightly concluded, in this year's National Heroes Day speech, that in the Barbados of that time the British Empire was seen as the custodian of human destiny and white racist myths were widely perpetuated and internalised.

The British colonial education given to black children in Barbados and the Caribbean placed little or no emphasis on the child's racial and ethnic identity. Instead, both formal schooling as well as what the Greeks called the "paedeia," those nonformal influences in the community and the culture, worked towards a denigration of negritude and a consequential alienation from the self . The eminent Barbadian novelist and social critic was profoundly accurate when he stated recently that "in Barbados there was a profound contempt for anything that was black." The result for many was what he posits as "a terror of the mind and a daily exercise in self-mutilation." The black Barbadian child of the period was told to value education as a path to social mobility and social respectability, but both mobility and respectability often required a rejection of negritude and Africanity and an embracing of self-defeating Eurocentric values and norms.

At Mona I believed I was fortunate in my teachers generally speaking and in making the acquaintance of Dr Walter Rodney and Dr Edward Brathwaite. My acquaintance with Dr Rodney was limited to a single speech at an after-dinner ceremony in Irvine Hall in 1968, but it was a critical turning point in the development of a positive racial consciousness. I remember well that Rodney Speech. The microphone was malfunctioning and Walter, putting the microphone aside, raised his voice and I will never forget the opening words of the speech which were: "It is the white man not the black man who has defined the parameters of racism." Rodney's address was a moral discourse on black redemption in which he indicated how the white race was historically in the wrong.

I am not sure what effect the speech had on others, but the scales had fallen from my eyes and I remember saying to myself "why hasn't anyone told me about this before?" That initial reorientation of consciousness that began with Rodney (shortly thereafter he was expelled from Jamaica by the Shearer Government) was continued under Edward Brathwaite in the course which he taught in the second year of the three year undergraduate course. Much of the substantive material for the course was based on Kamau's research into the nature of creole society and we were introduced, many of us for the first time to the importance of the African presence in Caribbean history and literature, a presence which I certainly had been led to believe was discontinuous or largely peripheral to the main stream and currents of West Indian history. Furthermore the impression had been given that what in Dr. Brathwaite's words had "survived the trauma" was not particularly worthy of study.

Two other rewards emerged from that course which was a compound of history and literature. Having done both history and literature at A-level, it was rewarding to take up the literature again and explore the creative literature of the region. I do remember however that the class had particular difficulty with the seemingly very esoteric works of Wilson Harris. Being a poet as well as an historian, Kamau Brathwaite was able to bring a certain sensibility to the human aspects of the script. As the famed educationalist Jerome Bruner has pointed out, "the scientist and the poet do not live at antipodes," there should always be a synthesis of cognition and sensibility.

The other dimension of change in understanding and sensibility which we the students of the class of 1970 derived from the teaching of Kamau was an appreciation of the imperative of viewing and indeed writing history from the bottom up. Having to that point studied mainly political, British constitutional history, it was a refreshing change to examine the discourse from the perspective of the folk, a motif that characterised much of the professor's teaching. Here for the first time, students became aware of what Sir Keith Hunte, the Principal of UWI Cave Hill, called "the people beyond the script." Here for the first time was a conscious attempt to legitimise the role of the slaves, the labouring classes and the women, the poor and the dispossessed of the Caribbean as the subjects rather than the objects of the history. Here for the first time was the culture of the folk, folklore, folk music and dance, folk dress, religion and language. I believe that history students today take this kind of focus for granted, but in the 1960s this focus was still relatively new. I am suggesting here that the contribution of Brathwaite to our education with regard to the discipline of history was not only a development of sensibility and awareness of our identity as young black West Indians, but also of the struggles of the class in which most of us had our social origins.

This new emphasis on what William Green calls "the underside of life in the Caribbean" was a natural corollary of the trend away from writing and studying history from the hegemonic imperial perspective. Philip Curtin observed in 1955 (in his *Two Jamaicas*) that Caribbean history could be written from two perspectives, either as an extension of the British experience or as the history of a distinctive and autonomous culture. Kamau Brathwaite belongs to a line of Caribbean historians, novelists, poets and social critics who have sought to repatriate our history or as Green again puts it, "to shift the historical centre of gravity from Europe to the Caribbean" ("Creolisation"). This new historiography begins with Eric Williams and includes the contributions of Elsa Goveia, Gordon Lewis, Walter Rodney and Hilary Beckles. I think it is fair to say that although there are variations on the theme, few if any West Indian historians currently write outside that perspective. This counter- Eurocentric discourse has done much to reverse the tragic innocence of the ideological imperialist delirium that once afflicted us as a people.

I believe that it was in one of Dr. Brathwaite's classes that we examined the concept of the "decolonised mind." I cannot claim to know Kamau Brathwaite, but I have long felt that of all the prominent persons I have met, Kamau best represents the concept of the decolonised mind, that is a mind-set and a persona shorn of the petit-bourgeois pretensions of the post-colonial Caribbean intelligentsia: the obsession with money, status and class and a hypocritical social distancing of themselves from the proletarian class they often claim to know, represent and defend.

Dr. Brathwaite is of course best associated with the notion of creolisation. Some academic theories appear often to defy linear logic and in spite of the authoritative and sometimes absolutist claims of their authors offer imperfect and limited instruments for the study of complex historical realities and what William Green calls "the kaleidoscopic diversity of human motives." As a student it seemed to me that the creolisation thesis not only possessed a certain intellectual coherence and integrity, but a common-sense plausibility: that transplanted peoples and culture cannot sustain the organic purity of their origins, that not only must they adjust to the new environment, but that they are likely to form in the process of interaction a new and distinct socially fashioned amalgam. Professor Rex Nettleford concurs. In his address "Caribbean Paradoxes and the Crisis of Change," a speech delivered in Barbados on Wednesday 29 May 1996 (The Sir Hugh Springer Memorial Lecture), he opined, "to this day genuine Caribbean expressions are regarded as those that have been creolised into indigenous form and purpose, distinctively different from the original elements from which those expressions first sprang."

Mervyn Morris

OBLATION

Then shall the poet say:

Draw near, and touch
my suppurating wounds.

This is my psyche
broken for you. Give thanks.

You have not cared enough.
But you may clap.

Kamau Brathwaite:
A Heartfelt Memoir

John La Rose

It was at the time that I was preparing to reprint John Jacob Thomas's *The Theory and Practice of Creole Grammar* (1869) and his *Froudacity* (1889) that I decided to contact Kamau. He was then Edward Brathwaite and we all called him Eddie. That was how his wife, Doris and friends then called him.

I thought he was in Barbados as his name appeared in *Bim*. I therefore knew him and his work through *Bim*. Making enquiries I discovered he was in London, at William Goodenough House where postgraduate and postdoctoral academics and researchers found accommodation.

In trying to come to grips with the complexity of Caribbean society, which we sought to transform, this political and cultural grouping in Trinidad, to which I belonged, had formed study groups where we studied, among others, one of the books of J. J. Thomas. Both of his main books were then out of print for generations. Getting hold of a copy of the *Grammar*, we had the complete text copied on a typewriter and used that for study. This book was popularly known in Trinidad, among aficionados, as the *Patois Grammar*. Among the other books we read and studied were Arthur Lewis's *Labour in the West Indies,* T.S. Simey's *Development and Welfare in the West Indies*. Eric Williams's *Capitalism and Slavery* and C. L. R. James's *The Black Jacobins* were also in the bundle of titles too numerous to mention in full. We were dedicated to the study and transformation of Caribbean society: its history, its creative literature, its folklore, its music and song, its culture, its politics, its social life, its institutions and its economy.

I wanted Elsa Goveia, the great historian whose work I admired and who had taught Walter Rodney and Gordon Rohlehr when they were both students at the University of the West Indies—UWI (the University College of the West Indies as it was then, an affiliate college of the University of London), to write the introduction to *Froudacity* which was, for me, a seminal defense of the Caribbean's ever widening aspirations for progress at the end of the 19th century.

As an historian, then working in the Department of History at the University of the West Indies, I thought Kamau would know where Elsa Goveia was and how to find her. In fact he did, but as she was otherwise busy on research for a history series for UWI courses, she could not write the introduction as I requested. I then asked C. L. R. James, who wrote a brilliant introduction and overview to *Froudacity,* which we at New Beacon published.

I telephoned Kamau's flat and we immediately agreed to meet. And that was the beginning of a close and lasting friendship. .

The year was 1966. In August of that year I, as founder and Sarah White as co-founder, launched the New Beacon publishing house with the publication of my first book of poems *Foundations*. New Beacon was named after the 1930's *Beacon* journal in which Albert Gomes, Alfred Mendes . and C. L. R. James had played the major roles. And, as it happened, the first meeting of the Caribbean Artists Movement took place in Kamau's flat in William Goodenough House in December of that same year, 1966.

Kamau and I knew of each other indirectly. I had been noticing his work in Frank Collymore's journal *Bim*. I had sent the last poem in *Foundations,* a long poem called "Song to an Imperishable Sunlight" to Norman Girvan then an academic economist at UWI Mona, Jamaica. I also sent it to John Maxwell, then editor of *Public Opinion*, for publication in the journal, founded and owned by O.T. Fairclough. Maxwell had published it but until I met Kamau I did not know this. Norman told me he had shown it to his close friend George Beckford, and to some others. He had also shown it to Kamau.

When we met, Kamau wanted to know more about "Song to An Imperishable Sunlight." I told him that was the end, that it was a complete sequence, there was nothing else. He told me of his book *Rights of Passage*, which was soon to be published by Oxford University Press in London. We met on common ground. I had been thinking of how to bring the novelists, poets, literary critics, painters and sculptors together. He too already had ideas of this type of interconnection between artists, which could be formed in London. I had mentioned something of this to Wilson Harris when we first met at the home of a mutual Guyanese friend in 1961. Wilson does not remember this. But Kamau and I agreed that he would contact Andrew Salkey, who knew everybody, and I would contact Wilson Harris and any others. That was the foundation of our triple alliance, Kamau, Andrew and I, and the building of CAM. Rather it was our quadruple alliance, including Doris, because she played such a pivotal role.

One night when we were meeting to discuss the future we were planning I was a few minutes late. As I entered his flat I heard a voice reading. It was a recording of Kamau's voice reading from his brilliant long poem *Rights of Passage*. Everybody was listening, as in a reverie.

Until that moment I had never heard a voice so beautifully modulated, reading poetry so movingly, with such transparent artistic vision and sincerity. I had known other readers and reciters of poetry but none with such an aesthetic sense and striving for perfection. Somehow I have a vague recollection of Orlando Patterson (then a lecturer at the London School of Economics) speaking in Kamau's flat about the admiration on the Mona campus for Kamau's reading of poetry. I immediately proposed to Kamau–that day–that Sarah and I and New Beacon would produce a reading of the whole of his *Rights*. I was so moved. I felt confident that he would do it beautifully and would hold the audience with the internal drama, rhythm and music of the poem.

We, Sarah and I, had been attending all the plays at the Jeanetta Cochrane Theatre which Jim Haynes was then producing there, and we knew him otherwise. He had been innovating in Edinburgh with his paperback bookshop and with his Traverse Theatre which became part of the Edinburgh Fringe Festival. He produced only plays by living contemporary playwrights and it was there at the Jeanetta Cochrane Theatre, with Jim Haynes's cooperation, that New Beacon produced Kamau's reading of *Rights of Passage*.

CAM was about to launch its regular monthly sessions and its members were highly stimulated and in a state of general intellectual excitement and they all helped to advertise the event. New Beacon invited all the connections we had, including Douglas Cleverdon who had produced the BBC radio performance of Dylan Thomas's *Under Milk Wood*. We had a distinguished audience of writers, artists and critics from the Caribbean and from Britain. And I produced the dramatized reading and performance. Kamau and Dermot Hussey also contributed suggestions to the production. There was a changing of positions on stage for different sections of *Rights* and pinpoint lighting of Kamau as he moved into different positions on stage. The whole event was a great success. Discussion and comment about what Kamau had achieved at this reading rumbled on into the public sessions of CAM when they began soon after.

The programme leaflet for the *Rights of Passage* reading and performance also announced the launch of public sessions of CAM at the West Indian Students Centre in London for just a week later. At the centre of all this were Eddie and Doris. They, Eddie and Doris, were like an undifferentiated, unbreakable word. Both played a pivotal role. And this was the beginning of Kamau's continuing influence on Caribbean poetry and letters as critic, historian, as poet.

This was a time of coincidence. New novels were being published and discussed at CAM sessions. The work of painters and sculptors were being displayed at art exhibitions. CAM sessions were full. Audiences included people of distinction. It was a kind of agora, a time of renaissance. The news of what was happening in London spread far and wide. The students at the Centre were energized into work with supplementary schools and public drama performances of plays like Ed Bullins's *Electronic Nigger* and the dramatization of Okot p'Bitek's *Song of Lawino*. Caribbeans in Britain were being influenced by the Black Power and Black Consciousness movements swirling around them. They were continuing in the direction that Caribbean organizations in Britain had initiated after the Notting Hill Riots of 1958. Education was of paramount concern. And we were in the anteroom of the Black Education Movement including the formation of the Caribbean Education and Community Workers Association (CECWA) and the Supplementary School Movement.

Kamau was concerned to know and observe all this resurgence in which Andrew and I were involved, I more than Andrew.

The first and second CAM conferences were held in 1967 and 1968 at the University of Kent at Canterbury. Louis James, one of our founders, taught there and facilitated arrangements. Kamau had urged New Beacon to set up a special bookselling event at the conference and we did so. It was also our first sortie into general bookselling and our first issue of a trilingual booklist in the main languages of the Caribbean: English, French and Spanish. The experience was invaluable for us and the conference participants. There was such a hunger for the books we had collected for the occasion. I was persuaded to open up late that night after the last creative session. The room was packed and I was there until about 2.00am. Kamau was happy and satisfied. It was his inspired suggestion. As we continued later on with book displays at CAM sessions and at other meetings, big and small, and at conferences, the hunger was the same. London and Britain were cauldron of challenge and change.

In one of the creative sessions of the CAM conferences I read from a bilingual edition of Aimé Césaire's *Cahier d'un Retour au Pays Natal* published by Présence Africaine and from Hampate Bâ's account of a creation myth taken from the proceedings of one of the conferences of Negro Writers and Artists organized by Présence. After that session Kamau was so enthused. Until then I did not know that we shared a passion for Aimé Césaire's work, especially for his *Cahier*. In a conversational aside amid banter he said: "I sleep with that book under my pillow."

Eddie and Doris again played central roles. But I knew that all intellectual, artistic and cultural movements like the *Beacon*, like *New World*, like CAM, like Surrealism eventually run their course; they leave their indelible mark on the artists and on the society, and having ingested and absorbed the experience the artists move on to new moments of intense creativity. CAM could not be replicated in the Caribbean or anywhere else. It was *sui generis* in place and time. Kamau had hoped for more but his immense creativity and originality now had a wider international reach.

This was also a time when Kamau was hard at work on his doctoral thesis at the University of Sussex supervised by the inestimable Donald Wood. When we read the thesis (published later as *The Development of Creole Society in Jamaicia 1770-1720*), we offered to publish a small section of it under the title *Folk Culture of the Slaves in Jamaica*, and he agreed. Kamau had left his PhD for later, when it mattered to him, just as Susan Craig, another island scholarship winner, also did; she an Island Scholar from Trinidad and Tobago, he an Island Scholar from Barbados.

It was during this time I discovered how lavishly he spent each week on jazz and other music records. In passing conversation, he mentioned how much he spent and I was amazed. But I shouldn't have been. The music and rhythm were embedded inside the heart of his poetry. And when he read it, he often drummed the rhythm with his fingers on any available spot or on the book and sometimes in the air like a conductor. He was a different drummer, with the mellifluous voice, a Haitian houngan as he imagined. He was a "marvel of reality" in the tradition of Alejo Carpentier's "lo real maravilloso" and Jacques Stephen Alexis's "le réalisme merveilleux."

Kamau would have liked New Beacon to publish more of his marvelous, voluminous literary oeuvre but we at New Beacon had decided to remain small to medium publishers and to expand our cultural activity in other directions with, for example, the International Book Fair or Radical Black and Third World Books and its accompanying Book Fair Festival, which we co-founded in 1982. Though we admired his genius and his fertile continuous innovation over the years we were like Leonard and Virginia Woolf with their Hogarth Press. Our work would be significant, influential and circumscribed. Others would be inspired to take up the baton.

Kamau had traveled far; from the Roundhouse and the sea, through thickets of jazz and cricket, thence to Cambridge, the university, another

Englishness indifferent to national pluralisms and emerging enthnicities, a variable Europe; from there to Ghana and the interior of Africanity and back; back to the Caribbean, ex Africa, X-self, back into the literature and wandering of history, of stories where it began, for him, for Derek Walcott, for Wilson Harris, for our Selves.

We met in midlife in London, each with years and volumes of experience. The visit I paid to his home, in the Roundhouse, was memorable insight and seeing. He was in his kumbla, in the midst of mother, father and aunt. We drove through Bridgetown visiting friends, reminiscing amid relics of his inheritance, the thread between his present and past. The house in Bay Street, opposite to the Roman Catholic Cathedral was now a little distant from the sea but in his time of childsplay the water almost lapped outside the house.

I was at Shop Hill years later and he at Dover Beach. We met in front of the conference centre on the sand and in the sea. He swam with the pleasure of a watersprite, returned to the Maresol to continue with his composition of *Sun Poem* while we vanished back into the beauty of Barbados.

By then, as "Pathfinder," in Gordon Rohlehr's phrase, Kamau had journeyed through the slings and arrows of outrageous criticism, not in silence, but with counterattack, creative self-affirmation and expansion of vision. I admired the resilience of his spirit. The great moment arrived, as it often does in the history of societies, unexpectedly. E. M. Roach, the gifted and largely ignored Caribbean poet, wrote witheringly in *The Trinidad Guardian* about *Savacou 3/4,* the Special Issue dated December 1970/March 1971 and devoted to "New Writing 1970." It had been edited by Kamau. Gordon Rohlehr wrote a devastating piece in reply. That was a landmark.

Kamau had clarioned the call in his introduction to the issue. He used another neologism from his armoury of neologisms: 'Foreward*'. The asterisk was his and at the bottom of the same page he wrote "*sic":

> At a time when the region is engaged in a serious, necessarily revolutionary questioning of West Indian values and their political, social and economic implications, it is very heartening to find that the imaginative literature of the region...reflects this crisis and indeed is often pragmatically involved in the debate. The way in which the number took shape is evidence of this inescapable fact, and the result is that although it was not put together according to any thematic masterplan, it demands, we think, to be read as a whole and single testimony.

These words, written by Arthur Drayton for the special West Indian number of *The Literary Half-Yearly* (Mysore, India, 1970) which

he guest edited, could apply with aptest justness to this first New
Writing issue from *Savacou*.

It was in relation to this work of cultural inspiration as well as to his historical researches and his shaping of a new poetry that Gordon Rohlehr used
the word "Pathfinder" to describe Kamau. As Gordon wrote in the foreword to his book of that title: "Pathfinder seeks to explore the various processes whereby Brathwaite has invested the word with dimension and den-
sity, on his journey from *Rights of Passage* through *Masks* to *Islands*.
This study places focus on the background and the contexts out of which
the poetry took shape, and on the actual process of shaping." The shaping
was that of his own creative and critical work and of Caribbean culture
more broadly.

Savacou was, to quote its own statement, "A Journal of the Caribbean
Artists Movement." It was started when Kamau left London and returned
to the Caribbean. He was its main inspiration.

CAM from its foundation in 1966 and Kamau and Gordon had consolidated the intellectual and artistic thrust of a new cultural paradigm in the
lands and waters of the Caribbean and beyond. The debate and public fra-
cas which occurred on the Mona campus of the University of the West
Indies during the 1972 Commonwealth Literature Conference, in which V.
S. Naipaul and others including Kamau were involved, was the tailend of a
hurricane blowing through Caribbean literature and society, which had not
yet died down. Andrew Salkey and I quite deliberately did not attend and
were later reproached for not taking our responsibilities seriously.

Whenever, over the years, Kamau visited London and stayed with us it
was like family reunion and renewal; the toing and froing of friend and
phonecall, laughing and talking, wideranging information and analysis,
perceptive discourse, serious conversation and ole talk.

It was during one of my many visits to the Caribbean that Sarah telephoned me with urgent news. Doris was dying of cancer. I wanted to know
what kind of cancer, and if Sarah could contact any of our friends or contacts in cancer research and see if they could find out the state of current
research and possibility of early breakthrough. I decided to cancel my travel
plans and headed immediately for Jamaica. I could imagine the inexpress-
ible turmoil that Kamau would be in and his need for unconditional help
and support from friends and family. His sister Mary was there and close.
Doris, smiling, loving and understanding, had given her all to Kamau.
Whenever he expressed his irritations or larger annoyances or hurt she
always soothed him. I sometimes heard her say: "but Eddie" to smooth
him.

I got there after he knew the end was nearing. I stayed with them in Irish Town. While there, Kamau and I learned from Sarah in London that there would be no breakthrough for that kind of cancer in the near future. Possibly in a couple of years, the researchers said. Kamau was devastated. I had wanted to see lovely Doris, to be with her, to be with them. She was the same beautiful, sensitive, thoughtful woman and companion to Kamau as I had always known her.

Doris was loved in the village and anxious about what would happen to Kamau. I had seen this concern and anguish before, with another husband and another wife, when Sarah's mother was dying of cancer. Doris died not long after.

Kamau's *Zea Mexican Diary* is one of the most moving and haunting testaments to love and parting. It is a great and enduring prose poem.

This was Kamau's greatest time of turmoil and distress. He hit out in all directions. But as Thucydides wrote: "Time softens grief". Time and the gift of creative genius with which Kamau is blessed.

I stayed with Kamau in his New York flat close to New York University after participating in a conference at MIT in the mid 1990s. He devoted himself to his work as if driven, writing and innovating on his computer late into the night and almost as soon as he rose early in the morning. I had to remind myself of his absorbing interest in and use of the latest and most up-to-date electronic equipment ever since we first met in 1966. His fertile artistic creativity was bolstered by the almost inexhaustible computerized devices. He played around as he explored its capacity for shape and aesthetic as he composed and recomposed anew.

We met again in the quiet of Barbados with Beverley and on Dover Beach again.

> Ever seen
> a man
> travel more
> seen more
> lands... ("Folkways," RP 34)

seen more love, seen more loss, seen more admiration and devotion, seen more in and into the world, seen and endured so much.

Peace and Love at 70.

Edward Kamau Brathwaite
Enfant Terrible or Kindred Spirit?
A Personal Commentary

Rex Nettleford

Every so often a generation throws up a crop of persons who live, have their being and, in doing so, manage to make a difference to that very generation by the exercise of the creative imagination. They bring to the existence, not only of their people but also of all humanity, iconic dimensions of growth and texture by the sheer excellence of their output as artists or as intellectuals, as conceptualisers or as cultural activists. The Caribbean in its post-Emancipation, Self-government and Independence dispensations has not been short on such a phenomenon. This region is a place of hilly, sandy spaces and cubic meters of salt-water concealing the "*submarine unity*" of an otherwise fragmented, hyphenated polity of diverse races (purish and hopelessly mixed), of classes, ideologies and myriad uncertainties. It is tenanted by a few million souls who are still emerging from the holocaust of slavery and protracted colonial abuse. It has depended for all of half a millennium on its creative workers to help it achieve that emergence from the obscurity of self.

In this regard Kamau Brathwaite stands head and shoulders above a great many others and abreast of the likes of Nobel laureate Derek Walcott, literary grandmaster George Lamming, the controversial Vidia Naipaul (who, he would agree, is part of the process even if they both differ on the vision of their people and their potential), the wondrous calypsonians Lord Kitchener and the Mighty Sparrow, the enduring and noble Jimmy Cliff and the great philosopher-lyricist Bob Marley who have all attracted from almost all of Planet Earth universal acclaim and prideful recognition.

Kamau Brathwaite, unlike some of his own peers, understands the process so deeply that he would not think of denying to popular artists in the reggae and calypso genres the legitimacy of stakeholding in that process. For to him, there are different kinds of poets, different kinds of artists, different kinds of creators each given to the flow of creative juices which result severally in different brews but offer no justification for the notion that a Brathwaite or a Walcott, a Lamming or a Naipaul belong to a better breed of players than others who may themselves be proven protectors of the patrimony. For all great art, of which poetry may well be both the essence and a nodal point in the creative process, is mediated by social reality and serves to extend human existence beyond mere survival.

But then Brathwaite is a *historian* as well as poet, literary critic, essayist, and cultural activist. His seminal work, *The Development of Creole Society in Jamaica, 1770-1820*, resonates with the voice of the creative imagination. The finest chapters are arguably those which plumb the depths of his own imagination and sensibilities in order to get at the deeper social forces that informed the dynamic survival of the majority of the population throughout slavery. For was it not the slaves who demonstrated the invincibility of the human spirit against all odds not simply by armed resistance but by the power of the mind, collective and individual? Had they not lived, they and their descendants of whom Kamau Brathwaite is inescapably one, to tell the tale?

So the chapters on the "Folk Culture of the Slave" and the penultimate chapter on "Creolization" give important clues to the extensive body of works produced since the Sixties by this insightful, creative and stubbornly courageous thinker on the formation of a society struggling *"to be."* Let him speak for himself: "The single most important factor in the development of Jamaican society was not·the imported influence of the Mother Country or the local administrative activity of the white élite, but a *cultural* action—material, psychological and spiritual—based upon the stimulus/response of individuals within the society to their environment and–as white/black, culturally discrete groups–to each other" (296, my emphasis). He supports this bold and seemingly insolent statement with material drawn from historical sources, and he found confirmation for his own hunches as a creative artist in plumbing the depths of Caribbean feeling and reality. His search for form to encapsulate this reality is part of his adventurous essay into poetic experimentation which prompts from at least one critic the view that he is "arguably the most original poet yet to emerge from the

Caribbean in terms of his technical experimentation with form and language and the sheer scope and ambition of his work...."

Such a statement is enough to fuel controversy, or rather *more* controversy, about this poet-historian who has never failed to engage his peers, friends and foes alike, in passionate discourse/debate on the *"publicness"* of his poetry (he has long performed his poems and addressed issues of the moment in trenchant prose, the deliberate exposure of rafters in an otherwise elegant poetic edifice, the *"exaggerated"* claims for the African Presence in a still emerging civilisation which owes everything not only to any one ancestor but also to all who, on Brathwaite's own insistence, is a civilisation of *"arrivants"* from a variety of "elsewheres."

But in fairness to Brathwaite, he felt that this is no excuse for his people to be distorted echoes of those elsewheres—Africa included. For he believes in the intrinsic ability of a people, the Caribbean people included, to be the creators of their own destiny, the *determiners* of life's mainstream rather than mere tributary-entrants into someone else's waterway.

Such is the vision and the conviction, pursued sometimes with a less than quiet missionary zeal, that leads him to that side of history which eschews notions of (European) *classical* versus ethnic *folklore* Other, of Great Tradition versus Little Tradition, with the output of his own people arbitrarily relegated as *aberrations* to the latter while the master's tongue, religion, kinship structures, artistic manifestations, philosophies, metaphysics, political arrangements and economic paradigms remain sole claimants to *"the norm."*

This established him as a kindred spirit the very first time we met in St Lucia—I as staff tutor in Political Education, he as Resident Tutor, and both of us as *"guerilla intellectuals"* in the employ of the University of the West Indies Extra Mural Department, the outreach wing of a still Oxbridge institution of higher learning in an erstwhile outpost of Empire—the British West Indies. His accent was unmistakably Bajan, but the spirit was the fighting one of the African diaspora with sense and sensibility rooted in the reality of a Caribbean still grappling with contradictions forged in the crucible of creative diversity and a kind of stable disequilibrium.

I wondered whether he was finding our arc of islands to be a greater challenge than Ghana, whether our islands did not challenge him in a way that ancestral Ghana, where he had lived and worked after a sojourn in the *"Motherland"* at Cambridge University, did not, despite the heterogeneity of Nkrumahland, tribe-wise (Akan dominance notwithstanding) and linguistically. His, for me, was an interesting journey *"back home,"* a literal return via the Middle Passage of historical memory and of particular significance to one like myself who had actually planned to proceed after

Oxford (that *"other place"* to Brathwaite's Cambridge) to the sister-University of Ibadan in Nigeria before taking up duties at UWI, Mona. The difference of course was that Kamau had not sampled the Caribbean through that undergraduate experience at the fledgling University College of the West Indies which spawned Caribbeanists of the ilk of Walcott et al. But now, I felt, he was filling that gap with an appointment (thanks to the foresight of Philip Sherlock) in the regional university. And though located in the threateningly marginalising outreach programme, he was well placed for the inward stretch that would take him through *Rights of Passage, Masks* and *Islands* to *Mother Poem* and all the other priceless poetic and prose gems he has produced to enrich a particular literature in English—the literature from the West Indies, which Ted Chamberlin, of Canada, was to see as long crying out to give its own language back to itself.

The journey—a kind of rite of passage—was in a way just beginning for a young Brathwaite blessed with the loyal support of best-friend Doris, his spouse and helpmate who stayed as companion and partner throughout that odyssey from Africa through St Lucia to Jamaica, where Brathwaite joined mainstream academia as Lecturer in the History Department at the Mona campus, until her untimely passing which left the mourning poet in virtual psychic disarray, but only for a while, albeit to some a longish while. His recovery may well have come because he remembered the shared vision of a mission to deal with the creative chaos of their region, to find form and purpose for his noisy beleaguered isles and Doris's mainland home of Guyana, which produced Wilson Harris and Martin Carter, fellow-poet to her beloved Kamau. He returned as quickly as he could, as if in memoriam to his and his "friend's" ritual quest for ideal, form and purpose for a budding civilisation which would know how to deal with what I have often referred to as the dilemma of difference, but without loss to the historical necessity of acknowledging and securing the centrality of the Africa Presence, transforming agent that it has been, to the Caribbean ethos.

Giving to this problematique a logical priority in the discourse about identity and the discovery of cultural certitude was clearly a recipe for a life of solitude, if not cultural marginalisation, in a region whose colonial pedigree took firm hold of consciousness among the brightest and the best long apprenticed, if not to take the region into independence, certainly to manage this longest colonised outpost of Empire—the West Indies—with autonomous efficiency often at the expense, alas, of autochthonous daring. Such contradictory omens he knew from early to be the stuff of the creative tension that issues from the region's cultural diversity coupled with the thirst for integration.

I remember wondering how someone so resolutely rebellious could manage to stand so firm in the wind rush of Shakespeare's language which has bent so many of his compatriots (with the glowing exception of Louise Bennett) to impeccable "Standard English" in the most banal of interpersonal exchanges or to "speaky-spokey" variations on the Queen's English. I further wondered why Kamau had not settled for composing music from neutral sounds or assembled movements into dance patterns–both modes of artistic expression long proven to be beyond the reach of the oppressor. But Brathwaite had no difficulty in using that *"Mother tongue."* As Walcott, Lamming, Wilson Harris and Aimé Césaire over in the French West Indies have themselves also demonstrated, liberal use of the imperial tongue and subversion of that monopoly claimed by the scribal writ on legitimacy and literary excellence are after all the *sine qua non* for the journey to a sense of place and purpose for the finest Caribbean writers. Kamau Brathwaite is firmly situated in this tradition.

For language, as he himself so well understood and repeatedly insisted, was more than a lexicon. It was rhythm, tone, pitch and more. It is the beat, it is music, it is dance! And for him the Caribbean voice draws naturally on its multivariate sources of energy to establish its own distinctive character evident in the dances of the peasant folk of the region as well as in the creations by Beryl McBurnie at the Little Carib, or in the *Kumina* of the Jamaican National Dance Theatre Company, in the music of the calypsonians of the Eastern Caribbean (his own Barbados now included) and the ska/rock steady/reggae complex of Jamaica, in the African diasporic blues, jazz and spirituals of the United States which is only one part of Africa-America of which his Caribbean is an integral and iconic part, and in the nation languages of the entire region which in turn feed the poetry, novels, dub and story-telling of all who tenant the lands ranging from the Bahamas to Guyana. The nation languages of the region have after all brought challenging richness to language generally, but specifically to so-called "Mother tongues" bearing such names as English, French, Spanish and Dutch. Without those nation languages there could be no srnan tonga, no papiamento, no kweyol, no Jamaica Talk, insists Brathwaite who would see them serving the purposes of a Robin Dobru, a Walcott, a Lamming, Louise Bennett, Samual Selvon, Vidia Naipaul, Vic Reid and, of course, himself! Did he not outdo himself with *Mother Poem* on this score? Talk about rhythm, tonality, texture and timbre! They—those motherpoems—are music to the ear!

Our paths crossed and criss-crossed for all of thirty and a little more years—as friends, as academic colleagues, in lecture and seminars, as fellow-artists, at Carifestas, backstage at performances, by letters (before and since email and fax). And indeed through that journal *Caribbean Quarterly* when as editor I feared the return of a Kamau-corrected proof-read manuscript since the entire (or most of an) already perfectly well-crafted piece was likely to disappear under not just corrections but a change of mind and sections to match. Perfectionist that he is and true artist, he knows so well how incomplete a work of art always tends to be for the creator and more so understands that one is only as good as one's last work.

Konversations in Kreole—Essays in Honour of Kamau Brathwaite, the theme of the Summer 1998 issue, was not only a collection of essays on the work of the prolific Kamau. This time it was to examine the theory of creolisation to which he has contributed seminal work. As I said then, it was fitting/significant that the guest editors Verene Shepherd and Glen Richards, beneficiaries of his tutelage, should be the ones to assemble the collection of essays in the form of serious critique and straightforward tribute by academicians drawn from such diverse disciplines as sociology, history, gender studies, literature, linguistics, musicology and poetry. This wide range of interests speaks to the interconnectedness of all knowledge and makes Kamau Brathwaite the kind of university teacher of whom more are needed to cope with the contradictory omens of the times, not only in the Caribbean but also in our Third Millennium world.

Back in 1982 a *Caribbean Quarterly* issue on *Critical Approaches to West Indian Literature* had guest editor Edward Baugh offering "*preliminary observations*" on Brathwaite as critic. But it was in the 1980 (March-June) issue of the journal in joint tribute to Brathwaite and Walcott that I described both literary luminaries as "two of the most distinguished and challenging of our creative writers writing in the English-speaking Caribbean today." The issue was timely. It came long before the Nobel Prize and the Neustadt International Prize for Literature, awards since won by both respectively. I felt that the "brilliant record at work so far [by both writers] and their contemporaneity in the vibrant, contradictory, and dynamic world of Caribbean letters and West Indian development quite rightly prompts...the dedication of the issue to them." Kamau's past work and all there is to come will continue to attract critical appraisal in his home region and far beyond to be sure.

In 1984 he generously consented to write a foreword for my effort to document the 21-year old history and development of Jamaica's National Dance Theatre Company in its quest for cultural definition and artistic discovery. He had been a keen follower, an astute and by no means indulgent critic of the Company's stated mission and the steps taken to realize that mission. He did not conceal his enthusiasm for the watershed appearance of the dance work *Kumina* in the repertoire of the NDTC in its performances at the first Caribbean Festival of Arts (Carifesta) in Georgetown, Guyana in 1972. He declared an epiphany for the ten-year old ensemble. I remember replying "Eddie (as I called him then), this is only the beginning." And so it was, as he agreed.

Ten years later he could write with characteristic poetic insight and linguistic elegance:

> It has become the body voice: brief but enduring signatures in space: of those who footstepped crouched leapt or were hurled onto what becomes the stage and drama of this book: the record of a people's cross & crossing: creative burden of colliding continents: reduced to necessary written word by this modestly masked "artistic director," who has him-singly done as much as anyone in these "blue scapes, Greek there" to articulate the pride & pain & passion brought us here, and more than most has worked far more than most toward that sense of style, vibration not missilic dictat; that cycle circle capsule contraction & release, that polyrhythmic contradiction we recognise as ours. ("Foreword" 11)

The passage is full of kinetic energy achieved in *"written word"* by this latter-day maroon who in flight from our locus of oppression constructs alternative habitats to plantation and plot back in a landscape where freedom is denied and movement restricted.

It is in this special sense that Kamau Brathwaite is a consummate "Caribbean man" and by so being is the "compleat" artist firmly rooted in the textured diversity of his Caribbean and a fine poet-scholar of universal proportions because of the depth and intensity he has brought to the specificity of Antillean history, his own experience and much that is the human condition.

The *"journey"* he joined as part of his artistic vision and his life's commitment has involved, as someone puts it, the challenges of "rebirth, rediscovery, reclamation of identity for West Indian people through an examination of their roots in the African past." To those marinated in European juices of the fermented obscenities of yore and who fail to grasp the significance of the meaning of that horrendous past, he remains an *enfant terrible*. But I am sure that he knows he has *kindred spirits* a-plenty among those who appreciate the acceptance of these roots as a necessity for the region to begin to "heal the negative self-images established by the experience of the middle passage, plantation and colonial life." For me, it is a kindred spirit who can articulate so effectively the despair that still lingers in all of this without a loss of faith or of hope in a future that depends on the proven creative potential of our Caribbean people.

History will indeed absolve the likes of Brathwaite; and generations to come will most likely intone *"it was good for him to have been here."*

Three Poems

Cynthia James

Beachboy

I watched you in the morning
look out across the ocean
sniffing like the wild horse
who knows but does not
know his ancient breath
that winds its way around the world

I saw you look
not knowing where or what to look
grasp a stick
scar sandpaper sand
run up the bronze beach
head for home

I watched you in the restless evening
back from school
return to try the dusky sky
to coax the wind
remove the rust
I watched you all the while

till one bank-holiday I heard you bugleing
there you were
cheeks bulging a lambi coral
bugleing to burst the blown world

broadcasting you had found the broken curl
blood running down your fingers

sieved grains of sand
leaved sea between the cut-lip coral
the little boy I watched
from far off standing on the gold
coast of little england looking to the other side
across a passage he thought he had forgot

sounding the syllables
in the porous crinkle of old bones
had found the message in the music
he was ready
to go out
and teach the world

CSN TV (Caribbean Satellite Network)

my friend
my friend
my absent friend

I wish you were here
to see the voyage
the voice has done

for sure the tribes still wail
in every manner of lament
but they enjoy

and I can sense
you'd like the revolution of the music
the Zouk, the Dub the industry of Dancehall

General Grant, young runaway
(some fear him, curse him!)
appoints himself protection

yes
the plantation's still alive
but instead of sugar metal grows

to suit
his boys no longer wear maroon
but sign now purple

and terror fabulous,
his second-in-command
refines what they left him of his tongue

these boys bad boys rude boys
don't hide no more Blue Mountain
but roam in open open jungle

bandana-d badmen
protected by their gansta anthem
ruling Kings and George and Bridge

such that some talk only
of their hate and contraband
and fear they runover all the towns

and plait their hair with hemp
and flex and sex with Patra
crying:
MUUUUURDERER!

O MUUUUURDERER!
Their miming fingers forking down
in shot call

time and time again in video
the ceaseless revolution
dubs and dubs and dubs

my friend my friend
I wish these times
my font were bit

as you would say
in time and tone
instead of heiro glyphic words

then I could transpose to you
these old and new and changeless
litanies

on which the new native has engraved
his soothing dove, his wind, his reed
his hope, his crashing ocean call

the tempest rages
STILL
yet no one dares dredge its midnight anger

the transplantation birthing
from top to bottom of the world
can no longer be ignored

and while I wake and wait
I take comfort in the new poet's
poetics

forgive my lack of faith
forgive me
Brother Caliban

Journey Mail
(Note to "Journeys" by Kamau Brathwaite)

Dear Mr. Kamau
(as one of the children say)
let me tell you about JOURNEYS

a journey is a milestone a teacher feel she pass
when she could stand up today
in a West Indian school
yes, in our schools
and teach Chaucer and Shakespeare and

"JOURNEYS"

by
Edward Kamau Brathwaite
same breath same breath
at last at last

a journey is when
the children's eyes light up
such that she feel we putting back
the brightness and the imagination
that you ask about
when you miss it and think it loss
scarce twenty years ago
when that teacher was in class
it wasn't so it wasn't so

a journey is when
she could be the link between
you and them and all of us
yes three of us
could continue the journey
into self-respect and experience
facing Amerindia
as you say
"gateway to the next millenium"

a journey is when
I hearing the History of the Voice
today along the way
blowing strong strong

and the children singing in all their tongues
and proud to stand up
and show those who only talking
because they have mouth
what is language creative language
including the oral songs

and of course
the best journey is when
my children could write to you
one of their poets
not wait until he dead
or only on a page
or in an archive
or removed from them in some wintry country
but feel you yes feel you
when they could write to you
and you answer back
and all of us in touch

for it is important
that the children see the makers of our songs
is people just like them
because all of us on the same journey
and they must know we could stretch out and
touch
because they have to feel
the corns and the blisters
and the warts
on the one hand so they will know
this is not
myth
this is not
storybook
but know they are makers too
and take up their pen
their pickaxe
whatever it is
for their own journey
alongside me and you

so I send the children's voices
like the voice of history
to tell you these journeys we make
and I know you will read these letters

and strengthen to see
why we can never forget the journey
you the poets make us make
even the boy who say
he real sorry
but he don't like your poetry

see how brave
and strong
the children get!

Walk with our blessing

Miss

The Word Walking Among Us:
Reading Kamau Brathwaite
with William Blake

Elaine Savory

> the Word becomes
> again a god and walks among us;
> look, here are his rags,
> here is his crutch and his satchel
> of dreams; here is his hoe and his rude implements.
> (Brathwaite, "Vèvè", *Islands, Arrivants,* 266)

> As a man is, So he Sees. As the Eye is formed, such are its powers.
> (*Blake's Poetry* 449)

> ... *we have to begin the great work of plan/tation psychocultural*
> *reconstruction by first knowing as clearly & carefully as we*
> *can wh/ere we each of us COMING from & the nature & complex-*
> *ity- often complicity of the BROKEN dis/possessed sometimes alien-*
> *ated GROUND on which we at 'first' find ourselves*
> (Brathwaite, "Post-Cautionary" 75)

Contributing to a festschrift for Kamau Brathwaite is an opportunity to give thanks for his work and inspiration, which in my life has not only been a crucial doorway into Caribbean literature and culture, but also the impulse to begin to write along the razor's edge of whiteness (Savory, "miranda"). Kamau Brathwaite's important work began when he turned from being simply a gifted young Cambridge poet to being committed to realizing the surviving and antihegemonic connection between Africa and the Caribbean. He has also much to teach an academy tempted to pride itself as above and beyond the community it should serve, and he has shown us that what we too often separate as creative and academic writing are in fact evident close relatives. Kamau Brathwaite reminds us, as we struggle to do our most inspired work in and for our ever-more corporate universities and publishing houses, that to take on the life of the writer may not be most importantly about the desire for rewards, financial or otherwise, of literary or academic stardom, but about being called to walk a pathway which may cost us a great deal, may in fact ultimately tear off those protective layers by which we distance ourselves from the most painful failures in our humanity. Because of that protection, we may, with the collusion of our audience, become entertainers and distractors, or cautious and comfortable educators and authorities, but in the eyes of our cultures entirely benign and harmless and therefore available for hire or sale.

It is Kamau Brathwaite who has brought me to understand how we as readers, as audience, can unwittingly contribute to the silencing of that which we do not want to hear, that which is too painful for common speech and too political for the quiet pages of the kind of book which fulfills expectations, never shocking, never destabilizing. It is Brathwaite, the eminent historian-poet, the griot, who is also the houngan (as spelled in Davis, *Serpent*), the priest of New World African spiritual tradition, who has taught me that there is no easy sloughing off of the past and, for us white people in particular, no quick volte-face from guilt to innocence without the journey through understanding and responsibility; that the inclusion of the personal journey is as important in discussing race and class as it has been known to be since the 1970's in discussing gender. Young poets in my poetry seminar, reporting on reading *The Zea Mexican Diary* (1993), over and over again identified its courage, as well as their awed discovery that this extraordinarily brave text could reproduce in them the exact contours of its brutally frank emotional landscape, speaking across thousands of miles in the rush and bustle of New York.

Brathwaite's work has always been about the pursuit of understanding the ways we call ourselves human: speaking firstly to his own community, people of African descent in a world fallen another time after transatlantic slavery, and then to all who will abandon their refusal to see what he is able to reveal. This is particularly personal for me, who left England in 1970 to spend two very important years in Ghana, and who was to read Brathwaite's representation of Ghanaian tradition and history in *Masks* (1968) after beginning to teach African literature in Barbados. My fulltime years in Barbados, (1973-1991) were years of my complete engagement with African and Caribbean culture, but I had no idea that the next stage of the journey would in a sense be that of bringing it all back home: beginning a revisionary crosscultural attempt to encounter once again some of the texts of my ancestral people in Britain, revisionary and cross-cultural in the context of being strongly informed by my twenty-five years of living and working in the Caribbean and West Africa.

So it is fitting that the first articulation of this revisioning in my critical writing is voiced in this festschrift honoring Kamau Brathwaite. Reading Brathwaite with the English visionary William Blake, my emphasis is on the first, on the ways in which his aesthetic and political journey not only revisions Caribbean and African diasporic culture but remaps English. Much post-colonial theory deliberately returns us to Europe via a foundational use of European theorists. It is not my intention to return us to Europe in that way, but rather, by reading Brathwaite with Blake, to see Brathwaite as a lens through which to re-view Blake and, more importantly, to use Blake as a lens through which to contextualize marginalization of Brathwaite's most recent iconographic work.

My purpose is not then simply to draw attention to some striking similarities between the two poets. The comparison, I argue, enables us to understand better why Brathwaite's more recent work is turning out to be controversial and relatively little understood, at least in some of the intellectual circles which were strongly appreciative of his first poetic trilogy, *The Arrivants* (1973). Although I have always been entirely committed to Caribbean-centered criticism as a response to Caribbean writers, there have been troubling signs lately of uncritical resistance to Brathwaite in some Caribbean literary circles: hastily judging his recent work in *video style* to be a dimming of creative power. Since the 1970's, Brathwaite has been misrepresented at times in simplistic racial terms. The frequent claim that he and Wilson Harris, for example, are very different from one another rests on the definition of Harris as a crosscultural antiessentialist and Brathwaite as a cultural nationalist-essentialist. Yet both have written eloquently of the creolization process, and to clarify the similarity of their positions, Brathwaite justifiably cites Nathaniel Mackey showing how both writers conceive of the "whole" as an endless creation from fragments (Brathwaite, *ConVERSations*).

Perhaps what seems to some readers radical is Brathwaite's brilliant realization since the 1970s of the creolized African subtext of the Caribbean. But if a focus on Africa in Brathwaite's work is read as racial exclusion instead of as a doorway into a powerful and crucial set of human mythologies and poetic metaphors by which to interpret our times and our histories, then it is completely misinterpreted. Hundreds of years of transatlantic racialized slavery and racism which has continued beyond it cannot be wished away: we all live with the consequences of that gross betrayal of human potential. Oddly enough, since Africa has so powerfully informed the Americas as a result of the slave trade, a deep affiliation with Africa is at times constructed by intellectuals–even some of Caribbean origin–as suspiciously political in a way willingness to urge European influence is not. Though evident racism, which served mercantile opportunism during the slave trade and British colonialism, is mainly silenced, we still live with the subtler kind which holds Africa apart and lesser at an entirely internalized, almost subconscious, level and believes that the continent is not central to the lives of people of all races in the Caribbean, not even central to the lives of those of African descent. It is Brathwaite who has brought us to see this, not only through what he has written and said, but through the responses his work has provoked.

It was quite some time after I began to think about this essay that I found Gordon Rohlehr's hints of a Blake/Brathwaite connection in his essay, "The Rehumanization of History," and although my own scale of comparison is far more extensive, it has been important to find such support from the most insightful Brathwaite critic (Rohlehr, *Pathfinder*; "George Lamming"). Rohlehr discusses a Brathwaite poem, "Kingston in the Kingdom of this World", as it appeared first in the collection *Third World Poems* (1983) describing Brathwaite's conception of prison, "either as Blakean 'mind-forg'd manacles' or physical lock-up" ('Rehumanization' 253). A little later, speaking of the same poem, Rohlehr says:

> "Kingston in the Kingdom of this World" dramatises the awakening of this historic consciousness; and though the voice in that poem has not yet called out to either the system's commissars or the lost children, such consciousness illuminates the necessity for action as, inevitably, the interior brooding of the subjugated Spirit becomes public and political. (Rohlehr, 'Rehumanization' 255)

This mention of the "subjugated Spirit" also calls Blake to mind. Furthermore, Rohlehr has confirmed for me that Brathwaite knew of an anthology of poems popular in Britain called *Children of Albion: Poetry of the Underground in Britain* (1969).

For most readers Kamau Brathwaite and William Blake may seem very much separated, by time, by nationality and ethnicity, by the borders we create in literary studies, by the borders we find ourselves negotiating in political and social space, and making a connection between them cannot ignore their differences. But they are both extraordinary visionary poets, who integrate the political, the spiritual and the creative into innovative epistemology and radical aesthetics. Both poets confront commodification and redefine revolution in their different cultures, speaking through the form of the book, but the book in their hands is reconfigured as politically, spiritually and aesthetically libertarian space, subverting boundaries between the verbal and visual, the scribal and aural. Both poets began innovatively, and for both, a continuing aesthetic revisioning is organically related to a developing sense of political context. Also the emergence of some significant reader-resistance contemporary with each poet marks not only a reluctance to understand their increasing aesthetic experimentation but a concomitant desire to avoid to each poet's radical spiritual and political readings of culture.

Blake was born in 1757. His young adulthood was informed by the American and French Revolutions; by the 1790's, British law had established precedents in ruling against slave traders (Blackburn). In 1792-3, Blake completed his illustrations to Stedman's *Narrative, of a Five Years Expedition, against the Revolted Negroes of Surinam, in Guiana, on the Wild Coast of South America*, translating Stedman's testimony into unflinching visual images of the sustained brutality of the plantation system at the end of the eighteenth century (Erdman 231). In his *Visions of the Daughters of Albion* (1793), Blake makes an explicit connection between the slaves in Surinam and the condition of women, between the "Daughters of Albion" and Oothoon, "the soft soul of America" (*Blake's Poetry* 71; see Vine for a response to Erdman's reading of this final Stedman illustration).

In *Visions*, Blake also takes on John Locke, the most influential philosopher of English mercantile expansion. Peter Ackroyd remarks (74): "Blake sees the connection between...Lockean theories of sensation and religious orthodoxy." Oothoon's lament, "(t)hey told me that I had five senses to inclose me up/ and they inclose'd my infinite brain into a narrow circle...", expresses Blake's view that Lockean theories of perception, which entirely privilege observable reality, were in fact a prison for the imagination (*idem*).

Blake thought genius, the most extraordinary manifestations of human thought and creativity, should be our standard of measure. Locke by contrast believed in a universally accessible kind of perception which could give rise to general terms and widely shared assumptions. In *Fearful Symmetry*, Northrop Frye remarks that Locke thought mediocrity the standard while Blake desired to measure from the extraordinary. Brathwaite's genius has been to understand that the extraordinary lives in a people's everyday survival strategies, which require them to revise and recreate, even whilst they often pretend to be abiding by the prevailing hegemonic norms of culture.

Locke's support for commerce went as far as substantial personal investment in the transatlantic slave trade, as well as importantly contributing to *The Fundamental Constitutions of Carolina* (1669) : "Every freedman of Carolina shall have absolute power and authority over his Negro slaves, of what opinion or religion whatsoever" (Locke, *Political* 180). Locke's assertion that "Slavery is so vile and miserable an estate of Man" was made in the context of landed Englishmen being freed of royal control: he thought only those people determined to be rational by the standards of European determination of the concept ought to have full freedom. His initial participation in the slave trade is the more tragic because he was such an influential political philosopher: he helped open the door to the seizure and shipment of enormous numbers of children and the consequent drastic reduction of the population of Africa (Walvin 320). Blake clearly understood the evil of slavery and made his work honest about it in the same ways that Brathwaite is honest about its aftermath.

By the time of Blake's youth, Locke's *Essay Concerning Human Understanding* (1689) had long been thought a major philosophical text perhaps in large part because Locke's work happened to be the most useful for the new political mercantile climate which developed after the so-called Glorious Revolution of 1688 when William III's accession benefitted mercantile interests and the West Indian planters. In Blake's scheme, the imagination was far more powerful a tool for human intelligence than Locke's memory or perception: it provided unique revisionings of both the visible and invisible worlds. But Blake, like Brathwaite, possessed a vision of poetry as deeply political and moral and as a liberating force, a vision inconvenient to those who wanted to celebrate only certain human advances and ignore painful realities which might come home to haunt them. Blake's poem "London" delivers a chilling portrait of a city in which the powerful ignore suffering: it is here that Blake's image of the "mind-forg'd manacles" appears (*Blake's Poetry* 53). Like Brathwaite, Blake responded to his world in ways which obeyed the integrity of his vision, not the literary conventions of his culture and time. T.S. Eliot thought, rather patronizingly, and perhaps subliminally because Blake was an artisan and not a man of formal letters, that Blake's philosophy inspired the same respect as "an ingenious piece of home-made furniture: we admire the man who has put it together out of the odds and ends about the house". Blake's understanding of human nature, his originality of language and its music, and, in late poems, his "hallucinated vision" would have been stronger if "controlled by a respect for impersonal reason, for common sense, for the objectivity of science." For Eliot, as a result, Blake remains "only a poet of genius," where Dante, who drew on a coherent framework of mythology, theology and philosophy built on the Latin tradition, is a classic. Eliot regards Blake as not sufficiently visionary, because he was too "occupied with ideas" (*Blake's Poetry* 509). This magisterial judgment is as breathtakingly sure as it is reductive: it is more useful for understanding Eliot and cultural politics than as a comparison of the two poets.

For Michael Dash (perhaps for temporary personal reasons, Rohlehr suggests), Brathwaite's visionary equivalence of poetry with music is also definitively understood as a major literary drawback: "(t)his reaching beyond language for pure sound is an admission of the inadequacy of words. However poetry must be an attempt to transcend the failure of language, not succumb to it" (Rohlehr, "Brathwaite" 221). Rohlehr rightly challenges another Dash complaint that Brathwaite has produced "a seemingly inexhaustible stream of publications" which are in effect an effort not "to surrender to silence" (*ibid.* 217). Behind Brathwaite's aesthetics lies the immensely functional metaphor of drum languages in West Africa, drawn from–grounded in–cultures where language was tonal. The metaphor of tonality, or of musical notation, could live only as a subtext in a culture which permitted no free linguistic expression by slaves or those made inferior in an irrational hierarchy by accident of birth. That Brathwaite often works on the border between poetry and sound or facility with words and the sometimes almost insurmountable silences around them is no more surprising than Blake's radical union of word and visual images. Rohlehr links Brathwaite and Blake in discussing the Brathwaite poem "Flutes", where a "Blakean, Romantic ideal" seems most appropriate to define Brathwaite's metaphorical understanding of "fiery form" ("Brathwaite" 222).

As Brathwaite has searched more and more innovatively, in both aesthetic and political terms, for a voice which speaks to Caribbean history and contemporary xperience, his critics and readers have struggled more and more to find innovative ways to read him, and some have not struggled long. Ted Chamberlin, after listing many important questions which Brathwaite's work raises, comments that they are related to "some fundamental epistemological as well as hermeneutical issues. Or not often connected–for Brathwaite is seldom taught in literature courses...We have neither the theory nor the practice to read him, or to listen to him" (*Come* 42). As one who teaches Brathwaite all the time, sometimes in conjunction with music and sometimes not, I beg to differ. I have no doubt that the bafflement which Chamberlin indicates as a disquieting aspect of experiencing Brathwaite's poetry has to be embraced rather than defeated in order for his most recent work to be enjoyed and understood.

Those who have drawn away from Brathwaite provide a particular litany of reasons: that since the early 1990's Brathwaite has become self-indulgent, losing the clarity and precision of form he used to have, has been overly repeating himself by revisiting old poems and resetting them in new contexts, is too reliant on distractions of form which interrupt a reader's desire to understand the content.

This recalls the increasing bafflement of some of Blake's audience, who whilst recognizing his great gifts, seemed to have mostly wished that he had stayed with his earlier, more cautious experiments with form: Samuel Palmer wrote to Alexander Gilchrist in 1855, eighteen years after Blake's death, that Blake's poems "...tested rather severely the imaginative capacity of their readers" (*Blake's Poetry* 505). John Thomas Smith wrote in 1828, the year after Blake died, that the "later poetry, if it may be so called, attached to his plates..," was "in some parts enigmatically curious as to its application" though "not always wholly uninteresting" (*ibid.* 484).

Despite some of his reservations about Blake, Eliot astutely saw in his work exactly what is difficult for some in Brathwaite's recent work, "a peculiar honesty, which in a world too frightened to be honest, is peculiarly terrifying. It is an honesty against which the whole world conspires because it is unpleasant. Blake's poetry has the unpleasantness of great poetry." Eliot understood, too, that it always takes great technical achievement to expose the underlying "essential sickness or strength of the human soul" (*Blake's Poetry* 506). In new poetry in progress, Brathwaite has engaged with the horrific genocide in Rwanda and the flight of poor Haitians in small, unseaworthy boats. He is working out how to make poetry out of the grimmest of human experience, a poetry which demands that his audience accept realization of human suffering beyond the point of polite social tolerance. In *Trench Town Rock*, Brathwaite writes of his own near-death experience at the hands of thugs in Kingston, communicating a hugely painful suffering of the spirit which, whilst intensely personal, comes to represent the ways in which materialism and its attendant cruelty have dehumanized people, not only slave-owners and their descendants, but slaves and theirs (in *ConVERSations*, Brathwaite comments further on the "increasing brutalization" of Caribbean society: 256-7).

To be able to read either Brathwaite or Blake, it is necessary to remove art from isolation: both poets make clear that art emerges from and responds to community, and that community is inherently political, always reflective of power relations, hierarchy, economic divisions. When Brathwaite and Blake think about politics, it is therefore frequently in relation to what they see as the crucial role of art in culture. When they think about art, it is with a strong emphasis on the importance of an innovative interrelation of form and content, which is in subtle or evident ways always political.

Two of this essay's epigraphs occur in the context of the poet defending himself against baffled or hostile criticism: Blake's in a letter to Reverend John Trusler in 1799, answering potential client Trusler's resistance to the poet's artistic opinions and methods; Brathwaite's in an essay answering Peter Hulme's criticism of his 1974 comments on Jean Rhys. These are the visionary remarks of wordsmiths, expressing strong views, but in a manner which requires the reader to appreciate the delivery system as much as the content. In their mature writing, Brathwaite and Blake rarely speak bluntly and plainly, though when they do it is usually with an acute political awareness and often placing art or language in the context of power relations: "The death of Rome signals the beginning of western expansion, which includes slavery and the slave trade and resultant disequilibriums throughout the world and within, therefore, the word" (Brathwaite, "Interview"15); "Revolts that are successful, like the French revolution and the Haitian revolution and, in a sense, the Russian Revolution—they all had a gestalt element about them. It was not simply that people were hacking down or destroying the Bastille of words, but they were also destroying physical and ideological Bastilles as well" (*ibid.* 17); "In a Commercial Nation Imposters are abroad in all Professions; these are the greatest Enemies of Genius" (*Blake's Poetry* 424).

Kamau Brathwaite's vision of Caribbean culture has always been informed by an acute sense of the way in which ideas and design, content and form fit together and by the realization that a Caribbean-centered, politically aware, anti-colonial aesthetic would need to develop new forms. As his vision has developed and changed over time, so has his poetry. Like Blake, Brathwaite crafts the design of a poem or piece of writing not only as a delivery system for its content, but as demonstration of the idea itself, intended also as a critique of power relations.

This means that Brathwaite's poetic style is exceptionally kinetic. Though he is not formally a visual artist, unlike Blake, he has increasingly sought in the *video style* to breach conventional boundaries between poetry and design, partly to facilitate the connection of poetry with sound and, he has recently said, to "make the words themselves live off -away from- the page" (*ConVERSations* 166). But that connection always has a social significance:

> The other thing about nation language is that it is part of what may be called *total expression*.... Reading is an isolated, individualistic, expression. The oral tradition on the other hand demands not only the griot but the audience to complete the community: the noise and sounds that the maker makes are responded to by the audience and

returned to him. Hence we have the creation of a continuum where meaning truly resides. (Brathwaite, *History* 18-19)

Blake was also clear about the need for content and form to be exactly devised to fit together:

> I have heard many People say, "Give me the Ideas. It is no matter what Words you put them into", & others say, "Give me the Design, it is no matter for the Execution." These people know Enough of Artifice, but Nothing of Art. Ideas cannot be Given but in their minutely Appropriate Words, nor Can a Design be made without its minutely Appropriate Execution. (*Blake's Poetry* 419)

Blake, in his *Songs of Innocence* and *Songs of Experience* (first published 1789; 1794), sought to turn words into visual designs and so to contextualise their ideas. In the process he was able to make powerful and radical political statements in some of the poems, partly by the juxtaposition of elements, as well as through verbal signifiers. Brathwaite, in his *video style* of recent years has found a medium in which the visual impact of the words on the page both adds to their signification and indicates rising and falling tones of voice.

Both poets often make the word strange as it appears in written form on the page. Blake's inventive development of copper engraving required that he write backwards on the copper plates with a quill pen, turning familiar words as he worked into new and mysterious designs. In this process, which required the plate to be "bitten in" by his aqua fortis of vinegar, salt armoniack, baysalt and vert de griz, Blake clearly saw a parallel with the poet's task of cleansing language and revisioning the world. In his delightfully ironical "Marriage of Heaven and Hell", he playfully reflects something of his own engraving process whilst subverting commonplace oppositions of good and evil:

> ...first the notion that man has a body distinct from his soul is to be expunged; this I shall do, by printing in the infernal method, by corrosives, which in Hell are salutary and medicinal, melting apparent surfaces away, and displaying the infinite which was hid. (*Blake's Poetry* 94)

This subversion is itself a form of epistemological inquiry, for the figurative construction of the idea prevents simple inversion, but rather complicates the relation of four concepts: body, soul, good and evil. Metaphor and compression here identify the language as close to poetic. Blake's conception of Poetic Genius is as the "true faculty of knowing": he thought that a visionary human imagination is also the source of all religions. The true poet, like the ancient European bard, possesses a capacity to perceive and understand which is beyond what Blake called "the ratio," or rational argument.

Brathwaite's vision of the Caribbean poet , whether as griot, voice of the African diasporic community, or as a subversive alienated single voice, Caliban (*Middle Passages*), has always understood the poet to be taking risks, both aesthetic and moral, in order to uncover and envision that which is hidden: first of all the history and identity of African cultures after transatlantic slavery.

Despite Brathwaite's training and role as an intellectual, like Blake he defines the poet as being able to see, and make others see, in a way which is markedly above and beyond mere rationality. Over and over again, he tells stories of discovering Africa underneath the colonial overlay of European culture: in *Barabajan Poems* he describes how during a visit to Belize, to the Garifuna, "the great Black Carib people," he notices their self-definition as "'ordinary' & Christian (like evvabodyelse)", but when he is taken to witness their drum ritual in the bush, he sees them differently:

> ....& it was as if those Black Carib?Christians had become Garifuna
> nation again since they have *unsubmerged* themselves & are giving
> me the greatest privilege of *seeing* them since in seeing them, I real-
> ize now, I was seeing *(learning)* myself/our*selves* (BP 167)

Later in the same work, Brathwaite revisions, in video style, a poem from his earlier collection, *Mother Poem*, in which a woman singing in a small Barbadian church meeting becomes the medium for the Yoruba god Shango. The video style version is able to get closer to the experience of hearing the poet read, for the poem on the page is only the score of the verbal music. In *Barabajan Poems*, Brathwaite extends and glosses the original poem, so that the reader understands the context of his vision of a hidden African spirituality manifestly in a "**whisper of a sound**," present beneath a colonized surface: "**That night it was Damballa . dancing with th/at whisper of a sound inside a simple unsuspecting shop in Mile&Q, Barbados**" (BP 182). The design of the words changes dramatically from *Mother Poem* to *Barabajan Poems* because Brathwaite is searching for a means to permit the music of the poem to be translated into a visual shape, which recalls Blake's determined attempt to fuse music, words and visual art in *Songs of Innocence* and *Songs of Experience*. At the end of the poem, in the later version, the elaborate, flourishing bold-type name Shango dominates the page just before the Spirit emerges through the overlay of singing.

Before the name a third of the page is a blank space, a substantial break of breath. In the *Mother Poem* version there is no pause.

The earlier form of the poem, coming as it does not long after Brathwaite's articulation of the identity of nation language, still relates to the familiar conventions of scribal poetry, despite its clearly oral identity. *Barabajan Poems* is like a series of riffs off a melody in which our experience of the poem and of the book are stretched and broken and recast, just as Blake, in his day, stretched and broke and recast the idea of the book: a reader looking for familiar conventions, for the observance of established boundaries between art forms and belief systems, will be disappointed in both.

Brathwaite and Blake both began as poets by making aesthetic experiments, and then built on this early work: the result in each case is experimentation taking the poet out of the realm of the expected and comprehended. Blake's early biographer, Frederick Tatham, who appears to have been partially motivated by a desire to sell some of Blake's work which he inherited from the poet's wife Catherine, wrote of *Jerusalem*, "...in reference to the authenticity of Blake's visions, let anyone contemplate the designs in this Book; Are they not only new in their method & manner, but actually new in their class & origin" (*Blake's Poetry* 491). But even this positive portrait contains some very strong, if rather bewildered, criticism: "The combinations are chimerical, the forms unusual, the Inventions abstract, the poems not only abstruse but absolutely, according to the common rules of criticism, as near ridiculous as it is completely heterogeneous" (*Blake's Poetry* 491). The trajectory of Blake's career, received in his day in England first as inventive engraver and ultimately as eccentric genius, has important parallels with Brathwaite's career, for as Brathwaite's visionary video style has become more evident, he has begun to experience difficulties with publishers (see Savory, "Returning") as well as with influential critics. For both Brathwaite and Blake, this uncompromising insistence on the poet as visionary, as spiritual journeyman who must follow wherever the imagination leads and be prepared to take great risks in order to break through to new ways of seeing, translates to a high cost in terms of their contemporary audiences.

Already in 1974, a relatively early stage of Brathwaite's mature work, his *Contradictory Omens* began to experiment with the form of the intellectual essay. He reports in the introduction to the published version that it met with some resistance among the academics who first heard it: "Handler, I remember, called it a 'melange', a 'personal poetic statement' ... he, like most delegates at this Conference, found it difficult to 'come to grips with its methodology'." But Brathwaite knew already that "**The style in** which this paper was written-and its form-are essential-and I hope necessary-aspects of its 'message'" (*Contradictory* 5). Using bold type for emphasis, as in this example, Brathwaite presaged his later development, via a Mac computer, of a highly variable use of typeface and spatial arrangement. The visual emphasis corresponds to oral emphasis, thus in one move disrupting the controlled, quiet, contemplative nature of academic writing (and later poetry), by the implied raising of the voice, as well as making a bridge to a sense of poetry as both visual art (design) and music. This unification of aesthetic forms symbolically equates to the complex historical relation between music and language in African cultures, and to use of symbols as verbal equivalents (for example, in the famous Adinkra cloth of Ghana, which Brathwaite mentions in *The Zea Mexican Diary*).

Following Brathwaite's theorising of Caribbean poetics in *A History of the Voice* (1984), a new voice began to emerge, especially noticeable in the "hurricane poem", *SHAR*, written in the late 1980s after his wife's death and after his beloved house in Irish Town, where he stored his huge and invaluable archive of Caribbean literature and culture, was hit by Hurricane Gilbert. The poem is also in memory of his niece Sharon. Here the hurricane is dramatically drawn on the page in enlarging bold lettering and words are blown into pieces. In *History of the Voice*, Brathwaite had written about the Caribbean poet's relation to the prevalence of pentameter in English poetry: "The hurricane does not roar in pentameters. And that's the problem: how do you get a rhythm which approximates the *natural* experience, the *environmental* experience" (10)?

Blake's famous definition of poetry as "Allegory addressed to the intellectual process, while it is altogether hidden from the Corporeal Understanding" (*Blake's Poetry* 478: Letter to Thomas Butts, July 6th 1803), is implicitly opposed to prevailing conventions, in this case Locke's notion of sensation which corresponds to Blake's Corporeal Understanding. What can be easily and generally observed on the surface is not what is important. Brathwaite, despite years of academic experience, has long suspected work which theorizes for a comfortable elite: even in intellectual writing, he has come to desire a holistic, iconographic vision speaking to all kinds of human intelligence and experience and demanding that things be seen beyond and beneath their surfaces.

In interesting ways, the class origins of both poets have something to do with their reception. Blake's origins were economically modest. His father had a hosier's shop in London's Soho. His parents were Dissenters, radical in their political views. His lifetime (1757-1827) saw huge political and cultural events: the war between the American colonies and the English and the establishment of the United States in 1776; the French Revolution in 1789; abolitionist debate in England in the 1790's leading to the abolition of the slave trade in the Atlantic in English law in 1807; the Romantic poets, Wordsworth, Coleridge, Byron, Shelley and Keats beginning to publish important work. He knew the English radical social writers William Godwin, Tom Paine and Mary Wollstonecraft. David Erdman points out how easily Blake wrote of "Republican Art" in a letter in the last year of his life and how disappointed he was that the revolutions in France and the American colonies had failed because they merely attacked a feudal order to establish a mercantile free-for-all (*Blake* 30, 226). In his work, Blake sought more and more to express the failures of human kindness and fellowship, and the spirit of genuine revolution. Part of the resistance to his poetry is no doubt its underlying support for for a drastic reorganization of society built up from a spiritual revolution: the secure middle-class, especially, which regarded art as primarily either entertainment or general moral uplift, found Blake too far out to be acceptable. Blake found support in his later years from young artists who understood his valuable example, something that is also happening among young writers in Barbados and the Caribbean who have no difficulty understanding Brathwaite's aesthetic innovations and importance.

Brathwaite, born in Barbados in 1930 into a middle-class family in Bridgetown, would grow up during the height of formal British colonialism and then witness its demise, as a formal structure though not as a hegemony, after the Second World War. In *ConVERSations with Nathaniel Mackey* (1999), Brathwaite recalls watching processions on Bay Street from behind the jalousies of his family house "at Christmas & Bankholidays the *African tuk bands came* out-the Bear & bag-cloth dancers, gargantuanly preganant *Aunt Sally*, the white-face backra puppet Mr *Harding destin for* the *pain* of canefield burning" (88), a description reminiscent of Jean Rhys's account of her own childhood experience in Roseau, watching Carnival processions from behind the jalousies (*Smile Please*), or Derek Walcott's childhood in Castries. But Brathwaite has not stayed behind the jalousies of the middle-class house: perhaps his most recent aesthetic experimentation seems, as did Blake's, too radically disconnected from middle-class priorities and cultural agendas to be acceptable by those who desire a different kind of artistic exploration.

Barbados became independent in 1966. Though Brathwaite wrote at first in a style which related him to modernist British poetry and knew Ted Hughes at Cambridge, where he might have been recruited into a lifelong elitism and affiliation with Britain, his experience in Ghana in the second half of the 1950s and early 1960s was formative and transformational. Ghana became independent in 1957. So he had a first hand experience of the anticolonial process working through to a successful conclusion and was much engaged by Ghanaian culture and history. He returned to the Caribbean in 1963 to teach history at the Mona campus of the University of the West Indies. Jamaica had become independent in 1959 and was already experiencing surging creative expression of the new nation. But Brathwaite's interest was never in the local ebb and flow of anticolonial and postcolonial politics. He has instead looked to uncover the larger hidden and denigrated presence of Africa in the Caribbean as well as in North America.

It was Brathwaite's highly original first trilogy, *The Arrivants*, which established his stature as a Caribbean poet. Though this is thoroughly informed by the presence of African diasporic cultural identities, most especially the presence of African music as a metaphor of subordinated but powerfully creative New World revisioning, it nevertheless can be read in the continuum of world poetry in English and bears the stamp of official Western approval in its publisher, Oxford University Press. The second trilogy (*Mother Poem* 1977; *Sun Poem* 1982; *X/Self* 1987), continues this affiliation, though in *X/Self* it is already clear that there are important new aesthetic imperatives. Since then, Brathwaite has gradually developed the innovative *video style,* which brings together intellectual and popular culture, most notably in recent times hip-hop sampling which cuts and pastes familiar elements together into a new whole. This is Brathwaite's method for revisiting not only his own previous poetry, but extracts from the works of other Caribbean writers, always acknowledged and woven into the texture of the new work. In this, and in the use of the computer to provide the *video style,* he has become more and more engaged in reaching an audience outside the Western-educated, and so his place as an icon of middle-class Caribbean literary culture has been questioned. Brathwaite's decolonization of his own poetic style has come at a great cost precisely because postcolonial writing has often affiliated itself in form, if not in content or accent, with prevailing Eurocentric identities of poetry, plays, fiction or criticism and theory. In *Contradictory Omens,* Brathwaite writes that there were three colonial systems of control: the mercantile, the plantation and the imperial government and that "[t]his retreat from an Afro- to a kind of Euro-orientated cultural disposition was made all the easier by the song and dance of emancipation" (30): in short the full promise of a transfer of power to the African-descended majority did not occur after slavery, and so the revolutionary potential of that change was thwarted by an alliance between the white Creoles and what Brathwaite describes as "their kith and kin overseas," as well as by the creation of a middle-class so saturated in British middle-class cultural values as to become "Afro-Saxon" (31). Instead of this, which Brathwaite sees as cultural inertia, a new and entirely Caribbean Creole way of seeing might develop: creolization is how-ever "cracked, fragmented, ambivalent, not certain of itself, subject to shift-ing lights and pressures." To apprehend the complexity of Caribbean cul-ture, it is necessary to turn to "a proliferation of images," a poet's visionary language which can explore political and social identities by means of meta-phoric patterns (6). This approaches Blake's disillusionment with the Ameri-can and French Revolutions and his desire to radicalize art as both aesthetic and moral-political statement.

Brathwaite even images thought as a visual artist might: as a spectrum of colours refracted through a prism. This way of thinking emphasizes func-tional complexity, yet recognizes, he concludes in *Contradictory Omens*, that the "unity is submarine" (64).

Blake and Brathwaite both understand that at certain times and places in human history, art must choose either to turn its face from the worst of human capability or to discover how to fracture its commitment to aes-thetic coherence in order to bring a society face to face with its own grave mistakes. Blake hoped that his people in England would realize what moral implications lay in the policies of their political leaders: "...grasping colo-nies and shedding blood whether in the name of royal dignity or in the name of commerce is not living at all, but killing" (Erdman 226). In much the same way, Brathwaite has wanted to bring his people in the Caribbean face to face with the breakdown of community: in *Trench Town Rock* he forces the reader to experience the moral anarchy which seizes a culture deeply scarred to this day by colonialism, slavery and racism. To do this, like Blake, he must violate the restraints and harmonies of previaling con-ventions of poetry or academic prose.

Brathwaite speaks of this journey to the edge of tolerance without any intellectual distancing. He understands the painful condition of the writer or artist who wants to be fully truthful and accountable:

> Nation language...is the *submerged* area of that dialect which is much more closely allied to the African aspect of experience in the Carib-bean. It may be in English: but often it is in an English which is like a howl, or a shout, or a machine-gun or the wind or a wave. It is also like the blues. And sometimes it is English and African at the same time. (*History* 13)

> ...so we have lyric slavery, romantic violence, rape as survival rhythm, peace as a hollow silence, howl's opposite, so that as writers...we remain trapped in the maelstrom of frustration, trapped and impris-oned within the detonations of our own fragmented words. ("Meta-phors"[3] 238)

Blake's poetry often lives on that same edge: "Every Wolfs & Lions howl/ Raises from Hell a human soul" (*Complete* 507). Like Brathwaite, Blake is willing to see past what is acceptable and tolerable to the worst than humanity can do.

This essay is merely a sketch for a longer study. Blake and Brathwaite have much to say to each other as originals, each with the courage to risk his public standing with those arbiters of creativity invested in not seeing what is difficult and agonizing. The comparison with Blake is most helpful in reading Brathwaite's work as it has evolved into the video style, from beginnings in the 1970s to the creative outpouring of the 1990s: when a great artist takes on his mercantilist society, the chances of resistance from those who do not want to see by the light of an alternative moral vision are high.

Kamau Brathwaite and T.S. Eliot: Inter-Dependencies of Metropolitan and Post-Colonial Texts[1]

Enrique Lima

History will not disappear. It reveals itself ubiquitously on the surfaces of objects, in the texture of landscapes, in the texts that name a culture. Everything that we recognize bears a mark, a mark that is historical, and it is precisely this mark that allows us to recognize it, to understand what it is. Kamau Brathwaite's poem "Crab" in *Black + Blues* engages the process through which history determines our place in and our understanding of the world. More specifically, it engages what centuries of colonization and slavery have reaped on the minds and bodies of displaced Africans. T. S. Eliot's poem "The Love Song of J. Alfred Prufrock" seems to be divorced from historical concerns, to be securely bounded by its own poetic imperatives, yet it cannot completely suppress the historical forces with which it is so intimate. These two poems brush together at an image and it is this brushing together that reveals what their relationship, a relationship of mutual histories, is.

It is brief. The image is ephemeral, a splash of an image really, surviving just past the couplet's length. I am referring to the image of a crab, the "pair of ragged claws/ Scuttling across the floors of silent seas" in "Prufrock" (6). The image of a crab resonates in the opening stanza of Brathwaite's poem. It reads, "From this cramped hand/ crippled by candlelight/ a crab scuttles" (BB[2] 64). The resonance between these two poems at these corresponding images signals a site of convergence. A conventional reading of the convergence might suggest that Brathwaite's poem is influenced by or is perhaps responding to Eliot's canonical text. Biographical research would confirm that there is a strong relationship between Brathwaite's and Eliot's literary production. Yet a reading that would limit "Crab" as derivative of or answering to "Prufrock" does little but confirm imperialist narratives of the colony's intellectual, cultural dependence on the metropolis. Brathwaite's text, like nearly all texts originating from colonized countries, is indeed intimately related to the literature of the colonizer but this relationship is much more complicated than mere dependency. Hence, I would suggest another kind of reading. Perhaps Eliot's poem had the possibility of Brathwaite's as a necessary component of its own creation. Perhaps the "ragged claws" in Eliot's poem mark the place where this necessity of Brathwaite's poem shows itself.

The "crab" in Brathwaite's poem is, among many things, the shadow of his writing hand thrown by the candlelight onto the writing surface. The shadow "scuttles" before the hand as it traces the horizontal motion of the act of writing. The shadow of the fisted hand seems "clenched armour," and the writing instrument thrusting from the fist resembles "mail'd dragonish swords" (64). Traveling before the writing hand and providing the source of the poem, the penumbric shell of the crab is a complicated nexus of past, present and future, all known partially, imperfectly, and all of which have the materiality of shadows: intangible but real. Unlike Eliot's "Burnt Norton," where time ("Time Present and time future/ What might have been and what has been/ Point to one end, which is always present," 4) offers alternatives to an individual for which the individual provides resolution, time in "Crab" is seen in terms of historical forces that drastically reduce alternatives and in so doing situate the individual in already determined social relations.

The history of slavery cannot be completely known. We can give approximate dates, approximate figures, we can read descriptions of slave conditions, we can read about the brutality of the Middle Passage, we can read slave biographies, we can read the prices offered for human beings sold at auction, and we can estimate the rising GNPs of nations involved in the slave trade, but none of these things will fully tell the story of the injustice of slavery. These facts will not tell what the destruction a people's history will do to them, what the loss of language means, what the arrogance of not being slaves leads to. "Crab" illustrates this truth. The poem reads, "the crab knows it all." Yet all that it knows is a "kernel of grit/ knowledge of the eaten edges of disaster" (68). What the crab knows is not the hard kernel of total knowledge but a "kernel of grit," the residue of complete truth. In other words, it does not know the historical disaster that has uprooted people from their land, language and culture to deliver them to slavery in its totality, but "the eaten edges" of this disaster. As a pearl grows in an oyster around an ingested bit of grit, so too has "Crab" grown around the "kernel of grit/ [the] knowledge of the eaten edges of disaster." The incomplete knowledge of the brutality of slavery and its consequences is the "kernel of grit" that has produced and is reproduced by "Crab".

The crab remembers the start of this disaster. It (Europe, the disaster) "set out" with "carrack. caravel/ galleons of spain" (66). It began with an invasion masked as exploration. Europe found itself "by the lake of invis-ible heritage/ heroless savages' civilizations" (66). Because Europe could not recognize what it "discovered," the civilizations that stood before it were "invisible" to the European eye. Europe could/would not recognize that what was before it was human culture, instead it saw in the brown and black skin of the people that it encountered "clay coloured coal" (67). Thus Europe turned dark-skinned people into fuel for its rise to global economic and military dominance. Europe's riches grew by transforming people into numbers on a ledger that could be balanced out at the end of the month, by shoveling mounds of people into the furnace of its economic machine. It was "these terrors" that built "the rockerfeller building/ on which i have found my church" (67). This is to say that the economic system that the slave trade fueled and that produced the wealth of the West is now dangled before the faces of those who were most victimized by it as the way to salvation, the means of deliverance. The crab remembers the edges of how this happened.

Brathwaite's crab carries in it the memories of the places from which people were uprooted. It "walks carefully on stones dreams" (68). This verse echoes an earlier verse that reads "pebbles became my continent of dreams" (66). Both of these verses seem to suggest that in the particulars of a place we recognize the memories of another place, as when in the geog-raphy of dreams we recognize a different geography. But this memory is incomplete, it is as when we wake from dreams and we struggle to remem-ber the specific details of the place that we dreamt. Uprooted people, no matter how many generations have passed since the uprooting, remember their homeland. They remember it imperfectly, the details are elusive, dream-like, but the memory never completely vanishes. History leaves its marks on the memories of people; it remains there as the kernel of grit around which their own personhood is formed.

The crab knows that the past, history, will not stay in its place. History not only marks us now but it is a central participant in the determination of our future. Capitalism, the economic system that owes so much of its pros-perity and power to the effective and lengthy enslavement of dark-skinned people, ensures that people from under-developed nations (usually those nations that provided or received the slave labor force) will continue to be exploited into the foreseeable future. "Crab" poetically delineates the effects of this exploitation. Brathwaite's crab "walks carefully on...cradles of children's skeletons" (68). The image of "children's skeletons" gives a sense of a future that is already dead in its infancy, of a future that is over-determined by the effects of an oppressive past. This idea is reiterated by the image of "the inheriting ghosts" (65). Again, through this image, we get the sense of a "dead" determined future ensured by the memories of a brutal past and by the material conditions that past has created. The writing of this poem, the inscription that the "cramped hand/ crippled by candle-light" makes on the writing surface, is the

> scavenging slowly through the hackles of grass
> *and the grass flesh*
> and the flesh memory
> *and the memory nodding* (68)

Thus in "Crab" writing is (re)presented as the exploration of a past that is written on the flesh. The flesh *is* memory, *is* a history that is as inescapable as our own flesh. We live this history, as will our "inheriting ghosts." Those that have benefitted and those that have been exploited by historical circumstances will likely continue to participate in them in their recognizable roles. It is this possibility that gives "Crab" its desperate, urgent tone. The urgency is reinforced by the setting off of the stanzas that begin "and crowd upon stammer..." and "and the grass flesh...." These stanzas disrupt the dominant voice of the poem through their use of different alignments and their different fonts as an attempt to jolt the reader into recognition of the material effects of history.

"Prufrock," on the other hand, is decidedly ahistorical. Eliot's poem seems free of "Crab's" concerns. The history of exploitative conditions, privilege and servitude, capital and power seems to play no role in organizing Eliot's poem. Instead, "Prufrock" is driven by poetic imperatives: the existential crisis of the narrator, control of rhyme and meter, the use of European cultural landmarks. But this kind of "poetic" unity could only be achieved by repressing the historical circumstances that allow its creation. Eliot cannot write history out of "Prufrock," rather, it scuttles across the entire surface of the poem.

One could say, by way of Freud, that because history is only suppressed in "Prufrock" it returns displaced into objects in the poem that bear the indelible stain of privilege. The poem's narrator's morning coat, his "neck-tie rich and modest, but asserted by a simple/ pin" (4), the bracelets and shawls that decorate the arms the narrator longs for but cannot have, "the cups, the marmalade, the tea, / Among the porcelain" (7), all these objects signify the social position that the narrator occupies. "Prufrock" is encoded in the vocabulary of social privilege. Porcelain, rich neckties and shawls are the markings of the luxurious world from which the narrator seeks escape in "certain half-deserted streets, / [and his] muttering retreats" (3). The narrator desires escape from his world, the world of wealth and privilege.

Not only these objects but also the use of rarefied cultural references (Michelangelo, Dante, Shakespeare, classical mythology) as poetic landmarks speaks volumes about the social circumstances that surround this poem. These references are dependent on a specific kind of reader, one who is versed in the cultural traditions of Europe. Without the right sort of cultural training (implying in the England of "Prufrock's" first publication a rather narrow intended readership), it would be very difficult to "understand" "The Love Song of J. Alfred Prufrock."

But why does the social position of the narrator or the cultural training needed to understand the poem matter? These considerations matter because they point to the historical circumstances that allowed the writing and the reception of "Prufrock." The wealth represented in the poem was created by the very same historical circumstances that are thematically dominant in "Crab." The accumulation of wealth that leads to the possibility of owning (and writing about) shawls, rich ties and porcelain can only happen through the exploitation of human beings through capitalist economic practices. The very history that spawns the "inheriting ghosts" of Brathwaite's poem renders possible the comfortable world that makes Prufrock's narrator so uncomfortable. The education needed to understand "Prufrock" also marks a place of social privilege that is indissociable from material wealth. An education that allows someone to decipher and to place European cultural products is a signifier of social status. Knowledge of Shakespeare, Dante and Michelangelo (and Eliot) carries cultural value because it marks a gentlemanly disposition towards the Arts, it marks social distinction that is always associated with material wealth.

The possibility of the poem "Crab" is constitutive of "The Love Song of J. Alfred Prufrock" not only by representing the historical circumstances that enabled the production of Eliot's poem, but by signaling the opposition, desired and repulsed, around which "Prufrock" is written. "Prufrock's" narrator says, "I should have been a pair of ragged claws/ scuttling across the floors of silent seas" (6). This "pair of ragged claws" that the narrator desires to be is the Other against which the narrator can define himself and through which he can judge his position in his social order. Brathwaite's and Eliot's poems arise from opposite sides of the historical divide between exploiter and exploited. It is this opposition that makes it possible to see "Crab" as the unnamed Other against which "Prufrock" is written. "Prufrock" opposes "Crab's" insistence on naming historical violence by affirming the gentility of culture. It opposes "Crab's" faulty and incomplete memory by asserting a memory that easily reaches back to the classical past by way of cultural landmarks. It opposes "Crab's" assertion of violent, multiple cultural origins with firm affirmation of its Westernness. Most importantly, I think, Eliot's poem counters "Crab's" ruptured, disjointed narrative with a cool, distanced, completely "rational" one. In order to define itself "The Love Song of J. Alfred Prufrock" needed that which the narrator desired he "should have been," for without the possibility of Kamau Brathwaite's poem, and the difference that it entails, Eliot would not have recognized himself.

Notes

1. This paper benefitted greatly from the help of Patricia Penn Hilden with whom I had a long conversation about the subject matter, Timothy J. Reiss who provided invaluable advice on how to strengthen my work, and Emily J. Swenson and her boundless support and patience.

The Lace People

(Excerpt from novel in progress)

Erna Brodber

One time, separated by now with a thin gauze, weathered into a substance like the hard plastic of the riot police men's shields but still looking like thin gauze, there was a kingdom in dream land where the people were the tallest ever, the slimmest ever, the darkest ever, so much so that they were silhouettes; they were frescoes; they were drawings in a pharaoh's tomb. To them was given the ability to fly. They were the prettiest things in flight. They were so thin and tall, the wind and the sunlight made holes in their bodies, transforming them into black lace floating up to the sun. The more holes each had, the more the wind wafted all the company up towards the heaven so that black lace could mask the sun, could mask the moon, could change the cycle of the elements, and keep the earth dark for months or years, as and if they wished.

Ascending as a community of fathers, mothers and children the lace people sometimes went up past the sun and the moon and into the very heavens and they heard things. Naturally: a sigh, the occasional grumbling. The sun and the moon, and the stars, fixed by nature could not move at will. How they understood the nature of the power of the black lace. How they admired and wished! How they loved the lace people and the new sense of life they brought! Understandably, they courted their friendship, and welcomed into their network these creatures who could float hither and thither and yon as the mood took them. You give gifts to friends you court. This one gave to the lace people a sparkling sun beam, the other a moon rock studded with diamond stones, the other gave a star emblazoned crown. It was a picture to see these black lace creatures floating above the earth, dressed now in sunbeams, and moonbeams and so on, sparkling and glistening, cutting caper together, a well organized dance troupe. So beautiful, especially when it was dark.

No one has been able to say why, Papa D said, but one day the lace people left their earth homes for a visit to the skies and did not return: their up and down movement ceased. Why, remains a mystery. The Book of Life merely records, he said, that for weeks on end the sky was dark, covered with black lace as black lace overlaid black lace filling the holes in each others bodies through which light used to filter on their occasional trips to the skies. It is recorded, and Papa D says his father who was a learned religious man saw the record, that they sometimes maneuvered close to the earth, if you were in Egypt you could almost touch them - making beautiful patterns; making sunlight now appear in the form of a triangle, a hexagon and so forth; writing words in the sky, arranging themselves so that the moon and the stars looked like camels, giraffes, peacocks, anything, as black lace allowed moonlight or sunlight or starlight to shine through.

The elements did not mind this new disruption at all; in fact they loved it. Today we watch on special occasions fireworks making sundry images in the sky. This was their special occasion, a kind of fair, a chance to rest a bit, to watch the spectacle, and to talk to their powerful friends. It was a holiday, one long party, a long one up there. Have you ever noted how relaxation can change things? How mutually disarming sharing in friendship can be? How holidays can carry with them the question why work and undermine former resolve? Just so it struck the sun – "These people are bright, are accommodating, why don't I ask them to do my work while I take a much needed rest." The lace people spoke with their usual one voice disarmed like their friends. "Why not? We will keep the shop for you." And they still consented with one voice even when the sun explained that only males could do this job. No problem-the Papas Lace would help out while the Mamas and the children, the Lacettes, would continue to play around with the moon and the stars.

The lace people weaving themselves into one powerful arm, strong black nylon thread, strong like the wires that bring you light and messages, prised Mr. Sun from his perch and off he floated to Northern climes where he needed to work only now and again.

The moon is female and given to changes. Her job is delicate. It involves cutting into halves, to quarters, dividing these portions of herself into smaller portions-rings and exposing herself subtly. If you look at the moon through a clean white handkerchief you can see the circles telling you her age, allowing you to deduce from that, when to plant peas or to cut bamboos. Her job also involves telling you when the rain will fall, how it will fall and she must be alert and change her colour accordingly. Hers was a woman's job, not just a female modeling job, changing dresses, as you might think, and she was very mindful of this, so when the Mamas Lace and the Lacettes urged the moon to take a break and leave them in charge, tempted though she was she found the courage to tell the Mamas Lace that much as she would like the break, it would be irresponsible of her to leave her job with them and their children, for you know what children give, but tired and tempted she remarked that if perhaps the children could be sent over to help the stars, then chances are she would consider it, but only consider it, mark you. No problem. The moon was not as fixed as the sun so the Mama Lace and the Lacettes could by themselves shift her and she too went off, a little like Eve, to the northern climes goofing off here and there and then settling down to less exhausting work than she had been doing formerly. Her goofing she did close by them, jumping into the sea, playing hide and seek behind the hills but watching to see that the Lacettes did go off to the stars and did not stay around to mess with their mothers' concentration.

It is a fact of life that hardworking people become their work. The new sun and the moon and the stars worked well; as well as the old had. Papas Lace were so much the sun that they like the sun before them became, fixed; it happened to Mamas Moon. They were now stuck and apart from the Papas. It was the rear eclipse that brought them together. So it was too with the stars: they too were fixed, for the Lacettes had followed their parents' example and offered to be the stars. There they were now blinking and twinkling away in fixed places in the heavens. It was the unusual star that shot across the skies now, falling to the earth. And was that little star happy? The family Lace was dispersed. Now and again the feeling that there was a time when things were different and more pleasant flashed through their minds but they were now too busy at their celestial work in that part of the world where the sun was required to shine for sometimes sixteen hours per day, where people looked at the moon to tell them all kind of things, from when to plant to who was mad, that there was no time to bring those memories in to consciousness. This little falling star was tired, overworked: blinking and twinkling and remembering that you belong to the great bear constellation and not the milky way, was not an easy task and that's precisely why he fell, exhaustion. What on earth would he do in this place, separated so totally from his workaholic parents and siblings. Papa D stopped here with his story-telling leaving us high and dry, up in the stars some might say , but not me. My mind was on the little star. Poor embarrassed little boy. How un-male to fall.

Establishing and Preserving an Identity: Brathwaite's 'Nation Language'

Korah L. Belgrave

Edward Kamau Brathwaite was not the first person to attempt to label the language variety spoken by Barbadians. It has been called "broken English," "bad English," "Bajan," "dialect," "Creole English", "semi-creole" and "native language." He was the first person, however, to give it a name that both linguists and laypersons could use and feel equally happy with - "nation language." Traditionally, speakers of the creoles or patois have generally accepted and maintained the characterisation of their speech as intrinsically inferior to the European languages. The label "nation language" carries none of the pejorative overtones of previous labels and it expresses the close association between language and nation or national identity as well as the pride that we feel, and should feel, in our language. It labels not only Barbadian language but all the other languages of "hearth and home." Brathwaite's use of words, idiomatic expressions, sayings and proverbs which we can identify as Bajan brings a certain measure of respectability and worth or merit to our language and thereby to us as a nation of people who speak the language.

A large part of our identity as a nation lies in acceptance of ourselves as who and what we are. Language is a very important part of that. Our language embodies our past and therefore acts as a rich storehouse of all the treasures that we have accumulated.

Linguists such as Sapir and Whorf suggest that the language we speak conditions our view of reality and of the world around us. Edward Sapir (1950) proposes,

> Human beings...are very much at the mercy of the particular language which has become the medium of expression for their society.... We see, hear and otherwise experience very largely as we do because the language habits of our community predispose certain choices of interpretation. ("Status" 207)

This suggests that failure to utilize all the varieties at our disposal diminishes us to the extent that we lose or avoid not only a language variety but the peculiar perspective which that variety embodies and become lesser persons for it.

Benjamin Lee Whorf goes further, to suggest that the role which language plays in our lives goes beyond creating a predisposition to view life in a particular manner. He sees it as being ultimately responsible for the way in which we perceive of the world around us. Whorf theorizes:

> We dissect nature along lines laid down by our native language.... The world is presented in a kaleidoscopic flux of impressions which have to be organized by our minds—and this means largely by the linguistic systems on our minds. We cut nature up, organize it into concepts, and ascribe significances as we do, largely because we are parties to an agreement to organize it this way—an agreement that holds throughout our speech community and is codified by the patterns of our language. (*Language* 137-8)

This means that were we to speak only European languages or even African languages, this would restrict our perception of the world and prevents us from tapping into the world view which our nation language affords us. An appreciation for these theories requires us not only to preserve our nation language but to seek as Brathwaite does in his poetry to celebrate it.

Brathwaite's contribution is especially important in light of opposing movements to suppress the use of nation language. Sentiments expressed by "learned" members of our society lament the spread of "sub-standard English" among the public. In an editorial in *The Barbados Advocate* of Tuesday, 30 June 1998, the editor quotes the following excerpt from a speech given at a Toastmasters' installation:

> Unfortunately, in a misguided effort to become "grass-rootsy" and "regular," radio personnel have of late been reinforcing and giving the stamp of institutional respectability and acceptability to forms

and standards of public speaking and communication that were once not considered the norm....

The editorial goes on to point out that

> It requires a certain preference for indiscipline to enable the wide scale entrenchment of downright *bad* language; something to do with personal laziness, indifference to appeals for excellence, even contempt for listeners and readers who are wrongly considered incapable of rising to higher standards. And once recourse to *linguistic coarseness* is repeated often enough by "better educated" individuals, it becomes a stigma identifying the careless, uncouth and weak-willed among us. (8: my emphasis, and paragraph brake suppressed)

Brathwaite's poetry in celebration of Barbados presents a rich source of language and culture and a view of our world that we cannot neglect. His writing runs the gamut from single-word lexical items to idiomatic phrases. It also includes those phrases which though analyzable, unlike idiomatic phrases, convey an "emotional intensity " not readily understood by an outsider, as Richard Allsopp remarks in the introduction to his *Dictionary* (xlix).

Representing spoken language

Attempting to represent a language which has no orthography of its own and which is only a spoken language is a problem that would have confronted Brathwaite.

Brathwaite uses both Standard English and nation language in rendering his poems—some poems are written in Standard English while others are written to reflect the nation language. For example, in *Mother Poem*, the first poem "Alpha" is written in Standard English while the second, "Twine," uses the nation language. In recreating the rhythms, intonations and pronunciations of the nation language, he uses an orthography which attempts to capture the essential features of Bajan while at the same time showing a basic adherence to the conventions of the English language. The orthography utilises the same symbols as those used in Standard English. In representing spoken language without resorting to the use of phonetic symbols he uses what can be called "eye" dialect.

"Eye" dialect tries to represent the precise sounds of the spoken word by altering the conventional spelling and by giving greater "phonetic significance" to symbols than they normally have. The following are the main characteristics of the "eye" dialect used by Brathwaite:

(i) The apostrophe is used to show the absence of a sound. For example: *t'ickets* (thickets), *rev'rent* (reverend), *'fraid* (afraid), *'bout* (about), *gi'* (give).

(ii) The apostrophe is also used to show consonant-cluster reduction. For example:

an' (and), *a'ready* (already), *fac'try* (factory)

In some cases Brathwaite shows does not use the apostrophe to show consonant cluster reduction. He simply presents the words as they are pronounced:

chess (chest), *duss* (dust), *bline* (blind), *hann* (hand)

(iii) The apostrophe is also used where the final sound has been replaced rather than a sound omitted. For example, in words such as *an'* the last sound has been omitted, but in *stannin'*, *bawlin'* and *cat'olic'* nothing has been omitted. In fact the single sound [ ] represented by *ng* has been replaced by [n] and in *cat'olic* the [th] has been replaced by [t].

For the most part, however he is true to linguistic conventions by representing a replacement of sound rather than an omission. For example:

countin (counting), *growin* (growing), *teet* (teeth), *tief* (thief)

(iv) Standard English spelling is altered to reflect differences in pronunciation. For example:

that ~ *dat*	Sunday ~ *Sundee*	out of ~ *outa*	listen ~ *lissen*
mother ~ *mudda*	dog ~ *dawg*	break ~ *brek*	can ~ *kin*
justice ~ *josstice*	woman ~ *umman*	could have ~ *cudda*	saltfish ~ *sawlfish*
here ~ *hay*			

In some instances he had to devise a spelling for words which did not exist in standard English. For example:

choopse   *conkey kukoo*   *bottsie*   *duncks okro*

The "eye" dialect offers the only choice for a literary work, especially one meant to appeal to a wide audience. To use Standard English is to obscure and misrepresent the nation language, while the use of phonetic symbols would alienate the majority of readers who lack the training required to understand them. "Eye" dialect also makes it easy easier to incorporate representations of spoken language into the novel using standard printing equipment since it uses the same symbols used in Standard English.

Furthermore, the use of "eye"dialect seems to be supported by native speakers' intuition. Many native speakers of creoles resort to using the "eye" dialect even where specialised orthographies have been developed for their nation languages.

Lexical features

Brathwaite's vocabulary offers a wide and varied menu. He covers the food and beverages we are most familiar with.

You can have a full course meal of soup—"split pea dumplin and salt beef" or enjoy a "batter of breadfruit kukoo" washed down with a glass of mauby or a sweet drink. If you prefer you can have some biscuits and sawlfish or some conkey, pone or jug-jug.

All black Barbadians (and dare I say, all black people) know of the value system attached to shades of colour which though seemingly covert is almost as serious as the caste system. Brathwaite covers a range of the colour gradations, namely, *black, copper-skinned, cobb-skinned, brown-skinned, red-skinned or red, and eccky-beccky* which we use in Barbados to place Black people in colour categories.

He also paints a vivid picture of a landscape of tamarind trees, shak shak, cherry, duncks, sapodilla, akee, gooseberry, hogplum which provided food or shelter and sometimes both. He reminds us of the silk cotton and sandbox trees which gave shelter and provided a regular meeting place for people to play games such as romie, whist, suck-de-well-dry dry, draughts, dominoes and so on.

The plot of land owned by most families provided sustenance in the form of yams, sweet potatoes, onions, shaddock, wild thyme, okro and green peas and of course there were the plants to stay clear of such as manchioneal, plimplers, cactus, and cowitch.

Brathwaite captures aspects of our culture in images of the rocking chair, the skillets of milk, the black coal pot iron, the standpipe, the wollaboa wood to build fires for cooking, the clay monkeys and the well known "chipped enamel bowl."

The images of the "cork-hatted sanitary inspector" and the old singer sewing machine evoke nostalgia in some of us (that is, those who lived in that era); and who could forget the clothes folded in mothballs and camphor in the padlocked sea chest or trunk as some of us called it?

Brathwaite's language in *Mother Poem* and *Sun Poem* (all my examples are from these two poems) also offers a course in folk medicine. Remedies for human ailments as well as other house hold jobs abound. There is Canadian healing oil for sore muscles, castor oil with lime or salt or sugar for extreme / distress and candle grease for sea-egg pricks and chigoes. There is also "shark ile for the de children colds" and miraculous bush for virtually all female ailments. The Bajan penchant for oil as a cure for just about every and anything is emphasized in the fact that there was also "Easing oil for crusty locks."

Of course one cannot forget the good old Bajan idiomatic phrases that capture so much of what was life was like then (and perhaps now) such as "boiling to buse somebody," or referring to persons as "poor great." We hear the voices of our grandparents in sayings such as "never trouble trouble til trouble trouble you," "follow pattern kill cadogan," "when crappau eat louse he left grass fuh de dog," and "Look me crosses now, nuh."

Through Brathwaite's use of the nation language, we can take out, dust off and admire those treasures which our language has bequeathed us. Brathwaite has managed to combine the roles of historian and poet to the extent that we realise that in African societies, the poet is indeed the historian and vice versa.

A New History of Reading:
Hunting, Tracking, and Reading

J. Edward Chamberlin

The one thing hunters know when they see the track of an animal is that the animal isn't there. That's all they know. And they know that's all they know.

This knowledge is at the heart of hunting and tracking; and it is at the heart of our understanding of representation. Learning about representation; learning to recognize the distinction between a thing and the representation of a thing–the difference between a bear and the word 'bear' or the spoor of a bear, for example; learning about the contradictions of signification . . . this is what tracking is all about. It's also what we do when we learn how to read.

Reading, 'Riting and 'Rithmetic. In the primer of civilization, R comes first. And second. And third. I want to focus on the first two right now, though I'll come to 'rithmetic by and by. But in any event it's typically reading and writing that are identified as the fundamental skills in a civilized society.

It wasn't always so; and, for this and many other reasons that will be the subject of this essay, it is usually assumed that reading and writing are relatively recent developments in the history of civilization. Many would say that they define it. Kamau Brathwaite's stern denunciation of this presumption, along with his clarion call for more work in the field, has been an inspiration to so many of us who are trying to understand the dynamics of both oral and written traditions (*History*).

In one of the most important aboriginal rights cases in recent jurisprudence, in which the Gitksan and Wet'suwet'en (Tsimshian-speaking peoples of the northwest of Canada) claimed jurisdiction over territory where they had lived for thousands of years, the judge said that since their ancestors had "no horses, no wheeled vehicles, no written literature" they were "unorganized societies"–that was his legal phrase–"roaming from place to place like beasts of the field." No writing. No civilization. No case.

That was in 1991. His judgment was later rejected by the Supreme Court, but even that court was unable to find a much better way of characterizing the oral traditions which constitute the history and philosophy and literature of aboriginal peoples than by saying they are not "steeped in the same notions of social progress and evolution" as written traditions. In other words, they are backward.[1]

The clear implication is that those who cannot read and write are less advanced than those who can. Nice enough people, perhaps–the judge described a couple of the most respected elders of the community as two old men who like fishing–but primitive. Illiteracy joins poverty and disease as insignia of underdevelopment.

Behind this, of course, is a familiar story line running from the Bible to the World Bank. "The history of nearly every race that has advanced from barbarism to civilization has been through the stages of the hunter, the herdsman, the agriculturalist, and finally reaching those of commerce, mechanics and the higher arts," said United States Colonel Nelson Miles in 1879, a few years before he accepted surrender from Chief Joseph and the Nez Perce and sent them off to school to learn to read and write. We scorn this sort of stuff as a cover for colonization; and yet most of us, even the most devoutly post-colonial, believe it.

For whether we admit it or not, we are deeply committed to the inevitable ascendancy of agricultural and industrial societies. We might not actually *say* so, of course (though I have heard it often enough over the past thirty years). Many of us would probably rail against this kind of hierarchy, celebrating the courage and creativity of hunters and gatherers clustered on the margins of our world, and envying what see as their freedom from the possessions and the belongings that plague our lives. But we are more like a nineteenth century advocate of progress than we care to admit.

For we are caught up in a deep and (for the hunter gatherers of the world) deadly contradiction. We call the people who wander around the world from place to place looking for land or labouring on it, and dreaming of the old country they left behind, we call these people, *our* people, 'settlers'; and we call the *other* people, those who live in one place hunting and gathering and dreaming of the ancestral spirits who have been there for thousands of years, we call them "nomads." If the truth were told, *we* are the nomads; *they* are the settlers. But we project our contradiction onto those whose "nomadic" lives we envy and whose land we want–for they are idle people and their land too remains idle until we come along to work it. We think about their children, and who's going to teach them to read and write, because their old ways are passing and it's a new world they are living in now, a world of farms and fences, a world with justified lines and clear margins. A world of books.

As though to confirm this, we classify them as "oral cultures" and praise the naturalness of their languages, with their clicks and grunts. We lament the ways in which we have moved away from this oneness with the world into the abstraction and alienation that supposedly come with the written word. We wonder how they recall things so clearly and how they reflect on ideas without the benefit of writing; and then we decide they really don't, they merely remember formulae. Just as scientists do, though we seldom say that, for after all these societies are "pre-scientific." Instead, we celebrate their naive consciousness–the kind that children display–and remark on how it is resonant with an openness to experience that we lose as we grow up and those "shades of the prison house," in Wordsworth's memorable phrase (from his poem "Intimations of Immortality"), close in upon us. And yet we know that with this new phase of our lives comes the compensation of self-reflexive intelligence, the kind capable of real thought. And so we end up thinking of aboriginal hunters and gatherers as not only pre-agricultural and pre-historical and pre-literate but pre-adult too. An early stage of human development.

Here's a contemporary description, by cognitive psychologist Gerry Altmann in a book published in 1997 by Oxford University Press: "The advent of the written word must surely rank, together with fire and the wheel, as one of mankind's greatest achievements," he proclaims with Promethean zeal, adding that "the only other time that evolution came up with a system for storing and transmitting information was when it came up with the genetic code." "Science and technology would hardly have progressed beyond the Dark Ages," he continues, "were it not for the written word" (Altmann 160).

It seems we're not so far away from those nineteenth century fatalists as we might think. Let's look at another version, one couched in more fashionably opaque terms. It's by Michel Foucault, one of the church fathers of our contemporary understanding of how we live in the world: only in the seventeenth century, he insists in *Les Mots et Les Choses* (*The Order of Things* [1966, 1970]), did sign systems such as language come to be seen as representations. Same message, since for Foucault knowledge of representation *is* knowledge.

Altmann and Foucault and almost every other chronicler of the wonders of European civilization (including those who bewail its colonial adventures) associate the major cognitive and cultural breakthrough that is exemplified in writing and reading with the late renaissance. And then the backfilling begins. The standard chronology of writing systems has them beginning with the use of counting devices to expedite trade in agricultural products. Reading–or at least the kind of reading we associate with what we call "literacy"–in turn accompanies the development of the technologies of paper and printing that coincided with the move from agricultural to industrial society in Europe and Asia and their colonial outposts in Africa and the Americas.

The only problem with this is that it's completely wrong. I won't say it's the product of malice and mischief, though there's been no shortage of both; but it certainly comes from ignorance and stupidity. It also makes for a good story, of course . . . such a good story that it has taken hold of almost all our disciplines.

It's not that these things didn't happen. But they happened a very long time ago. Instead of 300 hundred years ago, Foucault should have said 30,000. The cognitive advances we associate with literacy were fully evident many millennia ago, and still are today in contemporary hunter gatherer societies. The complex balancing of the letter and the spirit of a text– or of a sign and its meaning (which may include the motive of its maker)– which we identify with reading practices that developed from classical through medieval to renaissance Europe was flourishing in a very sophisticated form in the intellectual dynamics of ancient tracking in indigenous societies around the world.

What then of the distinction between oral and written traditions? All societies, agricultural and hunter gatherer, have both, as Kamau Brathwaite insisted in *History of the Voice* and many other essays. (It is also, of course, a fundamental premise of his poetry and its various forms of publication.) It is in the relationships between oral and written traditions that the differences are to be found; and it is in paying attention to listening and reading that we realize this. Reading involves a sophisticated appreciation of the contradictions of representation, in which we are (at best, wonderfully) unsure whether something is there or not, whether something is present or absent. An understanding of this contradiction–which is what reading is all about–is just as important in hunter gatherer societies as it is in agricultural and industrial ones, and maybe even more important.

Listening, on the other hand–which also takes place in both societies– involves a no less sophisticated but differently directed appreciation of what I call the contradictions of communication, the contradictions not of visual representation but of verbal communication in which we are always uncertain about whether it is the teller or the tale, the singer or the song, that we believe. This is an old uncertainty, right at the centre of many great traditions of pronouncement and performance such as those of religion and poetry and law. It is also one that Brathwaite's poetry relies on for much of the unsettling ambivalence that constitutes its imaginative power.

We negotiate these two contradictions all the time. But we need to decide which contradiction we are dealing with, and how. It is in *this* negotiation that the interesting questions about the relationships between oral and written traditions emerge. And some troubling misconceptions about them too, misconceptions that have obscured the significant cognitive and cultural achievements of hunter gatherer societies and encouraged us to treat them with a blend of condescension and contempt.

Tracking as a form of reading has long had currency, but always with a primitive cast. "Reading, like speech, is an ancient, preliterate craft," writes Robert Bringhurst in a book of Haida tales that he has carefully translated:

> We read the tracks and scat of animals, the depth and lustre of their coats, the set of their ears and the gait of their limbs. We read the horns of sheep and the teeth of horses, the weights and measures of the wind, the flight of birds, the surface of the sea, snow, fossils, broken rocks, the growth of shrubs and trees–and of course we read the intonations of speaking voices. We read the speech of jays, ravens, hawks, frogs, owls, coyotes, wolves and, in infinite detail, the voices, faces, gestures, coughs and postures of other human beings. This kind of reading antedates all but the earliest, most involuntary form of writing, which is the leaving of prints and traces, the making of tracks. (*Story* 14)

It is a lovely piece of prose. But it doesn't even nod in the direction of tracking as a form of "literate" reading, which is to say serious reading of the sort he is asking us to undertake in his book. And Bringhurst, writing in 1999, is as good as it gets.

Well, not quite. Others have certainly deepened our understanding of oral traditions: scholars such as Julie Cruikshank (*Dan Dha Ts'edenintth'e*), and Richard Dauenhauer and Nora Marks Dauenhauer, with their series of books outlining the sophisticated material and spiritual dynamics of Tlingit oral performance (see bibliography 4.). But most of what passes for scholarship in this field is filled with the same old generalizations, with the recent stuff simply dressed up in new age fashions.

The University of Toronto, where I teach, has a lot to answer for in the characterization of oral cultures as more or less backward. Harold Innis,

Eric Havelock, Marshall McLuhan and Walter Ong (who was McLuhan's sometime student), for all their admirable contributions to the study of the technologies of the word, did much damage in arguing that writing–alphabetic writing in particular–marked an evolutionary advance which set us apart, "us" being all those who are saved by the "first world" development of reading and writing from "third world" benightedness or what McLuhan called a "return to the Africa within" us (McLuhan, *Gutenberg* 45).

Writing frees the mind for original, abstract thought, insisted Havelock. The eye analyzes, the ear tribalizes, chimed in McLuhan. And Walter Ong added a list of additional limitations. Oral cultures are imprisoned in the present, uninterested in definitions, unable to make analytic distinctions, incapable of separating knowledge itself from the process of knowing, and incorrigibly totalizing ("sight isolates, sound incorporates" is the catch phrase he uses, echoing McLuhan). Oral cultures understand the world in magical rather than scientific terms; and those in such cultures who have any acquaintance whatsoever with writing are agonizingly aware of the "vast complex of powers forever inaccessible without literacy," and realize that literacy "is absolutely necessary for the development not only of science but also of history, philosophy, explicative understanding of literature and of any art, and indeed for the explanation of language itself" (Ong, *Orality* 15).

This catalogue is from Ong's *Orality and Literacy*, which has become a primer for the current generation of post-colonial commentary. It is deeply misinformed and dangerously misleading. It has been taken on and written off by scholars such as Leroy Vail and Landeg White (in "The Invention of Oral Man," their polemical introduction to *Power and the Praise Poem*). But it continues to be extraordinarily influential in the humanities and social sciences, and by extension in public debate about the land and livelihood of those who have these co-called oral cultures. It entrenches not only racist ideologies that, God knows, have enough purchase already, but also the truly idiotic notion that there *are* such things as "oral cultures" and "written cultures." Just to take the most obvious point: to argue that European and its various settler cultures in Asia, Africa and the Americas are "written cultures," at least since the renaissance, ignores the fact that the central post-renaissance institutions of these supposedly *written* cultures–their churches, courts, parliaments and schools–are defined by *oral* traditions. And it rather more deliberately discounts the forms of writing that are typical of so-called "oral cultures": non-syllabic and alphabetic forms such as woven and beaded belts and blankets, knotted and coloured strings, carved and painted trays, poles, doors, verandah posts, canes and sticks, masks, hats and chests, and so forth.

There *are* differences between cultures, to be sure, structural and stylistic and substantive differences of immense importance. And there *are* differences (as I will suggest below) in the ways in which different cultures apprehend and understand the world. But these differences are not binary, at least certainly not according to the oral/written dichotomy which, as Leopold Peeters recently argued, has been the regrettable result of an academic preoccupation with the formal and functional rather than the ontological and epistemological dynamics of language and expression ("Beyond"). Rather, cultures and their primary forms of expression are situated along a spectrum, with hunters at one end and farmers at the other. And the stages–or what we might call the "frequencies"–are non-sequential, the same way the colours in the light spectrum are; that is, they do not "precede" or "cause" each other according to some morphology or teleology.

Despite the ways in which they are characterized by Ong and others, "oral cultures" are all the rage these days. There are many reasons for this, among them the remarkable range and power they display (again differently in different cultures); and the ways in which they illustrate uses of language that we associate with the poetic and the religious. In the eighteenth and nineteenth centuries, discussions of poetry almost always turned to the speeches of Indian chiefs for examples of "pure poetry" because of their primitive "boldness", "originality" and "enthusiasm"–these are the terms used in an entry in the *Edinburgh Encyclopaedia* of 1830, quoting an unidentified Iroquois leader. Ong and his many followers use almost the same terms a hundred and fifty years later.

And there's the more political reason that written traditions are identified as symbols of imperial power and instruments of legal, commercial and cultural exploitation. So oral traditions, and the cultures that supposedly embody them, are embraced for their . . . their what? Their difference. Their naturalness. Their survival . . . but also their vulnerability.

The trouble, as I have said, is that this typology is just plain wrong. Speech and writing are so entangled with each other in our various forms and performance of language that we are like Penelope, weaving them together during the day and unweaving them at night. Our current theories and models illustrate none of this, with the result that studying oral and written traditions using existing paradigms is an exercise in pushing a string or herding cats. And for all of our post-colonial self-consciousness, our take on oral and written traditions has done next to nothing to diminish the dispossession of land, the displacement of livelihood and the destruction of languages that has been the story of colonial encounters between agricultural and hunting peoples for millennia, and which I believe is linked to our misconceptions about their cognitive and cultural achievements, and its basis in a misunderstanding of oral and written traditions.

I want to avoid the development politics and the evolutionary historicism that have created these misunderstandings and distracted so many scholars. So instead of speaking and writing, I will focus on listening and reading. And because cultural studies has such a hold on the academic as well as the popular imagination, and is so simple-minded in its account of oral and written traditions, I will begin by shifting attention from the cultural to the cognitive. At the end of the day, I hope that a new understanding of reading and listening may encourage a new appreciation of the cognitive and cultural achievements of both agricultural and hunter gatherer societies. It may even go some ways towards explaining the pathological fear and loathing of the languages of indigenous peoples by so-called settler societies, their determined efforts to destroy them, and their casual disappointment as they disappear. In this century, while hundreds of distinguished Comparative Literature departments dedicated to working in original languages have enlivened the study of literary traditions in universities across the Americas, over a thousand aboriginal languages have died. More people in the academy, not to mention outside it, worry about the spotted owl than about the languages of indigenous people. This disregard, I am convinced, flows from cognitive as well as cultural misunderstandings.

Reading,"Riting and"Rithmetic. I am obviously not the first to reverse the usual order that has reading *follow* writing. But I want to argue a more radical case, which is that reading comes before writing–historically as well as pedagogically–and that the cognitive advances we associate with the late renaissance were fully achieved millennia ago, long before the development of syllabic or alphabetic scripts, in the sophisticated dynamics of tracking.

I have some allies, especially among a group of contemporary psychologists who, although they don't concern themselves with historical chronology, do give *cognitive* priority to reading over writing. They have brought together the findings of historians, anthropologists and literary critics with those of cognitive psychology to offer a new way of thinking about this, and to demonstrate how the cognitive developments to which Altmann refers coincide with the development of new reading practices rather than merely with writing technologies.

This is the burden of the pioneering work done during the 1980s and early 1990s by historian and literary critic Brian Stock on the emergence of new reading techniques in late classical and medieval Europe, and the organization of "communities" of readers around a text, an interpreter and an interpretation–imagined communities of a different sort than Benedict

Anderson conceived, but with perhaps just as much power. A new kind of attention to the "letter" of a text produced new interpretations–or what I will be calling hypotheses–about its "spirit" or meaning, Stock argues; and when this kind of reading was applied to the Bible–the book of God–it had important historical ramifications, for it produced groups of dissenters and heretics who paved, or burned, the way to the protestant reformation. When it was applied to the book of Nature, it produced modern science.

Based on research they did in the 1930s, psychologists such as Lev S. Vygotsky and Alexander Luria showed how cognitive developments–higher mental processes they called them–were always dependent on cultural changes such as the invention of sign systems. Jerome Bruner (*Child's Talk* and *Acts of Meaning*) took up these ideas and provided new insights into the character of these cognitive developments; and Roy Harris has extended the understanding of cultural developments that coincided with them. There are of course many others who have been part of this scholarly enterprise, and this list provides just a sketch. But it is David Olson, especially in his *World on Paper*, who has most effectively brought together the work in the field, and in doing so provided some guidance on how to take the work of the "Toronto School"–as the anthropologist Jack Goody has labelled that earlier generation that includes Innis, McLuhan, Ong and Havelock (*Interface*)–onto new ground.

Olson joins Stock in concluding that it was not writing but reading that signalled a revolutionary change in European, west Asian and north African cultural practices. Olson is careful not to ascribe superior intelligence to those who made this cognitive advance, but proposes instead that they have what anthropologists might call a more complex tool kit. And although he focuses on alphabetic writing, Olson is also open to the suggestion that non-alphabetic forms may require differently complex reading practices, and therefore promote different cognitive developments.

He is in a minority among social scientists in his account of all this, for despite all cautions many scholars seem unable to avoid identifying cognitive change with cognitive superiority, or at least with evolutionary advance. And then it's an easy slide into the logic of the law of recapitulation (ontogeny recapitulates phylogeny), a nineteenth century fallacy which has shaped so much twentieth century social science and which presumes that the cognitive development of the child from speech to writing mirrors the cultural development of the society from primitive to civilized. While this line of thinking–I don't even like to call it that–is less obvious now than it was fifty years ago, it is still evident in many of our disciplines.

But this aside, a preoccupation with the connections between writing and reading is shared by most commentators, who assume that alphabetic writing of the sort we associate with European literacy is where the sophisticated and subtle reading that Foucault talked about takes place. I want to argue, on the contrary, that while new writing technologies may provide one occasion for new reading practices, there *are* others. In particular, reading practices almost exactly analogous to those celebrated by Olson and his colleagues emerged emerged under quite different conditions among ancient hunting peoples.

But we might not recognize this were it not for the insights of the very same scholars with whom I am disagreeing. So I need to outline in some detail the cognitive developments which they associate with the reading practices of modern European society, in order to provide a framework for considering the kind of reading that I believe also constitutes the achievement of tracking in hunter gatherer societies tens of thousands of years earlier.

David Olson outlines two fundamental points. The first is that the development of syllabic and alphabetic writing technologies and the cognitive changes associated with reading their new texts can best be understood by challenging the traditional assumption that writing is merely "visible speech." He is hardly alone in making this challenge, of course, though for most of this century, certainly since Ferdinand Saussure, the idea of writing as a technology for recording speech has had a remarkable hold. On the contrary, Olson argues, writing is much more: it is a cognitive agent that turns speech back on itself, making us aware of aspects of language that speech itself does not convey by displaying the *presence* of certain structural and substantive characteristics of language, and drawing our attention to the *absence* of other elements, such as the illocutionary markers of speech, the gestures and rhythms and tones which constitute much of its meaning and value.

The second point, which follows directly from the first, is that the ways in which we understand the relationships between speaking and writing and the theories of language which are generated by our reading practices then "serve as models for the world and for the mind" (Olson, *World* 258). It is, obviously, what writing does *not* display as well as what it does that is important; and the real achievement of reading is in negotiating this move from what is there to what is not there, from the sign to what is behind or before (in the sense of what causes) the sign. And while writing provides an occasion for this, it is in reading that the cognitive and cultural changes actually happen.

Recognizing this, which–as Foucault reminds us–is recognizing the dynamics of representation in language, has for Olson practical as well as theoretical implications, for it can usefully inform the teaching of reading and writing to children. Also, bringing into consciousness the lexical, syntactic, and logical consequences and the corresponding categorical determinants of language creates something else, something immensely important to us in both cognitive and cultural terms–a consciousness of difference.

One difference has to do with the primary forms of language, oral and written. It is sometimes said that speech *expresses* and writing *reveals* meaning. However we designate this difference, Olson argues that there *is* one. Reading involves first of all an attempt to compensate for what is lost in expression, and revelation, if it comes at all–and of course it always does in some measure for the competent reader–comes second. It depends on close initial attention to what is there–to what is expressed–in the written text, in order to achieve some eventual revelation about what is *not* expressed.

The other difference has to do with language itself, and how its modes of representation generate our models of reality. Like most theorists of language, even those dedicated to linguistic absolutes such as Noam Chomsky, Olson accepts that there is some element of relativity present in all language communities. He understands this in the way it was advocated earlier in this century by Benjamin Lee Whorf and his mentor Edward Sapir (picking up a long line of speculation from Wilhelm Von Humboldt to Franz Boas), and was given currency by the immensely popular mid-century writings of Samuel Hayakawa (*Language in Action*) and others. According to the theory of linguistic relativity, language *creates* as well as *conveys* thought and feeling, and to a greater or lesser degree determines the categories–of self, space, time, and matter–according to which we understand the world, categories which in turn shape our behaviour. It"s a strong version of McLuhan's dictum "the medium is the message."

And it is why aboriginal peoples are taught European languages, or more often forced to learn them. It's to alter the way they think and feel. To turn them into farmers. "The language which is good enough for a white man or a black man ought to be good enough for the red man . . . Teaching an Indian youth in his own barbarous dialect is a positive detriment to him. The impracticability, if not impossibility, of civilizing the Indians of this country in any other tongue than our own would seem obvious," said the United States Commissioner of Indian Affairs in his Annual Report in 1887. "Kill the Indian and save the man," added Richard Pratt, founder of the Carlisle Indian School in the United States, about the same time. It is both the grimmest terrorism and the highest tribute to the power of language to see it as the key to cognitive and cultural change; and insofar as they were inspired by a mission to civilize the savages, colonial policies were committed to this kind of social engineering.

Now to the heart of my argument. Reading as I have described it is an old, not a new, habit. (I use the word habit in its Latin sense, in which it used to be said that when one learned a language one had the "habit" of it.) Reading is just as closely linked with the development of ancient hunter gatherer societies as it is with modern agricultural and industrial ones. And the reading I am referring to involves precisely the same understanding of representation that Foucault celebrated, an understanding of how something can be both there and not there, can be both surface and symbol at the same time.

Tracking not only constitutes a form of reading that can be compared with the reading of other written texts, but it involves all of the cognitive innovations identified with the development of modern European culture, especially in relation to science and religion. I certainly acknowledge the formidable achievement of writing, from the pictographic to the alphabetic (though I would argue for a much wider acceptance of non-alphabetic script than many scholars recognize); and I agree that reading, especially reading of alphabetic scripts, involves a shift in the understanding of both reality and its representation. But I do not believe that the shift is an exclusive product of modern reading practices, coinciding (and this is usually part of the equation) with the developments of protestantism and what we call modern science. On the contrary, I believe that it was coincident with the development from simple or systematic to speculative tracking; and *this* occurred not hundreds of years ago in Europe, but thousands of years ago around the world, probably at different periods in different climatic zones.

In using these tracking terms–simple, systematic and speculative–I am particularly indebted to Louis Liebenberg"s *Art of Tracking*. Simple or systematic tracking, as he describes it, involves taking information from animal signs in order to determine what an animal was doing and where it was going: *following* the tracks, where possible; *finding* them, when necessary. Even in its more systematic form, this mode of tracking does not go beyond evidence into opinion; but trackers must, of course, know undisturbed terrain in order to "read" disturbances, and this requires what Liebenberg describes as "intermittent attention, a constant refocussing between minute detail of the track and the whole pattern of the environment" (103). Memory is crucial, since the tracker must be able to recall a wide range of knowledge both significant and meta-significant in order to place the signs in the appropriate semiotic context. But the key is attention to detail. In fact, this kind of tracking highlights a point often made about reading written texts: one must carefully read what's *on* the lines before one can read between or behind them. I suggest tracking also often involves the recognition of what might be called style and genre, for each animal has a style–predator or scavenger, individual or herd, young and old, male or female, in different seasons; and each animal may work in what for want of better terms might be called lyric, dramatic and narrative modes. (Incidentally, there are important connections to be made between written and oral *styles*. By far the best work on the latter comes from Marcel Jousse during years between 1925 [when his book *Le Style Oral* was first published] and 1957; and more recently from Edgard Sienaert at the University of Natal, who has edited and, with Joan Conolly translated Jousse's magisterial *The Anthropology of Geste and Rhythm*).

The very skill of a tracker in recognizing signs may be part of the reason hunting societies have been misconceived by those who observe them. For this is where both anthropological and popular attention is usually focussed, on the remarkable ability of trackers to recognize–literally to *see*–animal signs. It *is* remarkable, rather as learning an exotic orthography or recognizing a difficult handwriting is remarkable. It involves seeing certain signs, often barely perceptible or distinguishable, and linking them to certain sounds or "speech acts." But it's not reading. It's a necessary preliminary to reading, the way recognizing a script is. It's the first half of the process, if you will. The other half–and for our purposes here the important half–is the way in which the signs are *read*. That's where speculative tracking comes in; and it's where my argument is directed.

In all societies that have moved beyond gathering and scavenging, systematic tracking is complemented by speculative tracking. Its mode of reasoning, the mode that characterizes speculative tracking, involves explaining observations in terms of hypothetical causes. Let me underline the difference. Simple or systematic tracking always precedes speculative tracking the way recognizing a script precedes reading it; that is, it is a necessary but not a sufficient condition. Simple or systematic tracking is based on what Liebenberg calls inductive-deductive reasoning, in which general premises are induced from observed particulars, and then the identity of a particular spoor is deduced from these general premises. The deduction requires logic; the induction requires empirical generalization derived from experience. It is based on the accumulation of facts and generalizations derived from them. It explains nothing; nor does it predict anything. That said, it requires great skill, intelligence and dedication; and it can be very effective.

But at a certain point it's not enough; and that's where speculation comes in. Speculative tracking, while it depends on skilled simple or systematic tracking, incorporates something new: working hypotheses. These are developed from an interpretation of animal signs and a knowledge of animal behaviour and of the terrain. Other signs are then looked for in order to confirm or refute the hypothesis, which is then revised or elaborated accordingly. This represents a fundamentally new way of thinking, one which involves an interaction between the critical and the imaginative faculties, between discovery and invention, and between mechanistic and teleological explanations; and a constant interplay between hypotheses and the logical consequences they give rise to.

One of the major shifts which theorists of European literacy identify with the development of renaissance reading practices is what Olson calls "the recovery, or management, of intentionality" (*World* 267). I don't much like the word management, because it conjures up agricultural society's preoccupation with the management of time and space; but Olson's focus on *intention* is useful. There is, he argues, a new understanding of the relationships between sign and cause that coincides with this kind of reading, a new recognition of the gap between what is said (in a written text) and what is meant, and a new set of agreements about how to "take" a text (along with a new sense of a logic–or pathologic–of mis-takes). Another way of putting it–again, this is Olson's formulation–is to say that interpretation is naturalized: the "spirit" of a text is now seen as available through a careful analysis of the letter, rather than as a gift from above or a more or less mysterious understanding from behind or below or within. In this context, knowledge *is* interpretation, and a clear distinction is assumed between the meaning of a sign and what it refers to. Phenomena, or signs, are seen, heard, touched, tasted, smelled–apprehended by the senses, that is–and agreed upon. Causes, or meanings, are then inferred or hypothesized in the mind--and more often than not disputed.

I can't think of a better description of speculative tracking. Beyond its unequivocal acknowledgement of a distinction between sign and cause and its sophisticated interpretative strategies for closing the gap between them, there is in the ancient practice of speculative tracking a deep and complex understanding of the nature of representation that exactly mirrors contemporary notions of both literacy and what we call modern science. Or more precisely *they* mirror *it*.

And so it is arguable–and I think demonstrable–that tracking in a hunter gatherer society not only constitutes one of the most important intellectual achievements of humanity, with powerful theoretical as well as practical implications that reflect a remarkable harmony of land and livelihood, but that it also constitutes a form of reading that can be compared with the reading of other written texts in what we call a literate society.

This sort of reading makes up for what Olson calls the limitations of writing (that is, of the tracks)–the absence of illocutionary indicators, the gap between signifier and signified, the illusory quality of the meaning embodied in the language–by speculating about causes, motives, intentions. In this, too, it combines literary with scientific intelligence. It explains the visible world by a postulated invisible world. It often does so, of course, by projecting anthropomorphic qualities onto/ into the animal; but this is essentially no different from many of the projections of order or pattern or purposefulness onto phenomena in modern science. As the Nobel laureate in physical chemistry John Polanyi once remarked in a speech in Toronto:

> it is not the laws of physics that make science possible but the unprovable proposition that there exists a grand design underlying the physical world. And not just any old "grand design" but one that is accessible to the limited sense and modest reasoning powers of the species to which we belong. Scientists subscribe with such conviction to this article of faith that they are willing to commit a lifetime to the pursuit of scientific discovery. ("Magic")

And reading ordinary written texts, after all, is also almost always anthropomorphic, with its artificial positing of an author for a text (even though we may of course not know who it is, and even if we do we may know almost nothing about him or her). It's an artifice that is so habitual it seems natural, as we discover when we encounter texts–such as in certain forms of divination–that seem intentionless. The anthropomorphism involved in hunting constitutes the "tradition" of the animal, like the anthropomorphism of literary traditions; and like all traditions it's the product of the imagination. As writing makes readers aware of the performative aspects of speech, tracks make hunters aware of the performance of animals; they may even assume that the animals are performing– speaking, as it were–to them personally. To borrow a phrase from Roland Barthes, they stage the problematic of reading. Or to pick up Olson's image for the distinction between a thing and the representation of a thing–the difference between a bear and the word "bear"–tracks are animals "in quotation" (Olson's theory is outlined in his chapbook *The Written Word*).

There is another element here, raised by Bruner and reflecting McLuhan's comment that "by the meaningless sign linked to the meaningless sound we have built the shape and meaning of western man" (McLuhan 50). We invest texts with arbitrariness; this arbitrariness, in turn, creates a performative or what we might call a "quotational" distance between text and reader, which then becomes the key to words or signs as representations. This element of arbitrariness is the most important element in distinguishing between a word and the thing to which it refers; it is the key to recognizing words and signs as representations. Just so, a hunter invests the tracks he sees with arbitrariness (of intention, meaning, cause) so that he can read them. *We* would be likely to invest the same track with naturalness. That would be fine; but it would not allow us to apprehend it with the speculative imagination that constitutes genuine reading. (With familiarity, of course, we effectively naturalize these signs whether we are engaged in hunting or Biblical hermeneutics. But we retain an appreciation of their artifice, their arbitrariness.)

Those who read contemporary literary theory know more about this than they may realize, for it is what Emmanuel Levinas and Jacques Derrida are talking about when they identify the sign as the site of a relationship between the self and the other. This merely confirms the elements of arbitrariness, of disengagement, of distance, that is an inevitable and indispensable understanding for a hunter; but instead of being the trace or vestige that Levinas talks about, the track is invested with literariness by the readerly imagination of the hunter and becomes what might be called a translation. And yet this still isn't the whole story, for the anthropomorphism of the hunter defamiliarizes (or denaturalizes) the animal, making it strange and giving it autonomy by the same act of the imagination; turning the animal from an object into a subject, the way we do when we talk about a crouching armchair or a lurking cloud; creating a presence that both extends perception (because it is absent) and eludes perception (also because it is absent).

Sometimes, it appears that the tracker *becomes* the animal, or at least that's what he says. But we need to be careful about interpreting such statements. They may perhaps be figures of speech, the same way the power of natural selection or the attraction of gravity are. But it is not always easy to disentangle figures of speech from facts of life. At the end of the day, it's perhaps impossible; because that's the way we understand things. In everyday speech, we talk about the mouth of a river, a neck of land, handfuls of one thing, the heart of another, veins of minerals, bowels of the earth, murmuring waves, whistling winds, smiling skies, groaning tables and weeping willows. (This catalogue is by the renaissance scholar Giambattista Vico, from his book *The New Science*, and it's quoted by Isaiah Berlin in his book on Vico and Herder.)

Mostly, these become cliches; "fossil metaphors," Ralph Waldo Emerson used to call them. He went on to say that poetry brings them to life again; or more precisely the reading of poetry. I think that they are brought to life in *all* forms of reading that move beyond the level of seeing; and I suggest that this involves something much more radical than it may appear, an imagining that is so familiar we lose a sense of its strangeness. The more precise we think we are, the more metaphorical we become, with equations and formulae being among our purest forms of metaphor. When hunters rely on dreams, or presentiments, or forms of divining, we might remember Wordsworth's account in his poem "Resolution and Independence" of the day he met another hunter gatherer, the leech gatherer: "Now whether it were by peculiar grace, a leading from above, a something given." We read (and listen to) all texts with exactly that kind of uncertainty, that hovering between intention and inevitability. And the strangeness, or arbitrariness, or hypothetical quality that defines this reading reverses the relationship between the imagination and reality, and between subject and object. I like to put it this way: instead of the word "bear" or the track of a bear being a metaphor for the bear, the bear becomes a metaphor for the track or the word.

I want to conclude with a few connections between tracking and science. It's a way to get 'Rithmetic in, as I promised I would. The process of speculative tracking is not illogical but hypothetical. It begins and ends outside logic, one of those "free inventions of the human intellect" that Albert Einstein once called science. Neither the force of gravity, nor the size and shape of an atom, nor the animal the hunter is tracking, can be seen. Only their signs can; particle "tracks," as nuclear scientists tellingly describe them.

There's another understanding that binds together trackers and scientists. Trackers, like good scientists, accept that they cannot prove the truth of their hypothesis; and even though it has been proven true every time in the past, the next time it may not. As Northrop Frye noted, making a connection between the hypotheses of the arts and the sciences:

> the poet, like the pure mathematician, depends not on descriptive truth, but on conformity to his hypothetical postulates. The appearance of a ghost in *Hamlet* presents the hypothesis "let there be a ghost in *Hamlet*." It has nothing to do with whether ghosts exist or not, or whether Shakespeare or his audience thought they did. A reader who quarrels with postulates, who dislikes *Hamlet* because he does not believe that there are ghosts or that people speak in pentameters, clearly has no business in literature. (*Anatomy* 76)

Or, by implication, in mathematics. A little later, Frye repeats this tenet. "Mathematics, like literature, proceeds hypothetically and by internal consistency, not descriptively and by outward fidelity to nature. When it is applied to external facts, it is not its truth but its applicability that is being verified" (93). Though it may seem counterintuitive for a society whose survival depends on the success of the hunt, the same is true of tracking.

This cognitive and cultural attitude–and the level of comfort it requires with uncertainties and indeterminacies–is one of the great cognitive and cultural achievements of hunter gatherer societies. It reinforces the affinity of tracking with both modern science and the modern arts, and it brings trackers into the company of those who negotiate the contradictions of representation every day in their reading practices–which is to say, of all those whom it is conventional to call literate. Making this connection also highlights a mistake in some discussions of literacy, where it is seen as a process of *reducing* the uncertainty and ambiguity in a text; and yet our most complex forms of reading–of poetry, for example, and of many religious texts–nourish just this indeterminacy.

Finally, the hypotheses of speculative tracking are always open to criticism from participants in the process, who may induce different hypotheses or who may deduce results that discredit existing ones. In hunter gatherer societies, disagreements over hypotheses are routine, and contrary to the stereotype of authoritarian elders (or what one African historian of oral traditions called "vieillesse oblige") discussion is typically not limited to certain age or class groupings. Furthermore, because meat is always shared, there is an often unrecognized licence among individuals hunter–or readers–to be unsuccessful, to be wrong, to make mistakes. As Liebenberg puts it, "the principle of sharing gave trackers a degree of 'academic freedom' to explore new ideas. The success or failure of new ideas, that is the predictive value of new ideas, would determine whether they would be taken up" (162). One other point I would make is that not all members of these societies could–or can–read in the way I am talking about . . . any more than all members of our society can.

So one might say that hunters are like members of a reading group; or a gathering of protestants; or a research laboratory of scientific collaborators. I like the first analogy best, of hunters as "Alexandrian," remarkably like the members of the community that gathered in the great library of Alexandria and developed a set of reading practices and interpretative strategies that were dependent on the closed body of texts that were available to them, and the knowledge they shared. Because of the clearly defined nature of territory in a hunter gatherer society, and the fact that they must know the place and its flora and fauna intimately (and typically name them in extraordinarily specific detail) if they are to survive, the hunter's store of texts is as clearly defined (and includes as remarkable a range of genres and styles) as the holdings of the ancient library of Alexandria. And it is often just as arcane. In both cases, their interpretative and evaluative methods, and their reading practices (including their intertextual enthusiasms) are determined and contained by the texts that are available to them and by the traditions they have inherited.

One of the classic statements of the supposed distinction between the primitive and the civilized, by Lucien Lévy-Bruhl (in *Primitive Mentality* [1923] and *How Natives Think* [1926]), emphasizes that the primitive's mind does not distinguish between sign and cause; has no difficulty at all in statements which to us are absolutely contradictory; and is unable, as Foucault reiterated a generation later, to manage the relationship between a thing and the representation of a thing. If what is meant by "primitive" is "hunter gatherer"–and that certainly *is* what is meant by Lévy-Bruhl–the first is nonsense, the second is fundamental to modern science (think of the scientific characterization of light as a wave *and* a particle, or an infinite series that both reaches *and* never reaches its limit), and the third is the sophisticated achievement of readers, which they were.

Furthermore, the contradictions that troubled Lévy-Bruhl are at the heart of any understanding of representation. Hunters read visible signs, but they know them to be signs of the invisible, almost exactly as other readers of signs such as nuclear physicists do. A track, even when it's very clear, tells you where an animal (or a neuron) was, not where it is. To figure *that* out, a hunter uses a combination of experience and imagination, or mapping and dreaming, to make up a story in which he and the animal will meet. The hunter's imagination shapes reality through re-presentation; it must happen first of all in the mind before it happens in the world. And when it does happen, when the hunter and the animal converge, the reading is over. The story is done. The catching and killing of the animal has nothing at all to do with the tracking and reading that I am talking about. It is uninteresting and irrelevant. If the track is the animal in quotation, the kill is the story in paraphrase. In Herman Melville's *Moby Dick* (1851), Ishmael says of Queequeg's home, Kokovoko, that "it is not down in any map. True places never are" (56). The true place of tracking has nothing to do with the reality of the hunt. It has everything to do with the imagination.

We can learn much about reality and the imagination, about reading and writing, about the relationships between oral and written tradition, from hunter gatherer societies. We are lucky. They are still with us; on marginal land to be sure, but that makes it easier for us since tracks are often clearer there in snow and sand. And we, dummies that we are, may be better able to understand about representation, about distinguishing sign from cause, and about what it is to be literate.

Notes

1. There is a fair body of material now available regarding this trial, beginning with the trial transcript itself. The text of the December 11, 1997 Supreme Court decision is available on the Internet at: www.droit.umontreal.ca/doc/csc-scc/en/rec/html/delgamuu.en.html *BC Studies* devoted a special issue (Autumn 1992) to the trial and judgment, with interesting articles by Julie Cruikshank, Dara Culhane and Robin Ridington, among others; and Don Monet and Skanu'u (Ardythe Wilson) have compiled *Colonialism on Trial*, a book of excerpts, cartoons and commentary from the trial. The most powerful single monograph is Leslie Pinder's *Carriers of No*. Works mentioned throughout this essay are listed in this book's general bibliography (**4.**): if only an author's name is given in the text, reference is to the only one or all the works listed there, except when the name simply indicates an entire lifework, which is not then listed.

Contemporary Native Resistance in Africa: The Cultural Factor[1]

Ngugi wa Thiong'o

If we want to understand the character and form of the contemporary native resistance in Africa, it is necessary for us to cast a quick glance at the nature and forms of resistance in colonial Africa. With the Berlin conference of 1884 during which Africa was carved into spheres of influence of the various European powers, the continent emerged from the boiling pot of the Atlantic slave trade into the frying pan of colonialism. By 1900 virtually the entire continent was under direct European rule in one form or another.

Colonialism was first and foremost a matter of economics and profit calculations long before it was rationalized as an altruistic, if a little zealous, export of Europe's version of Christianity and civilization. People do not dominate others for the sake of aesthetic pleasure and moral rectitude. The resources of Africa both natural and human were the primary objects. This was to be effected through the establishment of actual white settler states as in Algeria, Kenya, Zimbabwe and South Africa or the non-settler type, the directly commercial, as in most of West Africa including Nigeria and Ghana. But the objects were the same: the enrichment of the mother country or the strategic control of the routes of such enrichment.

Economic control would have impossible to sustain without political and military control, and this was effected through military conquests, or pacification–to use the parlance of the times–and the subsequent establishment of the colonial state. Economics and politics walked arm in arm like Siamese twins, for one was really a condition of the other.

But economic and political control, however massive and well-organized, could never be effective without that of culture: hence the colonizers' attempts to control the realms of education, language, literature, dances, songs, religion, and performance through banning or in other ways discouraging those of the natives and elevating those of the conqueror to a desirable universality. If successful, this would inevitably lead to control of the entire ethical and aesthetic systems of a community; leading in turn to control of its individual and collective minds, its sense of who they are in relationship to themselves and the universe. And this would necessarily lead to the colonization of their perception of who exactly was enemy and friend. It was in fact through cultural engineering that colonialism was able to produce a class of natives who saw the colonizer as a friend and liberator from their own past of savagery. These were deliberately produced when they were not anyway an inevitable consequence of domination. One can readily give the example of Thomas Babington Macaulay who, as a member of the Indian Supreme Council, wrote in 1835 of the aim of Indian education as that of producing a middle-class of Indians who would be Indian in color and blood but otherwise British in mind and outlook. Macaulay's type of thinking is what is reflected in one of the European characters in my novel *A Grain of Wheat* who sees himself as a latter-day Prospero producing eternally grateful natives.

Macaulayism was an earlier British variation on what came to be systematized, in the hands of the French, into a policy of cultural assimilation. The purpose of colonial cultural engineering was not the disinterested inventor's delight in the act of invention as an aesthetic challenge, but rather, the very practical delight of having a class of natives who would stand between the dominating imperialist bourgeoisie and the vast majority of colonial subjects. In a way, cultural control, if ever it had been successful, would have been the perfect way to reduce the cost of maintaining an expensive police and military presence. A people who have been colonized in the mind would become their own policemen.

If colonialism did not produce auto-enslavement it was not for want of trying, but rather because right from the beginning it had generated its dialectical opposite: resistance. Like the plantation slave before him, the colonial slave was a most restive creature. He kicked out with his legs, he thrust out his arms, he yelled resistance, and in some cases he opted for death rather than life in servitude. There were highs and lows of this resistance, there were victories and defeats, but it was always there, continuous and unbroken, sometimes reaching magnificent heights–as in the armed struggles of the Mau Mau in Kenya and the FLN in Algeria, feats that were later followed and driven to loftier heights in the liberation struggles of Angola, Mozambique and Guinea Bissau in the seventies, and of Zimbabwe and South Africa in the eighties. The heyday of the triumph of African anti-colonial resistance was in the fifties and sixties, when one colony after another fell to its blows, like the celebrated house of cards. By the end of the sixties, the power map drawn largely in British, French, Portuguese and Belgian colors had been reversed, and now there were only a few territories which had not yet been liberated from direct colonial rule. Not surprisingly and not without some truth, the sixties were often described as the decade of Africa's independence.

But this independence was seriously flawed by the quick mutation of the old colonialism into a new form: what now goes by the name of neo-colonialism. Neo-colonialism was a situation where a country had all the trappings of sovereignty–the flag, the national anthem, the state–but where its economy, politics and culture were still dictated from the outside. Such a country was independent in political form but not in political, and certainly not in economic, content. Neo-colonialism was not a unique phenomenon which suddenly reared its ugly head after the Second World War. It was there in the late nineteenth century, though completely overshadowed by a triumphant colonialism engulfing Asia and Africa at the time. It was first noticed in the relations between the USA and the Latin American states which had emerged from European control. Most of these countries may have been independent, but their economies were certainly under the dominant sway of their giant neighbor who in fact flexed his political muscle by frequently intervening in many of these countries, often dictating who would exercise state power. The legal basis for these interventions was the protective umbrella unilaterally raised over these countries under the various guises of manifest destiny, finally assuming the name "the Monroe doctrine," but they had their real basis in US economic control.

The main difference between the pre- and the post-World War Two situations was the fact that neo-colonialism as a form of international relations of domination was clearly in its nascent stage in the prewar period, as against the global reach of the old colonialism. But after the Second World War and with the new independents of Africa and Asia, it became the dominant form, with its character now shaped not by the old rivalries between America and Western Europe but by the nuclear-armed rivalries of the Cold War led by the Soviet Union and the USA. The arms race became one of the military instruments for waging the war, and the Breton Woods institutions of the IMF and the World Bank were some of the economic instruments for doing the same. Both armed and economic might were used to control the nature and practice of the new states in their internal and their external relations. This was reflected in the arming of rival camps between nations, regions, and even within nations, and in the hostility of the West towards any state that tried to change and reshape its economy to meet the needs of the people. Every act in Africa was seen through the prism of the Cold War. In other words, every attempt, however modest, by Africa to disengage its economies from the strings that tied them to the West was seen as a giant stride towards the Soviet camp. Democracy in any form, let alone in its Lincolnian sense of government of the people by the people for the people, was seen as a dangerous weapon in the hands of Communists in the making. We can in fact characterize the period between the independence euphoria of the sixties and the end of the Cold War as one of political stagnation and economic decline.

For the period was indeed one of political stagnation. This came from the very fact that there had not been any genuine radical reform in the economies for the benefit of the people below. Like their colonial predecessors, these regimes quickly became politically isolated from the people. Not that this isolation led to sleepless nights on the part of the neo-colonial leadership. The regimes which came to power through western-backed military coups do not see themselves as being beholden to the country and to the people for the simple reason that their route to power and the key to their continued hold on that power were through the bullet and their client relationship to the dominant powers of the West. To maintain stability for western interests, these regimes often resorted to the same measures as those of colonial yesteryear. They deliberately cultivated and then exploited regional and ethnic divisions to keep the population divided in its response to their rule. In some places this resulted in government-engineered ethnic clashes with genocidal consequences for the people. The unity of anti-colonial resistance had been replaced by the divisions of neo-colonialism.

At the cultural level, most of these regimes identified themselves with the worst aspects of western bourgeois culture. Tourism becomes the foundation of the culture of servility and national self-abnegation. Frantz Fanon once accused neo-colonial regimes of becoming the brothels of Europe and their leaders of being the brothel-keepers who ensured that the countries under their control were ready to receive the tourist with open arms and legs. What they paraded as African dances and music, for instance, were performances completely emptied of their old living and often revolutionary content into empty bodily gyrations and servile voices of spiritual surrender. From the people they simply wanted a collective homage of servitude. Often they suppressed national creative initiatives and when they praised African cultures it was only the most backward elements of traditionalism, or culture as a static museum piece. The regimes often tried to Africanize or nationalize the colonial view of their history. Reminders of the heroism of anti-colonial resistance or any stories of people's resistance became an embarrassment. The education systems were often the same colonial ones dusted over and given grandiloquent-sounding names like "Education and National Development." European languages became the national arbiters of success and failure, and African languages were seen as unfortunate reminders of our backwardness. In fact there is a way in which it can be argued that it was under neo-colonialism that colonial culture really triumphed as an exercise in the reproduction of the values of servility, silence and fear.

We are still in the neo-colonial era and the post-Cold War situation has not radically changed the situation. We should be wary of terms like "post-colonialism" when they gloss over the realities of the neocolonial character of much of Africa's relationship to Europe and the West as a whole. Genuine national liberation is when the wholeness of a people's economy, politics and culture is free from external control as the determining factor in their development. But as in the case of colonialism, where there was a long process of anti-colonial resistance for our countries' independence, so now, in this era, there has been a continuous struggle against neo-colonial distortions of our realities and for genuine national liberation. It takes various forms in different places and situations.

I want to illustrate aspects of this struggle with particular reference to Kenya not only because it occupies a significant position in the imagination of Africa as the first country on the continent to take up the path of armed struggle to oust a settler colonial regime, but also because Kenya is my country and my own journey through life has been decisively shaped by the politics of repression and resistance in neo-colonial Kenya. I will illustrate with a focus on struggles for the definition of the soul of the country through cultural practice. But we need to bear in mind that the cultural is just one aspect, intertwined with the political and the economic.

One of the areas of intense contest in Kenya was the independent government's attempt to bury the history of the anti-colonial resistance and particularly that of its heroes. Kenya, facing the Indian Ocean and Somalia to the east, Ethiopia and Sudan to the north, Uganda to the west and Tanzania to the south, became a British sphere of influence and control as part of the 1884 Berlin division of Africa and a white settler colony from about 1895. Although its white population was relatively small compared to white immigration into similar settler colonies like Zimbabwe and South Africa, it was nevertheless being developed to become a white dominion in the tradition of the similar cases of New Zealand, Australia and Canada. Indentured labor from Asia was also brought into the country. Kenya, a place the British settlers used to call a Whiteman's Country, thus became a kind of race/caste pyramid social structure with corresponding rewards and privileges: the Whites at the narrow top, the Asians in the narrowing middle, and the Africans at the broad base. The anti-colonial resistance of the African peoples, aided by a small section of the Indian community, reached its most dramatic stage in 1952 when Jomo Kenyatta and other leaders of the anti-colonial national resistance were jailed and a 22 year-old ex-school teacher by the name of Dedan Kimaathi led some youth into the mountains and forests in an armed struggle against the British colonial settler state. This is what became known in history as the Mau Mau. They themselves called their movement the Land and Freedom Army, the very title embodying their aims. Kimaathi was captured in 1957 and hanged by the British. But the war he led continued, and although the Mau Mau leadership was later sidelined in the negotiations for independence, it was their sacrifice which had brought about our independence in 1963. The general sense of euphoria and hope generated by the entire anti-colonial resistance is captured in my two novels, *Weep Not Child* and *The River Between*, published in 1964 and 1965.

Kenya became an independent state under the leadership of Jomo Kenyatta as Prime Minister and later President, but unfortunately, as elsewhere, this independence took the form of the removal of racial barriers to social mobility instead of a removal of the structural barriers. That meant a small black middle-class literally joining their European and Asian counterparts at the top of the former colonial pyramid. The former militants were sidelined in everything and it was almost as if they had become an embarrassment to a regime that was in desperate need to prove to the West that it had truly abandoned its violent past, that it was now civilized in the western sense. The history of resistance was reduced to the heroic activities of Jomo Kenyatta. Now, Kenyatta was definitely in prison throughout the years of the armed struggle and although he was an important symbol, he was definitely not the only pebble on the beach of the anti-colonial resistance. The regime encouraged silence over the former militants.

The sense of disillusionment is captured in my third novel, *A Grain of Wheat*, published in 1967. While the preface cautioned readers that the personages in the narrative were fictitious, it also insisted that the issues themselves were very real for the peasants who had fought against the British but who now saw all they fought for being put on one side. This was probably the beginning of the antagonism between me and the new regime, but it was also a measure of the immediate post-independence tolerance that nothing really happened to me. In fact the same year that the novel came out I got a job in the English Department at the University of Nairobi. I was hardly there a year when I became involved in a controversy and debate which illustrate very well the ideological struggle in the field of education. Bits and pieces of the account of what has been called the Great Nairobi Literature debate can be found in most of my books, including *Homecoming*, *Decolonising the Mind* and *Writers in Politics*.

The debate was over the organization of English studies at the University of Nairobi. Many English departments in Africa at the time were organized around the centrality of English literature from Spenser to Spender, or Bill Shakespeare to Bernard Shaw. But by 1968 there was already a thriving tradition of literatures produced in Africa, the Caribbean, Afro-America, third world, and this was not reflected in the syllabus. We called for the abolition of the English Department as then organized and run. We wanted a reorganization so that African literature and its related literatures from the Caribbean would be at the center, and then European literatures orbiting around that center instead of the other way round. What was the debate really about?

It was about two assumptions concerning education. The colonial tradition, which was the basis of the education system in Kenya, assumed the primacy of that which was furthest removed from the people. An African child had to know itself via Europe. European history, European culture, European civilization, European geography, European Literature first. But our position was based on a pedagogical process rooted in common sense of how people ordinarily acquire knowledge. The normal cognitive process starts with where one is and then adds to it. You start with the familiar and progressively integrate the unfamiliar to that familiar so as to demystify reality. In our view, instead of this colonial education tended to mystify reality rather than open it out to our apprehension and integration into self. Under colonial education, the outside became the inside and annexed us to itself.

The result of this annexation of our history and literature to the European mainland, making us view ourselves through western eyes, was soon visible in some of the writings by Kenyan scholars and writers which were beginning to come out. The last straw was when certain kenyans started writing histories and theater pieces which denied Kimaathi and Mau Mau their central place in the struggle.

That was when some Kenyan intellectuals came forward and started recording the true history of the struggle. History and how to read it suddenly became an arena of fierce ideological struggle. This struggle over the interpretation of history was also waged in the area of performance, both popular and in the corridors of formal theater. That was how I came to join another colleague at the University of Nairobi where I was then teaching in the literature Department. We wrote and staged what we called *The Trial of Dedan Kimaathi*. In what has now become a landmark literary intervention, we posed the question, in the preface to the play: whose history and whose deeds were the historians and creative writers recording for our children to read? We were on the offensive. The collaborationist writers and historians had depicted Kimaathi as he had been depicted by the British, as a bloodthirsty tyrant who had no clearcut political goals. We took up the challenge of depicting Kimaathi as the embodiment of the will of Kenya people to be free. We organized the dramatic narrative around the actual trial of the historical Kimaathi in 1957, but interpreted it freely. Through him we wanted to dramatize the defiance and the resistance tradition of Kenya's history. For instance, when Kimaathi is brought into court to face the white colonial judge, he refuses to enter any plea. The judge, who is eager to demonstrate the fairness of the British legal system, is very angry, and he repeats the charge. An argument ensues between him and Kimaathi. Their outlook on the law, justice and proof are utterly different. Yet from within their different concepts of justice, both think they are speaking the truth. The point expressed is the same as that played out in the earlier Nairobi Literature debate: what should have first place in *this* land are *its* concepts of justice, not the self-universalized ones of a different and unfamiliar place. Here Kimathi's resistance involved fighting for a Kenyan, not a British, concept of justice, and the court scene here sought to *stage* that resistance. So it was perhaps not surprising that there was in fact a fierce struggle for an actual space (as opposed to a staged one) in which to stage the play–giving rise to another narrative of resistance which I have tried to theorize as the politics of performance space in my *Penpoints, Gunpoints and Dreams* (1998). The director of the play and I had later to answer questions at the Headquarters of the Criminal Investigation Department. Performance of our heroes has now been criminalized.

In a way it was the politics of performance space which led me and other intellectuals into the countryside to work with peasants and workers at Kamiriithu Community and Cultural center at Limuru about thirty kilometers from the capital city of Nairobi, which then became the beginnings of my struggle over the issue of African Languages. I was still Professor of Literature and chairperson of the same Department, and I had then written all my works, including *The Trial of Dedan Kimaathi* and *Petals of Blood*, in English. But involvement in the community made me take 180-degrees turn in my attitude to African languages. We had written *The Trial* in English. The question we had posed in the preface surely also applied to us despite our sympathetic treatment of the character of Kimaathi. For whom were we writing our history? from whose base?

Together with the workers of the village and the peasants, we developed the performance in Gikuyu language that came to be called *Ngaahika Ndeenda*, which in English is *I Will Marry When I Want*. The story is simple. A rich African landlord, who is also on several management boards of foreign multinationals, wants to get property for one of those companies to build a factory for insecticide. Because such a factory produces dangerous gases, it has to be built away from the wealthy and put where ordinary people live. And that is how he comes to eye the land owned by some of his workers. He wants their prime piece of property because of its location, and the best way of getting it is by tricking the peasant to acquire loans with his land as collateral. If he fails to pay back, well, you know what.... But first he has to persuade the peasant to take the first step towards his downfall. The landlord and his wife one day decide to visit their worker in their home, a thing they had never done before. Naturally the peasant family is overawed by the honor and will do everything possible to make the landlord and his wife feel at ease in their home. But still the peasant Kiganda and his wife Wangeci keep wondering about the whys of the visit. Suddenly Wangeci remembers the rumors that their own daughter was dating the landlord's son and she wonders loudly whether indeed his parents might not be coming to ask their daughter's hand in marriage. There follows an exchange between husband and wife in which they recall their youth and their role in the struggle. Their present contains their past, the landlord's oppression repeats that of the colonial power, his behavior typifies that of the neo-colonial authorities, directly recalling the older struggle and its purpose.

Well, you know the consequences. The play was stopped and I myself was later arrested and put in a maximum security prison for a year.

I came out in 1978 after the death of Jomo Kenyatta and the accession to power of his vice-president, Daniel Arap Moi, who may be remembered as the same guy who in 1954 was working schemes with the British on how to annihilate Mau Mau. He had now been reinvented as a post-colonial leader à la Mobutu Sese Seko and others of his ilk. I was banned from access to colleges and universities. Quite happily I stayed on in the village where in 1981 we tried to put on another performance of our history, this time in a play I did called *Mother Sing for Me*. But this time it was not allowed even *any* space. In fury, the government of Daniel Arap Moi sent three truckloads of armed police to our village to raze to the ground our open-air theater. That was 1982, the year Kenya became a *de jure* one-party state under the decree of Arap Moi. It was also the period which saw many academics killed., thrown into jail or forced into exile. I had to go to London in June 1982 to help in the London publication of the English translation of my novel *Devil on the Cross*, the play *I Will Marry When I Want* and the prison narrative, *Detained*. There I learned that I was due for another arrest or worse on my return. I had once again been too outspoken about the regime for my good. So I stayed on in exile, where I have been to this day. But I did join forces with other Kenyans for the release of political prisoners and for democratic and human rights. It was while I was in London that I wrote the novel *Matigari* in Gikuyu language.

Matigari came out in Kenya in 1986. It depicts a former freedom fighter who puts down his arms, wears a belt of peace and comes out of the forest only to find that the house for which he had been fighting had been occupied by the sons and daughters of those whom he thought he had conquered. He is so struck by the injustice of it all that he goes around the country raising issues of social justice. At one time he is arrested and put in a mental asylum from which he later escapes. The entire police force is now after a man of peace whose only problem is that he has been asking the same question over and over again: where can a person armed with peace find justice in this land? The radio station stops normal programs to acquaint people with the progress of the hunt.

The fate of the novel tells more about the nature of a neo-colonial regime than anything I can say about it. The novel came out in 1986, a year when there were even more arrests and killings than usual. Daniel Arap Moi had even issued a decree that people should not talk politics in public transport. Reports now reached him of this man going round the country asking awkward questions, whose name was Matigari. "Go and arrest him." But the police with their warrants found that Matigari was only a fictional character. Moi was so angry that he ordered the book removed from all the bookshelves in the country. This was done in a well-coordinated police action in February 1987. Matigari in an African language original is still unable to walk the streets of Nairobi and Kenya. But in his English voice, in translation, that is, he is able to walk those same streets.

And this is happening in the post-Cold-War Kenya, where now the democratic forces are demonstrating in the streets demanding a level playing ground. Actually what they are asking and demanding is abolition of the colonial laws which were passed by the colonial state with Moi's participation during the heyday of Mau Mau, and which have governed post-independence Kenya for thirty years. One of those laws says that it is illegal for more than five people to meet without a police licence. Under this law, any policeman can break up any gathering, even a family one of more than five people, and successfully charge them with illegal assembly.

Need I say more? The struggle in Kenya continues as in other parts of Africa. We may hear of massacres committed by regimes in the West who then turn around and talk about the savagery of Africa. We may hear of starvation brought about by policies demanded by the IMF and the West as a whole, who then turn around and talk about African mismanagement. But however bad things may look, there is always hope. When in 1967 in my novel *A Grain of Wheat* I wrote that sentence about the betrayal of promises, nothing happened one way or another. For many years arguments for democracy and calls for the end of colonial type laws were only in books, and in performance and in classrooms. Today, under the hail of government bullets, under the shadow of government murder squads organized by Dictator Moi as this trusted friend of the West, people are marching in the streets demanding their space.

There are as yet no dramatic victories. But even the fact that dictators like Mobutu of Zaire, Hastings Kamuzu Banda of Malawi or Idi Amin Dada of Uganda have been thrown out of power by movements which have at least the merit of not being part of the continuity of the colonial armies, gives us hope. And keeping hope alive in whatever fashion has to be a good part of what the struggle is all about.

Notes

1. The earliest version of this essay was given as a talk at the Center for Hawaiian Studies at the University of Hawaii, Manoa, 9 Oct. 1997

The Role of Africa in the Construction of Identity in the Caribbean

Mervyn C. Alleyne

The first assertion that this paper wishes to make is that in the Caribbean we are really speaking about "identities," rather than "identity." There is no all-embracing Caribbean identity. There is some degree of a common consciousness among Caricom countries of having been British colonies and there are a few common institutions which support this consciousness in this group, the most significant of which are the West Indies cricket team and the University of the West Indies. The concept of a Caribbean identity (or a West Indian identity) may also be strong in the imaginings of some Caribbean ideologues.

The claim here is that a "Caribbean identity" is yet to be constructed as a psychological reality. A Bajan feels very little affinity with a Dominican (from the Dominican Republic) and vice versa. Indeed, the Bajan hardly ever uses the term "Caribbean" in reference to his wider identity, preferring the term "West Indian." Similarly, when the Dominican refers to himself as "*caribeño*," this wider identity includes only the Hispanic territories of the Caribbean. The unity of the Caribbean is not in terms of psychological reality, but in terms of common historical processes and a certain degree of common objective cultural forms (including behavioural forms and even phenotype) which, when displayed together, may lead different Caribbean persons to recognize a commonness. The Dominican, when he sees a Trinidadian, observes his behaviour, and hears his music, may suddenly realize that the Trinidadian is really, like himself, a *"caribeño."*

The Caribbean is perhaps more diverse than it is integrated, and it is also this diversity in such small geographical space that I find intellectually interesting. At one point in the intellectual history of the Caribbean, quite apart from the ideological history, the idea of a common history and common destiny may have been dominant. But there is a growing interest in diversity. Paradoxically, the most common feature, what unites the Caribbean, is its diversity. Diversity among units, and diversity within a unit. The continuum of variation, which has been most studied for language, exists in macro form across units, and in micro form within a unit. To take one example in language, at one end of the macro continuum in the Caribbean, there are instances of African languages which are tonal; this tonality also supports communication by drums and conch shells which replicate the tones of the language; then there is the creole language Saramaccan of Suriname, based on English, in which every word has its distinctive tone pattern. The continuum then goes through other creole languages like Jamaican, Guyanese, etc. with tone playing an ever diminishing role, until it ends up with Bajan in which tone is merely vestigial. It distinguishes only very few pairs of words, such as Baker, the personal name, and baker the artisan.

This continuum of variation also exists microcosmically and macrocosmically for religion, music, and of course phenotype. There is no region on earth with such diversity in language type, religion type, music type and phenotype, in such small geographical space. However, the fascinating thing about the Caribbean is also that, in spite of the existence of linguistic, religious, phenotypical and other continua, there are elements of bipolarity still existing.

The role of Africa is another aspect of Caribbean diversity. This role is different in different places, in different individuals within the same place. But historically its presence was everywhere, uniting the Caribbean. It is still today present everywhere psychologically, either being denied, avoided or embraced.

Africa has been savaged in history. First of all, if Europe was the centre of the world (cf. Mediterranean), the norm against which all the other cultures were to be evaluated, then Africa south of the Sahara was on the distant periphery, the abode of monstrous peoples, grossly misunderstood, misvalued or undervalued. Africa was represented by the colour term black and the whole range of pejoration, which in European symbolization going back to Graeco-Roman Antiquity was associated with black, fell upon Africa.

Once brought to the New World, Africans lost their ethnic individuality as Yoruba or Ewe or Kikongo, and lost their regional cultural identity as Africans, and became simply blacks, *negros*, *nègres* or *neger*. At the next stage of evolution, black or *negro* or *nègre* became synonymous with slave. And later, designations such as "negro" and "coloured" were employed as euphemisms to avoid "black" and "African."

"Black" has been revived in Anglophone Afro-America; and so has "African," particularly in the USA where the term "African American" is the latest in the history of such representations. But why is there still a preference for "black" over "African"? There may be simple psycho-linguistic reasons. Identity entails popular definitions of "Who am I?," "What am I?." In some political circumstances (such as existed or exist in the Caribbean), self-other definitions become specified by colonial classifiers. Europe has seized the prerogative of naming and of symbol creation with their meanings and values. Perhaps the major achievement by Europe in this regard has been to seize the positive connotations of the colour white (whether these connotations are natural/universal or themselves contextually constructed) and to apply this colour and its connotations to themselves. Whether by a process of antithesis, or through some natural universal association, or whether contextually constructed, Europe assigned negative connotations to the colour black, and when Africa was "discovered," the colour black was used to represent Africa.

The Europeans who are first recorded as using colour terms to refer to people are the Greeks and Romans of Antiquity. But they, quite amazingly, are the Europeans furthest removed from the colour white and they held the more truly white Europeans from the North in contempt. Many Africans are far from black, particularly the first Africans encountered by the Greeks and Romans. But there was this obsession with naming people by colour.

Interestingly, the Chinese and Japanese, at home or in their Diaspora, have not accepted the colour characterisation of themselves as yellow, also negative in its connotations; they certainly do not refer to themselves as "we yellow people." And, similarly, the indigenous peoples of this hemisphere do not generally refer to themselves as "we red people." The evidence that all these colour terms with ethnic reference are contextually constructed is that the Chinese and Japanese, if they are forced to represent themselves by a colour, will use "white." But African Diaspora people have now largely accepted "black" and seem to prefer it to "African."

Of course, in the highly conflictual reality of the world and of the post-Columbian Caribbean, it has become an act of defiance for African Diaspora peoples to use the term "black" to refer to themselves. Indeed, there are many other cases where a group triumphs psychologically over a pejorative label by accepting it and using it defiantly. The use of "nigger" as a term of endearment is one example. The use of "yankee" by Northern Americans to refer to themselves is another such example.

In addition, in trying to account for the current preference for "black," we must note that "black" has been undergoing redefinition and is no longer a simple race/colour/ethnic category. There has been an ideologizing of "black" which now endows it with ideological features lacking in "African." And this adds to making it more appealing than "African." For example, by using "black" rather than "African" to represent themselves, Black Power leaders in Trinidad and Jamaica were able at least to invite Indians to join the movement. It is true that the attempt failed, obviously because the Indians saw "black" not as an ideological or class signifier but as a racial, ethnic category. But "black" stood a much better chance than inviting the Indians to join an "African" movement.

The precise ideological profile of "black" in Jamaica is Jamaican nationalism, socialist or radical political orientation, identification with Jamaican popular culture, opposition to Europe and the United States. A most illustrative case is that of the late Michael Manley, former Prime Minister. Racially, he is the son of a white British mother and a father who is at least three-quarter white. Michael Manley himself is phenotypically white/light-brown, socio-economically upper middle class, and culturally, in language, aesthetics, behaviour, tastes in food, music, etc., very European. In spite of all of this, he was, at least at one stage of his political career, considered "black." His opponent, Edward Seaga, son of an Arabic father and a white mother, lived and did sociological field work among inner-city residents, was one of the pioneers of the commercialisation of Jamaican popular music, and now represents an inner-city constituency with a virtually 100% black population; but he was never considered "black." In fact, his party lost the 1997 General Elections in some measure because he was seen as white and anti-black. Later in Michael Manley's political life, when he shifted his ideological position, made his peace with the United States and espoused free market policies, he lost his "black" status.

Finally, for those who wish to avoid "African," whether because they are uncertain about their origins, or because they do not wish to be associated with the stereotype and media image created about Africa, or because representing themselves as "African" would be, in their estimation, an act of disloyalty to their present national affiliation, "black" appears more acceptable. But there remains some semantic overlap between "Black" and "African."

The Caribbean dilemma has been how to reconstruct an identity, avoiding a representation and definition imposed from outside. This process has been complicated by the arrival of populations from Asia which have now become majority in some cases and have also added to the racial mixing.

One of the options of reconstruction has been to use, as one of the foundations, the reappropriation of a large vague geo-cultural identity based on Africa, given the complete impossibility now of reconstructing or reappropriating a more particularistic identity based on a specific ethnic group. Let us note in passing that this last option may be impossible for the general populations (since we can't all do the Alex Haley thing), but it is a reality for certain sub-ethnic groupings of Caribbean people: The Maroons of Jamaica have no doubts about their Twi-Asante (Coromante) ancestry; Cuban and Trinidadian groups similarly proclaim their Yoruba ancestry; Haitian Vaudoun faithfuls know their Ewe-Fon links. These are continuous unbroken links of identity for which there really is no need for reconstructing and reappropriating. The dramatic case of reconstructing and reappropriating is that of the Rastafari who have built an identity around a perceived Ethiopian ancestry.

So while post-modernism is busy trying to deconstruct African (and other) essentialisms, there are a number of Caribbean groups busy reconstructing it. While concepts (and I suppose in some cases movements based on the concepts) such as *créolité*, *métissage*, hybridity, and even globalisation, are busy projecting a new liberal middle class culture and identity order on the world, the cultural proletariat is still seeking ways to triumph over the savaging which it has undergone and continues to undergo in the modern world. Africa often plays a role, variously ambivalent, uncertain, aggressive, timid.

There are a number of different problems in the role of Africa in the construction of Caribbean identities that merit investigation. At what point, among whom, and by what process, did the memory of Africa and of its specific ethnicities become generally lost, to be replaced by the local perspectives subsumed under the concept "creole"? We know that the creole vs. *bozal* distinction was important in the plantation social order; but we also know that creole slaves led and participated in rebellions and general marronage. We know too that the equanimity with which some slaves faced death after the most cruel torture, or the merriment displayed on the occasion of natural death and burial were in part the consequence of a belief that the spirits of the departed would return to Africa to dwell among the ancestors. But we need to know more about the many organizations that were formed to encourage the continuity of a memory of Africa. We know a lot about the Garvey movement and the Rastafari movement of this century. But little of the African Free School in New York City or of the African Benevolent Societies and lodges and Brotherhoods of earlier centuries. And there is the remarkable establishment of the African Methodist Episcopal Church by Richard Allen in 1793.

The range of psychological adjustments to Africa is another area requiring attention because this is the source of great psychological tension in the Caribbean arising out of ambivalence. In Puerto Rico, Africa benefits from the presence of the United States as a competing pole for Puerto Rican cultural and national identity. In seeking to avoid the perceived threat of assimilation to a North American cultural identity (which is seen as the inevitable result of North American economic and political domination), Puerto Ricans may turn to emphasizing a Hispanic identity. But this is also unsatisfactory to some since it links Puerto Ricans with a former colonial power. So some Puerto Ricans look to the Caribbean and to Africa as sources and bases, contemporary and historical respectively, for the construction of a national identity. Some nationalist ideologues searching for an expression of Puerto Rican distinctiveness may even over-emphasize the Africanness of the island. *Lo africano* in Puerto Rico is a kind of corollary to the Puerto Rican Hispanic cultural identity in its opposition to threats of North American assimilation. And *lo africano* is also very much tied to *lo antillano* or *lo caribeño*.

In Puerto Rico, there is, on the one hand, a denial of and distancing from Africa; and yet, on the other hand, Africa constantly lurks in the background or in the closet, and there is great fear that she may be released and displayed to the public. *Y tú, dónde está tu abuela?* "And what about you, where is your grandmother?" is about the worst put-down delivered to uppity mulattoes.

In Martinique, the socio-psychological space of Africa has been undergoing a process of being vacated by a process of denial of Africa similar to what has been taking place in Puerto Rico (I will mention later the case of Negritude in the intellectual history of Martinique). The arrival of indentured African immigrants in the post-emancipation period in Martinique allowed that space to be once again filled. But these new Africans were called *nèg Congo*; they were considered to be phenotypically alien and bore the brunt of black/African pejoration. This then strengthened the Martinican notion of an identity which was essentially brown and mixed.

On the other hand, there was a similar arrival of Congo Africans in Jamaica in the latter half of the 19th century, but the effect of this was to add a new African infusion into the religion, music and dance of Jamaica. This strengthened the notion of an African-based heritage and identity in Jamaica.

Finally, the other aspect of the role of Africa that merits further investigation is the very validity of the hypothesis of African continuities. Although the contesting hypotheses have been widely studied in the area of creole language genesis, other areas have been ignored. As examples, I begin with the simplest. The Suriname Maroons keep their farms far from their villages. Is this an African continuity or did the practice develop in order to ensure food supplies if and when the village was burnt by the Dutch military? Or was it a tradition from Africa selected from among others under the pressure of the new conditions? As it turns out, this particular custom is not confined to Suriname Maroons, but is to be found in Jamaica both among the Maroons and the general population.

Were the new religious forms such as spirit possession and the high degree of musicality and dance a release from the day to day world of work and a refuge in the promise of salvation, a psycho- and physio-therapeutic device for dealing with anxiety? Or were they a precise body of beliefs, rituals and religious behaviour brought from Africa which expressed the world-view and cosmology of Africans? They could then be mobilised to serve a number of non-religious needs—some psychological to relieve stress and anxiety, some political to support resistance movements.

Do the animal stories featuring Anansi or Brer Rabbit owe less to African origins, as one anthropolgoist put it, than to the circumstances of slave life? Were they, as he continued, a psychic adjustment to slavery insofar as they show how the weak must make their way in a world of hypocricy and superior power by tricking not only the strong but also each other? Or did these stories exist in the pre-slavery culture of Africans, and already express a complex often paradoxical and ambivalent morality which Africans brought into slavery? In which case, were they also a part of an African picaresque narrative tradition many of the elements of which are hard to square with the image of down-trodden slaves triumphing over their oppressors? This of course is not incompatible with the idea that other moral elements expressed in these tales must have helped Africans deal with their existential circumstances. And another reason why these tales persisted would have been that their performance, also a possible African continuity, was an important part of African communal interaction that helped to mould new African Caribbean and New World communities out of diverse African elements.

Everywhere in the Caribbean, Africa is being ideologized. Ideology and objective cultural reality may coexist harmoniously (as in the case of the Maroons) or they may clash. The claims of the persistence of African cultural continuities in the New World can be used and indeed have been used to serve different and opposite political and ideological ends. This persistence of African cultural continuities may be acclaimed by Black cultural nationalists; but may be used by right wing extremist racists to propose that Blacks are intellectually incapable of assimilating European culture, including language, after more than 300 years of exposure. The African link has been a pillar of Rastafarian ideology; but is used by Rastafarian detractors to deny Rastafarians a legitimacy in the national identity construction.

There has therefore been considerable controversy surrounding this question of African-based ethnicity and identity in the Americas, corresponding to the many interpretations which have been proposed to account for the culture or cultures of the African Diaspora. These range from the "stripping" of Africans of their culture and ethnic identity to the continuity of African culture(s), in some cases virtually intact with "normal" processes of evolution. It is becoming more and more evident that one single theory of Afro-American culture or Diaspora culture cannot encompass all the different cases that exist in the Americas, and indeed we shall see that if we take the three modalities most copiously examined in this paper (Martinique, Puerto Rico, Jamaica) each presents a particular case as far as an African-based ethnicity is concerned.

There are groups or individuals for whom it might be argued that they were "stripped" of their African culture or at least of some aspects of it. There are other groups and societies who have preserved and consciously recognise an African culture and ethnicity (although it is obvious that this culture has undergone some measure of change and is not simply an intact survival). Indeed, even on the African continent, there is no culture that is "an intact survival" of the African cultures of the 16th century. I earlier mentioned the most notable cases of this: the Maroon societies of Jamaica and Suriname, the Lucumí of Cuba and the Shango of Trinidad, the Vaudoun faithful of Haiti.

There have also been attempts to reaffirm or reconstruct ethnicities based on the notion of Africa as the motherland and on a recognition that "we are Africans" (for example, the Garvey movement of the thirties, the Negritude movements of the forties, the Black Power movement of the sixties). But these have not prevailed or succeeded in binding people together in a common pursuit of cultural or political interests.

In the non-Maroon societies of the Caribbean, the African was a slave and became a "negro" in English and Spanish, and a *"noir"* or a *"nègre"* in French. His descendants have become "West Indian," "Caribbean," "creole," etc. They are the only racial group which is no longer simply identified by their ancestral origins. In Caribbean societies, there are Europeans (including Scots, Irish, French, British, German, Portuguese, etc.), Indians, Chinese, Javanese, Caribs, Lebanese, Syrians. But no "Africans." Individuals may, on a purely personal level, assert an African identity and call themselves "African Jamaican," "Afro-Cuban," etc. In some territories, like Barbados for example, such individuals are a rarity, and the term and concept "African Barbadian" virtually does not exist. It may seem that the numerical majority status of African Antilleans might explain this peculiar situation. But they are no longer majority in Trinidad and Guyana and in Suriname. And more importantly, whether numerical majority or not, African Antilleans still have all the trappings of a minority group.

Among this general Caribbean population of African descent, the picture is very complex and ambiguous. This population has come under the severe assaults of the race and ethnic hierarchy and it has emerged extremely scathed. They have been unable to construct and define freely their own identities, and have had to accept definitions of themselves imposed from outside. Europeans had, immediately on the founding of these post-Columbian societies, seized the prerogative of naming, and thereby of defining, of symbol creation and of setting the normative semantics of Caribbean experience and indeed that of the world.

Even where some attempts are made to correct the absurdity of these significant symbols, they often fall short of what is required. Thus "black" in the Jamaican flag is supposed to be, not an ethnic symbol recognising the majority ethnic group, but a symbol of "hardships faced."

There is also the important area of onomastics, which in the Caribbean was controlled by masters and resulted in African slaves acquiring new, often mocking and ridiculous eurocentric names. Given the important role that the word and the name in particular play in African world view, this control of personal names again was a masterful strategy for psychological control, for control of identity, for control beyond the simple control over life and death. This led as usual to resistance, in this case in the form of a proliferation of nicknames to which only the community was privy, and more recently to a fashion for non-Western European, and particularly for African or African sounding names. There has been among some Caribbean peoples and persons of African descent a continuous struggle to reject such external definitions and to re-appropriate the prerogative of self-defining.

Aimé Césaire, confronted with, and reacting to, Shakespeare's portrayal of Caliban as the monumental representation of the primitive in humanity, sought, in his play *Une Tempête*, to rescue Caliban, or sought to have Caliban rescue himself, by recasting a conversation between Caliban and Prospero in which Caliban declares that he will no longer be called Caliban. The name Caliban, indeed, is either an unwitting or a very clever corruption on the part of Shakespeare of the word "cannibal," itself a distortion of one of the variant names (*Calina, Carina, Caribali, Calibali*) of the indigenous people of the Caribbean region. Shakespeare's Caliban is in fact nearer the form of the original word, and, as well, is less of a semantic and humanistic degradation than is implied in the phonological and semantic distortion "cannibal." Césaire's Caliban rejects the name; nor will he accept the other name which Prospero suggests: Hannibal (Césaire's cynical approximation to "Cannibal"). And here Césaire is alluding, whether consciously or unconsciously, to the tendency of some Africans and Afro-Americans to attempt to rescue their humanity by evoking and invoking great African heroes of the past, of whom Hannibal is one. Césaire rejects this in favour of a process by which ordinary "primitive" individuals can rescue their own humanity by re-appropriating the prerogative of naming and therefore of defining. Caliban renames himself X, by which Césaire expresses the importance of naming and language in the process of self-appropriation, the reclaiming of one's self; but he also expresses the bind in which Caliban, and Caribbean people in general, find themselves due to the absence of a language in which this renaming and reclaiming can be communicated. It is the Caribbean dilemma. And it is interesting to observe how Malcolm X relived Césaire's Caliban in another time and another place.

There has been in Martinique an ideological distancing from Africa. This takes on a completeness surpassing that of Puerto Rico. In Martinique there is no widespread recognition of Africa either as a phenotype, religion, or music. In the case of Martinique, the only perceived threat is France, the purveyor of material benefits and guarantor of social order.

There have always been movements of cultural resistance in Martinique seeking to construct and assert a Martinican cultural identity separate from French. One of these "movements" was what has come to be known as Negritude, a largely literary posture that contained a literary discourse about the glorification of blackness and Africa. But this did not have any appreciable echo in the population at large and never developed a social praxis as the Garvey movement did in Jamaica. Martinique is different from Puerto Rico and Jamaica, where the issue of Africa is more than a literary trope but is examined at academic and more significantly at journalistic levels.

Negritude did challenge the concept and policy of cultural assimilation and the acceptance of European forms as universal canons. It affirmed black identity and solidarity among all black peoples, and espoused Pan-Africanism. All of these are also basic tenets of Garveyism.

Césaire recognised the role of Africa in the formation of Martinican society and culture; but he was not positively assertive about it, and neither he nor anyone else in Martinique ever pushed this recognition to the point of advocating a return to Africa. Césaire assessed the situation in the following way:

> One may speak of a great family of African cultures that merits the name of Negro African civilisation and that binds together the separate cultures of each of the African nations. Furthermore, one realizes that, because of the vicissitudes of history, the range and extent of this civilization have far outspread Africa, and thus it may be said that in Brazil and in the West Indies, and not only in Haiti and the French Antilles, and even in the United States, there are, if not centres, at least fringes of this Negro African civilization. ("Culture" 191)

It may be claimed that Martinique represents the highest degree of assimilation to the European norm in the Caribbean. It is in Martinique where primordial subordinate groups have been most thoroughly erased both materially and in the consciousness of the people. Very few phenotypical or cultural traces of the indigenous inhabitants; very few pre-Columbian onomastic influences; absence of groups of African origin still claiming African ancestry or openly recognised as having such (with the exception of the *Nèg Congo* group which dates back just to the second half of the nineteenth century and which no longer exists as a well-defined recognizable group).

If it may be said that the dominant ideology of race and ethnicity in Puerto Rico and Martinique is *mestizaje, metissage*, that of Jamaica would be marronage and blackness. Other competing ideologies in Jamaica are being eroded by the dominant one. But they still exist, and this leads to a situation of considerable racial/ethnic ideological complexity. The result is contradiction, ambivalence and ambiguity, as Jamaica wrestles with the problem of enhancing and asserting its black ideology and identity in the context of a world and a Caribbean where "white" values dominate and are still rampant.

Jamaica's official ideology as expressed in the motto "Out of Many, One People" may seem to be proposing an ideology of ethnic assimilation and unity. But this is largely considered to be an ideal yet to be concretely realised. It also represents some degree of denial of, and distancing from, the concrete reality of the dominance of black in the ethnic composition of Jamaica.

Jamaica has been constantly challenging the European canons, seeking to replace them with local ones not only in popular representations but also in the construction of the national identity (*pace* post-modernism). The Rastafarians have boldly constructed a black God; and Pukumina and Revival have created a pantheon which includes both African and Christian saints and deities. Black Messiahs and Prophets have dotted Jamaica's history, with Marcus Garvey and Alexander Bedward being the best known. The National Dance theatre Company has developed a Jamaican dance idiom based on the Afro-Jamaican anatomical structure and restoring the symbolic and aesthetic values of movements such as pelvic thrusts and others centered on the buttocks, many of them taken directly from folk dance.

In Jamaica, the role of Africa in the construction of identity has always been relatively very significant and is likely to become more so in the future, given the current political and cultural dynamics. In the general population , the consciousness of a Twi ancestry is lost, and the allegiance to Ethiopia has not spread beyond Rastafarian ethnicity. It is a general African ancestry concept that is adhered to by those persons who have either maintained a continuous conscious tradition of Africa as their original place of origin and as the source of their cultural identity or have intellectually now developed an ideology which has recreated this consciousness.

Jamaica has witnessed throughout its post-Columbian history a counterpoint of rejection of blackness and Africa in the construction and representation of personal and ethnic identity on the one hand and an assertion of it on the other. These two ideologies may separate groups; they may separate individuals, siblings, twins within the same family. And finally, the same individual may exhibit both identities organized in terms of public vs. private behaviour , surface vs. deep structure, and even moral vs. immoral (as in the case of code-shifting between "eat" and "nyam"). A parent may show off an offspring with a European-leaning phenotype (brown complexion, straight nose, "good" hair, for example), but feel stronger affective bonds with the offspring of African phenotype (something akin to the "ugly duckling" syndrome). Women are both proud of their full bottoms (and deride flat ones) and ashamed or embarrassed by them. Code-switching is a phenomenon that goes beyond language behaviour where it has been most widely studied. It is to be observed in other aspects of behaviour as Jamaicans endeavour to operate two (idealised) cultural and value systems.

Thus the Caribbean shows different processes of racial and ethnic construction and representation, albeit within a very common framework. As in other parts of the world, there is still considerable resistance to globalisation and cultural assimilation, which suggests that not everyone and not every society are "buying into" that model. Jamaica's dilemma has been, and is, how to manage the imperatives of global economics, while defending and asserting its African heritage, very often perceived as incompatible with economic modernisation. Martinique's dilemma is exactly the opposite, how to protect the rewards of political and economic assimilation (or dependency, if you like) with France, Europe, and therefore the globe, and at the same time develop a separate identity. Africa is entering only very marginally in the construction of this separate identity.

I could not end this brief, highly selective treatment of the subject without going back to the issue adumbrated earlier: how does this question of identity, primordial allegiances, especially African allegiances, fit into the modernising globalisation model and fit into the goals of multi-racial harmony?

Ian McDonald sums it up in this way:

> The test is whether or not the fundamental allegiances, be it race, religion, or heritage or whatever variety, can be absorbed but not lost in a wider allegiance. I believe in the West Indies we have proved over time that fundamental allegiances can be, and have been, so absorbed. That is not to say that all is sweetness and harmony. Far from it. There have been, there are, there will be resentments and suspicions. Tensions will rise and grow, certainly, but they will pass again. We have learnt enough about each other, we have grown used to making the essential basic accommodations, so that tensions will never tear us apart as they have torn apart Lebanon, Yugoslavia, Sri Lanka and may yet tear apart more than one African state... ("Katha" 2)

There may be some measure of idealism, or wishful thinking here. However, he makes the precise error that many advocates of racial/ethnic harmony make and which is at the root of the social psychological problems of the Caribbean. He accepts the fact of "East (sic) Indian" allegiances to their heritage and considers this a positive factor, but he seems to have some problem with analogous allegiances to an African heritage. He berates the captain of a former West Indian cricket team for having referred to the team as "African" in their racial/ethnic heritage. The team indeed had some East Indian and mixed-race members. But the captain was merely referring to what he saw as the dominant component both of the team and of the West Indies in general and was asserting that he was not one of those who denied or was uncertain or embarrassed about the African heritage.

Other heritages do not suffer from the same uncertainty and they can be preserved and celebrated even outside the particular ecology and social class where they are best manifested. That is to say that, relatively speaking, Indians and Chinese carry their heritages with them as they move through the social strata to the upper classes and from a rural agricultural context to a modern urban context. In the case of the African heritage, it remains a class phenomenon. Diaspora Africans tend to lose connection with this heritage as they move into the upper classes. This continuing association between black/African and lower class status and low social and esthetic value is the critical problem. Take the very important area of phenotype, unless the solution is to erase the African phenotype by mass miscegenation, there will be, especially in places like Jamaica, but really everywhere in the Caribbean, persons with African phenotypical features of skin pigmentation, nose, hair, lips, etc.

Black Power movements have tried to revalue some of these, or most of these (skin pigmentation, hair particularly). Other features, real, such as size of bottom (or maybe the absence of flat bottoms), imagined, such as size of penis, or as the skeletal and muscular structure that leads to rhythm and the ability to "wine," have always been appreciated. But there is still a lot of work to be done to achieve the total revaluation without which it will be impossible to fully harness all the human resources, paradoxically for the goal of modernisation.

Libre Sous la Mer—Submarine Identities in the Work of Kamau Brathwaite and Edouard Glissant

J. Michael Dash

For there is no landscape more suitable for considering the Question of the sea, no geography more appropriate to the study of exile. And it is that ruthless, though necessary wreck, which warns us that we are all deeply involved in the politics of intrigue.
(George Lamming, *The Pleasures of Exile*)

We need another time of *writing* that will be able to inscribe the ambivalent and chiasmatic intersections of time and place that constitute the problematic 'modern' experience of the Western nation.
(Homi Bhaba, *The Location of Culture*)

At the end of the poem "The Cracked Mother" from the 1969 collection *Islands*, Kamau Brathwaite asks the following questions

...how will new maps be drafted?
Who will suggest a new tentative frontier?
How will the sky dawn now? (TA 184)

Five years later, in his 1975 essay "Caribbean Man in Space and Time" (first presented as a lecture in January 1973 at UWI, Cave Hill), he provides an answer in the form of a poetic prologue to an essay in which he evokes Caribbean space as apparently unmappable archipelago, suggesting a world that is so convulsively unregimented, so irreducibly plural that it seems to resist any attempt at ideological or discursive closure:

> archipelago: fragments: a geological plate being crushed by the pacific's curve, cracking open yucatan; the arctic/north american monolith; hence cuba, hispaniola, puerto rico: continental outriders and the dust of the bahamas. atlantic africa pushing up the beaches of our eastern seawards. ("Caribbean Man" 1)

The Caribbean archipelago is projected in images of apocalyptic genesis, an unstable, primordial zone, tense with invisible forces waiting to be named. In the same way that in the mid Twenties the French Surrealists redrew the map of the world to relocate center and periphery so that France disappears and Mexico and Polynesia become centers of world culture, Brathwaite redraws a map of the Caribbean which emphasizes a series of submarine tensions and seismic confluences. More importantly perhaps, with the names of individual islands written in lower case letters, the archipelago is not asserted in terms of island specificity but defined through geographically contingent contours. Indeed, island enclosure or static meaning gives way to a chaotic text that is subject to hidden explosive forces, which suspend the possibility of fixed meanings or labels. Brathwaite seems, in this prologue, acutely aware that the role of the postcolonial artist is to wrest free national space from the constraining labels inherited from the colonial past which fixed and divided the Caribbean archipelago, and by extension the collective psyche, in terms of domination and power.

This convulsive vision of archipelagic Caribbean space is arguably a paradigm central to Brathwaite's poetics. Brathwaite's historical vision resisted from the very beginning easy manichean divisions in colonial society. In his mapping of the archipelago, the cross-cultural dynamic that he first perceived in the behavior of contending groups in plantation society is now tied to place. His view of Caribbean space does not privilege easy dichotomies between island and continent, land and sea, past and present, independent and dependent. The new Caribbean map, therefore, exhibits a violently forged site where Old and New Worlds collide, where North and South America dramatically encounter each other. It is difficult to overestimate the importance of this vision of cultural location in Brathwaite. The theorists of post-colonial literature, Bill Ashcroft, Gareth Griffiths and Helen Tiffin are correct when they assert that "a fundamental aspect of the cross-cultural dynamic is the relationship to land, to place. For Brathwaite, Creolization is a cultural action based upon the 'stimulus-response' of individuals to their environment" (147). The frenetic convulsions of

Brathwaite's archipelago are not constraining. They do not favor frozen or self-sufficient units or islands of meaning. Instead, these images facilitate the abolition of boundaries and redistribute meaning in terms of new conjunctions and oppositions.

The ideological implications of this new Caribbean mapping are enormous for the Seventies. The profoundly dynamic system conceived by Brathwaite zeroes in on an ideological crisis of representation that prevailed in Caribbean thought at the time. Brathwaite's model reaches beyond the image of the Cesairean shipwreck, which dominates the epic poem *Cahier d'un retour au pays natal*, and even more significantly that of plantation society in the Caribbean as uncreative and sterile. The strength of Brathwaite's ideas in the Seventies is tied to a seminal vision that privileges the creative confluence of contradictory forces and a poetics that requires that a new sign system be invented to represent this vision of repressed tensions and unvoiced interactions. He himself advocated a movement towards self-possession through an externalized, emancipated discourse in the 1970 essay "Timehri." Here he proposed that the Caribbean artist turn silence into language, indeed, use the process of imaginatively uncensored utterance as a collective form of therapy, a salutary transcendence of atavistic taciturnities. The structure or structuring forces are hidden and "we become ourselves, truly our own creators, discovering word for object, image for the Word" ("Timehri"[1] 44).

The logic of this model would seem to push Brathwaite not towards an integrating text or a reestablishment of lost continuities, but towards an anti-essentialist concept of radical incompleteness. However, there is a tension between such a radically transgressive idea and another impulse that haunts his poetic imagination, that of wholeness and reintegration. Chaotic surfaces and disjunctive horizontality are always prey to a structuring verticality, to shaping forces of depth. He expresses this problematic very clearly in his prologue to "Caribbean Man in Time and Space": "our problem is how to study the fragments/whole." And as this opening sequence proceeds, the free verse of this poetic prologue is twice punctuated by a line that expresses a desire to introduce symmetry and order into the opening vision of infinite diffraction. The poet repeatedly asserts, "the unity is submarine." The entire text ends or, perhaps, the dramatized poetic trajectory of the essay comes to a climax, with the triumphant assertion "the unit is submarine." Brathwaite seems, consequently, as much fascinated by the dazzling surface fragmentation of the archipelago as he is transfixed by submarine, structuring forces. As he admits in an interview with Nathaniel Mackey, "one is haunted that there is more there. Underground and under the water there are larger forms which have deeper resonance and we haven't yet reached them" ("Interview"[2] 21). This belief in powerful, deeper presences on Brathwaite's part is not just a rhetorical gesture. It is a basic modus operandi—as he makes clear towards the end of the essay on "Caribbean Man in Space and Time": "My own inclination is to establish a base in the inner plantation and proceed outwards: connection with the inner metropole, with the ancestors, with the outer plantation" (11).

Indeed, one can go even further and speculate that the archipelagic space is so constructed that it begs to be read and interpreted in terms of some deeper, integrating vision, that is "an inner metropole." To this extent, we can see distinct similarities between Brathwaite's inner, integrative vision and that of another Caribbean theorist, Wilson Harris, whose ideas are sometimes opposed to those of Brathwaite. Harris's paradigm may not be archipelagic but his view of eclipsed selves, phantom presences and fossil identities in the Americas are not all that different from the cataclysmic submarine structures envisaged by Brathwaite. Harris's language is more psychic and Jungian and his attitude less triumphant but the thrust of this theorizing is always towards fulfillment and reconciliation beyond fragmentation. Resolution is envisaged by Harris through a healing process that joins victor and victim, self and other in a moment of mystical oneness. (In this regard, it might be worth reconsidering the excessive claims made for Harris's work by the authors of *The Empire Writes Back*, and reinserting Harris, Brathwaite, Glissant and Derek Walcott in a continuum of postcolonial thought in terms of their positions in respect of such "resolution").

What Harris and Brathwaite seem to share is the need to contain and stabilize that which is fragmented and unstable. What they both have in common in their evocation of a telluric subtext is a tendency to conflate history and landscape, culture and nature. The New World is a foundational site, even if the bedrock is concealed in the ocean's depths. Ruins are surprisingly absent from this convulsive world that requires the poet to give voice to a hidden, primordial wholeness. Even if ruins are present, as in the case of a New World poet such as Pablo Neruda, the ruins are the timeless relics of an original people, the Incan monument of Machu Picchu. This is the space of a New World genesis, which removes the Americas from an Old World imperialist mapping to relocate the new center of origination in American space. This tropological structure is attributed by Roberto González Echevarria to "an anxiety for origins" which sought "access (in the New World) to the very origin and fountainhead of all signification, an origin that in the specific case of the Latin American novel took the form of the 'primitive' cultures of the continent, be it Mayan in the case of Asturias or African in that of Carpentier" (*Voice* 83).

It is his concentration on depth and origination as opposed to an exploration of the contingencies of creolization that create contradictory tensions in Brathwaite's work. He is invariably drawn to the unifying ideal of aboriginal, unchanging presences and foundational ground, which would normally be opposed to the process of transformation implied by the creolization process. This ideal of a New World genesis is the main idea in his major poetic "profession de foi," "Timehri." In this essay, the reduction of history to nature is full-blown and Brathwaite is effusive in his praise for the work of the Guyanese painter Aubrey Williams. The latter is presented as the quintessential New World artist who can bring visibility, quite literally, to an aboriginal culture whose graphic signs are inscribed in a timelessly permanent way in the primordial rock of the Guyanese interior.

> He didn't only come to an understanding of tribal custom and philosophy—although that too was essential to him as continuing creator. But he could actually see the ancient art of the Warraou Indians. Living with them placed him in a significant continuum with it; for high up on the rocks at Tumatumari, at Imbaimadai, people, who were perhaps of Maya origin – the ancestors of the Warraou and others in the area – had made marks or timehri: rock signs, paintings, petroglyphs; glimpses of a language, glitters of a vision of a world, scattered utterals of a remote gestalt; but still there, near, potentially communicative. ("Timehri"[1] 43)

The two aspects of Williams's art that are celebrated are its primordially "grounded" nature and the related ideal of text as inscription in the rock. Brathwaite's ultimate aim is to express an overwhelming empathy with an ancient New World people who are constructed as indestructible emanations of the rock. "We become the Maya who were already us." The genealogy of Caribbean man is hereby fixed in terms of a lost tribe whose vision of the region is a rupestral inscription that dissolves time and all the violent intrusions of Europe to survive in the paintings of Aubrey Williams.

This image of the transcendental leap forward of an ancient New World tribe allows Brathwaite to relate pre-colonial to post-colonial, to assuage the doubts and skepticism of the latter with the abiding certitudes of the former. The artists's role is defined not in terms of postcolonial anxieties but as a mediating presence or living link between aboriginal substructure and future belonging. The referential validity of the literary text, the vital connection between world and word, is tied to the dramatized presence of the lost aboriginal tribe and their rupestral inscriptions. This is a key issue in Brathwaite's poetics as the past is not made up of contending narratives but textuality gives way to geographic presence, visions (glittering

"petroglyphs") of ancient cultures that survive in a state of suspended anima-
tion and voices ("scattered utterals") that the artist triggers into audibility.

Williams's aesthetic has an authorizing power for Brathwaite. It is an
exemplary vision of geographic hinterland and aboriginal culture, which
the island poet longs to adopt for an island space that has neither one nor
the other. The double consciousness of Brathwaite's poetic vision pushes
him away from the paradoxes of fragmented archipelagic surface towards
the truth of an ancient communal tradition. The lure of the latter is so powerful that Brathwaite configures African culture in the New World in largely
pre-colonial, pre-Columbian terms.

> Williams' choice of the Amerindian motif does not exclude the Afri-
> can. For one thing, Williams claims ancestry from both peoples—he
> is spiritually a black Carib... what Williams' work has revealed—and
> what in my analysis of it I have largely unconsciously stressed—is
> that the distinction between African and Amerindian in this context
> is for the most part largely irrelevant. What is important is the primor-
> dial nature of the two cultures and the potent spiritual and artistic
> connections between them and the present. ("Timehri"[1] 43-4)

The artist then becomes a medium, to use Brathwaite's terminology,
which gives him access to this Afro-Amerindian past. Possession is a central aspect of a spiritual journey beyond cultural dispossession and the dis-
sociation of sensibility, which the poet increasingly associates with the fragmented archepelagic psyche. A flash of vision, an extreme state of feeling
open the gateway between an uncompromised past and communal present.

> In the Caribbean, whether it be African or Amerindian, the recogni-
> tion of an ancestral relationship with the folk or aboriginal culture
> involves the artist and participant in a journey into the past and
> hinterland which is at the same time a movement of possession into
> present and future. (*Ibid.* 44)

Brathwaite's poetics have proved troublesome to those wishing to include him in a creolizing, post-colonial process. The authors of *The Empire
Writes Back*, for instance, lament that his emphasis "on the importance of
the African connection has sometimes obscured his increasing concern with
Creolization" (147). The fact is that archepelagic thought in Brathwaite is
constructed around the tensions between hidden homogeneities of depth
and the transformative pluralities of the surface. He sometimes leaves the
resolution of these contradictory forces tantalizingly open. For example, he
concludes his "Caribbean man in Space and Time" by warning that "[w]e

shall also have to bear in mind the possibility that the resolution of this process may, but will not necessarily, be socio-cultural homogeneity. Our new models should leave us open to the possibility of permanent co-existent plurality" ("Caribbean Man" 11). However, one senses that Brathwaite, the cultural critic, has almost gotten carried away with the dizzying possibilities of this new interactional, multi-dimensional model and the admission comes a few lines later that "[m]y own inclination is to establish a base in the inner plantation and proceed outwards." Brathwaite's impulses privilege foundational space, the "classic norm," as he says in reference to nation language, the ancient watercourses of "Black Sycorax" who ceases to be the "Cracked Mother." His vision is invariably an evocation of apocalyptic genesis, of a grounded archipelago.

If we can now reread Brathwaite's archipelagic discourse deconstructively, it is due to the theoretical interventions of the Martinican theorist Edouard Glissant whose poetics are also sited in the Caribbean's archipelagic space. If the location of their poetics is similar their imaginative exploration of this zone of convulsive creativity is very different. Glissant himself confuses the issue of differing theoretical perspectives by citing approvingly, one is led to believe, Brathwaite's "Unity is submarine" as one of the epigraphs to his book of essays, *Poétique de la Relation* (A Poetics of Relating). Indeed, this was not the first time Glissant made reference to Brathwaite's formulation, using "the unity is submarine" in *Caribbean Discourse* to describe "submarine roots; that is floating free; not fixed in one primordial spot"—an early meditation on the image of the rhizome. (He also uses as epigraph to *Poétique de la Relation* Walcott's "Sea is History" and his poetics of Caribbean creolization may actually be as different from Brathwaite's as it is from Walcott's.) From the outset, however, Glissant's readings of Caribbean space have been provokingly transgressive. For instance, the lamented image of the cracked mother in Brathwaite's *Islands* is arguably reread by Glissant in terms of the cracked "pays natal" of the latter's first novel *La Lézarde* (1958). But in Glissant's construction of island space, the crack is conceived as fertile fissure complicating any temptation to uniformity or homogeneity. In his second novel, *Le Quatrième Siècle*, inside and outside, hinterland and littoral are problematized in a narrative that Homi Bhaba might well qualify in terms of chiasmatic reversals. What Glissant demonstrates in these early narratives is the fallacy of aboriginal inner space, of paradisal wilderness for a bewildered protagonist, Mathieu, whose profession, not coincidentally, is that of historian. What Glissant provides us with in his subversive constructions of Caribbean space is a salutary critical distance that allows us to rethink other Caribbean paradigms. In a sense, where a poet like Brathwaite dramatizes, Glissant problematizes.

Glissant's evocation of the archipelago orients him away from a poetics of origination and foundation towards an exemplary relationality, a negation of poles and metropoles. The image of the archipelago that appears in *Poétique de la Relation* is tellingly different from that of Brathwaite. Like his Anglophone counterpart, Glissant focuses on a definition of the process of creolization in the Caribbean, on tensions between inner and outer, depth and surface, but with a different emphasis. Glissant poetically and philosophically savors the creative tensions and avoids the temptation of legitimating submarine bedrock:

> What happened in the Caribbean, what we could sum up in the word creolisation, comes as close as one possibly can to the idea we have in mind. Not only an encounter, a shock (to use Segalen's term), a metissage, but an unprecedented dimension which allows each individual to be both there and elsewhere, rooted and open-ended, lost among the mountains and free under the sea, in harmony and in errancy. (*Poétique* 46)

The prevailing thrust of Glissant's poetics is not towards resolution of contradictory impulses. The dominant image is not of apocalyptic genesis but of the evocation of multiple, unpredictable trajectories that result from a relentless diffraction and scattering across an open sea, exploding an old discourse founded on an exclusionary rootedness. The image of relating and not synthesizing opposites is equally dominant in Glissant's recent monumental novel of errancy, *Tout-Monde*, where the Caribbean is defined by the image of "l'eau du volcan":

> The volcano's waters streamed through the tormented geography of these ocean depths, between the islands, and maybe they linked in one huge body of Water one continent to the other, the Guyanas to Yucatan, across this trajectory of craters placed one by one through the islands, on these shuddering heights where the earth questions the earth. (*Tout-Monde* 224)

Glissant's focus on Caribbean man "in time and space" in his "Poetics of Relating" revisits and complicates Brathwaite's archipelagic allegory. The aboriginal seabed and privileging of geographical depth over historical "transversality" that we see in Brathwaite is re-read in terms of a geography which cannot provide a genesis, of history that so impregnates nature as to provide the experience of multiple repeating experiences of genesis.

This meditation on multiple genesis or *digénèse* is the main idea in *Faulkner, Mississippi*, in which the Southern novelist is merely a pretext for a continued meditation on Caribbean space:

> In our lands shaped by History, where the histories of different peoples are ultimately intertwined, works of nature are the true historical monuments. The Island of Gorée, where all those Africans were flung into the depths of the slave ship, Mount Pelée and the disappearance of the town of Saint Pierre; the buried dungeons of Dubuc Castle at Caravelle Point in Martinique again, where those same Africans arrived, at least those who had survived the journey, the Sierra Maestra and the adventure of the Barbudos, the Bois Caiman where the oath of the Haitian Revolution was first taken, a wood with tree trunks scarred by erosion and in whose depths the wind no longer howls. (*Faulkner, Mississippi* 25)

Such a landscape, cannot sustain Creation and foundational myths in Glissant's view. This pattern of archipelagic thought leads away from ethnocentrisms and legitimizing genealogies. As he elaborates in his analysis of the art forms of the archipelago, a poetics of diffraction is invariably the product of this creolizing space. (Caryl Phillips's recent review of this novel provides useful insight on how a major Anglophone Caribbean writer from the generation after Brathwaite's sees Glissant's work.)

Glissant also chooses his exemplary painters of a region that is defined by exemplary relationality. As opposed to the aboriginal depths of Aubrey Williams, he is drawn to the visualizing of horizontal multiplicity in the Cuban painter Wifredo Lam and the Chilean artist Matta. It is the painterly text that is emphasized here not artistic intuition:

> In Wifredo Lam the poetics of the American landscape (accumulation, expansion, power of history, the African connection, presence of totems) is part of the design. From the dense layers of the jungle to those clear spaces hardly touched by color, where so many birds alight. Paintings of both rootedness in the earth and ascent upwards. Roberto Matta represents the intense conflicts that shape men's minds today. Paintings of multiplicity; I even dare to say: multilingualism. I feel in this a visible continuity between inside and outside, the dazzling convergence of here and elsewhere. (*Caribbean Discourse* 117)

The same is true of a traditional art form like the folktale, which either mocks or contests the possibility of a legitimizing Genesis:

> The language of the Tale is not dictated by a God nor derived from a
> Law. It is the language of the composite, of contesting, even without
> saying so, any idea of Genesis, of a creation of the world, of a legiti-
> mate genealogy guaranteed by lineage. This is my way of describing
> the Creole tales of the Americas. (*Faulkner, Mississippi* 265)

Chris Bongie is perfectly correct in emphasizing, in his recent *Islands and
Exiles*, the contradictory tension that pushes Brathwaite back and forth
between epistemological polar opposite views. What he says with regard to
Alejo Carpentier could also be referred to the Anglophone poet: "Carpentier's
text suggests, at least to this reader, that no matter how refined our notion of
transculturation, it will always fall short of what it points toward. A reliance
upon, and a reversion to, fixed and ultimately fictional (ethic, racial, national,
and so on) identities is inescapable, notwithstanding our ever greater im-
mersion in and sensitivity to a creolized creolizing world" (*Islands* 10).
Whether the falling short is always unavoidable is open to debate. However, in the wake of the excessively triumphant anti-essentialism of
postcolonial theory we may want to rethink the links that bind pre- and
postmodernism in Caribbean thought. Christopher Miller's effort in his recent *Nationalists and Nomads* to look at the opposition between nationalist models and hybrid paradigms in francophone literature may also be useful here.

In Brathwaite's and Glissant's Creole poetics we witness the tensions
of a crucial transitional moment in Caribbean literature, as they struggle to
define two key aspects of archipelagic thought, the closed insularity of an
essentialist identity politics against the diffracting possibilities of Creole
openness, an issue of "open" versus "closed" insularity that I have sought
to examine in the conclusion to my own *The Other America*. Could this
struggle be what George Lamming had in mind when he referred to "the
politics of intrigue" that are provoked by "that ruthless, though necessary
wreck" (*Pleasures* 96), a marker not of historical catastrophe but a point of
contact where island contours are constantly shaped by tidal detours?

Roberto Fernández Retamar

Sólo tu Nancy Morejón

A Marta Valdés

Sólo tú vestida de campana y cocuyos deslumbrabas así a mis niñas
Convencidas de que habíamos recibido la visita multicolor
De una pájara de cristal de fósforo de aire
Sólo tú escuchaste algunas notas dibujadas por la flauta de Richard
Sólo tú podías devolverme a Rosa mi abuela jamaiquina
Llevada en alas del pasaje Alfonso a la calle Peñalver
Sólo tú me regalaste la claridad romántica en la frescura de la patria
Sólo tú hiciste cruzar la más bella cotorra ante nosotros
Sólo tú eras capaz de escribir el epitafio de la inconsolable Ana Mendieta
Con la atroz infancia como un túnel sin fin en la memoria
Y el ávido sexo de pequeña golondrina añorando su tierra
Sólo tú viste ciertos paisajes célebres
Del Caribe de México de los Estados Unidos de África del Sur
Sólo para que tú los trasladases a tu lengua de ojos entrecerrados
Se inventaron en lugares distantes los enigmas del francés y el inglés
Y hermanos como Édouard Glissant y Kamau Brathwaite los aclimataron en
nuestras islas
Sólo tú mujer negra hecha de amor y de dolor de risa y de tristeza
Sólo tú hija grande
Sólo tú Nancy Morejón
Eres hoy esta muchacha de sorprendente tiempo que ilumina
Con la poesía de Felipe el padre mientras contempla un barco en la tarde
De Angélica la madre princesa del señorío absoluto
En la casa pobre y lujosa a la cual se asoma lo más puro del cielo estrellado

La Habana 14 de octubre de 1994

Roberto Fernández Retamar

Only You Nancy Morejón

For Marta Valdés

Only you dressed in bells and fireflies used so to dazzle my daughters
Convinced we had received the multicolor visit
Of a she-bird of crystal of phosphorus of air
Only you heeded a few notes sketched by Richard's flute
Only you could bring back to me Rosa my Jamaican grandmother
Borne on wings from Alfonso Lane to Peñalver Street
Only you offered me romantic clarity in the cool of the native land
Only you made the most beautiful parrot pass before us
Only you were able to write the epitaph of the inconsolable Ana Mendieta
Her brutal childhood like an endless tunnel in memory
Her avid sex a tiny swallow pining for its land
Only you saw celebrated landscapes
Of the Caribbean Mexico United States South Africa
Only so that you might translate them to your tongue of half-closed eyes
Were enigmas of English and French invented in distant places
And did brothers like Edouard Glissant and Kamau Brathwaite fit them to
our islands
Only you black woman made of love of pain of laughter of sadness
Only you great daughter
Only you Nancy Morejón
Are today this young woman of surprising time who lights up
With father Felipe's poetry while he gazes on a boat in the evening
Of Angélica mother princess of absolute dominion
In the luxurious hovel where the starry sky shows its clearest

Havana, October 14th 1994

Trans. Timothy J. Reiss, Isabel Balseiro and the author

Towards a "New Parochial Wholeness": Brathwaite's Dialectical Model of Creolisation

Richard L. W. Clarke

In an important essay, Nigel Bolland provides a very useful history of the concept of creolisation in the Caribbean as it has been deployed in recent times by a variety of sociologists and cultural theorists. The notion of creolisation, which denotes basically a "process of cultural interaction" (52), is in essence, he writes, a "version of the old 'melting pot' hypothesis, which conceives of a new cultural unity evolving from the blending of diverse original elements" (51). He argues rightly that the concept of creolisation has made it impossible to read Caribbean societies and cultures as the "result of a one-way process, of the unilateral imposition of European culture upon passive African recipients" (52).

Bolland is also correct to underline the neo-Hegelian dialectical problematic which generally informs the "creole-society thesis" (53). Implicit here, he writes, is a "dialectical view of social dynamics and cultural change" (64), that is, the "idea that the synthesis of new cultural practices emerges from the struggle between conflicting social forces" (64). What this means has been made more precise by Karl Popper, who offers a useful summary of the main tenets of dialectical logic. It is, he writes, a

> theory that maintains that something–more especially human thought–develops in a way characterised by what is called the dia-

lectic triad: *thesis, antithesis,* and *synthesis.* First there is some idea or theory or movement which may be called a "thesis." Such a thesis will often produce opposition, because, like most things in this world, it will probably be of limited value and will have its weak spots. The opposing idea or movement is called the *"antithesis,"* because it is directed against the first, the thesis. The struggle between the thesis and the antithesis goes on until some solution is reached which, in a certain sense, goes beyond both thesis and antithesis by avoiding the limitations of both. The solution, which is the third step, is called the *synthesis.* Once attained, the synthesis in its turn may become the first step of a new dialectic triad.... The dialectic triad will thus proceed on a higher level.... (313-4)

The logic of the dialectic, Popper correctly points out, as such "amounts to an attack upon the so-called 'law of contradiction' (or, more fully, upon the law of the exclusion of contradictions) of traditional logic, a law which asserts that two contradictory statements can never be true together" (316). Appealing in this way to the fruitfulness of contradictions, dialecticians claim that the law of non-contradiction at the heart of traditional logic must be discarded.

Bolland points out that the "process of decolonisation and nation-building" (52) in the Caribbean has been almost entirely predicated upon this dialectical model of creolisation: the "creation of a creole identity and the vision of the nation as a creole community," he writes, "constitute a *synthetic* mode of nationalism" (64, his emphasis). Bolland warns, however, that some versions of creolisation, while often overtly dialectical, have often lapsed back into more "dualistic" (53) or "dichotomous" (64) frameworks of thinking. And here, too, another recent thinker lets us be more precise: Herbert Marcuse offering a useful definition of this "dualism" to which Bolland thinks proponents of creolisation are sometimes prone.

In an influential account of Hegel's philosophy, Marcuse contends that common sense (what Hegel calls "understanding") views the world "as a multitude of determinate things, each of which is demarcated from the other. Each thing is a distinct delimited entity" (44). It "conceives a world of finite opposites, governed by the principle of identity and opposition. Everything is identical with itself and with nothing else; it is, by virtue of its self-identity, opposed to all other things. It can be connected and combined with other things in many ways, but it never loses its own identity and never becomes something other than itself" (44). In this scheme of things, the "qualities the thing has distinguish it from other things, so that if we want to separate it off from other things we simply enumerate its qualities" (67). From this perspective, the world consists of "irreconcilable opposites" (44), "numberless

Richard L. W. Clarke

polarities," "polar concepts" and "antagonisms" (45).

It is with something like this in mind that Bolland makes the specific claim that creolisation, "as exemplified in the work of Edward Brathwaite, is *not dialectical enough*" (53, my emphasis). He criticises a number of what he deems blindspots in Brathwaite's thinking (64), and while there certainly are aporia (which thinker is immune to them, I wonder?), many of Bolland's particular criticisms here do not hold water, in my view. I do agree that there is a potential for dualism in Brathwaite's work (this is something to which all dialectical thinking may be prone), but my thesis here is that Brathwaite's *Contradictory Omens: Cultural Diversity and Integration in the Caribbean* (itself to a large degree culled from his *The Development of Creole Society in Jamaica, 1770-1820*) is in fact a supreme example of applied dialectical thinking or, to put this another way, of dialectical theory and praxis conjoined. Moreover, my argument is that Brathwaite's signal achievement here consists precisely, at a purely theoretical level, in his seminal revision, with the aid especially of W. E. B. Du Bois's notion of "double consciousness," of the purely economistic conceptual framework which informs Georg Lukács's *History and Class Consciousness*, the *locus classicus* of neo-Hegelian dialectical historical materialism in the twentieth century. My point is that *within the field of vision permitted by a dialectic problematic* Brathwaite offered here a seminal account of the complex dialectic of identity, class, nationality, ethnicity and race to be found in the Caribbean (and, by extension, in any multicultural/multiracial society) as well as a persuasive map of the way forward. He was able, in other words, to show that economic class is not the only basis for social inequality which in fact manifests itself in many forms, nationality, ethnicity and race being three other and inter-related determinants (gender not figuring prominently in either of these studies).

Furthermore, Brathwaite may not have been the originator of the concept of creolisation but it is one with which his name has become more or less synonymous. If Hans Robert Jauss is right that the classic stature of a work is determined by the significance of its reception as well as its continuing impact, then Brathwaite's *Contradictory Omens* is as much a classic as *The Development of Creole Society in Jamaica* and deserves as such to be republished. Both these works may be said to have set the scholarly agenda for a whole generation of Caribbean historians, cultural theorists and cultural critics in particular, not to mention sociologists and political theorists, during the 1970s, 1980s and 1990s. This dominant dialectical problematic may be, as I have argued elsewhere, in the throes of giving way (an arduous process in that epistemic shifts are always discomforting affairs) to an emergent way of conceptualising Caribbean culture that is informed by (post-)Saussurean modes of difference and epitomised by the work of Stuart Hall, among others. However, dialectical modes of thinking about personal and collective identity, inextricably intertwined with a residual organicism that is arguably European Romanticism's most telling legacy, remain deeply entrenched, for good and for bad, in Caribbean discourse. (I have further explored the epistemic shift in Caribbean discourse in "From Dialectic," and organicism in "Root versus Rhizome" and "'Roots'.")

Bolland offers a useful summation of what a "dialectical analysis of society" (65) or problematic of the kind inspired by Lukács permits one to see. Firstly, each of the constituent groups which comprise a society are seen to be "parts of a whole, constituting a unity of opposites. They are parts of a system that have no independent existence, but are defined in their relation with each other" (71). Lukács puts it this way in *History and Class Consciousness*: "[i]deologically, no less than economically, the bourgeoisie and the proletariat are mutually interdependent" (68) and, as such, each is incomprehensible apart from the other and from their relationship to the whole. Secondly, a dialectical approach underscores the inherently conflictual nature of the relationships that exist between these groups which are. as Bolland puts it, "defined and differentiated in terms of power, between the dominant and the subordinate" (65).

It is important to remember in this respect that Lukács's Hegelian brand of Marxism revolves less around the familiar Base/superstructure trope than Hegel's metaphor of the "expressive totality." In *History and Class Consciousness*, Lukács explains: the "category of totality, the all-pervasive supremacy of the whole over the parts is the essence of the method which Marx took over from Hegel" (27). The "expressive totality" involves, Frederic Jameson argues, the "construction of a historical totality" (27) and the "isolation and the privileging of one of the elements within that totality ...such that the element in question becomes a mastercode or 'inner essence' capable of explicating the other elements or features of the whole in question" (27-8). Althusser asserts that the "expressive totality" consists of "so many '*total parts*', each expressing the others, and each expressing the social totality that contains them, because each in itself contains in the immediate form of its expression the essence of the social totality itself" (94). The "inner essence" expressed by all the constituent elements which comprise the "totality" is evidently, in the Marxist scheme of things, in the final analysis the economic. Within a purely Hegelian and, thus idealist schema, each stage of history and the human communities therein is conceptualised, of course, in terms of the "Zeitgeist," that is, as the expression or manifestation of Spirit. Lukács's stated desire being, like Marx's, to translate the "whole mysticism of the 'spirit' into materialist historical reality" (*Histori-*

cal Novel 119), he argues that each social totality as well as everything that comprises it is comprehensible, rather, as a function of its location along the dialectical sequence of the economic modes of production that constitute history. All the elements which comprise a given social totality are understood to have a common relation not to a static and self-sufficient economic base corresponding to an isolated moment of the dialectical development of human history but to a dynamic history always in the throes of change and, thus, of conflict.

The essence of the social totality is that essential contradiction at its centre which is construed, as Tony Bennett puts it, as the "clash between the dynamic momentum of new forces of economic production and the restraining hand of old social relations of production. This essential clash is then said to be present in, and therefore capable of being deduced or read off from, each of the constituent parts which, taken together, comprise the social totality" (*Formalism* 40). In short, every element within a given social totality expresses the "world-historical" forces pertinent to a particular time and place, that is, the conflict between the ruling class fighting, on the one hand, to maintain its dominance in the face of changing forces of production and the other classes struggling, on the other, to attain social ascendancy.

Thirdly and perhaps most importantly, as Bolland points out, the dialectical conflict between the groups that comprise the social totality is the engine of social change: "social forces and social systems...are characterised by conflicts and contradictions...that consequently give rise to their own transformation" (53). To put this another way, out of the contradiction of thesis and antithesis arises a synthesis which is tantamount to progress and amelioration. However, change is impossible without the development of what Lukács terms the "class consciousness" of the proletariat which, he writes, "has been entrusted by history with the task of *transforming society consciously*" (*History* 71). If social transformation is to occur, Lukács argues, the working class must *become* "class conscious" or "self-aware," that is, conscious of its objective location as a class in the social totality of which it is part. The bourgeoisie as a class is unable to do this, he argues, because, given its social dominance, it is unable to look beyond its own narrow self-interest. It is, as such, a victim of "false consciousness." Lukács puts it all this way: class consciousness is not an empirical "description of what men *in fact* thought, felt and wanted at any moment in history and from any given point in the class structure" (51). It is not, moreover, a given: indeed, precisely because of the dominance of the ruling class and the pervasiveness of their outlook, it is something which must be arduously striven for. Class consciousness is, in fact, an acquired objective awareness of the proletariat's position within *"society as a concrete totality,* the system of production at a given point in history and the resulting division of society into classes" (50). It is, in other words, the *"sense, become conscious, of the historical role of the class"* (73). The "superiority of the proletariat" (69), he writes, resides in the resulting "ability to see society from the centre, as a coherent whole" (69), that is, to "lay bare the nature of society" (70), an ability that results precisely from its disenfranchised location. The development of class consciousness on the part of the proletariat, enabling it to "act in such a way as to change reality" (69), is the indispensable prerequisite for the ushering in of a classless society. With the rise to ascendancy of the proletariat, this argument goes, classes are abolished.

(Bolland hints at much of this when he underscores that a dialectical problematic "draws attention" [65] to the "interrelated and mutually constitutive nature of 'individual,' 'society', and 'culture,' and of human agency and social structure" [65]. These are not dichotomies. Rather, emphasising the "mutually dependent relationship between social structure and human agency" [65], Bolland contends that "[c]ulture and society, in the form of traditions, ideas, customs, languages, institutions, and social formations, shape the social action of individuals, which in turn maintains, modifies, or transforms social structure and culture" [65].)

In short, in the Lukáscian scheme of things, there is no question of pluralistic relativism in that the characteristic experiences of different social groups do not provide divergent but equal grounds for reliable knowledge claims. It is for this reason that a distinction is drawn between "class consciousness," on the one hand, and mere "perspective," on the other. It is a given for Lukács that the lived realities of the lives of the working classes are profoundly different from those of the ruling class. Given that material life is structured in fundamentally opposing ways for different classes, it is only understandable that the vision of each will represent an inversion of the other. As a result, as Nancy Hartsock claims, "in systems of domination the vision available to the rulers will be both partial and perverse" (153) while the opposite is true for those who have been marginalised. However, precisely because the dominant ideology, to wit, the world view of the ruling class necessarily "structures the material relations in which all parties are forced to participate" (153), the standpoint or consciousness of the proletariat is an achievement, not a given, emerging only through the battles waged against the dominant/oppressive group. It is through the struggles against domination, this argument goes, that the experience of the oppressed can be made to "yield up a truer (or less false) image of social reality than that available only from the perspective of the social experience of men of the ruling classes" (169). This change in consciousness is the necessary prelude to social amelioration.

At least one other important influence on Brathwaite's concept of creolisation in this respect is worth noting at this point: Du Bois's seminal notion of "double consciousness" (Brathwaite's work is involved in a complex negotiation with that of several other non-European intellectual precursors but the majority of these are beyond this chapter's focus). The dilemma of being both American and black at the same time is most famously articulated in Chapter One of his *The Souls of Black Folk*, "Of Our Spiritual Strivings" (written in 1897). Openly drawing on Hegel's notion of the Master/Slave dialectic, he addresses what he describes as the "double consciousness" (102) with which the African American is afflicted:

> this sense of always looking at one's self from through the eyes of others, of measuring one's soul by the tape of a world that looks on in amused contempt and pity. One ever feels this twoness,–an American, a Negro; two souls, two thoughts, two unreconciled strivings; two warring ideals in one dark body. (102)

Du Bois evidently conceives of the American negro's psychomachia in terms of a struggle between two races and the two cultures that they represent, between innate endowment and the Eurocentric forces of acculturation to which the American negro is inevitably subjected. The "history of the American Negro is the history of this strife–this longing to attain *self-conscious* manhood, to merge his double self into a *better and truer* self. In this merging he wishes neither of the older selves to be lost" (102, my emphases).

Brathwaite's signal achievement in *Contradictory Omens*, at a theoretical level, consists in his use of Du Bois in particular to transform Lukács's purely economic or class-based mode of analysis, especially his notion of "class consciousness," in order to stress the overdetermination of nationality, ethnicity and race within the Caribbean context. Brathwaite underscores that these determinants exist in a dialectical relationship with each other, as a result of which each is incomprehensible without reference to the others, the question of class, for example, being inextricable from that of race. Brathwaite's thesis is that, from at least 1770 and extending long after 1820, the social totality that is the Caribbean has been defined in its entirety by and thus "expresses" in each of its parts an essential clash that is similar to but not identical with that described by Lukács. At the core of Jamaican society (as well as other societies, like Barbados, with a similar demographic distribution), Brathwaite argues, there has historically existed a dialectical conflict between social groups configured simultaneously in economic, national, ethnic *and* racial terms which has entirely shaped the social totality of which it is part. On the one hand, there is the numerical minority of white European colonisers/slave-masters and their descendants who continued in the course of the twentieth century to comprise the ruling class and thus to wield effective economic, social and (at least initially) political power. On the other hand, there is the enslaved black African majority and their descendants who continued to serve as the working masses in the post-Emancipation period but who have, more recently, increasingly tasted of social mobility. The former has battled continuously to maintain its hegemony, the latter to attain equality, if not dominance in turn.

As Brathwaite states in *The Development of Creole Society in Jamaica*, creole Jamaica was a society in which there was a *"juxtaposition* of master and slave, élite and labourer, in a *culturally heterogeneous* relationship" (xvi, my emphases). The question which this consequently posed for Brathwaite is this: exactly how should the heterogeneity of West Indian culture be conceptualised? Precisely how, in other words, ought one to comprehend the relationship that exists between master and slave, white and black? To answer this, Brathwaite alludes in *Contradictory Omens* to several inter-related models of cultural interaction, each of which he finds useful in some respects but unsatisfactory in others. He rejects, for example, the economic reductivism inherent in the so-called "plantation model" (associated with George Beckford) which, by virtue of its abstract economism and its reliance on a simplistic Base/superstructure model, does not do justice, he seems to feel, to the economic, social, and political diversity of social totalities such as Jamaica. These, he stresses, cannot be reduced to being merely something akin to a plantation "writ large." He distances himself similarly from what he describes as the "classical 'plural' paradigm" (25) advanced by the sociologist M. G. Smith which, because "based on an apprehension of cultural polarity...on an either/or principle; on the idea of people sharing fixed divisions instead of increasingly common values" (25), fails to do justice to the cultural "give and take" or intermixture that is the hallmark of Jamaican society. Brathwaite also rejects what he terms the "syncretic/synthetic ideal" (58) (one which he possibly associates with the work of Wilson Harris and Derek Walcott, among others) which envisages the emergence of a "'new' racial type" (58) that is the product of miscegenation between the races. What seems to make Brathwaite uncomfortable with the syncretic model is, firstly, the way in which it privileges biology over the social construction of race and, secondly, the way in which it effaces the original races (the thesis and antithesis, as it were) thought to be synthesised in this way.

It is no doubt for this reason that, instead of biological race, Brathwaite prefers to emphasise what he terms the "common somatic image" (22) which a race has of itself. Brathwaite draws here upon the concept of the "somatic norm-image" advanced by Harry Hoetink in "'Colonial Psychology' and Race." In a manner analogous to the Feminist distinction between anatomical sex and gender, Hoetink proposes to replace what he describes as the biological term "race" with its "social-psychological" (149) counterpart: the latter meets the "sociological demand of being transmissible by communication, instead of being biologically tied to hereditary substance" (149). To this end, he proposes that every "race" possesses what he calls a "somatic norm-image," to wit, the "total of somatic characteristics...considered by a group as its esthetic norm and ideal" (149). This, he argues, is the "embodiment of a socially determined narcissism" (149). Sidney Mintz defines it this way: it is the "mental concept that individuals have of the appropriate (or ideal or preferred) way to look" (442). For Hoetink, "somatic distance," by contrast, is the "distance subjectively experienced between one's own somatic norm-image and a different somatic type" (150).

Brathwaite suggests that the best way to conceive of the heterogeneity of Jamaican (and by extension West Indian) culture, especially during the period 1770 to 1820, is in terms of the process of cultural interaction which he calls "creolisation." In Brathwaite's famous formula, this is a "cultural action–material, psychological and spiritual–based upon the stimulus/response of individuals within the society to their environment and–as white/black, culturally discrete groups–to each other" (11). Brathwaite uses the term "creole" to denote all "born in, native to, committed to the area of living" (10) in question and thus to refer to "both white and black, free and slave" (10). However, he is at pains to emphasise that, by "creolisation," he has in mind less the individuals or the groups they represent than the dialectical relationship between these groups, "not white but black / white: mulatto; the 'white' and the 'black' still *locked in competition for ascendancy*" (6, my emphasis). Creolisation is, he writes in *The Development of Creole Society in Jamaica*, a "way of seeing the society, not in terms of white and black, master and slave, in separate nuclear units, but as contributory parts of a whole" (307). Brathwaite's point is that white and black, master and slave may be forcibly segregated from each other by virtue of the complex overdetermination of economics, nationality, ethnicity and skin colour (this is the thrust of the "plural-society" thesis of M. G. Smith), but the defining characteristic of Jamaican society, the essential contradiction which Jamaican society in its totality expresses, is the relationship that each group shares to the other. This relationship, he stresses, may be a conflictual, rather than harmonious one, a relationship of difference rather than similarity, but it is a defining relationship all the same.

Brathwaite is keen to point out that Jamaican people have historically interacted with each other with results that vary from identification and accommodation at one extreme, to rejection and hostility at the other. But there is also a common *cultural* middle ground of sorts which is occupied not only by the offspring of racial miscegenation. That these may occupy it in a particularly clear way is why Brathwaite argues in *The Development of Creole Society in Jamaica* that the "area of sexual relationships" (303) was one of the most potent *facilitators* of the process of creolisation: the "visible and undeniable result of these liaisons was the large and growing coloured population of the island, which, in its turn, acted as a bridge, a kind of social cement, between the two main colours of the island's structure, thus further helping (despite the resulting class/colour divisions) to integrate the society" (305). By virtue of their miscegenation those whom he describes as "'mulatto culturalists'" have been "*essentially* concerned with the *integration* of the society" (305, my emphases).

But that there is a *common cultural* middle ground is why Brathwaite stresses that "creolisation," by contrast to the stark binary oppositions envisaged by Smith's pluralism, seeks to capture the historical fact that there existed in Jamaican society

> a historically affected socio-cultural *continuum,* within which...there are four *inter-related* and sometimes *overlapping orientations.* From their several cultural bases, people in the West Indies *tend towards certain directions, positions, assumptions and ideals.* But *nothing is really fixed and monolithic.* Although there is white/brown/ black, *there are infinite possibilities within these distinctions* and many ways of asserting identity. A common colonial and creole experience is shared among the various divisions, even if variously interpreted. (25, my emphases)

The four principal orientations he defines as "European, Euro-creole, Afro-creole (or folk), and creo-creole or West Indian" (25). (Brathwaite emphasises that creolisation, because it commenced "as a result of slavery" (11), involved "in the first instance...black and white, European and African, in a fixed superiority/inferiority relationship" (11). However, with the arrival of other racial and cultural groups in the region, principally Indians and Chinese, it came to take on other configurations.)

To account for this continuum in Jamaican society, that is, the tendency towards certain directions, orientations and positions rather than hard and fast, monolithic divisions, Brathwaite seeks to define the relationship between the dominant and subordinate groups in Jamaican society more precisely in terms of two simultaneous and inter-related processes of cultural interaction. He speaks, firstly, of "ac/culturation": this is Brathwaite's term for the "yoking (by force and example, deriving from power and prestige) of one culture to another (in this case, the slave/African to the European)" (6). Elsewhere, he defines this as the "process of absorption of one culture by another" (11). Brathwaite speaks, secondly, of "[i]nter/culturation" (6), the process of cultural 'give and take' that historically occurred between white and black, master and slave. This has been a "reciprocal activity, a process of intermixture and enrichment, each to each" (11). In other words, it denotes the

> unplanned, unstructured but *osmotic* relationship proceeding from this yoke. The creolization which results (and it is a process not a product) becomes the tentative cultural norm of the society. Yet this norm, because of the complex historical factors involved in making it (mercantilism, slavery, materialism, racism, superiority/inferiority syndromes, etc.) is not whole or hard...but cracked, fragmented, ambivalent, not certain of itself, subject to shifting lights and pressures. (6, my emphasis)

In other words, by virtue of its dominant economic, political and social position, the ruling group was able to impose its culture upon the ruled (this is the acculturation of which he speaks). However, creolisation also implies a two-way process of "give and take" by which the ruled were able in turn to shape the culture of the rulers (interculturation). The outcome was a complex, hybrid, creole culture which, as a (not always acknowledged) mixture of European and African, forever changed the respective identities of the participants in this social totality. The result is that the white Jamaican was as different from his/her "pure" European counterpart as was the black Jamaican from his/her African, the subjectivity of each having been profoundly moulded by the creolised socio-historical environment that was Jamaica during this period.

It is from this point of view that Brathwaite in *The Development of Creole Society in Jamaica* likens creolisation to an "obscure force" (297) compelling all members of Jamaican slave society to "conform to a certain concept of themselves; makes them perform in certain roles which, in fact, they quickly come to believe in" (297). False consciousness, Brathwaite seems to suggest, has historically been a fact of life in the region for all parties concerned. The false consciousness of the ruling white (and "whitish") group–Brathwaite has in mind what he calls in *Contradictory Omens* the "Euro-centered elite" (29), the "Euro-orientated creole upper class" (29), and the "small creole intellectual elite" (29)–is largely the product of their privileged location within the social totality. Trapped within what Lukács might term the false "antinomies" (110) which infect their world view, this group as a whole was unable to see beyond the boundaries of its own narrow self-interest and historical origins. The "[c]ohesiveness and direction" (32) of the first two "orientations" came, Brathwaite avers, from a "sense of being 'European', derived from their metropolitan origin or memories; and a sense of being white, 'civilised' and superior, derived from the 'philosophy' elaborated to justify slavery" (32). In a manner not unlike Lukács's treatment of the bourgeoisie, Brathwaite asserts that the Euro-orientated's

> cultural contribution...was essentially structural / functional and materialistic in quality. Its objective was to perform well within the "raw materials" sector of the mercantilist framework. Its great achievement was the plantation and the evolution of highly efficient political Assemblies. Its aesthetic achievement was the Great House and the "civilisation of the wilderness." (32)

Although he acknowledges that there was "among the best of them, a certain measure of commitment to creole as opposed to European/imported values" (33) and that, because "of the concern for what was being created, some Europeans in the West Indies during the period of slavery came to know and love the landscape" (33), Brathwaite alleges that "their sensibilities never reached deep enough to possess it in other than a superficial, economic sense" (33). He blasts them, moreover, for practising what he calls in *The Development of Creole Society in Jamaica* a "bastard metropolitanism" (307), rather than embracing more fully the phenomenon of creolisation which has necessarily altered their identity in the Caribbean. In so doing, had they acknowledged the humanity of and forged a strategic alliance with the ex-Africans, the history of the West Indies might have taken a different course. The last "orientation" in this list, the so-called "small creole intellectual elite," he also dismisses in *Contradictory Omens* because, being without "real roots or vision...[w]ithout a concept of 'Caribbean,'" they really had nothing to orient towards" (29).

It is from this perspective that Brathwaite stresses the necessity of performing "psycho-social analysis" (33) upon all views expressed about West Indian culture, especially those which emanate from the aforementioned groups. The diversity of perspectives upon West Indian society and culture, he writes, "result[s] essentially from a subjective apprehension of 'reality', based upon the particular individual's socio-cultural orientation" (34). That is, each individual's perspective derives from his/her location within a particular group, configured simultaneously and complexly in economic, racial and other terms, and the relationship of that group to the others which comprise the social totality. In other words, in the Lukácsian schema which evidently informs Brathwaite's argument here, the members of each group share a communal vantage-point or perspective upon society but the validity of any given perspective is dependent upon that group's precise location within the social totality. Not all truth-claims are, consequently, accurate.

The segment which Brathwaite describes as the "Afro-Caribbean (black) population" (30) is also not immune to false/double consciousness. In their case, however, this is not inherent in their structural/functional location within the totality, as it is in the case of the white and "whitish" ruling classes, but is the tragic consequence of their acculturation. He is particularly concerned with the negative impact of acculturation upon the "orientations" he labels "elite blacks and the mass of free coloureds" (22) (he calls the former "Afro-Saxon" [39]). Although he acknowledges that the "[m]imicry" (15) in which the elite blacks and free coloureds were forced to engage was one of the necessary "conditions under which creolization had to take place" (15), Brathwaite views it as "one of the tragedies of slavery" (15):

> "Invisible," anxious to be "seen" by their masters, the elite blacks
> and the mass of free coloureds conceived of visibility through the
> lenses of their masters' already uncertain vision, as a form of "grey-
> ness"–an imitation of an imitation. Whenever the opportunity made
> it possible, they and their descendants rejected or disowned their
> own culture, becoming..."mimic-men". (22)

These blacks, he argues, were doubly mimic-men in that they were guilty, firstly, of an "imitation of an imitation" (308) (rather than, presumably, of the "real thing," the "true" European). More importantly, however, for the (ex-)African to imitate the (ex-)European at all was in effect not to be "true" to his/her "real" self. The key element in the acculturation of the black élite and free coloureds was an education system the object of which was, Brathwaite stresses, "'civilisation', and the eradication of all existing or remaining African traits that might have been found among the 'lower classes'" (30).

However, Brathwaite stresses that the "friction created" by the "confrontation" of white European and black African, master and slave, "was cruel, but it was also creative" (22), involving "both imitation (acculturation) and native creation ('indigenization')" (16) with the "blacks giving as much as they received" (17). Indeed, he contends, "our real/apparent imitation involves at the same time a significant element of creativity, while our creativity in turn involves a significant element of imitation" (16). As a result, Brathwaite is equally concerned to underscore the positive contributions made to the process of interculturation by that component of the black population especially which he describes as "the folk" (39), the "orienta-

.tion" towards whom he is, arguably, most favourably disposed. He identifies the "folk" as the "peasants, labourers, illiterates: the majority" (39) who have not only "managed to survive" (30) but, precisely because they are "in most direct line of descent from Africa" (39), also managed to hold "within themselves the potential of a real *Alternative Tradition* since they have successfully replaced the Amerindians as the folk or "little tradition" of the society" (30, my emphasis: the idea of "great" and "little" traditions is one Brathwaite draws from Robert Redfield's *Peasant Society and Culture*: *Development* 213).

Although, Brathwaite laments, the "folk" have since at least Emancipation found themselves "losing ground fast" (30) and, as a result, in "retreat from an Afro- to a kind of Euro-orientated cultural disposition" (30), he is at pains to emphasise that historically, it was the so-called "folk" who were responsible for the fact that a "strong Afro-creole element continued to persist within West Indian society" (31) in several ways: it "expressed itself in the Africanization of Christianity, ...in Garveyism after 1900, in the Rastafari movement (in Jamaica) since the 1930s, the Black Power of the 60s" (31). As Brathwaite points out, these are

> indications (only) of an *African consciousness* in the West Indies, the possibility of *a tradition alternative to the European*. At a deeper, though less articulate level, there is an actual African *presence* in the Caribbean based on a continuous African tradition passing into the present through the period of slavery. (39-40, my emphases)

Brathwaite has in mind in this respect the "continuing African forms of marketing habits, family practices, speech (dialect), magic-medicine (obeah), and religious practices" (31), among others.

In short, Brathwaite stresses, mimicry leads to false/double consciousness rather than that collective consciousness or self awareness which reveals the true nature of one's objective situation and thus identity, as well as induces one consequently to undertake the process of changing an unfair status quo. He blames the "black élite" (308) especially in this regard who "failed, or refused, to make conscious use of their own rich folk culture (their one indisputable possession) and so failed to command the chance of becoming *self-conscious* and *cohesive as a group* and consequently perhaps winning their independence from bondage" (308, my emphases). Brathwaite's point is that it is precisely the folk's location on the margins of Jamaican and West Indian society, however, that has allowed them as a group to maintain a strong bond with Africa and thus to preserve within themselves that flame of self-awareness which only needs to be rekindled

to burn brightly again. It is precisely this vantage-point which, once cultivated, will grant them the ability to "see society as a coherent whole," that
is, to "lay bare the nature of society" and initiate social change. In
Brathwaite's eyes, it is with them that hope for a West Indian future un-
marred by class, racial and other divisions lies.

The question with which Brathwaite concludes *The Development of
Creole Society in Jamaica* is a significant one. He wonders

> whether the society will remain conceived of as "plural"–the histori-
> cal dichotomy becoming the norm–or *whether the process of
> creolisation will be resumed in such a way that the "little" tradi-
> tion of the (ex-)slaves will be able to achieve the kind of articula-
> tion, centrality, prestige and influence–assuming that it is not by
> now too debased–that will provide a basis for creative reconstruc-
> tion.* Such a base, evolving its own residential "great" tradition,
> could well support the development of a *new parochial wholeness*,
> a difficult but possible *creole authenticity*. (311, my emphases)

The choice, he is clear, is between social apartheid and cultural interaction in which the African contribution is given its true weight. He sounds a
similar note in *Contradictory Omens*. Here, assuming that "all societies
ideally move towards norms based upon certain significant core values"
(52), he wonders "what are the norms in our society, or, ...what are the
'cores' from which they might derive" (52) in a multi-racial society such as
the West Indies. The core values which Brathwaite envisages are explicitly
those pertinent to the ex-African majority: he yearns for the "acceptance of
the culture of this black ex-African majority as the paradigm and norm for
the entire society" (30). In much the same way that an ultimately classless
society paradoxically come about only with the rise of the working classes
to social ascendancy, so too, Brathwaite seems to suggest, will only the rise
to ascendancy of the black population usher in a Caribbean society free
from ethnic, racial and other rifts.

For creolisation to turn from tragedy into romance, Brathwaite seems to
say, it must be predicated upon the rise to dominance and the move to
centre stage within Caribbean society of the ex-African majority. For this to
occur, the black segment of the population must grow into self-awareness
or class/race consciousnness. An integral part of this process is the recu-
peration of the "knowledge of ancestral cultures" (61) which only the "folk"
historically kept alive. Gesturing, arguably, to Friedrich Engels's famous
(but controversial) use of corn to illustrate the dialectical process (the ger-
mination of the plant [antithesis] is the negation of the seed [thesis] because
the seed ceases to exist when the plant begins to grow, while the production

of new seeds by the plant is the negation of the negation [synthesis]), Brathwaite expressly advocates that for the black West Indian, the synthetic product of creolisation, to arrive at a properly dialectical self-understanding, a return to cultural "roots" must be undertaken in order to discover the African "thesis" negated by the European "antithesis." Such a "return" is indispensable, Brathwaite writes, because the "virtue of a plant...is in its seed; and however elaborate, and however beautiful a plant might become, it cannot escape its essential beginning–the mysterious , triumphant life that goes on beneath its surface; the origin of all things" (59). For the ex-African majority, a return to the cultural seed from which it springs, Brathwaite asserts, is indispensable. It is this, he contends, which will "take us forward to the definition of our own authentic life/styles and the bodying-forth of 'great' and 'little' traditions from our own milk" (61), traditions that are residential rather than located elsewhere. In this regard, he posits that in the Caribbean there have historically been "two 'great' traditions, one in Europe, the other in Africa," but concludes that "neither was residential." "Normative value-references were [thus] made outside the society," while cultural homogeneity "demands a norm and a *residential* correspondence between the 'great' and 'little' traditions *within* the society" (24, my emphasis).

Brathwaite lauds modern Jamaica which, he feels, is well on the way to bringing the process of creolisation to a successful conclusion: it is, he writes, "in the course of developing a National Tradition by *blending* different *racial geniuses*" (56, my emphases). This is what Brathwaite means by his paradoxical concepts of "parochial wholeness" and "creole authenticity": a national identity necessarily forged out of diversity but in which the African component has attained its rightful and *central* place. Brathwaite's model of creolisation is evidently a paradoxical one, stressing simultaneously both wholeness and parochialness. Perhaps, however, we should bear in mind in this respect Orlando Patterson's distinction between "segmentary" and "synthetic" modes of creolisation. In his view, the synthetic creolisation of thinkers like Wilson Harris "seeks to unite all the different segmentary cultures into a unified national culture; it is, indeed, the dialectical synthesis of the various antithetical segmentary Creole cultures." By contrast, segmentary creolisation, which he associates with thinkers like Brathwaite, "by its very nature, resists such unification" (334). Can wholeness be parochial? Is such a term a contradiction or a paradox? The answer to this question will determine whether Brathwaite is guilty ultimately of lapsing back into dualism or whether his concept of creolisation is truly dialectical.

M. NourbeSe Philip

Upon Considering the Possibility of Friendship Between Tia and Antoinette
(In Progress)

a cheek split
in two wrongs can't
make it right
between history and
a hair-splitting
cheek-splitting
truth

"the cheek of her
taking my dress!"

undressing the theft
the take and took
in history

can't draw blood from
a stone
or a tear
spill the causes
of a cheek
      white
      split
by the hard in stone
the me and she
in black words
on a white page
where a stone lands

the cheek
split by the
hurl
pelt
the fling in stone
in history
        heals
not the heart
smashed ground
in the between of past
and future
        grindstones
exacting a finely
powdered present
to scatter wide
to the winds.

Friends, you say?
Only a stonethrow away.

Caliban's Betrayal:
A New Inquiry into
the Caribbean

Silvio Torres-Saillant

Tout botpipel yo se botpipel
(All boatpeople are boatpeople)
　　　　　(Félix Morisseau-Leroy 149)

Columbian Language and the Trauma

The figure of Caliban remains unrivaled as a signifier of the tensions existing at the core of the human experience in the Caribbean. Though invented
by the Elizabethan William Shakespeare, the Western poet *par excellence*
whom Harold Bloom's feverish fancy has rendered "inventor of the human," Caliban still commands value as a native topos that points to the
epicenter of historical complexity on the Antillean archipelago. Foreign
birth notwithstanding, the figure competes unabashedly with the most genuine of the region's symbols, qualifying unequivocally as a Caribbean "cultural synecdoche" (Palencia Roth 21). It matters little that Bloom should
zealously wish to guard Shakespeare against "mock scholars moaning about
neocolonialism" who have turned Caliban into "an African-Caribbean heroic Freedom Fighter" (Bloom 662-3). Reproaching Caribbean appropriations of Caliban by "despoilers of *The Tempest*," he ridicules their treatments as "not even a weak misreading; anyone who arrives at that view is
simply not interested in reading the play at all. Marxists, multiculturalists,
nouveau historicists–the usual suspects–know their cause but not

Shakespeare's plays" (662). As the cantankerous quality of his dismissal indicates, Bloom's ideological veil enfeebles his vision, hampering his ability to see exactly what kind of use Antillean artists and scholars have made of the Bard's play. Rather than advancing interpretive readings of *The Tempest*, the likes of Aimé Césaire, George Lamming, Roberto Fernández Retamar, and Kamau Brathwaite have mined the text for its rich ore of historically relevant symbols for the Caribbean. The play has lured them because of its wealth of metaphorical possibilities, its payloads of cultural and political paradigms whose deployment can prove enormously fruitful in eliciting the storms and calms that have shaped the Caribbean as a differentiated culture area.

It is Bloom's rabid Eurocentrism, no doubt, that makes him gape in disbelief at the audacity of the so called "despoilers of *The Tempest*" to utilize the priestly Shakespearean text in their Third World disquisitions. Conversely, however, a certain zeal for the cultural authenticity of their symbols may cause Third World spokespersons to deny Caliban the power to connote their reality given the European extraction of the figure. They may also object on the basis of the differential ethnology implicit in the coinage of Caliban's name. We know that Shakespeare made up the name as a near anagram of the word "cannibal," the appellation used by Michel de Montaigne in the essay "On Cannibals," from his famous collection *Essais* (1580), to designate a society of New World natives. A copy of the 1603 English rendition of *Essais* found copiously annotated among Shakespeare's papers indicates that the Bard had indeed read Montaigne's text (Fernández Retamar 17). Certainly, also, in creating the character of Caliban to pose as Prospero's antagonist in *The Tempest*, Shakespeare drew on the ideological baggage that at the time located the New World "savage" in a sort of moral antipodes vis-a-vis the "civilized" Christian, hence the unflattering coarseness displayed by the character in the play.

But one can argue against the objections by Third World voices just as one would against Bloom's. One could contend that, problematic as it may be, the birth of Caliban brings along a fair degree of native authenticity. Montaigne, for instance, did not simply echo the binary relation that assumed a moral dichotomy in the cultural disparity between Christian Europe and the newly conquered territories that had received the name of West Indies. The French sage did not succumb to the enticement of the contrastive ideology then current. With mordant irony, Montaigne took advantage of the distance between the two cultural poles to venture a critical glance at the presumed superiority of sixteenth-century Europe with respect to the people who had fallen in the course of the colonial transaction. His essay did not demonize the indigenous populations of the Americas. Instead, it scoffed at the common practice of every individual to call "barbarism whatever is not his own practice" (Montaigne 152). Montaigne criticized the scornful attitude of Europeans who rushed to place New World natives on a plane morally beneath them, while remaining "so blind to our own faults" (155). In that sense, the French author steered clear of the Columbian tradition that by the sixteenth century had already reified the conquered peoples of the Americas, relegating them ontologically to a sub-human level, stressing their anthropophagy as a salient marker of their identity. Through that denormalizing ideological maneuver, the conquerors established the rationale that justified their domination of the "savage." That thought pattern. served an invaluable function. Used to advantage initially by the Spanish pioneers of the colonial transaction, it warranted the physical violence deployed against the aborigines in each of the lands newly explored and colonized.

By intervening in the Columbian tradition through the creation of a character informed by Montaigne's evocation of New World "cannibals," Shakespeare rendered the Caribbean and Caliban rhetorically inseparable. Columbus inaugurated in his *Diary* the language that gave rise to all subsequent nomenclature to refer to the region and its people. The Diary applies the terms *"caribes"* and *"canibales"* interchangeably to those indigenous populations that most decidedly resisted the voracious encroachment of the Spanish conquerors beginning on 12 October 1492. In due time the stigmatizing web of Columbus's language enveloped a whole archipelago, a region, and the sea that delimited them. The word Caribbean, derived from the name *caribes* which the Admiral used to designate the natives, whom he also called "cannibals," meaning "eaters of human flesh", in time came to refer to the Antillean archipelago along with the coastal zones that mark the boundaries of the region and the sea that sustains the islands. At the end of that discursive cycle the Spaniards had conveniently resolved their labor scarcity to complete the colonial enterprise, as Palencia-Roth has noted (18). Given the undercurrent of genocidal violence that lies at the root of the Columbian nomenclature, one cannot ignore the plea by Colbert Nepaulsingh that urges us to rethink the colonial names for the Caribbean region and its people. Regarding the Columbian terminology as a stumbling block that obstructs efforts to explain the Caribbean as an autonomous culture area, Nepaulsingh emphatically calls upon us to adopt a "new name for the Caribbean." (Nepaulsingh "Things" 14; "New" 5-10). He proposes the term "New World islands," entreating us also to abandon "continental modes of thought" and their attendant view that "continents are by definition superior to islands" (Nepaulsingh "Islands" 8).

Yet, though sharing Nepaulsingh's disquiet about the troubling baggage contained in the Columbian nomenclature, I see a grave risk in any project aimed at correcting colonial misnomers. I believe we need to preserve the erroneous language in so far as it contains clues that preserve the memory of our trauma. Europe's intrusion in the archipelago unleashed a process of naming, renaming, and misnaming whose pugnacity paralleled the military raids on the indigenous populations of the region. I doubt that one could find a sensible way of evading the problematic heritage of the Columbian discourse without seeming to dissemble the Caribbean's inescapable–albeit painful–ties to the West. The effort to liberate the region from the linguistic violence of the colonial transaction might inadvertently privilege too civil a parlance that would lessen the gravity of the archipelago's traumatic history. We cannot epistemologically afford to deflate the harshness of that past, the grim images that stand out as we perform the unsavory act of remembering: Taino women raped, Taino men disemboweled, indigenous temples of worship reduced to ashes by the invader's torch, and countless uprooted Africans doomed permanently to slavery's social death. The existing Columbian vocabulary easily evokes the shock of the Caribbean's beginning with all of its baleful brutality: the cracks of the whip, the hangings, and the compulsory inferiorization included. Through it, we can also better value the actions occasionally taken by the besieged natives, from self-immolation in hopeless battles to running away to the mountains as a means to assert their contested human dignity. The Caribbean as we know it began by undergoing what Brathwaite has termed a counter-Renaissance. Brathwaite uses the term to designate the deplorable dark side of the European Renaissance, a period during which Western capitals witnessed dazzling achievements in sculpture, painting, architecture, and literature while simultaneously exporting death and destruction to peoples overseas.

Understanding the Caribbean past as "a *history* of catastrophe," Brathwaite has advocated a "*literature of catastrophe* to hold a broken mirror up to broken nature" (Brathwaite, "Metaphors"[2] 456-7). Similarly, I would argue for an approach to Caribbean reality that marches head-on toward the epicenter of the trauma as the best way to capture the gist of the human experience in the region and to grab at the crux of the evasive notion of Caribbeanness. A receptacle of good and evil, a crucible of human histories, a confluence of disparate legacies, the Caribbean boasts great originality in cultural expression. But that does not alter the fact that the constituent elements of Caribbean culture correspond to the convergence of distinct heritages that coincided in the region during the conquest and colonization. Africa, Europe, and the aboriginal Americas then and there encountered one another in a dreadful embrace, resulting in torrential blood-shed. The blood that ran fertilized the soil of the islands and the coasts, giving rise to the creolizing process whence the Caribbean would emerge as a new product in the history of human culture. But the advent of that new cultural entity responded primarily to an instigation by Western impe-rial expansionism. Elsewhere I have argued that "the West literally created the Caribbean" following the dynamic unleashed by the conquest starting in the fifteenth century (Torres-Saillant, *Caribbean* 5).

The Amsterdam-based Surinamese author Edgar Cairo stresses the patent form in which the baggage of the past reflects itself daily on the lives of contemporary Caribbean people. His novel *Dat vuur der grote drama's* [That Fire of Great Dramas] (1982) explores the inextricable connection of the Dutch-speaking Antilles and the Netherlands through the centuries. The text dramatizes the difficulty of evading a former colonial life, the legacy of slavery included, whose burden oppresses the individual experience of "each contemporary Caribbean person who has left the colony and settled in the 'mother' country" (Rutgers 551). Of course, recognizing the inter-connection between the metropolis and the colony or former colony should in no way lead to doubts regarding the fundamental difference between the two sites. By no means should one view the Caribbean as a mere cultural extension of the European nations that marshaled the colonial transaction no matter how many points of contact we might identify between here and there. Indeed, when Caribbean thinkers and artists have wished to stress the distinct contours of their identity they have often had recourse to accen-tuating their substratum of difference with respect to the Christian West (Torres-Saillant, *Caribbean* 5).

The phenomena that combined in the region to produce Caribbean cul-ture resulted in a peculiar contraption that harbored two seemingly contra-dictory qualities: inevitable derivativeness and stark authenticity. Similarly, the grievous historical experience that befell the region from 1492 onward, the fractured past that seems to repeat itself *ad infinitum*, has not hindered the Caribbean mind's ability to imagine a restorative future reality. Despite the ethnic and linguistic fragmentation occurring in countries like Suriname, for instance, poets still envision the presence of wholeness. Robin Ewald Raveles (1935-83), who used the *nom de plume* R. Dobru in his writings, rendered in his 1965 poem "Wan bon/Een boom" [One Tree] an evidently willful integrative vision. The speaker in one of the stanzas sees: "One tree/so many leaves/one tree" (Kempen 634). In another stanza, the nature imagery gives way to ethnic signifiers to rephrase the vision of unity "One Suriname/so many hair types/so many skin colors/so many tongues/one people" (Rutgers 548). Hopelessness regarding the region's geographical and historical balkanization has not taken hold of Caribbean thought pervasively.

Even among those who, like the Surinamese poet Henry de Ziel, better known by his pseudonym Trefossa, had to abandon their native soil to find refuge in the metropolis, one finds an adamant affirmation of their world. Trefossa's poem "Kopenhagen" presents us with a speaker beholding the famous Edvard Eriksen statue of a mermaid sitting on a rock. Instead of distracting him from the home country, that European figure is culturally transfigured in his eyes, with the siren turning into the legendary Watermama, the water deity from Suriname's folklore. The first stanza has the bedazzled speaker address the sculpture thus: "what is this by the sea?/ see - see!/ Watermama, is that you sitting on/that stone?" (Trefossa 519). With similar obduracy, an impressive number of voices uphold pan-Caribbean, unitary world-views culturally and otherwise. Themes connected to visions of regional unity recur, for instance, in the English-language writings coming from Saba, St. Eustace, and St. Maarten, the three territories that make up the Dutch Caribbean Windward Islands. (Badejo 679). By the same token, the publication in Sranan Tongo of Brathwaite's poetry volume *Rights of Passage* (1967), translated by D. France Olivieira as *Primisiô* (1997), represents a telling gesture of the prevailing intent to imagine the Caribbean holistically. That the translator should choose to render the text into a vernacular language rather than into Dutch manifests a desire to access the sort of cultural autochthony that Brathwaite himself has explored through his commitment to the search for an authentically Caribbean way of saying (Kempen 642).

Caliban, Contingency, the Caribbean

I subscribe to the use of Caliban as a vehicle via which to delve into the depths of Caribbean life in a manner that unabashedly confronts the tensions, contradictions, and frustrations inherent in the public history of the region. A critical glance at Caliban can enable us to organize a set of themes and variations on Caribbean society's past, present, and future. My use of Caliban as cultural synecdoche for the region will differ from previous treatments in my emphasis on his inconsistencies, which bespeaks a willingness to focus on historical contingency–the accident-prone texture of human events in the region–as a means to apprehend the complexity of the Caribbean experience. I concur with Fernández Retamar's appraisal of the hermeneutic power of Caliban as a metaphor that captures "our cultural situation," but would prefer to restrict its application to the culture area of the Caribbean while he applied it to the whole of Latin American and the Caribbean (30-1). I circumscribe its use to the Antillean zone of the hemisphere because I believe that discrete culture areas warrant their own differentiated symbols, and I would argue that the Caribbean merits a specific understanding in terms of its difference from the Latin American mainland no less than from Europe. This holds true despite the dual identity of the Hispanophone Antilles which simultaneously share the cultural orbits of the archipelago and of the mainland, moving between the poles that Milan Kundera has called "mediating contexts" (48). I myself have examined the Caribbean's distinct contours as a differentiated cultural zone in spite of its inexorable links to Africa, Europe, and Latin America (*Caribbean*). I would add that the relative marginality of Dominican, Puerto Rican, and even Cuban literatures in the panoramic vistas woven by mainland Latin American scholars may have to do with a reticence provoked by the peculiar texture of Caribbean writing. The academics in charge of constructing the Latin American canon may find the texts from the Spanish-speaking islands difficult to accommodate fully in the socioaesthetic and cultural framework that informs their tabulation.

Another reason for limiting the use of Caliban to a symbolization of the Caribbean is the connection of Shakespeare's *The Tempest* to events in the region. Roger Toumson points to a Caribbean news item that reached England in 1609 as one of the catalysts for the Bard's composition of the play. In that year, in the course of an expedition headed for Virginia, a ship that had become separated from the rest of its fleet capsized near the coast of one of the islands forming the Bermudas cluster. The crew members managed to find refuge on the island and several months thereafter succeeded on their own in arriving in Virginia, from where they were sent back to England (Toumson 27-8). Because of the dramatic texture of the incident, whose details resembled the events of a fictional adventure story, the shipwreck fostered abundant literary coverage. The Bermudas occurrence, then, created the context which informed Shakespeare's construction of the plot of *The Tempest*. Textually speaking, therefore, the character of Caliban was born in a Caribbean cradle.

A native of the Caribbean, Caliban accords with the region's reality in the contingent nature of their common trajectory. Caliban's problematic legacy translates, as it were, into a failure of leadership in the archipelago. The present essay posits the working hypothesis that Caliban has lost the fight with his formidable domesticator, Prospero, the awesome magician, having allowed the oblique and sinuous Ariel to confound him. He has also lost the fight against himself, proving incapable of distancing himself from the forces and patterns of conduct that have historically oppressed his people. We can begin to flesh out the foregoing hypothesis by appealing to the prism of the literary imagination to evoke the genesis of things Caribbean.

Skipping the initial arrival of the Admiral on the Amerindian shore, we may go back to a crucial point of origin. The conquest and colonization started in Santo Domingo–or Quisqueya, to honor one of the indigenous names for the island that subsequently became known as Hispaniola. At the incipient Antillean moment, the fleeting instant during which the native Tainos and the invading Spaniards were still equal, skirmishes and more sizable battles took place on the island. But as the unequal relations of force increased their gap, warfare gave way to genocide. Around the year 1513, in the district of Xaragua, one of the five chiefdoms that comprised the political units of the island, the first great massacre took place.

The episode involved the death of queen Anacaona, the widow of Chief Caonabo and sister to the late Behechio, from whom she inherited the rule of Xaragua. Along with her, died the men and women of her court as well as the guests she had convened "to receive, celebrate, and give their reverence to the *Guamiquina* of the Christians" (Bartolomé de Las Casas, cited in Wilson 133). The title *"Guamiquina"*, a Taino word for Lord, referred to the distinguished visitor Governor Fray Nicolas de Ovando, who had given the queen to understand that he came in peace, hence the generous hospitality bestowed upon him and his 300 Spanish soldiers in Xaragua on that fateful day. Then, at one point, after having enjoyed Taino food, drink, entertainment, and cordial conversation, Governor Ovando gave the lethal order. The swift motion of swords, spears, and shields started, and the deafening gunpowder smothered the screams of the astonished natives. Thus did violence put an end to Spanish-Indian communication. The mass murder perpetrated by Ovando's troops inaugurated the tradition of silencing the interlocutor to the advantage of monologic expression. In so far as "Xaragua was the last stronghold of pre-Hispanic power on Hispaniola," its genocidal destruction meant the completion of a context wherein the word would only command respect when uttered by the voice of the masters (Wilson 134).

In 1880, poet and educator Salome Ureña de Henríquez, the reputed founding mother of Dominican poetry, published the long narrative poem *Anacaona* to commemorate the courage of the martyred queen and pay tribute to the human dignity of the Tainos who fell victim to the gory onslaught of the "strange visitors/whom the sea hurled on the island's shore" (Ureña 185). Narrated in the third person and aiming for epic loftiness in content and diction, the text celebrates the spirit of resistance attributable to the indigenous population while lamenting the loss of the edenic world that the Spanish fractured upon their arrival in 1492. Ironically, Ureña felt too deep a sense of kinship with the Hispanic heritage that nineteenth-century Dominican society boasted to launch a really radical indictment of

Spanish violence. A mulatto who occupied a place of distinction among the country's literati, she harbored too much admiration for Spain's legacy in the New World to take issue with the colonial transaction systemically. The poem depicts the carnage of Xaragua as a deviation. Anacaona and her people die on account of the individual iniquity of Governor Ovando. Other than such isolated instances of misconduct, the Spanish retain their essential goodness. The noble spirit of Columbus remains unaltered throughout the poem. To maintain this portrayal, Ureña had to overlook the historical fact that the Admiral himself had unleashed grievous violence against the Tainos prior to the Xaragua killings. Columbian violence explained the death of Caonabo and Anacoana's widowhood. But the poet insists in exalting the "discoverer." Witness the unfavorable picture she draws of Columbus's squire Francisco Roldán Ximeno, who led a rebellion against his boss to demand a greater share of the gains amassed by the island's authorities from the colonial enterprise. A pertinent stanza in the poem says: "Infamous Roldán who withheld from Columbus / the tribute of love and respect that was due him / furiously raising his seditious voice / marshaled his troops in baneful revolt / with the myriad tedious turmoil that followed breaking the hear of the great Genoese" (Ureña 234).

As an ideological, historical, and literary counterpoint, nearly a century after the text by Ureña appeared, the Haitian poet Jean Métellus published his dramatic poem *Anacaona* (1986), which offers an alternative evocation of the Taino queen and the devastation of Xaragua. As one would expect, Métellus updates the historical content of the poem. The text represents Ovando's treacherous slaughter as an action consistent with the political and economic logic of the conquest rather than as a deviation stemming from the moral deformity of an individual functionary. We gather from the poem that the destruction of Xaragua occurred because the Spanish authorities wished to avert the possible alliance between the two ethnic groups that shared the common brunt of colonial subjection on the island. Métellus has Governor Ovando warn that "Ce serait une catastrophe si jamais se / produisait la moindre collusion entre / Indien et Nègres." The Spanish commander moans over the frequency with which black slaves have already escaped to the mountains and their ensuing hostility against the colonial regime (150). Conversely, the Taino queen is aware of the condition of blacks on the island and voices her solidarity with their cause. Whether or not the historical Anacaona may have known about blacks, the awareness that Métellus gives her is consistent with the demands of verisimilitude. For blacks had arrived in Santo Domingo in July 1502, in the same fleet that brought Ovando as Governor of the island, when the Catholic monarchs Ferdinand and Isabella gave him the rule of their first colony in the western hemisphere. Also, within a year of their arrival, black slaves had begun to run away to the mountains and to interact with the Indians, much to the chagrin of Governor Ovando (Deive 20). The inter-ethnic solidarity that Métellus assigns to the character of Anacaona, then, has a measure of historical plausibility. Shortly before the queen dies, she expresses the wish that she could add to her glory the title of "Champion of the black and Indian maroons" (Métellus 155).

While Ureña nostalgically recreates in her text the memory of a lost world, Métellus seeks to infuse the events of Xaragua with the genesis of a legacy of resistance against colonial oppression in the Caribbean. The Dominican poet in that sense looked solely to the past while the Haitian poet has his eyes set on the future. The closing lines of Métellus's poem allude clearly to the insurrections that Indians and blacks would subsequently embark upon in their quest to shake off the chains of their subjection. The character of Yaquimex, who acts as a sort of collective conscience of the Taino community, announces his people's determination to "head for Bahoruco," reach the mountaintops where their "African brothers" have already gone, and launch from there their common offensive against "these monsters ejected by the sea" (154, 156, 158). They thus will avenge the deaths of their queen and their compatriots. The poem's ending, charged with righteous emotion and anticipating coming liberation struggles, makes for a pervasive optimistic outlook. The last two lines "L'Afrique est venue / Aya bombe, Aya bombe" (Africa is here / Better dead than slave), would seem to connect this moment of potential insurgency with the black slave rebellion that almost three centuries later would dismantle the French colonial structure in Saint Domingue.

No doubt Ureña sins from ideological naiveté in her problematic intent to repudiate the Xaragua massacre without condemning the political and economic project that informed the conquest and colonization of Quisqueya by the Spanish. However, despite enjoying access to the added perspectives afforded by the fact that he wrote almost a century later, Métellus sins no less woefully in so far as he succumbs to the temptation to evoke the history he would have liked rather than the one that actually happened. The sad historical fact is that the genocidal action perpetrated by Ovando did not trigger a movement that would subsequently advance the cause of equality and justice. History did not register the revolutionary virtues that the poem wishes to attribute to the descendants of the Xaragua victims. Just as Ureña's late nineteenth-century poem misrepresented historical data to flatter Columbus, Prospero's progenitor, so Métellus's late twentieth-century poem misrepresented the known facts to flatter the Taino leadership, ancestors of Caliban. An uprising did occur in the mountains of Bahoruco around 1519 led by the young warrior Guarocuya, a member of the conquered Taino nobility. But that insurrection had hardly a glorious outcome. The event did not bequeath a legacy that could inspire subsequent freedom fighters in the Caribbean.

For many generations, Guarocuya, better known as Enriquillo, a diminutive of his Christian name Enrique, has enjoyed great prestige in the historiography of Hispanola. The Dominican author Manuel de Jesus Galván, in a novel entitled *Enriguillo: Novela histórica* (1882), which became a classic of *indigenista* literature in Latin America, almost singlehandedly established the tradition that venerates Guarocuya as a heroic standard-bearer of equality and justice. Haitian schoolbooks also subscribed to the historiographical lore that celebrated "le cacique Henri" as a "vaillant défenseur de sa race opprimée" whose "tenacité avait triomphé de l'injustice" (Dorsainvil 24, 26). But the outcome of the Bahoruco rebellion would not seem to justify the apotheosis of Enriquillo.

One should note that Galván's novel, like the poem by Ureña, manages to extol Guarocuya's armed struggle against the colonial authorities without challenging the *raison d'être* of the conquest itself. His text also explains the injustices that the Tainos fought against as caused by isolated acts of cruelty committed by individual Spaniards. The venerable José Martí, who sang the book's praises in a letter to the author that editors have conventionally used as a prologue in the successive reprints of the novel, failed to catch the insidious duplicity that informed Galván's evocation of the Bahoruco rebellion. We owe to the Dominican poet and historian Pedro Mir an interpretation of Guarocuya's story that sets the record straight.

The second chapter of Mir's *Tres leyendas de colores* explores the Taino leader's trajectory from his early upbringing as the protege of a Spanish landowner named Valenzuela, who nurtured him and saw to his education in a Franciscan convent. Baptized with the Christian name Enrique, he received the socialization befitting a Spanish lad (Mir 130). The death of his good master Valenzuela, whose heir treated Enriquillo with contempt and removed the privileges he had previously enjoyed, awakened the young Taino to the lugubrious plight of his people. In time he led a band of native insurgents to the mountains of Bahoruco, starting an insurrection that for fifteen years the colonial regime could not defeat. Mir minimizes the personal nature of Enriquillo's grievance, reasoning that whatever its catalyst the young warrior's action ceased to be personal once his community validated his leadership, putting their lives on the line in order to advance the cause he had articulated for them (Mir 145). However, Enriquillo proved unworthy of that trust. He lacked the moral mettle of authentic leadership. When the Spanish authorities, whom he had defeated militarily, sent as emissary the spiritual guide who had instructed him in the Catechism as a child, he could not resist. The religious offensive was too formidable, and shortly thereafter he brought his troops down from the mountains, the Spanish having offered to restore his social privileges, including the added distinction of addressing him thenceforward as Don Enrique. The prodigal son of the colonial regime then signed an infamous peace treaty whereby his mighty guerrilla forces would from then on employ their martial adroitness in the service of the Spanish power structure. Their service included pursuing other insurgents who challenged the colonial regime and capturing runaway black slaves at a *per capita* price (Mir 156).

Viewed through the prism of the Shakespearean triad, Enriquillo's political inconsistency follows these stages. A momentary loss of privilege brought him into opposition to Prospero, causing him to locate himself in the role of the dissenting native, namely Caliban. But, Hispanized and Christianized by an earlier socialization, his instincts placed him closer to the sensitivity of Ariel. The Ariel that informed his neutralized conscience got the best of him. As soon as Prospero restored his blessing, the Taino chief quickly gave in to the allurement of his former privileged condition. Yet, the chameleon-like nature of his trajectory did not disqualify him for the heroism ascribed to him in the history textbooks. Mir express no surprise at the glorification of Enriquillo, which even today holds sway over the national imaginary in Dominican society. Deconstructing Galván's psychopathology, Mir understands that the architects of official Dominican discourse elevated the Taino chieftain as an immaculate symbol of Dominican nationality because of their own ideology and class positioning. Simply put, a historian or a novelist with Ariel's mentality will most likely identify with the Ariels of the past. For instance, Galván's glorification of Enriquillo perfectly matched his support of the 1861 annexation of the Dominican Republic to the Spanish crown. He belonged to an entrenched creole oligarchy that was willing to exchange their nation's sovereignty for the preservation of their social privilege. As Mir has succinctly put it, Galván was a modern-day Enriquillo (Torres-Saillant, *Caribbean* 166).

Anatomy of Disillusionment

The Haitian poet Georges Sylvain (1866-1925) once characterized the historical experience of his people in a manner applying equally well to the Dominican side of the island. He spoke of a recurring pattern consisting of a series of "exultations of popular sentiment, [which] then change, with every new leadership that rises to power, from the most ecstatic effusion of hope to the most hopeless disillusionment" (Sylvain 14). One would concur that the pattern describes the history of Hispaniola beginning with

Enriquillo's disappointing performance when he rose to power. A glance at the present would suggest that the pattern has proven enduring. The case of Dessalines reveals a history of liberation that culminates in authoritarian rule. Incontestably heroic as leader of the anti-colonialist revolt of the Saint Domingue slaves and subsequent founder of the Haitian Republic, Dessalines also inaugurated the native tradition of Caribbean dictatorship. Abusing his power and showing a flair for cruelty, he implemented a development model that in many respects replicated the slave economy that the uprising had come to dismantle. He also proclaimed himself emperor. The painter Édouard Duval Carrie delves into the irony of that history in his work "Le Nouveau Familier," a portrait of Dessalines who appears sitting with his legs vulgarly spread. He wears the eerie black spectacles that became a trademark of the Tonton Macoutes, the paramilitary terrorist band that Duvalier employed to maintain all dissidence in check. Carrie's portrait painfully connects Duvalier to Dessalines, drawing a long line of dictatorial kinship.

Henry Christophe, another great hero of Haiti's revolutionary saga, reached the pinnacle of the grotesque in uncritically aping the luxuriousness and pomp of European courts. Having come to power in 1806 as chief of the North, when Dessalines died and the government bifurcated, with the South going under the command of the mulatto Alexandre Pétion, Christophe crowned himself king in 1811. This black leader of the Revolution did not hesitate to commit atrocities against his people, whose condition resembled their previous slavery. According to General Pamphile de Lacroix, who at the time authored a report on Haiti for presentation to Napoleon Bonaparte, under Christophe's rule farm workers could not leave the area designated for their labor without a written authorization from their foreman (Lacroix 411). Though far less picturesque than Christophe, Pétion had no lack of authoritarian flair. Declaring himself President-for-life, he invested himself unreasonably in the pursuit of French approval. He consented to an arrangement whereby Haiti would pledge to indemnify French planters for the loss of their plantations and their privilege in the course of the slave uprising that culminated in the new country's independence. France would receive compensation also for the expenses incurred in sending troops to Saint Dominque to try to defeat the insurgents and preserve the slave economy (Nicholls 51). The subsequent government led by Jean Pierre Boyer reunified North and South under one rule and marched on the Spanish-speaking side of the island to bring the whole of Hispaniola under one sole juridical order, with Port-au-Prince as its seat of government. Boyer's unification scheme was initially well received when it occurred in 1822, but the financial debt to the French that his administration had inherited from Pétion led him to implement unpopular and unreasonable fund-raising measures that hurt the commercial class of Santo Domingo. A separation movement emerged that succeeded in rallying widespread support for their cause, which materialized in the declaration of Dominican independence in 1844 (Moya Pons, *Dominación* 38, 45).

One should not ignore implications of the fact that Boyer, like Pétion, arrived in Hispaniola from France to fight the insurgents and return them to abject slavery. They both came as French soldiers with the invading army commanded by General Leclerc against the black rebels. Lacroix's report to Napoleon contained a profile of Boyer describing him as a "visceral enemy of Toussaint's regime", as a "good Frenchman," and someone capable of playing a crucial role "as intermediary in the advances that we might make to the rebels" (Lacroix 390). Ironically, despite the circumstances of their arrival in Saint Domingue, Boyer and Pétion moved in time to occupy positions of power as leaders of the people whose desire for freedom they came to crush. Here we see another pattern that recurs in the Caribbean, whose political history often provides a stage for Ariel's ubiquity to put on its show. We see myriad political turncoats relishing the embrace of God and the devil. Their type recurs in Caribbean history more often than Fernández Retamar's *Caliban* acknowledges. On the Dominican side, Buenaventura Báez and Máximo Gómez come to mind. Both served as officers of her Majesty the Queen of Spain and fought Dominican nationalists from 1861 to 1865, a period when the Spanish army invaded the Dominican Republic to consolidate the Caribbean country's annexation to the Madrid government after a creole oligarchy surrendered their nation's sovereignty to its former colonial master. The Spanish empire gave Báez the title of Field Marshall for his service fighting the patriots who took up arms against the invaders and their creole allies. However, no sooner had the Dominican nationalist forces won the war for the restoration of independence than Báez had made himself palatable to compete in the political arena as a presidential candidate, reaching his goal in less than three years. Gómez, for his part, remained as a soldier of the Crown till the end and had to leave Dominican soil when the nationalists won, landing in Cuba, which still lived under Spanish colonial rule. There he experienced a change of heart. He identified with the Cuban struggle for independence, joining the nationalist forces against Spain and achieving distinction as a commander of the liberation army. For many, his services rendered to the anticolonialist struggle in Cuba erase his annexationist record in his home country. But I will contend that letting the two facets of Gómez's public history stand side by side, unreconciled and unresolved, can put us in closer contact with the pervasive contingency of human events in the Caribbean.

The foregoing discussion points to only a few of the memorable cases of turncoats, conflicting legacies, antipopular leaders of the people that crowd Caribbean history. Caribbean leaderships, with an acute case of moral ambivalence, make Caliban suspect. Evoked as symbol of the leader in the region, Caliban exhibits multiformity and a series of mutations so rapid that none can predict the ideological path he will take. Caliban has worn the trappings of Ariel at times and appeared indistinguishable from Prospero at other times. Nor has race or class origin mattered much to explain his conduct. Blacks, mulattos, and whites have acted alike, in keeping with the legacy of the Indian Enriquillo. Similarly, those coming from the gutter have no less misconduct to their credit than the offspring of privilege. The Haitian Faustin Élie Soulouque, who proclaimed himself emperor, and the Dominican Ulises Hureaux, who ruled tyrannically for over fifteen years, both shared blackness and humble origins. Yet, they exhibited neither less corruption nor greater regard for the well-being of the oppressed masses of their countries than their well-to-do and light-skinned counterparts.

The best known twentieth-century tyrants from Hispaniola, the Dominican Trujillo and the Haitian Duvalier, came from deprived backgrounds. Yet they perpetrated the most odious regimes against their compatriots. Rarely in human history have rulers displayed greater depravity in trampling the bodies and souls of their people than they did in their prolonged dictatorships. Duvalier attained popular appeal by offering himself as champion of black Haitian culture. But his branch of negritude soon revealed itself as nothing but "an Antillean form of Fascism, a totalitarian neo-racism whose main victims [were] the millions of black peasants and black workers of Haiti" (Depestre, *Pour* 69). Trujillo, for his part, was the grandson of Ercina Chevalier, a Haitian woman who had settled on the Dominican side of the island. However, he ordered a horrendous massacre of Haitian migrant workers at the border in October 1937 and his government made rabid anti-Haitianism a prominent feature of official discourse on Dominican identity. Duvalier and Trujillo illustrate the gamut of contradictions and inconsistencies that the history of leadership–cultural and political–presents us with in the Caribbean. Caliban has changed colors, exchanged allegiances, and changed his mind too often for one to tell his story in a smooth, forward-looking narrative. His Protean behavior makes him difficult to place, leaving the observer at a loss for race, ideology, or class signs that could help to make an intelligent guess regarding what his next step will be.

Homo Migrans

As a concrete, glaring, and deplorable result of Caliban's problematic legacy, the contemporary Caribbean, often the site of economic injustice, political oppression and corruption, has large portions of the population reduced to poverty and helpless neglect. No wonder that emigration has become the strategy par excellence for people to wrestle with the demands of survival. Leaving the archipelago has become a norm. The speaker in the poem "Nabel String" by Merle Collins suggests that people leave "because things not so good / and something better is always somewhere else." The former Haitian Ambassador to Washington Jean Casimir describes the current historical moment in the region as one in which "the whole population savors expectantly the opportunity to migrate to the rich countries. Migration is probably the only survival strategy shared by all social groups. No government seems capable of arresting the current depopulation and, at the same time, sustaining, directing, or accelerating social change internally" (Casimir 257). One could argue that Caliban, though sharing responsibility for the decline of contemporary Caribbean societies, has also suffered destitution. This view would advise us to look for Caliban not only among leaderships controlling power structures but also among the downtrodden who leave their homelands in order to secure their material well-being. Victim as well as victimizer, Caliban heads the inefficient and perverse State that has made almost every Caribbean country dependent on tourism–the economy of sand, sun, and sex that has virtually replaced agricultural production–while he also wears the pained countenance of the expelled, the excess workers who venture across the ocean in pursuit of receding job markets. In other words, the desperate passengers of Haitian "boats," Dominican "yolas," and Cuban "balsas" who regularly defy the dangers of the unharvested sea for a chance at a decent life represent the other face of Caliban. I would contend that in that fact lies the Caribbean's greatest repository of hope. As the experience of the diaspora may foster a new kind of agency, Caliban is likely to undergo a sort of spiritual rebirth that might put him on the path to a restorative future.

The title story in the collection by Ana Lydia Vega entitled *Encancaranublado* has three archetypal characters representing distinct Caribbean national experiences. The three end up sharing a fragile boat in the middle of the ocean. A Haitian man named Antenor, seeking to escape his country's asphyxiating poverty, has put to sea in a fragile skiff that seems unlikely to withstand the severe movements of the waves and the long journey on his way to Miami, Florida. He has no reason to look back: "The putrid mangoes, emblems of diarrhea and famine, the war cries of the macoutes, the fear, the drought–it's all behind him now. Nausea and the threat of thirst once the meager water supply runs out–this is the here and now. For all its menace, this miserable adventure at sea is like a pleasure cruise compared to his memories of the island" ("Cloud" 1). From out of nowhere come the Dominican Diógenes and the Cuban Carmelo to join Antenor's eerie voyage. Their common wretchedness induces a sense of circumstantial solidarity, which subsequently withers as they begin to taunt one another recalling national antipathies from their fractious Caribbean historical experience. Their ventilating feelings coming from their insidious legacies escalates to near-physical aggression, causing their boat to capsize. Just before they are to fall to their deaths out of the boat, a U.S. ship comes to their rescue. Once under the protection of an American captain, "Aryan and Apollonian," our three Antilleans receive instructions from the mouth of a fellow Caribbean, a Puerto Rican sailor member of the crew, who reminds them that in order to eat they would have to work "and I mean work hard. A gringo don't give anything away. Not to his own mother" ("Cloud" 6). Evidently an allegory of the plight of contemporary Caribbeans, the story presents us with the dark side of transnational mobility from the islands, an ironic realization of the Antillean Federation gone awry. Haiti, the Dominican Republic, and Cuba meet Puerto Rico on the American ship. They share a common dependency on and a common subservience to the United States. They also share the compulsion to leave home to ensure their material survival.

Another story from the same collection by Vega, "El día de los hechos" depicts a possible outcome of the legacy of animosity between Haitians and Dominicans once they meet in the diaspora. The Dominican emigré in Puerto Rico Filemón Sagredo loses his life at the hand of his Haitian nemesis Félicien Apolon, who has tracked him down in the neighboring island to avenge an age-old offense. The fatal resolution of Félicien shooting Filemon brings closure to several generations of conflicts between their respective families in a feud nurtured by a long history of Haitian-Dominican tensions (*Encancaranublado* 21-7). The events related in the story suggest the possibility that the inter-ethnic conflicts that have hampered regional cohesion at home might follow Caribbean migrants abroad to the detriment of unitary projects in the diaspora. However, the alternative outcome appears no less plausible. Something in the shared uprooting of Haitians and Dominicans who must leave home for a chance to dream would seem most conducive to stimulating pan-Caribbean solidarity. The majority of Haitians residing in the United States arrived after 1957, during the repressive regimes of Papa Doc Duvalier and his son Jean-Claude. The combination of factors that propelled their emigration included political persecution, administrative corruption that resulted in a continuous decline in the quality of life, and the progressive deterioration of the national economy (Laguerre 21).

Concomitantly, the massive exodus of Dominicans began in the 1960s, following the death of Trujillo, whose firm control of foreign travel by Dominican nationals had kept the number of emigrants low. A military coup against a democratically elected president, a popular armed uprising to restore the constitutional order, and a U.S. invasion later, Joaquín Balaguer, who was serving as puppet President when Trujillo died, returned to power as president of the Republic on 1 June 1966. Balaguer not only resorted to unrestrained political repression, murdering and incarcerating most prominent dissidents, but his regime also embraced economic policies that restructured the job market, displacing low-skill urban workers and farmers. For economic and political reasons, then, leaving home became the thing to do for Dominicans who could. Also contributing to fuel the instinct to escape was the prevailing sense of hopelessness that dominated the country. How could the people hope in light of the bitter fact that, despite the struggle, the sacrifice, the many lives lost for the cause of freedom and equality, the Trujillo power structure had returned with the backing of the United States and wearing the guise of democracy. Then came too the 1965 immigration law which increased the number of Caribbean migrants who could enter the United States every year. That combination of push and pull factors catapulted Dominicans massively to the North American mainland, triggering a migratory flow that has continued unabated (Torres-Saillant and Hernández 30-1).

Dominicans and Haitians represent the epitome of the condition that the contemporary Caribbean person faces: a scenario where compulsory exile shapes the people's visions of tomorrow. The Haitian creole poet Félix Morisseau-Leroy has evoked that fateful predicament in the poem "Botpipèl," which dramatizes his people's compulsion to leave home: "We are all in a drowning boat / it happened before in St. Domingue / We are the ones they call boat people /...We set out in search of jobs and freedom/ Piled on cargo boats–direct to Miami / They began calling us boat people" (Morisseau-Leroy 149). One of the poem's closing stanzas stresses the equalizing force of diasporic uprooting: "We don't raise our voices or scream / But all boat people are equal, the same / All boat people are boat people" (149). The scenario Morrisseau-Leroy evokes, discrete national specificities notwithstanding, also describes the plight of Cuban *balseros*, Dominican *yoleros*, and all others for whom staying in the native land has become hazardous to their well-being. Occupying the space of the diaspora has not come without a measure of ontological discomfort, stemming most likely from the sense that one has lost a homeland without necessarily gaining another. The listless, circular, transnational mobility that many scholars have been pastoralizing since the 1990s may in the Caribbean case result from this ontological discomfort. Luis Rafael Sánchez has explored the Puerto Rican side of the phenomenon in his often quoted, lyrical essay "The Flying Bus." The easy travel between here and there–which because of modern aeronautics Puerto Ricans can now experience the Atlantic Ocean as a "blue pond"-- paradoxically points to a split with potentially sad consequences (Sánchez 24). The flight between New York and San Juan provides Sánchez with a stage that displays much of the angst of his people's national condition: "Puerto Ricans who cannot breathe in Puerto Rico but catch a lung-full in New York can achieve a ballpark average of four hundred.... Puerto Ricans who want to be there but must remain here.... Puerto Ricans who live there and dream about being here"(24). The essay's closing sentence succinctly describes the predicament evoked here, namely "the relentless flow of a people who float between two ports, licensed for the smuggling of human hopes" (25).

But irrespective of how one construes the psychology and existential drama behind the back and forth mobility that Sánchez investigates in his essay, all Caribbeans must deal with the fact of having to trade home for elsewhere. The responsibility for the compulsory dispersion, we have said, falls partly on the shoulders of a leadership that the governed have neglected to hold accountable. The above cited poem by Merle Collins suggests a sort of suicidal leniency on the part of the people who have to leave: "Because the landless somehow becoming / more landless yet but still loving / some leader because of a memory" (91). They leave grumblingly, though. They resent their virtual banishment. They continue to hurt on account of the homeland. Their emotional attachment to their native soil, exacerbated by the hostility that might meet them in the receiving society, may induce in them an ambivalent state of mind regarding the here and there dialectic. The Surinamese writer Astrid H. Roemer has articulated one of the manifestations of the ambivalence in a passage from her book *Nergens ergens* (Nowhere, somewhere, 1983): "I have a love-hate relationship with Suriname. Hate because history shows how I ended up here. My ancestors were dragged here by force and emigrated under false pretenses. They suffered and never bequeathed Suriname as their native country to their offspring...yet I love Suriname because I was born there...Holland's material wealth was gained partly at the expense of my native land. After five generations of legitimate oppression I have the right to choose to which country I belong. I have chosen Holland, even though Holland has not chosen me" (Rutgers 552).

We cannot lose sight of the salutary potential inherent in the ontological discomfort of Caribbean emigrants. The awareness that their compulsory exile, and the grievous suffering therein, occurred on account of the ineptitude and indignity of their homeland ruling elites makes them judgmental and vigilant about their history and culture. The diasporic experience induces a desire to supervize Caliban, scrutinize his behavior, control the quality of his service, reward and censure him according to dessert. The diasporic experience gives Caliban himself a second chance to think through his career and seek to repair the damage. As a site of ontological renewal, the diaspora may bring about a change of direction in the history of Caribbean leadership while the governed accept their responsibility to hold the leaders accountable. The Caribbean diaspora, in putting legacies under the lens, may sponsor the overhaul of official nationalist discourses and fraudulent patriotisms encouraged by entrenched ruling elites. The logic born of the diasporic experience may create conditions in which the denouement of Ana Lydia Vega's "El día de los hechos" would seem inconceivable. At the level of popular culture, for instance, we see the opposite trend. Diverse groups from the English-speaking West Indies, where the politically unifying West Indian Federation project failed miserably, have managed to privilege regional over national interests in their joint celebration of Carnival. Currently over forty U.S. cities have Carnival celebrations that stress regional symbols, suggesting a meaningful "potential of Caribbean unity and identity" (Belcom 191). Referring to the most famous Carnival celebration, the one held on Labor Day in Brooklyn, New York, sociologist Patricia Belcom says that "On Eastern Parkway there are no Jamaicans, no Bajans, no Trinidadians–we are all 'Caribbeans.' We benefit from our solidarity as we learn to leave parochial squabbles behind" (193).

Caliban Reformed: A Vision of the Future

History is the story of things that actually happened irrespective of how unsavory the results may have been for us. We may frown at the unfavorable outcome for us of particular past events. But we cannot change what actually was. Our power lies in the ability to change our understanding of things past with an eye on affecting the future. When we identify past wrongs and wrongdoers we might learn enough to promote behavioral modifications in the present so as perhaps to promote a restorative future, hence the belief that by updating our understanding of Caribbean traumas through the examination of failed native leadership we may reach the point of stimulating improvement and making hope tenable. The Caribbean imagination, empowered by the experience and the learning of its diaspora, can chart new historical ground. By essaying new–albeit painful–interpretations of the culture and history underlying the present state of affairs in the region (not by merely coining neologistic vocabularies nor wielding new tropes to signal familiar knowledge), Caribbean discourse has a chance to restore cultural self-confidence and historical possibility. But a truly new inquiry into Caribbean history and culture necessitates a measure of intellectual disruption. Problematizing the familiar metaphors and tropes to penetrate the core of the trauma in the history and culture of the region presupposes a willingness to dissect the ideologies and myths that have dominated analysis of the human experience in the archipelago. The focus on Caliban's ideological duplicity and moral deformity along with his legacy of insurrection and resistance accords with that willingness.

The idea here is that Caribbean discourse should become emancipated just as Caliban in repairing his historical misconduct ought to overcome his ontological dependency. With excessive and lethal frequency, Caliban has justified himself by simply brandishing his opposition to Prospero. Proclaiming his difference with respect to his former master has mattered more than showing virtues of his own. Needless to say, he has often failed even at that meager feat. But on the whole, he has hardly needed to show concrete proof of his commitment to the well-being of his society. Nor has he suffered the consequences of his dereliction of duty or even his crime. The Caribbean has a long history of impunity for leaders who commit atrocities and then leave power. A list focusing solely on Hispaniola would include the Trujillo family, Balaguer, Jean Claude Duvalier, and Raoul Cedras. Unlike the other three, Balaguer has not even needed to abandon the scene of his crime. After his initial escape from the Dominican Republic following the death of Trujillo in 1961, he came back shortly thereafter, gaining the presidency in 1966. Neither the thousands of political murders committed by his regime between 1966 and 1978, nor the corruption of his governments up to 1996, nor his complicity with the genocide of Haitians at the border when he served as henchman of the dictatorship have caused him any discomfort.

The thought that he will have to pay for his wrong-doing can orient the actions of the new Caliban. The vigilance of the governed would help to keep him honest. Aware that the oppositional stance with respect to Prospero will not suffice, he would have to make a more creative, more genuine, greater effort to individuate his worth. Concomitantly, intellectual production around historical development and cultural identity would do well to pay heed to Brathwaite's proposal beginning over fifteen years ago when he posited an alternative model of Caribbean self-definition. Drawing on the Shakespearean paradigms, Brathwaite summoned Caliban to delve deeply into the realm of his own self in search of native roots. That descent into self, Brathwaite contended, could give Caliban access to the subterranean plane where his mother Sycorax lies buried. Addressing the matter of Caliban's derivative, oppositional, and therefore dependent ontology, Brathwaite speculates that if instead of learning to "curse" Prospero in the master's own language, Caliban "had listened to his mother's voice; if he could speak her [sic] in their *language* / He might have had a better chance when the chance for revolt came his way" ("Caribbean Culture" 35). Sycorax does not appear as a physical presence in Shakespeare's text and to Brathwaite that invisibility suggests further symbolism. In other words, her absence has protected her resources, which remain submerged as historical subtext and cultural potentiality (*Colonial Encounter* 44). To reach his mother, to reap the benefit of a legacy that because of its long concealment has managed to preserved its vitality, he has to reconnect with the autochthonous heritage of his land.

Consistent with Brathwaite's instructions to assist in the rehabilitation of the leader in the archipelago, the intellectual discourse that follows Caliban's trajectory as cultural synecdoche of the Caribbean might enhance its focus on the wavy course described by his career. As the foregoing pages insistently highlight, Caribbean history, as encapsulated in the fluctuation of agents and events, follows a zigzag path that defies the narrative logic discernable in the teleology of either Hegelian or Marxist dialectics. Brathwaite's alternative paradigms would seem to contribute an analytical model capable of accounting for the Caribbean's fluctuating pattern of mobility and unassailable careers of the leadership. In 1990 father Jean-Bertrand Aristide–Titid to the people–rose to visibility in Haiti with a message of justice and equality, illuminating Haitian society as a beacon of hope. Today, a coup d'état having overthrown him and a U.S. invasion having restored him, he has lost his shine and possibly his moral rectitude, as reports of his huge mansion and spectacular land acquisitions suggest. On the other side of the island, events have taken a no less magical turn. Ninety three-year-old Balaguer, blind and hardly able to walk, with a record of murder and corruption that few organized crime clans could equal, not only holds in his hands enough power to decide political elections in the country but in September 1997 was proclaimed by the multipartisan legislature of the Dominican Congress "Great Builder of Dominican Democracy." The year before, Balaguer, representing the Trujillo oligarchy, held hands with Juan Bosch, a reputed democrat who had opposed Trujillo and Balaguer, flanked by young political leaders whom the dictator and his heir had rendered orphans and widows, standing next to the military chiefs who had killed their parents and their spouses, forging an alliance called "Patriotic Front," to bring Leonel Fernández, candidate of the Dominican Liberation Party, to the presidency of the country, and block the most popular leader in the race, José Francisco Peña Gómez, who had Haitian ancestry. Such sinuous history, which reads like experimental fiction, needs a method that can fit the unexplainable, the unsavory, the horrific.

Brathwaite has proposed the notion of *tidalectics*, a theoretically alluring paradigm promising to account for the uncanny, for trauma, and stasis, for hope and catastrophe in the archipelago. Tidalectics accords with the wavy movement of Caribbean events, the dialectics of the tides, "the movement of the water backwards and forwards as a kind of cyclic, I suppose, motion, rather than linear" (Mackey, "Interview" 44). Conceived from the perspective of a centripetal approach to the philosophy of history of the Caribbean, detached from Western teleological inexorability, Brathwaite's *tidalectics* avoids simplification and distortion. Perhaps here the complexities of the human experience in the region have found the autochthonous paradigm they needed. Constructed from a Caribbean positionality, the model provides the porous framework required to assess the seemingly contradictory ordering of events in the region. Tidalectics can perhaps help to harmonize the hallucinating Haitian-Dominican rapport in Hispaniola, thus pointing to the possibility that we might confidently tackle the development of a coherent and believable theory of Caribbean unity in history and letters. Should we find the fit between the two contrasting narratives on both sides of Hispaniola, the foundation for a pan-Caribbean vision of wholeness will have been promisingly laid.

Three Poems

Honor Ford-Smith

The Theif

The orange sun is hovering
over the Old Hope Road

I am chasing a child in the twilight.
he has stolen my day's work
my tape recorded histories
my informants lives, my critical questions
and the harvest of their answers.

I am chasing the child in a car fast fast
and the child is outrunning the car.
A crowdapeople is coming behind.
Quietly. There is only the song
of the car engine and the drumming
of their angry feet.

He knows he will be killed.
He is running for his life.
My heart is beating to see an ending
I have read before in **The Star**
"Theif beaten to death by citizens."

Behind the nun's lodgings
the empty chapel, the open school room
he is racing, devil's horsewhip
whipping his legs. And I
want him to escape, but

I can't leave the chase.
There is blood in my throat
and salt on my tongue.

Ahead the gully spins its keloid cells
between mansion and shack.
It opens like an old sore sprouting blooms
of callalloo, pumpkin, ganja and peas.
Spreading his thin arms, the boy jumps
into the darkening gully leaving the recorder,
its tape intact, enfolded in the dry bush at the edge.

We stop. The boundary marked by cactus:
the earth falling away to the zinc maze,
the cardboard castles, car carcasses
and the food growing in the rich mountain run off,
city of the murdered, bones and body parts,
bagged and tagged and forgotten.

I stand looking into the living gully
a killer dog at the land's edge
end of a chrome chain, panting,
my neck craned for the blood of children,
a tape recording of their short life histories
playing in the background
as the sun plops down
in the sea and
night comes
down.

The Archangel

WHEN THE CAR HIT THE IRON PIPE holding aloft the sign at the crossroads, she saw the dark shape at the edges of her vision. She scolded herself as the car that had hit her flashed and zoomed away out of sight toward St. Thomas. "That's what you get for making house calls in this day and age."

And the angel with the large wings who had been there all along waiting to open them, to dip and sway, emerged from the flash, fluttered and cooed like the sisters at Mother Henry's yard in Jones Town and eased her against that ice-cold bosom. At that moment her life seemed to her only the dull pink of the blotting paper given out at St. Hilda's Diocesan High School on Monday mornings, the dull pink of the photograph of a cell she customarily surveyed at office. Then the blotting paper absorbed something red from the outer edges in.

She looked at the circle of faces gathered over her as she lay in the wrecked Honda Civic. She blinked back the red and said "I have fractured a hip."

When a man looked sceptical, she informed him that she was a physician. And if he knew what that meant, he would realize she knew what she was talking about and call this number immediately to tell her patient she had been unavoidably detained and notify her daughter to come at once to the roundabout at Harbour View.

Other faces came then. Familiar faces, but hazy. All was a bright redness. Then dark.

II

It comes softly
from the spine, through the blood
drums rising at a kumina
rising, rising, then the cutting breaks.
Cut. Cut. Cut. Cut.

Yes balance yourself between the rhythm
hold to that other self like a piece of bamboo
in big sea then the sheets of water lick you
lick you lick you   Turn the raft a weapon gainst you
drive it through the spine
chip. chip. chipping bone

A bulldozer smashes the boarded up shacks
marking the trail of where you have been
1939 with your father on deck the banana boat
en route to England colliding with 1976
"socialism is love" rally; with that Saturday
in '46 when Bellevue strikers and police clashed,
and at the Kingston Public Hospital

the male doctors had a meeting to discuss
"what's to be done" while downstairs
you worked the wounded with the nurses,
and the puppy at Rock Hall disappearing under the massive
boogoodum of the flat steel bearing down
on the face of your daughter the day she married that American.

Thin tiny hairlike roots of your life
dark light under a microscope the solid bright
merciless blue of the sky uninterrupted
stretching blankly nothingly on

Bulldozer come again
blade power open remembrance's shack
smash the last egg shell round
the wriggling montage of faces.
Fingertips calling those
you tried hardest to forget
wizened ancients thought dead
bubble up like drowning things
in their pitchy patchy scrapsy clothes
dressed as people once feared or
heard of but never really known

Bulldozer scooping again
(Call to the angel there, do. Call s/he. call s/he
have mercy. Have mercy. Lord have mercy)
they rise up from the blue darkness
noiselessly, steppin, steppin
to a mix up of mento or waltz or
tambo or dub. Open mouths grin holding
small heaps of things from their time and place,
shack-shacks, mouths of blood

You had imagined dying a soft harmonious chord
which enveloped pain as quietly as you once
went into the still sea at dawn
for a constitutional bath.
Now dying is a crowd of ragamuffin, stink
with a scent of flesh fired on the bone,
of infected gashes from clashes between Tivoli and Jungle
from yaws and chiga, choleric retching
a stone-throwing crowd like those unseen ones
who stoned your mother from her Orange Hill house.

III

you have worked
48-72 hours at a stretch
sleepless night on day on night
you have worked to develop a gaze
which sees beyond the surface of
the flesh you examine spread on the steel table
you have endured the physical abuse to the healer's body
delivering, suturing, scrubbing, stitching
injecting, lancing, blood on the white
boot beneath the green gown night after night
dying for sleep collapsing cracking open your skull
on the door of the operating theatre.
And what emerged?

Give account. Did it work?
You have not healed with your medicine
the wounds of centuries' habitual cruelty.
Embalmed in your body shut tight
locked up are the things
you could not fix or face.
And so they are liberated now.

IV

And that humming in the shadows like doves
funny how comforting those songs are
I try to hum along with tunes I heard before,
but cannot remember singing ever
though now I hear the words

Fly away home to Zion
Fly away home
One bright morning
when my work is over
gonna fly away home.

Old Girls Reunion 1999
(in memory Dennyse Dempster King 1951-1999)

Then the Cancer ambushed her - merciless
divisions devoured her body uncontrolled.
Her little boy was ten.
"No sir." we said, resistance rising
resonant as the hymns we sang
crowded in that hot old hall on St Cecilia Avenue.
At 8 am sharp every school day for seven years,
the chorus of nice-girls' voices would
up up up to the heights of Zion,
down down down to the black rockstone
under that former slave plantation
that was our school: along the airless secret passage
from the Great House to Port Royal
and then stop and softly switch to "Our Father ....."

No Sir.
Death will not be simply -
death -
The End.
Boom   Power cut   Water lock off   Blackout.
And Jack Mandora me no chose none.

No sir. We chose.

A flock of birds on white ice - on cold ground
and in flight from many places
singing - thirty years matured,
crowded into that chilly hospital cell in Missisauga
to soothe her body's ruptions
read the bad card a different way
sweeten the bitter gall and
let it rise, ban yuh belly, let it rise
O Lord hold her tight and let it rise.

All we had to bring were stories - so we told and told:
She of the too rich family and the gold toothed chauffeur,
the one with the easy laugh, married a man
who murdered a prostitute and lives now on welfare,
in a rooming house by the Kingston Penitentiary, Ontari - O.
She who sends weekly remittance home (plus glaucoma drops)
honoured the generosity of the desperate poor

but never named her own. She who should have been
a Nuclear Physicist, but is a Single Mum instead,
smiled and never mentioned it. A Science woman still
she rose at 5 am to curry the chicken,
scoveitch the fish and bake the bammy
for the banquet of menopausal lovelies.

Those who'd put on fifty pounds, but carried it graceful
as bulging bankras on bodies patterned with cellulite
and those who'd mawga'd down and shriveled
stood as if recoiling from the deceitful·memory of their beauty
in that old school hall   in that hospital room
we stood round Dennyse who always wanted
to be thin and now was, wired to the bed,
morphined and signing semafore
to the spirits like a lost girl guide,
we stood, as we had stood, not here but there
uniformed and belted, reciting worlds
blown like feathers, disappeared,
that chorus of women's voices chanting
that chorus of girls voices dipping

down down down to the black rockstone
 under that old plantation school
 - notes hopping like birds
along that secret airless passage to Port Royal
bursting up up up with her
to the mountainous waves of Zion:
life more abundant - at last.

Black W/Holes:
A History of Brief Time

M. NourbeSe Philip

event: A point in space-time, specified by its time and place.[1]
*Immersed in a recently bought newspaper, I exit a variety store and almost
collide with a man walking west along St. Clair Ave West. I am immediately apologetic. His response is swift. And contemptuous. "You fucking
people are all over the place!" I suggest he do something to himself which
is anatomically impossible. I am angry - very angry. I am also afraid. He
is white. He is male. In a big city interactions like these can easily become
fatal. I quickly duck into a another store. Some minutes later I emerge and
am relieved to see his figure a block or so ahead of me.*

Quark: A (charged) elementary particle that feels the strong force.

"You fucking people are all over the place!" The white man's words remain with me for a long time. They reverberate within - "all over the
place...," "all over the place..." If nothing else, it was clear that he felt I
ought not to be on St. Clair Avenue West. The further implication of his
statement was that my being on that street in Toronto was evidence that we
- African people, I suppose - were "all over the place." The corollary being
that we ought not to be. I could easily dismiss that man's statement, were
it not for the fact that the notion of illegitimacy contained in his words is
carefully nourished, cultivated and brought to splendid fruition in the white-
supremacist immigration practices of all the western, so-called democracies. The main job of these countries - formerly the Group of Seven, now
the Club of Eight - appears to be figuring out how best to club the rest of

the world into submission, while keeping darker-skinned peoples physically corralled. Meantime capital, which is in fact our capital, wielded by multinationals, runs rampant and rough-shod all over the world. Indeed, all over the place!

big Bang: The singularity at the beginning of the universe

for five hundred years the essence of being black is that you can be transported. anywhere. anytime. anyhow. for five hundred years a black skin is a passport. to a lifetime of slavery. a guarantee that the european can carry out terrorist acts against the african with impunity. for five hundred years the european moves the african "all over the place." at his behest and whim. and then one bright summer's morning, he looks me in the eye and tells me: "you fucking people are all over the place."

ever since the holds of the slave ship, the european attempts to curtail the every moving of the african:
the moving in time
the moving in space
the moving into their own spirituality
the european forbids the african language; forbids her her spirituality; forbids her her gods; forbids her her singing and drumming; forbids her the natural impulse to cling to mother, father, child, sister and brother - forbids her family. leaves her no space. but that of the body. and the mind. which in any event they deny. cut off from their own histories and History, the african moves into a history that both deracinates and imprisons her. in the primitive. in the ever-living present absent a past or a future.

uncertainty principle: One can never be exactly sure of both the position and the velocity of a particle; the more accurately one knows the one, the less accurately one can know the other.

I live in a starter home. On a starter street. For two decades I have lived in a starter home. The street remains a starter street for many who buy their first home there - a starter home - then move on. There are a few like me and my family, however, who defy the very meaning of start which intends always to lead to somewhere else. We remain. Stay put. In a starter home. Away from home. Defying the wanderer, the lost, the unbelonging in Black. The spore at the root of Africa.

today - the black skin is not so much a passport as an active signifier to those manning borders of the brave new world order of everything that must not be allowed in. crime, drugs, AIDS, sex, ebola,... into these self same western democracies whose spawn - the metastasizing multinational - is all over the place.

Robina, Winona, Alberta. Three women's names. And the names of three streets in the neighbourhood in which I live. The same one with the starter home. The story is that at one time - in the past - is there such a thing? - a Black man owned the land on which these streets are now located. That man had three daughters whose names were Robina, Winona and Alberta. I have never verified this story, maybe fearing its inaccuracy. Somehow I feel more connected to this area, knowing? believing? that a long time ago Robina (I had an aunt called Rubina), Winona and Alberta, three Black women, grew up here. In this neighbourhood. And that their father once owned this land.

Which in turn begs the question. How did he own it? How do you, as a blackman - an African man, or woman 'own' land in a space e/raced of its native peoples, bounded "from sea to shining sea" by the ligaments of white supremacy? A space. Our home and native land - our stolen, native land. A space. Still being warred over by the descendants of two European powers. How do you own land, a house, even a starter home in a space and place where a minor encounter with an/other gives rise to the challenge of your legitimacy in this space. A space of massive interruptions. And disruptions. Mostly fatal for the First Nations people. That is the new world. That is the space we call canada.

magnetic field: The field responsible for magnetic forces, now incorporated, along with the electric field, into the electromagnetic field.

Goethe was of the view that the negative space around which leaves develop influenced the shape of a plant as much as their genes. Something in the surrounding emptiness, he believed, gave shape to the leaf.

What is the space - the negative space - that is Canada, around which I grow? Around which African people - Black people - grow? How does that negative space shape us? And do we, in turn, shape that space - moulding it to fit our specificities?

in this space we call canada, blackness serves as a cypher. a tool. the means by which the larger, white space shapes and ritually purifies itself. blackness becomes the most effective way in which the essence of canadianness - is there such a thing? - is articulated and the purity of canadian space is ensured. so that the refrain - "you fucking people are all over the place" is modified - parsed into "you people will **not** be allowed to be all over this place called canada. except and in so far as we allow you to be."

spin: An internal property of elementary particles, related to, but not identical to, the everyday concept of spin.

Time and again in the media, the involvement of African men and women in crime becomes the excuse to question the effectiveness of the immigration act. As if white men and women do not commit crimes. As if the very space that is canada is not founded on profound and unforgivable crimes against First Nations people. Against humanity.

"Why are we letting these kinds of people into **our** country?" the editorials question. Deportation becomes the most favoured tool to deal with that speciality, "black crime." Despite the fact that many, if not most, of these people convicted of crimes may have spent their most formative years here. In this space called canada.

At least once a year white Canadians ritually define and purify themselves and their space by going through this public process - ably assisted by their media handmaidens - of ensuring that indeed "you fucking people are **not** all over the place."

Every two or three years these rituals culminate in the high mass of a commission of inquiry into the state of immigration. The recommendations of these commissions invariably narrow the manoeuvrable space allowed Africans and other peoples of colour. Head taxes, extended waiting periods for refugees, genetic testing of family members - the list of punishments for those who have sinned by desiring to enter the space called canada is long and exquisitely tortuous.

1973 was just such a year: Canadians would examine how immigration practices were affecting the country. In a country built primarily on white immigration, it is significant that in the 1974 Green Paper on Immigration, all the worst case scenarios used examples of African peoples: for instance, how would parents feels about the "fate of their offspring if their children were to marry a black person." All material showing the potential effect of demographic changes resulting from **immigration** used examples of **domestic** migrations of Black Americans **within** the United States - a country convulsing in response to challenges to its governing ideology of white supremacy.

The black body becomes **the** measurement - the point at which absolute difference is established.

acceleration: The rate at which the speed of an object is changing.

an emptiness - an absence
shapes me shaping it
as the space around
the leaf serrates
the oak
fringes the willow
needles the larch

you may be born here - your mother's mother and father's father - you will still get asked where you're from. if your skin is black. you answer here. which is where? but if the minister of immigration gets her way - even being born here, in the space called canada, will be no guarantee that you can claim canadian citizenship.

the white that is snow
shapes itself around the silence
of cree and ojibwa - a hardness
in the face of something new
strange

primordial black hole: A black hole created in the very early universe.

"all over the place!" is there anywhere in this world - this brave and newly ordered world - to which a white skin does not become an automatic passport? all over the place, indeed! from the fifteenth century on, columbus, pizarro, hawkins, drake and others of that ilk - robber barons all supported by their robber-baron monarchs - run around the world terrorising africans and other peoples of colour. this is how they repay the hospitality of their hosts wherever they land. their most effective weapon is the company. there is a plethora of companies: the dutch east india company, the company of royal adventurers, the french east india company, the royal african company and on and on. and they deal in bodies. black bodies. what they call pieces of black ivory. today the ceo sons of these same robber barons and buccaneers sit atop multinational corporations whose work has not changed in five hundred years. they still deal in bodies. yours and mine. "you fucking people are all over the place!" talk about role reversal and projection.

Take the Ossington bus - say at Dundas. Ride north on it to Eglinton. Observe how the bus goes through a chromatic shift from light to dark as you enter the space of Blackness. That 'exotic' space of Blackness as rendered by Atom Egoyam. Up on Eglinton. Heartland of exotica. Exotic from whose perspective? (No review or critique of this film challenges the use of Blackness as nothing more than a signifier. For the exotic.) Then take a walk down Bay. Not so much heartland as engine of the capitalist machine. Observe how monochromatic that space is. Its beat that of a metronome.

rhythm is simply space divided by time. "up on eglinton" at oakwood is rhythmed in the same time as port of spain, trinidad; as accra, ghana; as scarborough, tobago; as kingston, jamaica; as harlem, new york.

event horizon: The boundary of a black hole

Canada is the cliched land of wilderness. Like all cliches it is also founded on truth - the space that is canada contains 20% of the world's wilderness. And yet in such vastness Africans and other peoples of colour are to be found by and large only in urban areas. Forty minutes outside of Toronto African peoples are invisible. Not present. Despite some four hundred years on this continent - in this land called canada. Cottage country remains a white enterprise in every sense of that word. Complete with power boats, jet skis and luxury cottages. It is, indeed, a strange way to be "all over the place" when African and other children of colour are noticeably absent from "wilderness" camps outside of the urban areas.

What is it about this experience of "wilderness" - this very Canadian experience - which Africans and other peoples of colour who have come here as immigrants do not participate in? Do our African brothers and sisters who have been here far longer than we fresh water Canadians have, engage in a different relationship with this twenty percent wilderness?

There appears to be some sort of psychic border which prohibits or limits our entry, as "Others," into this particularly Canadian aspect of life. Considering that most immigrants are at most one generation away from the land, their lack of engagement with it in Canada is significant. For many peoples from Africa and Asia, the land remains integrally linked to their life: not only is it the source of food, but also of healing and spirituality. With European settlement in Canada, however, the "wilderness" has developed a language which we cannot penetrate, unless we enter the world of whiteness - possess a cottage and boat. With the e/racing of the First Nations presence and their removal to reservations, their wisdoms, their languages, their manner of relating to the land have all been unavailable to us. The "wilderness" has indeed been racialized.

Safety lies in numbers. This is why we African peoples coalesce in cities. We know we will find others like ourselves there, we will find foods we're used to. We can hear our languages spoken. There is an immediate sense of connectedness which cannot be underestimated. It recreates the illusion of home and belonging.

imaginary time: Time measure using imaginary numbers.

I am a child, sitting in a darkened movie theatre. This is our regular Saturday treat. .A matinee. The cowboys and white settlers are on the lookout for Indians. The beautiful scenic river becomes ominous: Indian savages may be hiding in the bushes just waiting to scalp white men, women and children. Several years later I paddle a canoe along a quiet lake in north Ontario, round a bend and for a split second am afraid, expecting a canoe of tomahawk-brandishing Indians. Maybe Tarzan will come and rescue me.

Long before I am aware of it the "wilderness" is racialized. In movies, books - fiction and non-fiction, and comic books. I am not from the American South, but as an African person the American South is in my psyche. Somewhere.

Walking up a back road in Southwestern Ontario - the sound of an engine behind me tenses my body; my thoughts - and fears - turn to rape, lynching and racist rednecks. Nor can I forget, while vacationing in Minden, Ontario, deep in the Haliburton Highlands, that white supremacists held a rally in that very town not that long before.

When you put an African person in the woods, in the "wilderness", one of the first images that comes to mind is that of being hunted. By dogs. By white men with shotguns.

The immediate and individual power of the redneck cannot be underestimated - one only has to think of the recent lynching in Texas of an African
American by three white men who tied his body to a truck and dragged him
to his death. As the most powerful purveyor of popular culture, however,
the movies have played a significant role in representing the "wilderness"
and rural areas as the heartland of the redneck. They also let the urban
redneck off the hook. One of the strongest screen images of the ur-racist is
that of poor, white trash riding shotgun in an old beat-up pickup truck.
Seldom do we ever see those three-pieced, pinstriped business men and
women (members of the Club of Eight) riding shotgun, hunting Black
people. But they are, indeed, the ones with the resources and commitment
to the policies and practices which have carefully nurtured and sustained
the belief system of white supremacy.

Meantime Africans are literally scared off the land, which the European
purchases and enjoys relatively free of any contact with African people.

*It is winter. I am standing on a frozen lake some two hours north of
Toronto. There is a still whiteness all around me. In this moment I
recognize something about the way in which First Nations people relate to the land. As a living, breathing force which one needs to interact with. Not to conquer, but to be in relationship with. Several hours
later I hear the First Nations scholar, Georges Sioui, speaking eloquently about the need for the newcomer - the european - to learn the
concept of Americity. Americity, he argues, encapsulates an approach
to the land which all the first peoples of the Americas share.*

**white dwarf: A stable cold star, supported by the exclusion principle
repulsion between electrons.**

in the brave and oh so new world where africans have no agency - can be
bought or sold at will, they turn their eyes to that large undifferentiated
space lacking any particularity for them. the singularity to the north called
canada, at the end of the north star. where harriet tubman took her people
and "never lost a single passenger." they was going to do some walking,
these africans, out of slavery. into freedom. or so they thought. into the
space called canada.

this space called canada is not a white, virgin space. it never was. it is a
space that was initially inhabited by brown peoples. and continues to be.
the black presence - the african presence - has been here for a very long

time - indeed ever since the blackman, matthew da costa, arrived with samuel de champlain in 1605. the space that is canada is linked to the black world, the african world as a space of refuge, hope and new beginnings, all too often unrealized. during the american revolution the crown promises freedom and land in canada to africans who would flee their owners and fight on the side of the loyalists. they receive their freedom and land; often it is the most barren land and their presence in this space is neither valued or wanted. in 1796 the colonial government of jamaica grows tired of trying to keep control of the maroons and ships them to nova scotia. once again freedom proves to be a mirage for africans - eventually the maroons emigrate to sierra leone. it is a space - this space called canada - enlarged by appetite - salted, east coast cod is sent to the caribbean to feed the bodies of enslaved africans; in return hogsheads of rum are shipped back to the east coast. for free europeans. the appetite for cheap labour: african caribbean men join their nova scotian brothers in the mines of sydney. in ontario african caribbean women enter the space we call canada as cheap domestic labour. doing work white women will not do.

mass: The quantity of matter in a body; its inertia, or resistance to acceleration.

Canada remains the place to which people flee. Good guys fleeing bad guys; bad guys fleeing good guys; white draft dodgers fleeing their abbreviated futures in the jungles of Viet Nam; Black draft dodgers - considerably fewer in number; wealthy businessmen and women who can buy Canadian passports. You name it, there's always a good reason to head for Canada. These people never go to the specificities of Vancouver, Toronto, or Sudbury. At least as represented in the movies. Sometimes - very sometimes - they go to Montreal which is French and, therefore, not really Canada after all. It is that undifferentiated mass - the same mass that Africans set out for a long long time ago - that is the space of Canada they head for. It is a space of becoming. All things to all people. Canadians on the other hand almost always never head for the United States, preferring instead LA or San Francisco, or New York or Chicago. Unless you're Black of course, and you're going Stateside. Which is a very different country.

weight: the force exerted on a body by a gravitational field. It is proportional to, but not the same as, its mass.

I am at a resort in the Hockley Valley - the land around it has been reshaped with the golfer in mind. There is an abundance of open space carefully mowed and shaped into an eighteen-hole golf course. Here white men get to drive around in little, white buggies (often followed by their women, also in little white buggies); they jump out, hit little, white balls around the green expanse, then jump back into their little, white buggies and drive off. The sense of expansive entitlement is palpable.

It is a very white space. Tiger Woods notwithstanding.

The buffet style meals continue this theme of largesse and plenitude bringing out the gluttonous, all-you-can-eat side in me.

It is the same approach of that quintessential marauder, the European, to the world. Eat all you can. It is the same approach the multinationals, supported by the "clubbers-of-eight" to the world today. The world and its resources have become a smorgasbord, a buffet, at which they are each expected to consume all that they can, go back for seconds, thirds and fourths, and hang the consequences.

The flash-point of the 1992 Oka crisis lay in an attempt by white Canadians to expand a golf course. Into an area that had spiritual significance for the First Nations people in Quebec. So that white men with their gulf clubs could run around in little, white carts, hitting little, white balls. Frances Cress Welsing, the African American psychologist, has argued that there is symbolic social and racial significance in the kinds of balls used in sports It is no coincidence, she suggests, that golf - a game involving little, white balls played over a vast expanse of land, is traditionally the elite sport favoured by rich, white men, and from which Black men have also traditionally been excluded.

So powerful is the sense of white space, I hesitate to walk on the green, walk instead on the paved roads linking these eighteen holes. My black and female body vibrates with the question: am I allowed? Not so my companion who is white and male. He too, although not a golfer, shares in this aura of entitlement. The space is his to occupy. Which is a microcosm of how our peoples inhabit this space that is canada. One with a sense of entitlement - even greater than that of the First Nations people; the other with a sense of being allowed in on sufferance.

strong force: The strongest of the four fundamental forces, with the shortest range of all. It holds the quarks together within protons and neutrons, and holds the protons and neutrons together to form atoms.

sing to me of africville where african nova scotians build a community. in the implacable face of white supremacy. then sing me the africville blues that tell of city fathers attempting to e/race the african presence. in this white space called canada. so that they can build a park! not a golf course. but a park. with a water fountain. what is the negative space called canada around which those early african canadians shaped themselves? into africville? into resistance? and into memory?

Listen to the sound of the river. I did. The Credit River. I sit, close my eyes and listen to the sound of the water flowing by. And within the sound of water I hear the sounds of the languages of the First Peoples. The liquid, mellifluous sounds of their languages. I listen and hear how the very sound of the space around us shapes us fundamentally - from the ground up so to speak, so that even the tongue must remain faithful to the language of the land.

space-time: The four-dimensional space whose points are events.

You cannot talk about space as it relates to Black people - to African people - without talking about movement or moving through space. And once you talk about moving through space as it relates to Africans, then you must confront the forces that prohibit or restrict that moving.

What happens when "you fucking people are all over the place!"? As in Caribana. Where hundreds of thousands of black bodies take over the streets of toronto. This collectivity of black bodies, that is truly all over the spe-cially allocated place, is always seen as a potential source of trouble. A threat. To the city fathers. And were it not for the 200+ million dollars Caribana brings into the city, it would have been stopped a long time ago.

Just as immigration has become the ritual purification ceremony for white Canada, so the yearly abasement of Caribana organizers before the city fathers, begging for money and permission to move, has become an impor-tant provincial aspect of that ritual. The white fathers control the space through which these black bodies will move and will to move: virtually every year the police flex their collective muscle and threaten to withhold permits and licences. The white fathers reaffirm their supremacy by por-traying the african organizers as being unable to manage money. Proof being the debt the organizers have incurred. No mention is ever made of the monies the province annually pours into European-based arts such as the opera, the ballet, the symphony, the Art Gallery of Ontario and the

Royal Ontario Museum. None of which generates the financial returns which Caribana does. No mention is ever made of the many financial fiascos of governments, both provincial and federal, such as the Sky Dome and Pearson International Airport for which taxpayers have had to pay. No mention is made of the $200+ million that Caribana brings into the province's coffers. But within this space allowed to African people, to black bodies, there must be the ritual scourging of those who will not be allowed to be all over the place. And ritual obeisance to those who are, indeed, all over the place.

photon: A quantum of light

the moving of african peoples within a white supremacist society from a space of longing. a longing to be free in that most basic of senses - freedom of movement. which is exactly what africans do not and have not had ever since the european moved their bodies from africa to the new world. and then told them that they could not move. or run. they could only die and even that was forcibly prevented at times. today, despite michael jordan flying through the air to do his slam dunk, or oprah travelling in the stratosphere of the wealthy, or cosby, or michael jackson. the black body moving through space - physical space and time - is still a threat. to be controlled. by those whose job it is to control the space. chief among whom are the police who harass african people, particularly african men, to a degree that the very concept of freedom of movement as it applies to black people is ludicrous.

wherever it takes place - notting hill, new york, montreal, miami - the route of this festival is, indeed, a route of memory, moving through the lower case historical space that is the african canadian community here in canada, as well as the upper case Historical space that is the trajectory from slavery to freedom. it is a route of memory that traverses and confronts the space that is canada which is essentially founded on white supremacist principles. the dynamics of this space functions so as to e/race the black presence - the african presence in this country, while enriching itself at the expense of those very black bodies. how else to explain the refusal of hotels in the city of toronto, some of the largest financial beneficiaries of the presence of thousands of black bodies in this space, to make any financial contribution to the staging of this festival in the form of sponsorships? the phototype for this present e/racing of the african presence is the earlier e/racing of the first nations presence. the white space we call canada is, indeed, a palimpsest scored by multiple e/racings.

how, in the space we call canada, do we explain that at the last juno awards ceremonies, black musicians were given their awards at an earlier, non-televised ceremony? how, in the space we call canada, do we explain that the canadian broadcasting commission (cbc), the supposed voice of the nation, does not have a single black television show? are we to conclude that in this so-called vast country of ours, there are no black screen writers, with stories to tell? or black actors needing work?

nucleus: The central part of an atom, consisting only of protons and neutrons, held together by the strong force.

The engine driving the popular music industry in the world today is African music. Given that it has the largest number of African peoples in Canada today, Toronto naturally becomes a happening city for black music. This was the argument Milestones Communications used to base its application to the Canadian Radio and Telecommunication Commission (CRTC) for a licence for a Black music radio station in 1998. For the second time the CRTC refused to award a licence for a Black-owned radio station. The last remaining FM spot went to the CBC. The previous one to a country and western station - CISS FM.

The issue was never truly about black music. Had that been the case Milestones Communications would have got its licence. To licence a black-owned radio station which opens up the possibility for the coverage issues of importance to the African Canadian community and to the world Afrosporic community is to hand the African Canadian communities a resource with enormous and unpredictable potential. To withhold the license is to ensure that African Canadian people will not have the cultural space necessary for them to flourish as a people. In this space we call Canada.

black hole: A region of space-time from which nothing, not even light, can escape, because gravity is so strong.

White society perceives the black body as dangerously transgressive. The black body is not only cypher, but metonym for danger, crime and subversion. To have thousands of these black bodies in the heartland of white Toronto is not exotica. For many, and particularly the police, it is nothing but a riot waiting to happen. Despite its aura of celebration, Caribana is symbolic of the discomfort the black presence creates in the falsely white space of Canada. In 1994, for instance, when the first Kiddies Carnival (for children) was scheduled to be held in the Oakwood/Eglinton area - a predominantly Black area - many of the area's Italian residents, ably supported by their Members of Parliament, vehemently opposed the event. Community meetings held to discuss the issue degenerated into shouting matches, and the newspapers quoted Italians as telling African organizers to hold their parade elsewhere. Where else? If not Oakwood and Eglinton.

neutron star: A cold star supported by the exclusion principle repulsion between neutrons.

I attend a funeral of an elder of the African Canadian community in Toronto. There isn't enough space for us in the funeral home. People spill out onto the sidewalk and again there is a sense of there never being enough room for us - not enough space. After such a long presence in this city, in this country, there are no Black-owned funeral homes, so that even in mourning our passing there remains the sense of being cramped and stifled.

Meantime the media allow us all the space we want, provided we show ourselves to be criminals and murderers, always looking for handouts, starving in africa, dying in africa, killing in africa. There is very little space for any other representation.

exclusion principle: Two identical spin-1/2 particles cannot have (within the limits set by the uncertainty principle) both the same position and the same velocity.

Where else should Africans and Black people free up? If not at Oakwood and Eglinton. Where else if not in the heart - centre is perhaps more apt - of the city? After 20 years of moving and dancing down (and sometimes up) University Avenue past the symbols and statues of a now defunct empire, past the US embassy - symbol of a very present empire, past the law courts that play a disproportionately large role in African life, past the hospitals where many Africans work, often in the lowest jobs, Caribana has grown too large for the city. Or so they tell us. In 1994. Its organizers move it to the Lakeshore. Africans will have more space to free up, is the argument. Sitting on the grassy areas along the Lakeshore, watching the lake shimmer in the summer sunlight, it is easy to imagine that one is indeed in the Caribbean. The resemblance to the islands is uncanny - a sort of simulated re-representation of the Caribbean with its coastal communities and villages. The water, albeit fresh water, reminds you of the salt waters those first Africans crossed. Both separating and connecting us to Africa.

There is a shadow side: participants and spectators alike have literally become littoral if not litter/al - marginal.

naked singularity: A space-time singularity not surrounded by a black hole.

Within the confines of the city Caribana cannot/could not be ignored. The wide open spaces of the Lakeshore work to dilute and dissipate the energy generated by the gathering of so many black bodies. This dilution and diffusion is one of the unique effects of Canadian spatiality. It might be one of the ways the negative space that is Canada helps to shape its inhabitants. The beauty of the scenic surroundings works to undercut the tension generated by black bodies. The parade nature of the festival increases along with greater police control. Complete with signs commanding the music to "stop here." A sort of public *coitus interruptus*. Barricades restrain people. It is more of a challenge to participate, to move from spectator to performer, as happened on University Avenue - an important aspect of carnival. Helicopters patrol the event in a way they were unable to on University: at the end of the day the Lakeshore has the feel of South Central, LA, circling helicopters, spotlights and all. Not to mention the garbage cleaners after the last band literally and ritually cleansing the white space of the stain of blackness. And heaven forbid there should be a disturbance of any sort, then people - African people - are boxed in between the expressway and the lake.

electric charge: A property of a particle by which it may repel (or attract) other particles that have a charge of similar (or opposite) sign.

the space that is canada - a space of refuge over which hangs the north star - to which those early africans fleeing. from the united states. leaving the past. moving into the imperfect present. believing it a racism-free space. the space we call canada: a respite - a hiatus - a pause - a caesura between the space of violence of the pilgrim fathers. and mothers all. and the space as yet unformed. the african - fleeing a space where black was not cypher or postmodern hieroglyph. but a thing. fleeing a space where even the so-called savage native could own an african slave. provided they - the native that is - were civilised enough. as in the five civilized tribes. this space that is. canada. a negative space. around which we? i? the african. the black. shapes herself - ourselves. a space of unrelenting, unforgiving whiteness. a tabula rasa which was never blank.

nuclear fusion: The process in which two nuclei collide and coalesce to form a single, heavier nucleus.

Note

1.   All definitions appear in Stephen Hawking's **A Brief History of Time.**

Three Poems

Pamela Mordecai

To No Music

That is my quarrel with this country.
You hear them say: "April?
April? Spring's on its way, come April."
And, poor things, believe it too.
See them outside, toes blue
in some skemps little cotton skirt
well set on making what don't go so, go so.
And think: this big April morning
it make as if to snow.
Serious!

That is something that must
make a body consider: if you can't
trust the way the world turn–
winter, spring, summer, autumn–
what you can trust?

When it reach April
and you been bussing your shirt
for eight straight month just
to keep warm, you in no mood
to wait one dege-dege day more.
Not when you poor
and cold in the subway
cold in the street
cold where you work

where you eat
where you sleep.

But you don't get a peep
of protest from these
people. "Well, it's late
this year," they say, toes blue
peeping out the open-toe shoe,
and hug the meagre little skirt
tight round them, shivering
for all they worth.

They don't agree with the coldness
and they don't disagree;
they walk to no music
and that is misery.

Will's Flowers

I never yearned for snow
though brand new clothes from fat
Sears-Roebuck catalogues
committed to the U. S. post
by Uncle Lannie's faithful hand
in Cincinnati's never never land –
those made me glad enough.
He stayed away for years
writing Aunt V long letters
casting box after box onto
the dead slow sea-mail waters
hoarding expiring pennies
for a car a house storing
for ever after the best time
of his life. Adult and old
I never thought, "Is how
him manage foreign? Not
a wife. No family, no kin."
And so of course I follow him...

Now when spring reach T.O.
and the wild blonde from up
the street that tend to endless
cats and her small garden
with fierce care come forth
with spade in hand to set
again this year pot upon
pot of yellow daffodils
I think how we ex-slaves
enfranchised manumitted
free of snow white queens
Britannic motherland
I think we still don't
understand the bard's
peregrinations and sake
of that we dis poor Will –
mightily do him wrong.

Niggers still coming North
lured by the siren song
of work and decent pay
the chance to quarry out
a little life. Meanwhile

as dog nyam dog cold
carving up your carcass
vampire cops hunt you
for your dark blood this drip
of light this skemps of flower
that God promote from grass
rooted in blackness bent
on breaching ice just
pushing pushing up to
celebrate sun summer
unrepentant livity...

To rass! What a misguided fuss.
The blasted daffodils is just like us.

Caliban Calypso or Original Pan Man

Chorus
And, too, we come from island
So we know you Prospero
Fancy yourself as high priest
Sporting cape and wand and so

Serve up you own-a pikni
As a hapless sacrifice
Is want you want you kingdom back
No matter what·de price

You never give the girl a chance
To organize she own romance
You fraid Miranda get to understand
That the island man-of-words is Caliban.
You fraid Miranda get to understand
That the shaman man-of-words is Caliban.

I

On·high hillsides or as he floats
over the blue in small bright boats
see *homo Caribbeanis* grin
at how he's fecund, revelling in
how the ting-ting can spring
the fire in him wire still crackling.

"So, how much pikni you make, man?"
Him can't answer you back
but him quick to tell you
woman is a leggo-beast – "so slack!"

Chorus

II

And Sycorax? Perhaps
each island woman
mated and devastated
by some regional ramgoat
persuaded that the family plan
is a conspiracy to kill black man?

See her in travail with her lot
She's had them out[1]—
they're all she's got
her witchery the alchemy
to conjure food inside a pot.

Chorus

III

Of course, till now we don't determine
who insprignant[2] Sycorax
a matter upon which the bard
not giving any facts. Hole in
him head as far as any memory of that.
But if you check the niggergram[3]
the chat have it to say
is backra massa rape her
put her in the family way!

Chorus

IV

As for the creole boy child
him tongue twining with curses?
Muttering glossolalic nonsenses
him find him can decline
him pain in verses; start spirits with words;
that the birds, if him call them, will come.

When him listen, him heart flutter
for him hear the calling stones;
the rattle of creation waking
bones reaching for bones.

The sound prickle him body,
it make him head start rise;
him bruck a stick and clean it off
and start lick galvanize.

Chorus

V

So man when the music reach you
and the rhythm start take hold

and you feel the need to bring
the little chap in from the cold,

consider meditation
and the fruits that it can bring;
remember breed and grind
is two very different someting.

Chorus
And too we come from island
So we know you Prospero
Fancy yourself as high priest
Sporting cape and wand and so

Serve up your owna pikni
As a hapless sacrifice
Is want you want you kingdom back
No matter what de price

So poor Miranda never understand...
But you better know say we understand
that the shaman man-of-words is Caliban—
that the shaman man-of-words is Caliban!
So we jumping when we hear him playing pan
for we love that man-of-words, that Caliban.

Notes

1. Caribbean notion that each woman is predestined to have a particular number of children, i.e., a "lot"
2. Impregnated
3. Informal black people's network for transmitting "information."

"Black Sycorax, My Mother": Brathwaite's Reconstruction of *The Tempest*[1]

Gordon Rohlehr

Mother Poem is about ancestry, ancestors and their legacy of labour, love, struggle, dreams and hope for future generations. In this long poem, the first book of Kamau Brathwaite's second trilogy, the contemporary Caribbean is portrayed as a new world of islands standing at a juncture or intersection of times; lost or drifting between two cycles, one the formative colonial era of the ancestors, the other the as yet unformed but already ominous dispensation of the so-called "post colonial" present. Choosing as his epigraph a quotation from Cristo's testament in Harris's *The Whole Armour* –"We're the first potential parents who can contain the ancestral house"–Brathwaite affirms, as Harris had done fifteen years earlier, that the first "post-colonial" generation has a special responsibility towards the ancestral legacy and the future. They are "the first potential parents" in the sense that they have been invested with the potential for engendering a new era, a new civilization which must accommodate ("contain") what the ancestors have built, shaped and bequeathed as legacy to the present generation. *Mother Poem* and its successors *Sun Poem* and *X/Self* seek to identify the complex and contradictory dimensions of this New World legacy, constantly measuring and reclaiming the contribution and the unresolved confrontation of still antagonistic ancestors.

The ancestors in *Mother Poem* are parents, grandparents, the family tree and the web of neighbours and close acquaintances who form the intricate network of the extended family throughout the Caribbean.

Brathwaite employs the term "ancestories" to describe the narratives that have sprung from these ancestral sources, and *Mother Poem* may on one level be read as an anthology of such narratives told either through the remembered voices of the various "mothers" of the extended family, or through the sympathetic eyes of the poet as omniscient narrating voice.

The Ancestor is also Barbados, the island which first nurtured the poet as sensitive consciousness. "This poem," Brathwaite writes in his Preface, "is about porous limestone: my mother, Barbados." The island with its landscape, geography, history and folklife, is as much his ancestor as is his flesh and blood mother, and part of the challenge that the poem posed the poet was that of unifying the various levels on which the "mother" concept exists. Such unification is achieved through imagery that alternates between representing the landscape as person and voiced persona and presenting the women in the poem as voluble muses of landscape and lived history.

Apart from landscape and parent the term "mother" connotes several other ideas. There is Mother Church – or the Christian religion in both its establishment Anglican Catholic and its African-Caribbean, Zion Revivalist, Myal grassroots dimensions. Each dimension generates its own aesthetic of prayer, liturgy and dramatic enactment and exerts a shaping force on the collective sensibility of the island to which the poet seeks to give voice. A significant part of the poem is dedicated to exploring the contradictions between these different versions of "Mother Church" as they impact on the consciousness of a desperately questing woman, whose journey from Anglo-Catholic pew to meeting-house and houmfort becomes a metaphor for the poet's oscillation between Anglo-European and Creole Caribbean registers in language and aesthetics.

The School is another version of "mother." Ideally, the School is conceived as one's "Alma Mater" or loving mother, a fostering, kindly agency. In reality, the School is an agency of colonialist indoctrination whose real objective, unmasked by the acrid voice of the narrating persona is: "to build a nation of forked sticks" (MP 20). As was the case with the Church, the School is confronted with, and is programmed to eradicate, native intelligence and mother-wit, rooted modes of knowing and apprehension. This unresolved antagonism between formal colonial education and native intelligence lies at the very centre of *Mother Poem*. "Lix" and "Occident" (MP 19-24) as well as "Nametracks" (MP 56-64), foreground this confrontation, whose dire consequences are depicted in "Woo/Dove" and "Hex" (MP 41-51).

At the centre of the battle between formal and natural education lies the question of language. In *Mother Poem*, this is depicted as an ancestral struggle between mother-tongue and the imposed lexicon and syntax of a patriarchal and authoritarian presence. Appropriating Shakespeare's last play *The Tempest* as a seminal and ancestral prototype, Brathwaite presents the acrimonious debate about poetic language registers in terms of an historic contest between Sycorax as Mother Tongue and Prospero as a malign sorcerer and spirit-thief disguised as the authoritarian schoolmaster "Ogrady." In the process, he reconstructs and reinterprets *The Tempest* as a founding New World myth in which Prospero, Caliban, Ariel and Sycorax are recognized as ancestors and are given a presence that is as real as any of the Barbadian women whose "ancestories" form the substance of *Mother Poem*.

Of the four characters Sycorax, about whom we are told very little in the play, becomes Brathwaite's unique invention. In Shakespeare, Sycorax is described as a "blue-eyed hag," a sorceress who finds prior refuge on the island where she imprisons Ariel. Prospero, who arrives some time later, himself a refugee from his dukedom in Milan where he has been deposed, proves to be a stronger magician than Sycorax. He releases Ariel from Sycorax's spell only to place him under a thraldom of his own. He also subjugates Caliban, Sycorax's half-human and, according to Prospero, half-demonic son who teaches Prospero the secrets of the island, including the art of surviving there, and is in turn taught Prospero's language. Caliban comes to grief when he presumes there to be a human equality in the exchange between himself and Prospero, tries to mate with Miranda, Prospero's daughter, and falls from the grace of being Prospero's apt pupil into the disgrace of being Prospero's slave.

Brathwaite, in his reconstruction of the play as a myth of imperialist encounter, "writes in" Sycorax as prior pristine resident and possessor of lore, language and spell which Prospero seeks to appropriate. Brathwaite's Sycorax, who is identified at one point as "black sycorax my mother" (MP 47) imparts her own language and a prior sense of identity and will to rebel in Caliban her son. These gifts initially sustain him in his encounters with Prospero after Sycorax's disappearance when, like Prospero, Caliban and Ariel, Sycorax is transmuted into a principle or a complex of qualities and attitudes buried deep in the subsoil of Caribbean consciousness and influencing the patterns of action and reaction in contemporary time.

She is first manifest as "the sunken voice of glitter," the pool or reservoir of pure water at the island's subterranean core, the vegetation or perhaps the rainclouds which sit upon the island's mountains and the rain which fertilizes and revivifies the dry cracked surface of the porous coralline landscape. "my mother rains upon the island with her loud voices" (MP 3) summarizes the major ideas around which the poet will construct Sycorax as archetypal Mother. Taken together with the image of the Mother *sitting above* the gullies and dry rivers "on her mountain," the word "rains" may carry connotations of the homonymous word "reigns," which suggests that the as yet unnamed Sycorax is associated with queenship, a certain divinity, a prior, pristine presence in her island. The clue to this aspect of her identity is provided immediately afterwards when she is described "with her grey hairs/with her green love" (MP 3) as manifesting simultaneously the qualities of age and youth. When she appears much later in "Hex" in the guise of an old demented witch, we learn that "she is alpha/she is omega" (MP 45) and that:

> she is as young as the pouis
> as ancient as dead leaves
> she will outlast the present season's thunder
> the ovens of august (MP 47)

As "sunken voice" of water and hidden soul of his island, Sycorax must be sought out, honoured and rehabilitated by the poet. It is she who "rains upon the island with her loud voices." As sorceress and shape-shifter she is a protaean presence visible in the island's women and audible in their loud voices. So in seeking Sycorax, who is alpha and omega, the eternal ancestor, the poet will present us with several memorable and clearly seen portraits as well as the accurately recorded voiceprints of women in his land.

Mother Poem begins with the dry, cracked, sterile landscape of the first fifty pages, but arrives at "Nametracks", the core of the poem, where Sycorax, the old withered hag of "Hex" is rediscovered as a potent naming force, in possession of word, name and *nam* which she imparts to the still inarticulate Caliban to equip him for his fights against Prospero, fights which she foresees will be taking place throughout all ages world without end. *Mother Poem*, then, moves backwards in time and place as did *The Arrivants* in its central book *Masks,* and then outwards and forwards again into present time and place. It is noticeable that the women and men who appear after "Nametracks" are all a little more daring, rebellious and self-assured than the ones who appear in the first fifty-five pages of text. Ann, the slave girl punished for insubordination, a character whom Brathwaite creates from an historical account, is identified as rebel ancestress, a daughter of Sycorax who wears splintered fingernails, a natty dread head that would have worried Edward Long, and "shoulder blades balancin quiet and straight like is brass/scales" (MP 70); she is the image, that is, of retributive justice. The narrator predicts that Ann will become the mother of rebels and fighters

> ann custom to kick and scratch in dis place
> jack johnson goin breed an born from she waise
> he goin carry on bad an mash up you face (MP 70)

This prophecy aims its threat at Prospero, who as contender with his black servant in the equalised space of boxing ring or playing field would have to cope with the skill and fury of his former slave. The narrator's voice is also the voice of all Black women – as portrayed by Brathwaite – who despite all evidence still look to their sons for some ultimate vindication of their historic suffering. Significantly, even the dying Mother/Grandmother of "Driftword" still envisages her sons as potential avenging angels of Apocalypses to come before she herself sinks into the landscape as corpse, as spirit, as the Sycorax principle of fertility, identity and renewal: Earth and Water.

It is therefore crucial that the reempowered Sycorax of "Nametracks" be understood as archetypal presence and Muse. Here Sycorax manifests as sorceress, powerful enough to pit her word against Prospero's book-learning. She is first described through a cluster of images which contrast dramatically with those that Caliban has employed to describe Prospero's world of great house, factory, machinery, technology and mechanical time-piece. Sycorax is mudda, mud—that is, of the Earth, a natural life-force. She is

> black fat
> soft fat man-
> ure

"Fatness" in the pre-aerobic age was often associated in the folk mind with health and fertility. The break in the word "man/ure" indicates Caliban's perception of Sycorax as the mother who fathered him: who was both nur-turing woman and "man" and who was also a fertilizing agency ("manure").

She is next associated with food—essential peasant food kukoo (cornflour, ochro—meal and slime/semen) cooking pot—i.e. her domestic function; "herb"—i.e. natural lore, obeah, healing; wollaboa wood (i.e. cook-ing, fire) and "eve/ning." Here the break in eve/ning counterpoints the ear-lier one in "man/ure." Caliban recognizes and names Sycorax as **Eve**, that is the Universal Mother and Ancestress who—so the archaeologists still tell us—was African. So Sycorax is everybody's ancestor, the original pro-genitor. She is, as Mother Earth, associated with both the beginning and the ending of life; hence "evening" carries with it connotations of death, "sleep, sleep rest"—the final resting place being the bosom of the Earth, Caliban's mother. Note how Caliban's description of his "mudda" has moved in a circle. For Caliban is also establishing his sense, and the poem's sense of time as cyclic, as ritual movement from life which begins as 'mud' to death which ends in mud, with the mother principle dominating the entire cycle— earth, food, faeces, fertilized, renewed earth.

The second movement of "Nametracks" is Brathwaite's imaginative construction of the pristine relationship between Sycorax and Prospero as witnessed by Caliban. Sycorax recognizes Prospero as a rival magician and an agent of emasculation and death, and tries to defeat him with her strongest magic. She draws an eye which represents Prospero's visionary power and spits into it, seeking perhaps to blind Prospero with her anger and contempt. She also unleashes language and spell upon him—

> she spite/in an spitt/in
> she curses upon him
> wid de sharkest toot o she tongue (MP 57)

In Shakespeare's *The Tempest*, Caliban curses Prospero by commanding the sun to suck up the diseases of fens, bogs and marshes and deposit them in foul vapours upon Prospero. Brathwaite, in his development of this literary source identifies Sycorax as the source of Caliban's curses, and as the rebel ancestor for whose voice and will Caliban becomes a channel. Caliban's memory of Sycorax's word has invested him with a sense of prior residence on his island which in Shakespeare's *The Tempest* he declares to be his "by Sycorax my mother." It is, however, not only this sense of prior residence but also a pristine acquaintance with Sycorax's mother-tongue, her language of spells and runes and riddles, and the aboriginal power of her naming that will preserve and inscribe in Caliban the will to rebel, in cycle after cycle of encounter with Prospero's spirit-thievery.

Thus the third movement of "Nametracks" portrays Sycorax in her role of bestower of pristine inscription—bearer of the engrafted word. First she names Prospero, fixing him for good in her definition as a breaker of men and a destroyer of "de lann o me faddah." Prospero's impact is devastating on both man-scape and landscape. This feature of Prospero will become clearer via the numerous illustrative examples provided in *X/Self* where Prospero emerges as a malign principle of History: a perverted masculinity, atrocious, acquisitive, parasitic and destructive of both ecology and civilization in the name of Empire.

But Sycorax tells Caliban that Prospero "doan possess we at all," by which she means that Prospero "owns" people in one sense but has never quite filled and can never quite fill their spirits; never quite reach or plumb their inner depths of soul, can never own their *nam,* a concept that will become clearer as her naming and indoctrination of her son proceeds. Prospero will die like a dog, she predicts. She then tells Caliban his name.

> ma ma ma: she is tell muh
> ma ma *man*:   she is tell muh

say *man:*   she is tell muh
say *man:*   she is tell muh

say *man*
say *manding*
say *mandingo* (MP 57)

The first point about this moment of naming is that it is done by stages and is bound up with Caliban's learning to speak. He must significantly learn to say "ma ma ma" before he can learn to say "man." That is he must learn to acknowledge the mother as presence and tongue and anima, before he can properly realize his own identity as *man*. If Prospero, wrecker of manhood and exploiter of mother and father land, is characterized by a deep divorce from the feminine principle that might have counterbalanced his hubris, his imperial will-to-power, Caliban must learn to acknowledge both the feminine (ma ma) and the masculine principles within himself—both anima and animus. Such recognition must precede any other kind of naming: tribal, ethnic or national "mandingo." Naming, then, begins with archetype and then proceeds to other layers of identity. Such is Sycorax's wisdom as myal woman, a healer whose word needs to be truer and hence stronger than Prospero's, since it must survive the centuries of his distortion.

The fourth movement of "Nametracks" is Prospero's rejoinder to Sycorax's act of pristine naming. It is at this point that he tries to teach Caliban language in the form of a children's word game called "O'Grady Says." Different versions of this word game have survived in the Caribbean, but the one that Brathwaite is using here requires a giver of the word "O'Grady," whose given word must be correctly repeated by the group of children. "O'Grady," however, is not to be trusted. Sometimes he disguises himself as "Ole Lady" in order to trick the other participants in the game into repeating the wrong word or "breaking the word" that O'Grady alone has the authority to deliver. In "Nametracks" though, Prospero's authority as O'Grady has already been usurped and anticipated by Sycorax's aboriginal act of naming. In the O'Grady game one must repeat only what O'Grady says and avoid what Ole Lady says. Sycorax reverses the rules of the game, subverting Prospero's rule(s), and Caliban, insofar as he remembers (but does not disclose) Sycorax's word(s) (mother tongue, mother as first language) will himself as poet or citizen be capable of both rebellion and creativity from what Brathwaite calls "centre-self" or "nam."

Prospero's strategy in his quest for Caliban's soul is first to get Caliban to say "I"—that is to practice individualism, Prospero's ideology, and in the process to lose vision ("eye"), world-view, wholeness or roundness ("globe"), a language of consciousness and perception ("seeing word") and with such loss to lose the myalistic or shamanistic qualities of the word ("priest/green voodoo doctor"); Sycorax's fertile and healing (green/doctor), magical and potent obeah words. Prospero tries to possess Caliban; to enter and displace his spirit. But before he can do this Caliban has to acknowledge Prospero's spiritual authority over him, Prospero's right to his *nam*. Hence Prospero's command: "Say/ i/am your world," a parody of the devil tempter's offer of the world to Christ if only he would bow down and worship him as God. Prospero's problem, however, seems to be the urgency of his desire to confuse. He changes the word, i.e. the rules of the game with such bewildering rapidity—quick, stick, dog, sick, good, god, wick, whip—that Caliban has no time either to repeat or to break the word. Even in a game that requires interplay between domineering word-giver and acquiescent responder, Prospero is so obsessed with his own importance that he can allow the other no room for response. He repeats his initial command to Caliban to say "i"and when Caliban fails to respond strikes him with the whip so that he cries out "aei."

Caliban's capacity to resist is reinforced in Section 5 when he remembers his mother's resistance. Sycorax not only breaks the word, but she savours it. Language for her is the bread of life, the word of life, essential and nourishing, and her message is one of life and hope

> dat de worl' rising in de yeast
> wid red wid cloud wid morning mist
> wid de eye: ron of birds

Like the mother of Blake's Black Boy, Sycorax directs Caliban's attention to the rising sun, a symbol of his own sonship/sunship. Her hope in her son will be repeated in the enormous investment in hope which future Black mothers will place in their sons, sometimes in vain. Sycorax predicts a rebirth and an uprising: a red rising of sons. "The eye:ron of birds" is problematic, a confusing image. Iron is Ogun's metal, symbolizing his warriorhood and inflexibility. "Birds" however usually signify the Muse, the creative process, while "eye" as usual connotes vision. Taken all together the phrase implies Sycorax's vision of a new dimension of consciousness in which insight will nurture rebellion and both will inform the poetry of the age.

Prospero/O'Grady's response in Section 6 to Sycorax's reordering of discourse is more hostile and less controlled. He threatens "lock bar bolt rivet" prison, privation and deprivation, lock and lack, ice, his medium, and murder, his mission, transplantation in slave ship, whip, torture "future wrack/ plantations greening," "scream" rather than dream, decay:

say rot
ogrady says

say rat

say right
say white
say wrong

say strong
ogrady says

not song

This is a good sequence. It illustrates O'Grady changing the word, sometimes employing minimal pairs of word-sounds to confuse—e.g. "hit hot" or
"rot rat" or "trip trap." At other times rhyme becomes the basis for change:
("right white") and "wrong strong" being particularly effective as rhymes
that have had a deeply embedded place in popular consciousness. (If you're
white it's right.) Here the closeness of "white/right" "wrong/strong" rhymes
to each other creates an unintentional irony on Prospero's part. "Wrong/
strong" contrasts with and unmasks white/right by revealing force as the
true ethic upon which Prospero determines right and by suggesting that to
be right and white is also to be wrong and strong: a comment ultimately on
the very basis of international affairs and on the ethic of imperialism in all of
its forms: political, economic or cultural. It is upon the paradox of white/
right/wrong/strong—that the world is governed. Prospero's voice is that of
History itself.

Ultimately, Prospero is working his way towards what he most desires,
the Soul/Spirit/Nam/Name of Caliban

say pain
say blame
say cane
say name

This triplet of sounds—pain, blame, cane—tells us something about the
psycho-social history of those worlds that were shaped by the sugar plantation. For not only did Prospero inflict pain, he also encouraged in the children of Caliban a spirit of self-recrimination in which they learned to blame
themselves for their condition. A large part of colonial education and certain aspects of post-colonial discourse have been devoted to a blaming of
the victim. When such discourses are propagated among the victims, they

learn to dislocate themselves from historical context. They are actively discouraged from reading or thinking "Black" or "Africa," learning Prospero's lesson of (self)-blame. So while pain becomes a major part of their tradition, they are discouraged from acknowledging, exploring and creating solidarities of suffering and triumphant transcendence, such as, for example, the Jews have. Prospero's triple philosophies of "cane" (i.e. the plantation as a total system—economic, social, agricultural, even spiritual) "pain" and "blame" (i.e. the negativising of liberation discourses: the discouragement of Caliban's self-exploration) have been overwhelmingly successful methods of maintaining the status quo. He later adds "shame" to the list of words he commands Caliban to say. This "shame" is not a quality that Prospero manifests in his own life, but rather the burden of self-recrimination that Caliban is being forced to bear. Colonized or subjugated people have had to live with a crippling sense of inferiority reinforced by a guilt (a) of having been ancestrally responsible for their own subjugation and (b) of having been too cowardly or too inefficient or too divided and weak to rebel successfully against their tormentors. Cane, pain, blame, shame : much of colonial history has been about these four words to which O'Grady adds "drain" and "maim."

"Maim" is the final result of all these words/processes. Hence the prevalence of the image of cripple, the wounded man, the disconsolate wanderer who bears a life-sore. Prospero warns the unanswering Caliban of what will be his fate if he does not surrender the last and in a sense first and only of his possessions, his name.

> i come
> ogrady says
>
> to strangle
> you maim
> in de grounn (MP 61)

Each of O'Grady's words of intimidation is a sign of who and what O'Grady is. The "nametracks" in this poem lead not only to Caliban's but also to Prospero's hidden identities. Prospero it may be said, makes no attempt to conceal who he is in this word-game. Using the boasting that is common to many traditions of inter-male confrontation—e.g. the heroic epic, the Western movie, the stickfighting music/word-games of Old Trinidad, the Oratorical Calypso, the Carnival Midnight Robber, and today's Rap and Dub spiels —Prospero signifies. His signifying may be a ploy to get Caliban to answer him in an equally frank and self-revealing, signifying speech. Boasting speeches, however, are normally a dialogue between equals; the inflated but mutual exchange of self-defining egotisms, a war between two self-glorifying fantasies. No such exchange can occur between Master and Slave, Prospero and Caliban. Instinctively the Slave knows this and remains silent when O'Grady signifies. His own bondage is all the testimony he needs that Prospero/O'Grady's words are not idle boasts at all but shamelessly accurate self-representation.

Sycorax in the seventh movement speaks up to reinforce Caliban in his silent resistance, or his resistant silence. Prospero has carried out his last threat and strangled Caliban "maim/in de grounn." Sycorax, the healing feminine restorative "myal" principle to Prospero's aggressive domineering and ultimately murderous masculinity, appears to Caliban in his broken, strangled, maimed, crippled and interred state—"She cumya to me pun de grounn." There is a cat-like essentially about her behaviour here. She "licks" Caliban like a cat cleaning her kitten. It is a powerful yet soothing image, and her voice with all its sibillance (issper; essssper) is hopeful, secretive and soothing. "issper" and "essssper" are both variations of purr, with "essssper" suggesting French "espoir": hope. "She comes to me years," says Caliban, meaning that she whispers in his ears but also that Sycorax's voice has remained with him throughout his "years"—the lifetime of his people. Sycorax also "lispers"

> she lisper to me dat me name what me name
> dat me name is me main an it am is me own an lion eye mane
> dat whinner men tek you an ame, dem is nomminit diff'rent an nan
> so mandingo she yessper you nam (MP 62)

This is Sycorax's longest and most complicated speech, particularly as heard by Caliban's confused ears ("years"). As usual, what Caliban hears is a shift and shimmer of sounds and meanings, an unsettled language in which the relationship between word-sounds and their connotations is as yet unstable. What Caliban hears and how Caliban hears are important dimensions of the poem, since Caliban here is Brathwaite's way of imagining a Creole Caribbean sensibility in its earliest process of formation. For Caliban, language is molten. Words shift their boundaries, flow into other words; word-sounds suggest other sounds. Meanings are approximate except the most fundamental meaning of them all; Caliban's *nam*. And that meaning is a silent, secret and sacred pact exchanged between Caliban and his mother Sycorax and beyond Prospero's parasitic appropriation.

Sycorax lispers (i.e. lisps and purrs) because of the Anansi nature of what she is about to communicate. Anansi is always depicted in Jamaica folklore (e.g. Louise Bennett's performance of folk tales) as having a lisp.

Black Sycorax as sorceress is about to speak with the ambiguity or the obscurity common to magical speech anywhere. Her aim is to confuse Prospero should he ever succeed in getting Caliban to disclose what his mother told him. Yet she needs to do this without confusing Caliban. Her message then must be both ambiguous and true, her language both obscure and clear. She truly needs Anansi's duality of consciousness and articulation here. As antidote to Prospero's heavy doses of threat, death and licks, she *licks* Caliban in an entirely different and opposite connotation of word and performance.

. She next tells him; "me name what me name." That is Caliban has been named for good and ever; his name, his secret identity, his *gros-bon-ange* (Haitian voudon) is definite, established and securely implanted within him. Her second message to Caliban on mourning ground or in the "grave" that Prospero has dug for him, a graveyard of consciousness, the cemetery of his crippledom, is the even more mysterious jumble of murmured sounds: "me name is me main and it am is me own." Decoded this says that Caliban's name is his strength. "Main" can be French *main*: hand or strength. "Am" may be English "am" as in "I am" which in this context would be a powerful signifier of identity. Or "am" may hint at French *âme*. Indeed, "ame" is actually used in the next line, though here it seems to imply a reduction of "name," i.e. name with the n eaten off or erased, elided. This is what happens when men, particularly those of evil intent, spirit-thieves such as Prospero, get hold of your name, warns Sycorax. Despite this negative connotation of "ame" it is still worth pursuing a possible link between "am" in the previous line and French *âme*, which means "soul" or "anima." Can not that line "it am is me own" mean something like "its soul," i.e. the true secret meaning of his name, the soul or anima of Caliban's name is his own, belongs to Caliban and Caliban alone; is his deepest innermost possession, that which Prospero cannot possess? This would confirm her initial declaration that "the man who possesses us all," despite his expertise at spreading dismay and crippledom, "doan possess we at all."

If "am" means *âme*/anima, Sycorax is saying something very powerful here. For the anima is the feminine dimension within the male psyche out of which the male creates. So even as Sycorax assures Caliban of his masculinity as force, power, might of arm ("main"), she also locates "soul," sensibility, sensitivity, a "feminine" dimension at the centre of that maleness. As we perceived earlier, "ma" precedes "man" and "mandingo" in the primal language that Sycorax teaches Caliban. Caliban will need both his "masculine" and feminine qualities: both man/*main* and ma/ *âme* anima, if he is not in the very fight against Prospero to become "manimal" (MP 81) that is, a replica of what he is fighting against. The fight against Prospero is a fight about "soul"/anima. In Caliban's case it will be a fight to affirm and assert the power of soul. In Prospero's case it is a fight to appropriate and consume soul, to catch and imprison spirit. It is the "Ariel" or the subjugated spirit of his victims that provides Prospero's magic with its force, rather than their enslaved bodies. Sycorax in delivering her second word – "dat me name is me main an it am is me own an lion eye mane" – is functioning as myal woman, a healer and strengthener of spirit and counterforce, as always, to Prospero's power to negate and devour.

Part of her myalism seems to involve a facility with more than one of Prospero's languages in addition to her own "nation language." She employs English, French, aspects of Latin, Creole English along with Akan and is obviously a projection of Brathwaite's personal concern with exploring possible interlinkages between the many aspects and dimensions of his experience and education. Sycorax is both his fabrication and his voice of many registers as, of course, are Caliban and all the "characters" and voices who speak in the text. Sycorax teaches Caliban a riddling language that would befuddle Prospero or anyone else. This is funny because Prospero is himself trying to confuse Caliban in the O'Grady word-game by rapidly changing the key-word that Caliban is required to repeat. But at another level, of course, the riddling is anything but funny. It is again Anansi's "lispering," that reworking or "misusing" of language by which the slave, Brathwaite once argued, created a language incomprehensible to the masters (*Development* 237).

Sycorax also leaves Caliban with word-images of her own, "lion eye mane." These word-images signal Brathwaite's awareness of Rastafarian consciousness as expressed in painting, music and invented language. Sycorax is trying to invest her son with heroic spirit and a sense of kingship ("lion") vision ("eye") and the physical and spiritual strength that Rastafarians believe to be lodged in dreadlocks ("mane"). She warns him about spirit-thievery, Prospero/Crusoe's power to appropriate and reshape one's name: to "nomminit different an *nan*," i.e. negate one's manhood, to replace "man" by "nan": that which is na man/not man. "So mandingo she yessper you nam." Her final purr is a sound of affirmation, a *yes* purr and her final word *nam* is a word that Brathwaite has invented from Akan ancestral roots: Onyame the Creator God, as active principle; yam, substantial and sustaining root crop; nyam; the act of eating and other related word sounds such as name, anima and even man of which "nam" is a disguised word-form. The very arbitrariness of the word's etymology in Brathwaite's several accounts of it, tells us something about his approach to language as a medium for expressing the fluidity of a New World sensibility that is still in the process of being formed. "Nam" means whatever he says it means: kernel, seed ...

irreducible core of being, that which however it may be encrusted with scars and rust, cannot be appropriated. It is a beautiful and hopeful concept and a sustaining one for all those beaten Calibans of the first, second, third or fourth worlds.

Prospero responds to Sycorax's powerful word-spells in a language that is beginning to resemble Sycorax's or even Caliban's in its register

> ku late
> cries o grady
> high year what she yell yuh
> an i tekkin you number down on i plate
> mek i tell yuh
>
> i learn
> says o grade
> what she bell yuh
>
> but i doan want no oo –
> ma nor congolese mudda
> to hell i in here
> leh me quell yuh (MP 62)

This almost deliberate shift towards Caliban's register is Prospero's now desperate attempt to appropriate this language in order to control Sycorax/Caliban. His rendition of "mooma" as "oo / ma" signals his intention of reducing Sycorax to a double cypher (oo) by devouring the "m" with which "mooma," the nation word for "mother" begins. But Prospero's adoption of nation-language is, ironically, also a sign that Sycorax has triumphed in her breaking of the word. Prospero is now forced to operate on her terms and in a simulation of her register. It happened with Jazz and African American dance: it happened with performance style in song, sport and vernacular. "Man," Archie Shepp, avantgardist Jazz saxophonist once complained of the host of white musicians who had appropriated and were living well off the style of their African-American counterparts, "it's like we're being pursued."

Prospero's adoption of Sycorax's/Caliban's register, however, doesn't mean that he is admitting defeat. If one magician can capture the word, spell or book of spells of another, he then gains power and authority over that rival. So Prospero is trying to show Caliban that he is stronger than Sycorax; that since he can command Sycorax's tongue, he is her master. So when he declares "I learn what she bell yuh" he is trying to show that he too is capable of double meanings, folk metaphor, anansi speech and all the rest. The bell is what the Zion Revivalist or Spiritual Baptist "Mother" uses to ring in or invoke the spirits as she pours out its sound in the vèvè (MP 15). So Prospero reveals that he knows something about the folk religion; but in so doing, he acknowledges Sycorax's word as a bell: a powerful vibration upon which the ancestral spirits awaken. Elsewhere in Brathwaite, "bell" is linked with the gong gong of annunciation or the alarum bell of rebellion.

Prospero's description of Sycorax as a "congolese mudda" (MP 62) confirms him as the direct cultural and intellectual ancestor of Chalkstick the schoolmaster (MP 21) whose vocation is to ensure that his hostages "don't push bones through each other's congolese nostrils." As is the case with Chalkstick's derogation of his pupils' African ancestry, Prospero's use of the term "Congolese" is meant to be one of direst insult, the stereotypical notion for centuries before Conrad's *Heart of Darkness* being, that the Congo was "darkest Africa," the most abysmally backward and dismal centre of darkness on earth. There may be, however, another reason for Prospero's ancestral use of "Congolese" as an abusive epithet. The diasporan Congolese were half-dreaded and half-derided by their African compatriots because it was believed that they were sorcerers (Warner-Lewis, *Trinidad Yoruba* 46). Prospero, then, may be trying to overcome Sycorax by deriding the tribal source of her magic and thereby teaching Caliban scorn for his mother, his mother's country, his mother's magical word and ultimately, inevitably, scorn for himself, a primal shame at his origins. This is why one of O'Grady's keywords that Caliban is commanded to repeat is : shame.

Prospero's failure to inscribe shame on Caliban's psyche is signalled by two things: the increasingly threatening nature of his language and the tacit admission that Sycorax's breaking of the word has upset his game plan

> but i doan want no oo—
> ma nor congolese mudda
> to hell i in here
> leh me quell yuh

Sycorax "hells" Prospero in the sense of raising hell in the Prospero household; messing up his O'Grady word-game. "Quell" deriving from Anglo-Saxon *quellan* or *cwellan* means "kill." Prospero threatens murder; an occupation at which he has had centuries of practice. But given the rule of "who vex loss," Prospero, like Papa Bois in Walcott's *Ti Jean and His Brothers*, may well be losing this contest for Caliban's name and soul.

He reverts to his original command to Caliban to say "i." Caliban, however, is by now sufficiently strong in Sycorax's word to break Prospero's.

For the first time he answers Prospero, and in language as complex and subtle as Sycorax's:

> but eye blind to the worl
> where you see mih
> cahn seh what me see when you say mih

Caliban, responding to Prospero's command to say "i," deliberately says "eye", a word with the same sound but quite different connotation. Caliban says that his eye is blind to the world. This could mean that he has developed inward and spiritual rather than outward and material vision. One recalls Harris's parable of the blind seeing eye and the open unseeing one. Brathwaite consistently represents Prospero as a supreme materialist, a man who is, like Harris's Donne, a mixture of pragmatism, pure rationalism, the supreme spirit of individualism and will-to-power which seeks to fulfil itself through acquisitiveness, conquest and imperialism. This aspect of Prospero along with its connection to capitalism, the industrial revolution, ecological pollution and the subjugation of the natural to the technological within the human person and in the world, will be developed in *X/Self.*

When Caliban defines his situation ("where you see mih") as that of one whose eye is blind to the world, he places himself outside Prospero's arena of contestation, negating Prospero's scheme of values. "Can't say what me see when you say mih" is obscure and riddling, but implies Caliban's rejection of the stereotypes through which Prospero has represented him. Prospero's "saying" of Caliban is his way of representing Caliban in fiction, film and the various media which Prospero has invented as a crucial aspect of his historical domination. When Caliban says that he can't say what he sees when he confronts Prospero's images of him, he probably means that he does not recognize himself in those distortions; that his inward seeing eye, the eye opened by Sycorax's word, illuminates his true self, the *nam* that Prospero has been unable to appropriate, the spirit that he has in all his rapacity been unable to steal.

At this point, the game—which Caliban isn't even playing—is lost for Prospero/O'Grady. The command to say "stick" evokes from Caliban not fear, but the memory of the African martial art of stickfighting and a typical stickfighter's boast that he is invulnerable to O'Grady's blows. O'Grady's stick breaks. This might imply a loss of potency or the breaking of Prospero's magician's wand. In either case, Caliban's defiance seems to have both unmanned and unmasked Prospero, whose voice becomes more and more that of the hoodlum who descends to cheap name-calling— "wog," "nigger," the "nig nog" of British Television race comedy[2]—and wilder threats.

Caliban's voice, in contrast, becomes more triumphantly defiant – ("when you kick me up me still tickin": MP 63). Like Dennis Brutus's persona, Caliban's sounds begin again beyond the sirens, knuckles and boots. Even Prospero's whip/wand of ultimate coercion now seems, under Sycorax/ Caliban's obeah to ricochet off Caliban's back and "rocket black up" (MP 63) against the oppressor.

The final three lines of Section 8 seem by the logic of how they are presented, to be O'Grady's final threat:

> so i keel you (ogrady)
> i diggin you coffin blox black in de brown
> an i livvin you dead in de grounn

(ogrady) in brackets may simply mean that O'Grady is the person speaking. He has lost the game of words and has only violence on which to restore authority. "So I keel you" could mean "so I kill you" or "so I keel (haul) you" or "so I enslave and transport you : i.e. chain you within the slave-ship's keel." The last two lines are gunfighter talk though; ironically, the final threat "an I livvin you dead in de grounn", by substituting "livvin" for "leavin" creates a play on the ideas of life and death. Thus the line could mean "and I shall be alive while you'll be dead underground."

If by an outside chance, however, it is Caliban who speaks these words, it would mean that he has begun to turn Prospero's spells against him. Just as the whip has turned "black" on its master, so Caliban will in his rebellion have turned Prospero's death-threat against him. The poem is a battle of spells culminating – if this line of interpretation is feasible – in Caliban's triumphant resurrection/survival (i livvin) and Prospero's death (you dead).

Section 9, though, rendered in the italics of Caliban's speech, seems to validate the first reading which attributes the last three lines of Section 8 to Prospero/O'Grady. Section 9 is Caliban's now jaunty rejoinder to Prospero's death threat, that since he (Caliban) is already dead, he cannot be killed anymore, and he has been freed from responsibility for his actions ("an me doan give a damm"). Caliban's elation is readily explained as the result of his transformation from a simple ruin to the ambiguous Legba state, simul-taneously crippled and potent, a symbol of both old age and green beginning, of direst erasure and most hopeful possibility. Such a reading is buttressed by all that Brathwaite has proposed about the death and resurrection/trans-formation of Gods (Legba, Ananse, Ogun, Shango, Erzulie, Damballah, Christ, Onyame, Jah, Olodumare, Odomankoma) in the process of forced crossing. Here, Caliban, quoting an old calypso, *Jumbie Jamboree,* is ex-ploring the death/ burial/underground metaphors that have become com-mon in Caribbean and some African-American writing. Like Ellison's invisible man, Caliban declares that his several cycles of encounter with Prospero have left him in the *bolom* state of being simultaneously dead and undead, defeated and yet possessing an ominous potential for resurrection and retaliation, a potential for recreation as Legba–whose sidekick representative or even sometimes equal, Anansi, is Sycorax's lispering speaker of undermining riddles.

This potential survives Prospero's attempts to devour or misrepresent Caliban's name. Caliban, remembering Sycorax's advice, identifies Prospero's naming as a form of laming: an imposed crippledom even when it seems to be acknowledging Caliban as Jazz and Blues man:

> lame me black
> lame me blue
> lame me poopapadoo
>
> lame me nig
> lame nog
> lame me boobabaloo
>
> but he never know what me
> main (MP 64)

This is a protest against the stereotype of the diasporan Black as performer, entertainer, coon, clown, dancing man, Bojangles; and against the highly suspect adulation that often accompanies these stereotypes. Caliban recognizes this as Prospero's most subtle ruse in the game of spirit-thievery; but knows that he will survive, since the inner soul of who he is behind dance, jibe or riff has never been appropriated.

> but e nevver maim what me
> mudda me name
> an e nevver nyam what me mane (MP 64)

Caliban's name has not been maimed, nor have his manhood, capacity for heroism and meaning ('mane') been consumed by Prospero. So far, Sycorax's word seems to have triumphed.

Notes

1. This essay is an excerpt from Gordon Rohlehr, "Sycorax as Ancestor, Archetype and Muse : Kamau Brathwaite's Mother Poem." Conference Paper, UWI, St. Augustine, March 1996.
2. The Television show alluded to here is *Love Thy Neighbour* which featured Trinidad Caliban Rudolph Walker. 'Nig nog' was a term of amicable (?) abuse employed by one of the white characters in the show.

K/Ka/Kam/Kama/Kamau:
Brathwaite's Project of Self-Naming
in *Barabajan Poems*

Rhonda Cobham

Brathwaite, Naipaul, and Walcott constitute the crest of the wave of West Indian literary achievement that began to build in the 1950s and 1960s. When they published their first literary efforts there was no such thing as a Caribbean literary tradition beyond the small circles of struggling writers in each of the separate British West Indian colonies. Today, their feel for words and their experiments with form help define the standards by which creative writing is assessed across and beyond the English-speaking world. In different ways and to differing degrees they have achieved the dubious distinction of becoming institutions within their lifetimes.

The work in progress from which this paper is taken examines the meaning of that achievement: the license it allows these authors to experiment with forms which in the work of writers of lesser repute might have been considered too eccentric for serious consideration; the protected space it makes available to them to face up to issues that in their earlier work they were too insecure or too inexperienced to confront. It is about the temptations of narcissism and isolation this license conceals, the seductive drift toward self plagiarism and aesthetic stagnation it can portend; the endless, tautological conversation of I with I. Ultimately, it is a reflection on the intimations of mortality one senses in the recent production of all three men. These writers already can see that their work will outlive them and in their recent literary projects all three are fighting for the right to influence the way in which that legacy will be read.

The present essay examines the ways in which Brathwaite names himself as poetic subject in *Barabajan Poems*. "Kamau" and "Son/Sun" have histories that originate in other poems. Embedded, here, in the fiction of an encompassing autobiography about the way they are spoken or rejected by the poet's interlocutors—be they the African American writer Carolivia Heron or Brathwaite's computers or Barbadian society—the names accrete new meanings to themselves. My reading of the politics of heteroglossia Brathwaite's "video style" enacts provides the point of departure for a reconsideration of the writer's assumptions about audience and subjectivity.

> *You have to be concerned with the sources of a poet's life a people's inspiration and try to protect care for as best you can, those sources. . . We have to be concerned with the poet's health well-being and comfort. yes; but above all there are the **archives**— that written memorialized recorded record of his/her life/hope/history/art. Because if you can applaud him/her ('clap a likkle') as he/ she stands before you, if, as I assume, you feel that he/she has something important to say, then you've got to be concerned with the **whole thing**. Don't wait until you hear that so-and-so dying of whatever, that so-an-so aint got no dunny, cast away in him garret or ghetto. . . Don't wait until you hear that fire or flood destroy Brathwaite house to say that you sorry an start runnin' arounn about what to do what to do how we can help etc etc etc (364)*

In this passage from "Saving the Word," Appendix V of *Barabajan Poems*, Kamau Brathwaite frames his own words from an earlier essay in two ways: Between the black lines within which his extravagant "video style" layout allows him to box his citation, as if it were a wedding announcement, or the epitaph on a gravestone; and in the frame of the novelist and critic Carolivia Heron's voice, as she cites Brathwaite in her introductory remarks to a lecture he gave at Harvard University in September 1988. Heron's citation of Brathwaite predates the *Savacou* publication date of the essay/ prose poem *Shar* from which the passage is taken by two years. The time lag suggests that a completed version of the essay must have been in circulation well before it finally appeared in *Savacou*, a chronically underfunded one-man publishing enterprise that Brathwaite has used to disseminate some of his most important essays as well as to produce *Barabajan Poems*.

These are the kinds of inefficiencies around the distribution and preservation of the written word in the Caribbean that cause the frustration so evident in Brathwaite's words. For Brathwaite is an historian as well as a poet. The kind of writer who understands the value of keeping everything – invitations, drafts, letters, invoices, manuscripts, bibliographies, journals – which later generations will need to reconstruct the achievement of a public figure. The fact that he must publish some of his most important works himself, and that he must have recourse to citing himself via an American critic to affirm the importance of his writerly legacy, underlines his bitterness at the way in which he perceives how his region's neglect of its artists perpetuates the collective cultural amnesia his work has tried so hard to counteract.

The near destruction of Brathwaite's archives in 1988 by Hurricane Gilbert, to which Brathwaite alludes in Heron's citation, was one in a series of devastating personal losses the poet suffered in midlife.[1] The worst of these was the death of his wife, Doris, in 1986, who for decades had been the poet's chief source of aesthetic inspiration and spiritual support, as well as his archivist and research partner. In 1990 Brathwaite's post-Gilbert Kingston apartment was invaded by robbers, who held the poet at gunpoint while they stripped him of all valuables, including his wedding ring. Their violation of his person severed the poet's last tenuous imaginative links to his adopted Jamaican landscape, which appears thereafter in the grimly disconsolate vision of "Trench Town Rock" as "a city smouldering [sic] in garbage & men & women plundering that monstrous HELL of stench & detritus & death, dead rat, live rat, for bread, bone, dead rotting flesh, dead rotting fish, the decomposing contents of yr kitchen sink & toilet bowl & latrine, of what you sweep off from yr floor & doormat, tabletop in greasy paper, plastic bags" (196).[2] Gordon Rohlehr has written perceptively in his introduction to *DreamStories* (1994) about the way in which each of these crises has informed Brathwaite's subsequent publications. He sees Brathwaite as transforming his personal trauma into meditations on guilt and loss; allegories of the dark night of the soul that announce a new severity in the poet's vision, hinted at in the earlier *The Arrivants* (1967) and more clearly enunciated in *X/self* (1987) but only fully articulated in the more recent prose poem/journal pieces like *Shar*, "Trench Town Rock" and *The Zea Mexican Diary* (1993). These texts write from within "the silent howl and scream of the straitened man," while his *DreamStories* chronicle "the events of an interior journey; to divine directions from the signposts of the dark valley: broken tree stumps, frowning rocks, thorns of darkwood" (vii).

For me, the most searing of these documents has been *The Zea Mexican Diary*, the poet's journal account of his wife's death and the changes her passing produced in his work and in his relationships with family and friends. The *Diary* is brutally autobiographical in an unmediated way that makes me want to lower my gaze, as one instinctively does when forced to stand eyeball to eyeball in a crowded train with a person one hardly knows. Until the publication of the *Diary*, I considered Brathwaite a very formal writer, that is, a writer whose most important effects depended on his ability to work through formal masks; through poetic personae whose appearance and perspectives were "obviously" not those of Brathwaite, the individual.[3] Like the absent white father, with whom the poet often competes in his work, Kamau Brathwaite was the man who possessed them all – Uncle Tom in *Rights of Passage*; Ogoun the carpenter in *Islands*; Esse the "forward" country girl in *Sun Poem*. Paradoxically transcendent and transparent, Brathwaite's public persona was that of the voice of the people; a shaman or mouthpiece through whom we were able to hear the submerged voices of Africa/the islands/history. In *The Zea Mexican Diary* this mask is ripped off, taking with it the first layer of skin on the public orator's face. We are forced to look directly at the raw, exposed flesh of Kamau Brathwaite, the man: a frightened man, at times, incapable of providing the wife who has supported him for decades with the support she now needs as she lies dying; a wise man, at times, capable of naming and writing this failure of will. Bereft of his reflection in Zea's gaze, incapable in the first terrifying months after her death of even retrieving his words from the bowels of her computer, Brathwaite presents himself in *The Zea Mexican Diary* and essays like *Shar* that follow as overwhelmed by the fear of extinction. He seems suddenly aware that no one actually may have known or heard him —the man behind the mask rather than the masquerade through whose orifices the voices of the collective issue.

Barabajan Poems is the most ambitious work in this series of confessional texts, torn out of the poet's consciousness in the aftermath of loss. In it, Brathwaite attempts to place himself and his message more securely within the reach of his readers. He does so by drawing together the explicitly biographical material from across his oeuvre, especially the poems rooted in the private Barbadian landscape of his childhood, as opposed to the public Jamaican landscape of the shaman/orator, or the reconstructed African landscape of the historian. He then embeds these "Barabajan" poems in the historical and intellectual apparatus he imagines will best facilitate their reading.

I like to think of Brathwaite's *Barabajan Poems* as a piece of virtual sculpture; a plastic artifact that enacts the process of creating an archive through its innovative form. The "video style" layout of the project quotes the stylistic conventions of the computer hypertext. It produces for its readers the illusion that they can consume with Brathwaite's words all the ramifications of the multiple landscapes that have produced his poet's sensibility: his family history; his aesthetic influences; his place within Barbados society and his relationship to the Barbadian landscape; his position within a Barbadian literary history that extends back chronologically to Chapman's eighteenth-century poem, *Barbados*, and outward to embrace other contemporaneous poets and makers of Barbadian culture. The text is set up to be read via the click of a mouse rather than the turn of the page. Its only concession to linear progression is the unfurling personal essay that runs through the entire document. Part memoir, part scholarly dissertation, the essay began as a lecture given in Barbados in 1987.[4] Into this prose banner, Brathwaite threads what he considers his most significant Barbadian poems from previously published collections as well as snippets of poems, memoirs, and interviews written by a range of other Barbadian scholars, athletes, and artists. Beyond the body of this narrative collage, the volume expands to include over fifty endnotes, as polymorphously perverse in their content and form as the main corpus of the text itself. There are also seven appendices. They include a listing of Shango train songs – secular and religious music from Africa and the African diaspora which makes use of the metallic effects and driving rhythms Brathwaite associates with the Yoruba /Dahomey god Shango – and a chronological checklist of poetry by Barbadians since the eighteenth century. "Finally finally finally " (377) as the narrator puts it, there is "a brief vertical interview" – the "I and I" trope par excellence – in which the author creates a whimsical conversation between himself as critic and himself as poet on the "meaning" of his work. Even then the text is not complete, however, as Brathwaite adds an index, cross-referencing every person, concept, and place name mentioned in his virtual archive. The text's interactive format allows the reader to scan it in a variety of ways: from cover to cover, like a conventional book; from text to endnotes, like a scholarly treatise; from poem to personal narrative, as one listens at a poetry reading, and from icon to text as a computer user would manipulate a program.

Brathwaite also produces dramatic visual effects on the page by making use of the full range of typefaces to which his computers give him access. His video style layout, as he names it, calls to mind the way in which Reggae and Hip Hop musicians have foregrounded the technology of the studio in their music by exploiting the acoustic possibilities of dubbing, mixing, and scratching, as well as the electronic distortion of sound itself. Like these musicians, Brathwaite is interested in breaking through the illusion of verisimilitude offered by more conventional forms of production. The technical details of presentation are no longer transparent to the reader. Instead, like the no longer invisible poetic persona, Kamau, they deliver the effects the artist desires by calling attention to themselves. Brathwaite constantly shifts the layout patterns of his text so that we are forced to register how and why they affect the words on the page. Thus, as the poet moves between commentary, bibliography, anecdote, chant, lyric, and endnote, the typeface of the poem expands and contracts to elaborate or blur the boundaries between different genres as well as to indicate a range of emotions.

Some of Brathwaite's visual effects are predictable. For example, in section VII, which brings together a number of poems that explore the metaphor of religious possession as a form of cultural affirmation, the poet interweaves a scholarly commentary on the process of possession as well as his subjective response to such phenomena. The heavy typeface of his commentary on "Angel/Engine," —a sequence he includes from *Mother Poem*—mimics the heavy-handedness of an academic presentation. It even highlights words like "loneliness," "disappointment," and "dispossession" in oversize black lettering, as a teacher working with an overhead projector might highlight the main ideas he expects his students to glean from his lecture. The first section of the poem, describing the mother's life, is rendered in small italics that seem to run together like the mundane details of the grinding poverty and dispossession that characterize her experience:

> *The yard around which the smoke circles*
> *is bounded by kitchen, latrine & the wall*
> *of the house where her aunt died, where*
>
> *her godma brought her up, where she was jumped*
> *upon by her copperskin cousin*
> *driving canemen to work during crop*
>
> *time, smelling of rum and saltfish*
> *who give she two children when, so she say,*
> *she back was turn to the man, when she wasn't*
>
> *lookin (185)*

Each new act of violence that pens the woman in, pushes the words away from the margins as if, over time, the woman's horizons have contracted to the point where, in the last line cited, there is nothing to look forward to beyond emptiness. Indeed, Brathwaite often uses empty space and esoteric symbols to make his reader "see" the extratextual powers at work in the poem. The passage from "Angel/Engine" cited above is prefaced by a grid that suggests prison bars or the closed gate of a cattle pen. Further on, the conventional typeface of the scholarly treatise on possession is interrupted by irregular runes—a circle, an arrow, a spiral. Like the vèvès chalked at crossroads in Haitian Vodun rituals, they announce the presence of symbolic elements drawn from beyond the boundaries of language. As the description of the woman's possession approaches the arrival of the gods Shango and Damballah, the scholarly typeface contracts and recedes, until it is crowded against the margins, mimicking the way the researcher now cowers on the periphery of the ritual he is describing, overwhelmed by the unseen forces released through the body of the possessed woman:

that was the night PROFESS-
OR ?slumming w/ us from the UNI-
VERSITY - recorder tape the camer
(a) the lot - becames embarrassed fr
ightened - *Erzulie too xtreme?* wh
en he meant 'obscene' - **K/Ka/
Kam/Kama/Kama/**
Kamau/too sacred = scared

He switched the light of the 'Niag
ara'(Nagra) off - xcuse? - *don't wa-*
nt invade the privacy ... (189)

Here the layout allows us to make a direct connection between the frightened, embarrassed professor and the poet K/Ka/Kam/Kama/Kama/Kamau as we later glimpse him confronting Africa's spiritual forces in the "Limuru" section of Part XII where he recounts his ambivalent response to the traditional African ceremony at which he received the Gikuyu name, Kamau. By consulting the entry "Kamau" in the index, the reader can "click" forward to the Limuru passage in order to develop the connection the poet is making. The cross referencing allows the poet to indicate his complicity in the professor's discomfort with the folk culture; to acknowledge in himself, the hitherto omnipotent creator of "Angel/Engine," the same human limitations that assail his *dramatis personae.*

When the text returns to the poem "Angel/Engine," after a detour through "Stone Sermon"—an earlier poem from *The Arrivants* describing a similar moment of religious transformation, but in terms of Christian imagery—the italic font is thicker and more assertive than in the earlier stanzas. The voice of the scholar/narrator also re-emerges, intermittently, tentatively, each line stretching a little longer, until its description of the way in which the sibilant spirit of Damballah enters the circle of worshippers can once more spread itself with confidence across the page in huge, oversized lettering that fills entire pages with just a dozen words or less. In the final downhill rush of the woman's possession, her signature italic font straightens up. The short lines beat out, in squat, upright boldface, the rhythm of the woman's breathing to which her entire body, stretched taut like a drum, moves, while the sibilant swish of the departing spirits continues to be registered in italics.

sh

praaaaze be to
praaaaze be to
praaaaze be to

shang

praaaaze be to

sh

praaaaze be to

gg

praaaaze be to
praaaaze be to
praaaaze be to

*sssssssssssssssssssssssssssssssss***hhhhhhhhhhhhhhhhhhhhhhhhh**

**an de train comin in wid
de rain**
['Angel/Engine', **Mother Poem**, pp98-103][52+] (202)

The association of visual computer effects with extra textual spiritual powers in *Barabajan Poems* is no accident. For Brathwaite's personal computers, Stark and Sycorax, have both become symbolic presences in their own right in the poet's private iconography. Brathwaite has written about how his inability to retrieve his manuscripts from his wife's computer seemed to portend the creative desolation he dreaded would overwhelm him in the aftermath of her death.[5] His subsequent mastery of the computer constituted a point of cathexis within the mourning process. It gave him new access to the qualities of nurture and preservation he associated with his wife's support of his artistic project.

Brathwaite's newfound understanding of the possibilities associated with "writing in light," as he has called it, and with electronic memory also enabled an illusion of total recall: a fantasy that his reader could attain unmediated access to his imagination; could move beyond language to the remembered wholeness of the womb. Not surprisingly, the symbol of that access is unmistakably gendered: Brathwaite's first anthropomorphic computer takes her name from Sycorax, Caliban's mother in *The Tempest* and one of the images for the submerged maternal principle in *Mother Poem*. In "Hex" in *Mother Poem*, for example, the poet invokes Sycorax to accomplish a shift in his presentation of the mother from sufferer to avenging force through a series of images that move from the domestic to the elemental:

> so she sits, bandana ikon
>
> stool in the corner
> that cool stone in the backyard
> that flat rock underneath the cotton tree
> that rocking chair on the enslaved verandah
>
> black sycorax my mother
>
> she is as young as the pouis
> as ancient as dead leaves
> she will outlast the present season's thunder
> the ovens of august
>
> and the september's breath of hurricanes;
> and when the wind from the east brings dust,
> brings crack, brings flowers,
> she will begin to creak and give the dry rot meaning (46-7)

The images here mirror and anticipate a similar series of shifts in the associations that accrue to Zea in *The Zea Mexican Diary*. Zea's portending death precipitates the poet's (and the computers') abandonment to the elements in images that make it increasingly unclear whether she is a protective muse or the vengeful elements to which the poet feels abandoned:

> For it was she who handled the French & Spanish & all the hazards
> of all the foreign travel Who navigated the car across Europe & into
> New York & Chicago & Edinburgh & from Massachusetts to the
> Miami shoreline & sometimes took over the wh/eel after midnight
> on those long crazy drives back from Accra on Nkrumah's new lonely

highways when possessed by the red firefly eyes of *sasabonsam* I
was dreaming the Minx up a tree or over th/(e) black redge of ravines
. . . dealt w/ people . . . from marketwomen to workmen to editors
professor/(s) madpeople & specialists . . . Whatever else may be fall
me now after 26 years can only be cola or coda/appendices - can
only be luck/ if a lucky/ if a don't get ill/ if a don't meet mi dessert or
deserts w/ an asp or an adder or a boa-constrictor or gorgon O poor
little helpless What will happen to Savacou & the computers Who
will love you so total/ly, friend (72-3)

The images in this passage present Zea as a bulwark of strength so fixed, so
impervious to the assaults of the elements that her absence, like Sycorax's
presence in "Hex," is the equivalent of a natural disaster: the ripping away
of a headland by an earthquake or volcano; the violence of a hurricane that
tears open the roof to let the forces of destruction into the home. In calling
his first computer—her computer, really,—"Sycorax," Brathwaite brings
together the creative and destructive aspects of the strength he associates
with Zea and with electronic memory. In the face of death his dependency
on her/it becomes a terrible curse, as he realizes that he does not know—
has never known—the command that would allow him to retrieve that part
of himself that is stored in/by her.

Brathwaite's second computer, however, whose programs have allowed
him to create his new video layouts, he calls Stark. The meanings that
accrue to Stark's name derive from both the English word "stark," meaning
spare or bold (in your face? womanish?) and its Germanic root, connoting
indefatigable strength. Stark is also the name the poet gives to Caliban's
sisters in the private iconography laid out in endnote 43 of *Barabajan Poems* where he discusses plantation personality types:

> STARK/Sister Stark, Caliban's sister . . . did not walk clearly away
> from me until the October evening in 1991 at NYU when I spoke of
> Paule Marshall's then new book, **Daughters** and recognized Stark
> in what Marshall was doing - the first time that the Plantation has a
> black woman w/ firm feet, sensitive/aggressive breasts and a space
> & plan if not always a room of her own She begins in James
> Carnegie's Mary **(Wages Paid)** and now makes her way in & through
> the wonderful efflorescence of STARK WRITING since Mary Prince
> since Mary Seacole since Walker since Morrison since Brodber since
> Kincaid since Condé since Warner since Carolivia Heron since
> Cynthia James/ to name only a few (316)

This is how Brathwaite imagines the personality of his second computer,
the one he acquires not as a terrified sightless child, searching vainly for

the lost words he has entrusted to Sycorax, the submerged mother, but as a man in control of his technological world, who can work with its creative possibilities rather than being overwhelmed by them. It is also the collective term he uses to describe the contemporaneous new school of black women writers whose current luminosity he could have read from a more paranoid perspective as having eclipsed his own. Whereas the supportive/submerged/subversive Sycorax communicates loved and feared Medusa-like magical powers which, if not contained or understood, could reduce the poet's gift of language from Prospero to silence and stone, Stark is the poet's comrade and creative equal. The emphasis is on kinship and solidarity rather than on a generational or an erotic opposition. Stark's femininity also is contained, however, by the interchangeability of the names for the women writers and Brathwaite's computer. Through the exchange, the poet inadvertently figures feminine creativity as synonymous with a technological resource available to the male writer. From this perspective, the poet's invocation of the writer Carolivia Heron's voice in "Saving the Word" to frame his own words renders her silent. Rather than speaking her own lines as an independent source of creative possibility, she becomes a mechanical recording device, returning the poet's own words to him; preserving them, like an archive or a faithful computer, from the corrosive indifference of the Caribbean community and the economic vagaries of indigenous publishing.

There is nothing inherently invidious about this utopian image of woman as supportive cyborg.[6] It arises out of Brathwaite's conceptual preoccupation with images of wholeness and complementarity; his search for a history that "will not always bleed on other people's edges" (MP 112). Where Naipaul sees first a landscape, wiped clean of past associations, and then a past so overwhelming in its ramifications that it defies representation and threatens to engulf the writer's subjectivity, Brathwaite sees his subjectivity as tied up with a submerged cultural landscape that the power of the word/computer/feminine principle/voice can help him raise intact to the surface. For him, the blank page *can* be filled. The problem is not the excess of infinite ramification but the threat of sabotage; the anxiety that somehow the page will remain blank because of indifference, denial, repression or the indirect violence of technical and economic constraints.

The artist in this scenario is always in search of allies. Rather than capitulating to the ravages of history, he combs the landscape for clues to the meaning of his community's past. He sees his enlistment of the creative powers and voices of his sister writers not as a form of self-aggrandizement but as part of what he imagines is their joint project and duty in relation to the plantation cultures that have produced them both. It is in this spirit of solidarity and communal retrieval that Brathwaite ends the main body of his text with a selection of Barbadian proverbs collected by another woman, Margot Blackman. Conversely, in his penultimate endnote, he presents *himself* as the archival conduit through which one of his female students of Barbadian descent discovers Margot Blackman's proverb collection in *Bim*. He reports that through her work for his class on "*Bim* and the development of Caribbean Literature through *Bim*, she began to learn & understand thi/ngs that she didn't know or rather things that she had SUBMERGED" (328). Like the community's archives and the personal computer, the creative and critical contributions of both male and female writers thus become the mediums/media through which the submerged memories of the Caribbean folk will possess, or become accessible to, a new generation of Caribbean initiates in search of their history.

But Brathwaite in this text is also in search of personal affirmation. The words he places in Carolivia Heron's mouth, about the community's responsibility to preserve its cultural legacy, represent the poet's life and personal well-being—his reputation and the critical apparatus that maintains it—as part of that legacy. For if it is true, as he says in his essay on "The New West Indian Novelist" that "for a [writer's] mind to be truly itself it cannot only be self-regarding, introspective and selfish, it must be out-going: aware of its responsibilities to others in society" (274), it is also true that society has a responsibility to "care if i-man never write another word another poem" (*Zea* 153).[7] For Brathwaite, the individual artist is incomplete if he cannot see himself reflected in the gaze of his society. But that community will only be whole and able to see the artist if it can remake itself in the image of the society which the artist lays down in his work. Brathwaite sees himself and his text as incomplete until both can come back to him through the understanding and appreciation of his listeners, just as the African American writer, Carolivia Heron, must first internalize the meaning of Brathwaite's text in order to return it to him as tribute or epitaph.

"One haan cyaan clap" (334), the poet remonstrates in a letter to the editor of the *Barbados Advocate*, reproduced in bristling, oversized calligraphy in Appendix I of *Barabajan Poems*. The letter takes the Barbadian community to task for neglecting the contribution of other Barbadian writers in the course of the Barbados Archive's 100th anniversary celebrations of the life and work of Frank Collymore, the founding father of *Bim*. Brathwaite is particularly distressed that his own contribution to *Bim* is not mentioned at any point in the anniversary exhibition. His letter invokes his services to the magazine as Collymore's associate editor for over thirteen years and his publications in the journal of some 60 poems and 20 critical articles as entitling him to recognition. Moreover, he notes that "what is most dismaying is that I—**myself a Bajan**—should have to make this point to **Barabados** at this stage of our development" (333).

Brathwaite uses the Barbadian proverb "One haan cyaan clap" to suggest that Collymore's editorial legacy is diminished when it is viewed in isolation from the contributions other Barbadians made to the achievement of *Bim*. Nevertheless it is difficult to avoid the implication that Brathwaite, too, is clapping with one hand. However necessary the mutual acknowledgement he demands for his work and that of other Barbadian writers within the celebration of Collymore may be, it is difficult for the poet to eulogize himself; to be both the grammatical subject and object of his own speech act; the transcendent I and I of Dread talk which, in its uncompromising appropriation of all subject positions, negates the possibility of an object/interlocutor and therefore of dialogue (on psychological implications of this grammatical move, see my "Colin Ferguson"). Brathwaite attempts to circumvent this problem by citing himself through the words of other writers and through his deployment of his anthropomorphic computers. But without the unsolicited support of his community, the poet's virtual archive runs the risk of becoming an empty, echoing hall of mirrors that gives back to the writer only the images of himself that he has brought to the text.

And yet. The act of naming oneself, of claiming and establishing one's own worth, is often represented by writers—and accepted by their readers —as the superlative act of literary instantiation. As critics we affirm that creative possibility each time we distinguish between the poet and poetic persona of a text; each time we allow the artist to be the agent of representation as well as the thing, the object represented; each time we refer to the act of writing as a process of self-creation. One sees the paradoxically tautological and creative possibilities of the dramatic monologue the poet performs in the absence of communal dialogue in the closing sections of the main text of *Barabajan Poems*. Section XII brings together a number of "endings" from previous long poems by Brathwaite as well as a new autobiographical sequence describing the ceremony in Limuru, Kenya where the poet was given the Gikuyu name "Kamau." The Limuru sequence is the linchpin of Section XII, as it is here that Brathwaite identifies himself most clearly as sharing the denials and repressions which produce the collective cultural amnesia he attributes to "the eternal victim of 'The Man Who Possesses us all'/" (222). He notes that, especially in the postcolonial Caribbean, this victim is "also increasingly victim of himself (like Prof, like Redman, like the Father of **Mother Poem**)" (222), and in the Limuru section he places himself briefly within this catalogue of self-victimization.

Brathwaite surrounds his description of his naming ceremony with other stories about the giving and claiming of names. He cites his own introduction of the concept of "nam," or inner name, in *Mother Poem* and *Sun Poem*, as well as biblical and Shakespearean precedents for the importance of names. He recounts the battles he has fought to have others call him Kamau rather than Edward and he quotes from the transcript of the film version of Alex Haley's *Roots*, where the overseer beats Kunte Kinte into accepting that his name is Toby. He then offers the reader an explication of each syllable of his new name, spelt forwards—K/Ka/Kam/Kama—and backwards—U/au/mau/amau/ama (239-40). Section XII ends with a re-rendering of the poem "Nametracks" from *Mother Poem* in which a deadly game of O'Grady (Simon Says) between the mother and "The Man Who Possesses us all" takes place. As "O'Grady makes a last desperate effort to dictate/nominate/re/name **eat** Mandingo" (263), we hear the child begin to sing in his mother tongue, "to unsubmerge, to begin the come/ the come/ the come back up assertion/reassertion of the **nam**" (264).

There is a point in his description of these heroic struggles, however, where Brathwaite stumbles in parenthesis: when he allows his reader to see him as more fallible than his mythic alter egos. It comes during the description of his surprise naming ceremony when, in tiny script enclosed in parentheses he glosses (over?) the emotions he felt:

> kneeling on the ground with the wind on my face & the great sky of Eden all around me in fro/nt of these old women who like ripped open my shirt & like spat upon my chest (the water of baptism/though I was very much alarmed to say the least at first) & began chanting deep deep down inside their chests & deeper down into their very bellies searching for my **nam** so they cd find my name (236)

There is a vertigo about the language in this passage, produced by the effect of the parenthesis, the diminution of the type script, and the use of slashes and ampersands to connect words. It is as if the poet is hurtling through the space between two modes of potential subjectivity—the incompletion of "Edward" and the aspiration of "Kamau." The force of his destinerrance may throw off either outcome at any moment just as in the process of birth the foetus/child must pass through a hypothetical moment where its connection to life comes neither through the lungs nor via the umbilical cord. Moreover, the understated neutrality of the word "alarmed," which Brathwaite places within parentheses, isolated from the rest of the sentence and written in extra tiny script, recalls the professor's euphemistic usage of the word "extreme" at the possession ritual discussed earlier:

wh/en he meant 'obscene' - K/Ka/Kam/Kama/Kama/Kamau
too sacred = scared (189)

Brathwaite's linkage of these two passages, through the insertion of his
name in the first one, draws attention to the poet's embarrassment and vulnerability in the face of the primitive, almost obscene elements of his own
naming ritual. The word "like," reiterated before "ripped" and "spat," registers, without naming, the poet's anxiety, like that of a rapist's victim, or a
woman in childbirth, that his body will be exposed and violated in the
course of the proceedings.

The use of parentheses and understatement to sequester the poet's admission of shame and fear calls to mind the stories of cultural refusal/
repression inserted into the earlier "Legba" section: about the embarrassment of the Garifuna in Belize, who tell outsiders they know of no African
survivals in their culture while hiding/hoarding their drums (167); or the
stubborn insistence with which the hired help at the poet's sister's home in
St Vincent denies her agency, refusing even to acknowledge the sound of
drumming in the hills when asked about its message:

she didn't hear anything - *me nevva hear nothin - me na hear
nuttn - mwen na rien,msieu* (167)

All these stories are about how people of African descent in the Caribbean
"bracket" memories and associations they are not ready to deal with, sub-
merging their cultural connection to Africa through slavery as a way of
circumventing its attendant shame and pain. Brathwaite, in announcing his
new name, and describing the entire naming ceremony as well as the meanings he imputes to each syllable, forces onto the page a series of associations which even he concedes he once found "alarming." In the process,
our sense that the poet is pushing it—overdoing the narcissism, being em-
barrassingly personal, clapping with one hand the syllables of his own name
—pushes *us* as readers through the whole messy, self-absorbed, introspective, exhibitionist, shameful business of watching someone (ourselves?)
giving birth *or* being pushed into existence. It draws us into the embarrassment of those self-confessional moments when we are forced to look too
closely at the poet, skin peeled away, without the masks of aesthetic distance, and find in his eyes our own reflections, repressions, and unnamed
fears.

When, in closing the poem, the poet begins to rewrite the opening
acknowledgements to the sponsors of the Sir Winston Scott Memorial Lectures as he wishes he might have been able to articulate them, it hardly
comes as a surprise that the symbol he fantasizes this virtual archive will

now have made possible turns out to be a plaque with the poet's new name placed over the door to his dressing room:

> **First of all** Mr Chairman, I must thank the Central Bank of Barbados for bringing me here at this time and for promoting me to labour what I have hear this out over all these years. Never befo/re in this island (and I am still standing to yr attention) have I been treated so royally. [There was even, I remember, The Artist's Dressing Room with NAME
>
> <KAMAU>
>
> on the legba door (remember?) and large photos all over the palace] It is something I never xpected but which, I can assure you, I am enjoying. It is good to feel that your own island and your own people have somehow . . . understood what you have been trying to do (268)

Here, the undersized script of the words in the brackets within brackets serve to frame the oversized <KAMAU> the poet longs to see inscribed in his community's imagination. It is the kind of detail, he contends, that a loved and respected artist should be able to expect without having to clap for it—"Because if you can applaud him/ her ('clap a likkle') as he/she stands before you, if, as I assume, you feel that he/she has something important to say, then you've got to be concerned with the **whole thing**" (364).

Brathwaite's project by this point seems at risk of being undone by its very success. For if his fantasy were indeed to have come true, and the talk he was giving could have started in the manner he now imagines, then there would have been no talk—certainly there would not have been this prose poem, whose whole purpose has been to educate a reluctant audience into accepting the poet's right to name himself; to be loved and respected on account of the image of himself he has created through/in his work for his community. In such a scenario, the consciousness that would have stood before that imagined audience, secure in its expectation of respect and applause, could not have produced that painfully elegiac plea for lost community and submerged self that propels *Barabajan Poems* at its finest. Nor could a society that no longer needed such an elegy have produced the artist Brathwaite presents himself as having become. Like the biblical paradise where "I shall know as I am known," such a society would recognize and honor its own prophets without prompting. And the fear of rejection, the necessity of grammar, the mourning of loss, and, thus, the possibility of poetry would be no more.

All writers play a version of this game, whereby the object desired is precisely the one whose presence would disable the possibility of narrative. What makes the strategy so fraught in Brathwaite's case is the inescapability of the autobiographical presence—our sense that for Brathwaite this is no mere game of words and that he genuinely imagines that an artist *should* be able to expect this kind of unconditional love from his community—*and* that his writing will be the better for it.[8] His predicament dramatizes the Sisyphean extremity of the postcolonial writer who, in the absence of an established literary tradition, has only him/herself as literary subject and pre-text. Even as his virtual archive invents a literary tradition for Barbados through its painstaking appendices, drawing attention to the way the poet's achievement has been part of a wider moment of cultural possibility, Brathwaite remains circumscribed; unable to write from outside the castle of his skin, the only literary subject position available to him in a community whose histories remain submerged.

And so the *Barabajan Poems* drift erratically between the tidal pulls of autobiography and the anchor of Art, creating a society for the poet as well as a poet for the society it attempts to represent; talking at times in circles to itself. Its insistence that the value of the poet's person be inseparable from the achievement of the poet's work seems wistful at times, but there is no question that the poems this virtual archive allows Brathwaite to re-present from other collections gain depth and texture as a consequence of their insertion into the framework of his autobiographical hypertext. The interaction between the poetic persona, Kamau, and dramatic persona like the protagonist in "Angel/Engine" enables a new level of dialogue between the poet's life and work. His anthropomorphizing of his computers and his introduction of historical and contemporaneous voices to situate his own writing create a provisional virtual community for the artist in a situation where the support and resonance of the island community remain elusive. As critics, we long for that moment when a writer of his stature will achieve the recognition he thinks he deserves. But as readers we continue to be moved most profoundly by the elegiac achievement of Kamau's work; the cathartic anguish of his mourning; his unerring ability to name his loss and ours.

Notes

1. For Brathwaite's personal and aesthetic responses to the destruction of the Hurricane, see *Shar* and his "Open Letter to the Vice Chancellor of the Uni-

versity of the West Indies" (18th November 1988) describing the threatened archive at his Irish Town home and pleading for help in its preservation and cataloguing. Cited in Gordon Rohlehr's "Introduction" to Brathwaite's *DreamStories* (iv).

2. Cited by Rohlehr in *DreamStories* (vi-vii). "Trench Town Rock" is built around the ordeal of the robbery. See also "Open Letter." Brathwaite mentions the detail of the wedding ring in *The Zea Mexican Diary* (183).

3. Winnie Risden echoes a version of this sentiment in her review of *Masks*, when she complains that "[t]he small private moments when the conscience is shattered through contact to new perceptions are excluded by the poem's very nature. Brathwaite's success is to have endowed a familiar theme with the dignity of public ceremonial. He offers no message to the heart." She wants to know who speaks from behind the masks, "which face is his among the strange and terrible" (147). I am less critical of this formal distancing of the poet because I see it as a useful strategy for addressing a pressing aesthetic dilemma in Caribbean writing—the absence of a literary tradition in which to ground the personal—that all too easily can become an excuse for endless narcissism.

4. In the preamble to the volume, Brathwaite explains that the lecture was one in a series of memorial lectures sponsored by the Barbados Central Bank and named for Sir Winston Scott, the first native Governor General of Barbados. It was held in the Bank's Frank Collymore Auditorium, named after the founder and editor of *Bim*, the literary magazine that gave both Brathwaite and Walcott their start as creative writers (11). Brathwaite says that he produced *Barabajan Poems* in frustration over the Bank's almost decade-long failure to produce a published version of his lecture. Sections of the talk may have existed for a much longer time in manuscript, however, as Rohlehr in *Pathfinder* quotes from personal communications with Brathwaite dated 1974 that reproduce almost verbatim some of the material now integrated into *Barabajan Poems* (5). Ironically, the Bank's version of the talk finally appeared weeks after the launching of the present volume. See also note 1 (286) where Brathwaite describes the historical context in which his speech was delivered.

5. See Rohlehr's comments in the "Introduction" to *DreamStories*, also X/S 80-7. See also the note to the reader at the beginning of the story "Chad" where Brathwaite's two muses, Chad and Zea, merge through his computer to warn him of the impending destruction of his Irish Town home (DS 47-50).

6. Brathwaite's poetic vision has been the butt of some feminist criticism, most notably Beverly Brown's "Mansong." She accuses Brathwaite of manufacturing exclusively male myths and reducing woman in his work to voiceless, passive, inert landscape. She is especially critical of what she perceives to be Brathwaite's recourse to "androcentric birthing, so that even foetal blood may be credited to a male figure and the sea is the recipient of Father-ancestor rivers" (70). In "Brathwaite with a Dash of Brown," Rohlehr mounts a spirited defence of Brathwaite from Brown's critique, which mostly faults Brown for not having read Brathwaite closely enough (229-43). Nevertheless, I think

Brathwaite's work is open to charges of male-centeredness—not because it is not sympathetic in its presentation of women but because he *does* (understandably!) write from a male perspective, and there is often an implicit opposition in his work between woman as place/land/ mother and man as intellect/alienated subject/keeper of the word of the father. I see this most of the time as a productive opposition. Given the poet's subject position and historical moment of insertion into Caribbean literary discourse, it seems inevitable that he would work best through such images—and predictable that eventually they would attract disapproving attention from feminist critics. What interests me here, however, is the way in which this dialogic process is extended and refracted by the reinscription of Brathwaite's poems within the latticework of autobiographical interventions provided in *Barabajan Poems*.

7. Brathwaite's statement about the individual's relationship to community is made in the course of a criticism of the narcissistic introspection he divines as a flaw in both the author and the protagonist of Lamming's *Of Age and Innocence*. I find it significant that both Naipaul and Brathwaite identify in this particular novel, which they both read in important ways as having failed, problems that become central to the aesthetic dilemmas of their own later work.

8. Rohlehr writes perceptively in "Brathwaite with a Dash of Brown" about what he perceives as the central irony of Brathwaite's life as a public poet who, in order to create, needed to remain the most private of persons, but who failed to understand this need in others. When, in the aftermath of his wife's death, Brathwaite upbraided the University community at Mona, Jamaica for their lack of support, Rohlehr contends, he was asking other equally private people in this "community of isolatos" to step out of their own needed private space: "Brathwaite was demanding from Mona far more than it could ever have given: a support system of continuous concern and caring, that is possible only within the warmth and immediacy of a family. And Brathwaite had lost his" (*Shape* 211-12).

This Silver Feather

Mary E. Morgan

" ... it is with great esteem that I present to you on behalf of the entire Neustadt family, this box made of native Oklahoma woods and containing our symbol of literary accomplishment: this silver feather ... "

In Oklahoma University's Memorial Union on Friday September 30, 1994, Walter Neustadt Jr presented Kamau Brathwaite with the **silver eagle feather,** sign of inspiration and victory to the native american peoples, symbol of spirit: of soaring and vision; and in the literary tradition, instrument of recording, writing: thereby signal of continuity.

The Neustadt International Prize for Literature is awarded every two years to an outstanding writer, following deliberations by a jury of eminent writers and critics brought together for a few days in March by OU's prestigious literary quarterly *World Literature Today*.[1] Some six/seven months later, members of the jury again meet at Oklahoma University (OU) to honour the laureate at a splendid university function, with the Neustadt family, the Journal's Board of Visitors and editorial staff, sustainers and friends.

The jury for the 13th Prize comprised the following literary personages:

Kofi Awoonor	Wlad Godzich
Zoya Boguslavskaya	Angel Gonzalez
Alan Cheuse	Githa Hariharan
J.M. Coetzee	Elli Peonidou
Nawal El Saadawi	Chris Wallace-Crabbe
Nuruddin Farah	Djelal Kadir - Chair

homecoming weekend

The 1994 Neustadt Award ceremony was timed to coincide with the home-coming weekend, when OU alumni and their families flocked back to the little university town of Norman, Oklahoma, filling the Sooners Hotel and its cottages on campus, crowding out the town's accommodations and reaching up to Oklahoma City, a ninety-minute drive away. That year's home-coming highlighted graduates of the 1930s and 1940s, who brought children, grandchildren and great-grandchildren back to their university home.

The staff of *World Literature Today* worked closely with the Office of the President to craft a truly memorable weekend. And it was wonderful—from the warm welcoming of Djelal Kadir and his beautiful wife Juanita (Classics Professor Juana Celia Djelal) on Thursday to the magnificent award banquet on Friday, through the idyllic picnic on Saturday forenoon hosted by the President for homecomers and Neustadt guests, the exciting football match of the year that same afternoon and the Kadirs' elegant reception in the evening; to Sunday's flurry of brunch and goodbyes...

On Friday afternoon, Tania Norris, a member of the journal's Board of Visitors, took Harclyde Walcott (then of the Philip Sherlock Centre for the Creative Arts at the University of the West Indies Mona Campus) and my-self to meet Camilla Secrest, who has made of her home a veritable mu-seum of native American *memorabilia* and art. There we perceived simi-larities to our African heritage: significance of animals; influence of sun and moon; importance of landscape and harvest; the durability of oral traditions; the centrality of ritual: ceremony and dance and movement and mime...

> reverence for the ancestors   the power of the dream   the aura of the feather...

neustadt thirteen

In recognition of the 1994 laureate's place of origin, Caribbean music was featured on Friday evening at the President's reception preceding the ban-quet. Members of the OU Steel-band were delighted to meet visitors from the Caribbean and to demonstrate their skill. After their performance, they proudly showed us the beautifully wrought leather cases which the Univer-sity had provided for the treble and alto pans, and the shining lightweight trolleys for the bass drums.

After the banquet, Master of Ceremonies Djelal Kadir, Journal Editor and Distinguished Professor of English, introduced the 1994 Neustadt Lau-reate: Barbadian poet, historian, essayist, literary critic, academic, Kamau Brathwaite, formerly Professor of Social and Cultural History at the University of the West Indies Mona Campus, currently Professor of Comparative Literature in the graduate program at New York University.

Brathwaite had been nominated by Kofi Awoonor—poet, novelist, dramatist, critic, and until that year Ghana's Permanent Representative to the United Nations. The company noted with regret that Kofi Awoonor himself could not be present, but heard part of his advocacy:

> *Brathwaite is a poet of the total African Consciousness who possesses a deep grasp of the tones and reflexes of the African Lingua, as it encompasses the aboriginal sounds of West Africa and the distinct but profound echoes that are still prevalent in the English speaking West Indies. His poetry constitutes a complex commentary in stylistics and aesthetics, as well as being an incredible set of recordings on the larger canvas of the totality of Africa's history....*
>
> (award ceremony program)

proclamation and presentation

The Governor of Oklahoma, David Walters, conferred on Kamau Brathwaite honorary citizenship of the state.

Walter Neustadt Jr presented the Silver Feather, recounting how his father, a German immigrant, had joined in the trek to Oklahoma in the 1880s. His money ran out at Ardmore near the Texas border, so he stopped there, and later became involved in the mercantile business. In 1917 oil was found on the lands at Ardmore. It was in 1917 also that Oklahoma Territory to the north and Indian Territory to the south were merged to become the State of Oklahoma.

The aura of ancient peoples still pervades the land—that vast country named by the Choctaw nation: *oklahoma land of the red man.* It whispers in the wind; you hear it in the place names, in the night sounds; you see it in the craftwork, it looks out from behind the eyes of people in the streets; it reaches out to touch you. For it was here that the nations had found refuge at the end of the *trail of tears*—that long sad flight of pain from their homes in Florida and elsewhere in the south.

Interim President Dr J. R. Morris presented the Award: a sheet of vellum appropriately inscribed, under the Arms of the University of Oklahoma -

> *civi et republicae   for the citizen and the state*

- and a cheque for forty thousand dollars. President Morris said that he had read a number of Brathwaite's works before the announcement of the award winner at the end of March, and that he was looking forward to reading the latest book, *Barabajan Poems*, a copy of which the author presented to him.

salutations

Barbados's then Ambassador to the United States, His Excellency Dr Rudi Webster, delivered the first Salutation. His country was proud of Kamau Brathwaite, he said, as attested by the National Honour conferred on him in 1987—CHB: Companion of Honour, Barbados. On behalf of the Government and people of Barbados, Ambassador Webster extended best wishes and warm congratulations to Professor the Honourable Kamau Brathwaite.

Dr Webster spoke of Kamau Brathwaite's role as Consultant to the Barbados Government in 1978, when he defined culture as *"historically influenced life-style and expression,"* taking into account the ancestral forces instinct in our region: those of indigenous peoples, Europeans, Africans, Asians. Rudi referred to the *Twelfth Sir Winston Scott Memorial Lecture* in 1987, when Brathwaite had identified the poet's place in Barbadian culture as being -

> *...My place among us...where I come from, how I come from.... What I get, gain. lose, fit in, take out, give & give back.... How I see it.... How you see I seeing it.... How I see you seeing I seeing it...we - all one: interfacts and interfaces....* (BP 22)

The second Salutation, from Jamaica's Ambassador to the USA, His Excellency Dr Richard Bernal, was read by Harclyde Walcott of the Philip Sherlock Centre for the Creative Arts at the Mona Campus of the University of the West Indies. Dr Bernal referred to other awards gained by Brathwaite, as academic and as writer: Guggenheim and Fulbright Fellowships, Commonwealth Literary Award, Casa de las Americas Prize, *inter alia*; and paid tribute to his immense contribution over 28 years at UWI Mona, as a teacher *par excellence*, stimulator of consciousness, former colleague—a poet who had left UWI as Professor of Social and Cultural History.

Ambassador Bernal tendered apologies for his absence and extended congratulations on behalf of the Government and people of Jamaica.

encomium

Kenyan novelist Ngugi wa Thiong'o delivered the *encomium.*

Ngugi spoke of the impact of Brathwaite's work and thinking on his own development as a writer. He evoked the vision of the diaspora which they both shared: consciousness of one's worth, acceptance of one's self, appreciation of one's heritage. He referred to the impact which Brathwaite's notion of nation language had on him—**nation language,** the submerged language of the enslaved, capable of asserting itself and *"claiming the right to name ourselves, our landscape, our struggle."*

Ngugi recalled their first meeting at a gathering in 1966 in London, when Brathwaite's ideas for launching the Caribbean Artists Movement (CAM) were accepted. Later, as a young lecturer at Nairobi University, Ngugi was among those spearheading efforts to have Dr Edward Brathwaite invited, in 1972, as first visiting scholar in the Department of Literature, on a City of Nairobi Fellowship—to teach literature in its social/historical milieu, merge literary and cultural studies, explore connections. And, said Ngugi wa Thiong'o, Brathwaite (then a Senior Lecturer in History at UWI, Mona) *"proved a great teacher."* He was happy that they were now colleague professors at New York University.

Ngugi recalled too, that Brathwaite's lectures and readings at the University of Nairobi in 1972 were recognised as the authentic voice of orature:

*His voice was returning us to our formative roots in **orature**.... This orality runs through Brathwaite's entire work and is what gives it its very distinctive quality. This comes out powerfully through performance...Brathwaite gropes for the word in its oral purity. In doing so, he is groping for the voice of the peasant, the submerged voice of the many who toil and endure.* ("Kamau Brathwaite"[1] 678)

Ngugi referred to the part which his own family had played in the deepening of Brathwaite's insights into the significance of ceremony and the meaning of ritual *"in the traditions of our people."* When he invited Brathwaite to his home in the beautiful Tigoni Limuru area,

an area hallowed by memories of intense struggles, ...the peasants from the villages and the men and women of letters from Nairobi...gathered in this rural outpost to celebrate Brathwaite's presence (idem)

- this brother from across the seas. - Led by Ngugi's mother, the village women singing

***Gitiiro**, a kind of dialogue in song and dance, ..Edward Brathwaite was given the name of **Kamau**, the name of a generation that long ago had struggled with the elements to tame the land....* (*idem*)

[Kamau remembers this occasion in *Barabajan Poems*: "...nurtured in a spiritual secret place."][2] Ngugi saw Kamau Brathwaite as a connecting spirit, keenly aware of the links which bind us to our past and release us to our future. He cited an occasion, personally significant, when at the naming ceremony of his infant daughter earlier that year, Kamau had recited a poem in which the repeated invocation of the child's name *Mumbi Mumbi Mumbi* was an indication that he not only vividly recalled his own naming by Ngugi's mother, Wanjiku, but that he perceived the spiritual nexus between mother and granddaughter. To Ngugi and his wife Njeeri Ndungu, his mother Wanjiku, who died in 1989, was reborn in his daughter, Mumbi Wanjiku.

Finally, the celebrated Kenyan writer reminded his distinguished audience that Kamau Brathwaite admits no barriers between history, geography, literature...

> *We are celebrating the voice of connections, because what is so remarkable about him is not that he is a great poet, historian, critic, and teacher, but that these are not separate entities in himself.*
> ("Kamau Brathwaite"[1] 679)

interlude
When the applause died down, Jahruba, a rastafarian trio from Oklahoma City, provided an authentic reggae, blues and drumming interlude, setting the tone for the laureate's response.

"haltering the landscapes of the wind"
In his "thanks-tune" Kamau Brathwaite referred to the heritage shared by the people of the Caribbean and of Oklahoma, both with multi-faceted and various roots-

> *here is a person from these small islands far south of here...brought all these prairie miles of northamerican heartland to the crossroads of the **"trail of tears"** for this honour by an african brother a further 10,000 miles away...and who... recognises...that there is time & space shared...by our three landscapes - antillean, okla**home**an, african....*
> ("Newstead" 679)

Kamau commented on the *fragility of life* in the Caribbean, an arc of astonishingly beautiful islands perennially threatened by floods, hurricanes, earthquakes and occasionally by volcanoes. He extolled the *resilience of the people* in face of those threats, comparing them with the people of Oklahoma, themselves so often under siege from another natural menace: that of tornadoes. He paid tribute to the *fortitude* of those in both places who had lived through the anathema of forced migration and slavery, and of those everywhere who continued to withstand the unnatural menaces of injustice and discrimination/unkindness based on race or colour.

Brathwaite spoke of the paradox of cultural continuity in face of the several discontinuities of our history. In a wealth of metaphor he linked a family house, *Newstead* in Mile & Quarter, St Peter, Barbados—*"the underside of the leaf of my childhood"*—with this prize for literature endowed to the University of Oklahoma, USA, by a German American family, *Neustadt*:

> *Here is open canefield caneland snuggled by the darker colour of trees, time, green waters of vegetation flowing around the islands of hills, Brevitor caves, windmills... & our warm sleepy cooking-smoke villages in the shallow valleys of sound. And at the centre... this house of the ancestors, Newstead, which is quietly preparing itself for the Neustadt Prize in a similar landscape of spirit & spirits sixty years later on, on the other side of the wall.*
>
> *I bring you therefore a very special greeting of the most intimate recognition,*

he said, and continued in a blaze of imagery:

> *I in a sense am sent to return to myself what you both give me: speech, shafts of canelight, a green silver feather, my ancestories coming to be born here again: planter & slave, Ogoun & buffalo,* **Newstead & Neustadt** *spiritdances of the native crossroads....*
> ("Newstead" 654)

Kamau Brathwaite spoke of community and consonance, of vision and symbol and spirit. He invited his audience to accompany him on a journey through *"the landscapes of the wind,"* to examine the metaphor of stone and light and circle and flute; to learn with him the mystery of ritual, *"to pour a brief libation at the foot of the several trees of memory I growing... in these beautiful landscapes"*; to feel the feather brush of healing; to recognise the power of music and painting and dance, the power of oral traditions, of poetry, of the word—which like a feather can soar and dip, and soar and dip and soar and settle and rise again to soar...

And so Brathwaite read, in his inimitable way, from some of his works: *Rights of Passage*; *The Arrivants*; *Soweto.* -

> *out of this dust they are coming*
> our eyes listen out of rhinoceros thunder...
> when all the lights of anger flicker flicker flicker...
>
>   ...and the fist
> clenching around that scream of your mother, bled

into a black head of hammers

and the light fell howl
on soweto
the night fell howl
on soweto... (*Soweto* 1-2 [unpaginated])

He analysed the development of his writing: change from Miltonic pentametre to "*... singing the genesis of these islands...in im own native ancient and modern riddim(s) of calypso*" - and read from "Kaiso":

The stone had skidded arc'd and bloomed into islands... (RP 48)

The rapt audience learned of the expansion of his horizons, his growing awareness of varied cultural influences from the various shango rhythms of our pasts-

so sistren & breddren
we is all gather here
tonight to praise
the Lord an raise
a anthem to his holy name ("Stone Sermon," IS 254)

Kamau read from *Mother Poem*; *Sun Poem*; *X/Self*; ...of ancestors and ceremony and cricket; of masks and islands; of circles and stones and pain and spirit...

It is a cultural thing with us, that we often slip into music when we are moved—a trumpet curl around a phrase; a fleeting whisper from a flute; an undergirding of drums; a hum. So that evening, Jahruba, the Rastafarian trio, interjected an occasional finger of music as Kamau Brathwaite read. When he began to read "Rasta" (formerly "Negus"), they spontaneously joined in with a palpitation of drums:

it
it
it
it is not
it is not enough
it is not enough to be free
of the red white and blue.... ("Rasta," IS 222)

Kamau identified certain metaphorical triggers—**pebbles**—associated with his growing consciousness of cultural roots

smooth voices like pebbles
move by the sea of their language ("The New Ships," M 124)

and awareness of the significance of ceremony, of the African ancestral gods/presences: Legba Ogoun Oshun Oya/Adowa...

here is a stool for you. sit ...
here is water. dip... (*ibid.* 124-5)

He explained his theory of *tidalectics*—movements of water or sound, tide rather than time, allowing him to use, build on and renew poems/structures.—Certain poems flow like corridors of water, reappearing in new settings of time or place; like the poem "South":

We who are born of the ocean can never seek solace
in rivers; their flowing runs on like our longing
reproves us our lack of endeavour and purpose
proves that our striving will founder on that... (RP 57; BP 84)

- which he used in *Barabajan Poems* to illustrate his coming full cycle home, after his seven years in Ghana:

But today I recapture the islands'
bright beaches: blue mist from the ocean
rolling into the fishermen's houses... (BP 83)

Kamau commented on the way the verse moves

in its accumulations of sound/sense (the way Oshun xpresses her-
self here in essesses, countering the ing sounds of the riverbank and
the dark ripple of rapids ... mark[ing] this for me as another of the
special **libations** *or signposts or stele - radar stations of a certain*
kind of tidalectic time/space. ("From Newstead" 657)

He spoke of a new corridor of movement between *Sun Poem* (1982) and *X/ Self* (1987) of *The Ancestors* trilogy. Some of the earlier poems reappeared in different forms in *Middle Passages* (1992, 1993)—after the period of personal suffering brought on by the death of his first wife Doris in 1986, the destruction by hurricane Gilbert of much of his home in the Irish Town hills in 1988, the hold-up by armed robbers in 1990.

During this period, which he had described to his friend Gordon Rohlehr as *"the time of salt the wasteland"*[3] he developed the *post modem Sycorax video style*; the computer became an instrument to facilitate his use of various fonts and letters/digits of different sizes on the same page, or even in the same line, thus reflecting his feelings of insecurity and loss. Prose became the medium. Many cheeks in the Memorial Hall glistened as he read from *The Zea Mexican Diary*, in which he recorded his anguish at Doris's death after an all too brief illness:

> *And as the dawn was coming up coming up...making it deeper &*
> *deeper & darker they came...& took her away in th(e) white wind-*
> *ing sheet her whole self wrapped away...as i following like help-*
> *lessly like helplessly this soft dark horse/ looking like any ordinary*
> *car or horse or hearse - but larger - longer - leaner - and so very*
> *very very different - so quietly quietly special w/ not a sound of*
> *wheels along the(e) russet-leaf-stained-almond-curve of the road...*
> *only this rise & foil as if they being careful down the now cold steps*
> *past perfume tree & cherry tree & the almonds & the jacaranda*
> *bush the broken little white Gibraltar Camp gate & then the darker*
> *darker river of the road away from me from me from me from me & the*
> *chill & silent & still darkness of that foreday morning & then nothing nothing*
> *nothing nothing nothing I cd do cd do cd ever do again ... for her for*
> *her...& the silence & the sky above me one alone here now like the*
> *now really lonely morning star...& faintest pin & pink of wind on*
> *all those other softly fading stars that somehow reach and touch*
> *the silver of my face (Zea 101-3)*

Brathwaite touched briefly on some of the nightmares he experienced in the period of desolation which followed, when, still in prose, he wrestled with guilt and self-reproach which found expression in *DreamStories*, parables of the poet/protagonist, portrayed as a simple soul, struggling for life/light against the powers of darkness:

> *what I felt when he struck didn't have the sensation of bodily pain.*
> *But ... I could hear myself groaning. ... But the groans didn't come*
> *from my physical self. It seems that each time Kappo hit me, he*
> *didn't actually hit my chin or my face, but he hit something bright*
> *like **nam** or a star or far like a jewel inside me - my innocence, it*
> *seems - my spirit or my soul - and it <was this xistence - inside -*
> *within me, which involuntarily groaned & cried out every time....*
> *(DS 15-16)*

> *Kappo's jacket was something living, a fabric inhabited by a dark*
> *insidious presence; a living form of something Other - Older - than*
> *itself; ...*

Mary E. Morgan

I rushed to the bunk bed where Delta lay like so
faded out & silent . tore the

Black Angel

from the dark moorings of his throat
and lifting it up and turning, threw it into the fire

....

. .. when I throw away the jacket the
stone was roll away & the great sun come
shining in/to my now known darkened
wood like a great gong... (DS 41-3)

He read from "Computer Legba," halfway into *X/Self*, beginning :

Why a callin it

X ?

a doan write.
ly know (X/S 12)

- everything seems "hung up" like a dysfunctional computer ("a cyaan
get nutten write...").

He is left *"stanning up hey...like i inside a me shadow...."*

F l u t e (s), he indicated, was his last *pre-modem* poem , *"but it had all
the premonitory elements of a post modem corridor"* - *"a new kind of Oya
corridor"* ("From Newstead" 659). The flute is also another parallel between the ancient peoples of the Americas, Africa and Asia. The great hall
in Norman, Oklahoma was hushed as he read, to the plaintive whisper of
flutes from Jahruba:

is when the bamboo from the clip of yellow groan and wrestle
begins to glow & the wind learns the shape of its fire
and my fingers following the termites drill
drip into their hollows of silence . shatters of echoes of tone

that my eyes close all along the walling . all along the branches .
all along the world

> *and that that creak of spirits walking these graves of sunlight*
> *spiders over the water . cobwebs crawling in whispers over the*
> *stampen green*
> ("Flute(s)," *Jah Music* 22)

The images are powerful: insidious destruction of termites; shivery crawling of spiders/cobwebs. But the music of the bamboo flute has power to shatter the nightmare's echo, and as he continues the poet finds

> *that the wind is following my footsteps*
> *all along the rustle all along the echoes all along the world*
> *and that that stutter I had heard in some dark summer freedom*
> *startles and slips from fingertip to fingerstop*
> *into the throat of the morning into the throat of its sound*

Kamau introduced his new "Xango at the Summer Solstice" - *each year upon this longest day...* - written for Neustadt, with the assertion that "*the great spirits of yr landscape...must have recognize & welcome me even before I reach here*" ("From Newstead" 660). He linked the ancient peoples of Africa and America, connecting them with the pioneers of the south west and the free villages of former slaves (Langston, Oklahoma, USA; Sligoville, St Catherine, Jamaica; and in Barbados: Sweet Bottom, St George; Rock Hall, St Thomas; Supers/*Souffrieres*, St. Philip). Jahruba provided an occasional murmur of sound as his words reached for the light of healing, the life of creativity:

> .. all winter wrong he store the sounds you hear now in these man-
> dolins. All through the cold hard dark he labour for this light
> & now he find it on im lip he blow the flute he string im
> lute im rise & go again looking for his Oya of the after-
> noon: im rose im pain the pale flame of im sunset in the western
> tree ... *("From Newstead" 660)*

And Jahruba's trumpet twirled softly as Kamau spoke again of the restoring power of music. As the drums had throbbed for *Soweto*, so during his poignant reading from =***SHAR*** =***Hurricane Poem*** (written after the 1988 hurricane and revised in 1990 after the death of my daughter Sharon), they pulsed gently, ending with a hauntingly beautiful *ceeyay*, that sound made by drawing a finger across the top of the drum, across the goatskin, while resonating with an elbow stop:

> ...sing. ing & sing. ing. the train

song of rain. fall & what's left of the

stone of the mourn. ing. the mount. ain
black.slide.ering. slide. ering. slide
ering. over the. pain and the valley
the sing. ing

still
there in the rise & rise of
the sorrel horizon & sing ing
& sing ing
the song
of the morn. ing
jah's . sym.bole & . flame in the rain.blow
out . of the tree
of ijs heaven

[njnnnnngn]

A brief silence.   Then a standing ovation.
And Djelal Kadir declared the proceedings at an end.
....

What better way can I end this essay than—with Kamau's permision—with his own words? Conceived in that moment of celebration in Oklahoma, encircled by echoes of other moments, other voices,[4] gestating these six healing years, this signal of consummate hope now comes, in this new century, from a new work still in the making—another kind of eagle:

Bird Rising

Until it come to the time for the great myriad bird the Mithurii[5]
to begin its ascent . its challenge against the earth
the paradoxical oracle of wind . the wings beating unchaining. out. boarding

as seamen might say . the great breast ruffled & rising . as in all the great legends
and this happening here before me under me now wonderfully surrounding me
the white silver louvered feather shift &˙chevron stretching out

across the sunlight into the pale almost like rainbow mist of its ending
the great terrible beauty & beating we have always heard about

beating beating beating upward & froward . the planks of its shape shivering
at first like a ship . like a dhow . then spheering down into smooth as we scool up.
wards...

......   *the sea below all shard & silver like*
our shadow . the beacon topaz eyes un-
blinking even through all the shudder . the wings now stretched across all space
*openly & awesomely . so that we are not beating any. more but **ahh** sailing .*
something
like singing . because at last I have been able to use all the wounds in the lan-
guage
as long as I lay them out softly & carefully . like these unfluttering feathers of
song
....
like the darkness no longer lingering above us . but we moving towards
it as part of its fuse & and its future . ...
......
the oars
of sleep through the silence . the metaphor at last afloat in the feathers . almost a
. light
in the darkness

mem   FETHEROU.wp
revised May 8, 2000 for Kamaufest
UWI Mona Jamaica

Notes

1. In 1970 the University of Oklahoma created an award known as the *Books Abroad* Literary Prize, carrying a cash award of $10,000. When this prize was in danger of being discontinued by 1972 due to financial constraints, Walter Neustadt Jr, then on the University's Board of Regents, persuaded his mother to continue it by endowing the prize with a gift of $200,000 in the Neustadt family's name. They later added sufficient to perpetuate a biennial award of $40,000. The name of the literary quarterly, *Books Abroad*, was later changed to *World Literature Today*.

2. "I wd like to share with you a little more about my Gikuyu name Kamau.... I was there, kneeling on the ground with the wind on my face & the great sky of Eden all around me, in front of these old women who like ripped open my shirt & like spat upon my chest...& began chanting deep deep down inside

their chests & deeper down into their very bellies searching for my **nam** so they cd find my name..." (BP 236). For the meaning of the name, each letter/ sound/meaning building on the one before, see also BP 239-40.

3. Quoted by Rohlehr in "Dream Journeys" [Introduction] iii, from a letter dated 14 Aug. 1986.

4. Echoes of "The Windhover" (outriding) by Gerard Manley Hopkins? "I caught this morning morning's minion, king-/dom of daylight's dauphin, dapple-dawn-drawn falcon, in his riding / Of the rolling level underneath him steady air, and striding / High there...."

5. East African eagle.

A New World Lament

Joan Dayan

> under de rattle & pain
> i de go
> **huh**
>
> i de go
> **hah**
> (Brathwaite, *Barabajan Poems*)

> "--the constriction in the throat, the snake pealing towards a
> new meaning of the skin--"
> (*Barabajan Poems* 192)

Ghosts and gods walk together in lands made waste by greed, drugs, and mammon. Brathwaite writes to get them going. These "gods of the Middle Passage," as Brathwaite calls them, mark his poetry both early and late with remarkable urgency. Moving from the gods of *Islands* that "can walk up out of the sea/into our houses" to the "ghosts, spirits, sky-juices, ancestors, immemorial memories" of *Barabajan Poems* to the bodies of "Dream Haiti," "all quite dead & bloated/by this time," we are invited to make the transit through desecration and violence, through dark blood and gunshots. The brute scenes of Brathwaite's later poems are apparently untouched by the saving graces of the gods, their sounds now muffled, no longer shaking the earth. Yet even in the desolate ruinscape of poems like *SHAR*, "Trench Town Rock," and *DreamStories*, the gods remain, as if to ask again, "How do we sing the Lord's song in a strange land?"

In thinking about Brathwaite's poetry, I am struck by the reinvention of notions of vengeance and grace. Brathwaite has reinterpreted and transformed the long poem or poetic sequence. How has that happened? What has he brought to bear on the conventions of epic? And how has he used religion–what he early claimed was the "focus of African culture in the Caribbean"–to write things of such unmediated horror that one turns away only to look again, to read, reflect, and know in the gut what it means to know. To know the face of the woman possessed by Damballa, "eyes now bulging bulbs of light, her breasts puffed out puffed out aggressive her breathing **engine**, the *hiss* become a howl where once was smiling mouth a broken cup or cistern (sistren) of a new world new world new world as the gutterals of god **ashamed astonished into stone and like surprised her face**" (BP 188). To know how this face looks taken up by the spirit only to turn to another woman's face, this one changed utterly by the slice of a knife:

> They break into our finest editor's home one night and place her carving knife between her teeth & force it forward. forward. forward. slicing the boundaries of skin that mark her lips that let her snark & smile & speak. until the dark blade reached the skull. You never knew a human tongue cd be so red & look so long & gurgle with such flame. ("Dis," "TTR" 196)

Is this prophet delivering a Jeremiad for the Canaan lost, the rivers run dry, the bones that will not rise on that great getting up morning? "This is a lamentation, and has become a lamentation." Ezekiel's warning begins with the appearance of winged human-headed creatures that gleam like burnished bronze. Under the wings are human hands, on the front of their faces, the look of a man and on the right side, the face of a lion, on the left side, the face of an ox, and at the back the face of an eagle. There are wheels rimmed with eyes, and "the spirit of the living creatures was in the wheels." Wheels within wheels. Chariots of fire. God's sapphire throne. Seeing the radiance of the Lord, Ezekiel falls on his face. He hears God's voice. Prophecy comes to Ezekiel in the form of a scroll which he must eat. The words of mourning and woe taste to him like honey. God orders that he eat bread baked on human dung. When Ezekiel objects, saying that he has never defiled himself, never eaten foul flesh, God allows him to substitute cow's dung. Throughout Ezekiel's oracles of warning, desolation is portrayed as pollution, whether the wanton flesh of harlots, the rot of bodies left unhallowed, the blood of the slain, the blood leak of women. Against images of blood, excrement, and the stink of seminal outpouring, God sets the whirling wheels, his cherubim, and the promise of purification, when the altars will be laid waste, the cities ruined, and the bones of the people of Israel scattered.

The wild admonishment, the rocking of God's sweet chariot forms a background against which we can read Brathwaite's annunciation of "late light duppy Kingston nights," "the valley of destruction filled with buzz," in his "hurricane poem" *SHAR*, or the "Age of Dis. Distress Dispair & Disrepect. Distrust Disrupt Distruction" in "Trench Town Rock" ("Dis" 196). Over thirty years ago, Brathwaite called for an "alternative history," unmediated by false idealism, but caught up in the stress and breakage of gods looking for their places. What I hope to demonstrate in this essay is how Brathwaite accomplishes not only the experience of "possession" in these late poems, but actually dramatizes, pulls us toward, gets us into what it means to take the givens, the shards, the fragments and out of them make belief. So that what first seemed lament becomes matter for creation. As in the early *Islands* (1969), the road is rocky, the burdens heavy, but what is new is not the invocation of loss and renewal but the staying close to rot and cruelty, without any sign of salvation. Yet the replaying, the taking to the limits the very thing that has killed the gods, brings them back in ways that go beyond their appearance on the page.

Brathwaite's poems of trauma force readers to know what it means to serve the gods: the grueling, sometimes demanding attachment to what is ugly or repugnant. He understands that service is nothing less than a peculiar brand of sensuous domination. A ritual of memory, these spirits return as deposits of history. In *Islands* Brathwaite reveals this historical streak, as well as the cost of remembering. Memory pierces through to the quick, carrying with it as the god mounts his horse, the insistent, undying past:

> I am water
> I am blood
> I am the hot rum leaking from green
> from the clanking of iron
> I bleed with the fields' sweat
> with the sweet backs of labour
> my steps take root in the worn shadows
> where the noon has burnt a harbour. ("Shepherd," IS 187)

Here Brathwaite calls upon the gods to walk on up out of the sea, find their places, and there combat the white master's arbitrary power, the swathe of whips, the lashed wounds. But in "Trench Town Rock," the forces of contingency and dispossession are located in a contemporary, urban, and drug-ridden Jamaica. The unspeakable acts are committed by gunmen, **duppies, warriors, drones**" ("The Mechanics, "TTR" 181). Relics and scraps of bodies return; they pulse through the darkest locales, "monstrous HELL of stench & detritus & death, dead rat. live rat. for bread. bone. dead rotting flesh. dead rotting fish," ("Dis," "TTR" 196). The poet turned prophet conjures, divines, and judges, naming the victims of the new, 20th century "Middle Pass." (196)

The crucial knot of images in this reclamation is that summoned by the Haitian spirit Damballa-wèdo (Danbala in Haitian Creole), the serpent god, who haunts rivers, springs, and marshes. He is represented as a snake, arched in union with his female counterpart Ayida to form the rainbow. In Haiti Damballa, spirit of fertility and force, is also lightning. He joins his whistling and staccato *tettetetete* with the chugging, locomotive rhythms of Shango, though Shango is not worshipped as a *lwa* (god, presence, or spirit) in the Haitian vodou pantheon. Once mounted (possessed) by Damballa, the "horse" darts out her tongue, crawls on the ground and climbs trees. The experience of the snake, whether green *coulevre*, python, boa, in its hiss and rattle slides through Brathwaite's pages. The face of the woman slit through to the skull turns into Damballa flambeau (torch) of the Petro ritual, flames jutting out of the tongue forked by the blade: "you never knew a human tongue cd...gurgle with such flame."

Let us trace the sound and movement of this spirit as if a thread through the contortions and complexities of poems from Brathwaite's New World Trilogy *Arrivants* (1973) to *DreamStories* (1994). If we take Damballah as "**seer & sayer**," whirling and wheeling through these poems, we understand how Brathwaite miraculously restores an experience of innocence and indefeasible gusto which the world–and an Old Testament prophet like Ezekiel–have rejected:

> so that Damballa
> at the centre of that circle slowly
> spread to the circumference of feeling
> into new more xplosive breath sounds:
> *huh*/intake/*hah*/intake/*huh huh*/intake/*hah*
> faster & faster & faster the snake of the train picking up speed
> & the Damballa *hiss* become wheel become whistle become wind.
> engine. power. howl (BP 190)

As early as "Homecoming" in *Islands*, the poet, "expecting nothing/my name burnt out," once possessed by the image of the snake, turns blood into drink, flesh into dry tongue of memory. This passage matters for its grip on how Damballa, known most often as the beneficent god of springs and rivers, knows ferocity. In Haiti the lwa–products of a purely local imagination– though identifiable in terms of their traditional traits, change and adjust to the peculiarities of their devotees. Damballa, though identified as a "white," benign Rada spirit (said to come from Dahomey) can "walk" in different rites, mix with other "nations" (the African ethnic groups of which Haitians are descendants), and take on traits that refute the idea of innate character. Damballa, the good Rada spirit, turns into the savage Petro presence Damballa flambeau. Here is Brathwaite's terse and ingenious expression of the violent and provisional locale for vision:

> even my skin
> now sheds its shame;
> like a snake
> the eyes do not wink
> away; whips do not flinch
>
> from what they will destroy:
> strips , strips of flesh,
> flash of the black forked tongue
>
> licking these scars,
> this salt red liquor,
> beaten labour. (IS 177)

In both *Mother Poem* (1977) and *Sun Poem* (1982), the snake remains. Like the sunken waters of Brathwaite's island Barbados, "echo of river, trickle, worn stone," sunken but ever ready to reemerge, the gods return, and customs and rituals survive though reappearing in new guises. In *Mother Poem* Brathwaite turns to the experience of a woman in Revival Church, possessed by the Haitian god of the sweet waters. Once celebrated in Dahomey as the great serpent who rises from the underworld to drink the fresh water of the streams, in "Angel Engine" Damballa returns in the blood of this woman speaking Afro-Bajan language: "i tek up des days wid de zion/we does meet tuesdee nights in de carpenter shop/praaze be to god/ *i hear the chapman hall preacher shout out*" (98). Suddenly, "de tongue curlin back," her "praaze be to god" of Revival zion is subsumed by the "seamless hiss/that does rattle these i:ron tracks," the "huh....hah/is a scissors gone *shhhaaaa*/under de rattle an pain" of Damballa, who joins with the "*shang,*" the "*sh,*" "*gg,*" and "*sssssssssssssssshhhhhhhhhhh*" of Shango ("Angel Engine," MP 98-103).

In *Sun Poem*, Brathwaite's origin poem "Red Rising" begins with the Fon cosmic serpent, since as *Da* or *Dan*, the origin and essence of life, Damballa presided over creation:

when the earth was made
when the sky first spoke with the voice of the rain/bow
when the wind gave milk to its music
when the suns of my morning walked out of their shallow
     thrill/dren (SP 2)

The very topography of *Sun Poem* takes on the curves and lineaments of the snake, whether the "Son" who "still knows that ice awaits him when the curve is done/down that descent he plotted on a rain-/bow: in the deep veins of neptune and uranus" (SP 10) or in Adam's reversal of the Middle Passage, his description of boys on a "sunday school excursion," before crossing over the heights of the island via Horse (Hearse) Hill, and then· traveling east "far far below," toward "the promised land," sinking down like a boa,

slowly they dipped up and dipped down
down steadied and slowly
dipped down again: be

coming part of the water: be
coming part of the dream

until they were almost not there
like old men...being forgotten...dozing away into silence (SP 42)

What happens to Damballa, lover of freshness and purity, in the dirty, stagnant regions of *SHAR*, "Trench Town Rock" and *DreamStories*? After hurricane Gilbert nearly destroyed his home, personal archives, and library up in Irish Town, Jamaica in 1988, Brathwaite wrote *SHAR* out of the landslide, mud, and rot. In Part I he laments the incredible waste after "the shattered cess of the storm," when the winds "began to reel . in circles . scream. ing like Ezekiel's wheel." The rip and the roar, the "lamentations of the stars . above these broken shingles," becomes more than apocalyptic catalog, as Brathwaite seems initially to renounce Eschatology, the idea that in the end lies salvation, ending the story of the end. As Part I draws to a close, Brathwaite waits, hearing "the sound of curses under this abuse of beauty left within me/under my forked foot. forked foot. foot print limp. that limps across this/land of five hundred thousand homeless on this night alone." Bearing God's curse, the poet walks alone through the debris, merging Legba's limp with Damballa's forked tongue. Suddenly redemptive vision comes along as praise song: "**song** at last **song**/from the throats of the five hundred thousand/the hands/clasped to bellies of pain & the rocking of agon/but/**song. song. song.**" (*SHAR*). This sinuous grace of singing announces Damballa's presence, "a new voice based on sibilance," as Brathwaite will describe it in *Barabajan Poems* (189). By Part 2, the **sing./ ing** conjures again the doubling of Shango and Damballa, "**the train./song of rain./fall,**" as we move through the "**slide./ering/slide/ering/slide/ ering,**" which I take to be the snake's slithering "**over the pain & the valley**" (*SHAR*). Reading through the fluid mutations of Brathwaite's video style, we are brought into the sound of the song and see the darkness arc with color, as if with every repeated "s"–and there are many–we are brought closer to the promise of the rainbow in the morning light:

> **jah's**
> **sym/bole &**
>
> **flame in the rain/**
> **blow**

"Trench Town Rock" takes us back to the the dump, the detritus that is backdrop to the tangled plot of economic greed, governmental stupidity, and poverty. "The Marley Manor Shoot/in" opens with "gunshatt," followed by "crack-like-firecracker-racket shats" ("TTR" 131). Brathwaite thus sets the scene for the corrupt, bloody Kingston of mutilation and murders, the new "Sodom & Gomorrah" ("TTR" 139). Twice describing the murder of "Early Bird," the young Glenford St Joseph Phipps (135-6; 137), Brathwaite forces us twice to witness with him the body, unforgettably ravaged. Early Bird's ravishment also prepares us for Brathwaite's own "turn" as victim, when armed robbers plundered his house, and he, gagged and tied, waited for death. The first rendition is a startling poetic lament that turns dreadlocks into the site of both cruelty and comfort. It is difficult is to show that this is not merely symbolic. Yet the words make us see how the dance of death is turned, even if just momentarily, into another kind of dance, perhaps the *yanvalou*, the dance especially liked by Damballa: body sloping forward, the shoulders undulate and hands fall to the knees. The dead man's hair, as if possessed, comes alive in the poet's pursuit of foulness:

> **his beautiful**
> **long hair like curled around**
> **his body making snakes like**
> **dance/like dancing...........**
> **& his hair**
> **- some of his hair - his locks**

>   - beside him - pulled out by
> the very roots by some stran
> ge/some strange stranger vio-
> lence - the gunmen had been
> *dragging* him away like that
> by all his loveliness. **("TTR" 135)**

Body stripped of bones, meat and muscle, face no longer familiar, all that remains is the astonishing redemption experienced by the poet as he imagines the Medusa locks quickening into beauty.

> **his locks had**
> **whirled around him as the bull**
> **ets made him dance his death**
> **& wrapped themselves around**
> **him as he fell. so now there**
> **was this eerie beauty in the**
> **barley light. his hair become**
> **his only perhaps comforter** ("TTR" 136)

In February 1988, during the transitional government of Haiti before the election of Jean-Bertrand Aristide in 1991, the *New York Times* reported in words I never forgot: "A cargo ship chartered in the United States has dumped about 4,000 tons of garbage on a Haitian beach." After many attempts to dump the cargo of waste in other Caribbean countries, the interim military rulers of Haiti gave the ship permission to dump Philadelphia toxic city waste near the port of Gonaïves. A few years later, after the overthrown Aristide had been suitably neutralized in the United States, President Clinton was ready to let "operation democracy" once again "save" Haiti by returning Aristide, though accompanied by U.S. troops. Jesse Helms castigated the President: "Don't send our troops to clean up the garbage in Haiti."

In "Dream Haiti" (DS) Brathwaite has wrought a powerfully Caribbean conversion narrative and there found anew the motive for epic poetry. The dream vision is, of course, more than mere dream. For vision to be granted there must be first "the shared collective conscious (and unconscious) xperience of a people" (BP 21). Though set as sea voyage, this journey comprises the prisons of the new America, the Haitian internment camps, the bitter gardens of the new multinationals, the criminal alien tracking centers for illegal immigrants, and, ultimately, the methodical exclusion of certain folks outside the pale of human relation and empathy. Recalling the Middle Passage and the mythical *Guinée* of the gods under the sea, these "slate-grey" waters mark a terribly circumscribed place: a container for contamination, the final receptacle for social undesirables–Haitian refugees drowning in a sea patrolled by the Coast Guard vessel "US Gutter."

Like the shape-shifting snake that sheds skin and moves as if without bones, the amphibious body of the dreaming poet initiates the journey. But what kind of body? I want to suggest that in these lines the poet dreams himself as already a living dead spirit:

> The sea was like slate grey of what was left of
> my body
> & the white waves
> I remember
> they was like very white
> on what was left of my skin
> & they kept comin in at this soft swishing diagonal
> against the
> bow & metal slides of my nerves (DS 95)

Inhabitant of the waters, his skin already beginning to slough off, he becomes vehicle of the merging of sea and body, waves and skin, as even the boat's bow and metal sides turn into the "slides" of his nerves. The dreaming and drowning become one as Brathwaite reveals to us that eternal place under the waters, where the spirits reside.

The perception or attitude demanded in following this drama demands our experience of *presentness*, and its demands are as rigorous as those of any spiritual exercise. Recall that moment in *Barabajan Poems* when Brathwaite places the gods in the minds of their people, and tells us how they travel, where they walk:

> and the hissing snake/steam Damballa - **gods of**
> **the Middle Passage** - who came over - who arrive -walking on the wa-
> ter of our conscience as they say in Gulla - rising from the silvers of
> our souls in Haiti - as they say from Guinea (BP 173)

"Dream Haiti," then, proceeds as a recurrent formation of consciousness, localizing and materializing the life of the spirit in the "up & down movement & soft ooze of/things creakin," in memories of Port-au-Prince, the painter Hector Hippolyte, Christophe on La Ferrière, Toussaint "on the glacial seas of the/Jura," the battle of "**la crête-a-pierrot**."

Whether on the US Gutter or the doomed Haitian *canot*, fighting for Haitian independence or trying to get to Miami, no matter, for this discipline of memory and task of imagination joins explicitly the experience of dreaming and drowning: "screaming to someone tryin to dream or drownin" (DS 97). But the pulse of conversion, based upon sound itself, takes us back to the call of the gods, and here Brathwaite turns the ship itself into a spirit with power to possess, when he remembers "going up &/down slowly & softly grey like the ship in my head." What that ship becomes, what we hear, is Damballa lending his healing to "muted agony": "w/the nerves breaking out sibilant & white like a /long line of lip rolling softly" (DS 96).

Roaring River of Reflections

Isis Costa

for Kamau Brathwaite who stood at the gateway
& when I thanked him for opening it
he told me about the reflections

his body now without its bones or musculature, without its meat without its clutch &
nomen of a face/ familiar creatures/ that someone somewhere somehow knew/ that
someone/somewhere loved & because the man himself had fled out through these
leaking holes, his locks had whirled around him as the bullets made him dance
his death & wrapped themselves around him as he fell.
so now there was this eerie beauty in the barley light (TTR 13)

But to whom will the stranger
return
when touched by disaster? (Sappho 42)

in new york I step on pieces of light shining through the pores of this rock
that doesn't know my name

nessa nova iorque eu descubro a encruzilhada estrangeira
on the ends of fork stems I nurse the mutilated sprout
acurralada nesse bêco êco éco ôco

i came to this crossroad and waited for permission
stretched fingers reaching for the
intersection of tongue and throat
learning the braille of foreign vowels, clusters

opening up windows, softly, slowly
I came to this language
acurralada nesse bêco êco éco ôco
desert

replacing glass with clay bricks and sturdy wood
to be safe and even so termites   ••
& through cracks: rain, draft, crows
and his shadow

devising shapes on the ceiling cracks of this dungeon
holding lullabies and the hands of my mothers
as the shadow of this unwanted body on top of mine
looms larger & larger & larger

i came to this crossroad and waited

carved a hole
found the *roots curled like shells* (X/S 105)
poured some honey
brought a turtle full of eggs
com a benção de minha mãe
and like moss this rock & i
like i and i
como?
this rock that didn't know my name
like is & is
like my mother
como é? como é?
say woman: she is tell muh (MP 57)

como mãe?
in my mother tongue
o que?
she lisper to me dat me name what me name
dat me name is me main an it am is me own an lion eye mane (MP 62)

spinning to New York drums
in this turtle nest full of eggs
and serpents pleased with honey
dancing, dancing   •

i wd leave house of bone
i wd leave moss & musk & musty corner/stone
i wd leave stone & dance (X/S 97)

344

retracing the route that brought me to this rock
girando, girando
so as to crack this rock
so as to let this trapped light
this trapped light coming out from the pores of these streets
so as to let this rock, so as to rock this rock
polindo a luz dessa pedra, nessa pedra, essa pedra
so as to let it

breath

and the stone wrinkled, cracked and gave birth to water (MP 16)
and all the fire of the sun
claypots igniting in flames
short circuit of spiritual coils
electricity sparkles in the wings of a butterfly
gravel frying lizards & frogs
& the 6am sand felt like larva

out of the long grass
out of the ancient forest (BB² 39)
vermilion dancer out of antelope
i summon you from trees
from ancient memories of forests
from the uncurling ashes of the dead
that we may all be cleansed (X/S 98)

veio de lado - refletindo o axé de folhas raízes caracóis. piscando os olhos em ventania. pisando em fohas estalando esparramando seiva os troncos em musgo refletindo luz e cada veia cada olho de cada tronco de cada árvore pulsava o coração em disparada. correria de animais buscando canto mas o zunido da flecha- ah o zunido.... o zunido da flecha de meu pai:

You see, there was once a mother who lived with her three children

Her womb could have given birth to many more children & it eventually did - some became animals, some became plants others turned out to be human. But Yemaya at first had three sons: Elegba, Ogun & Oshosi. Elegba was the first one to leave her, and his departure, it must be said, was quite a relief for her, "this one is always up to something, always creating confusion" Her other two sons were very close. Ogun seemed rough in his heavy built body always working and down to himself. Oshosi was smaller and looked more like a boy or a bird. Ogun would march ahead into the woods clearing up paths with his iron tools. Oshosi would follow him very quietly, following invisible cues, guiding his brother. That's how they hunted, and that's how they insured the nourishment of their village. Those two were quite unfit for the village life. They would drink too much, or laugh too loud. They would say things that didn't make much sense and which would make people uncomfortable, or just stay quiet showing no interest in ordinary lives. But since they brought food to the village, people tried their best to cope with the strange ways of the brothers

Once while Ogun was busy trying to clear a path which Oshosi believed they needed to follow, Oshosi got distracted with a bird song that was unlike anything he had ever heard. He followed the song until he reached the heart of the woods. There he met Osayin who offered him some amúniméyè: "come, come, archer, see if you can you look beyond your targets." Oshosi went further and further away in his amúniméyè visions. He was dressed in feathers and could no longer remember who he used to be. Osayin showed him all the visions, all the roads of each and every leaf, each and every root. But Oshosi could no longer remember what an arch was for. He couldn't remember there were people living outside the woods waiting for him

Since the day Oshosi disappeared Ogun had been walking down all tracks, opening up new ones, looking for his brother all over the woods. He never stopped to drink, eat or sleep. He never thought he should go back to his village, to his mother and tell the others what was happening. Years went by, and Ogun finally found his brother. He was dressed like a bird. His eyes looked as if he belonged to the òrun, not to the àiyé which is the space of the living. Ogun put Oshosi on his shoulders and took him back to their village. When Yemaya saw them she said she no longer wanted to mother Oshosi. Ogun got furious with her lack of compassion: "if he is not your son, I am not either." And they left, back into Osayin's woods.

Yemaya cried for the loss of her children
She cried until she became a river

asuo merensen ("Oya" 240)

KAM
meaning chief or sun, something solid, something on which you can clamber, hold, depend on, sustain yourself with or on
MAU
wood, womb, grove or secret place, hence Mau Mau, Maroon etc and

AMAU

which is a spiritual secret place or source (BP 239-40)

They hopped off the bus in a suburb of Salvador and started walking on the narrow trail along the highway. the sun was still asleep. two small women. one half the age of the other. The younger one kept on looking down the bushes fighting against the concrete. zig zagging along her path, fighting against unwanted thoughts, she took a sigh, tightened up her head tie & rubbed her eyes. The older one, head straight up, steady gaze & pace, looked beyond this world. from where the sun sets in the water to where the sun sets behind the mountains, she knew all the roads & yet she seemed too slim shouldered for certain burdens. she shook her head and sucked her teeth as she approached the police station at the entrance of São Bartolomeu

São Bartolomeu once home to the maroons, now backyard to thousands of destitute slums. each & every herb one might need for the healing of the body and the strengthening of the spirit was there. a bundle of sacred medicine waiting to be untied, combined & activated. but the agony of destitution demanded immediate relief. a quick fix. illusions of conquest: a blade, a cutlass, a gun. denied manhood. raping young bodies of girls, your daughter, sister. denied womanhood. spirits amputated by man-made chemicals. life not as a gift but as an incursion into the darkest alleys of hell. denied light & potential destiny. the sole north: possession - by force, over bodies & land & anguished spirits. a cynic smile & a minute of pleasure, coming, coming, in further, and yet further - destruction

an we burnin babylone: (BB² 9)
caliban blind, tortured, twisted, bent/ reduced (BB² 18; TTR 47)
victim of the cities' skin and trinkets (BB² 18)

these crimes we all embrace
the victim & the violate
the duppy & the gunman
so close on these plantations still
so intimate
the dead/undead (TTR 22)

São Bartolomeu, for centuries touching & sheltering & opening up & speaking to sprouting spirits of newly initiates. healing ground for priests & priestesses of Salvador. living library & archive for all of those who could read between stems. São Bartolomeu, now bordered by the highway, secured by military forces. Osayin's sacred realm encroached by modernity, urban violence & fear. Katende's healing cosmos misunderstood, abused, violated. ancestral maroon ground obscured by engendered disorientation

The two women were greeted by a policeman. he touched the ground and asked for blessings from the older one. from the inside of the improvised police station came sounds of guns being loaded. the younger one clenched her teeth. Alafia... wishing for peace almost seemed like a contradiction. the policeman standing still, looking down & with her gentle piercing eyes the older woman brought his head up & captured his eyes & smiled. he thought his mission was to protect us. she knew her mission was more complicated than that

"kò si ewé, kò si òrìsà" - without herbs there are no orishas

Three policemen followed the two women. loaded guns sticking out from their belts. they kept a distance from them, out of respect, out of fear of unknown forces immune to bullets or uniforms. as concrete turned into dirt, the women opened their bags and put on the ground some coins, to-bacco leaves, poured some honey & spit some rum. chewing on a shared kola nut they started singing, almost in a whisper, asking for permission to enter those grounds-

"àwa dàgò l'ojú ewé, àwa dàgò l'ojú e mò oògùn,
a dàgò l'ojú ewé, a dàgò l'ojú e mò oògun"
on behalf of our eyes we ask your permission Herb
we ask permission for our eyes to look into yours
and see all your wisdom

The younger woman offered her arm to the older one. they had arrived in good time, way before the sunrise & they walked into the woods, slowly and carefully as if they didn't yet wish to awaken that world. the boots of the policemen echoing in unison made the older one stop and look back and with her gaze she froze them for a minute or so before they turned back & walked away

When I was a child - started the older one in a low, slow, voice - we didn't have so much concrete, we didn't have so many walls. when my grand-mother was a child she didn't keep the orishas in rooms, framed by walls, this is where she would come to be with them and as she greeted them, her forehead would touch the warmth of the earth. don't know child, I see diseases today that didn't exist before and people know less & less about these herbs. everything that exists on this earth, everything that sprouts from this bundle of coiled energy, looking at us from inside out even when we cannot see them, eyeing us the way they do - everything here, was given to us with a purpose. the loss of the knowledge of the world in which we dwell is what creates the unbalance. so what you are dealing with is not the disease of one individual, it is not the physical or spiritual unbalance of one body, it is not something one individual brought on to himself or a part of his journey in this world - it is much more complicated than that, much deeper child, much deeper...

The younger woman stopped and picked up a small leaf from the ground. she licked it & stuck it to her forehead as if parading a third eye, as if showing the winning card in her deck, as if saying "it's better than it seems, here she is, etiponla, right on our path." and she sang in a smile "etiponla wa fi pá burúrú, a fi pá burúrú..." etiponla: the herb that pushes away all that is evil. the eyes of the older woman brightened up, the tradition would be kept, had to be kept, she continued

So as you walk on this world of the living and see what you see, and hear what you hear, beyond this àiyé, there is an òrun which is the source of the reflections of everything you may feel over here. everything is connected like each grain of corn has a string to its husk. now the umbilical cord for each ará àiyé to each ará òrun is an ewé. without these herbs the connection between us - living - and them - our ancestors - is lost

"Kò si ewé, kò si òrìsà" - said the young one

Bèè ni omo ode. bèè ni... each herb offers a map that directs us to one ancestral family. their wind, their strength, is all around us. before receiving we need to attract. before attracting we need to be clear. in order to be clear we need to listen to this silence and understand it. everything has a counterpart in this world omo ode. you, child of the hunter, child of the King of Keto, you are part of him, as he is part of you. alékèsì, is one of the leaves that allows you to exist into each other. it is the one which allow us to be with him & him with us. for these shores of Salvador to be kept at arm's reach to Dahomey, for your feet to be kept on this àiyé & your head to be launched to the mysteries of the òrun, alékèsi needs to sprout from the earth without the help of men. agriculture feeds the body, the touchable flesh, that's Oko's wisdom. but no man can plant the road to his belly. only the wind, the rain, the kindness of Olodumare. the herb is what creates the paths which lead us to the òrun. as this highway expands, potential paths are shattered, spirits yet to come already shipwrecked, unimaginable diseases like curses weakening & destroying strong men & women

The young woman turned her face from the path to the first arrows of light being shot up the horizon. she looked for a soothing word, an answer, an affirmation of alternatives an *affir-nation* ("Oya" 242). she chose to remain quiet, to look into they eye of the hurricane, breath it in, give it time

On the sky a small òpeèré took flight, direct as an arrow yet not rushing to get to no final destination

"òpeèré òsáyìn s'ibú
kúrú ìde akàkà"
osayin's bird flies deep: the tiny one won't change his nature

Because he knew
a multitude
of raven's feathers
could not restrain the sky from being blue

He'd xamined every raven's feather
so he knew (Sappho 51)

Caliban in Y2K?—
Hypertext and New Pathways

Cynthia James

What happens when an artist publishes his conversations? Is it wisdom, a sign of retirement, or at the close of the century, a second coming statement? Kamau Brathwaite has published *ConVERSations with Nathaniel Mackey* on the eve of Y2K with an UPPER-casing of the VERS in *ConVERSations*. The work is described as "layered with subsequent ruminations arising from [Brathwaite's] lifelong engagement with world literature and expressive cultures" (cover review). It can be noted though that, *SHAR* and *Middle Passages* apart, in this last decade of the 20th century Brathwaite has produced a host of multi-styled conversations, prominent among these being: 1) *The Zea Mexican Diary*, a record of his wife and poet's life plus an account of his relationship with his friends and the Jamaican academy; 2) *Trench Town Rock*, a report on crime in Jamaica as it gruesomely impacts on man, artist and society; 3) *DreamStories*, which according to Gordon Rohlehr, the writer's best-known critic, "should be read alongside the testimonies, letters, cries for help and documentation of nightmare" of the artist (Preface iv); 4) *Barabajan Poems*, a restylised lecture on the making of the Caribbean artist; 5) the *WASAFIRI* document, "A Post-Cautionary Tale of the Helen of our Wars," a critical assessment of the representation of Caribbean literature by critics outside the region; and 6) *MR*, Brathwaite's latest unpublished work on Caribbean criticism for which he won the Casa de las Americas prize in 1998.

This essay posits that Brathwaite's work of the present decade of the 1990s is a stocktaking and a way forward into 2000. The work evaluates birth, work, death and rebirth, not for the artist alone but for Caribbean literature and Caribbean society as a whole. This analysis of the decade's work focuses on three salient features: (1) Brathwaite's review of the Caribbean and its relationship with Miranda and the Caribbean aesthetic; (2) his re-voicing of the metaphoric tempest principally in the ignored *SHAR*– a task the poet had indirectly set himself since *History of the Voice*; and (3) as he enters the new millennium, the artist's engagement with hypertext through multiple linkages of subconscious text by the click of the hand guiding the cursor to the hard-drive of the reader's and the artist's collective brain. The centerpiece of this essay is *ConVERSations with Nathaniel Mackey*, a work with the theme "new pathways," a phrase Brathwaite invoked almost ten years ago in *The Zea Mexican Diary*. Amid these three tangents, however, the *cause célèbre* is the old avatar Caliban who remains as active as ever in the writer's consciousness in his latest work; so, first a word on the centrality of Caliban to Brathwaite's project of the present decade.

Caliban

In *Barabajan Poems* Brathwaite pulls together the various strands of his evolutionary usage of the protean manimal:

> For many years now in my writing research & teaching have I been (hopefully) developing the Mannoni-Geo Lamming PROSPERO/ CALIBAN concept (**Prospero y Caliban-The Pleasures of Exile** out of Shakespeare's **Tempest**) & the Elkins/Orlando Patterson SAMBO/QUASHIE complexes or syndromes (out of **Slavery/Sociology of Slavery**) into quite a wide and I think useful range of PLANTATION PERSONALITY TYPES
>
> ....
>
> Caliban/ Prospero's slave and symbol of the Caribbean rebel or more accurately wd-be rebel. A whole range of types develop out of this: the SAMBO/QUARSHIE, the ANANCY, the TACKY/SAM SHARP/TOUSSAINT LOUVERTURE/TOUSSAINT LEGBA rebels, the Cudjoe & GrandeeNanny or Palmares type Maroons, the Rastafari or Contemporary Maroons, the Bob Marley artistic & psychological Maroons; with all these personality types wrought or fraught with DICHOTOMOUS sometimes SCHIZOPHRENIC CONFLICTS (Mitt, Rhys, Fanon, DW, ?Michelle Cliff) result of the drama of 'creolization' (culturation, acculturation, deculturation, interculturation, reculturation, out & in culturation, culturation as ornament sometimes orNAMent etc etc etc) (BP 315-6)

This is primarily Caliban from within the regional spectrum. *ConVERSations* supplements the picture with another version of Caliban–Caliban in the self-reflexivity of the European imagination. Here Caliban is outward and other:

> ('Carib', 'Caribbean', 'cannibal'/representing Europe's primitive in-accurately nostalgic sense of 'Nature'; the 'natural person' of the play/best express perhaps by Robt Browning in the poem 'Caliban upon Setebos' (1864)) (*ConVERSations* 188)

In Brathwaite's manipulation of the Caliban mask, he has never professed to love the tortured fellow. Caliban is a reflection of historical changes and adaptations–at once maroon on behalf of his all nurturing society, and at the same time the product of Prospero's imagination. Yet other reflections show Caliban criminally turned upon himself. So Caliban can be rebel; he can be two-faced traitor, mulatto and opportunist. He can be mindless, danc-ing hedonist of the Carnival "Jou'vert," dancing to "bambalula bambulai" all the while solemnly forging "something torn and new" (TA 267-90). Caliban is the Rasta and Bob Marley figure; he is the rat-trapped recurring poet/prophet of "Wings of a Dove." He is the metaphorical eye of the hur-ricane located in the prayerful middle of "Kingston in the Kingdom of this World" in *Trench Town Rock*, reduced to his gospel, suffering the little children to come unto him out of their society's self-created Mammon. In *Trench Town Rock*, though, the prophet is inseparable from his twin, the drug-mafia attacker. The victim, the prophet and the beast are conjoined in their polpot society. Caliban is the victim and the victimizer, the misguided Abu Bakr named in "Dream Chad" of *DreamStories* (64) who decides to free his society in the Trinidad 1990 coup, raking up death in the name of peace and love.

One notices, then, that as the century closes, Brathwaite takes stock of the recent actions of Caliban as both terroriser and terrorized. In *ConVERSations* the artist sums up wryly Caliban's latter-day record in the fifth and sixth stages of Caribbean independence (50) under the umbrella of "The New Day Vic Reid sang in 1950":

> . . . Caliban coming into im own in a series of momentous socio-political cultural events that shook—no doubt—the world Yet by the decade of this our first millennium—in the 500th year of Christophere Columbus' precipitation of us here—Caliban has be-come Cannibal if not 'again' then pretty close to it . so that our lib-eration & the sense of freedom in our hearts & homes earned by rebellions & maroons has been so gravely washed away to what

some call 'our flawed but not yet failed society'- *(ConVERSations* 276)

Finally, Caliban is the author himself *conVERSing* about his familial people, "celebrating [mother and father and "the caliban people old and new [he] grow up with, [he] know and get to know" *(ConVERSations* 44). Caliban is the poet's mask, X/Self of the 13 string-stone island provinces of the Caribbean. Writing as he is at the end of the century under the Sycoraxian totem in video style, the artist has donned a complex mask. "Letter to Sycorax" becomes the centerpiece of this phase. Caliban is border man, Black man, colonial man, exiled man. Also, as man launched out of a great odoum, Caliban is hacking and chiseling his way into new-age visibility, using both missilic and cenote technology to find a vantage point of selfhood. In sum, Caliban's historical continuity is ever-present. Having shown that *ConVERSations* gathers his multifarious disguises and facets to date,let us examine some of his "new pathways."

Recognizing Miranda But Continuing the Battle Over the Helen of our Wars

As the *WASAFIRI* exchanges from 1995 to 1996 indicate, Brathwaite's position on the White Creole continues to engender controversy. However, both *Barabajan Poems* and *ConVERSations* indicate that the evolution of Caribbean society has brought white Creoles into greater integration within the regional fabric. In *ConVERSations*, this integration is discussed in the context of the revival of Emancipation Day celebrations in many Caribbean islands at the close of the 20th century after some 160 years in abeyance (175-88). The rapprochement comes from what Brathwaite perceives as the white Creole's readiness at the close of the century to "nativize" himself. As reported in *ConVERSations*, the nativization process in Barbados, the artist's home country includes societal discussion on issues such as "Who is white/Who is still white . . . hybridity/miscegenation" (181); on expressions of "contrition" by Creoles for their "forefathers' contribution to the evil/horrors of slavery" (181); issues such as slave descendants asking for "reparations for the holocaust" (181); on issues of ?apportion[ing] blame (182); and on "acceptance, reconciliation, redemption" (184). In *ConVERSations*, the redleg sisters Ealene Downie and Nita Gibson report "they are scorned because of their friendliness with black people" (187). Nita continues: "We does mix up with coloured people . . . My father raise up with them, my mother raise up with them, an(d) they have to kill me to come out of it . . . We ain't begging for family" (187-8).

The significance of this social integration to the evolution of the Caribbean aesthetic becomes clear in Brathwaite's description of what he regards as a symbol of the nativization of the Creole: the "white maroon" or white Rasta Julian Hunte swimming around Barbados psychically claiming identification with his island home:

> Those of you who read *Barabajan Poems* will not be surprise at this—that Hunte wd be an exception. Because he nativizes him-self in swimming (solo) around—in this way possessing, -the sea-island; & expressing his love for it not only in the act of courage & endurance in so swimming; but in his knowledge of what he was doin & in the way he xpress in words that knowledge & love. He knowa by sight/by feel/by name/ by memory/ every beach, rock, reef, tide of the island   (*ConVERSations* 182-3)

Thus, sections of the society previously deemed alienated from each other have moved closer to each other; so that whereas Brathwaite's 1970 essay "Creative Literature of the British West Indies During the Period of Slavery" regards the narratives of 19th century Caribbean white maroons, not as Caribbean literature but as "tropical English" because of their tourist or observer stance (*Roots* 130), by contrast, *ConVERSations* records, albeit with caution, Caribbean society's rapprochement towards the white maroon who relates to the Caribbean not as superior and expatriate artist, but as citizen and native artist.

Revisioning the Caribbean Aesthetic and Renaming the Tempest (SHAR)

One of the wrestling points of Caribbean poetics over the past fifty years has been: what exactly is Caribbean literature and how can it be identified? At the 1992 CARIFESTA Brathwaite reviewed some of the issues that had occupied him for years and were subjects of discussion in early documents such as *History of the Voice*. His Carifesta 1992 lecture entitled, "The Search for a Caribbean Aesthetic," is a progress report on the old project: A Caribbean aesthetic cannot be measured in a count of years and in terms of nominal power changes; an aesthetic is not created by willing it to appear, nor is it an elusive construct; aesthetic measurement begins with a process of discovery and according to him the discovery has just begun. So, questions about "the new [Caribbean] aesthetic" at the close of the 20th century are premature. Brathwaite says:

> I'm not even going to be able to talk about the new aesthetic, because we have not even begun an aesthetical exercise as yet for the

last 500 years. We are only in the business of beginning to know what the aesthetic is. The definition is as follows: the aesthetic is a critical communal sense of the essence of one's culture.

That is how you begin. It has to be critical, it is not an accepting, you have to be able to say, "Is this good, is this average?" ... I would say that a working definition would be a critical communal sense of the essence of one's culture which would involve an awareness of style, how that style became style. What is good style and how that style became style. In other words, what is Caribbean? If you write a poem or a piece of music how do you know it is Caribbean? How do you know it is not fusion? African-American? How do you really speak about these things? ("Search," October 25, 37)

The article goes on to raise specific tasks for the critic of Caribbean literature in the 21ˢᵗ century:

But again, what makes a good dub poem? We don't know! We go by personalities: you like Lutha, you like Okun? You like Brother Book, you like Brother Resistance, and therefore they make good poets. But what is a good dub poet? What is a good dub poem? What are the qualities that make up this kind of expression? How did we access it? How do we therefore make it part of ourselves?

You see, what is happening always is that we are spectators to our own culture. That is what happens, we sit down and we applaud our own culture. But we are not taking part in the business of mediating its qualities, we are not able to say, "Yes, it is good, because..." We can quarrel about it: "Yes, because I like it..." But we cannot say, "Yes, because this person has adhered to a tradition that you can define as a Garifuna or a Garifuna derivative."

There are all sorts of things like that. And that is what the 21st Century will have to begin with. ("Search", November 8, 29: emphasis added)

Brathwaite's own work of the 1990s shows an implementation of such heightened consciousness about the Caribbean aesthetic. In *History of the Voice*, he had expressed a worrying concern about the lack of psychic resonance in Caribbean poets' treatments of elemental facets of the indigenous landscape:

But still no 'proper' hurricane; no volcano except Shake Keane's *Volcano Suite* (1979) no earthquake; drought only in Walcott and Brathwaite's *Islands* (1969) and *Black + Blues* (1976) ... But we have been trying to break out of the entire pentametric model in the Caribbean and to move into a system which more closely and inti-

mately approaches our own experience. So that is what we are talking about now. (12)

In this 1970s extract, Brathwaite compares poems written about the hurricane, the most recurrent and most devastating element in the Caribbean
landscape and finds, with the exception of Anthony Hinkson's on Hurricane Janet, that Caribbean poetic depictions are too few and too Anglo-
Saxon in style.

By contrast, Brathwaite's own *SHAR: Hurricane Poem* of 1990 is an
example of the Caribbean poetics the artist has in mind. Having put out an
indirect mandate in the *History of the Voice* for Caribbean versification of
the exact measure of the hurricane's roar, the poet could hardly have thought
he would so cruelly be put to the test. A brief comparison of the two best
known versions of the Caribbean tempest–Shakespeare's and Aimé
Césaire's–with Brathwaite's can help to evaluate his effort in *SHAR*.

Shakespeare's 17th century tempest is make-believe. It is a figment of
the imagination, a raising of the wand to effect imperial retribution.
Prospero's play with the Caribbean waters clears the deck for a tourist
surfboard of goodies for all but Caliban. For Miranda it ushers in a Brave
New World–a man who becomes her royal husband and the magical descent of goddesses for her nuptial. Shakespeare's tempest forms a theatrical backdrop for the reconciliation between family members who make up
and voyage back to their element. This tempest is a metaphorical construct
of the European mind.

Césaire changes the definite article to the indefinite "A"–Une Tempête.
By this change Césaire suggests that tempests are different according to
the perspective of the persons experiencing them. Césaire's 1969 tempest
is an early West Indian reply to the Empire. Its subtitle reads "based on
Shakespeare's *The Tempest*: adapted for black theatre."

SHAR shows continuity with the negritude project of Césaire, but by
contrast with the two other versions, *SHAR* is the tempest experienced with
the English word "tempest" sonorously replaced by the onomatopoeic
SHAR. Laying down his magic mantle, the basis of his "Art," Prospero can
comfort his Miranda:

Lie there, my Art [his mantle]. Wipe thou thine eyes; have comfort.
The direful spectacle of the wrack, which touch'd
The very virtue of compassion in thee,
I have with such provision in mine Art
So safely ordered, that there is no soul—
No, not so much perdition as an hair

Betid to any creature in the vessel
Which thou heard'st cry, which thou saw'st sink.

By contrast, Brathwaite contemplates tempestuous Caribbean devastation
from a personalized view with the potency of graphic cultural knowledge:

For the stone of this island to be bombed
by this wind & all this. all this. water
O longshore late light duppy Kingston nights
wood
has become so useless. stripped. wet .
fragile . broken . totally uninhabitable
with what we must still build

a half-a-million shaved off from the auction block
curled & cut off from their stock
without even that sweet scent of resin on a good day
O Saviour Saviour Sav-la-Mar

It is not a question of whether the 1611 European-styled "tempest" is better
than the 1990 Caribbean-styled "shar." The point is that in terms of a Caribbean aesthetic *SHAR: Hurricane Poem* reflects its own cosmology, its
own particular and momentous cultural Caribbean.

From Timehri to Hypertext

In *ConVERSations*, Brathwaite offers the most comprehensive explanation
to date of his controversial video or Sycorax style. A study of his remarks
indicates that his experiment with the word can be viewed from at least
four perspectives: (1) as an outcome of personal and societal violation; (2)
as a form of cultural signification; 3) as an ideological blueprint of fragmentation reflecting the status of the Caribbean writing from the margins;
and (4) as an understanding of how the oral tradition and present-day technologies complement and enhance each other in returning kinesis to the
word which has lost its cultural substance since Guttenberg. These four
aspects of Sycorax are worth exploring individually.

On one level, Brathwaite explains his video style in personal and societal terms as emanating from personal trauma. In other words, the artist's
latterday Sycorax imprint is a personalized configuration of his cross from
within a personal life and from within a society plagued by mayhem. On a
second level, in *ConVERSations*, the video-style is explained in artistic
and cultural analogies. Its equivalent is the video or movie (210), the news
clip–"a counter-cry for redemption, visibility–re-muralization" (208) of the
daily torments of a Somalia, a Bosnia, or a Rwanda. Another equivalent is

the mural (207), visual art or societal painting (210) such as one finds in the ravaged Haiti. The video-styled mural is like a "cinema-painting" on the go, "thr (u) these senses, becom[ing] more public in the sense of more shared, more part of the community"—large-scale statements shared at important visible levels by all" (207). The Sycorax style is also approximated to Amerindian *timehri* or primeval imprints (201). The markings indelibly signify this moment in Caribbean history just as Amerindian marks on caves were etched on the Caribbean landscape in their time and moment (210). The video-style finds its equivalent, too, in inner-city art-graffiti (207) as a continuous "wall of memory" (208), as cultural statement that cannot be suppressed:

> All these sufferations we familiar with thru the video of television, are experienced in this—anelike devastation. And people are expressing about it and against it in these little signals that they have put up upon some wall or bus or subway or on a motorcar; on their bicycles as they glide past, you know, And somewhere I feel that this poetry, whatever you might think of its texture. . .the message of i/ (t), the essence of it, increasingly becomes imbedded upon th (e) wall of memory - the only ancient way it has always been preserved; the only way that it can be shared within the shadow of the ruins... (208)

Third, Brathwaite draws ideological parallels for his video style. He is hesitant to accept the approximation of his video style to hieroglyphics (195-96), seeing hieroglyphics as an "abstraction" that people on the margins have not been able to afford. By contrast, "the pressure of [his] content—[his] received information—requires...the need for us to celebrate marginality by making it a centrality" (195). Returning to long-standing theories of Caribbean fragmentation and devastation (199), Brathwaite argues that the Caribbean offers Caribbean people no ready archaeological heritage for exploration, except in the case of the Guyanese who have an instinctive sense of continuity that comes from their being part of an ancient primordial continental mass.

Finally, in *ConVERSations* Brathwaite integrates his video style and the orality usually attributed to Caribbean culture into a video-styled communication theory. For him his video style bridges (1) orality, (2) the flat print tradition and (3) the missilic technology of the present and future. The technological aspects of the video style are the kinetic aspects the griot has never been able to set to enduring print. Brathwaite calls on analogies from the performance world—from rap, calypso, Kumina, film (*Daughters of the Dust*)—to explain his point. He sees no contradiction between the development of his video style and his status as oral poet. Sycorax is his attempt to return the sound system to print. Stories like "Dream Haiti" embody a mixture of print and voice. Thus the artist is reluctant to read from *DreamStories* to his audience "because to get the full insomnia of it, you've got to *see* it as much as *hear* it—that's why it's 'video', okay? (210).

> What I'm saying – the thing about 'oral poetry' – the Oral Tradition [OT] today - in a world of electronic (s) is that it's allowing us at last to mix the two 'traditions' into sound/ visual; to convert script into sound via the spirit – the mkissi – of timehri/mural/graffiti –The ancients, the ancestors, the griots, had to commit it all to memory because they had no useful script or cursor or camcorder or other extra sortilege to aid/illuminate their passion of composition. And so they did it wonderfully, homerically, heroically, ogotemmelically, imperishably, classically, with breath and memory alone (*ConVERSations* 215-17)

Hypertext

Alongside his video style and more revolutionary than it in the 1990s is Brathwaite's infusion of the notion of hypertext into Caribbean writing. The hyperlinks in a story like "Dream Chad," for instance, connect a Caribbean literary history through the subconscious, activating memory through highlighted font and print. The superimposed slides simultaneously expose myriad montages each with its own archive. The highlighting of "**the Empire Windrush**" (52), for example, links on one hand to the "pilgrim father" analogy of the Caribbean writers setting sail for England to found their literary careers in the 1950s and on the other side to Orlando Patterson's seminal sociological work. In the same paragraph "'the green academies' of lamming leaves" recall George Lamming as one of the early pioneers, his landmark success and his initial excursion into poetry. "Banana Republic" (54), "The Cockpits" (55), the invocation of the female runners Merlene Ottey, Wilma Rudolph, FloJo control mental links with maroon histories reaching beyond the specific lacings of intertextuality. Superman's "Gotham City" (56); the "Eyes on the Prize" (64), Yassim Abu Bakr; and CLR James' pamphlets, "Facing Reality" (69) open up hyperlinked analogies that hold archives of their own. In his emphasis on quick mental linkages, Brathwaite indicates that he has gone beyond the word-elisions, puns and word-slippages that characterized his early work, into interactive scenarios lacing a wealth of multi-dimensional memory where the past present and future are encapsulated simultaneously to form a literary and social continuum on interlocking pages. In "Dream Chad," the dreamer explains the sensation and action joining reader, author and culture in terms of the control of a VCR: "push/in a/head like he pressin the key on a VCRs **fast far. ward mode/** to the dark front door of my head" (63).

Brathwaite is a writer who pays attention to cycles of development. The impending *MR* alongside *Roots* in criticism and the *Ancestors* trilogy alongside *The Arrivants* in poetry will certainly enhance Caribbean literary history and scholarship as compendium volumes indicating the passage of Caribbean Literature over its first official fifty years. In his conVERSations of the decade of the 1990s Brathwaite addresses Caribbean poetics in his capacity both as artist and as critic. In all these conVERSations, Caliban his alter-ego is repeatedly being reassessed and renamed. This is both a stocktaking of Caribbean literature and a preamble to his way forward into Y2K.

Mystic Man: Irations/Jahrations

Opal Palmer Adisa

De   mystic man
Lives inside his head
    He beats out words
        and his voice rumbles and stumbles
        crawls over rocks
        cascades down falls
            but still he drums on and on
            trying to still the hullabaloo in his head

De mystic man
Stays focused on dreams
    His pain is deep
        and his ache is raw
        his heart is an open wound
            but still he ponders and contemplates
            until his head is the tail of a hurricane storm

De mystic man
Rants and wails
chants and prays
        until we are all under his spell
        numbed from being fed so much

        and his hoarse voice pleads

Dem belly full but dem hungry
Too full on the work that's ahead
So full we dare not speak
We been knowing how to tie up we jaw and band we belly
Hard times not new to us
Sometimes we wrap up so close
Hard times seems like a bosom friend

So De mystic man
continues on
drumming and drumming
trying to quiet
de noises in his head
de wailing in our eyes
de chorus of litanies

De mystic man
continues on
leaving us behind

For many years he - Brathwaite- was just a name to me, a phantom spirit. He was real yet larger than life. He seemed out of reach, removed from the mundane, yet I knew I should, would have to meet him one day if I was going to take this path– the word lore kept seducing me to follow. The first time I saw him was on UWI campus at Mona with uncombed hair and straggly beard. Who is taking care of him? I wondered, knowing that he was not capable of these daily tasks, his head was too full of ideas. I could tell where his mind was, was not on what was before him or who. Would he hear me if I say I am a poet? Would he care? Not about me being a poet, but about my earnestness to write. How deeply buried was his head in the misery of his people or snagged somewhere in the envelope of history? I paused and waited and watched.

I heard him
He was chanting irations and Jahrations
about de down trodden and de dis trodden
about corruption and lack of cooperation

Irations /Jahration
Raking up feelings
Stirring up reason
Chanting skanking
De river dun come down
De river dun come down

In a bayblon town
no mercy fah de poor
no food fah de hungry

How we get over
How we get over

Dese isms and scheming
Des schisms and separatism

Irations/Jahrations
Confusing the African in us
Shaming the Africa that we are

He was raking   and skanking
Stirring things up
Soup boiling
Pot too full
Stirring up things
Questioning and redefining
Rejecting and realigning

How we get over
How we get over

Irations   /Jahrations
de beat of de words
Irations   /Jahrations
de pulse of conscience

Him seh

    look suh   *look suh*
    See suh   *be suh*
    Swim suh   *float suh*

    Til you get over
    Til you get over

And de pot bubbles and boils
Steaming the coals
and the fire sneezes and quivers

Mystic man and his irations
Thumping and thumping
Droning on until we hear
Until he feels the words in our bodies
Until we move into irations and jah rhythms

Because bravery sometimes stalks me, I sent him—Brathwaite—some of my poems in 1976 and found myself in his office, unprepared to speak to a real man. No questions came to mind. Not even small talk. I could drink in his silence. Listen my inner voice said. So I prepared to sit still. But here before me was a man who was a man. A soft man in looks and touch. Almost frail and I loved him like only a green woman can love such a man. Such a gently voice, like an evening breeze in December, soft and lazy and cool, ginger and pineapple juices combined. I was hooked. He had no rough edges and I could tell he was pliant. Cornmeal dumpling is what came to mind; he is cornmeal dumpling with a little mackerel-run-down on the side.

There is a way that conversation happens between two people who see eye to eye, even when the vantage point is different. It is not a dialogue that takes place, more like a an ancient yet spontaneous dance, *a peel head john-crow sitting on the tree top/let we prance and dance boy/ let we prance and dance.* We danced, sometimes alone in the same space, sometimes together, but always we applauded each other's dancing. He would be a friend my inner voice said, a friend who is admired, someone worthy to aspire to excel beyond. And he would want that—that the dreamee outstep the dreamer—he would want that.

I cannot say how and when our friendship took the avenue it took; it was not a frequently traveled road. However, every so often I would hear from him, that he liked something I sent him and that he would publish it and that I should send it here or there and keep writing. It was enough and yet never enough these all too brief and hurried scribbles or messages that I spent more time deciphering. We never had what we needed or what I desired—leisurely time, alone, to muse over and confront the things that he saw that I too saw, I thought; the things the he felt, that I too felt, I was certain; the great longing that was his and mine and for all those we called our people. And it was then that I suspected that I might have loved him, been in love with him, not to make him my lover—though if he had asked I would have surrendered—I imagined us like both Picasso at eighty with his young wife and Rilke with his young writer/admirer. What I was feeling was not a common Blackie mango that you bit into then tossed before going onto the next one; their numbers so abundant that scarcity was never a thought. No! My feelings were not so simple or clear. This was not going to be a passionate affair with a bitter after taste. No way! Words stood be-tween us, wrapping us in their nuances, committing us with their meaning, branding us with their power. Words anchored us beyond the slippery feel-ings, before we could embark on or descend into what? A marriage of languages. A sentencing of words. A soaring of poetry-spirit.

I remember sitting down to read *Black + Blues*, his—Brathwaite's—1976 Casa De Las Americas poetry volume. It was like walking in his boots, large black rubber ones that farmers wore to the field. This volume was a sharp machete chopping away at the overgrowth in my path. I needed to hear the words part my lips in the drone I imagined to be his. This way I could be with him, inside his head, next to his heart, flowing in his blood vessels—wherever the words came from. I wanted to be there. Yet I didn't always feel as he felt, or saw as he saw, but I could clearly see what he saw and I understood his fever because my own was churning. And I think then, I wanted him to be a mentor because I thought that was all there could be. After all, there was Doris his wife. Kamau was and still now, is the idea of a mentor, but he was never the mentor I wanted. Perhaps he could never be what I wanted, my expectations exceeded both of us. But still he hovered, always, like an afterthought that is actually the idea before the thought. He is the reflection of that part of the back of the head that you can never see, but you know it is there, and if you hold the mirror at the right angle you will see the spot you have been seeking. But I would be a liar, if I were to say, I didn't still long to have him to myself, for a long week, or a couple of days. For us to walk through the greedy growth of the Caribbean landscape and wind out way to a river where we would spend the day, sunning, catch-ing cray-fish, boiling a pot of soup and not staying a word to each other. However, we would hear each other's thoughts through the silence of lan-guage that was creating epic poems. I wanted us to collaborate and write poems together, to read together and have our breaths mingle and spew the air with our rhythmic magic—words evoking, making real the desires of the poets—Brathwaite and Adisa. Then, when dusk crawled in, he would take my hand, and his palm would be like I remembered them, soft, not a mushy softness but a gently softness, a tenderness that says, yes there is still yearning here, yes, there is still hope here, yes there is anger and even deep disappointment, but my soul is still tucked under my sleeves, and with the coming night, I can let it out, give it some breeze, and even let it warm you. With hands clasped, we would walk to the little cottage in which we were staying, with its veranda that faced the sky, and we would cuddle in the hammock that hung there and write each other poetry, not of poverty and the abyss of cruelty into which we have descended, but of love and beauty and tranquility and oneness with ourselves and each other. Am I the dreamer or the dreamee, trying to supplant and replant old admiration.

> Mystic man
>   do you know me now
> Or have I revealed a secret
> best left buried
>
>   It is de dub rhythm that took me there
>   undressing me
>   releasing me
>   stripping me of all fantasy
>   shattering de mask
>   sending me to de river of babylon
>
> I hear Shango panting
> He is whispering to a woman
> through a cracked window
> She is not his woman
> He's only interested in someone else's woman
>
>   Am I Oya
>   Ruthless about her need
>   -woman who will have her man
>   no matter the price

It is not permanency she seeks
Goddess of conquest and passion
Guardian of all words and their meanings

And the storm was beating at your window
Long before you took heed
And with Doris went your foundation
Who else could take care of you like her
Who else could love you so
without asking
without demanding reciprocation
and your letters were one liners   undecipherable
and my heart bled for you
feeling you slipping
moving beyond my reach

And next came Gilbert with the rains
and the mud took your house
and ·ravished my island that was your home
my land that sheltered you was now a thorn stuck between your big toe
and my heart reached out
searching for you
trying to find you within the limbo-limbo-limbo like me
rhythm you were working through
my heart sensing /knowing you were in limbo
balanced on one foot, scanning for a place to find ground
limbo-limbo-limbo like me
I too was dangling on one foot and wanting to ground with you
needing to talk heart to heart with you
Wanting you to hear me   but knowing you couldn't   not fully
Whatever time there might had been or could have been was   gone

Mystic man with your irations/Jahrations rhythm
I have heard you
Have listened keenly to all you have said
Have sat with others mesmerized at how well
you sing our songs discordant and harmonious
And I know to feel as deeply as you do you must be mad

369

To keep all those rhythms in your head and hum and recite them
is to join forces with Ogun
is to exile yourself from those who have known you all along,
to cut yourself off or allow yourself to be cut off
is to become lost in the words as urgently as you try to hold on...

limbo   limbo   limbo like me
limbo   limbo like me

What shame, if any, is there in admitting now to myself that all along, without even fully knowing it, I loved you, even in the belly of the poem? What shame or lack of heart can there be to say to you mystic man, that to choose to love you is to resolve to take the rough and long road, not unrequited –just imperceptible. I have often asked myself, although I don't anymore, what do you mean to me? What having met and known you for two decades and three years, mean? Why do I feel so honored to know you, to have been encouraged by you, to have been praised by you? The honor is in itself. Who would shun walking in the path where a great truth has traveled? Not I. I would have gladly walked in your shadow, and perhaps that is where I've been in your eyes, except when you see me in my work. Your work is like acupuncture to me. When I hear you read there is jahrations moving in my stomach and I don't need to ponder what that means. My stomach knows before I do, my navel still receives nourishment from the world. Your words are pomegranates and avocado, flame-tree and waves, fish and festival. Your iration rhythm is an ancient language that swirls at my feet and beat at my heart. What shame could there be to love a St Vincent yam man like you? The shame is the fear to love or worse ignore it, pretend it's not there, as if there is smoke without a fire. So I give you these three letters that I could not have written until now, but which I had composed to you all along.

Letter 1

My Dear Eddie:

I can't tell you how much it means to me to be in your presence, to hear you talk about my poems, to see them being held in your hands, and hear your voice pick at a line, a phrase. I can't tell you what this friendship that we have developed means. I can't tell you. You making time for me to come and see you, you returning my call, you telling me to submit my poems here and there. I can't describe to you the language of my feelings to witness you in quiet disarray; something about you always a little off tempo—you move to a beat only you hear. But I hear it too, really. I do and I want you to know that I know the music that plays inside your head; it drones inside my head too. I feel it fingering out a rhythm on my body. So I know you through the cadence of your words, the journey of your poems.

Can't tell you how it feels to have you do a private reading of your poems, and just be present in your office as you talk about what occupies you. Sometimes, while you are speaking and busily searching through piles of papers, I take you distracted moment to fix on your lips and I wonder how they would feel writing a poem on my body. And I want to offer myself to you for the experiment, but before I can muster the nerves to present myself to you, you look up at me and my eyes quickly wander to the sights out the window: it is after all the middle of the day and life as ordinary as a light breeze tossing leaves and blowing dust has been happening as I sat in your office entertaining my own private fantasy. And did I say that my longings were never really sexual; I never thought of us in that way, although some part of me must have locked into the geography of our relationship, the dash and alliteration of our poetic connection and the fantasy of a young woman pressed up close enough to be enfolded in the arms of her admirer/mentor.

Thanks for welcoming me, and not turning me away when I came to visit you that first time. I remember you were busy, having errands to do, but I sat patiently in your office, scanning your shelves of book and stacks of paper while you escaped to do your thing. And after tiring of studying your office while I waited for you to return, I looked out the widow at the mango tree. I was not going to be dismissed,. Patience is knowing what you want and not allowing circumstances to redirect you. So I kept coming back until you knew me, and knew that the work you received in the mail was mine and that I was serious, and as crazy about words and using them to transform and motivate, to heal and liberate as you were.

I just can't tell you the simple complexity of my emotions from being in your space and hearing the words from your mouth tease my ears before your spittle had dried. Just can't tell you, but you know. The dub rhythm beats for us.

I hold you close to my heart.
One Love,

Opal

P.S. I have enclosed some new poems that you haven't seen yet. I welcome your feedback. I'll be happy to meet you on campus to discuss - just let me know when.

1978, Kingston, Jamaica.

Letter 2

My Dear Kamau:

I understand why you want to throw off Eddie. I imagine some of the same desires propelled me to take Adisa. Besides, Kamau suits you and when I visited Nairobi University I met a man who knew you and who said that he was among those who named you when you were there a decade or more before me. Like me, they were impressed with you, captured by the sensibilities of your words, the conviction of your politics, the energy of your poetry. Do you have a favorite prose writer? I don't think we ever discussed our favorite writers.

My short story collection is out. Did you receive your copy yet? I welcome your response. You haven't seen any of these stories. I am a poet whose poetry is getting longer, so I seeking to know this or genre? It allows me the room I am needing to tell our stories.

What is happening with <u>Savacou</u>? What is happening with you? You know I hold my breath to receive your letters. I am all out of breath, dare I not breathe? What are these new poems that you mentioned you were working on. I haven't seen any? Will you send me some or will they be published soon?

I miss seeing you. I miss those times we had in your office talking, being silent, reading poems, talking politics. I think you did most of the talking and I listened. I think I mentioned how put off I was by Salkey when I met him years ago before I started teaching. He had warned me to not even think in that direction, but I was not ready to understand what he was saying. Now I know. I get very little writing done during the semester, and I am thinking of pursuing my doctorate? Do you think that's a good idea or should I just focus my energy on writing? With a child, security is pressing in on my mind. Yet you have combined scholarship and poetics. I will try on your shoes, if they get too cumbersome, I can always toss them off.

The enclosed card represents the disconnection I have been feeling and the need for home. I plan to come home for the Holidays so hope you will be around.

I miss the ocean smell and the mangoes. I miss the voices of my people and the sight of familiar places. I miss you, our time together, someone who knows my work and encourages it. Missing is the alphabet of exile, voluntary or forced
Stay strong and wrapped in my love.

Walk Good,

Opal

P.S. I have enclosed some poems so that you know what occupies my mind these days. Do let me hear from you with more details about how you are. Sometimes, I am certain you forget about continuing to live...

1986, Oakland, CA.

Letter 3

Dear Kamau:

Sometimes words are acid eating at my tongue. I try not to swallow or judge, and surprise is not a strange, just an unexpected guest.

How are you? I suppose I don't have to worry anymore about you taking care of yourself. That was never meant to be my job, but over the years, every so often, especially after Doris' death, I did wonder/worry about how and if you were taking care of yourself. I am truly happy that someone has stepped forward and you are being loved. A man such as you should always have love in his life.

The last time I saw you, you said your house was a mess, papers were scattered everywhere and that you needed someone to help you organize things. Why did I not know what you mean? Why did I not want to know that a man like you need a wife to take care of the daily, routine tasks of life. I didn't want to acknowledge what you were saying because I knew then that I couldn't be your wife. I needed a wife of my own, to take care of my children and I, and all the many other life's task that I have to cope with. Where am I supposed to find uncluttered space s and time to write. I wanted to ask you to be my wife? I knew it wouldn't work, but what the hell. We could try. A comma might interrupt the flow of a sentence, but it doesn't destroy it –, yes, it can shift the meaning or confuses the reader, but it still remains, always, a useful child ready to be placed in service.

Now was to have been an opportunity for us to finally have that time I have been dreaming on, but I knew I couldn't/didn't want to nurture you – any man again – in the way that I knew you needed a wife for your work. But it still should have been our time. Not to wrap legs around thighs, or arms around shoulder and press chest to breast. The words are relentless and greedy too. They demand attention. Want to see you frolic with them, hear them in private audience, help to redirect their path.. This was to have been our time.

I am not wine, just a woman who listens to the tempo of life and learns to run with it. I am many things, but foolishness holds no claim to me. I insist on being free and true to myself. I step from the shelter of your shadow and walk with certainty, confident of my own language and the way it moves in the wind.

Why is it one can never reach back into the past and change it? What would you change, not then, but this moment, the history that you're in the act of writing?

Finding home is a useless pursuit. You carry it so well with you, and you are being called to be a gypsy, to give light to what you experience and interpret. Know that I will always be home for you.

Irie and Nuff Respect,

Opal Palmer Adisa
1999, Oakland, CA.

P.S. I am not enclosing any new work. But know that we are writing about the same subject. Our paths might have veered in different directions, but the geography of our poetry coincides.

Mystic man
Word healer
    The waves splash ashore
    Bringing the bones and memory
    Of those who paved the way for us

Listen oh
Listen oh
      De song they sing is a map
      De song they sing is our journey

Mystic man
Rhythm maker
    The wind sweeps over the mountains
    Taking our dreams and struggle with it
    Reminding us that only this day   this moment is promised
      Listen nuh
      Listen nuh
         De tune is jahration
         De tune is iration

Mystic man for whom passion is cloak
I recite in your honor
I chant and wail and dub out the sound of your words
      Dem get over
      I know dem get over...

Kamau:
Notes from the Barbadian Underground

Hilary McD. Beckles

The socially self-defined white inhabitants of Barbados, some 15,000 of them in 1930, called their island home "Little England." They, in turn, effectively encouraged "their" black inhabitants, almost 200,000 of them, to share the use of the word "Bimshire"as a popular name for the island. It was an agreed upon nomenclature that reflected the colonial desire to promote the "shire" identity in England's first farflung island colony which was built upon the strikingly new idea of white supremacy and the institution of black chattel slavery.

Such anglophone representations of the society fashioned the ideological context within which Kamau Brathwaite grew to historical consciousness. The meanings of his inward and outward journeys, mind, land and sea voyages, constituted the vital, driving energy of a locally and globally fought struggle of detachments from the colonial scaffold of the shire. Collectively, they amount to an endemic war waged by a native son and his folk for X/Self respect, cultural freedom and spiritual reconstitution.

My perspective as an historian on this process of rediscovery, as intellectual unhinging and reconnection, differs from that of the literary critic in so far as it discriminates against literariness in favour of social history narrative. The argument is presented in a less critical fashion, and asks fewer questions of an existential nature. In this regard I begin by invoking the insights of Gordon Lewis into the adamite "Bimshire" of Brathwaite which serve to illuminate the site from which this "war of respect" was conceived and fought.

Bimshire, Lewis tells us, was a world that meant what the "white plantocratic" inhabitants wanted it to mean, no more and no less. They mimicked the culture of "an English market town, Cheltenham, as it were," and revered a social world that gave way in 1914 throughout the United Kingdom. Determined to preserve the shire they dug in with the power of nostalgia, and prepared to rule the folk for ever. Other parts of the colonised world watched this "reactionary conceit" in amazement. But one overarching result, Lewis tells us, was that in 1966, when the colony crept into constitutional Independence, it remained "difficult to speak of [it] except in mockingly derisory terms" (Lewis, *Growth* 226).

The Bimshire of Brathwaite's birth, then, was more than the physical world of the plantation, and the merchant houses, churches, courts, and political councils that served it. It was an "inner place" where ideological discourses and cultural contestations for the soul were waged relentlessly as if all could be won or lost with the changed meaning of a word. And the "words" were policed by official powers since to "speak" was to subvert the "law and order" of the surface or to unearth the worlds beneath.

Barbadians from Bimshire, as a rule, could not speak freely; they whispered and spoke in tongues about things "heard" but never "seen." There were no first eye accounts, no witnesses, only old news kept current as a past time to entertain tourists in the day and children at dusk. Lewis, again, tells us that neither could the lords of the land "write" about their home or themselves, except to tell of things that once mattered. He says:

> When, therefore, Barbadians do write about themselves it usually turns out to be, like Louis Lynch's *The Barbados Book*, an odd assortment of items, from historical details about the local churches, through a large section for the tourists, to an antiquarian nostalgia for the old folk ways and pastimes losing out.... Thus does the Barbadian climate of opinion live under the omnipresent shadow of a romanticized past. (Lewis, *Growth* 227)

One of their enduring favourites, says David Lowenthal, relates to World War II when "Barbados sent a telegram to England, saying: 'Go in England, Barbados is behind you'.... Hitler, on being informed of this message, sent a signal to Barbados, saying, 'If you stay out, we will give you Trinidad'"(Lowenthal 10).

The rupture of this tradition of silence was nourished, in a way as a contradictory omen, by the womb that was *Bim* (shire!), a discursive arts/literary journal edited for locally exiled and ignored Caribbean artists/writers by Frank Collymore who, within the colour vernacular, narrowly escaped whiteness. In the beginning, then, there was *Bim*, where Kamau and George Lamming, among others, were cuddled and cared for. Kamau, in flight to freedom from the police of the "pure" plantation system, and knowing the evidence of things seen and felt, had *Bim* as a haven, a kind of maroon town. The tensions of this refusal to stay confined determined the dynamic and range of Kamau's military modalities, the trajectories of his voyages and journeys, and the kinky texture of this thought.

To begin with, there was the dispossession of the people. Black Barbadians received what historians have described as the worst deal at the hands of the local elite and its imperial backers during the emancipation reforms and legislation of 1838 and after. In effect, they experienced a cold blooded "landless freedom" which ensured, a hundred years later, that Kamau would be natally trapped within a plantation sector that offered the lowest wages within the region.

The "divorce of the people from the land"—no peasantry nor small farmer culture emerged here—guaranteed the "economic and social subserviency of the black majority...to a degree unknown elsewhere," says Lewis. The "stranglehold of the resident whites" created a "cramped and introspective" mentality among the "folk" who lived within their skin beneath the shadow of the plantation "castle." Little did they know, though that suspicion was always there, that guy fox was in the making (Lewis 227, 228).

The midday, middle passage sweat of the dispossessed, and their silent struggles within Bimshire, fertilised the seed of all Kamau's work, starting in *Bim* in the early 1950s. At this time he knew the personalities that postured as the politicians of the poor; he watched them as they constituted themselves into an organisational process called the "labour movement." The local stirring of a workers' civil rights campaign, the discourse of black redemption, middle class self-mobilisation through the rhetoric of democracy, and all such like politics represented a formal, surface challenge to the makers of Bimshire. While in effect it widened the space for cultural discourse within civil society, the depth of an inner sense of black alienation, of subjection, the feeling of being kept prisoner, remained unattended.

Lewis has no time for the political challenge of this kind, but places his hope in the archaeology of the artist. He sums up the limits and the language of the political signifiers in this way: "They fought for single causes rather than for a complete reconstruction of Barbadian life. In different ways, they opposed the oligarchy, but they had no clear idea of what they wanted to replace it with"(Lewis 235). On this score there was disquiet; a quiet defeat that drowned out the drum by an orchestrated numbing of the

African mind promoted by incessant afternoon chamber music that dominated the radio waves.

The Mandingo drum had been banned by the colonial government since 1688 when the slaveowners' legislature codified laws for the "good governing of negro slaves." Blacks took to the few remaining woods to beat the criminalised skin, but did so under the canopy of silence. This was how the young ones were schooled and scolded; "hush ya mout fore ya get yaself and we in trouble."

The orderliness of Kamau's youth was the sum of 200,000 silences, private closures sealed in fear of life and death. The alternative was not evident, certainly not visible, and Kamau began by breaking the barrier with words, rhythmic sounds, using the drum and invoking the spirits that respond to it. In short time his talking drum was being heard all over the land, including neighbouring lands, and across the triangle of the great crime.

Kamau's use of poetry and prose fiction as cultural media enabled him to declare "unbanned" the Mandingo drum that had come to know only rippling sounds under gentle hands. The pulsating acoustic effect of his public performances brought back to a people the taste of a terrifying sound that had been foreign in formal places. The release of the hand had a hurrying effect upon the community that was seeking, especially after 1966, to imagine and invent new ways to live culturally as a constitutionally independent identity. No easy matter was it to come back from a de- historicised past with confidence, certainty, and poise.

Suddenly, there was the sound of gushing young blood steaming within the symbolism of the liberated drum. But the experience of complete spiritual renewal, the ancestors had said, could only be attained with an untying of the tongue to disclaim the chains of history. In the beginning there was the "word," and the word was in *Bim*, and it was war. But every word needed a home, a place of its own. Kamau's calling was to remove the surface of the killing fields, redefine the space, and speak to the architecture of the rebirth. The rhythm of texts and sound were the digging tools and building blocks of the emerging folk on whose souls the enterprise was hinged.

Rooting his resistance in the spiritual world of the common people, the folk who fished, fetched, and felled canes, was in full measure the core mission of Kamau's social philosophy. It transcended debates about the natures of literatures and the anxieties of the artist. Connectivity and commitment informed his moral aesthetic. His view was that the artist had a duty to bring in "the voices of the people of the new nation making patterns of sound in hammer, engine, power saws, and the movement of earth and water." This is what he said. This was what he did.

It was here in this well that Kamau chose to drop his bucket. Within the still tentative politics of the folk he devised a strategy to establish an enduring, authentic alliance that enabled him to live his own law that the artist should have a committed sense of social and moral values. How else could he have used the voice to verse the alienation of landlessness and give visibility to the culturally submerged?

Kamau offered a pedagogy of the rootless as notes from the underground. Their response to endemic fluidity was the building technology of the "chattel house," a stoneless castle that was send packing from "his" land when the plantation "man" was mad. The ex-chattel would pull apart his wooden world and journey to a less angry estate in a humbled state. There were a million such rightless middle passages; the chattel house was the "sign and symbol of their rejection by society" (Torres-Saillant, *Caribbean Poetics* 94, 95).

Chained to the shack that had no roots of its own, the folk could make no sound. Kamau rattled the gaggle, banged the walls, and make noises that still haunt the plantation's peace, both day and night. He unleashed the spirits of Ta Mega, Negus, and Ogun with sounds remembered at a Ghana gathering. But the villages here and there, across the triangle, could not house the echoes of his voice. The man of words from the woods had created a new context, the site where he fixed history and established the terms of resistance. The villager, then, was the folk, both modern and traditional, who like the sankofa bird flies forward while looking back.

The sankofa, we know, is rooted in the Ghana that called upon Kamau to trace (back-back) the passage as part of the beginning of the inward voyage in search of a "rights." The village of Bimshire was a place of beginning in the search for "a sense of belonging." The inner part of the journey was through a sunken well, deep beneath the living space, where secrets were buried and kept burnished by trickling sounds of through limestone. Emerging, we recognised and claimed him with the restlessness he represented; the "arrivant"who could never settle, reconstituted as the creole in eternal motion.

The middle passage for Kamau, then, was no healing place with wholesome hopes. It was too tearing an exploration of the flesh and the soul; the former absorbed the terror of the lash until the blood ran cold, and the latter, like a cracked mirror, reflected broken pieces of splintered dreams. Criss-crossing the passage, between island and continent, ocean and rivers, Kamau the creole claimed all the history that made his mould. Fully embracing the Atlantic shores he found his centre, however, in the primordial clouds of Sahara dust that arrives annually to cover and connect the submerged Africa of Bimshire.

He is a Barabajan, the son of a mother whose poem is that you cannot turn back because there is never a going back. "Home," says Billie Holiday, is filled with pain, but for the Barabajan the homelessness of landlessness *is* the "pain." But voyages and journeys of rediscovery can only begin at the new home. It is a place made by history and inhabited by the youngest ancestors. Bimshire, submerged Iboland, both occupied layers of the same space under the same sun. "Islands and Exiles" and "Mask" are the antithesis in the story of this rising son that penetrates like rays of steel the places beneath. Taking a stance, standing for Africa, the themes explored as spiritual liberation in "The Making of the Drum," are the calls to arms associated with "naming."

The power to name a public place was never within the grasp of submerged Africa. The "Edward" of birth that gave way to "Kamau," like all the folk, was invisible in voicelessness. His focus on language and sound in search of the power to name things gave direction to the missile which he launched to breach the apartheid wall. Like Jamaica Kincaid's Antigua, the landscape and mindscape of Bimshire were named in celebration of the shire. "Edward" was conceived in the language hegemony of the imperial monarchy. The wearing of the name, "Kamau," given him by Ngugi wa Thiong'o's mother in a Gikuyu ceremony, was an Abeng that signalled the arrivant.

Jamaica Kincaid, speaking of Antigua, exposed the naming heresy that the shire had called into effect. She had this to say: "In the Antigua that I knew, we lived on a street named after an English maritime criminal, Horatio Nelson, and all the other streets around us were named after some other English maritime criminals. There was Rodney Street, there was Hood Street, there was Hawkins Street, and there was Drake Street" (Kincaid 8). Brathwaite's Bimshire, likewise, in 1813 had constructed as its proud centre piece a monument of Nelson, Lord Nelson if you please, an edifice offered in victorious support of Englishness, or at least the colonial version of it.

But the acquisition of the capacity to name things in such contexts was a long and painful process of "de-education" and resurgence. It was acquired only after a thousand voyages "back back/to Af-/rica" where common folks discovered themselves buried beneath the bloody soils on which they stood. Scaling the walls of an imperial education required all the strengths of self and ancestral spirits; to rise was to laugh at, to mock, and to trample on the ideas that held the bricks of Bimshire together. Kincaid, speaking for Kamau, said: "We were taught the names of the Kings of England." Edward was a King. She continued: "In Antigua, the 24th May was a holiday—queen Victoria's official birthday. We didn't say to ourselves, hasn't this extremely unappealing person been dead for years and years" (Kincaid 8).

Kamau, furthermore, was schooled in the ideas of Rome and the values of Christian saints. There was nothing of importance and consequence in between. The name "Tom" came to signify all there was to know about the black mind that absorbed and tried to live it all. A Tom, it was said, never raised his voice to the white man. Tom never said, "hey I saw ya!" The journey from Edward, around and beyond Tom, to Kamau was therefore a removal of the mask, a voyage through the middle, into the awaiting ancestral space.

On this voyage, Kamau has never allowed his feet to leave the ground. He remained planted, rooted realistically, even if elevated by cultural ritual. Behind the masks were the many fractured souls, broken, battered and bruised, some beyond healing. He understood how this reality was easily translated into a politics of treachery and divisiveness. The public murders of Michael Smith in Jamaica and Walter Rodney in Guyana came like flashes of flames that left ashes for the winds. There was always the dread of the oppressor's "fire next time." He was to receive a kind of stoning. In the Bimshire of his time, unlike before, there was no need for the flame, and public stoning instead awaited all the pathfinders who rose from the underground.

Kamau used the metaphor of being a "stranger in one's land" to illuminate the cycle of denial that accompanied the stoning. The voyages of discovery, the hearing of the drum, the basking in the healing feeling of the spirits, and being a bloodied arrivant, speak to the silencing power of colonialism. How easy it was to be declared "mad" by the empowered few above and sanctioned by the dispossessed many below. The villagers would shun you, and ask of you to be quiet in "their" place. Their children are instructed not to hear you, and they would laugh with pointed fingers. The voyage, you soon discover, could so cruelly take the life it is meant to give.

The historian's eye had seen it all before. Kamau's navigation, then, benefitted from the privileges of this knowledge and he returned "alive," even if not "well." But Bimshire took its beating, and in short time the drum became louder as the folk stood taller. The Ogun became an icon for the few whose tongues were unleashed enabling the "Mighty Gabby" to sing "Take down Nelson, Take down the Sea Dog." The government has now agreed. Gradually, the people are remembering the places where the secrets were buried, and the underground is slowly yielding them from an ancient time.

The rediscovered voice, unearthed, now roams the sugar lands mingling with the water gods of the passage—land and water connected by petals of blood. The spirits at the rising, called by Kamau's "dread locked" invocation, no longer dwelled as pebbles in the sand but as poems in the land chanting down the stone walls of the "high" church that blessed the deaths. Kamau wore his "Tam" as a Muslim bore his "Mat"—turned around —a first step to send and receive the "WORD." Here, the limestone could not bear it all. The pocomania and kumina fell through, but the Ogun, the Vodun, the Obi remained—waiting for the call, the Spiritual Baptism, to trickle up to a dawn. Kamau, standing at the cross roads, tapped his feet, hummed and hissed, called and waited. One response that came took the form of an echo. It was the announcement by Errol Barrow, a native "sun," that told the villagers the time had come to "no longer loiter on colonial premises." The Union Jack came down on November 30, 1966. Gordon Rohlehr, who has followed Kamau closely, tells us that "Independence," if a meaningful concept, "must mean a new language, a redefinition of self and milieu"("Islands" 197). It meant that Barbados had been pushed, torn and tortured to the junction. Kamau was standing there with Attibon Legba, the vodoo god of the crossroads. And he said, "fill me with words/ and I will blind your god....Att/Att/Attibon!!!."

But it was the midwife with the knife who had the final word on the new life. Raped, plundered, and denied for 300 years, the womb had served as a tomb, and as the sugar men straddled the open legs of 1966 they found composure within their discomfort. Kamau looked around and saw that they too had a firm grip on the hand that guided the knife; the screaming cord they whispered was also a silencing rope. The new life received no slap; it breathed quietly and gazed through the bars of the crib that resembled the old world. Kamau remained at the crossroads, going nowhere, anchored to the limestone, calling again "Att/Att/Attibon!!!."

The refusal to fall, and the courage not to bend, did not blow with the common wind. Kamau says that those who did not stand were those who ran: "My husband/if you cud see he/fragile, fraid o'e own shadow." The Queen of England remained the "mother," still the bosom of first resort. The landless remained in the castles of their skin, the only inns within. Nelson also stood his ground, demanding an Official Commission of Enquiry and a public referendum. Kamau unashamed, and stoned again, stands his ground undefeated: "and I will dwell in the house of the merchants For NEVER."

Brathwaite was right and precise. The strategy adopted by the planter-merchant houses, especially after 1966, was two-fold. First, to regroup and examine what role, if any, they could play in shaping and controlling the politics of the new nation. They chose to finance the new ruling labour parties, demand positions on the boards of statutory corporations, and manipulate economic policy in such a manner as to convince government of the still effective political power of big business. They also impressed upon government that any discussion about "development" should involve their members and more importantly, that the cultural and intellectual climate of the country should favour them if their economic cooperation was to be assured.

Black government developed no policy on land redistribution. The agenda of democracy did not include a discourse on ownership. The independent Prime Minister stressed the importance of government's partnership with the landed elite. There was no attempt at transforming race and managerial relations in the work place; debates were confined to the need for black tellers in the commercial banks. No campaign was launched to address the redress of unequal resource ownership. This was a political betrayal of the arrivants—capitulation in the face of refashioned mercantile mastery.

Tourism was promoted as a major industrial sector during the first four years of the regime, and government revenues earned from this sector increased at a remarkable rate. A hotel construction boom assisted in stimulating the manufacturing sector that contributed to drift of the landless into the city. The planter too had come to town, completed his metamorphosis, and emerged as a stronger force. Those who ruled did not govern and Black government seemed in pursuit of the "elusive pimpernel."

The black community, though, appeared more confident in expressing its still stultified racial consciousness. In general, there was widespread feeling that society was posed for a push away from its colonial foundations and government had the potential, and support, to chart a new and independent path. But black politicians who had grown up under the Union Jack with Kamau, some of whom had walked with him during the anti-colonial nationalist surge of the post-war years in support of liberation causes in Africa and Asia, remained silent on the question of white economic and racial domination.

When the all-black government in 1970 found it necessary to prevent Trinidadian-born, American black power activist Kwame Toure (then Stokeley Carmichael) from addressing public audiences during his short and well-policed visit, the formal rationale was that government was committed to non-racialist politics and the defence of white minority rights. A Public Order Act was passed that year which sought to suppress the black power movement, and to escalate police surveillance of known black-consciousness radicals.

Unable or unwilling to implement structural changes in the ownership of productive land, government resorted to a wide range of social politics designed to create the potential for black redemption. These included free secondary and university education, national insurance schemes, incentives to small black businesses, and a comprehensive health policy. These policies, however, were about the politics of capitulation of which Lewis spoke with disdain as the despicable seeking to be acceptable to the respectable.

Kamau was not silent on the persistence of institutional anti-black racism. He made references to discrimination against blacks in the cultural economy that had been tugged to the centre of popular social discourse. He challenged the emergent black middle-class to facilitate culture as a transforming force. It remained divided, unwilling to challenge the merchant in the market, it developed a dependency ideology and consciousness which compromised its social potential. According to Cecilia Karch:

> The black middle class embraced the prevailing ideological system; many were proponents of Empire. The majority sought access to the system; they did not seek to destroy it. Status as a middle class and their dependency on the paternalism of the oligarchy, and the colonial system, blunted the nationalist revolutionary spirit of black middle income groups and go a long way in explaining the recent political history of the island. Individuals from this class, not the class as a class, became political leaders and spokesmen for the majority population. It was the massive unrest of the black working class which propelled them into the limelight. Where leadership emerged from the ranks of the working class, it was repressed. (Karch 224)

Deep-seated dependency and fear among the black professional class, then, intensified the stoning.

Other voices now liberated also poured scorn on the independent arrangement. Crippled behind the crib the young nation did not burst force with the rashness of its age. The energy of freedom contained, and promise unfulfilled, the Court of St James remained. The poet Bruce St. John saw this clearly when he wrote "Political Progress':

> We got democracy!
> Man shut you mout.
> We en got democracy?
>
> Who in de assembly now?
> Who sheltering who now?
> Backra telling we wuh to eat,
> Backra telling we wuh to wear,

Backra telling we wuh to live in,
Backra telling we when.
Backra out o'de assembly
But backra mekkin' 'e money!

Slave got government,
Slave got opposition,
Slave defending labour,
Slave opposing slave,
Who defending backra?
Backra making money!
Money without Assembly?
Slave making joke. (Beckles and Shepherd 536)

There are no longer any guarded secrets St. John tells us. Ownership pattern and control mechanism now move like soldiers on parade. The commanding heights of the economy are the home of a minority white elite which wields levels of power far in excess of what its demographic proportion suggests.

Over time a counter attack was launched. Critics of the new dispensation were labelled by its media sentinels "undesirables" and "misfits." Offers were made to a few who came on board as legitimisers in the market place. Academics became the new validating elite. But there was a sting in the tail. Some board room blacks feel a sense of both gratitude and resentment. They are made to feel outsiders since, by and large, they work for, or under the man with the land. They all know where their ceiling is located; they all know on which doors they cannot knock.

The status quo was also rationalised with a rhetoric of white supremacy ideology. Blacks are incompetent in an age of management, they say. Their tutelage incomplete they should continue to serve as best they can. Dr. Waldo Waldron-Ramsey, former Barbados ambassador to the United Nations, and a popular newspaper columnist, articulated the historicised reasoning in an article published in the Barbados *Daily Nation*, July 6, 1989. Entitled "De-mystification of the legend," it reads:

There is a legend, of a sort, that in Barbados only Euro-Barbadians or caucasoid Barbadians can manage and run business enterprises here. That they are better at it than any other race. That they have had many years in the experience of management, and so, almost as a group, they are now, ipso facto, experts at business.

On the other hand, people of African origin have no such tradition and acquired expertise to rely upon. That Africans or people of the black race have other strengths and expertise as a people. But man-

aging business is not one of them. Our colonial education and experience have been so contrived and devised, that they lend a certain
credence to that myth. And worst still, many of the Africans in Barbados would seem to have been seduced by this facile, weak, and
unsubstantiated argument. There is no truth in it all. But this had
been part of the colonial plot to weaken the sinews of the majority in
the colonial population, and to render the imperium infinitely more
secure by augmenting the faith of that section of the population
which could more readily identify with imperial masters.

The journey from colony to country, then, as Kamau had seen, kept class
and race relations intact and ensured continuance of the basic division within
the society.

These developments in social structure had a significant impact upon
the process of cultural institutionalisation that had been stimulated by
Kamau's stance in public places. Radical elements within the student community, encouraged also by the wider influence of the Pan-African black
consciousness movement, socially rejected some formal aspects of
Eurocentric cultural dominance and joined the community movement for
the redemption and validation of the Afro-Barbadian heritage. The rural
villages and urban slums gave form to vibrant social expressions in song,
dance, art, theatre, drama and language.

Elton Mottley, privileged son of the black mayor of the city who was a
principal political spokesman for the merchant-planter alliance, followed
Kamau in a voyage of discovery. He emerged as Elombe Mottley, and in
the leadership vanguard of the Afro-Barbadian cultural renaissance. The
formation and development of "Yoruba House," an organisation dedicated
to cultural understanding and revival, under Mottley's directorship, provided a forum, as *Bim* did, for cultural activity and a home of sorts.

In 1978 Kamau was invited by the government to conduct a survey of
indigenous cultural activities and to draw up proposals for a national development plan for the cultural sector of the country. In his report,
Brathwaite stated that despite individual efforts in various sections of the
arts, it could not be said that Barbados had developed any significant institutional cultural infrastructure in the period prior to political independence.

Daphne Joseph-Hackett was critical in the establishment of the Barbados National Theatre Workshop, and Anthony Hinkson, poet-playwright,
had pioneered the formation in 1969 of the Barbados Writers Workshop.
Black Night, a grass-roots forum of writers, poets and dramatists, also under Mottley's guidance, led the way in the early 1970s, in the development
of community/street art which drew upon the folk tradition. But also in
June 1978, Mottley, along with the Ministry of Education and Culture,

mounted an islandwide community and theatrical event. The traditional "Crop-Over Festival" was unearthed and brought back to social life (Beckles 209).

This development was a major achievement for the project driven by Kamau's energies and visions. The Crop Over festival was a site of cultural expression for the enslaved since the early 18th century. The tightening of police control over the cultural activities of blacks, and the rapid pace of demographic creolisation, served to drive the festival underground. Between 1750 and 1834, Barbados had a larger percentage of creole blacks in the population than any other sugar colony in the West Indies. It became common for whites to argue that creoles were less culturally vibrant than the African born.

The impact of social creolisation upon the black community was profound. It meant that the African cosmology came under greater internal pressure as a result of the diminishing percentage of African recruits and external assault from the degradations of the white community. One effect was that blacks learned to avoided severe penalties by not adhering too closely to it. But they responded in other ways. One was by taking underground those elements of culture which could survive without public display. These include aspects of religion and philosophic world views. Obeah, for example, survived underground in spite of legislation which outlawed its practice as a social ritual or religious construct.

In spite of intense anti-African pressures, enslaved creole blacks were able to enhance and defend aspects of their ancestral heritage. The creative arts, religious social philosophical ontology, as well as language, survived as cultural institutions. Far from concealed, these elicited condescending or frankly hostile reactions from Europeans. In 1796, Dr. George Pinckard, an English military medic, thus gave an example of the prejudiced attitude held by Europeans towards the display of African social culture in the Crop Over festival. He wrote:

> They assemble in crowds, upon the open green, or in any square or corner of the town, and forming a ring in the centre of the throng, dance to the sound of their favourite African yell. Both music and dance are of a savage nature, ...their songs which are very simple, [are] harsh and wholly deficient in softness and melody.... While one negro strikes the Banjar, another shakes the rattle with great force of arm, and a third sitting across the body of the drum, as it lies lengthwise upon the ground, beats and kicks the sheepskin at the end, in violent exertion with his hands and heels, and a fourth sitting upon the ground at the other end, behind the man with the drum, beats upon the wooden sides of it with two sticks. Together with the

> noisy sounds, numbers of the party of both sexes bawl forth their
> dear delightful sound with all possible force of lungs, ...a spectator
> would require only a slight aid from fancy to transport him to the
> savage wilds of Africa. (*Notes* 264-5)

Frederick Bayley, another Englishman, visited Barbados during the 1820s
and stated how the enslaved blacks, to the annoyance of whites, would "sit
up during the greater part of the moonlight nights, chattering together, and
telling 'nancy stories'" (*Four Years'* 436). "A nancy story," he said, "is
nothing more or less than a tale of ghosts and goblins, which pass with the
negroes by the appellation of Jumbees" (*idem*). He then commented on the
slaves' "grand day of jubilee, which they call 'crop over'." During this
festival, he wrote, "it was common to see the different African tribes forming each a distinct party, singing and dancing to the gumbay [an African
drum], after the rude manner of their native Africa." He added that the
festival had now been made less African, with the fiddle and tambourine
being used instead of drums, while "black and white, overseer and book-
keeper, mingle together in dance" (*idem*).

African culture, then, in becoming Afro-Barbadian, absorbed elements
of Euro-creole ideas and practices. This was undoubtedly a circumstantial
response to power inequality. But by virtue of its inner vitality in the survival quest African culture remained the dominant popular form. There
can be no doubt that Crop Over, now an annual event, is the most remarkable rediscovery of the Kamau project. Together with the National Independence Festival of Creative Arts which began in 1973, it has become the
beacon of the postnational cultural upsurge.

The institutionalisation of African cultural identity since the mid-1970s,
in the form of the Crop Over festival, a proliferation of theatre workshops,
dance and musical groups, professional artists, writers and storytellers, all
working within the social experiences of the folk, attests to the extent to
which Kamau's notes from the underground have refashioned the Bimshire
of his birth allowing for a new Barbados to emerge. Kamau, then, has provided the main pathways for outer voyages and inward journeys.

At no juncture, however, did Kamau attempt to set aside the vitality or
the importance of Eurocentric traditions. His use of the bass and the drum
as the base line was not intended to eradicate or deny the melodies of Europe, but merely to mark a place of beginning, a home, from which his
journeys departed. He provided, as a result, no dichotomised vision of culture but accepted the role of the dialectic in reading the creolising force of
all histories. For him the Caribbean X/Self is best understood as a cultural
melange in the tradition of all creole creation. On this score Derek Walcott
joins him, the evidence of which is his *Omeros* (1990) that embraces the

discursive vision of *X/Self* (1987).

While the logic and intellectual force of X/Self are cast as everlasting subversions of imperialists' construction of what is the hegemonic "West," Kamau accepts that Africa and Europe had been hinged culturally together by direct human interaction long before the crime of the middle passage. The militant assertion of Europe within the ancient relationship is read however as a betrayal of that engagement and a sin of an oedipal nature.

The West Indian, says the X/Self, denied none but seeks truths in moral and philosophical discourse. One compelling truth is that Europe in enslaving the African bit the hand that bore and fed it. The use of the Christian God as a wicked weapon in the armour of the pro slavery military and technological assault, placed the recast "jet white" Christ at the disposal of slave traders, genocidal conquistadors, and their financial and political sponsors. The recall of slavery by the European mind at a time of self- proclaimed "enlightenment,"globalised the cultural erasure that is racism. Racialised chattel bondage was their invention for the African; for the Asian at a later date it would be bomb of Nagasaki and napalm of Vietnam.

The oppression of the colonial heritage, then, is not for Kamau an abstraction but a living condition. This perspective is in opposition of reading of his work that denied him, as an artist, socio-political agency. No one from or in the Barbados underground, trapped in the prison of Bimshire, has expected of Kamau any political prescription for liberation. But they followed his light with a hammer in hand. He showed us then how and where to dig; and he told them why. His message is a missile, powerful and "smart." THE VOYAGE TO THE PAST IS THE JOURNEY TO THE FUTURE. He is no "playing" politician, but a self-confessed "cultural gorilla" fighting for the "alter Native."

As I end this intervention in the discourse the island has moved away from debate over the removal "Nelson" from the city centre to the illegalising of "dub music" in public places. The youth are up in arms against this attempt by the State to silence their drum. Neither has the State removed Kamau from its gaze. The stoning continues as he wages a battle in the public media to prevent government from acquiring the land on which his "house" stands in order to make way for an extending airport. The blasts of jets will, it seem, drown his sound, and fill the space that he has set aside for a library in honour of General Bussa, the enslaved leader of 1816 anti-slavery rebellion in Bimshire.

Elaine Savory

miranda: the first voicing

i

> Europeans, you must open this book and enter it...it is you who will
> feel furtive, nightbound and perished with cold. (Jean-Paul Sartre,
> Preface to Frantz Fanon, *The Wretched of the Earth*. 11, 12)

i am old now & burdened with memories.

four hundred years
& my young arrogance

& beauty merely
the salt bone of the wind
flaying my understanding.
no more balm of forgetting.
i look for pretty words &
find only a tunnel of mirrors.

this face-mask of old lies
i have never looked behind:
what is there left of me?
i can only hear caliban's
words in my words.
i am a small stone on the parched floor
listening to the dam burst.

i am double-divorced from language
& an outsider. loss & denial
my brittle companions whose shapes
silently hollow out
my chill cell of remembering.
i speak without speaking
as through flowing water & dying

bizarre & stubborn fragment of love survives
a frail leaf clinging to a withered stem.

i was careless once, i could speak
comfort, quietly lethal as butter.
i loved my coils of blonde curls
dazzlingly shed & reclaimed my skin.
i was an ordinary petulant girl,
a doorway for the wind.

i want to tell now. & the
drawing of feeling. in a
language which has faced & understood.
i have no nation. no breathing language
only my father's words rotting in the shell
& my own brutal & inarticulate misgivings.

ii

                    ...I have bedimmed
The noontide sun, called forth the mutinous winds
                    ...graves at my command,
Have waked their sleepers, oped, and let 'em forth,
By my so potent art...
           William Shakespeare, *The Tempest*, 67, 68.

four hundred long & mostly lying years:
this island's green & turbulent graces
cut & remodelled in my father's hand.
four hundred years of silent masquerades.

like an old photograph, an old
self is a closed window, an old life
too easily lights as fable. if i believe,
i'll hear only the whores of language.

my voice is fashioned to celebrate prospero
& so i have long silenced myself
only one choice
i flower as betrayal or swell as his savage fruit.

there have been centuries of my forgetting.
lifetimes of wandering after i betrayed my father.
i am half-crazy with lives i could never enter.

but as i stepped mischievously
onto the dangerous edge of motherless womanhood
my young skin glowing like a living marble
dusted with anticipated & unknown pleasures
i ruled my father & i tormented him.
barefoot & innermost
wielding the cruel imperative of a young, full smile.
i grew princess of all princesses
in my father's loneliness
& no mother to rival me & jibe.

my choices always lines already interpreted.
my father sometimes conjured me
as a book & read my unrestrained images of desires,
read longing and language hunted one another.

i learned division as i learned to speak
i was my father's son & daughter
fragile heir & summation
cause & explanation in the

guarded & fortressed name of miranda.

i harboured shrill & secret resentment
like the cruel blood of the manchineel
bitterness rooted in salt.
the motherless & wayard miranda
thought only to hold her hands empty & receive.

my father stilled the idea of his daughter
possessed it with the violence of injured spirits.

my father who smelled of spices & high rank.

iii

> You're trapped in this fantasy, that someone like him could melt you
> and take you down to the thing you've lost touch with...
>
> (Marina Warner, *Indigo* 368)

we turned over unprotected palms
letting clear water run over back to the pale sand:
the island's sacred mornings, blue & delighted.

the coral slabs glistening greens & browns
and ochres and the crabs attentive.
caliban in his embrace & freedom of a voice
translating other worlds for me
morning after glorious morning.
the high surf shaped a barrier of sound
my father who delivered no possibility of alternatives
out of his great magic
could not hear our voices.

the skins laid down. hands over hands
scarred on sharp rock. we were copper
& sand. we were ochre & earth.
the harsh hard cliffs of the north
the island's point into ocean bare & callous
,forbidden consciousness. i was constructed
freedom. my father slept on
images of my obedience.

i thought i could laugh then
enough to give the winds
sense of redrawing
the entire map of feeling.
i saw ideas turning their colours
a true anarchy in a shining air
owning themselves & nothing.

the wet cutting coral of the northern cliffs
a passage spiralled down to the mysteries
a cave the ocean devours every high tide
sweeping all sacrifices into its hungry mouth.
suddenly & all the colours of creation
the spray hot & brilliant in the uncanny sun
& caliban would draw in his breath
& bright complexities: his mother's
chest of word gems. sycorax
rainbow magician arching her brilliant
palette over the wounded &
ruined conception the island
erasing old failures
to begin new memory of endless
transformations. before the captivity of
thought, before my father jealous &
savage with half-decided fear.

iv

> "She is the white light that paralysed your mind, that led you into
> this confusion."
>
> (Derek Walcott, *Dream on Monkey Mountain* 319)

just before flame & purple sunset.
caliban was tapestries of words
figured extraordinary silks of imagining
full of singing in his mother's words
which i knew then
& which wrapped us in possibilities of transition.
the moment lay on my tongue
& i began to taste its many fragrances.
but he said, first in his words,
then in my father's harsher fabric
i helped him fold into his inner sense

there is no more loss worse than this.
& i knew he spoke of sycorax.

& i demanded *speak to me.*
words cannot be demanded.
he looked for the rainbow
& for me every word was opaque
& my tongue sought weapons
& i allowed a shadow
between the sun & my longing.
i spoke
& sycorax held my words
smothered & tied & dropped into deep water
carried on the high white waves
silent & divorced
& i could not
say.

v

> It was the Atlantic this side of the island, a wild-eyed, marauding sea
> the colour of slate, deep, full of dangerous currents, lined with row
> upon row of barrier reefs, and with a sound like that of the combined
> voices of the drowned raised in a loud-unceasing lament- all those
> the nine million... who... had gone down between this point and the
> homeland lying out of sight to the east. (Paule Marshall, *The Chosen
> Place, the Timeless People* 106)

outwards into memory
sycorax gathered her daughter.
voices & language singing through space.
but i only turned the shells that i was given,
turned them & turned them, listening.
i could not hear the echoes of the dead:
my silence was too brazen & too long.
i write their names where ocean washes them:
stiff fingers cannot shape connection.
i am brought here.
i come to this bare beach & beg for words:
the crowds of memories refuse them.
behind my life the ships furl sails,
there out beyond this violence of waves,
where poetry is ended. this is plain:
lives which i might have loved, cast overboard.
the ships glide on to market. veils &
gasps of tears do nothing. the dead
speak only as the waves can breach
masks & amnesia.
                    a faint voice a footfall.
who can bring back the dead? what
penance buries them with honour?

i set my white hand at the water's edge:
a novice of surrender ignorant of vows.
my breath caught in the voices of the waves.

vi

            ...I pitied thee,   .
Took pains to make thee speak, taught thee each hour
One thing or another: when thou didst not- savage!
Know thine own meaning, but wouldst gabble like
A thing most brutish... (Shakespeare, *The Tempest* 19)

old i am now & burdened with memories.

harm reaps such unbridled interest
doubling & tripling & quadrupling its power.
i remember although for these numb centuries
i have refused to have to remember

my father's cobalt eyes
clouded with questions
his voice razored with insecurity.
under the scarlet fire-tree's blossoms
under the warm dangerous kisses of the wind
amidst thin bush on the faded clay mountain
rivered with self-doubts. behind my father's cabin
his wooden palace: blinding authority:

i denied, with my own words, my brother.

miranda, palest and youngest & most dangerous
thinking to enter caliban's ancient knowledges
without surrender. to design new gods
without giving libation. i turned from shadows
thousands deep in my blue eyes
afraid of strong light.
as if it were possible
though i have bitterly learned
over many lifetimes
skin sometimes tells you
little of its stored secrets
we do not always serve
the new lifetime in the same surface
honour it or not.

vii

> So the god,/mask of dreamers/ hears lightnings/stammer,
> hearts/ rustle their secrets.
> (Kamau Brathwaite, Masks, The Arrivants 131)

strict white & starched jewels
out of the thin rain & the mud.
painted roof sheltering celebration
then the shone bell & shell trumpet:
so the belonging is traced & signed

fragrance for cleansing
clove cinnamon glimmering nutmeg
bowled in a young girl's hand.
threads unwinding the step
back to first self unfolded

from the chill eyes of the week
only guarded by Sunday's freedom.
& the frangipani & oleander
for clear eye & fierce touch
when past centuries & promises leap up in the incense smoke

weary & divided child of the spirit
faded & weathered the blood diverted
brought for this witness.
i stand apart
in unaccustomed purity of garments
hold long fractured connections
buried shards of old angers
& the wound is empty & grey.
origins of silence lit like
candles with flames &
they know me through
spirit eyes hard laughing
not yet not yet not yet:
blessing only to strengthen.

consciousness drop by crimson drop
may bring colour & feeling
pain in the long-dead flesh
so they determine:

weave again alone the
long frayed hope of
rediscovery & so begin
the journey back to source

the ancient
smiles
of elders.
& i must speak:

i have been the raindrop
which contaminates the leaf
i have been the ray
which must devour the cell
i have been the silent
wishing to decipher
the lost alphabet of connections
half-erased with bloodstains
carved with names

there is dust on the world
& it no longer shines
& i am old & remarkably burdened with memories.

& worse i am always outsider
so i can only watch
the children of our savageries
nurture their stubborn plantings
injured selves until they are choked
& exhausted with the elaborate fatigues of hating
children of our cleverness & failure ·
gaming with words hoping for signs
& beginning to despair of all signing

there is only
to testify &
to acknowledge
& finally to know
four hundred years of lifetimes
try as i might
to image easily enough
to escape.
there is only
to gather
scattered word embers
so they may light questions
dark & pale
a thought who is a woman
holds my hand.

it is for me to turn
& confront that prison:

prospero's daughter.

Note

For those who do not know Shakespeare's play *The Tempest*, its Caribbean iconography, or Kamau Brathwaite's important development of both, it is necessary to say a word about the characters in the following poems. Each one has an incarnation which is slightly different in England, Africa, the Caribbean and the United States. Some of these have been already established by other writers.

Prospero: Ruler of the island, which he took away from Sycorax and her son Caliban. The European prince and the great magician; in Caribbean iconography, the white colonialist and slave-owner.

Miranda: The daughter of Prospero, the European princess; in the Caribbean, the cossetted white lady of the plantation. Raised by her father alone, with Caliban as her companion, until as she claimed to her father in Shakespeare's play, Caliban tried to seduce her. In Marina Warner's novel, *Indigo*, Miranda also has several lifetimes, and is an upper-middle-class English woman most recently.

Caliban: In Shakespeare's play the eloquent slave, fully aware of Prospero's abuse of power. In the Caribbean, the enslaved and dispossessed but defiant and subversive African man, as in the work of Kamau Brathwaite, George Lamming and others.

Sycorax: In Shakespeare's play, merely a few mentions, but in Kamau Brathwaite's work, the powerful source of anticolonial creativity which sustains both Caliban, and also the African woman, Caliban's woman, Caliban's sister, named Stark. Sycorax is an important presence in Marina Warner's *Indigo*.

"Til Indian Voices Wake Us...."

Patricia J. Penn Hilden

This is a love story. It is about two kinds of love: the love we share, Kamau Brathwaite and I, of a home place, though our homes are so distant, so different; and the love of a person, a man, who, ten years ago, on a rainy night in Canterbury, handed this exile a light, a map of the path back home, and a lexicon with the words I needed to speak about the journey and the arrival. Like so many of us in this volume, I, too, followed Brathwaite, became an arrivant.

Home at last, I wrote, I taught, I continued to read. Then I visited Kamau Brathwaite in Barbados. Interested in my trajectory homeward, Kamau took me to look for Indians:

> "Now, final, Bathsheba. But we must include the
> whole wild Maroon coast from RiverBay right
> round to Pico & the miracle of Cove the ancien
> (T) Amerindian religious settlement, through Ca-
> ttlewash to Martin's Bay and congoRock & Con-
> setts in the distance...." (BP 228)

We drove around most of one morning, Kamau driving the little yellow moke, Beverley beside him, Tim and I in the back seat, my Indian straight hair blowing wildly into my face, sticking to my eyelids, my mouth, my ears, and we could not get to that holy site where those Arawaks (and, I dream, those Pequots and Wampanoags, those Natchez and proud Powhatans) prayed to the sun and the sea and sent their canoes (or their dreams) skimming out over the reef into that wild wild sea (turning North, toward home)

I did learn then and on a later trip when we, Tim and I, found Pico, found that place, lingered there and took its picture

that most such "Amerindian sites" (like those all over North America) are the focus of archaeological excavations, the results of which end up in the new, post-independence Barbados National Museum in the "Prehistory" section. Here they are assuming another familiar role: "our (Barbadian) heritage," a role that differs little (except in its scope) from that played by North American Indian artifacts in U.S. museums.

> [And so the naming - **pre**-history - once again highlights who is "us", and who lives only as "them." Michel-Rolph Trouillot: "Contact with the West is seen as the foundation of historicity of different cultures. Once discovered by Europeans, the Other finally enters the human world" (*Silencing* 144).]

I wondered about this, about the spread to its empire of European prejudices that assign the lives of indigenous peoples to a static, a-historical world. I wondered, too, at the evident ease of their erasure. I knew, from teaching Native American history, from reading Caroline Foreman and Jack Forbes (see biblio. **4.**), as well as from tantalizing references in many colonial history books—about those enslaved North American tribal people who were sold into colonial-era slave markets. I had heard, too, about boatloads of restive African slaves traded from the West Indies for cargoes of similarly locally troublesome North American Indian slaves. Was Barbados involved in such exchanges? Did some North American Natives, captured by the English or their Indian allies find themselves working in Bajan cane fields? Especially after ambitious, land-hungry planters from the island founded the South Carolina city of Charles Town where they took an enthusiastic role in the trans-Atlantic and Caribbean slave trades?

Despite doubts fostered by both histories and historians of Barbados, my curiosity drove me to seek a familiar refuge. Following a tiny wooden sign, spotted along the highway just north of Bridgetown, I turned a corner and drove up a narrow road to the "National Archives, Barbados." I didn't have much time: this trip was not planned for this kind of research. But aided by a skeptical but willing archivist, I started in on the records of the Barbados Assembly, beginning in the middle of the seventeenth century when the first of North America's Indian slaves were captured and sold south.

Several hours of fascinating reading provided many hints. All slave regulations, for example, referred to "African and other slaves." Still, I knew that Indian slaves had also been brought from Guyana and from Venezuela, so perhaps *these* were the "others"? Then I came across the following act, dated June 1676:

> "Act to Prohibit the Bringing of Indian Slaves to this Island"
> "This act is passed to prevent the bringing of Indian slaves and as well to send away and transport those already brought to this island from New England and the adjacent colonies, being thought a people of too subtle, bloody and dangerous inclination to be and remain here..."

So there it was: clear evidence that North American Indian peoples had worked in Barbados's sugar plantations. I next took up Richard Hall's *Acts Passed in the Island of Barbados from 1643-1762* (London, 1764). Inside lay several tantalizing titles:

-27 October 1692. "An Act for the encouragement of all Negroes and other slaves that shall discovery any conspiracy...."

--------------------. "An Act for prohibiting sale of rum or other strong liquor to any Negro or other Slave...."

--------------------. "An Act for the encouragement of such Negroes and other slaves that shall behave themselves courageously against the enemy in time of invasion (manumitted if two white men proved that they killed an enemy)...."

-6 January 1708. "An Act to prevent the vessels that trade here, to and from Martinico or elsewhere, from carrying off any Negro, Indian, or Mulattoe slaves or persons indebted or contracted servants...."

-8 August 1727. "An Act for the punishment of runaway slaves and of slaves who shall wilfully entertain, harbour, and conceal any runaway slaves. Whereas divers Negroes and other slaves do often run away and absent themselves from the service of their owners and are willfully entertained, harboured, and concealed by other slaves....

[The punishments? Running away or concealing a runaway = 21 lashes on the bare back for the first offense; 39 for the second offense; 39 plus branding "R" on right cheek, then for any further offenses, "any punishment the owner sees fit save execution."]

-11 November 1731. "Act for amending an Act...entitled 'Act for the Governing of Negroes and for providing a proper maintenance and support for such Negroes, Indians, or Mulattoes as hereafter shall be manumitted or set free....'"

I left Barbados then and began a journey. This is the narrative of my going from that day to this.

A diversion:

Had I known (as Kamau knew - why didn't I ask him?) that Jerome Handler had been in those archives before me, I should have discovered the 1676 law much sooner. In 1968, in *Caribbean Studies*, Handler had quoted the Assembly's record of the act ("Amerindian" 57). Still, had I accepted Handler's conclusions about that Act, or about the origins of Indians enslaved in Barbados, I should not, perhaps, have undertaken this research. For Jerome Handler (as for many other historians), North American Natives formed only a minuscule and insignificant number of Barbadian slaves. In Handler's mind, all references to "Indians," any Indian place-names in Barbados records, indicated Native peoples brought either from the coast of South America or from other islands. In both cases these Indians were primarily, in Handler's view, either Caribs or Arawaks. His work, then, altered only slightly the "pre-historic" portrait of Barbados's indigenous people, adding Caribs and Arawaks from neighboring islands and relocating both groups from "prehistory" to Euro-historical time. When North American Natives *were* sold to Barbados, he argued, they were too few to matter. Even those Arawaks and Caribs from elsewhere in the Caribbean, called for no further study. As Handler put it, "Indian slaves always formed a very insignificant minority of Barbados' population and by the end of the first few decades of the eighteenth century there are few traces of them existing as a distinctive sub-cultural group" (39).

Traces

Stubbornly ignoring Handler and the others, I continued collecting my fragments, piecing together the little stories that make up this essay.

There were words:

At the beginning of the eighteenth century, when Native slaves provided South Carolina with some one-third of its slave population, "mustee" meant people born of Indian, African, and European parents. And then there was the word "mulatto." In 1771, a Society of Gentlemen in Scotland produced an *Encyclopædia Britannica: or a Dictionary of Arts and Sciences*. Here is their version: "Mulatto: a name given in the Indies to those who are begotten by a Negro man on an Indian woman, or an Indian man on a Negro woman" (3.314).

There were facts:

James Axtell, writing of seventeenth and early eighteenth-century North American colonies, noted that there was profit to be made in trading in Indian slaves. "The English," he wrote, "incited 'civil' war between the tribes" and then "rewarded one side for producing Indian slaves who were then sold to the West Indies, often for more biddable black slaves" (*The European* 239). Axtell's assertion that "black slaves" were more desirable because more tractable reflects a view, born in the practice of African slavery, that has many echoes. Here is Yasuhide Kawashima, writing of the Pequot warriors captured after escaping the Puritans' genocidal attempt to exterminate their people in the 1630s. After capture they were "sold to the West Indies in exchange for more docile Blacks who became the first Negro slaves in New England" ("Indian Servitude" 404). Gordon Wood agrees: "before 1640, colonists in Massachusetts and Virginia...bartered captive Indians for Blacks in the West Indies" ("Bloodiest" 43). Wilcomb Washburn, once "dean" of US historians of Native America adds a subtler version:

"The use of Indian slaves was rarely successful and in most instances was soon supplanted by black slavery" ("Introduction" 4). How did this stereotype of willing Black slaves and rebellious Indian slaves arise? Mason Wade offers this clue: "The French...at Biloxi and New Orleans attempted to use Indian slaves to work the tobacco plantations but these ran away and it was decided to import Blacks from the French West Indies" ("French-Indian" 26).

Of course Indians *could* run away - to their own tribes, to other Indians, to escaped Black slaves in the many maroon communities that grew up wherever there was African slavery. So long as they were *home*, Indians knew where they were - much better than any European, as the records of Indian rescues of witless Europeans attest. Rather than trading boatloads of rebellious Indians for cargoes of "biddable" Africans, it is surely more likely that the English - in New England, Virginia, Barbados, and elsewhere - rounded up and exported *any* leaders or fomenters of rebellions, whether African or Indian. Removed from whatever place and community they knew, they were perhaps more easily subdued, more easily reduced to a state of hopeless exhaustion characteristic of any dislocated, enslaved peoples. (But, it should be reiterated, the laws of the Barbados Assembly testify to the extent that enslaved peoples still rebelled, still ran.)

This stereotype also justified the importation of vast numbers of Africans to "replace" the "disappearing" Indians. But however "troublesome," or increasingly scarce, these latter, their enslavement, and their sale to Barbados, continued. After the 1670 founding of Charlestown by Sir John Colleton and his fellows, dozens more landless Barbadians soon flocked to the area, eventually settling what became South Carolina. That these new invaders would quickly replicate Barbados economic and social practices was soon apparent. Anthony McFarlane tells us, "there was...an ominous sign that [Carolina] would eventually follow this path [of Barbados's social and economic structure], in that the settlers took Indians as slaves, both for their own use and for export to the West Indies" (*The British* 111). As commodities on the slave market, they were quite valuable. In neighboring Virginia, "a child was worth more than her weight in deerskins; a single adult slave was equal in value to the leather produced in 2 years of hunting...By the latter half of the 17th century, if not before," Joel Martin reports, "slavery was big business in Virginia, an important part of the English trading regime" ("South Eastern" 308).

Marking the historical moments when the British sold captive Indians into the slave trade is possible. Every single rebellion against the invaders, starting with the first organized resistance to the Virginians at the beginning of the seventeenth century and continuing through the Pequot genocide (1630s), Metacom's Rebellion (1675-76), the Tuscarora Revolt (1711), the

Yamassee war against their former English allies (1715-28), Pontiac's Rebellion (1763-66), sent still more Indians on their way to the Caribbean cane fields. From other invaded regions of North America came more rebellions, more slaves. The Carolinians' conquest of Spain's Florida Indian missions in 1702-1707 garnered hundreds for the Caribbean slave markets, these "missionized" Indians already trained to serve and readily captured.

And all the years between these markers, and all over North America, slave raids and violent conflict produced humans for sale. The "Plantation Records" of the Barbados Museum and Historical Society carried these fragments: In 1630, John Winthrop sold an Indian to John Mainford of Barbados; in the 1660s, Narragansetts from Connecticut (once the Puritans' loyal allies in their war of extermination against the Pequots) were sold to Barbados; in 1668, an Indian slave was sent from Boston to the island; in 1700 a "big sale" of Indians from North America to the West Indies occurred; and, in 1701, Acolapissa Indian captives were sold by Virginians into the Caribbean. But the early eighteenth century did not see a gradual end to the Indian slave trade as Handler and others have claimed. In 1729, the French, together with their Choctaw allies, put an end to constant Natchez Indian revolts, capturing "hundreds" and selling them to the West Indies. These captures and sales to the islands continued until, one historian notes bleakly, by 1742 "the Natchez tribe had virtually disappeared" (Usner 109).

.Small additional markers, perhaps, but markers nonetheless of a vast dislocation, a terrible colonial "trail of tears" as later forced removals came to be known. Indian slaves were useful; Indian slaves were profitable; Indian slaves left behind land for the English to steal.

More recently, colonial Indians—including slaves—have become an important aspect of the career-making trajectories of younger colonial-era historians. These "new" US historians, according to Gordon Wood, are paying "new attention...to the Indians.... A century ago, historians of early America scarcely acknowledged their existence.... Through the efforts of a squadron of scholars, the Indians have now made their presence felt in early America" ("Bloodiest" 41). One of this "squadron" noticing Indians is Jill Lepore, who has studied the massive 1675 rebellion of Northeastern Natives led by Metacom (who, together with his war, was renamed "King Philip" by the colonizing English). As was customary in those colonial days, the victorious English slaughtered the captives they considered dangerous. They then beheaded Metacom and put his head on extended public display, a grisly warning to all other would-be Indian rebels. Those captives deemed less dangerous faced another fate, this shared by Metacom's wife and children (Lepore 173-5). Ever in pursuit of profit, the English sold some 1,000 Natives into the West Indian slave trade (Axtell 148).

At least Lepore *mentions* Indians. But do they "make their presence felt" in her text? Alas, in her work Indians merely add background color, despite the book's claim to explore "King Phillip's War." What matter to this historian are not the indigenous people or their reasons for taking up arms against the Puritan invaders, but rather the English and their motives for barbarous acts. Seeking explanation for what most would-be descendants of these same Puritans would find a startling revision of their national origin myths, Lepore argues away the most appalling behaviors: selling Metacom's wife and children into Caribbean slavery was driven, she argues, not by material greed or even by vengeance, but rather by Biblical imperatives which taught that sons should be punished for fathers' transgressions. (Wives and daughters were evidently accidental inclusions.) Lepore further cites Cotton Mather's 1703 Bible-supported approval for selling other Indians into the African slave trade (his justification beginning "tis a Prophesy in Deuteronomy 28:68. The Lord shall bring thee into Egypt again with ships...") and concludes that what happened to the thousands of Indians sold after "King Philip's War" might also have elicited such citations as this one from Jeremiah 22:12: "But he shall die in the place whither they have led him captive and shall see this land no more." Even absent any Biblical justification, the Puritan clergy, in Lepore's view, considered "slavery...to be just this kind of compassionate compromise: notorious Indians, like Philip himself, were executed; harmless enemies, mainly women and young children, were forced into servitude for a period of years; and those who were neither notorious enough to be hanged nor harmless enough to remain in New England were routinely sold into foreign slavery" (153).

What then happened to these transported Indian slaves? Lepore shows little interest. "Of...the hundreds of other Algonquians shipped out of the colonies, including Philip's son," she assures her readers blandly, "**we** know precious little. By the time Philip's son left the colonies, Barbados and Jamaica had both passed legislation preventing the importation of Indians from New England...." Without any further research, she assumes that these laws were completely effective. This assumption justifies a flight of fancy: "Turned away at port after port it is possible that slave ships from New England simply dumped their now valueless cargo somewhere in the Caribbean Sea, or abandoned groups of New England Indians on uninhabited islands. Perhaps some number of them were illegally smuggled into English colonies in the West Indies. Yet one small piece of evidence, a letter from John Elliot to Robert Boyle written in 1683, suggests that at least some New England Indians, after being bounced from port to port, were shipped all the way to Africa..." (170). This young and much-celebrated denizen of the "new, Indian-noticing US historians" concludes her portrait of the Puritans by asserting that colonial era Indian slavery was not as bad as African slavery, resulting solely from the Puritans' and other Europeans' inability to understand the nature of Indian societies (which neither worshipped the Puritans' god nor possessed other human beings as property) rather than from more material factors, such as lust for Indian land or greed for the money to be made in the slave trade.

Despite its shortcomings, her book offers some material of interest. She notes that Nathaniel Saltonstall's *Continuation of the State of New-England, together with an Account of the Intended Rebellion of the Negroes in the Barbados* was published in London in 1676 and thus linked - for "readers in London" at least - the revolt of African slaves in Barbados to the revolt of New England Indians. She creates the following links among events: "Terrified English colonists in Barbadoes (sic) believed that the Africans had 'intended to murther all the white people there,' just as panicked English colonists in New England feared that the Indians had 'risen almost round the countrey.'" And so, she concludes, "the parallels between the two uprisings were uncanny and profoundly disquieting" (167-8). (She notes further that Virginia also experienced Indian revolts in 1676 when Governor Berkeley complained that the "New England Indian infection" had spread. And so Barbados's governor, Jonathan Atkins, had earlier warned London: "the ships from New England still bring advice of burning, killing, and destroying daily done by the Indians and the infection extends as far as Maryland and Virginia": 168). That her linkages among rebellions of enslaved peoples might have been real - not grounded in "disquieting" coincidences but rather in plans shared amongst enslaved Africans and Indians, does not occur to her. Like most historians writing from the "outside" - from a European-American perspective - she simply cannot imagine a world in which enslaved and conquered peoples communicated amongst themselves, plotting the overthrow of *all* Europeans, wherever they enslaved others. But of course it is clear from dozens of sources that the indigenous peoples of the Americas, together with enslaved Africans, communicated constantly and in sometimes wildly imaginative ways: through songs that encoded routes to freedom, through messages carried by captives sold into exile, through weapons and intelligence (sometimes stitched into fabric or decorated onto objects) shared by boatloads of slaves exchanged between Barbados and Virginia or the Carolinas, through conversations between the personal attendants who accompanied white men wherever they traveled between the West Indies and the North American coast. As the whites always feared (as their laws and restrictions and punishments attest), enslaved peoples of color worked exhaustively and collectively to end their servitude, to expel the invaders, to go home.[1]

Had Lepore actually been interested in Indians, and not in painting a colorful background against which to set the struggles of her fearful English colonists, she might have explored more deeply, delving into archives which, as the above shows, record numbers of North American Indian arrivals before, during, and after the outbreak of King Philip's War in 1675. Moreover, she might have concluded that the laws she'd heard about - including that 1676 law I came across at Cave Hill - were direct results of the arrival of "infected" war captive slaves as well as of the "diseased" news carried by ship's officers. Looking still deeper, she might quickly have seen that far from halting the lucrative trade in Indian slaves, the law did nothing to prevent its spread well into the next century.

———

Indian voices, then, however muted, however mixed in the "Negroe, Indian, and Mulattoe" slave worlds of the seventeenth and eighteenth centuries, formed an as yet little heard chorus mixed into the complicated sounds of Barbados that Kamau Brathwaite has given that nation and the world. Even as I listened to Kamau sing us the drumming sounds of Mile and a Quarter that drizzly night in Canterbury I heard, too, the softer sounds, audible nearby at "Indian Groun(d)" (now a Seventh Day Adventist Church),

the sounds of the houmfort, the tonelle, the music of his Great Uncle Bob'ob, the Ogoun (and the sounds of the prejudice: "white man better than red man better than black man": BP 129), even as I thought: but I am hearing our

Indian sounds, too, the drumming, the sounds of moccasined feet dancing the earth. (An Indian voice, speaking English so slooowly, asks "Hey, why wud they call Esse's father 'Red Man' if he wuzn tun Indi'n?") I wondered: how to track their notes, map their footsteps, record their voices mingled with those many others from Africa, from South America, the Caribbean, and Europe?

And even here some suggestive fragments, more links. Here is Duke Ellington's sister, Ruth, telling Modoc Indian jazz musician Dave Brubeck, "All the credit's gone to the African for the wonderful rhythm in jazz, but I think a lot of it should go to the American Indian." And it is true. Carl Fischer, called a "full-blooded Indian" by óne jazz historian, wrote "an orchestral suite called "Reflections on an Indian Boy," while Brubeck himself began and ended "They All Sang Yankee Doodle" with Indian songs he had learned from other Native jazz musicians. And here are more jazz artists whose heritage was Indian as well as European and African: Kay Starr, John Lewis, Joe Williams, Bobby Scott, Art Farmer, Lena Horne, Benny Golson, Ed Thigpen, Ben Thigpen, Earle Warren, Jim Hall, Doc Cheatham, Kid Ory, Big Chief Russell Moore, Joe Mondragon, Oscar Pettiford, Trummy Young, Mildred Bailey, Lee Wiley, Horace Silver, Sweets Edison, Frank Trumbauer, and Duke Ellington himself. There are hundreds of other players known mostly only to other Indians: Jim Pepper - whose life is the subject of my friend Sandy Osawa's documentary, *Pepper's Powwow*, and the "Nez Perces" who featured the guitarist grandfather of another friend, Beth Piatote. Connecting again to Africa, Dave Brubeck's son Darius (named after Brubeck's teacher, Darius Milhaud) has for many years been teaching jazz at the University of Natal in Durban (Lees, *Cats* 40, 57, 39).

In Barbados again, a few years later, this time in May. A guidebook told the existence of "Yarico's Pond" where an "Amerindian woman" had either drowned herself in despair or given birth. The despair scenario had her lover, the Englishman Inkle whom she had rescued from her tribe's killing of his fellows, taking her to Barbados where he callously sold her into slavery. The birth occurred during her time working as a slave on an island plantation. This was the tale we found, a few words, a crude map. This, we soon discovered, pointed only to a patch of bare ground, stripped by developers building holiday homes for Europeans who come to Barbados now not for the profit in sugar and slaves but to find sun in what is touted as the "safest" of the Caribbean nations, the most like "home", Kamau's loved/despised "Li'l England."

But my Yarico was not this guidebooked figure. Standing then by the empty ground the map had designated "Yarico's Pond" I paused "for them...for those who have gone before...'*once you were here...hoed the*

earth...and left it for me.........that I may attempt here...that may I hav
strength to attempt here...strength enough to attempt here..."

And Kamau's words once again sent me questing. I wanted—still want—
to find Yarico—to hear her voice, or, failing that, to walk in her moccasins
—off the ship, along the Bridgetown wharf, up the road

seeing the colors of the earth: white (from the coral she wouldn't know
grounded the island, gave it its white white sands, held its fresh water, fed
its long strands of sea grapes running down the beaches to the sea), ma-
hogany red (though if she came from the Southern North American coast
she would know this color, red Georgia clay), deep brown, almost black (the
fertile home of the cane) and, here and there, a strange mauve, soft tone,
almost of the desert (the earth dug now by archaeologists, the homes of the
Arawaks), ending in the dark closed road leading into the plantation's slave
quarters.

I wanted to look behind me at the vanishing sea: home. I wanted to smell the island, heavy with sweet strangeness, to see with dread the dark little house where I - used to the air, used to my body's freedom, used to the open sky - would live.

I wanted to watch the tiny hungry finches who chased crumbs then as they do now, the losers gesturing their anger with spread and lowered wings and tails, hissing at their fellows. And I wanted to find the real pond, Yarico's

Pond, where she worked, washed, drew water for the household and its foreign guests and perhaps died.

A little narrative of Yarico:
(Kamau knows all this story, knew it before I did. But he never told. I never asked.) Richard Ligon traveled to Barbados in the middle of the seventeenth century. Back in England, he wrote his *True and Exact History* of the island. He recorded his many encounters with Indian slaves who worked in the houses of his hosts. One nameless woman taught him how to make corn pone by "searing it very fine (and it will fall out as fine as the finest wheat-flower in England) if not finer" (29-30). Other Indian men made "Perino", a drink "for their own drinking and is made of Cassavy root, which I told you is a strong poyson; and this they cause their old wives, who have a small remainder of teeth, to chaw and spit out into water (for the better breaking and macerating of the root). This juyce in three or four hours will work, and pure it self of the poysonous quality" (32).

Ligon liked these Indians:

> As for the Indians, we have but few, and those fetcht from other Countries; some from the neighboring islands, some from the Main, which we make slaves; the women who are better vers'd in ordering the Cassavie and making bread, then the Negroes, we imploy for that purpose, as also for making Mobbie: the men we use for footmen and killing of fish, which they are good at; with their own bowes and arrows they will go out; and in a dayes time, kill as much fish as will serve a family of a dozen persons two or three dyes...They are very active men, and apt to learn any thing sooner than the Negroes...they are much craftier and sutiler then the Negroes; and in their nature falser; but in their bodies more active: their women have very small breasts and have more of the shape of the Europeans than the Negroes.... (55)

Having approved the Indians and disapproved the Africans, Ligon then offered the first of the references others would shape into dozens of later narratives of Yarico:

> We had an Indian woman, a slave in the house, who was of excellent shape and colour, for it was a pure bright bay;...This woman would not be woo'd by any means to wear Cloaths. She chanc'd to be with Child, by a Christian servant, and lodging in the Indian house, amongst other women of her own country, where the Christian servants, both men and women cam; and being very great, and that her time was come to be delivered, loath to fall in labour before the men, walk'd down to a Wood in which was a pond of water, and there by the side of the pond, brought her self abed; and presently washing her child in some of the water of the pond, wrapped it up in such rags

416

as she had begg'd of the Christians; and in three hours time came home, with her child in her arms, a lusty Boy, frolick and lively. (55)

And then *the* narrative:

This Indian dwelling near the Sea-coast, upon the Main, an English ship put in to a Bay and sent some of her men to shoar, to try wat victuals or water they could find, for in some distress they were: But the Indians perceiving them to go up so far into the country as they were sure they could not make a safe retreat, intercepted them in their return and fell upon them, chafing them into a wood and being dispersed there, some were taken and some kill'd: but a young man amongst them stragling from the rest was met by this Indian Maid, who upon the first sight fell in love with him and hid him close from her Countrymen (the Indians) in a cave, and there fed him till they could safely go down to the shoar, where the ship lay at anchor expecting the return of their friends. But at last, seeing them upon the shoar, sent the long-boat for them, took them aboard, and brought them away. But the youth, when he came ashoar in the Barbadoes, forgot the kindness of the poor maid, that had venture her life for his safty, and sold her for a slave, who was a free born as he: and so poor Yarico for her love, lost her liberty. (55)

Where did he find this curious tale, so strangely familiar to English readers of American stories, so appealing to English men who wanted to believe that their rape of indigenous women and girls was desired by their victims?

It was Ligon's countryman, John Smith, who had fabricated the first story of male desire and rescue, this the story cooked up in 1624, decades after his departure from Virginia in 1609. Evidently unhappy with the published version of his time in North America, a long letter to a friend printed in London in 1608 as *The True Relation.....*, John Smith decided to embroider his story. In *The General Historie of Virginia, New-England, and the Summer Isles*, Smith added one of the most re-told scenes of early American history, that of his capture by Powhatan and subsequent rescue from death by Powhatan's beautiful daughter, Pocahontas. Just as Yarico's embellished story would prompt hundreds of echoes amongst European commentators narrating the history of their Caribbean empires, so Pocahontas's tale quickly stimulated North American poets, playwrights, and fiction writers into action. Most recently, her story has achieved the American apotheosis: Walt Disney Company's myriad animators have given us the movie-length cartoon version, suitably complete with cunning hummingbirds and talking trees. Although Yarico has yet to find herself luring audiences into her Pocahontas's universalizing (animated) "colors of the wind," she has elicited dozens of portraits, each re-telling an increasingly lurid and romantic story.

Like Yarico's first appearance in print thirty years after, Pocahontas's emergence in Smith's 1624 tale was quite brief. Writing in the second person, Smith described a bound captive, brought before Powhatan, the King of the Powhatans. After "two great stones" had been placed before the King, "as many as could laid hands on him, dragged him to them, and thereon laid his head, and being ready with their clubs to beat out his brains, Pocahontas, the King's dearest daughter, when no entreaty could prevail, got his head in her arms and laid her own upon his to save him from death: whereat the Emperor was contented he should live..." (*Capture* 18).

It seems likely that Richard Ligon had read these words before he wrote his similarly abbreviated story. Even if he had not, however, his short tale of a Caribbean John Smith and Pocahontas clearly resonated in English breasts, ready to imagine a "New World" peopled with beautiful, naked young women anxious to rescue from their fellow Natives these invading blond, blue-eyed European men.

So popular was Ligon's little story of his Englishman and Indian that Richard Steele re-told it in the *Spectator,* no.11, Tuesday, March 13, 1711. Here the tale took on the details that have clung to it through the centuries: one Thomas Inkle of London, 20, left for the West Indies on "the 16th of June, 1647, in order to improve his Fortune by Trade and Merchandize." He was "a Person every way agreeable, a ruddy Vigour in his Countenance, Strength in his Limbs, with Ringlets of fair Hair loosely flowing on his Shoulders." When he and some comrades put ashore "on the Main of America" seeking provisions, they were attacked by Indians who killed all but Inkle. Fleeing into the forest, "he threw himself, tired and breathless, on a little Hillock." Here "an Indian Maid rushed from a Thicket behind him." They discovered the requisite mutual attraction: "If the European was highly Charmed with the Limbs, Features, and wild Graces of the Naked American; the American was no less taken with the Dress, Complexion, and Shape of an European, covered from Head to Foot." Of course this naked, wild being reacted more primitively, untroubled by "civilization's" racial and sexual constraints. "The Indian," Steele assures readers, "grew immediately enamoured of him and consequently solicitous for his preservation." In the cave to which they repaired, Yarico produced all kinds of "New World" wonders for her lover - and in odd moments, charmed him still more by playing with his golden hair and wondering at the contrast between her darkness and his whiteness. Moreover, like Pocahontas, whose royal pedigree helped mitigate the consequences of her inferior race, Yarico soon showed Inkle that she, too, was "A Person of Distinction."

Steele's early eighteenth-century Yarico and Inkle spent some considerable time together, she caring for him, he promising her a home with him and the all-important share in his worldly goods. "In this manner did the Lovers pass away their Time, till they had learn'd a Language of their own.... In this tender Correspondence these Lovers lived for several Months...." Yarico then discovered a ship on the coast and together they set out for Barbados. Once there, however, Inkle reverted to his English mercantile self, beginning "to reflect upon his loss of Time and to weigh with himself how many Days Interest of his Money he had lost during his Stay with Yarico.... Upon which Considerations, the prudent and frugal young Man sold Yarico to a Barbadian Merchant; notwithstanding that the poor Girl, to incline him to commiserate her Condition, told him that she was with Child by him: But he only made use of that Information to Rise in his Demands upon the Purchaser" (Addison, Steele 1.38-9). From this point it was but a short distance to the version in which Yarico, now enslaved, either bore Inkle's child beside her pond or, in more romantically satisfying terms, drowned herself, despairing.

Steele's version, however, already remote from Ligon's simpler tale presaged what was to come. From that moment any echo - however slight - of Yarico's own voice vanished as she was turned first this way and then that - first into an embodiment of anti-mercantile sentiment, then into an icon of the anti-slavery movement (when she moved through racial stages from "Amerindian" to "Mulatto" to "Nubian" to "African"), then into a romantic, "wild" and noble heroine. Recently, Beryl Gilroy's England-written re-telling, her 1996 novel *Inkle and Yarico*, abandons Yarico again in favor of the supposedly self-told tale of the immoral Inkle, forced by his poverty and natural indolence to sell his Carib wife, Yarico, once his many years of exile amongst the Indians ended with his rescue by his countrymen. Except to act the stoic Indian princess and wife, silently pained by Inkle's passion for a child captive from another tribe but protesting only in a sullen, passive-aggressive stereotype of a 1950s television sitcom housewife, Yarico hardly exists at all in this text. Only her cover picture suggests a corporeal presence and this shows only a naked, bow-and-arrow carrying Diana, holding a parrot aloft to site her in the exotic western hemisphere. Her world inside the novel is nothing but stereotypes, these racial. Gilroy's Inkle relates, "She was pure instinct, for to survive in her world, to be at one with Nature's rhythms and to heed its customs, there was no place for thought and reason." Later, "I called her by name but never would she address me as Tommy because she said, 'Spirits would call you away to their land of death.'" In fact in this indigenous world, "All activities were surrounded by superstition and ritual, and many times I was scolded by Paiuda, the irascible priest, for violating some rule which they had absorbed into their spongelike natures from birth" (20, 28, 29: one cannot help wondering if some of this stereotype, of the nasty-tempered, unpredictable evil Indian shaman did not stem from Gilroy's viewing of the awful film, *Black Robe*, based on the deeply racist account of the French invasion of Canada written by the English novelist, Brian Moore, and based, by his account, on the notorious *Jesuit Relations*). The women in Gilroy's Carib world are a disgrace: will-less, they serve the Carib men, already enslaved. So no Yarico here. Rather this novel - like its European predecessors, is Inkle's tale, the narrative of his collapse from a youthful a-morality into an adulthood of hot pro-slavery passions.

But the story has not ended. Just two years ago Yarico played again, this time on a Caribbean stage, here the beautiful, (white) be-feathered protagonist of a musical, performed for white Barbadians and their tourist cousins, featured - together with a "Caribbeanized" *Tempest* - in the annual Season held at Holders Plantation House in March, 1999.

Then, in 1999, Yarico entered yet another realm, this one almost as absurd as Disney's. With Inkle, she has become the object of heavy, post-modern academic analysis. Frank Felsenstein has introduced and edited *English Trader, Indian Maid: Representing Gender, Race, and Slavery in the New World*, just published in 1999.

While the Barbados-produced musical version of the story was titled, simply, "Yarico," Felsenstein returns matters to their earlier state: Inkle is first, described by occupation. Yarico comes second, described only by a sexualized body. Together they "represent" a world "new" only to Inkle.

[Michel-Rolph Trouillot notes: "The lexical opposition Man-versus-Native...titled the European literature on the Américas from 1492 to the Haitian Revolution and beyond. Even the radical duo Diderot-Raynal did not escape it. Recounting an early Spanish exploration, they write, 'Was not this handful of *men* surrounded by an innumerable multitude of *natives*...seized with alarm and terror, well or ill-founded?'" (*Silencing* 82)]

Here is Felsenstein explaining:

"Current critical interest in the tale reflects a growing awareness of the value of studying the often intangible points of contact between oral traditions and written or printed cultures. Described by David Brion Davis as one of the great folk epics of its age, 'Inkle and Yarico' provides just such a site of mediation between the oral and the literate." (2)

But: who "studies", producing "value" to whom?

Thanks to Richard Steele, one oral Indian assumed a privileged place. Felsenstein tells us that Steele's Yarico is special. "As a festishized native, a Noble Savage, reduced to a mere possession, Yarico is perhaps unique among such figures in being given [by Steele] the opportunity to answer back" (5). Answer back? Pleading with Inkle to keep his promises to marry her? Confessing to a pregnancy that raised her price? Or is it simply that she has a name and a story that Europeans could read, remember, re-tell, re-imagine, represent, albeit entirely in their own terms?

Despite his dubious assertion that Yarico speaks, Felsenstein elsewhere unknowingly gives readers an Indian woman who actually does answer back, more insistently, more stridently than Yarico managed with her soft, impotent pleading. *This* Indian woman - nameless - reminded me of those the old people meant when they warned us "Never mess with Indian women."

This Indian woman lives in a French text, Jean Moquet's early seventeenth-century *Travels and Voyages into Africa, Asia, American and the East and West Indies*, where he recounted the story of one English pilot, lost on the shores of Newfoundland:

> He had found an Indian woman, of whom he was enamoured, making her fine promises by signs, that he would marry her; which she believed and conducted him through these desarts; where she shewed him the fruit and roots good to eat and served him for an interpreter amongst the Indians.... They had a child together; and found there an English ship.... He was very glad to see himself escaped from so many dangers and gave these English an account of all his adventures...but being ashamed to take along with him this Indian-woman thus naked, he left her on land, without regarding her any more.... But she seeing herself thus forsaken by him, whom she had so dearly loved, and for whose sake she had abandoned her country and friends, and had so well guided and accompanied him through such places, where he would, without her, have been dead a thousand times. After having made some lamentation, full of rage and anger, she took her child, and tearing it into two pieces, she cast the one half toward him into the sea, as if she would say, that belonged to him, and was his part of it; and the other she carried away with her, returning back to the mercy of fortune and full of mourning and discontent. (Felsenstein 294-5)

And thus this "New World" Medea wreaks vengeance!

Reading without the European male ego-commentary—the promise of European marriage so meaningless to any indigenous woman, the selfless passion this man believed she must have felt, the abandonment of him she "so dearly loved" - there stands an angry woman. She replies - rejecting the rape, the theft, the conquest. Saying no

> that children above all others would be like the sun.
> rise   (Brathwaite, *Middle*[1] 46)

Edward Said in *Culture and Imperialism*:

> European geographical centrality...is buttressed by a cultural discourse relegating or confining the non-European to a secondary, racial, cultural, ontological status. Yet this secondariness is, paradoxically, essential to the primariness of the European.... For natives to want to lay claim to that terrain is, for many Westerners, an intolerable effrontery, for them actually to repossess it unthinkable. (Quoted Felsenstein 42)

So let us "affront", offend; let us lay claim to this terrain.

Gordon Wood, still praising Lepore's book, worries a little that "we" shall take too seriously the young historian's implied condemnation of Indian and African slavery. "She never mentions the fact that during the English Civil War the English likewise sold Scottish and Irish prisoners into bondage in the West Indies. It was a cruel and brutal age, and human life was a good deal cheaper than it is for *us* today" (43, emphasis added).

I'll leave aside his implication that if white people were sold into "bondage" (*not* slavery) then the enslavement of North American Indians (or Africans) was not so bad. I'll also ignore his "two-other-wrongs-make-the-first-wrong-less-wrong argument. I cannot overlook his entire dismissal of those whose lives "we" - U.S.ers - continue to "take cheaply," those millions, some so close by, just across the (barricaded) U.S. southern border, who labor for "our" wealth, "our" greed for an endless supply of ostentatious commodities, to fill the shopping malls where we satisfy "our" lusts - and *for our time and money to travel to "their" world*, albeit a world protected, sanitized for "our" protection by the Hilton Hotel Corporation.

> "[In order to construct the Hilton Hotel at Needham's Point in 1960, Nature itself, it seems, had to be altered....]" (BP 115)

What also cries out for reply is Wood's evident inability to imagine what slavery - ownership of body, your life - meant to Indian people. Wilbur Jacobs, another white man, another eminent historian of the United States, at least worked hard to move his in-born Euro-imaginary closer to that of the Indians he wrote about. Noting that hundreds, maybe thousands of Native peoples killed themselves (throwing themselves from departing ships and so on) rather than endure slavery, Jacobs asked himself: "Why would the average woodland tribesman [women did it too - and in the face of impending rape as well as enslavement] choose death as an alternate to being a white man's slave?" His reply? "Freedom was the Indian's element: freedom of movement, freedom of speech, freedom of action, freedom to do whatever he pleased whenever he chose to do it" (*Dispossessing* 167).

---

if yu cyaan beat prospero
Whistle,"   (*Middle*[1] 77)

They have always wanted to possess the women of the Americas, these Europeans. But not every woman proved as willing as Pocahontas or Yarico. In 1524, Giovanni da Verrazano "attempted to capture an Indian family consisting of an old woman, a young girl, and six children on the northeast coast of North America. But the girl proved so intractable that the soldiers were forced to give up the attempt to take the whole family to the ship, and finally carried away but one small boy who was too young to make any resistance" (Lauber 71). [You know what they say: Don't mess with Indian women! And so, when Verrazzano and his brother landed at a Caribbean island - probably Guadaloupe - in 1528, "the fierce cannibal Caribs killed and ate Captain Verrazzano" (Olexer 18).]

Again, Yarico:
The walk:

The glimpse:

The home place:

Escape:

Richard Ligon gives us a picture:

"But there is a Bird they call a Man of War and he is much bigger than a Heron and flies out to Sea upon discoveries (for they never light upon the Sea) to see what ships are coming to the island; and when they return, the Islanders look out and say, a ship is coming and find it true." (Ligon 61)

Did Yarico watch these great birds? Did she follow her eyes seaward? Home? Did she watch the new ships unload their captives and weep?

Yarico was a "house slave" and as such the keeper of male visitors. Here was one of her tasks, performed on this occasion for Richard Ligon, afflicted with the chiggers (called "chegoes") that buried themselves in the soft European skin:

> This vermine will get thorough your stocken and in a pore of your skin in somepart of your feet, commonly under the nail of your toes and there make a habitation to lay his offspring, as big as a small Tare, or a bag of a Bee, which will cause you to go very lame, and put you to much smarting pain. The Indian women have the best skill to take them out, which they do by putting in a small pointed pin or needles, at the hold where he came in, and winding the point about the bag, loosen him from the flesh and so take him out.....some of these Chegoes are poysonous and after they are taken out, the Orifice in which they lay will fester and rankel for a fortnight after they are gone. I have had ten taken out of my feet in a morning by the most unfortunate Yarico, an Indian woman. (65)

Daily Yarico went to her pond - to wash (Indians startled the dirty Europeans when they insisted on bathing every day) to get water for the household, to wash the household's laundry, to dream.

Her pond:

Water, its sounds and its silences....in this place of still water... Did she hear, too, Kamau's coral springs? The silvery fall of fresh island water coming up from underground? Did she gather with the others at Indian Spring? Still there, beside the plantation great house but down the hill from Indian Town...
    And did she run?

There are the caves—all along the wilder Atlantic Coast (looking to ward Africa, Kamau says as he looks East). Tim and Kamau climbed dow and around and through a labyrinth of caves while Beverley and I waited watching, up on the cliffs above. If she did run to these caves, Ligon give us an idea of life there:

> These caves are very frequent in the island and of several dimen-
> sions, some small, others extremeley large and capacious: the run-
> away Negroes, often shelter themselves in these coverts for a long
> time and in the night range abroad the countrey and steale pigs,
> platins, potatoes, and pulling and bring it there; and feast all day
> upon what they stole the night before and the nights being dark and
> their bodies black they escape undiscerned'd.... (98)

Or did Yarico find that bay - the little Arawak settlement among the tall palms, shivering and clattering in the strong winds blowing from Africa? The smooth flat rocks climbing down in flat wide terraces to the bay where they had once launched their canoes into the Atlantic beyond? Did she walk on that shore and long....?

Silences.

What can Yarico tell us - herself - now?
Perhaps these words will give a small voice to all the Yaricos, all the war captive women, all the children who walked the earth of Barbados, who ran away to the Arawaks' caves, who died in the tiny dark slave houses set

back from the main plantation roads. Perhaps too the story still to be told will complicate all our understanding of origins. Now the stories begin in Africa, cultural manners and modes traced to present day African worlds. It will not be easy to uncover the connections between the North American Native cultural worlds and those of Africa. There exist now only traces of North America-Caribbean ties: the use in Santería ceremonies (in New York *and* in Latin America) of a North American Plains Indian plaster bust, weirdly pink, and a "gold dust Indian spray", available in every Washington Heights *bodega*. Plains Indian costumes appear in Crop Over parades - and coloring books - in Barbados.

Neighboring Trinidad's carnival celebrates North American Indians - as does the all-"black" "Indian Crew", parading through the streets of New Orleans, every year (Bellour and Kinser). There are all those stories still to be found in the law books, the plantation sales and tax records, the parish lists of deaths and baptisms, and in the archives of colonial South Carolina, Massachusetts, Connecticut, in those of Bridgetown and Cave Hill.

And then there is Yarico.

Notes

1. This kind of Euro-ignorance is well-known amongst historians of color who invariably find themselves confronted by those who simply cannot imagine real agency amongst those who are not white. That the indigenous peoples of the world communicated with each other - across vast distances - about the awful, stinking, and hairy Europeans, long before many had encountered those creatures, is well-known to indigenous intellectuals. It still seems impossible, however, to many white people. Recently, I heard a Samoan historian, Toeutu Fa'aleava, describe the extensive knowledge of whites that had spread across the Pacific decades before Samoans first encountered the invaders. Several white anthropologists present, all self-described "authorities" on the Pacific, denied the possibility of such sharing of information across such vast distances, despite both Fa'aleava's evidence and the histories of the vast trading networks, thousands of years old, that they knew existed across the Pacific's vastnesses, drawing thousands of Pacific Island sailors into their routes. They did not wonder why they thought people might trade goods and so on but not information. Apparently, knowledge (especially, to these anthropologists, knowledge of "other people") is a European phenomenon.

Lorna Goodison

Angel of Dreamers

Angel, ever since I came back here trying to reopen this dream shop
I get so much cuss-cuss and fight down, these merchants don't want me
to prosper in this town.

Seraph mine you supervised and trained me, inspected my goods
declared it celestial first quality. But cherubim what a cherubam
since I land.

I set up my shop in this big sprawling bazaar, central, to draw them
from near and from far. Well the first thing I notice all around
and about me

is other sellers living in fear and under necromancy. Every morning
they get up they squeezing lime to cut and clear and all I using
is the power of prayers.

Some consulting with D lawrence (darkness) writing down my name on
parchment. Some have taken to attacking my name in malcrafted,
lopsided, imitations of my creations

all because of bad mind. Angel, if you see the spoil-goods they peddle
as dreamwares. Chuh, I leaving them to count the proceeds from their
bankruptcy sales.

For seraph, you should see how I fix up my shop, nobody around here
ever see a shop fix up like that. When I throw open the doors not even
the most bad-minded

could come out with their usual naysaying, carping and fault finding.
For I have painted the walls in a deep evergreen, and all around the
cornices and along the ceiling

I have picked out the subtle patterns in the mouldings in the indigo
of discernment so what was hidden has now become clear, illuminate,
and prominent.

Along the walls I have placed some low cane-seat couches.
The cushions all covered in the lavender of lignum vitae. It is there
that dreamers sit and drink rosemary tea.

On the floor I dropped a rug of lagoon blue with feathers floating
free on its surface, and if you look long and your eye is clear, you see
schools of goldfish swimming down there.

And my extraordinary dreamshop was opened with no fanfare,
not one high official, Pharisee or Tappanaris was there. I just threw
open the doors and sat there quietly

till some dreamseeker pass by and noticed me. Someone well-parched
from too much hard-heart life, they look up and see my sign a crescent
moon with a single star fixed

and dreamseller lettered in font Gazelle, lower case, sans serif.
And so they stumble in weary, having tried various health schemes
and bush medicines and ask me for a dream.

As soon as they ask me I go to work like Attar, the darwish chemist,
my ancestor. In a clean crucible I mix the fallout from stars and the
fragrant dyestuff of roses.

I add to this, then, various elements for the restoration of lost shining.
Only one or two hearts that have lived too long in the dark professed
dissatisfaction with the dream they bought.

But most of the ones who acquire them always come back in to report
how acquiring their dream has alchemically changed and altered their
way of seeing and being.

They say to all visitors, "Come see this dream I have received from
the seller in the bazaar, godchild of Ghazali, student of
Attar, the love child of Rumi and Asi Itra.

One of the ancient keepers of dreams and songs, great granddaughter
of a psalmist and griot Guinea woman. They say if you deserve one of
these she will mix you one

to quicken your hopes and tune your heart to hear songs of bliss.

All she takes for payment is sincerity and red roses."
I have received many referrals in this way.

The ones who acquire these dreams are inspired to light candles of
understanding which illuminate all they do thereafter with a clear
pervasive shining.

I am writing this to you seated at the shop door where the simurgh,
that cinnabar talisman of a bird, has just flown in and perched upon
one of the bunches of wine-fruit

which hang ripe from the ceiling. Sometimes ground doves fly in and
Barbary doves too. Let me attempt to describe the transcendent
Barbary dove song for you.

❀

The Transcendent Song as Taught by a Passing Tuareg Woman

A Tuareg woman passing once taught me a song.
It was really a series of intricate notes
urgently sounded, like the fast-forward call
of a rising flock of Barbary doves.

The song, if correctly and effectively done,
can lift me up to a cool place
above the burning chamber of the sun.
The woman said it is the transcendent song

known only to the ones like us.
I caught the song and held it.
I feel it is not wise to use it too frequently.
Just so, I have learned to save it for unbearable days.

First a series of fluttering notes
then a long low fluting coo.

Then a series of fast-forward notes
till there occurs a wild breakthrough.

Then a joyful, joyful gurgling
like a full-throttle rain replenished stream

and after that it's just pure sweet cooing.

❋

The only way that I have been able to withstand
the undermining efforts of the other sellers
is to sound this transcendent song.

Until I see you face-to-face, I ask you to pray that God grant
me celestial insurance from the arsonist efforts
of the job-lot sellers.

Bibliography

This list is not exhaustive. That needs another book. I list Brathwaite's most important titles, reprints, major translations and recent uncollected poetry and dreamstories, with secondary bibliographies of most writings on his work (part 3) and all others cited here (4). I do not list other translations or the myriad anthologies, journals and other places (including the London Underground) where his poetry appears, and list dissertations only when his work is the sole or major focus of analysis (his theoretical and historical work is a growing catalyst for scholarship and to use even long allusion as a listing criterion would be sisyphean). Nor do I list most brief reviews: I know of over forty of *Rights of Passages* alone. The basic order of Brathwaite's writings in the sections of part 2 is by year, but those published in the same year are listed alphabetically by title, while interviews (section 2.11.) are listed alphabetically by interviewer. Reprints are mostly kept together. They are distinguished in this book's chapters by a superscript arabic numeral matching their publication order. To ease location, titles in part 2 cited in this collection are in boldface. Cross-references are within a same section unless otherwise indicated.

1. Bibliographical Sources on Kamau Brathwaite

Brathwaite, Doris Monica. *A Descriptive and Chronological Bibliography (1950-1982) of the Works of Edward Kamau Brathwaite*. London and Port of Spain: New Beacon, 1988.

____. *E. K. B.: His Published Prose and Poetry 1948-1986, a Checklist*. Mona, Kingston: Savacou Cooperative, 1986.

Carnegie, Jeniphier R. *Kamau Brathwaite: A Selected List of Materials in the Main Library, University of the West Indies, Cave Hill*. Cave Hill: Main Library, UWI, 1995.

2. Works by [Edward] Kamau Brathwaite

2.1.1. Poetry – Books

Rights of Passage. London: Oxford UP, 1967.

Sranantongo trans.: *Primisi-ô*. Trans. France Olivieira. Paramaribo: Stanpupe Vaco P, 1997.

Masks. London: Oxford UP, 1968.

Islands. London: Oxford UP, 1969.

Penguin Modern Poets 15. Harmondsworth: Penguin, 1969. [With Alan Bold and Edwin Morgan.]

The Arrivants: A New World Trilogy. Oxford: Oxford UP, 1973.

German trans.: *The Arrivants: A New World Trilogy/Die Ankömmlinge: Eine Neue Welt- Trilogie*. Trans Rainer Epp, mit Glossar und Nachwort Jürgen Martini. Bremen: Ubersee-Museum, 1988

Days & Nights. Mona, Kingston: Caldwell P, 1975.

Other Exiles. Oxford: Oxford UP, 1975.

Black + Blues. Havana: Casa de las Americas, 1976; rpt. Benin, Nigeria: Ethiope Publishing, 1976.

Spanish trans.: *Black + Blues*. Trans. David Chericián. Havana: Casa de las Americas, 1977.

Black + Blues. 2nd edn. New York: New Directions, 1995.

Mother Poem. Oxford, London and New York: Oxford UP, 1977.

Soweto. Mona, Kingston: Savacou, 1979.

Word Making Man: Poem for Nicolás Guillén in Xaymayca. Mona: Savacou, 1979.

Afternoon of the Status Crow. Mona, Kingston: Savacou, 1982.

Sun Poem. Oxford, New York, Toronto and Melbourne: Oxford UP, 1982.

Third World Poems. London: Longman, 1983.

Le détonateur de visibilité/The Visibility Trigger. Ed. and trans. Maria-Francesca Mollica and Christine Pagnoulle. Intro. M.-F. Mollica. Louvain: Cahiers de Louvain, 1986.

Jah Music. Mona, Kingston: Savacou, 1986.

Korabra. [Poems with paintings by Gavin Jantjes.] London: Edward Totah Gallery, 1986. *See also* 2.1.2.

X/Self. Oxford and New York: Oxford UP, 1987.

Sappho Sakyi's Meditations. Mona, Kingston: Savacou, 1989.

SHAR: Hurricane Poem. Mona, Kingston: Savacou, 1990. *See also* 2.1.2.

Middle Passages. Newcastle upon Tyne: Bloodaxe, 1992.

Middle Passages. [New edn.] New York: New Directions, 1993.

Words need love too. Philipsburg, St. Martin: House of Nehesi, 2000.

Ancestors. New York: New Directions, 2001.

2.1.2. Poetry – (Anthologized, recent and/or uncollected)

"Clips (for Frank Collymore, 1893-1980) (in Caribbean Literature)." *Callaloo* 34 (Winter 1988): 52-73.

"Korabra." In Kwesi Owusu, ed. *Storms of the Heart : An Anthology of Black Arts and Culture*. London: Camden, 1988. 253-62.

"Shar (Huracane Poem)." *Anales del Caribe* 10 (1990): 247-53. *See also* **2.1.1.**

"I Cristóbal Colón." *The Page* (literary monthly in *The Northern Echo* [Darlington]), March 1993: 6-7

Spanish trans.: "Yo Cristóbal Colón." Trans. A. Z. ("versión libre"). *Casa de las Américas* 191 (April-June 1993): 67-69. (A. Z. = Adelaïda de Juan and Roberto

Fernández Retamar.)

"**I Cristóbal Colón.**" *Vniversity* (New York University Newsletter), Winter 1994: 18-21.

"**I Cristóbal Kamau.**" *Review: Latin American Literature and Arts* 50 (Spring 1995): 5-11.

"The Dream Sycorax Letter." *Black Renaissance/Renaissance Noire* 1.1 (Fall 1996): 120-36.

"**Oya Continues Towards the Source & Sounding(s) of the Nile.**" In *Fertile Ground: Memories & Visions 1996.* Ed. Kalamu ya Salaam and Kysha N. Brown. New Orleans: Runnagate P, 1996. 237-42. (First and only issue of planned annual journal.)

"The Mmusiowatuunya Dream Mountain (for Tom Dent)." *Black Renaissance/ Renaissance Noire* 2.3 (Winter 1999-2000): 38-49.

"Esplanade Poem." *Xcp: Cross-Cultural Poetics* 7 (2000): 84-8.

"My Funny Valentine." *Hambone* 15 (Fall 2000): 55-9.

"My Funny Valentine." In Nalo Hopkinson, ed. *Whispers from the Cotton Tree Root: Caribbean Fabulist Fiction.* Montpelier, VT: Invisible Cities P, 2000. 299-302.

2.1.3. Poetry into Music

The Making of the Drum. By Bob Chilcott [to poems of KB]. Oxford: Oxford UP (Music), 1997. (Music for voices and percussion: 0 19 3355221.)

2.2.1. Fiction, Memoir, and Dreamstories – Books

The Zea Mexican Diary, 7 Sept 1926-7 Sept 1986. Madison: U of Wisconsin P, 1993.

Barabajan Poems 1492-1992. Kingston and New York: Savacou North, 1994. *See also* 2.6.1. (*The Poet and His Place.*)

DreamStories. Harlow: Longman, 1994.

Trench Town Rock. Providence, RI: Lost Road, 1994.

Dream Haiti. New York: Savacou North Limited Editions, 1995. *See also* **2.2.2.** French trans.: *RêvHaïti.* Trans. Christine Pagnoulle. Forthcoming.

2.2.2. Fiction, Memoir and Dreamstories – (Earliest publication and recent uncollected)

"The Black Angel." *Bim* 6.22 (1955): 79-87.

Rpt. in Andrew Salkey, ed. *Stories from the Caribbean: An Anthology.* London: Elek, 1965. 227-39. (Rpt. New York: Dufour, 1965, 1968; 2nd London edn. 1972.)

"El angel negro." Trans. Blanca Acosta. In Blanca Acosta, Samuel Goldberg and Ileana Sanz, eds. Havana: Casa de las Américas, 1977. 231-50. (With English.)

"Law and Order." *Bim* 6.23 (1955): 193-200.

"Christine." *Bim* 8.32 (1961): 246-50. (Chapter from unpublished novel *The Boy and the Sea*, some more of which now incorporated into *Barabajan Poems*.)

"Cricket." In Andrew Salkey, ed. *Caribbean Prose.* 1967; rpt. London: Evans, 1973. 60-7.

"The Crossing." In Velta J. Clarke, ed. *Native Landscapes: An Anthology of Caribbean Short Stories*. New York: Caribbean Research Center – Medgar Evers College, CUNY, 1989. 33-41.

"The 4th Traveller." *Callaloo* 12.1 (Winter 1989): 184-91.

"Meridian." *Kunapipi* 11.2 (1989): 60-74.

"Dream Chad". *Landfall* 46.4 (Dec. 1992): 441-8.

"Scapeghosts or The Whole Lindisfarne Dream Warning." *The Page* (literary monthly in *The Northern Echo* [Darlington]), Nov. 1993: 6-7.

"**Trench Town Rock**." *Hambone* 10 (Spring 1992): 123-201.

"Days & Nights or Jean Rhys & Cynthia Wilson [the part of the poem in this performance is played by Christophine]." *Wasafiri* 22 (Autumn 1995): 79-81.

"Dream Haiti." *Hambone* 12 (Fall 1995): 123-85.

"Dream Haiti." In Stewart Brown and John Wickham, eds. *The Oxford Book of Caribbean Short Stories*. Oxford: Oxford UP, 1999. 169-86.

"Dream Orange." *The Caribbean Writer* 9 (1995): 117-34.

"*Limuru* and *Kinta Kunte*." In Charles Cantalupo, ed. *Ngugi wa Thiong'o: Texts and Contexts*. Trenton, NJ: Africa World P, 1995. 1-11.

"Scapeghost(s)." *Xcp: Cross-Cultural Poetics* 4 (Spring 1999): 7-27.

"An Excerpt from *Limbo*." *The Caribbean Writer* 14 (2000): 97-111.

2.3. Plays
Four Plays for Primary Schools. London and Accra: Longmans Green, 1964.

Odale's Choice. London: Evans, 1967.

Sun Poem. Dir. Margaret Wilkins. Lead Ian Walcott. Bridgetown, Stage One, 1989. (Best play in MEGOB awards. Also toured England.)

Barabajan. Script and direction G. Arthur Smith. Performed. Port-of-Spain: Carifesta VI, 1995.

How Music Came to the Ainchan People. KB's script after Timothy Callender. Barbados Carifesta presentation by Stage One. St. Kitt's, August 2000.

2.4. Films
Ogoun. Root & Water. London: BBC2, 1999. (Broadcast, Jan. 1999; video ISBN 0 563 462290 6)

2.5.1. History – Books
The People Who Came. See 2.10.

Folk Culture of the Slaves in Jamaica. London and Port of Spain: New Beacon Books, 1970; revised edn. 1980.

The Development of Creole Society in Jamaica, 1770-1820. Oxford: Clarendon, 1971.

The Development of Creole Society in Jamaica, 1770-1820. Revised edn. Intro. Barry Higman. Kingston: Ian Randle, 2001. (Besides two new chapters, the text is much changed.)

Caribbean Man in Space and Time. Mona: Savacou Offprint, 1975. *See also* **2.5.2**.

Wars of Respect: Nanny and Sam Sharpe (Nanny, Sam Sharpe and the Struggle for

People's Liberation). Kingston: Agency for Public Information, 1977. *Caribb[ean] Wo[men] during the Period of Slavery*. Forthcoming.

2.5.2. History – Articles

[Review of *A Century of West Indian Education* by Shirley Gordon.] *The Voice of St Lucia,* 24 May (4), 1 June 1963 (4, 9).

[Review of *History of the People of Trinidad and Tobago* by Eric Williams.] *The Voice of St Lucia* 29 (4), 6 July (4, 9), 27 July 1963 (4).

"Jamaican Slave Society." [Review of *The Sociology of Slavery* by Orlando Patterson.] *Race* 9.3 (1968): 331-42.

[Review of *The Confessions of Nat Turner* by William Styron.] *Frontier* (Wrexham) (1968): 234-5.

"Jamaican Society" [excerpt from *Development of Creole Society*]. *The Periodical* (Winter 1970-71): 343-5.

"Writing for Young West Indians: History, Geography and Slavery." *Torch* (Jamaica Teachers Association) 20.2-3 (Summer and Christmas 1970): 6-9.

"Dialect and Dialectic: A Review of *How Europe Underdeveloped Africa* by Walter Rodney." *African Studies Association of the West Indies Bulletin* 6 (1973): 89-99.

[Review of *Social Control in Slave Plantation Societies: A Comparison of St. Domingue and Cuba* by Gwendolyn Midlo Hall.] *American Historical Review* 78.1 (Feb. 1973): 183-4.

[Review of *Sugar without Slaves: The Political Economy of British Guiana* by Alan Adamson.] *Caribbean Quarterly* 20.3-4 (Sept.-Dec. 1974): 84-5.

[Review of *The Unappropriated People: Freedmen in the Slave Society of Barbados* by Jerome S. Handler.] *Caribbean Quarterly* 20.3-4 (Sept.-Dec. 1974): 85-8. [Also in: *Hispanic American Historical Review* (May 1975): 350-4.]

[Review of *The West Indian Nations* by Philip M.. Sherlock.] *Jamaica Daily News,* 21 April 1974: 5.

"**Caribbean Man in Space and Time.**" *Savacou* 11-12 (1975): 1-11. *See also* **2.5.1.**

"Caribbean Man in Space and Time." In John Hearne, ed. *Carifesta Forum: An Anthology of 20 Caribbean Voices*. Kingston: Carifesta 76, 1976. 199-208.

"Submerged Mothers: Militant Black Women in Historical Perspective." [On *The Rebel Woman in the British West Indies during Slavery* by Lucille Mathurin.] *Jamaica Journal* 9.2-3 (1975): 48-9.

"La criollización en las Antillas de lengua inglesa." *Casa de las Américas* 96 (May-June 1976): 19-32. [From *Development of Creole Society.*]

"Caliban, Ariel and Unprospero in the Conflict of Creolization: A Study of the Slave Revolt in Jamaica in 1831-1832." In Vera Rubin and Arthur Tuden, eds. *Comparative Perspectives on Slavery in the New World*. Annals of the New York Academy of Sciences 292. New York: New York Academy of Sciences, 1977. 41-62. (Rept. 1994.)

"Caliban, Ariel and Unprospero in the Conflict of Creolization: A Study of the Slave Revolt in Jamaica in 1831-1832." In Verene Shepherd and Hilary McD. Beckles, eds. *Caribbean Slavery in the Atlantic World*. Kingston: Ian Randle;

Oxford: Currey; Princeton, Marcus Weiner, 2000. 879-95.

"Caribbean Slave Society: Commentary on the Conference." In Vera Rubin and Arthur Tuden, eds. *Comparative Perspectives on Slavery in the New World.* Annals of the New York Academy of Sciences 292. New York: New York Academy of Sciences, 1977. 694-6. (Rpt. 1994.)

"Afro-American Slave Culture." In Michael Craton, ed. *Roots and Branches: Current Directions in Slave Studies. Historical Reflections* (Waterloo, Ontario) 6.1 (1979): 150-55.

"The Geography of the Rebellion: The Great River Valley of St. James 1831/32." *The Daily Gleaner Supplement,* 28 Dec. 1981: n.p.

"Rebellion: Anatomy of the Slave Revolt of 1831/1832." *Jamaica Historical Society Bulletin* 8.4 (1981): 80-96.

"The Slave Rebellion in the Great River Valley of St. James 1831/32." *Jamaica Historical Review* 13 (1982): 11-30.

"Confrontations in the Caribbean." [Review of Michael Craton's *Testing the Chains: Resistance to Slavery in the British West Indies.*] *Times Literary Supplement,* 23 Dec. 1983: 1425.

"Caribbean Woman During the Period of Slavery." *Caribbean Contact,* May 1984, 2, 13; June 1984, 13-14.

"World Order Models: A Caribbean Perspective." *Caribbean Quarterly* 30.1 (1985): 53-63.

"Maroons and Marooned." [Review of *The Maroons of Jamaica 1655-1796* by Mavis C. Campbell.] *Jamaica Journal* 22.3 (Aug.-Oct.1989): 5-6.

"Nanny, Palmares & the Caribbean Maroon Connexion." In Kofi Agorsh, ed. *Maroon Heritage.* Mona: Canoe P, 1994. 119-38.

"Creolization in Jamaica." [Extract from *Development of Creole Society.*] In Ashcroft, Griffiths and Tiffin, eds.(*see* **4.**). 202-5.

2.6.1. Literary and Cultural Criticism – Books

Contradictory Omens: Cultural Diversity and Integration in the Caribbean. 1974; rpt. Mona, Kingston: Savacou, 1985.

Bajan Culture Report and Plan. Barbados: UNESCO/Ministry of Education and Culture, March 1979.

Kumina: The Spirit of African Survival in Jamaica. Savacou Working Paper 4. Mona: Savacou, 1982. *See also* **2.6.2.**

National Language Poetry. Savacou Working Paper 5. Mona: Savacou, 1982.

The Colonial Encounter: Language. Mysore: Dept. of Commonwealth Studies, U of Mysore, 1984.

History of the Voice: The Development of Nation Language in Anglophone Caribbean Poetry. London and Port of Spain: New Beacon, 1984.

Roots: Essay. Havana: Casa de las Américas, 1986.

Roots: Essay. 2nd edn. Ann Arbor: University of Michigan P, 1993.

Gods of the Middle Passage. Mona: Savacou, 1989. *See also* **2.6.2.**

Barabajan Poems. See **2.2.1.**

The Poet and His Place in Barbadian Culture. The Twelfth Sir Winston Scott

Memorial Lecture. Bridgetown: Central Bank of Barbados, 1994. (The lecture was given in 1987, and became the core of *Barabajan Poems*.)

ConVERSations with Nathaniel Mackey. Staten Island: We Press; Minneapolis: Xcp: Cross-Cultural Poetics, 1999. (Written almost entirely by KB, starting from Mackey interview.)

Love Axe/l. 2 vols. Leeds: Peepal Tree, 2001.

MR. New York and Kingston: Savacou North, 2001.

2.6.2. Literary and Cultural Criticism – Articles

"A West Indian Culture?" *The Harrisonian* (Bridgetown), Dec. 1949: 50-2.

"Letter from Cambridge." *Bim* 5.20 (1954): 256-7.

"Sir Galahad and the Islands." *Bim* 7.25 (1957): 8-16. Revised and enlarged in *Iouanaloa*. 50-9. *See* **2.10.**

[Review of *The Faces of Love* by John Hearne.] *Bim* 7.25 (1957): 63-4.

"The Controversial Tree of Time." *Bim* 8.30 (1960): 104-114.

"The New West Indian Novelists." *Sunday Advocate* (Barbados), 21, 28 Feb., 6, 13, 20 March 1960.

"The New West Indian Novelists, Part I." *Bim* 8.31 (1960): 199-210.

[Review of *The Autumn Equinox* by John Hearne.] *Bim* 8.31 (1960): 215-17.

[Review of *A Quality of Violence* by Andrew Salkey.] *Bim* 8.31 (1960): 219-20.

[Review of *Voices of Ghana* by Henry Swanzy.] *Bim* 8.30 (1960): 131-4.

"Composition and Creative Writing." *Ghana Teachers' Journal* 32.4 (Oct. 1961): 14-22 [Part 1]; *GTJ* 33.1 (Jan. 1962): 30-7 [Part 2]; *GTJ* 34.2 (April 1962): 26-9 [Part 3]; *GTJ* 35.3 (July 1962): 25-32 [Part 4].

"The New West Indian Novelists, Part II." *Bim* 8.32 (1961): 271-80. Both parts in: *The Voice of St Lucia*, 19 Oct. (4), 26 Oct. (4), 2 Nov. (4), 9 Nov. 1963 (4, 9).

[Review of *Tamarack Review* 14 (Winter 1960).] *Bim* 8.32 (1961): 288-9.

[Review of *The Last Enchantment* by Neville Dawes.] *Bim* 9.33 (1962): 74-5.

[Review of *In a Green Night* by Derek Walcott.] *The Voice of St Lucia*, 13 April 1963: 4.

"The Role of the University in a Developing Society." *The Voice of St Lucia*, 9 March 1963: 4. Rpt. in Brathwaite, ed. *Iouanaloa*. 13-18. *See* **2.10.**

"Roots." *Bim* 10.37 (1963): 10-21.

"The Use of Radio in a Developing Society." *The Voice of St Lucia*, 9 March 1963: 2. Rpt. in Brathwaite, ed. *Iouanaloa*. 34-6. *See* **2.10.**

[Review of "Syrop" by Garth St. Omer (in Faber's *Introduction 2: Stories by New Writers*).] *Caribbean Quarterly* 10.1 (March 1964): 68-9. Rpt. in *Bim* 10.40 (1965): 290-1.

[Review of *Nebucadnezzar and Other Poems* by Jacqueline Pointer.] *Bim* 11.41 (1965): 69-70.

[Review of *The Scholar-Man* by O. R. Dathorne.] *Bim* 11.41 (1965): 68-9.

"*Kyk-over-al* and the Radicals." *New World Quarterly*. Guyana Independence Issue (May 1966): 55-7.

[Review of *The Castaway* by Derek Walcott.] *Bim* 11.42 (1966): 139-41.

[Review of *Caribbean Literature*, ed. G. R. Coulthard, and *From the Green Antilles*, ed. Barbara Howes.] *Bim* 11.43 (1966): 222-3.

"CAM Comment on Gordon Rohlehr's 'Sparrow and the Language of the Calypso'." *CAM Newsletter* 4 (Aug.-Sept. 1967): 8.

"Jazz and the West Indian Novel." *Bim* 11.44 (1967): 275-84 [Part 1]; *Bim* 12.45 (1967): 39-51 [Part 2]; *Bim* 12.46 (1968): 115-26 [Part 3].

"Jazz and the West Indian Novel". In Ashcroft, Griffiths and Tiffin, eds. (*see* **4.**). 327-31.

"Kent Conference on Caribbean Arts." *CAM Newsletter* 4 (Aug.-Sept. 1967): 1.

"West Indian Prose Fiction in the Sixties." *The Critical Survey* (London) (Winter 1967): 169-74.

"West Indian Prose Fiction in the Sixties: A Survey." *Bim* 12.47 (1968): 157-65. [Also published in *New World Quarterly* 1969; and revised in *The Sunday Gleaner* 8, 15 and 22 March 1970: each issue, page 27.]

"West Indian Prose Fiction in the Sixties." *Caribbean Quarterly* 16.4 (1970): 5-17. ("Final" version.) [Also in *West Indies Chronicle* (London) 86.1482 (July 1971): 298-301, and 86.1484 (Sept. 1971): 400-1; and *New Community* (London) 1.2 (Jan. 1972): 142-8.]

"West Indian Prose Fiction in the Sixties." *Black World* (Chicago), Sept. 1971: 15-29. (Further extended.)

"CAM Comment on 'Sparrow and the Language of the Calypso' by Gordon Rohlehr." *Caribbean Quarterly* 14.1-2 (1968): 90-96. (Discussion between KB and Rohlehr.)

"The Caribbean Artists Movement." *Caribbean Quarterly* 14.1-2 (1968): 57-9.

"Caribbean Report." *CAM Newsletter* 6 (Jan.-March 1968): 2-5.

"Themes from the Caribbean." *Times Educational Supplement* 2781 (6 Sept. 1968): 396.

"Priest and Peasant." [Review of *The Schoolmaster* by Earl Lovelace.] *Bim* 12.48 (1969): 273-7.

"Priest and Peasant." *Journal of Commonwealth Literature* (July 1969): 117-22.

"Reflections on West Indian Literature." [Review of *The Islands in Between: Essays on West Indian Literature.*] *The Southern Review* 3.3 (1969): 264-72.

Rpt. as "Caribbean Critics." *New World Quarterly* 5.1-2 (1969): 5-12.

"Caribbean Critics." *Critical Quarterly* 11.3 (1969): 268-76.

"**Creative Literature of the British West Indies During the Period of Slavery**." *Savacou* 1 (1970): 46-73.

"Foreward." *Savacou* 3-4 (Dec. 1970-March 1971): 5-9.

"Rehabilitations: A Study of Paule Marshall's *The Chosen Place, the Timeless People.*" *Bim* 13.51 (1970): 174-84.

Rpt. corrected (and with different titles) in *Caribbean Studies* 10.2 (1970): 125-34; *Journal of Black Studies* 1.2 (Dec. 1970): 225-38; and *Critical Quarterly* (Summer 1971): 175-83.

[Review of *The Expatriate: Poems* by Faustin Charles.] *Caribbean Quarterly* 16.2 (1970): 65-9.

Also in: *CAM Newsletter* 12 (Aug. 1970): 6-9, and *Bim* 13.52 (1971): 252-5.
"**Timehri**."[1] *Savacou* 2 (1970): 35-44.
"**Timehri**."[2] In *Is Massa Day Dead? Black Moods in the Caribbean*. Ed. Orde Coombs. Garden City, NY: Doubleday Anchor, 1974. 29-44.
[extract in] *Caribbean Perspectives* 28 (1984): 2.
[extract in] In E. A. Markham, ed. *Hinterland: Caribbean Poetry from the West Indies and Britain*. Newcastle upon Tyne: Bloodaxe, 1989. 117-9.
[extract in] Anne Walmsley, ed. *Guyana Dreaming: The Art of Aubrey Williams*. Aarhus: Dangaroo P, 1990. 82-5 ("Timehri" began as introduction to an Aubrey Williams exhibit.)
"Timehri." In *The Routledge Reader in Caribbean Literature*. Ed. Alison Donnell and Sarah Lawson Welsh. London: Routledge, 1996. 344-50.
[extract in] *The Harrisonian: The Sir Grantley Adams Commemorative Issue*. [Ed. Ralph A. Jemmott.] Bridgetown: Harrison College, 1998. 50
"Art and Society: Kapo a Context." In *Jamaica Folk Art*. Kingston: Institute of Jamaica, 1971. 4-6.
"Introduction" to Melville J. Herskovitz, *Life in a Haitian Valley*. New York: Doubleday Anchor, 1971. v-viii.
"Race and the Divided Self." [Review of *A Rap on Race* by Margaret Mead and James Baldwin.] *Frontier* 14 (Nov. 1971): 202-10. Revised and expanded as:
"Race and the Divided Self." *Black World* 21.9 (July 1972): 54-68. Final version ·in: "Race and the Divided Self." *Caribbean Studies* 14.3 (1974): 127-39.
"West Indian Culture." *The Jamaica Churchman*, April 1971: 3, 7.
"Carifesta 72." [Eight articles in] *The Advocate-News* (Barbados), 16 Oct.-3 Dec. 1972.
"The Contribution of M.J. Herskovitz to Afro-American Studies." *African Studies Association for the West Indies Bulletin* 5 (1972): 85-94. (Original version of "Introduction," 1971.)
"Festival Poetry: Report on the Jamaica Festival Poetry Competition." *Jamaica Journal* 6.3 (Sept. 1972): 27-9.
"Ronald Moody, Jamaican Sculptor." *Sunday Gleaner*, 6 Aug. 1972: 41. .
"Laters: A Tribute to Frank Collymore." *Savacou* 7-8 (1973): 19.
"The African Presence in Caribbean Literature." *Daedalus* 103.2 (1974): 73-109.
"The African Presence in Caribbean Literature." In Sidney Mintz, ed. *Slavery, Colonialism, and Racism*. New York: Norton, 1974. 73-109.
"Presencia de Africa en la literatura del Caribe." In Manuel Moreno Fraginals, ed. *Africa en América Latina*. Mexico City: UNESCO/Siglo Veintiuno, 1977. 152-184.
"The African Presence in Caribbean Literature." *Abbia: Revue Culturelle Camérounaise/Cameroon Cultural Review* 34-37 (1979): 133-75.
"The African Presence in Caribbean Literature." *Bim* 17.65 (1979): 33-44; 17.66-7 (1983):165-85.
"The African Presence in Caribbean Literature." In *Africa in Latin America: Essays on History, Culture, and Socialization*. Ed. Manuel Moreno Fraginals. Trans. Leonor Blum. New York: Holmes & Meier, 1984. 103-44.

"Brother Mais." *Tapia* (Tunapuna), 27 Oct. 1974: 6. (Final version of "Introduction" [1974] *below.*)

Extract in: *West Indies Chronicle*, May-June 1975: 66-9.

"Doing It Our Way: Carifesta: '72." *West Indies Chronicle*, April 1974: 104-5. [From first article of 1972 *Advocate-News* series above; also in *New Community* 3.4 (Autumn 1974): 343-8; selection then reprinted in *Jamaica Daily News*, 23 July 1976: xxix.]

"Introduction" to Roger Mais, *Brother Man*. London: Heinemann, 1974. v-xxi.

As "Nachwort" in Roger Mais, *Bruder Mensch*. Trans. Janheinz Jahn. Zurich: Unionsverlag, 1981. 219-33. (Trans. Marlies Glaser and Gil Tucker.)

Selection (English) in Sharon K. Hall, ed. *Twentieth-Century Literary Criticism*. Detroit: Gale Research, 1982. 246-7.

"Postscript" to *Writing Away from Home*. *Savacou* 9-10 (June 1974): 132-3.

"Antigua Black." [Review of *Antigua Black: Portrait of an Island People* by Margo and Gregson Davis.] *Jamaica Daily News*, 30 May 1976: 7.

"Houses in the West Indian Novel." *Literary Half-Yearly* 17 (1976): 111-21. Revised as: "Houses: A Note on West Indian Literature." *First World* (Atlanta) 1.2 (1977): 46-9.

Final version: "The House in the West Indian Novel." *Tapia* 3 July 1977: 5-7.

"The Love Axe/L: Developing a Caribbean Aesthetic 1962-74." In Houston A. Baker, Jr., ed. *Reading Black: Essays in the Criticism of African, Caribbean and Black American Literature*. Ithaca: Cornell UP, 1976. 20-36.

"Introduction" to Jean Goulbourne, *Actors in the Arena: Poems*. Mona: Savacou, 1977. 9

"The Love Axe/L: (Developing a Caribbean Aesthetic 1962-1974)." *Bim* 16.61 (1977): 53-65 [Part 1]; *Bim* 16.62 (1977):101-106 [Part 2]; *Bim* 16.63 (1978):181-192 [Part 3]. (Much expanded version of above. *See too* **2.6.1.**)

"Preface" to *Caribbean Women*. *Savacou* 13 (1977): vi-vii.

"Resistance Poems: The Voice of Martin Carter." *Caribbean Quarterly* 23.2-3 (1977): 7-23.

"Caribbean Writing Today." *Nam Speaks* (Kingstown, St. Vincent) 2.3 (Aug.-Dec. 1978): 17-38 [Part 1];. 2.4 (Sept.- Dec. 1979): 20-6 [Part 2].

"Explosion of Caribbean 'Sound Poetry'." *Caribbean Contact* (Bridgetown), Oct. 1978: 9.

"The Continuing Explosion of Caribbean Sound Poetry." *Jamaica Daily News*, 6 Oct. 1978:16.

"Foreword" to Daniel P. Kunene, *Pirates Have Become Our Kings: Poems*. Nairobi: East African Publishing House, 1978. ix-x.

"Introduction" to Hazel D. Campbell, *The Rag Doll and Other Stories*. Mona: Savacou, 1978. iv-vii.

"*Kumina*: The Spirit of African Survival in Jamaica." *Jamaica Journal* 42 (1978): 44-63.

"Kumina." In Adelaide Cromwell Gulliver, ed. *Proceedings of a Symposium on the African Dispersal...*sponsored by the Afro-American Studies Program, Boston University, 24 April 1976. Boston: Boston U, 1979, 57-72. *See also* **2.6.1.**

"Roger Mais' *Brother Man* as Jazz Novel." In Baugh, ed. *Critics* (1978: *see* **4.**). 103-12 (*see above* "Introduction" 1974)

"Alejo Carpentier 1904-1980 (A Tribute)." *Sunday Gleaner Magazine*, 6 July 1980: vi.

"English in the Caribbean: Notes on Nation Language and Poetry." In Leslie A. Fiedler and Houston A. Baker, Jr., eds. *English Literature: Opening Up the Canon*. Baltimore: Johns Hopkins UP, 1981. 15-53.

"Martin Carter's Poetry of the Negative Yes." *Caliban* 4 (Fall-Winter 1981): 30-47.

"Gods of the Middle Passage: A Tennament." *Caribbean Review* 11.4 (1982): 18-19, 42-4. *See also* **2.6.1.**

"Introduction" to Tony Kellman, *In Depths of Burning Light*. Barbados: Kellman, 1982. 3-5.

"**Caribbean Culture: Two Paradigms.**" In Jürgen Martini, ed. *Missile and Capsule*. Bremen: U of Bremen, 1983. 9-54.

"Dionne Brand's *Winter Epigrams*." *The New Voices* 11.22 (1983): 23-38. [also as] "Quick radicle of green: to see and overstand the voice." *Fuse* (Toronto) 7 (Nov.-Dec. 1983): 179-83.

"Dionne Brand's *Winter Epigrams*." *Canadian Literature* 105 (Summer 1985): 18-30.

"The First International Book Fair of Radical Black and Third World Books, London." *Carifesta Writers Newsletter* [Georgetown] 3 (1983).

"A. J. Seymour: '*And deserving of his country's honour*'." In Ian McDonald, ed. *AJS at Seventy*. Georgetown: private publication, 1984. 58-62.

"Caribbeanspeak." [Review of *Dictionary of Bahamian English*.] *Times Literary Supplement*, 3 Feb. 1984: 102.

"Helen and the Tempest-Nègre: René Depestre's *A Rainbow for the Christian West*." *Caribbean Quarterly* 30.1 (1984): 33-47.

[Comment on *Jamaican Folk Tales and Oral Histories* by Laura Tanna.] *Daily Gleaner* 27 Dec. 1984: 3 [unattributed, corrected *Daily Gleaner*, 28 Dec. 1984].

"Metaphors of Underdevelopment: A Proem for Hernan Cortes."[1] In *Festival européen de poésie/European Poetry Festival*. Ed. Eugene van Itterbeek. Leuven: n.p., 1984. 35-57.

"**Metaphors of Underdevelopment: A Proem for Hernan Cortez.**"[2] *New England Review and Bread Loaf Quarterly* 7.4 (Summer 1985): 453-76.

"**Metaphors of Underdevelopment: A Proem for Hernan Cortez.**"[3] In Brown, ed. *Art* (*see* 3.). 231-53.

"Foreword" to Rex Nettleford, *Dance Jamaica: Cultural Definition and Artistic Discovery. The National Dance Theatre Company of Jamaica 1962-1983*. New York: Grove, 1985. 7-11.

"The Monkey and the Submarine [a comment on the contemporary Caribbean]." *Caribbean Perspectives* (Georgetown) 29 (1985): 12-13.

"Chronicles of Unchaos: Rex Nettleford's *Dance Jamaica*." *Jamaica Journal* 18.4 (Nov. 1985-Jan. 1986): 46-51.

"Preface." In Anne Walmsley and Nick Caster, ed. *Facing the Sea: A New Anthology from the Caribbean Region for Secondary Schools*. Preface Edward Kamau Brathwaite. Illustrated Errol Lloyd. London and Kingston, Jamaica: Heinemann Educational Books, 1986. i-ix.

Rpt. with correctios in 1992.

"The Unborn Body of the Life of Fiction: Roger Mais' Aesthetics with Special Reference to *Black Lightning.*" *Journal of West Indian Literature* 2.1 (1987): 11-36; 2.2 (1988): 33-5.

"Open Letter to the Vice Chancellor of the University of the West Indies." 18th Nov. 1988. [A plea for help after the hurricane damage to his house and great archive of West Indian writing, orature and music, and its consequences for the historical memory and historiography of Caribbean culture during its era of greatest expansion.]

"Poetry Presentation." Transcription of a talk to the Fifth Annual Conference of West Indian Literature, College of the Virgin Islands, 1986. In Jackson and Allis, eds. (*see* **4**.). 153-82.

"Ala(r)ms of God: Konnu and Carnival in the Caribbean." *Caribbean Quarterly* 36.3-4 (Dec. 1990): 77-107.

"History, the Caribbean Writer, and *X/Self.*" In Geoffrey V. Davis and Hena Maes-Jelinek, eds. *Crisis and Creativity in the New Literatures in English.* Amsterdam and Atlanta: Rodopi, 1990. 23-45.

"Pam Mordecai's *Journey Poem.*" *Caribbean Quarterly* 36.1-2 (1990): 127-40.

"John the Conqueror." *Foundations of a Movement: A Tribute to John La Rose on the Occasion of the 10ᵗʰ International Book Fair of Radical, Black and Third World Books.* London: John La Rose Tribute Committee, 1991. 20-3.

"Bruce St. John and the Bajan Oral Tradition." Public lecture. Bridgetown, 1990.

"Caliban's Guarden." [A version of Lecture I of *Conversations w/Caliban*, the T. S. Eliot Memorial Lectures at the U of Kent, Canterbury, 1990.] *Wasafiri* 16 (1992): 2-6.

"The Mighty Sparrow—Slinger Francisco." *The New Voices* 20.39-40 (1992): 110-29.

"**The Search for a Caribbean Aesthetic**." *Sunday Express* [Trinidad]. Viewpoint. Oct. 25, 1992: 37-44; Nov. 8, 1992: 29-36; Nov. 15, 1992: 33-40.

"Words by Kamau Brathwaite." Kamau Brathwaite and the Caribbean Word: A North-South Counterpoint Conference. Bronx, NY: Hostos Community College, CUNY, 24 Oct. 1992.

"The Literary Crisis in the Caribbean: Dead-End or Fewture Beginnings?" Typescript, Jan. 1994.

"**Newstead to Neustadt**." *World Literature Today* 68.4 (Autumn 1994): 653-60.

"The Adugo Onuora Interview w/Kamau Brathwaite: New York 25 October 1993." *English Caribbean Literature and Arts.* Special Issue, *Review: Latin American Literature and Arts* 50 (Spring 1995): 38-51.

"**Editor's Note**." *English Caribbean Literature and Arts.* Special Issue, *Review: Latin American Literature and Arts* 50 (Spring 1995): 4.

"Nation Language." [Extract from *History of the Voice*.] In Ashcroft, Griffiths and Tiffin, eds. (*see* **4**.). 309-13.

"**A Post-Cautionary Tale of the Helen of Our Wars**: Kamau Brathwaite Replies to Peter Hulme on *Wide Sargasso Sea* His History of the Crit in *Wasafiri.*" *Wasafiri* 22 (Autumn 1995): 69-81.

"MR". In Brathwaite and Reiss, eds. (1997) 1-28. *See* **2.10.**

"MR" [in sycorax style]. In Timothy J. Reiss, ed. *Sisyphus and Eldorado: Magical and Other Realisms in Caribbean Literature.* 2nd edn. Trenton, NJ and Asmara: Africa World P, 2001.

"El MR como aspecto del cosmos dislocado." Trans. Alfredo Alonso Estenoz. [Excerpt from *MR* (**2.6.1.**) on occasion of 1998 Casa de las Américas prize for criticism.] *Casa de las Américas* 213 (Oct.-Dec. 1998): 37-40.

"Prolo" to Elizabeth F. Watson, *From "Ma boy" to a King: John King, 1982-1998: An Annotated Discography of Popular Music from Barbados.* Barbados: Research Riddims, 1999. i-v.

"Fragments of African culture must be carefully preserved." The *Daily Herald* [Philipsburg, Sin Maarten], 28 Feb. 2000; 6-9. [Report of lecture, with first person material included.]

2.7. Encyclopedia and Dictionary Entries

Contemporary Poets of the English Language. Ed. Rosalie Murphy, with James Vinson. Chicago and London: St. James P, 1970. Entries on: Martin Carter 179-80; Frank Collymore 215-18; Wilson Harris 475-7; E. M. Roach 926-7; A. J. Seymour 979-81.

"Caribbean Literature." *Encyclopædia Britannica.* 24 vols. Chicago and London: Encyclopædia Britannica, 1971. 1.314G-H.

"Caribbean Literature in English, French and Spanish." *Encyclopædia Britannica.* 24 vols. London: Encyclopædia Britannica, 1974. 10.1233.

Contemporary Poets. Ed. James Vinson. 2nd edn. London and New York: St. James P., 1975. Entries on: Martin Carter 235-6; Frank Collymore 275-8; Wilson Harris 638-41; Anthony McNeill 1027-9; A. J. Seymour 1377-9.

Contemporary Poets. Ed. James Vinson, with D. L. Kirkpatrick. 3rd edn. London and Basingstoke: Macmillan, 1980; New York: St. Martin's P, 1980. Entries on: George Campbell 230-2; Martin Carter 236-7; Frank Collymore 273-6; Wilson Harris 645-7; Anthony McNeill 1015-17; Bruce St. John 1321-3; A. J. Seymour 1367-70.

Contemporary Poets. Ed. James Vinson and D. L. Kirkpatrick. 4th edn. New York: St. Martin's P, 1985. Entries on: George Campbell 123-4; Martin Carter 126-7; Wilson Harris 350-2; Anthony McNeill 560-1; A. J. Seymour 765-7.

Contemporary Poets. Ed. Tracy Chevalier. 5th edn. Chicago and London: St. James P, 1991. Entries on: George Campbell 134-5; Martin Carter 138-9; Wilson Harris 384-6; Ian McDonald 622-4; Anthony McNeill 633-4; The Mighty Sparrow 653-5; Mervyn Morris 676-8; Bruce St. John 839-40; Dennis Scott 863-5.

"Roger Mais." In Bernth Lindfors and Reinhard Sander, eds. *Dictionary of Literary Biography,* vol. 125: *Twentieth-Century Caribbean and Black African Writers.* Second Series. Detroit and London: Bruccoli Clark Layman, 1993. 78-81.

Contemporary Poets. Ed. Thomas Riggs. 6th edn. New York [etc.]: St. James P, 1995. Entries on: George Campbell 149-50; Martin Carter 152-3; Wilson Harris 439-40; Ian McDonald 710-11; Anthony McNeill 721-2; The Mighty Sparrow 744-5; Mervyn Morris 768-70; Bruce St. John 943-5.

2.8. Government Report
Bajan Culture Report and Plan (1979). *See* **2.6.1.**

2.9. Bibliographies
Our Ancestral Heritage: A Bibliography of the English-Speaking Caribbean. Kingston: Carifesta Jamaica: 1976; rpt. Kingston: Savacou, 1977.
Barbados Poetry ?1661-1979: A Checklist. Mona: Savacou, 1979.
Jamaica Poetry: A Checklist. Books, Pamphlets, Broadsheets, 1686-1978. Kingston: Jamaica Library Service, 1979.

2.10. Edited Collections
The People Who Came. 3 vols. London: Longman, 1968-72. Several reprints, and 2nd revised edn. 1987-93. (General ed. and author.)
Iouanaloa: Recent Writing from Saint Lucia. Castries: UWI, Dept. of Extra-Mural Studies, 1963.
Savacou nos. 1-14/15 (1970-79). First as co-editor with Kenneth Ramchand, then as general editor and publisher.
New Poets from Jamaica: An Anthology. Mona: Savacou, 1979. [*Savacou* 14-15.]
Dream Rock: A Collection of Poems. Kingston: Information Service, 1987.
English Caribbean Literature and Arts. Special issue of *Review: Latin American Literature and Arts* 50. New York: Americas Society, 1995.
____, and Timothy J. Reiss, eds. *Sisyphus and Eldorado: Magical and Other Realisms in Caribbean Literature. Annals of Scholarship* 12.1-2 (1997).

2.11. Interviews
[Brathwaite] "Author Answers Questions from Students of Mico Teacher's College." *JET/Journal of English Teachers* (Jamaica) 11-12 (Oct. 1977): 17-35.
____. "De calypso tegen de slaverij." *Poeziekrant* (Brussels?) 7-8 (Sept.-Oct. 1984): 16.
____. "EKB on Nation Language: The Second Vertical Interview with Kamau Brathwaite." *The New Theater Review: A Lincoln Center Publication* 8 (May 1993): 19-20.
____. "Hotels Are Squatting on His Metaphors: The New York Newsday Interview with Kamau Brathwaite." *New York Newsday*, 4 April 1994: A25 ("Viewpoints NY").
Brown, Stewart. "Interview with Edward Kamau Brathwaite." *Kyk-over-al* 40 (Dec. 1989): 84-93.
____. "'Writing in Light': An Interview with Edward Kamau Brathwaite." *Planet* (Tregaron, Wales) 75 (June-July 1989): 58-66. (Edited version of preceding entry.)
____. *See also* **3.**
Bruner, Charlotte H. *See* **2.12.2.**: "Anglophone, Francophone" (tape).
Chang, Victor, ed. *Three Caribbean Poets on Their Work.* Kingston: Institute of Caribbean Studies, UWI, 1993. 1-29.
Cooper, Vincent O. *See* Fenwick, M.J. and Vincent O. Cooper, below.

Bibliography

Dorn, Georgette M.. *See* **2.12.1.**: "Barbadian Poet" (tape).

Fenwick, M.J., and Vincent O.Cooper. "Geological Connection/Poetic Perception": An Interview with Kamau Brathwaite: Part I." *The Caribbean Writer* 14 (2000): 76-84

Gilkes, Michael. "Barbados Heading for Revival of African Cultural Traditions." *Caribbean Contact* (Feb. 1979): 10-11.

____. [as "Our Correspondent"?] "A New Development for Caribbean Writers." *Caribbean Contact*, Sept.-Oct 1991: 19. (About major Caribbean writers' workshop at the U. of Miami, based in part on interview with KB.)

James, Sybil. "Edward Brathwaite Answers Questions on His Poem *Rights of Passage.*" *Journal of English Teachers* (Jamaica) 4.2/3 (1977): 17-35.

Korley, Nii Laryea. "Brathwaite Home Again." *West Africa* (London) 3627 (16 March 1987): 514-15.

Mackey, Nathaniel. "An Interview with Edward Kamau Brathwaite." *Hambone* 9 (Winter 1991): 42-59. Rpt. as "An Interview with Kamau Brathwaite." In Brown, ed. *Art* (*see* **3.**). 13-32.

____. *See also* **2.6.1.** *and* **3.1.**

Onuora, Adugo. *See* **2.6.2.** ("The Adugo Onuora Interview" [Spring 1995].)

Rigby, Graeme. "Improvisations and Dreams." *The Page* (literary monthly in *The Northern Echo* [Darlington]), June-July 1992: 3.

____. *See also* **3.**

Santana, Joaquín G. "La cultura del tambor." *El Caimán Barbudo* (Havana) 89 (1975): 7-9. Rpt. in: *La Gaceta de Cuba* (1979), 21-3

Searle, Chris. "Message to Grenada." *Race and Class* 22.4 (1981): 387-94.

____. *Words Unchained: Language and Revolution in Grenada.* London: Zed Books, 1984. 232-9.

Smilowitz, Erika. "Interview with Edward Kamau Brathwaite." *The Caribbean Writer* 5 (1991): 73-8.

Stamberg, Susan. *See* **2.12.1.**: [Interview] (tape).

Stephenson, Olivier. "A Talk with Kamau Brathwaite, a Leading Caribbean Writer." *Amsterdam News* 83.49 (5 Dec. 1992): 4, 41.

Taitt, Andrew. "Savacou Survives." *Caribbean Contact*, Nov.-Dec. 1990: 18. (Review/commentary on Savacou publications and situation, based largely on interview with KB.)

Van der Wal, Andries. "Wij moeten elkaar leren kennen." *Mandala* (Rotterdam) 4 (1976): 3-6.

2.12. Discography
2.12.1.

Rights of Passage. Mona: Radio Education Unit, REU/124/55a, 1965. [Full reading of pre-published draft of *Rights.*]

Rights of Passage. Mona: REU/124/55b, 1967. [Recording of Noel Vaz production of *Rights.*]

Rights of Passage. London: Argo, DA 101, 102 (1969)

Kamau Brathwaite Reading His Poems with Comment in the Recording Labora-

tory, Sept. 11 1970. US Library of Congress, Archive of Recorded Poetry and Literature, DC T 6115.

Masks. London: Argo, PLP 1183, 1972.

Rights of Passage. London: Argo, PLP 1110/1, 1972.

Islands. London: Argo, PLP 1184/5, 1973.

Reading with and for Nicolas Guillén. Mona: UWI Assembly Hall, REU/164/24, 1974.

Poemas. Havana: Casa de las Americas, 1976.

Edward Kamau Brathwaite's Mother Poem. London: National Sound Archive, British Institute of Recorded Sound, BIRS T 4309 WR 25 Sept. 1980.

Masks. London: British Council, 1980.

Guyana Readings. Turkeyen: U. of Guyana, 1980. (UG recording.)

Mother Poem Workshop. London: Association of Teachers of Caribbean and African Literature, 1980.

Mother Poem (with Chinua Achebe). At Cambridge Poetry Festival 1981. BIRS uncat.

Edward Kamau Brathwaite in Conversation with Yolande Cantú. London: British Council, 1981. Audio-cassette CW03.

Barbadian Poet Edward Kamau Brathwaite Reads from His Poetry and Is Interviewed by Georgette M. Dorn. US Library of Congress: Archives of Hispanic Literature on Tape, 1982.

Edward Kamau Brathwaite Reading His Poems. Introduction Anthony Hecht. 2 tapes. US Library of Congress, Archive of Recorded Poetry and Literature, 1982.

[Interview with Susan Stamberg]. Washington, DC: National Public Radio, 1988.

Atumpan. Washington, DC: Watershed Tapes, C-229, 1990.

Kamau Brathwaite and Allen Ginsberg, 1994. Intro. Eliot Weinberger. New York: Academy of American Poets, 1999.

2.12.2. In Anthologies

The Poet Speaks 10. Ed. Peter Orr. London: Argo Records, 1968.

Poetry International '69. Ed. Peter Orr. London: Argo Records, 1969.

Poets of the West Indies Reading Their Own Works. Ed. John Figueroa. New York: Caedmon, 1971.

Poetry International '72. London: National Poetry Centre, 1972. British Institute of Recorded Sound [BIRS] T 989 R.

Anglophone and Francophone Talks with and about Third World Writers, by Charlotte H. Bruner. 6 tapes. WOI Radio, Ames, IA, 1979. Tape 4.

Caribbean Anthology. Ed. Joan Goody. London: Inner London Education Authority Learning Materials Service, 1981.

An Evening of International Poetry, recorded live at the Camden Town Hall, 30 March 1982. (First International Book Fair of Radical and Third World Books). Ed. John La Rose and Linton Kwesi Johnson. London: Alliance Records, 1983.

2.13. Symposia on Brathwaite's Work (Recorded, with KB's taped participation)

"Kamau Brathwaite and the Caribbean Word: A North-South Counterpoint Conference." Hostos Community College, CUNY, Bronx, NY, 24 Oct. 1992. Or-

ganized by Silvio Torres-Saillant.
[Neustadt Prize Award Symposium.] University of Oklahoma, Norman, OK, 30
Sept. 1994. Organized by Djelal Kadir and *World Literature Today*.
"Symposium in Celebration of Edward Kamau Brathwaite's 70th Birthday." University of the West Indies, Cave Hill, 12 May 2000. Organized by Tony Phillips.
"Flashes of Kamau's Spirit: An Evening of Poetry and Drama in Honour of Kamau
Brathwaite." Barbados Community College, 9 July 2000. Organized by Yvonne
Weekes.
"Between Caliban and Sycorax: Kamau Brathwaite and Caribbean Culture." New
York University, 9 Dec. 2000. Organized by Timothy J. Reiss.

3. Secondary Materials on—or substantially on—Kamau Brathwaite

Acosta, Blanca. *The Literature of the English-Speaking Caribbean*. Havana: Editorial Pueblo y Educación, 1988.
Adcock, Fleur. "The Bajan Beat." [Review of *Sun Poem*.] *Times Literary Supplement*, 18 Feb. 1983: 160.
Aidoo, Ama Ata. "Akan and English." *West Africa* 2677, 21 Sept. 1968: 1099.
Aiyejina, Funso. "The Death and Rebirth of African Deities in Edward Brathwaite's
Islands." *World Literature Written in English* 23.2 (Spring 1984): 397-404.
Allis, Jeanette B. *West Indian Literature: An Index to Criticism 1930-1975*. Boston: G. K. Hall, 1981.
____. *See also* Jackson and Allis, eds. (In **4.**)
Angmor, Charles. "Black Consciousness in the Poetry of Edward Brathwaite". In
Ikonne, Eko and Oku, eds. (*see* **4.**). 113-28.
Anonymous. "How Far Are Derek Walcott and Edward Brathwaite Similar? Is It
Impossible for the Caribbean to Choose between the Two, If So, Which Way
Should They Choose and Why?" *Busara* (Nairobi) 6.1 (1974): 90-100.
Anonymous. Review of *Rights of Passage* by Edward Brathwaite. *Times Literary
Supplement*, 16 Feb. 1967: 125.
Anonymous. Review of *The Zea Mexican Diary: 7 Sept 1926-7 Sept 1986* by Kamau
Brathwaite. *The Village Voice*, 7 Dec. 1993: 11.
Asein, Samuel Omo. "The Concept of Form: A Study of Some Ancestral Elements in
Brathwaite's Trilogy." *African Studies Association of the West Indies Bulletin*
4 (1971):19-34.
____. "Symbol and Meaning in the Poetry of Edward Brathwaite." *World Literature Written in English* 20.1 (Spring 1981): 96-104.
____, ed. *Comparative Approaches to Modern African Literature*. Ibadan: Ibadan
UP, 1982.
Badejo, Fabian Adekunle. "Introduction" to KB, *Words need love too*. Philipsburg,
St. Martin: House of Nehesi, 2000 (*see* **2.1.1**). ix-xx.
Baugh, Edward. "Edward Brathwaite as Critic: Some Preliminary Observations."
Caribbean Quarterly 28.1-2 (1982): 66-75.
____. "Poetry as Ritual: Reading Kamau Brathwaite." *Journal of West Indian Literature* 8.1 (Oct. 1998): 1-9.

_____. "Questions and Imperatives for a Young Literature." *Humanities Association Review* 24 (Winter 1973): 13-24.

_____. [Review of *Masks.*] *Bim* 12.47 (1968): 209-11.

_____. [Review of *Rights of Passage.*] *Bim* 12.45 (1967): 66-8.

_____. *West Indian Poetry 1900-1970: A Study in Cultural Decolonisation.* Kingston: Savacou, 1970.

_____. "The West Indian Writer and His Quarrel with History." *Tapia*, 25 Feb. 1977: 6-7; (27 Feb. 1977): 6-7.

_____. *See also* **4.**

Best, Curwen. "Affecting and Interpreting the Tone that Smiles." In Salick, ed. (*see* **4.**). 148-58.

_____. "Text, Tradition, Technology: Crossover and Caribbean Popular Culture." In Brown, ed. *Pressures* (*see* **4.**). 75-82.

_____. *Unmasking X/Self.* Lecture at the 10th Annual Conference on West Indian Literature. St. Augustine: Dept. of English, UWI, 1991.

Biancolini, Paola. "The Experience of Recognition in Brathwaite's *Roots.*" *Caribana* (Milan) 5 (1996): 173-8.

Bloom, Valerie, and Douglas Bloom. "The Development of Caribbean Dialect Poetry." *Cambridge Journal of Education* 14.3 (1984): 21-4.

Bobb, June D. *Beating a Restless Drum: The Poetics of Kamau Brathwaite and Derek Walcott.* Trenton, NJ: Africa World P, 1998.

_____. "Kamau Brathwaite's New Poetry." In Carol P. Marsh-Lockett, ed. *New Critical Essays on Caribbean Literature: Caliban's Turn.* New York: Garland, 2001. Forthcoming.

_____. "'Minefield(s) of Unmemory': The New Poetry of Kamau Brathwaite." In E. Anthony Hurley, Renee Larrier and Joseph McLaren, eds. *Migrating Words and Worlds: Pan-Africanism Updated.* Trenton, NJ: Africa World P, 1999. 175-82.

_____. "The Recovery of Ancestry in the Poetry of Edward Kamau Brathwaite and Derek Walcott." Ph.D. diss., City University of New York, 1992.

Bodunde, Charles A. "The Black Writer and the Multicultural Caribbean: The Vision of Africa in Edward Kamau Brathwaite's *The Arrivants.*" *Matatu* (Mainz) 12 (1994): 17-33. Glaser and Pausch, eds. (In **4.**)

Breiner, Laurence A. "Edward Kamau Brathwaite." In Bernth Lindfors and Reinhard Sander, eds. *Dictionary of Literary Biography*, vol. 125: *Twentieth-Century Caribbean and Black African Writers.* Second Series. Detroit and London: Bruccoli Clark Layman, 1993. 8-28.

_____. "How to Behave on Paper: The *Savacou* Debate." *Journal of West Indian Literature* 6.1 (1993): 1-10.

_____. *An Introduction to West Indian Poetry.* Cambridge: Cambridge UP, 1998.

_____. "Lyric and Autobiography in West Indian Literature." *Journal of West Indian Literature* 3.1 (Jan. 1989): 3-15.

_____. "The Other West Indian Poet." *Partisan Review* 56.2 (1989): 316-20.

_____. "Tradition, Society, the Figure of the Poet." *Caribbean Quarterly* 26.1-2 (1980): 1-12.

Brown, Beverly E. "Mansong and Matrix: A Radical Experiment." *SPAN: Journal of the South Pacific Association for Commonwealth Literature and Language Studies* (Murdoch, W. Australia) 21 (Oct. 1985): 56-74. Rpt. in Kirsten Holst Petersen and Anna Rutherford, eds. *A Double Colonization: Colonial and Post Colonial Women's Writing.* Aarhus: Dangaroo P, 1986. 68-79.

Brown, Lloyd W. "Brathwaite, Edward Kamau." In *Contemporary Poets.* Ed. James Vinson, with D. L. Kirkpatrick. 3rd. edn. London and Basingstoke: Macmillan, 1980; New York: St. Martin's P, 1980. 156-60. (And in subsequent editions with occasional changes, notably in KB's "statement.")

____. "The Cyclical Vision of Edward Brathwaite." In his *West Indian Poetry.* Boston: Twayne, 1978. 139-58. (2nd edn. London: Heinemann, 1984.)

Brown, Stewart. "Dreadtalk: Caribbean Poetry Now." *Planet* (Tregaron, Wales) 53 (1985): 70-80.

____. "Introduction." In Brown, ed. *Art* 7-12.

____. "Middle Passages." *Poetry Wales* 29.1 (1993): 56-8.

____. "A Rainbow Sign." *Poetry Review* 72.4 (1983): 59-61.

____. "Sun Poem: The Rainbow Sign?" In Brown, ed. *Art.* 152-62.

____. "'Writin in Light': Orality-thru-Typography, Kamau Brathwaite's Sycorax Video Style." In Brown, ed. *Pressures* (*see* **4.**). 125-36.

____, ed. *The Art of Kamau Brathwaite.* Bridgend: Seren, 1995.

____. *See also* **2.2.2** ("Dream Haiti"), **2.11.** and **4.**

Bruner, Charlotte H. "The Meaning of Caliban in Black Literature Today." *Comparative Literature Studies* 13.3 (1976): 240-53.

____. *See also* **2.12.1.** ("Anglophone, Francophone" [taped interview with KB].)

Busia, Abena P. A. "Long Memory and Survival: Dramatizing *The Arrivants* Trilogy." *World Literature Today* 68.4 (Autumn 1994): 741-6.

Calder, Angus. "Walcott's 'The Schooner Flight' and Brathwaite's 'Nametracks': Two Short Verse Narratives." In Jacqueline Bardolph, ed. *Short Fiction in the New Literatures in English: Proceedings of the Nice Conference of the European Association for Commonwealth Literature and Language Studies.* Nice: Faculté des Lettres et Sciences Humaines, 1989. 109-19.

Carruth, Hayden. "Poetry Chronicle." *Hudson Review* 27 (Summer 1974): 308-20.

Chamberlin, J. Edward. *Come Back to Me My Language: Poetry and the West Indies.* Urbana and Chicago: U of Illinois P, 1993; Toronto: McLelland & Stewart, 1993.

____. "The Language of Kamau Brathwaite." In Brown, ed. *Art.* 33-51.

____. "Myself Made Otherwise: Edward Kamau Brathwaite's *X/Self.*" *Carib* (Kingston, Jamaica) 5 (1989): 19-32.

____. "Speaking in Tongues: The Language of West Indian Poetry." *Brick* (London, Ont.) 26 (Winter 1986): 14-20.

Chang, Victor, ed. *Three Caribbean Poets on Their Work.* Kingston: Institute of Caribbean Studies, UWI, 1993.

Chukwu, Augustine. "Bridging the Gulf: The Ancestral Mask and Homecoming in Edward Brathwaite's *Masks.*" *Ufahamu* (Los Angeles) 11.2 (Fall 1981-Winter 1982): 131-9.

Clarke, Richard L. W. "The Psychopathology of Transplantation: Towards a Gene-alogy of Brathwaite's Concept of the Deracinated West Indian Creole." Forthcoming.

____. *See also* **4**.

Cobham, Rhonda. "Teaching Brathwaite's 'Wings of a Dove'." *Okike* (Enugu) 15 (1979): 23-6.

____. *See also* **4**.

Cobley, Alan G., and Alvin Thompson, eds. *The African-Caribbean Connection: Historical and Cultural Perspectives*. Bridgetown: Dept. of History, UWI Cave Hill, and the National Cultural Foundation, 1990.

Collett, Anne. "Edward Kamau Brathwaite, the Wordmaking Man: An Exploration of Edward Brathwaite's Philosophy of Word." M.A. thesis, University of Queensland, 1988.

Collier, Gordon. "Artistic Autonomy and Cultural Allegiance: Aspects of the Walcott-Brathwaite Debate Re-examined." *Literary Half-Yearly* 20.1 (1979): 93-105.

____. "Edward Kamau Brathwaite und das Selbstverstandnis der Schwarzen in der englischsprachigen Karibik." In Eckhard Breitinger, ed. *Black Literature: Zur afrikanischen und afroamerikanischen Literatur*. Munich: Fink, 1979. 214-54.

Connor, William. "Edward Brathwaite's Symbolic Use of Water Imagery in *The Arrivants: A New World Trilogy*." *Literary Half-Yearly* 21.2 (1980): 13-21.

Cooper, Carolyn. *Noises in the Blood: Orality, Gender and the "Vulgar" Body of Jamaican Popular Culture*. London: Macmillan, 1993.

Coppleston, Fenella. [Review of Kamau Brathwaite, *Middle Passages* (1992).] *P. N. Review* 89 (19.3: Jan.-Feb. 1993): 61.

Coulson, Sheila. "Roots." *Jamaica Journal* 21.3 (1988): 52-3.

Coulthard, G. R. "Edward Brathwaite y el neo-africanismo antillano." *Cuadernos Americanos* 184.5 (1972): 170-7.

Criswell, Stephen. "Folklore and the Folk in Derek Walcott's *Omeros* and Edward Kamau Brathwaite's *The Arrivants*." Ph.D. diss., University of Southwestern Louisiana, 1997.

Cudjoe, Selwyn. *Resistance and Caribbean Literature*. Athens: Ohio UP, 1980.

D'Aguiar, Fred. "Lines with Their Knots Left In: *Third World Poems* by Edward Kamau Brathwaite and *Midsummer* by Derek Walcott." *Wasafiri* 1.2 (1985): 37-8.

Dabydeen, Cyril. [Review of *Middle Passages*.] *World Literature Today* 67.2 (Spring 1993): 425-6.

____. [Review of *Zea Mexican Diary: 7 Sept 1926-7 Sept 1986*.] *World Literature Today* 68.3 (Summer 1994): 617-8.

Dabydeen, David, and Nana Wilson-Tagoe. *A Reader's Guide to Westindian and Black British Literature*. London: Hansib, 1997.

Dash, J. Michael. "Le cri du morne: La poétique du paysage césairien et la littérature antillaise." In Jacqueline Leiner, ed. *Soleil éclaté: Mélanges offerts à Aimé Césaire à l'occasion de son soixante-dixième anniversaire par une équipe internationale d'artistes et de chercheurs*. Tübingen: Gunter Narr, 1984. 101-10.

____. "Edward Brathwaite." In King, ed. *West Indian* (*see* **4**.). 210-227. (In 2nd edn. 194-208.)

____. "Psychology, Creolization, and Hybridization." In King, ed. *New National* (*see* **4.**). 45-58.

____. [Review of *The Visibility Trigger* and *Jah Music.*] *Journal of West Indian Literature* 1.2 (1987): 87-90.

Dathorne, O. R. *Dark Ancestor: The Literature of the Black Man in the Caribbean.* Baton Rouge: Louisiana UP, 1981.

Dawes, Kwame. "Christianity in *Islands*: An Introduction." In Jackson and Allis, eds. (*see* **4.**). 195-200.

Dayan, Joan. "The Beat and the Bawdy [Review of *X/Self*]." *The Nation* 246.14 (9 April 1988): 504-7.

____. "Who's Got History? Kamau Brathwaite's 'Gods of the Middle Passage'." *World Literature Today* 68.4 (Autumn 1994): 726-32.

D'Costa, Jean. "The Poetry of Edward Brathwaite." *Jamaica Journal* 2.3 (Sept. 1968): 24-8.

DeRose, Michelle Diane. "Caliban Takes Up His Pen: The Epic Poetry of Kamau Brathwaite, Derek Walcott and Andrew Salkey." Ph.D. diss., University of Iowa, 1996.

Donahue, Joseph. "Kamau Brathwaite's Videolect: Spirit and Letter." In Charles Cantalupo, ed. *Ngugi wa Thiong'o: Texts and Contexts.* Trenton, NJ: Africa World P, 1995. 271-81.

Durix, Jean-Pierre. [Review of *Le détonateur de visibilité/The Visibility Trigger.*] *Commonwealth* 9.2 (1987): 114-5.

Edmondson, Belinda. "Race, Tradition and the Construction of the Caribbean Aesthetic." *New Literary History* 25.1 (Winter 1994): 109-20.

Eko, Ebele. *See* Ikonne, Eko and Oku, eds. (In **4.**)

Elisabeth, Léo. [Review of *Development of Creole Society.*] *Revue Française d'Histoire d'Outre-Mer* 59.215 (1972): 337-8.

Ellis, Paula Ann. "Nation-Builders in the Works of Kamau Brathwaite." M. Phil. diss., University of the West Indies, St. Augustine, 2000.

Ezenwa-Ohaetu. "From a Common Root: Revolutionary Vision and Social Change in the Poetry of Brathwaite and Chinweizu." *Journal of Caribbean Studies* 8.1-2 (Winter 1990-Summer 1991): 89-104.

Fido, Elaine Savory. *See* Savory, Elaine.

Fraser, Robert. *Edward Brathwaite's Masks: A Critical View.* London: Collins, in Association with the British Council, 1981. 2nd edn. 1985.

____. "Mental Travellers: Myths of Return in the Poetry of Walcott and Brathwaite." In Vera Mihailovich-Dickman, ed. *"Return" in Post-Colonial Writing: A Cultural Labyrinth.* Amsterdam and Atlanta: Rodopi, 1994. 7-13.

Freeman, Richard. [Review of *Masks.*] *Ambit* 36 (1968): 34-5.

Gallardo, Ximena. "Representing Shakespeare's 'Brave New World': Latin American Appropriations of *The Tempest*." Ph.D. diss., Louisiana State University, 1997.

Gaunt, Darren. "Mother and Son: Reading Brathwaite's *Mother Poem* and *Sun Poem.*" Ph.D. diss., The Flinders University of South Australia, 2000.

Gershator, Phillis. [Review of *SHAR: Hurricane Poem.*] *The Caribbean Writer* 6 (1992): 136-8.

Gikandi, Simon. "E. K. Brathwaite and the Poetics of the Voice: The Allegory of History in *Rights of Passage*." *Callaloo* 14.3 (1991): 727-36.

Gilmore, John. "Seeing with Both Eyes: The Poetry of Edward Kamau Brathwaite." *The New Bajan* (Jan. 1988): 14-15.

Goldberg, Samuel. "El desarrollo de la sociedad criolla en Jamaica." *Casa de las Américas* 91 (1975): 196-200.

Goodwin, K. L. "Invective and Obliqueness in Political Poetry: Kasaipwalova, Brathwaite, and Soyinka." In C. D. Narasimhaiah, ed. *Awakened Conscience: Studies in Commonwealth Literature*. New Delhi: Sterling, 1978. 251-60.

Gowda, H. H. Anniah. "Creation in the Poetic Development of Kamau Brathwaite." *World Literature Today* 68.4 (Autumn 1994): 691-6.

____. "Edward Kamau Brathwaite: A Profile." *Literary-Half Yearly* 23.2 (1982): 40-6.

Graham, Sheila. "Three Responses to the Caribbean Experience: Césaire, Brathwaite, Guillén." Caribbean Studies Paper, UWI Mona 1976. (Typescript.)

Grant, Damian. "Emerging Image: The Poetry of Edward Brathwaite." *Critical Quarterly* (Manchester) 12.2 (1970):186-92.

Greene, James W. [Review of *Development of Creole Society*.] *Journal of Interamerican Studies and World Affairs* (Jan. 1973): 491-2.

Griffith, Glyne A. "Kamau Brathwaite as Cultural Critic." In Brown, ed. *Art*. 75-85.

Griffith, Paul Anderson. "The Liberating Imagination: Politics of Vision in the Art of Edward Kamau Brathwaite and Henry Dumas." Ph.D. diss., Pennsylvania State University, 1995.

____. "Metaphorical Designs in the Poetry of Edward Brathwaite." M.Phil. diss., University of the West Indies, Cave Hill, 1985.

____. "*Mother Poem*: Art and National Consciousness." In Baugh and Morris, eds. (*see* **4.**). 193-206.

Griffiths, Trevor R. "This Island's Mine: Caliban and Colonialism." *Yearbook of English Studies* 13 (1983): 159-80.

Habekost, Christian. "Dub Poetry—Culture of Resistance." In Thomas Bremer and Ulrich Fleischmann, eds. *Alternative Cultures in the Caribbean*. Frankfurt: Vervuert, 1993. 205-16.

____. *Verbal Riddim: The Politics and Aesthetics of Afro-Caribbean Dub Poetry*. Amsterdam and Atlanta: Rodopi, 1993.

Hart, Richard. [Review of *Development of Creole Society*.] *Race* 14.3 (1973): 356-7.

Hearne, John. "The Jig-Saw Men." [Review of *Development of Creole Society*.] *Jamaica Journal* 6.1 (1972): 12-14.

Herdeck, Donald, ed. "Edward Kamau Brathwaite." In *Caribbean Writers: A Bio-Bibliographical Encyclopedia*. Washington, DC: Three Continents P, 1979. 33-9 [entry by John Figueroa?]

Holmes, Timothy. [Review of *Rights of Passage* and *Masks*.] *The New African* 51 (1968): 23-4.

Hoppe, John K. "From Jameson to Syncretism: The Communal Imagination of American Identity in Edward Brathwaite's *The Arrivants*." *Weber Studies* 9.3 (Fall 1992): 92-105.

Huggan, Graham. "Opting Out of the (Critical) Common Market: Creolization and the Post-Colonial Text." *Kunapipi* 11.1 (1989): 27-40.

Irele, Abiola. "The Return of the Native: Edward Kamau Brathwaite's *Masks*." *World Literature Today* 68.4 (Autumn 1994): 719-25.

Ismond, Patricia. "Walcott versus Brathwaite." *Caribbean Quarterly* 17.3-4 (1971): 54-71. Rpt. in Robert D. Hamner, ed. *Critical Perspectives on Derek Walcott*. Washington, DC: Three Continents Press, 1993. 220-36.

James, Cynthia. "The Unknown Text." *World Literature Today* 68.4 (Autumn 1994): 758-64.

James, Louis. "The Black Utopia of Edward Kamau Brathwaite." In Raffaella Baccolini, Vita Fortunati and Nadia Minerva, eds. *Viaggi in Utopia*. Ravenna: Longo, 1996. 303-8.

_____. "Brathwaite and Jazz." In Brown, ed. *Art*. 62-74.

_____. "A Caribbean Poet Questing." *Third World Quarterly* 10.1 (March 1988): 334-7.

_____. "Caribbean Poetry in English—Some Problems." *Savacou* 2 (1970): 78-86.

_____. "The Island as Mother: Matriarchy and Identity in the Work of Kamau Brathwaite and Jamaica Kincaid." In Jean-Pierre Durix, ed. *Literary Archipelagoes/Archipels littéraires*. Dijon: Centre de Recherches Image/Texte/Langage, Éditions Universitaires de Dijon, 1998. 13-18.

_____. "The Poet as Seer." In his *Caribbean Literature in English*. Harlow: Addison Wesley Longman, 1999. 185-91.

_____. [Review of *Rights of Passage*.] *Caribbean Quarterly* 13.1 (1967): 38-41.

_____, ed. *The Islands in Between*. London: Oxford UP, 1968.

James, Sybil. "An Approach to the Teaching of *Rights of Passage* to Students Pursuing a Course in Caribbean Literature in Teachers' Colleges in Jamaica." *Journal of English Teachers* (Jamaica) 6.2-3 (1977): 1-17.

[Jemmott, Ralph A.] "The Poet Laureate of Harrison College." *The Harrisonian: The Sir Grantley Adams Commemorative Issue*. [Ed. Ralph A. Jemmott.] Bridgetown: Harrison College, 1998. 49.

Jones, Bridget. "'The Unity Is Submarine': Aspects of a Pan-Caribbean Consciousness in the Work of Kamau Brathwaite." In Brown, ed. *Art*. 86-100.

Kadir, Djelal, ed. See *World Literature Today*.

Kaminjolo, Althea. "The Trilogies of Edward Kamau Brathwaite as Post-Colonial Discourse." M.Phil. diss., University of the West Indies, St. Augustine, 2000.

Kell, Richard. [Review of *Masks*.] *Critical Survey* 4.2 (Summer 1969): 127-8.

Kellman, Anthony. "A Historical and Musical Experience: Edward Kamau Brathwaite's *X/Self*." *Trinidad New Voices* 16.32 (1988): 88-94.

_____. "Projective Verse as a Mode of Socio-Linguistic Protest." *Ariel* (Calgary) 21.2 (1990): 45-57.

_____. "A Rich Plural Heritage as a Tool for Survival: Edward Kamau Brathwaite's *X/Self*." *Callaloo* 11.3 (Summer 1988): 645-8.

Kemoli, Arthur. "The Theme of the Past in Caribbean Literature." *World Literature Written in English* 12 (1973): 304-25.

King, Bruce Alvin. "West Indies II: Walcott, Brathwaite and Authenticity." In his *The New English Literatures: Cultural Nationalism in a Changing World*.

London: Macmillan, 1980; New York: St. Martin's Press, 1980. 118-39.
____. *See also* **4.**

King-Aribisola, Karen. "*The Arrivants*: Brathwaite's Elemental Directive." In Ikonne, Eko and Oku, eds. (*see* **4.**). 129-40.

Kortenaar, Neil ten. "Where the Atlantic Meets the Caribbean: Kamau Brathwaite's *The Arrivants* and T. S. Eliot's *The Waste Land*." *Research in African Literatures* 4 (Winter 1996): 15-27.

Kubayanda, Josaphat. "On Discourse of Decolonization in Africa and the Caribbean." *Dispositio/n* (Ann Arbor) 14.36-38 (1989): 25-37.

Lawrence, Leota S. "From Cultural Ambivalence to the Celebration of the African Heritage in British West Indian Literature." *College Language Association Journal* (Atlanta) 23 (1974): 220-33.

Lazarus-Shepherd, Verene A., and Glen L. Richards, eds. *Questioning Creole: Creolization Discourses in Caribbean Culture: Essays in Honour of Kamau Brathwaite*. Foreword Rex Nettleford. Kingston: Ian Randle, 2001. (A revised edition of Shepherd and Richards, eds. [*see below*]: with added essays by Cecil Gutzmore, Paul Lovejoy and David Trotman, Pat Mohammed and Glen Richards, and a comment by Lovejoy)

Lieberman, Lawrence. [Review of *Masks*.] *Poetry* 114.1 (April 1969): 56-7.

Lindo, Cedric. [Review of *Jah Music*.] *The Caribbean Writer* 2 (1987): 85-7.

Lucie-Smith, Edward. "West Indian Writing." *The London Magazine* 8.4 (July 1968): 96-102.

Mackey, Nathaniel. *Discrepant Engagement: Dissonance, Cross-Culturality, and Experimental Writing*. Cambridge: Cambridge UP, 1993.
____. "Edward Brathwaite's New World Trilogy." *Caliban* 3.1 (1979): 58-88.
____. "Other: From Noun to Verb." *Representations* 39 (Summer 1992): 51-70.
____. "*Sun Poem* by Edward Kamau Brathwaite" [book review]. *Sulfur* 4.2 (Fall 1984): 200-5.
____. "Wringing the Word." *World Literature Today* 68.4 (Autumn 1994): 733-40. Rpt. in Brown, ed. *Art*. 132-51.
____. *See also* **2.5.** (*ConVERSations*) *and* **2.11.**

Malcolm, Livingston Rudolph. "Theological Reflections on Edward Kamau Brathwaite's *Arrivants*." M.A. thesis (submitted 1990), University of the West Indies, Mona, 1993.

Martini, Jürgen. "Literary Criticism and Aesthetics in the Caribbean, 1: E. K. Brathwaite." *World Literature Written in English* 24.2 (Autumn 1984): 373-83.

Mathurin, Lucille. "Creole Authenticity: A Review of Edward Brathwaite's *The Development of Creole Society in Jamaica 1770-1820*." *Savacou* 5 (1971): 115-20.

Maxwell, Marina. "The Awakening of the Drum: A Review of *Masks*." *New World Quarterly* 5.4 (1971): 39-45.
____. "Towards a Revolution in the Arts." *Savacou* 2 (1970): 19-32.

McDougall, Russell. "Something Rich and Strange in the Poetry of Edward Kamau Brathwaite's *The Arrivants*." In A. Taylor and R. McDougall, eds. *(Un)Common Ground: Essays in Literatures in English*. Adelaide: CRNLE, 1990. 63-74.

McLeod, A. L. [Review of *Middle Passages* by Kamau Brathwaite.] *Choice* 30.9 (1993): 1460.

McMorris, Mark D. "Subjects in a Classical Labyrinth: Tradition, Speech and Empire in English-Language Poetry (T. S. Eliot, Kamau Brathwaite, Derek Walcott, Louis Zukofsky)." Ph.D. diss., Brown University, 1998.

McWatt, Marc A. "Edward Kamau Brathwaite." In Daryl Cumber Dance, ed. *Fifty Caribbean Writers*. New York: Greenwood P, 1986. 58-70.

____. "The Preoccupation with the Past in West Indian Literature." *Caribbean Quarterly* 28.1-2 (1982): 12-19.

____. "Re-collecting the African Ancestor." *Catholic Communicator* [Bridgetown] (July 1993): 6-7.

____. [Review of *Mother Poem*]. *Bim* 16.62 (Dec. 1977): 137-40.

____. "The Two Faces of El Dorado: Contrasting Attitudes Towards History and Identity in West Indian Literature." In McWatt, ed. (*see* **4**.). 33-47.

____. *See also* **4**.

Monahan, Jennifer. "Edward Brathwaite Reading." [Review of recital.] *Times Literary Supplement*, 3 Oct. 1980: 1099.

Moore, Gerald. *The Chosen Tongue: English Writing in the Tropical World*. 1969; rpt. New York: J. & J. Harper, 1970.

____. "Confident Achievement [Review of *Masks*]." *Journal of Commonwealth Literature* 7 (1969): 122-4.

____. "The Language of West Indian Poetry." Baugh, ed. *Critics* (*see* **4**.). 130-36.

____. [Review of *Contradictory Omens*.] *Times Literary Supplement*, 14 Nov. 1975: 1369.

____. [Review of *Islands*.] *Bim* 13.51 (1970): 186-9.

____. [Review of *Other Exiles*.] *AFRAS Review* 2 (1976): 50-1.

____. "Use Men Language." *Bim* 15.57 (1974): 69-76.

____. "West Indian Poet [Review of *Rights of Passage*]." *Transition* 32 (1967): 62-3.

Mordecai, Pamela Claire. "The Image of the Pebble in Brathwaite's *Arrivants*." *Carib* (Kingston, Jamaica) 5 (1989): 60-78.

____. "Prismatic Vision: Aspects of Imagery, Language and Structure in the Poetry of Kamau Brathwaite and Derek Walcott." Ph.D diss., University of the West Indies, Mona, 1997.

Morejón, Nancy. "Brathwaite: identidad y poesía." *Bohemia* (Havana) 68.27 (2 July1976): 28.

____. "E. Brathwaite y su poesía antillana." *Bohemia* 69.22 (3 June 1977): 10-12. Rpt. in *Fundación de la imagen*. Havana: Letras Cubanas, 1988. 234-44.

Morgan, Mary. *A Gathering of Threads*. Kingston: n. p., 1991.

____. "Highway to Vision: This Sea Our Nexus." *World Literature Today* 68.4 (Autumn 1994): 663-8. Also in: *Caribbean Quarterly* 44.1-2 (March-June 1998): 169-76.

Morris, Mervyn. "Niggers Everywhere: Edward Brathwaite, *Rights of Passage*." *New World Quarterly* 3.4 (1967): 61-5.

____. "Overlapping Journeys: *The Arrivants*." In Brown, ed. *Art*. 117-31.

_____. "Some West Indian Problems of Audience." *English* (Oxford) 16.94 (Spring 1967): 127-31.

_____. "This Broken Ground: Edward Brathwaite's Trilogy of Poems." *New World Quarterly* 5.3 (1971): 14-26.

_____. *See also* Baugh and Morris, eds. (in **4**.) *and* **4**.

Morris, Sandra E. "Kamau's Spider." [Poem] *Calabash: A Journal of Caribbean Arts and Letters* 1.1 (Sept. 2000): 26-7

Motion, Andrew. "Self and Scenery." [Review of *Mother Poem* (and other poets).] *The Times Literary Supplement* 20 Jan. 1978: 66.

Mott, Michael. [Review of *Islands*.] *Poetry* (May 1971): 108-9.

Mugo, Micere Githae. "'Patterns of Communication' in Edward Brathwaite's *Masks*." In Eddah Gachukia and S. Kichamu Akivaga, eds. *Teaching of African Literature in Schools*. Nairobi: Kenya Lit. Bureau, 1978. 240-5.

Nanton, Phillip. "Making Space for Orality on Its Own Terms." In Brown, ed. *Pressures* (*see* **4**.). 83-90.

Naylor, Paul. *Poetic Investigations: Singing the Holes in History*. Evanston: Northwestern UP, 1999.

Nelson, Emmanuel S. "Black America and the Anglophone Afro-Caribbean Literary Consciousness." *Journal of American Culture* 12.4 (Winter 1989): 53-8.

Nelson, Lowry. [Review of *Development of Creole Society*.] *American Academy of Political and Social Science* 405 (Jan. 1973): 173-4.

Ngugi wa Thiong'o. "Kamau Brathwaite: The Voice of African Presence." *World Literature Today* 68.4 (Autumn 1994): 677-82. Rpt.: "Kamau Brathwaite: The Voice of Pan-African Presence." In: *Writers in Politics: A Re-Engagement with Issues of Literature and Society*. Revised and enlarged edn. Oxford: James Currey; Nairobi: EAEP; Portsmouth, NH: Heinemann, 1997. 132-7.

_____. *See also* **4**.

O'Callaghan, Evelyn. "Jumping into the Big Ups' Quarrels: The Hulme/Brathwaite Exchange." *Wasafiri* 28 (Autumn 1998): 34-6.

Oku, Julie. *See* Ikonne, Eko and Oku, eds. (In **4**.)

Osman, Jena. Reading the Theatrical Inanimate: Brechtian Possibility in Contemporary American Poetry." Ph.D. diss., State University of New York at Buffalo, 1998.

Pagnoulle, Christine. "Kamau Brathwaite: A Voice Out of Bounds." In Gilbert Debusscher and Marc Maufort, eds. *Union in Partition: Essays in Honour of Jeanne Delbaere*. Liège: L3-Liège Language and Literature, U de Liège, 1997. 225-39.

_____. "'Labyrinth of Past/Present/Future' in Some of Kamau Brathwaite's Recent Poems." In Geoffrey V. Davis and Hena Maes-Jelinek, eds. *Crisis and Creativity in the New Literatures in English*. Amsterdam and Atlanta: Rodopi, 1990. 449-66.

_____. "Profil et épaisseur des mots: Kamau Brathwaite, *RêvHaïti*," *Palimpsestes* 12 (2000): 31-7.

_____. "The 'Voice' of E. K. Brathwaite into French: Grappling with the Untranslatable." *Le Langage et l'Homme* (Louvain-la-Neuve) 23.3 (Dec. 1988): 245-52.

_____. *See also* **2.2.1.** (*Détonateur; RêvHaïti*)

Panel Discussion. "History in E. K. Brathwaite and Derek Walcott." *The Common-wealth of Letters* 1.1 (June 1989): 3-14.

Paquet, Sandra Pouchet. "Foreword" to Kamau Brathwaite, *The Zea Mexican Diary.* v-xi. *See* **2.2.1.**

Parker, Michael. "His Island's Voice: Kamau Brathwaite's *Middle Passages.*" *Times Literary Supplement,* 27 Nov. 1992: 27.

Parris, Trevor. [Review of *Barabajan Poems.*] *The Caribbean Writer* 10 (1996): 212-14.

Pattanayak, Chandrabhanu. "Brathwaite: Metaphors of Emergence." *The Literary Criterion* (Bangalore) 17.3 (1982): 60-8.

Pearn, Julie. *Poetry in the Caribbean.* London: Hodder & Stoughton, 1985.

Perrier, Paulette. "Harmattan: Whose Ancestor Am I?" *Journal of Black Poetry* 1.17 (1973): 22-4.

Pollard, Charles Williams. "Cosmopolitan Modernism: T. S. Eliot, Kamau Brathwaite and Derek Walcott. Ph.D. diss., University of Virginia, 1999.

Pollard, Velma. "'The Dust' — An Analysis." *JET - Journal of English Teachers* 8 (1976): 6-14.

_____. "'The Dust' — A Tribute to the Folk." *Caribbean Quarterly* 2.1-2 (1980): 41-8. (Preceding, rewritten.)

_____. "Language in the Poetry of Edward Brathwaite." *World Literature Written in English* 19.1 (1980): 62-74.

_____. "Other Exiles." *Caribbean Quarterly* 23.2-3 (1977): 91-103.

_____. [Review of *Contradictory Omens.*] *Teacher Forum* 1 (Spring 1975): 68-72.

Povey, John. "The Search for Identity in Edward Brathwaite's *The Arrivants.*" *World Literature Written in English* 27.2 (Autumn 1987): 275-89.

Questel, Victor D. "Blues in Caribbean Poetry." *Kairi* 78 (1978): 4-6.

Ralston, Richard D. [Review of *Development of Creole Society.*] *Journal of Negro History* 58.4 (Oct. 1973): 475-9.

Ramchand, Kenneth. *Acts of Possession: The New World of the West Indian Writers.* The Ninth Eric Williams Memorial Lecture. Port of Spain: Bank of Trinidad and Tobago, 1991.

_____. "Edward Brathwaite." *An Introduction to the Study of West Indian Literature.* Sunbury-on-Thames: Nelson Caribbean, 1976. 127-42.

_____. "The Fate of Writing." *Caribbean Quarterly* 28.1-2 (1982): 76-84.

_____. "Parades, Parades: Modern West Indian Poetry." *Sewanee Review* 87.1 (1979): 96-117.

_____. "The Pounding in His Dark: Edward Brathwaite's Other Poetry." *Tapia* 7 (2 Jan. 1977): 5-7.

_____. *See also* **4.**

Reiss, Timothy J. "Reclaiming the Soul: Poetry, Autobiography, and the Voice of History." *World Literature Today* 68.4 (Autumn 1994): 683-90.

_____. *See also* **2.10.** (*Sisyphus*), **2.13.** ("Between") *and* **4.**

Rigby, Graeme. "Publishing Brathwaite: Adventures in the Video Style." *World Literature Today* 68.4 (1994): 708-14.

____. *See also* **2.11.**

Risden, Winnefred. [Review of *Masks.*] *Caribbean Quarterly* 14.1-2 (March-June 1968): 145-7.

Rodríguez, Emilio Jorge. "Oral Tradition and Recent Caribbean Poetry." In Glaser and Pausch, eds. (*see* **4.**). 1-16.

Rohlehr, Gordon. "Afterthoughts." *Tapia*, 26 Dec. 1971: 8, 13. Revised in *Bim* 14.56 (1973): 227-32.

____. "Black/ground Music to *Rights of Passage.*" *Caribbean Quarterly* 26.1-2 (1980): 32-40.

____. "Blues and Rebellion: Edward Brathwaite's *Rights of Passage.*" In Baugh, ed. *Critics* (*see* **4.**). 63-74.

____. "Brathwaite, L. Edward." *Contemporary Poets of the English Language.* Ed. Rosalie Murphy, with James Vinson. Chicago and London: St. James P, 1970. 128-30. (And in 2nd edn., 1975:136-7.)

____. "Brathwaite with a Dash of Brown: Crit, the Writer and the Written Life." In his *Shape* 209-47.

____. "Bridges of Sound: An Approach to Edward Kamau Brathwaite's *Jah.*" *Caribbean Quarterly* 26.1-2 (1980): 13-31.

____. "The Carrion Time." *Tapia* 4 (June 1974) 5-8, 11. Revised as "A Carrion Time" in *Bim* 15.58 (1975): 92-109.

____. "The Creative Writer and West Indian Society." *Kaie* (Georgetown) 11 (Aug. 1973): 48-77.

____. "Dream Journeys." [Introduction to] *DreamStories.* Harlow: Longman, 1994. iii-xvi.

____. "Dream Journeys." *World Literature Today* 68.4 (Autumn 1994): 765-74.

____. "George Lamming and Kamau Brathwaite: Nationalists, Caribbean Regionalists, Internationalists." Central Bank Lecture, 1999. Typescript.

____. "Gordon Rohlehr Talks to E. A. Markham about Edward Brathwaite's *X/Self.*" *Artrage* 18 (Autumn 1989): 27-9.

____. "The Historian as Poet." *Literary Half-Yearly* 11.2 (1970): 171-8.

____. "History as Absurdity." In Orde Coombs, ed. *Is Massa Day Dead? Black Moods in the Caribbean.* Garden City, NY: Doubleday Anchor, 1974. 69-109.

____. "Introduction." In S. Brown, M. Morris and G. Rohlehr, eds. *Voiceprint: An Anthology of Oral and Related Poetry from the Caribbean.* Harlow: Longman, 1989. 1-23.

____. "Islands." [Review.] *Caribbean Studies* 10.4 (1971): 173-202.

____. "Megalleons of Light: Edward Brathwaite's *Sun Poem.*" *Jamaica Journal* 16.2 (1983): 81-7.

____. "Metaphors of Making: Art, Craft and the Creative Process in Brathwaite's Poetry." In Knowles and Smilowitz, eds. 71-94. *See* **4.**

____. *My Strangled City and Other Essays.* Port of Spain: Longman, 1992.

____. "New Dimensions in West Indian Poetry: *Rights of Passage.*" *Pivot* 2 (25 Oct. 1968).

____. *Pathfinder: Black Awakening in* The Arrivants *of Edward Kamau Brathwaite.* Tunapuna: Gordon Rohlehr, 1981. 2nd impn. 1992. (Also contains essays additional to some listed here.)

_____. "The Problem of the Problem of Form." *Caribbean Quarterly* 31.1 (1985): 1-52.

_____. "The Rehumanisation of History: Regeneration of Spirit, Apocalypse and Revolution in Brathwaite's *The Arrivants* and *X/Self.*" In his *Shape*. 248-92.

_____. "The Rehumanization of History: Regeneration of Spirit: Apocalypse and Revolution in Brathwaite's *The Arrivants* and *X/Self.*" In Brown, ed., *Art*. 163-207.

_____. [Review of *Islands*.] *Caribbean Quarterly* 16.4 (1970): 29-35.

_____. [Review of *Rights of Passage*.] *Moko*, 9 April 1969: 2.

_____. "Rohlehr on Brathwaite." In E.·A. Markham, ed. *Hinterland: Caribbean Poetry from the West Indies and Britain*. Newcastle upon Tyne: Bloodaxe, 1989. 109-16.

_____. *The Shape of That Hurt and Other Essays*. Port of Spain, Longman, 1992.

_____. "Songs of the Skeleton—A Poetry of Fission." *Trinidad and Tobago Review* (1980): 12-13 [Part I: "Petit Careme"]; (1980), 10, 15, 20 [Part II: "Divali"].

_____. "Songs of the Skeleton: Part III. Flowers of the Harmattan: Brathwaite's *Black + Blues* Examined." In Jackson and Allis, eds. 201-17. *See* **4.**

_____. "'This Past I Borrowed': Time, History, and Art in Brathwaite's *Masks*." *Caribbean Studies* 17.3-4 (Oct. 1977-Jan. 1978): 5-82.

_____. "West Indian Poetry: Some Problems of Assessment." *Tapia*, 29 Aug. 1971: 11-14. Revised in *Bim* 14.54 (1972): 80-8 [Part 1]; 14.55 (1972): 134-43 [Part 2].

_____. "'When Gullstone Clash with Hop-a-long Cass' or Cricket and the Colonial Experience: A Reading of Brathwaite's 'Rites'." *Trinidad and Tobago Review* 1.2 (31 July 1977): 9-12.

_____. *See also* **2.6.2.** ("CAM Comment")

Saakana, Amon Saba. *The Colonial Legacy in Caribbean Literature*. London: Karnak House, 1987. 103-7.

Sail, Lawrence. "Poetry Chronicle II (*X/Self*)." *Stand* (Leeds) 29.2 (Spring 1988): 73-4.

Samad, Daizal R. "Wholeness and Home in Edward Brathwaite's *Rights of Passage*." *World Literature Written in English* 35.1 (1996): 99-110.

Savory, Elaine. "Africa in the Caribbean: The Literary Case." In Cobley and Thompson, eds. 123-43.

_____. "Jean Rhys, Race and Caribbean/English Criticism." *Wasafiri* 28 (Autumn 1998): 33-4.

_____. "Returning to Sycorax/Prospero's Response: Kamau Brathwaite's Word Journey." In Brown, ed., *Art*. 208-230.

_____. "Spectrum and Prism: The Language of Contemporary Caribbean Anglophone Poetry." *Bim* 18.69 (1985): 73-8.

_____. "The Word Becomes Nam: Self and Community in the Poetry of Kamau Brathwaite, and Its Relation to Caribbean Culture and Postmodern Theory." In John Hawley, ed. *Writing the Nation: Self and Country in the Post-Colonial Imagination*. Amsterdam: Rodopi, 1996. 23-43.

_____. "Wordsongs & Wordwounds/Homecoming: Kamau Brathwaite's *Barabajan Poems.*" *World Literature Today* 68.4 (Autumn 1994): 750-57.

_____. *See also* **4.**

Savory, Jenny. *Glossary and Notes on Poems by Edward Kamau Brathwaite.* London: Inner London Education Authority, 1988.

Scott, David. "An Obscure Miracle of Connection: Discursive Tradition and Black Diaspora Criticism." *Small Axe* 1 (March 1997): 19-38.

Senenu, K. E. "Brathwaite's Song of Dispossession." *Universitas* (Stuttgart) I (March 1969): 59-63.

Shepherd, Verene, and Glen Richards, eds. *Konversations in Creole. The Creole Society Model Revisited: Essays in Honour of Kamau Brathwaite. Caribbean Quarterly* 44.1-2 (March-June 1998). (This collection's essays use KB's work as point of origin, not usually as sole focus, and are not listed separately: O. Nigel Bolland, Carolyn Allen, Maureen Warner-Lewis, Rhoda Reddock, Veronica Gregg, Verene Shepherd, Hilary Beckles, Swithin Wilmot, Lucie Pradel, Carolyn Cooper, Mary Morgan; poems by Jean Small and Lorna Goodison.)

_____. *See above*: Lazarus-Shepherd and Richards, eds.

Slemon, Stephen, and Helen Tiffin, eds. *After Europe: Critical Theory and Post Colonial Writing.* Mundelstrup: Dangeroo P, 1989.

Small, Jean. "Po'm for Kamau." *Caribbean Quarterly* 44.1-2 (March-June 1998): 177-82.

St. John, Janet. [Review of *Black + Blues.*] *Booklist* 92.3 (1 Oct. 1995): 246.

Thomas, Kathryn. "Sunken Treasure" [Review of *Middle Passages*]. *CRNLE Reviews Journal* (Adelaide, Australia) 1 (1994): 142-5.

Thomas, Sue. "Sexual Politics in Edward Brathwaite's *Mother Poem* and *Sun Poem.*" *Kunapipi* 9.1 (1987): 33-43.

Torres-Saillant, Silvio. "Caribbean Poetics: Aesthetics of Marginality in West Indian Literature." Ph.D. diss., New York University, 1991.

_____. *Caribbean Poetics: Toward an Aesthetic of West Indian Literature.* Cambridge: Cambridge UP, 1997. 93-155

_____. "The Trials of Authenticity in Kamau Brathwaite." *World Literature Today* 68.4 (Autumn 1994): 697-707.

_____. *See also* **2.13.** ("Kamau Brathwaite")

Tuma, Keith. "Edward Kamau Brathwaite's *X/Self* and Black British Poetry." In his *Fishing by Obstinate Isles: Modern and Postmodern British Poetry and American Readers.* Evanston, IL: Northwestern UP, 1999. 244-64.

_____. "What Did I Do To Get So Black and Blue?" [Review of *Black + Blues*[2].] *American Book Review* 17.3 (Feb.-March 1996): 8.

Walcott, Derek. "Tribal Flutes: Review of *Rights of Passage.*" *Sunday Guardian Magazine* (Trinidad), 19 March 1967: 2-3.

Walmsley, Anne. *The Caribbean Artists Movement 1966-1972: A Literary and Cultural History.* London and Port of Spain: New Beacon, 1992.

_____. "Dimensions of Song: A Comment on the Poetry of Derek Walcott and Edward Brathwaite." *Bim* 13.51 (July-December 1970): 152-67.

____. "Her Stem Singing: Kamau Brathwaite's *Zea Mexican Diary: 7 Sept 1926-7 Sept 1986.*" *World Literature Today* 68.4 (Autumn 1994): 747-9.

____. "A Sense of Community: Kamau Brathwaite and the Caribbean Artists Movement." In Brown, ed. *Art.* 101-16.

____. *See also* **2.6.2.** ("Timehri" [extract])

Warner-Lewis, Maureen. "Africa: Submerged Mother." In Brown, ed. *Art.* 52-61.

____. E. *Kamau Brathwaite's Masks: Essays and Annotations.* Kingston: Institute of Caribbean Studies, UWI: 1992. [Reissue of *Notes* (below), with revised version of "Odomankoma"]

____. "Image and Idiom in Nationalist Literature: Achebe, Ngugi, and Brathwaite." In Eckhart Breitinger and Reinhard Sander, eds. *Studies in Commonwealth Literature.* Bayreuth: Günter Narr, Tübingen, 1985. 105-114.

____. "The Meaning of Religious Metaphor in Edward Brathwaite's *Islands.*" In Jackson and Allis, ed. (*see* **4.**). 183-94.

____. *Notes to* Masks. Benin City: Ethiope Publishing, 1977. [Reissued as E. *Kamau Brathwaite's* Masks (*above*).]

____. "Odomankoma 'Kyerema Se'." *Caribbean Quarterly* 19.2 (1973): 51-99.

____. [Review of *Islands.*] *Black Orpheus* (Ibadan) 2.5-6 (1970): 72-4.

Waters, Erika J., ed. "Birthday Tribute: Kamau Brathwaite." [Fenwick/Cooper interview (see **2.11**); poems by Opal Palmer Adisa ("Head in Idea"), Lelawattee Manoo-Rahming ("email to Kamau Brathwaite"), June Owens ("The Spinning in the Rock"), Middleton Wilson ("We Salute Our Griot"), Geoffrey Philip ("to an exiled poet"), Elaine Savory ("Wishing for Fire: for Therese"), Kwame Dawes ("Holy Dub"), Kamau Brathwaite ("Limbo")]. *The Caribbean Writer* 14 (2000): 75-111.

Webster, Rudi. "Salutation...to Kamau Brathwaite on the Presentation of the 1994 Neustadt Prize." *World Literature Today* 68.4 (Autumn 1994): 661-3.

Weinberger, Eliot. "Kamau Brathwaite." In his *Written Reaction: Poetics, Politics, Polemics, 1979-1995.* New York: Marsilio, 1996. 170-1.

____. *See also* **2.12.1.** (*KB and Allen Ginsberg*)

Weinstein, Norman. "Jazz in the Caribbean Air." *World Literature Today* 68.4 (Autumn 1994): 715-18.

Weiss, Jason. [Review of KB, *Barabajan Poems.*] *Review: Latin American Literature and Arts* 51 (Fall 1995): 92-4.

Wheeler, Elizabeth Anne. "Unthinkable Cities: Kingston and Los Angeles." Ph.D. diss., University of California, Berkeley, 1996.

Williams, Emily Allen. *Poetic Negotiation of Identity in the Works of Brathwaite, Harris, Senior, and Dabydeen: Tropical Paradise Lost and Regained.* Lewiston, NY: Edwin Mellen P, 1999.

____. "Whose Words Are These? Lost Heritage and Search for Self in Edward Brathwaite's Poetry." *College Language Association Journal* 1 (Sept. 1996): 104-11.

Williams, Marvin E. [Review of *The Art of Kamau Brathwaite*, ed. Stewart Brown.] *Caribbean Writer* 11 (1997): 262-3.

Wilson-Tagoe, Nana. "The Backward Glance: African Continuities a Gateway to Definition in Caribbean Writing: Harris, Lamming and Brathwaite Re-Examined." In Ikonne, Eko and Oku, eds. (*see* **4.**). 43-54.

_____. "Edward Brathwaite and Submerged History: The Aesthetics of Renaissance." In her *Historical Thought and Literary Representation in West Indian Literature*. Gainesville: UP of Florida; Barbados, Mona, Jamaica, Trinidad: PU of the West Indies; Oxford: James Currey, 1998. 182-222 (Chapter 8).

_____. "Edward Brathwaite: Poems." In David Dabydeen, ed. *A Handbook for Teaching Caribbean Literature*. London: Heinemann, 1989. 105-15.

_____. "Tradition and the Creative Imagination: The Poetry of Christopher Okigbo and Edward Brathwaite." In Samuel Omo Asein, ed. *Comparative Approaches to Modern African Literature*. Ibadan: Ibadan UP, 1982. 133-52.

_____. *See also* Dabydeen and Wilson-Tagoe.

Winship, Janice. "The River, Sea and Time: With Special Reference to Edward Brathwaite, Alejo Carpentier, and Wilson Harris." *Sussex AFRAS Journal* 1 (Spring 1972).

World Literature Today 68.4 (Fall 1994). Ed. Djelal Kadir. (Special issue on KB in honor of his winning the Neustadt Prize.)

4. Other Secondary Materials Cited in This Collection

Achebe, Chinua. *Conversations with Chinua Achebe*. Ed. Bernth Lindfors. Jackson: UP of Mississippi, 1997.

Ackroyd, Peter. *Blake: A Biography*. New York: Ballantine, 1995.

Addison, Joseph, Richard Steele, *et al. The Spectator*. 4 vols. Ed. Gregory Smith. 1909; rpt. London: Dent; New York: Dutton, 1979.

Allsopp, Richard. *Dictionary of Caribbean English Usage*. Oxford: Oxford UP, 1996.

Althusser, Louis. "Part One: From *Capital* to Marx's Philosophy." In Althusser and Étienne Balibar. *Reading Capital*. Trans. Ben Brewster. London: NLB, 1970. 11-69.

Altmann, Gerry T. M. *The Ascent of Babel: An Exploration of Language, Mind and Understanding*. Oxford: Oxford UP, 1997.

Ashcroft, Bill, Gareth Griffiths and Helen Tiffin. *The Empire Writes Back: Theory and Practice in Post-Colonial Literatures*. London: Routledge, 1989.

_____. *Key Concepts in Post Colonial Studies*. London and New York: Routledge, 1998.

_____, eds. *The Post-Colonial Studies Reader*. London: Routledge, 1995.

Axtell, James. *The European and the Indian: Essays in the Ethnohistory of Colonial North America*. New York: Oxford UP, 1981.

Bacon, Francis, Lord Verulam. *The Essayes or Counsels, Civill and Morall*. Ed. Michael Kiernan. Cambridge, MA: Harvard UP, 1985.

Badejo, Fabian A. "Introduction to Literature in English in the Dutch Windward Islands." *Callaloo* 21.3 (1998): 676-9.

Barthes, Roland. *The Pleasure of the Text*. Trans. Richard Miller. New York: Hill & Wang, 1975.

Baugh, Edward. "Ripening with Walcott." *Caribbean Quarterly* 23. 2-3 (1977): 84-90.

____, ed. *Critics on Caribbean Literature*. New York: St. Martin's P, 1978; London: Allen & Unwin, 1978.

____, and Mervyn Morris, eds. *Progressions: West Indian Literature in the 1970s*. Kingston: Dept. of English, UWI Mona, 1990.

____. *See also* **3**.

Bayley, Frederick. *Four Years' Residence in the West Indies, 1826-29*. London: William Kidd, 1833.

Beckford, George L. *Persistent Poverty: Underdevelopment in Plantation Economies of the Third World*. New York: Oxford UP, 1972.

Beckles, Hilary McD. *A History of Barbados*. Cambridge: Cambridge UP, 1989.

____, and V. Shepherd, eds. *Caribbean Freedom: Economy and Society from Emancipation to the Present*. Kingston: IRP, 1998.

Belcom, Patricia. "All Ah We Is One: Caribbean Connection in New York." *Caribbean Connections: Moving North*. In Sunshine and Warner, eds. 191-4.

Bellour, Helene, and Samuel Kinser. "Amerindian Masking in Trinidad Carnival: the House of Black Elk in San Fernando." *TDR: The Drama Review* 42. 3 (Fall 1998): 147-69.

Bennett, Tony. *Formalism and Marxism*. London: Methuen, 1979.

Blackburn, Robin. *The Making of New World Slavery: From the Baroque to the Modern 1492-1800*. London: Verso, 1997.

Blake, William. *Blake's Poetry and Designs*. Ed. Mary Lynn Johnson and John E. Grant. New York: Norton, 1979.

____. *The Complete Poems*. Ed. Alicia Ostriker. London: Penguin, 1977.

Bloom, Harold. *Shakespeare: The Invention of the Human*. New York: Riverhead Books, 1998.

Bolland, O. Nigel. "Creolization and Creole Societies: A Cultural Nationalist View of Caribbean Social History." In Alistair Hennessy, ed. *Intellectuals in the Twentieth-Century Caribbean*. Vol. I. London: Macmillan, 1992. 50-79.

Bongie, Chris. *Islands and Exiles*. Stanford: Stanford UP, 1998.

Breeze, Jean 'Binta'. *Spring Cleaning*. London: Virago P, 1992.

Bringhurst, Robert. *A Story as Sharp as a Knife: The Classical Haida Mythtellers and Their World*. Vancouver: Douglas & McIntyre, 1999.

Brown, Stewart, ed. *The Pressures of the Text: Orality, Texts and the Telling of Tales*. Birmingham: Centre of West African Studies, U of Birmingham, 1995.

____. *See also* **3**.

Bruner, Jerome S. *Acts of Meaning*. Cambridge, MA: Harvard UP, 1990.

____, with Rita Watson. *Child's Talk: Learning to Use Language*. New York: Norton, 1983.

Casimir, Jean. *La invención del Caribe*. San Juan: Editorial de la Universidad Puerto Rico, 1997. (Spanish version of *La Caraïbe: Une et divisible*.)

Césaire, Aimé. "Culture et colonisation." *Présence Africaine* n.s. 8-10 (June-Nov. 1956): 190-205.

____. *Une Tempête: d'après "La Tempête" de Shakespeare. Adaptation pour un théâtre nègre.* Festival d'Hammamet 1969. Paris: Seuil, 1974.

Clarke, Richard L. W. "From Dialectic to Différance: Rethinking Caribbean Creolisation." *Social and Economic Studies.* Forthcoming.

____. "'Roots': A Genealogy of the 'Barbadian Personality.'" In Don Marshall and Glenford Howe, eds. *The Empowering Impulse: The Nationalist Tradition of Barbados.* Kingston: Canoe P, Forthcoming 2000.

____. "Root versus Rhizome: An 'Epistemic Break' in Caribbean Thought?" *Journal of West Indian Literature.* Forthcoming.

____. *See also* 3.

Cobham, Rhonda. "Colin Ferguson, Me and I: Anatomy of a Creole Psychosis." *Transition* 67 (Fall 1995): 16-21.

Coleridge, Samuel Taylor. *Biographia Literaria or Biographical Sketches of My Literary Life and Opinions.* Ed. James Engell and W. Jackson Bate. 2 vols. (*Collected Works* 7.1-2.) Princeton: Princeton UP; London: Routledge & Kegan Paul, 1983.

Collins, Merle. "Nabel String." In Sunshine and Warner, eds. 90-1.

Craig, Susan. "Sociological Theorising in the English-Speaking Caribbean: A Review." In Craig, ed. 2.143-80.

____, ed. *Contemporary Caribbean: A Sociological Reader.* 2 vols. Maracas, Trinidad and Tobago: College P, 1981-82.

Cruikshank, Julie, with Angela Sidney, Kitty Smith and Annie Ned. *Life Lived Like a Story: Life Stories of Three Athapaskan Elders.* Lincoln: U of Nebraska P, 1990.

____. *Reading Voices / Dan dhá ts'edenintth'e: Oral and Written Interpretations of the Yukon's Past.* Vancouver: Douglas & McIntyre, 1991.

Dash, J. Michael. *The Other America: Caribbean Literature in a New World Context.* Charlottesville: UP of Virginia, 1998.

____. *See also* 3.

Dauenhauer, Nora Marks, and Richard Dauenhauer. *Haa shuká / Our Ancestors: Tlingit Oral Narratives.* Seattle: U of Washington P; Juneau: Sealaska Heritage Foundation, 1987.

____. *Haa tuwunáagu yís / For Healing Our Spirit: Tlingit Oratory.* Seattle: U of Washington P; Juneau: Sealaska Heritage Foundation, 1990.

____. *Haa kusteeyí / Our Culture: Tlingit Life Stories.* Seattle: U of Washington P; Juneau: Sealaska Heritage Foundation,1994.

Davis, Wade. *The Serpent and the Rainbow.* New York: Warner Books, 1985.

Dayan, Joan. "Introduction." In René Depestre. *A Rainbow for the Christian West.* Trans. and intro. Joan Dayan. Amherst: U of Massachusetts P, 1977. 1-106.

Deive, Carlos Esteban. *Los guerrilleros negros: Esclavos fugitivos y cimarrones en Santo Domingo.* Santo Domingo: Fundación Cultural Dominicana, 1989.

Depestre, René. *Journal d'un animal marin.* Paris: P, Seghers, 1964.

____. *Pour la révolution. Pour la poésie.* Collection Francophonie Vivante. Quebec: Lémeac, 1974.

Donoghue, Denis. "Fretting in the Other's Shadow" [review of Colm Tóibín, ed. *The Penguin Book of Irish Fiction*]. *Times Literary Supplement*, 19 Nov. 1999: 21.

Dorsainvil, Justin Chrysostome. *Manuel d'histoire d'Haïti*. Port-au-Prince: Henri Deschamps, 1934.

Du Bois, W. E. B. "Of Our Spiritual Strivings." *The Oxford W. E. B. Du Bois Reader*. Ed. Eric J. Sundquist. Oxford: Oxford UP, 1996. 101-7.

Eliot, Thomas Stearns. *Four Quartets*. New York: Harcourt, Brace & World, 1943.

_____. "The Metaphysical Poets." In *Homage to John Dryden: Three Essays on Poetry of the Seventeenth Century*. London: Leonard & Virginia Woolf at the Hogarth P, 1927. 24-33.

_____. *The Varieties of Metaphysical Poetry. The Clark Lectures at Trinity College, Cambridge, 1926, and The Turnbull Lectures at The Johns Hopkins University, 1933*. Ed. And Intro. Ronald Schuchard. New York, San Diego and London: Harcourt Brace, 1993.

_____. *The Waste Land and Other Poems*. 1930; rpt. New York: Harcourt Brace Jovanovich, 1962.

Encyclopædia Britannica: or a Dictionary of Arts and Sciences...by a Society of Gentlemen in *Scotland*. 3 vols. Edinburgh: A. Bell & C. Macfarquhar, 1771.

Erdman, David V. *Blake: Prophet Against Empire*. New York: Dover, 1977.

Fanon, Frantz. *The Wretched of the Earth*. Pref. Jean-Paul Sartre. Trans. Constance Farrington. Harmondsworth: Penguin 1963.

Felsenstein, Frank, ed. *English Trader, Indian Maid: Representing Gender, Race, and Slavery in the New World: An Inkle and Yarico Reader*. Baltimore and London: Johns Hopkins UP, 1999.

Fernández Retamar, Roberto. *Calibán: Apuntes sobre la cultura en nuestra América*. 2nd. ed. Mexico City: Editorial Diógenes, 1974.

_____. 'Caliban: Notes Toward a Discussion of Culture in Our America'. Trans. Lynn Garafola, David Arthur MacMurray, and Roberto Marquez. *Caliban and Other Essays*. Trans. Edward Baker. Minneapolis and London: U of Minnesota P, 1989. 3-45.

Fiet, Lowell, ed. *West Indian Literature and its Political Context*. Rio Piedras: Sargasso, 1988.

Forbes, Jack. *African and Native Americans: the Language of Race and the Evolution of Red-black Peoples*. Urbana: U of Illinois P, 1993.

Foreman, Caroline. *Indians Abroad, 1493-1938*. Norman, U of Oklahoma P, 1943.

Foucault, Michel. *The Order of Things*. London: Tavistock, 1970.

Froude, James Anthony. *The English and the West Indies or, The Bow of Ulysses*. 1888; rpt. New York: Charles Scribner's Sons, 1892.

Frye, Northrop. *The Anatomy of Criticism*. Princeton: Princeton UP, 1957.

_____. *Fearful Symmetry*. Princeton: Princeton UP, 1947.

Galeano, Eduardo. *We Say No: Chronicles 1963-1991*. Trans. Mark Fried and others. New York: Norton, 1992.

Gates, Henry Louis, Jr.. *The Signifying Monkey A Theory of African American Literary Criticism*. Oxford: Oxford UP, 1988.

Gilroy, Beryl. *Inkle and Yarico. Being the narrative of Thomas Inkle concerning his shipwreck and long sojourn among the Caribs and his marriage to Yarico, a Carib woman.* Leeds: Peepal Tree P, 1996.

Glaser, Marlies, and Marion Pausch, eds. *Caribbean Writers: Between Orality and Writing. Matatu* (Mainz) 12. Amsterdam and Atlanta: Rodopi, 1994.

Glissant, Edouard. *Caribbean Discourse: Selected Essays.* Trans. J. Michael Dash. Charlottesville: UP of Virginia, 1989.

____. *Faulkner, Mississippi.* Paris: Gallimard, 1996.

____. *Poétique de la relation.* Paris: Gallimard, 1990.

____. *Tout-Monde.* Paris: Gallimard, 1993.

Gombrowicz, Witold. *Diary.* Ed. Jan Kott. Trans. Lillian Vallee. 3 vols. Evanston: Northwestern UP, 1988-93.

Gomez, Michael A. *Exchanging Our Country Marks: The Transformation of African Identities in the Colonial and Antebellum South.* Chapel Hill and London: U of North Carolina P, 1998.

González Echevarria, Roberto. *The Voice of the Masters.* Austin: U of Texas P, 1985.

Goody, Jack. *The Interface between the Literate and the Oral.* Cambridge and New York: Cambridge UP, 1987.

Green, William A. "The Creolisation of Caribbean History: The Emancipation Era and a Critique of Dialectical Analysis." *The Journal of Imperial and Commonwealth History* 14.3 (1986): 149-64.

Hall, Richard. *Acts, passed in the island of Barbados. From 1643-1762....* London: For R. Hall, 1764.

Handler, Jerome. "The Amerindian Slave Population of Barbados in the Seventeenth and Early Eighteenth Centuries," *Caribbean Studies* 8 (1968): 38-64.

Harris, Wilson. *The Guyana Quartet.* London and Boston: Faber & Faber, 1985.

____. *The Womb of Space: The Cross-Cultural Imagination.* Westport, CT and London: Greenwood P, 1983.

Hartsock, Nancy. "The Feminist Standpoint: Developing the Ground for a Specifically Feminist Historical Materialism." In Sandra Kemp and Judith Squires, eds. *Feminisms.* Oxford: Oxford UP, 1997. 152-160.

Hawking, Stephen W. *A Brief History of Time: From the Big Bang to Black Holes.* New York and Toronto, 1988.

Hayakawa, Samuel I. *Language in Action.* New York: Harcourt Brace, 1941.

Hoetink, Harry. "'Colonial Psychology' and Race." In Jerold Heiss, ed. *Readings on the Sociology of the Caribbean.* New York: MSS Educational, 1970. 147-51.

Horovitz, M., ed. *Children of Albion: Poetry of the Underground in Britain.* London: Penguin, 1969.

Ikonne, Chidi, Ebele Eko, and Julie Oku, eds. *Black Culture and Black Consciousness in Literature.* Calabar Studies in African Literature 2 (General Editor, Ernest N. Emenyonu). Ibadan: Heinemann Educational, 1987.

Jackson, J., and Jeanette B. Allis, eds. *West Indian Poetry: Proceedings of the Fifth Annual Conference on West Indian Literature.* St. Thomas: College of the Virgin Islands, 1989.

Jacobs, Wilbur. *Dispossessing the American Indian*. Norman: U of Oklahoma P, 1972.

James, Cyril Lionel Robert. *The Black Jacobins: Toussaint L'Ouverture and the San Domingo Revolution*. 2nd edn., revised. New York: Vintage, 1963.

Jameson, Frederic. *The Political Unconscious: Narrative as a Socially-Symbolic Act*. Ithaca and London: Cornell UP, 1981.

Jauss, Hans Robert. "Literary History as a Challenge to Literary Theory." *Toward an Aesthetic of Reception*. Trans. Timothy Bahti. Minneapolis and London: U of Minnesota P, 1982. 3-45.

Jousse, Marcel. *The Anthropology of Geste and Rhythm: Studies in the Anthropological Laws of Human Expression and Their Application in the Galilean Oral Style Tradition*. Trans. Edgard Sienaert with Joan Conolly. Durban: U of Natal, Centre for Oral Studies, 1997.

Joyce, James. *Portrait of the Artist as a Young Man*. 1916; rpt. New York: Viking, 1960.

Karch, Cecilia A. "The Growth of the Corporate Economy In Barbados: Class/ Race Factors, 1890-1977." In Craig, ed. 1.213-41.

Kawashima, Yasuhide. "Indian Servitude in the Northeast." In Washburn, ed. 404-6.

Kempen, Michiel van. "Vernacular Literature in Surinam." *Callaloo* 21.3 (1998): 630-44.

Kincaid, Jamaica. *In a Small Place*. London: Virago, 1988.

King, Bruce Alvin, ed. *Literatures of the World in English*. London and Boston: Routledge & Kegan Paul, 1974.

____, ed. *New National and Post-Colonial Literatures: An Introduction*. Oxford: Clarendon; New York: Oxford UP, 1996.

____, ed. *West Indian Literature*. Hamden, CT: Archon, 1979; London: Macmillan, 1979. 2nd edn.: London: Macmillan Educational, 1995.

____. *See also* **3**.

Knowles, Roberta Quarles, and Erika Sollish Smilowitz, eds. *Critical Approaches to West Indian Literature*. St. Thomas: College of the Virgin Islands, 1981.

Kundera, Milan. "The Umbrella, the Night World, and the Lonely Moon." *The New York Review of Books*, 19 December 1991: 46-50.

Lacroix, Pamphile de. *La Revolution de Haiti*. Ed. Pierre Pluchon. Paris: Karthala, 1995. (1st edn. 1819.)

Laguerre, Michel S. *American Odyssey: Haitians in New York City*. Ithaca and London: Cornell UP, 1984.

Lamming, George. *In the Castle of My Skin*. 1953; rpt. New York: Schocken, 1983.

____. *Of Age and Innocence*. London and New York: Allison & Busby, 1981.

____. *The Pleasures of Exile*. London: Michael Joseph, 1960.

Lauber, Almon. *Indian Slavery in Colonial Times within the Present Limits of the United States*. New York: privately printed, 1913.

Lees, Gene. *Cats of Any Color*. New York: Oxford UP, 1994.

Lepore, Jill. *The Name of War: King Philip's War and the Origins of American Identity*. New York: Knopf, 1998.

Lévy-Bruhl, Lucien. *How Natives Think*. Trans. Lilian A. Clare. New intro. C. Scott Littleton. Princeton: Princeton UP, 1985.

____. *Primitive Mentality*. Trans. Lilian A. Clare. London: George Allen & Unwin; New York: Macmillan, 1923.

Lewis, Gordon K. *The Growth of the Modern West Indies*. London: MacGibbon and Kee, 1968.

____. *Main Currents in Caribbean Thought: The Historical Evolution of Caribbean Society in Its Ideological Aspects*. Baltimore and London: Johns Hopkins UP, 1983.

Liebenberg, Louis. *The Art of Tracking: The Origin of Science*. Clairemont, South Africa: D. Philips, 1990.

Ligon, Richard. *A True and Exact History of the Island of Barbadoes: illustrated with a map of the island and also the Principal Trees and Plants there, Set forth in their Proportions and Shapes, drawn out by their several and respective Scales....* London: Frank Cass, 1970. (1ˢᵗ edn. London: privately printed, 1657; 2ⁿᵈ edn. London: for Peter Parker & Thomas Guy, 1673.)

Locke, John. *Political Essays,* Cambridge: Cambridge University Press, 1997.

Lowenthal, David. *West Indian Societies*. Oxford: Oxford UP, 1972.

Lukács, Georg. *The Historical Novel*. Trans. Hannah and Stanley Mitchell. Boston: Beacon, 1962.

____. *History and Class Consciousness: Studies in Marxist Dialectics*. Trans. Rodney Livingstone. London: Merlin, 1971.

Marcuse, Herbert. *Reason and Revolution: Hegel and the Rise of Social Theory*. 2ⁿᵈ edn. London: Routledge & Kegan Paul, 1955.

Marks, Emerson R. *Taming the Chaos: English Poetic Diction Theory since the Renaissance*. Detroit: Wayne State UP, 1998.

Marshall, Paule. *The Chosen Place, the Timeless People*. New York: Vintage, 1984.

Martin, Joel. "Southeastern Indians and the English Trade in Skins and Slaves." In Charles M. Hudson and Carmen Chaves Tesser, eds. *The Forgotten Centuries: Indians and Europeans in the American South, 1521-1704*. Athens: U of Georgia P, 1994. 304-24.

McDonald, Ian. "Katha; or a culture for the world." *Vista* (NCB Group with the Faculty of Arts, UWI) 4.2. (June-August 1997): 1-4.

McFarlane, Anthony. *The British in the Americas, 1480-1815*. London: Longman, 1994.

McKay, Claude. *Selected Poems*. New York: Bookman Associates, 1953.

McLuhan, Marshall. *The Gutenberg Galaxy: The Making of Typographic Man*. Toronto: U of Toronto P, 1962.

McWatt, Mark A. *The Language of Eldorado*. Sydney, Mundelstrup and Hebden Bridge: Dangaroo P, 1994.

____, ed. *West Indian Literature and Its Social Context*. Cave Hill: UWI, 1985.

____. *See also* **3.**

Melville, Herman. *Moby Dick: An Authoritative Text; Reviews and Letters by Melville; Analogues and Sources; Criticism*. Ed. Harrison Hayford and Hershel Parker. New York: Norton, 1967.

Métellus, Jean. *Anacaona*. Paris: Hatier, 1986.

Miller, Christopher L. *Nationalists and Nomads: Essays on Francophone African Literature and Culture*. Chicago and London: U of Chicago P, 1998.

Mintz, Sidney W. "Groups, Group Boundaries and the Perception of 'Race.'" *Comparative Studies in Society and History* 13 (1971): 437-50.

Mir, Pedro. *Tres leyendas de colores: Ensayo de interpretación de las tres primeras revoluciones del Nuevo Mundo*. 2nd edn. Santo Domingo: Editora Taller, 1978. (1st edn. 1969.)

Monet, Don, and Skanu'u (Ardythe Wilson). *Colonialism on Trial: Indigenous Land Rights and the Gitksan and Wet'suwet'en Sovereignty Case*. Gabriola Island: New Society Publishers 1992.

Montaigne, Michel Eyquem de. *The Complete Works of Montaigne*. Trans. Donald M. Frame. Stanford University Press, 1957.

Morisseau-Leroy, Félix. "Botpipèl." In Sunshine and Warner, eds. 148-49.

Morris, Mervyn. *"Is English We Speaking" and Other Essays*. Kingston: Ian Randle, 1999.

_____. See also Baugh and Morris, eds. and 3.

Moya Pons, Frank. *La dominación haitiana: 1822-1844*. Santiago: UCMM, 1972.

Mphahlele, Ezekiel [Es'kia]. *Down Second Avenue*. 1959; rpt. London and Boston: Faber & Faber, 1980.

Nepaulsingh, Colbert I. "Things Fall Apart; The Center Cannot Hold." *Latino Review of Books*. (Winter 1998): 13-17.

_____. "A New Name for the Caribbean." *Latino Review of Books* (Spring 1996): 5-10.

_____. "Islands and Continents." *Latino Review of Books* (Fall 1996): 8-10.

Ngugi wa Thiong'o. *A Grain of Wheat*. London, Ibadan and Nairobi: Heinemann, 1967.

_____. *Matigari*. Trans. Wangui wa Goro. 1987; rpt. Oxford [etc.]: Heinemann, 1990.

_____. *Penpoints, Gunpoints and Dreams: Towards a Critical Theory of the Arts and the State in Africa*. Oxford: Clarendon, 1998.

_____, and Micere Githae Mugo. *The Trial of Dedan Kimathi*. 1976; rpt. Oxford [etc.]: Heinemann, 1977.

_____, and Ngugi wa Mirii. *I Will Marry When I Want*. Trans. by the authors. London, Ibadan, Nairobi: Heinemann, 1982.

Nicholls, David. *From Dessalines to Duvalier: Race, Colour and National Independence in Haiti*. Revised edn. New Brunswick, NJ: Rutgers UP, 1996.

Olexer, Barbara. *The Enslavement of the American Indian*. Intro. Stephen Paul De Villo. Monroe, NY: Library Research Associates, 1982.

Olson, David R. *The World on Paper: The Conceptual and Cognitive Implications of Writing and Reading*. Cambridge and New York: Cambridge UP, 1994.

_____. *The Written Word*. Toronto: Ontario Institute for Studies in Education, U of Toronto, 1999.

Ong, Walter J. *Orality and Literacy: The Technologizing of the Word*. London and New York: Methuen, 1982.

Ormerod, David. "Bad Talk and Sweet Speaking." [rev. of Andrew Salkey; *Anancy's Score*, and Edward Baugh, ed., *Critics on Caribbean Literature.*] *CRNLE Reviews Journal.* 1 1979, 42-45.

Palencia-Roth, Michael. "Mapping the Caribbean: Cartography and the Cannibalization of Culture." In A James Arnold, ed. *A History of Literature in the Caribbean.* Vol. 3: *Cross-Cultural Studies.* Amsterdam and Philadelphia: John Benjamins, 1997. 3-27.

Patterson, Orlando. "Context and Choice in Ethnic Allegiance: A Theoretical Framework and Caribbean Case Study." In Nathan Glazer and Daniel P. Moynihan, eds. *Ethnicity: Theory and Experience.* Cambridge, MA: Harvard UP, 1975. 305-49.

Peeters, Leopold. "Beyond Formalism in Oral Studies." *Voices: A Journal for Oral Studies* 2 (Jan. 1999): 5-21.

Philip, Marlene NourbeSe. *Frontiers: Essays and Writings on Racism and Culture 1984-1992.* Stratford, Ontario: Mercury P, 1992.

____. *A Genealogy of Resistance and Other Essays.* Toronto: Mercury P, 1997.

____. *Looking for Livingstone: An Odyssey of Silence.* Toronto: Mercury P, 1991.

____. *She Tries Her Tongue, Her Silence Softly Breaks.* Charlottetown, P.E.I.: Ragweed P, 1989.

Phillips, Caryl. [Review of Glissant, *Faulkner, Mississippi.*] *The New Republic,* 27 Dec. 1999, 33-8.

Pinckard, George. *Notes on the West Indies; written during the expedition under the command of the late General Sir Ralph Abercromby....* 3 vols. 1806; rpt. Westport, CT: Negro Universities P, 1970.

Pinder, Leslie. *The Carriers of No: After the Land Claims Trial.* Vancouver: Lazara P, 1991.

Polanyi, John. "The Magic of Science." *The Canadian Federation for the Humanities Bulletin* 16.3 (Winter 1994): 6-11.

Pollard, Velma. *Considering Woman.* London: The Women's P, 1989.

Popper, Karl R. "What Is Dialectic?" *Conjectures and Refutations: The Growth of Scientific Knowledge.* London: Routledge, 1992. 312-35.

Ramchand, Kenneth. "Introduction." In C. L. R. James, *Minty Alley.* London and Port of Spain: New Beacon, 1971. 5-15.

____. *See also* **3.**

Redfield, Robert. *Peasant Society and Culture: An Anthropological Approach to Civilization.* Chicago: U of Chicago P, 1956.

Reiss, Timothy J. *The Discourse of Modernism.* Ithaca and London: Cornell UP, 1982.

____. *The Meaning of Literature.* Ithaca and London: Cornell UP, 1992.

____. *See also* **2.10.** (*Sisyphus*), **2.13.** ("Between") *and* **3.**

Rutgers, Winn. "Dutch Caribbean Literature." *Callaloo* 21.3 (1998): 542-55.

Said, Edward. *Culture and Imperialism.* New York: Knopf, 1993.

Salick, Royden, ed. *The Comic Vision in West Indian Literature.* St. Augustine: UWI, 1993.

Sánchez, Luis Rafael. "The Flying Bus." Trans. Elpidio Laguna-Díaz. In Asila Rodríguez de Laguna, ed. *Images and Identities: Puerto Ricans in Two World*

Contexts. New Brunswick and Oxford: Transaction Books, 1987. 17-25.

Sapir, Edward. "The Status of Linguistics as a Science." *Language* 5 (1929): 207-14.

Savory, Elaine. "miranda: the first voicing." *The Caribbean Writer* 12 (1998): 63-72. (Revised version in this collection.)

____. *See also* **3.**

Shakespeare, William. *The Tempest.* Cambridge: Cambridge UP, 1948.

Skanu'u (Ardythe Wilson). *See* Monet and Skanu'u.

Smith, John. *The Capture and Release of Captain John Smith. Including his rescue from death by Pocahontas. In his own Words from The Generall Historie of Virginia as published at London in 1624.* [Ann Arbor, MI]: Reprinted for The Clements Library Associates, 1960.

Smith, M. G. *The Plural Society in the British West Indies.* Berkeley: U of California P, 1965.

Stock, Brian. *The Implications of Literacy: Written Language and Models of Interpretation in the Eleventh and Twelfth Centuries.* Princeton: Princeton UP, 1983.

____. *Listening for the Text: On the Uses of the Past.* Baltimore and London: Johns Hopkins UP, 1990.

Sunshine, Catherine, and Keith Q. Warner, eds. *Caribbean Connections: Moving North.* Washington, DC.: Network of Educators on the Americas, 1998.

Sylvain, Georges. *Confidences et mélancolies.* Port-au-Prince: Henri Deschamps, 1979. (1st edn. 1898.)

Thomas, John Jacob. *Froudacity: West Indian Fables Explained.* 2nd edn. London: J. Fisher Unwin, 1889.

Thomson, James. *The Seasons and the Castle of Indolence.* Ed. James Sambrook. 1972; rpt. Oxford: Oxford UP, 1984.

Torres-Saillant, Silvio. *Caribbean Poetics: Toward an Aesthetic of West Indian Literature.* Cambridge: Cambridge UP, 1997.

____, and Ramona Hernández. *The Dominican Americans.* Westport, CT: Greenwood P, 1998.

____. *See also* **2.13.** ("Kamau Brathwaite")

Toumson, Roger. *Trois Calibans.* Havana: Casa de las Américas, 1981.

Trefossa [Henny de Ziel]. "Kopenhagen." *Callaloo* 21.3 (1998): 519. (Rptd. from *Trotji Püema.* Amsterdam, 1957.)

Trouillot, Michel-Rolph. *Silencing the Past: Power and the Production of History.* Boston: Beacon, 1995..

Ureña de Henríquez, Salomé. *Anacaona.* [1880.] *Poesías completas.* Santo Domingo: Ediciones de la Fundación Corripio, 1989.

Usner, Daniel H., Jr. "American Indians in Colonial New Orleans." In Peter H. Wood, Gregory A. Waselkov, and M. Thomas Hatley, eds. *Powhatan's Mantle: Indians in the Colonial Southeast.* Lincoln and London: U of Nebraska P, 1989. 104-27.

Vega, Ana Lydia. "Cloud Cover Caribbean." Trans. Mark McCaffrey. In Marcela Brown, ed. *Rhythm and Revolt: Tales of the Antilles.* New York: Plume/Penguin, 1995. 1-6.

_____. *Encancaranublado y otros cuentos de naufragio*. 3rd ed. San Juan, PR: Editorial Antillana, 1987.

Vine, Stephen. "'That Mild Beam': Enlightenment and Enslavement in William Blake's *Visions of the Daughters of Albion*." In *The Discourse of Slavery: Aphra Behn to Toni Morrison*. Ed. Carl Plasa and Betty J. Ring. London: Routledge, 1994. 40-63.

Vail, Leroy, and Landeg White. *Power and the Praise Poem: Southern African Voices in History*. Charlottesville: UP of Virginia; London: James Currey, 1991.

Wade, Mason. "French-Indian Policies." In Washburn, ed. 20-8.

Walcott, Derek. *Another Life*. New York: Farrar, Straus & Giroux, 1973.

_____. *Dream on Monkey Mountain*. London: Jonathan Cape, 1972.

_____. "The Muse of History: An Essay." In *Is Massa Day Dead? Black Moods in the Caribbean*. Ed. Orde Coombs. Garden City, NY: Doubleday Anchor, 1974. 1-27.

Walvin, James. *Black Ivory: A History of British Slavery*. London: Fontana, 1992.

Warner, Marina. *Indigo*. New York: Simon and Schuster, 1992.

Warner-Lewis, Maureen. *Trinidad Yoruba: From Mother-Tongue to Memory*, Tuscaloosa and London: U of Alabama P, 1996.

_____. *See also* **3.**

Washburn, Wilcomb. "Introduction." In Washburn, ed. 1-4.

_____, ed. *Handbook of North American Indians: vol. IV. The History of Indian-White Relations*. Washington, DC: The Smithsonian Institution P, 1988.

Whorf, Benjamin Lee. *Language, Thought, and Reality: Selected Writings of Benjamin Lee Whorf*. Ed. J. B. Carrol. Cambridge, MA: MIT P, 1956.

Wilson, Samuel M. *Hispaniola: Caribbean Chiefdoms in the Age of Columbus*. Tuscaloosa and London: U of Alabama P, 1990.

Wood, Gordon S. "The Bloodiest War." [Review of *The Name of War: King Philip's War and the Origins of American Identity* by Jill Lepore.] *New York Review of Books*, 9 April 1998: 41-4.

Contributors

Opal Palmer Adisa is a roots woman who is stepping boldly into the light. A teacher in her former life, a writer in her new life, a mother in her present life and a bringer of the healing medicine in her reincarnation. She is author of *It Begins With Tears* (1997), a novel, and *Leaf-Of-Life* (1999), a collection of poetry.

Mervyn C. Alleyne is Professor Emeritus, Linguistics, at the University of the West Indies, Mona. He was founder and head of the Language Laboratory and first head of the Department of Linguistics. He has also been Visiting Professor at a number of Universities, including SUNY (Buffalo), Yale, Indiana, Stanford, Amsterdam, Antilles-Guyane, and Puerto Rico. His major book publications are *Comparative Afro-American, Roots of Jamaican Culture, Syntaxe Historique Créole, Theoretical Issues in Caribbean Linguistics, Studies in Saramaccan Language Structure, Construction and Representation of Race and Ethnicity in the Caribbean and the World* (in press).

Isabel Balseiro is Associate Professor of Comparative Literature at Harvey Mudd College, The Claremont Colleges, California. Her work on African and Caribbean writing and film has been published in journals in the United Kingdom, the United States, and South Africa, and she has edited *Running towards Us: New Writing from South Africa* (Heinemann, 2000). Currently she is co-editing a volume on South African cinema and working on books on South African cinema and Caribbean literature and culture.

Hilary McD. Beckles is Professor of Economic and Social History at the University of the West Indies, Mona, and Pro-Vice Chancellor, Undergraduate Studies. A member of UNESCO's international task force on the Slave Route Project, he has published many books on slave society in Barbados, with special focus on women, gender and resistance. These include: *Black Rebellion in Barbados: The Struggle against Slavery 1627-1838* (Carib

Research & Publications, 1987); *Afro-Caribbean Women and Resistance to Slavery in Barbados* (Karnak House, 1988); *Natural Rebels: A Social History of Enslaved Women in Barbados* (Rutgers UP, 1989, and Zed Books, 1989); *A History of Barbados: From Amerindian Settlement to Nation-State* (Cambridge, 1990); *White Servitude and Black Slavery in Barbados, 1627-1715* (Tennessee UP, 1990); *Centering Woman: Gender Discourse in Caribbean Slave Society* (Marcus Wiener, 1999). He has an interest in the cultural history of cricket, and besides being Director and Founder of the Centre for Cricket Studies at UWI, Mona, has recently published, *The Development of West Indies Cricket*: vol. 1, *The Age of Nationalism*; vol.2, *The Age of Globalisation* (UWI Press, 2000).

Korah L. Belgrave was born and educated in Barbados at the Boscobelle Girls' School, The St. Michael Girls' School and the Combermere School. After her Bachelor's Degree in English (Literature) and Linguistics with Education at the University of the West Indies, she did a Master's Degree in Modern English Language at the University of Leeds. She started teaching as a part-time tutor at the University of the West Indies Cave Hill in 1990, and joined the staff as a full-time lecturer in 1995. In 1998, she was appointed Coordinator of the Foundation Language courses, which she teaches as well as Level One Linguistic courses. She is presently writing her PhD thesis at UWI Cave Hill on acceptability in Barbadian Language, and also has research interests in teaching English to speakers of other languages and as a second language, in nation language, and in language and identity.

Erna Brodber has been lecturer/researcher at the University of the West Indies and visiting professor at several US universities. Author of three novels, *Jane and Louisa Will Soon Come Home*, *Myal*, and *Louisiana*, as well as papers and several monographs in history and sociology, her political practice is devoted to helping the African of the diaspora find a social space. Currently resident in rural Jamaica, raising her son, and helping the community via a program called *blackspace*, she is completing a fourth novel and two texts for college students in the study of Africa and its diaspora.

Ted Chamberlin was born in Vancouver, and educated at the universities of British Columbia, Oxford and Toronto. Since 1970, he has been on the faculty of the University of Toronto, where he is now Professor of English and Comparative Literature. He has been Senior Research Associate with the Royal Commission on Aboriginal Peoples in Canada and Poetry Editor of *Saturday Night*. His books include *The Harrowing of Eden: White Attitudes Towards Native Americans* (1975), Oscar Wilde's *London* (1987), and *Come Back to Me My Language: Poetry and the West Indies* (1993). He is currently directing a project on oral and written traditions.

John Chioles divides his time between teaching Comparative Literature at New York University and Philosophy of Culture at the University of Athens. His most recent academic books are *Aeschylus: Mythic Theatre, Political Voice* and *Theory of Literature* (in Greek). He is currently working on a collection of his short stories, on a novel, and another historical and critical work, *Historiography and the Greek Novel*.

Richard Clarke is a Lecturer in Cultural and Critical Theory at the Cave Hill campus of the University of the West Indies. His research interests include rereading the canon from alternative perspectives, the study of postcolonial literatures, the history of ideas, the history of cultural and critical theory in general, and post-structuralist, feminist, and postcolonial theories in particular. He has published essays in all these areas, focusing most recently on the deficiencies of cultural nationalism.

Rhonda Cobham teaches English and Black Studies at Amherst. She has edited the Sistren Theatre Collective's play *Bellywoman Bangarang*, a collection of *Contemporary Caribbean Culture and Art* (*Massachusetts Review* 35.3-4), and co-edited *Watchers and Seekers*, an anthology of writing by Black Women in Britain. Her critical essays have appeared in *Research in African Literatures Callaloo, WLWE, Women's Review of Books, Transition, Annals of Scholarship* and in various critical anthologies. A collection of her essays is forthcoming.

Maryse Condé is well-known as novelist, playwright, critic, cultural commentator and teacher. Among her novels are *Hérémakhonon, Une saison à Rihata, Ségou* (2 vols.), *Moi, Tituba, sorcière noire de Salem* (Grand Prix Littéraire de la Femme), *La vie sclérate* (Prix Anaïs Nin de l'Académie Française), *Hugo le terrible, Traversée de la mangrove, Les derniers rois mages, La colonie du nouveau monde, La migration des coeurs, Désirada* (Prix Carbet de la Caraïbe). Her plays include *Dieu nous l'a donné, La mort d'Oluwéni d'Ajumako* and *Pension les Alizés*; her short stories and novellas, *Pays-mêlé* and *Nanna-ya*. Most are available in English. Recently her childhood memoirs, *Le coeur à rire et à pleurer: contes vrais de mon enfance* won the Prix Marguerite Yourcenar (1999). She is also the author and editor of many academic works, among them *La poésie antillaise, Le* *roman antillaise*, a commentary on Césaire's *Cahier, La parole des femmes*, the edited collections *L'héritage de Caliban, Penser la créolité*, and many essays. *Entretiens avec Maryse Condé* appeared in 1996. She currently teaches at Columbia University and divides most of her time between New York and Guadeloupe.

Isis Costa was born in Brazil and educated there and at New York University. She has lived in the US since 1989. She became a student of Kamau Brathwaite in 1992 and worked as his graduate assistant since 1993. In 1994 she started to administer Brathwaite's Savacou North. She is currently a Lecturer at Rutgers University and a doctoral candidate at NYU on the final stages of her dissertation entitled "xéNgolo Poetics: A Socio-Semiotic Reading of Afro-Brazilian Creative Texts."

J. Michael Dash, born in Trinidad, has taught in the Caribbean, Africa and the US. He has worked extensively on Haitian literature and French Caribbean writers, especially Edouard Glissant, whose work he has translated into English. After 21 years at the University of the West Indies, where he was Professor of Francophone Literature, he is now Professor of French at New York University. His publications include *Literature and Ideology in Haiti* (1981), *Haiti and the United States* (1988), *Edouard Glissant* (1995). His most recent translation is *The Drifting of Spirits* (1999) by Gisèle Pineau. His most recent books are *The Other America: Caribbean Literature in a New World Context* (1998) and *Libète: A Haiti Anthology* (1999) with Charles Arthur.

Joan Dayan, Regents Professor of English at the University of Arizona, is author of *A Rainbow for the Christian West: The Poetry of René Depestre*, of *Fables of Mind: An Inquiry into Poe's Fiction*, and many critical essays. Most recently she has published *Haiti, History, and the Gods* (University of California Press, 1995) and is now completing *Held in the Body of the State: Prisons and the Law* and a memoir called *The Law is a White Dog*. For the year 2000-1 she is a fellow in the Princeton Program in Law and Public Affairs.

Roberto Fernández Retamar was born in Havana in 1930. From *Elegía como un himno* (1950) through *Aquí* (1995), which received Venezuela's Pérez Bonalde International Poetry Prize, he has published fourteen volumes of poetry. He is also author of several books of essays, among which are *Caliban* (1971: *Caliban and Other Essays*, 1989) and *Algunos usos de civilisación y barbarie* (1989). His work has been translated into more than a dozen languages. Among his many awards are Cuba's National Prize for Literature, the rank of Officer in France's Order of Arts and Letters, and honorary doctorates from the Universities of Buenos Aires and Sofia. He has been visiting professor at Yale University, and is Emeritus Professor at the University of Havana and President of the Casa de las Americas.

Honor Ford-Smith is a writer, performer and teacher. She was founding director of the Jamaican theatre Company Sistren with whom she wrote several plays and a collection of life histories called *Lionheart Gal*. Her most recent publication is a collection of poems called *My Mother's Last Dance*. Presently she teaches at the University of Toronto at Scarborough and is completing her PhD at the Ontario Institute for Studies in Education at the University of Toronto.

Lorna Goodison was born in Jamaica and now lives in Toronto and teaches in the English Department at the University of Toronto. Recipient of many awards in poetry and prose, including Jamaica's Musgrave Gold Medal in 1999, she has been a central figure at international conferences and festivals, among them a special evening in her honor sponsored by the Research Institute for the Study of Man and the Commonwealth of Letters (Yale University) in New York, which published a chapbook of her work. She regularly reads at schools, cultural centers and hospitals in rural as well as urban communities throughout the world, to children, workers and others whose lives are not often shaped by poetry. She has conducted special workshops in the United States, Canada, Europe and the West Indies, and taught previously at the University of Toronto, the Sitka Summer Institute in Alaska, the University of Miami Caribbean Summer Institute, the University of the West Indies Caribbean Writers Program and, for the past seven years, the University of Michigan. Her poetry has been translated into several languages, published widely in magazines and included in the major anthologies and collections of Caribbean poetry published in the West Indies, Europe and the United States, and most recently in the *HarperCollins World Reader*, the *Vintage Book of Contemporary World Poetry*, and the *Norton Anthology of World Masterpieces*. Her paintings have been exhibited throughout the Americas and in Europe. Her collection of short stories, *Baby Mother and the King of Swords* appeared in 1990. Her books of poetry include *Tamarind Season* (1980), *I Am Becoming My Mother* (1986), *Heartease* (1988), *Selected Poems* (1992), *To Us, All Flowers Are Roses* (1995), and *Turn Thanks* (1999). Carcanet published her latest collection, *Guinea Woman*, this year.

Patricia J. Penn Hilden is Professor of Comparative Ethnic Studies at the University of California, Berkeley, where she teaches Native American history and comparative ethnic studies. Holder of a Ph. D. from Cambridge University, she is a descendant of Chief Joseph's band of Wolowa Valley Nez Perces. She is the author of *Working Women and Socialist Politics in France, 1880-1914* (Oxford 1986), *Women, Work, and Politics: Belgium, 1830-1914* (Oxford 1993), and *When Nickels Were Indians: An Urban, Mixed Blood Story* (Smithsonian 1995, 1997). Author of many essays on both European and North American history and represented in anthologies of American Indian writers, she has most recently published essays and book chapters on issues of race and representation in Europe and the Americas. Her principal ongoing projects concern the history of race and ethnicity in the western US, the representation of ethnicity in museums, and North American natives in the Caribbean slave trade.

Cynthia James is a Trinidadian writer whose work has been published in regional and international journals such as *World Literature Today, Massachusetts Review*, *The Caribbean Writer*, *Sisters of Caliban*, *The Lincoln Theatre Review* and the *Trinidad and Tobago Review*. She graduated with a Ph.D. in Caribbean literature from Howard University, Washington D.C. Her novel *Bluejean* was published this year by GreenTree Press (Port of Spain).

Ralph Jemmott is currently Head of the History department at Harrison College in Barbados, Brathwaite's alma mater. He was one of the first students to take EKB's groundbreaking course at the Mona campus of UWI of which he writes in his contribution. He is a regular commentator on social and historical affairs in the Barbadian media. In recent years, although a historian by training, he has devoted much of his academic energy to educational and pedagogical issues, his most recent essays appearing in *The Journal of the Barbados Museum and Historical Society*.

Linton Kwesi Johnson was born in Jamaica in 1952 and moved to London in 1963. He early joined the Black Panthers, helped organize a poetry workshop in the movement and worked with Rasta Love, a group of poets and drummers, later studying Sociology at London University. In 1977 he won a C Day Lewis Fellowship and was that year's writer-in-residence for the London Borough of Lambeth. He then worked as Library Resources and Education Officer at the Keskidee Centre, first home of Black theatre and art in Britain. In the 1980s he worked as a journalist closely with the Brixton-based Race Today collective. BBC Radio 1 broadcast his 10-part radio series on Jamaican popular music, *From Mento to Lovers Rock*, in 1982, repeating it in 1983. From 1985-8 he was a reporter on Channel 4's *The Bandung File*. Today he tours the world, runs his own record label, and is renowned as the world's first reggae poet. He has published four volumes of poetry, *Voices of the Living and the Dead* (1974), *Dread Beat An' Blood* (1975), *Inglan Is A Bitch* (1980) and *Tings An' Times* (1991) and twelve albums, *Dread Beat An' Blood* (1978), *Forces of Victory* (1979), *Bass Culture* (1980), *LKJ in Dub* (1981), *Making History* (1983), *LKJ Live in Concert with the Dub Band* (1985), nominated for a Grammy Award, *Tings and Times* (1991), *LKJ in Dub: Volume Two* (1992), *LKJ Presents* (1996), *LKJ A Cappella Live* (1996), *More Time* (1998) and *Independant Intavenshan* (2 CDs, 1998). *Dread Beat An' Blood*, a documentary film on his work, was released in 1978. He is an Associate Fellow of Warwick University (1985), Honorary Fellow of Wolverhampton Polytechnic (1987), winner at the XIII Premo Internazionale Ultimo Novecento (Pisa 1990) and of the Premio Piero Ciampi Citta di Livorno Concorso Musicale Nazionale (1998).

John La Rose was born in Trinidad in 1927, and has been school teacher, trade-union leader, insurance executive, documentary film-maker, tv producer and broadcaster, editor and on editorial committees of literary, cultural, social and political journals, and publisher. General Secretary of the West Indian Independence Party and Executive Member of a leading trade union before going to Britain in 1961, he is still tied to the Caribbean trade unions and currently honorary European representative of the Oilfield Workers Trade Union. In 1966, with Brathwaite and Andrew Salkey, he founded the Caribbean Artists Movement. In 1969 he founded the Black Supplementary Schools Movement, co-founding accompanying organizations, including the Caribbean Education and Community Workers Association, the Black Parents Movement and the National Association of Supplementary Schools. He chaired the Institute of Race Relations from 1974-75 and the New Cross Massacre Action Committee in 1981, which brought 20,000 onto London streets to demand action on the racial murder of 13 youths that January. He is now Chairman of the George Padmore Institute and on the board of the Talawa Theatre Company. A broadcaster in Trinidad in the 1950s, he continued in Britain, and his documentaries include the *Mangrove Nine* (with Franco Rosso) and *The Black Church in Britain* for the BBC TV program "Full House." La Rose has published two books of poetry, *Foundations* (1966) and *Eyelets of Truth Within Me* (1992); *Kaiso Calypso Music* (with David Rudder) and *Attila's Kaiso: A Short History of the Trinidad Calypso* (with Raymond Quevedo, the calypsonian Attila).

His work appears in several anthologies. Founder and publisher of New Beacon Books (since 1966), he has brought to public attention innumerable Caribbean works.

Enrique Lima was born in El Salvador and emigrated to the United States as a child. After years of manual labor, he continued his education at community college and then at the University of Oregon where he received his B. A. He is a published poet whose most recent work appeared in *La Expresión*. His awards include the University of Oregon Diversity Building Scholarship, the Executive Grant for undergraduate research from the Center for the Study of Women in Society and the Stanford Divisional Fellowship in Literatures, Cultures and Languages. He is currently a graduate student in comparative literature at Stanford University.

Mark McWatt was born in British Guyana and grew up in various interior districts, as his father was a district officer in the colonial government of the time. The family migrated to Canada in the mid-sixties because of political and racial disturbances and McWatt attended the Universities of Toronto and Leeds. Since 1976 he has taught Literatures in English at the Cave Hill campus of the University of the West Indies, where he is currently Professor of West Indian Literature. He has published extensively on West Indian Literature, especially Guyanese Literature. He has also been writing poetry since undergraduate days and has published two volumes: *Interiors* (1989) and *The Language of Eldorado* (1994), which received the Guyana prize for poetry.

Pamela Hitchins Mordecai is a poet and short story writer, award-winning children's author, anthologist (especially of the writing of Caribbean women), and compiler/co-compiler of some fifteen language arts textbooks for the Caribbean. Her most recent children's books are *The Costume Parade* and *Rohan Goes to Big School*, both from Oxford UP in 2000. She recently completed *Jus' a Likl Lovin'*, her third book of poetry. She has written on language education and Caribbean literature, in particular on the work of Kamau Brathwaite and Derek Walcott. She co-edited *Jamaica Woman* (1980; 1985) with Mervyn Morris and *Her True-True Name* (1989) with Betty Wilson, and edited *From Our Yard: Jamaican Poetry Since Independence* (1987). *The Culture and Customs of Jamaica*, co-authored with her husband, Martin Mordecai, was published by Greenwood Press this year. Other books include *Journey Poem* (1989) and *De Man a Performance Poem* (1995), an eyewitness account of the crucifixion of Christ in Jamaican Creole. She lives in Toronto.

Mary E. Morgan is the first of Kamau Brathwaite's three sisters. Born in 1933, she took her English degree at the then University College of the West Indies at Mona (London University) in 1957. Besides writing and work in theater, she has been an academic administrator and teacher in Barbados, Guyana, St Vincent and Jamaica, beginning as a High School teacher—notably at Rusea's school in Lucea, Jamaica and St. Joseph's in Georgetown, Guyana—and ending with twenty-five years at UWI, Mona. She was General Secretary of Jamaica's YWCA in 1958-9, Training Officer in the Government Service of St Vincent & the Grenadines from 1967-74, and retired last year from UWI as Senior Assistant Registrar. For the past fifteen years she has been on the Synod of the Methodist Church in Jamaica and sub-editor of *The Jamaica Methodist Link*. She sits on the Board of the United Theological College of the West Indies, is a member of the Jamaica Association for Training and Development and on that association's Research and Publications Committee.

Mervyn Morris, Jamaican poet, teaches at the University of the West Indies, where he is Professor of Creative Writing and West Indian Literature. His collections of poetry include *The Pond, Shadowboxing* and *Examination Centre* (New Beacon Books) and *On Holy Week* (Dangaroo Press). In 1976 the Institute of Jamaica awarded him a Silver Musgrave Medal for poetry. He was a United Kingdom Arts Council International Writer in Residence at the South Bank Centre in 1992. In 1993 and 1994 he was Poetry Workshop Director at the University of Miami's Summer Institute for Caribbean Creative Writing. He is the author of *"Is English We Speaking" and Other Essays* (Kingston: Ian Randle, 1999).

Rex Nettleford is Professor and Vice-Chancellor at the University of the West Indies, and founder and artistic director of the National Dance Theatre Company of Jamaica. After taking a history degree at the UWI, he pursued graduate studies in politics at Oxford as a Rhodes Scholar, later becoming well-known as a trade union educator, social and cultural historian, political analyst, and authority on the performing arts. He has served on international bodies treating development and intercultural learning, been consultant to UNESCO (and member of its Executive Board), OAS, and the Government of Jamaica and is now Rapporteur of the International Scientific Committee of UNESCO's Slave Route Project and its Regional Coordinator for the Caribbean. He heads Jamaica's National Council on Education and serves on numerous other commissions in his country. Recipient of the Order of Merit, Jamaica's Gold Musgrave Medal, the Living Legend Award (Black Arts Festival, Atlanta), the Zora Neale Hurston-Paul

Robeson Award and others, he also holds honorary doctorates from many universities. He has authored several government reports, edited collections, written many scholarly essays, and is editor of *Caribbean Quarterly*. Among his books are *The Rastafarians in Kingston, Jamaica* (with F. R. Augier and M. G. Smith); *Mirror, Mirror: Identity, Race and Protest in Jamaica*; *Manley and the New Jamaica*; *Roots and Rhythms*; *Caribbean Cultural Identity*; *Dance Jamaica*; *The University of the West Indies* (with Sir Philip Sherlock); *Inward Stretch, Outward Reach: A Voice from the Caribbean*.

Ngugi wa Thiong'o is one of Africa's principal writers and intellectuals. Most celebrated as a novelist (*Weep Not Child, The River Between, A Grain of Wheat, Petals of Blood, Devil on the Cross, Matigari*), dramatist (*The Black Hermit, This Time Tomorrow, The Trial of Dedan Kimathi, I Will Marry When I Want*), and prison diarist (*Detained*), he is also noted as a short story writer, a writer of children's tales, poet, editor (*Mutiiri*), and film-maker. Besides these activities, he has been no less globally influential as a cultural, political, and literary critic: *Homecoming, Writers in Politics* (whose much-revised–fully redone–second "edition" appeared in 1997), *Decolonising the Mind, Barrel of a Pen, Moving the Centre*, and, most recently (1998), *Penpoints, Gunpoints, and Dreams: Towards a Critical Theory of the Arts and the State*, the 1996 Clarendon lectures. His newest novel is in press. Ngugi teaches Comparative Literature and Performance Studies at New York University, where he is also Erich Maria Remarque Professor of Languages.

M. NourbeSe Philip, born in Tobago, worked for many years as a barrister and solicitor in Toronto, where she is also prominent in equal rights struggles. She is the author of two novels, *Harriet's Daughter* and *Looking for Livingstone: An Odyssey in Silence*, of three non-fiction volumes, *Frontiers: Essays and Writings on Racism and Culture, Showing Grit* and *A Genealogy of Resistance and Other Essays*, and three volumes of poetry, *Salmon Courage, Thorns* and *She Tries Her Tongue, Her Silence Softly Breaks*, the last of which won the 1988 Casa de las Americas Prize for Poetry.

Velma Pollard spent her teaching career at the Mona campus of the University of the West Indies, from where she retired very recently. Her major research interests are in Creole Languages, language in Caribbean literature, and women's writing, fields in which she has published widely, both locally and internationally. She has also trained teachers to teach English in Creole-speaking environments and to teach literature at primary and secondary levels. As a creative writer she is author of a novel, *Homestretch*, of two collections of poetry, *Crown Point and Other Poems* and *Shame Trees Don't Grow Here*, and of two collections of short fiction, *Considering Woman* and *Karl and Other Stories*. The novella *Karl* won the Casa de Las Americas fiction prize in 1992.

Ras Akyem Ramsay is one of Barbados' premier artists. Born in 1953, Akyem studied at the Jamaican School of Art (1979-83) and later at the Instituto Superior d'Arte in Cuba (1995-7) with his associate Ras Ishi Butcher. He presently teaches at Barbados Community College. Co-founder with Omowale Stewart of De People's Art Movement (De Pam, inaugurated in 1977), he has also been active in the 1990s with the "anti-establishment" Representing Artists (RA). Inspired by the Rastafarian movement, Akyem has been concerned with social and political liberation, and art as embodying "a passionate impulse to create or destroy" within that context. Since 1981, his work has been exhibited through the Caribbean, in the US, England, Switzerland and elsewhere–including many solo shows. In 1985, his *House of King David* won the Tom Adams Award for Excellence and the Dr. and Mrs. H. Richard Sonis Purchase Award. In 1990, his and Ras Ishi's *Roots and Soul* received an Honorable Mention at the Tiburon California Sausalito Art Festival, and in 1991 he won a gold Ivan Payne Award at Barbados' National Independence Festival of the Creative Arts. Over the last decade he has been much influenced by the Haitian artist Jean-Michel Basquiat, whose graffiti sources and style furthered Akyem's incorporation of a pictorial "version" of Brathwaite's nation language into his art. "Peligroso," on the cover of this collection, joins these influences. It won a gold medal at the 3rd Biennial of Latin American and Caribbean Paintings held in the Dominican Republic in 1996.

Timothy J. Reiss, Professor of Comparative Literature at New York University, has most recently published *Knowledge, Discovery and Imagination in Early Modern Europe: The Rise of Aesthetic Rationalism* (1997). *Mirages of the Selfe: Patterns of Personhood in Ancient and Early Modern Europe* is nearing completion. *Against Autonomy* will be published in 2001. He is also the author of *The Discourse of Modernism* (1982, 1985) and other books. *The Meaning of Literature* won the 1992 Forkosch prize in intellectual history. He is editor or co-editor of several collections, among them *Sisyphus and Eldorado: Magical and Other Realisms in Caribbean Literature* (1997) with Kamau Brathwaite, whose revised second edition has just been edited by Reiss and will be published by Africa World Press in 2001.

Gordon Rohlehr, Professor of West Indian Literature at the University of the West Indies, Trinidad, was born in Guyana in 1942. He graduated in 1964 from UWI, Jamaica with an Honours degree in English Literature and wrote a doctoral dissertation entitled, "Alienation and Commitment in the Works of Joseph Conrad" at Birmingham University (1964-7). He is author of *Pathfinder: Black Awakening in* The Arrivants *of Edward Kamau Brathwaite* (1981), *Calypso and Society in Pre-Independence Trinidad* (1990), *My Strangled City and Other Essays* (1992), *The Shape of That Hurt and Other Essays* (1992), and co-editor of *Voiceprint: An Anthology of Oral and Related Poetry from the West Indies* (1989). Recipient of a Fulbright Award (1985), a Mellon Foundation Award (1997) and the University of the West Indies Vice-Chancellor's Award for Excellence in the fields of Teaching, Research, Administration and Public Service (1994-5), he has been visiting professor at Harvard, Johns Hopkins, the University of Miami, York University (Toronto), Tulane, and Stephen F. Austin State University, Texas.

Elaine Savory taught for many years at the University of the West Indies, Cave Hill, and now teaches at the New School University in New York. She co-authored *Out of the Kumbla: Caribbean Women and Literature* (1990), with Carol Boyce Davies. Her collection of poems, *Flame Tree Time*, was published in Kingston, Jamaica in 1993, and her *Jean Rhys* came out with Cambridge UP in 1999. She has written extensively on Caribbean and African literatures.

Olive Senior was born and spent most of her life in Jamaica and now lives in Toronto, Canada. She is the author of eight books including three collections of short stories, two of poetry and non-fiction works on Caribbean culture. Her first short story collection, *Summer Lightning*, won the Commonwealth Writers Prize. She was most recently Writer-in-residence at the University of Alberta, Canada and Internet Poet-in-residence on the "Common . . . Places" web site launched by the Commonwealth Institute in London, England. She reads her work and conducts writing workshops internationally and is on the faculty of The Humber School for Writers, Humber College, Toronto. Another collection of poetry, *Over the Roofs of the World*, is forthcoming.

Omowale Stewart is a Caribbean self-taught artist who has been drawing and painting since 1972. Embedded in Barbados life, he was a major part of the Black Conscious movement of the 1960s and 1970s. Founder of DePam, he has led the movement away from traditional approaches to Barbadian art, brought in influences from Trinidad, and been generally inspired and motivated by his varied Caribbean experience. Omowale embraces the union and power of sight and subject as he makes his journey. He has exhibited widely in the Caribbean, North America and Europe, with drawings and paintings in many private and public collections. He is also a costume designer and producer. He has designed the National Male Costume, won the Crop Over Costume Band of the year prize no less than four times, and executed numerous murals, including the U.N. - S.I.D.S. Mural at the Sherbourne Conference Centre and the Cable and Wireless Mural at the B.E.T. Sports Club. Omowale recognises that art must be emotionally, intellectually and technically sound, it must be powerful, important, enriching culture while impressing the eye, the mind and the soul.

Silvio Torres-Saillant, a native of the Dominican Republic, taught until recently at the City University of New York, of whose Dominican Studies Institute he is founding Director. He is now Associate Professor of English at Syracuse University and heads its Latino-Latin American Studies Program. Author of *Caribbean Poetics* and of the recent *El retorno de las yolas: Ensayos sobre diaspora, democracia y dominicanidad* (Santo Domingo: Ediciones La Trinitaria & Editora Manati, 1999), he co-authored *The Dominican Americans*, has edited two volumes on Latino literature in the U.S., and contributes to many anthologies and such journals as *Caribbean Studies, World Literature Today, Research in African Literature*, among many others. He is also editor of *Punto 7 Review: A Journal of Marginal Discourse*.

Index

People are listed only when named for more than a simple bibliographical reference. Citations of and commentary on Kamau Brathwaite's writings are listed under his name. The poems and books of *The Arrivants* are not indexed separately when they are part of a discussion of the entire trilogy. Terms constantly invoked (colonialism, diaspora, migration, slavery, United States...) are not indexed.